William Taylor, Charles G Moore

William Taylor of California, Bishop of Africa

An Autobiography

William Taylor, Charles G Moore

William Taylor of California, Bishop of Africa
An Autobiography

ISBN/EAN: 9783743386204

Manufactured in Europe, USA, Canada, Australia, Japa

Cover: Foto ©Raphael Reischuk / pixelio.de

Manufactured and distributed by brebook publishing software (www.brebook.com)

William Taylor, Charles G Moore

William Taylor of California, Bishop of Africa

WILLIAM TAYLOR

WILLIAM TAYLOR

OF CALIFORNIA

BISHOP OF AFRICA

AN AUTOBIOGRAPHY

REVISED, WITH A PREFACE

BY

THE REV. C. G. MOORE

LONDON
HODDER AND STOUGHTON
27, PATERNOSTER ROW
1897

Printed by Hazell, Watson, & Viney, Ld., London and Aylesbury.

PREFACE

In preparing the English edition of this remarkable auto-biography, it has been my single aim to select those portions of the original work, edited by Dr. Ridpath, likely to be most interesting to the English reader. The course of the narrative has nowhere been broken, and I have altogether left Bishop Taylor to tell his story in his own way. Nor have I added anything to his words.

The repeated perusal of this life story has left a deep and gracious impression upon my own heart. I commend these pages to the reader in the confident anticipation that he will glorify God both in the worker and in his wonderful work —"and they glorified God in me."

CHARLES G. MOORE.

November, 1897.

CONTENTS

PART FIRST

EARLY LIFE AND TRIAL PERIOD IN THE MINISTRY

CHAPTER I

PART SECOND

PLANTING THE CROSS IN CALIFORNIA

CHAPTER V

CHAPTER VII

CHAPTER VIII

CHAPTER IX

CHAPTER X

CHAPTER XI

CHAPTER XII

PART THIRD

IN THE OLD STATES AND CANADA

CHAPTER XIII

CHAPTER XIV

PART FOURTH

MY WORK IN AUSTRALIA

CHAPTER XV

PART FIFTH

MISSION TO SOUTH AFRICA

CHAPTER XVIII

CHAPTER XXIII

CHAPTER XXIV

CHAPTER XXV

CHAPTER XXVI

CHAPTER XXVII

PART SIXTH

ENGLAND AND THE INDIES WEST AND EAST

CHAPTER XXVIII

CHAPTER XXIX

CHAPTER XXX

PART EIGHTH

MY AFRICAN EPISCOPATE

CHAPTER XXXIX

CHAPTER XL

CHAPTER XLI

PART FIRST

EARLY LIFE AND TRIAL PERIOD IN THE MINISTRY

CHAPTER I

MY ANCESTRY AND BOYHOOD

My grandfather, James Taylor, was one of five brothers who emigrated from County Armagh, Ireland, to the colony of Virginia, about one hundred and thirty years ago. Their names in the order of their birth were George, James, William, John, and Caufould. On their arrival they invested their money in land and slaves in Rockbridge County. They were fine specimens of that hardy, energetic race known as Scotch-Irish, of the old Covenanter type. They all fought for American freedom in the Revolution of 1776. John was killed in the war, and Caufould was a prisoner for a year or two. He was liberated by the birth-throes of the new nation. George and James both married daughters of Captain Audley Paul, of the same hardy clan, the Scotch-Irish. Audley Paul was a fellow-lieutenant of George Washington in General Braddock's army, and was present when Colonel Washington ventured to suggest to the British general that to conquer the Indian forces combined against them the colonial soldiers should be allowed the protection of the trees of the wood and to fight the Indians in their own fashion. But the general called him a "young buckskin," and reproved him for his presumption. That was in the morning of the day noted as the day of "Braddock's defeat." Audley Paul, with many others, in their retreat swam the Alleghany River near the site of Pittsburg. The sword he carried in that engagement and in his years of marching and fighting as captain in the War of Independence hung in my father's bedroom through all the years of my youth.

The Pauls were religiously opposed to slavery, and so indoctrinated the rising generation of the Taylors into anti-slavery sentiment that as fast as they came into possession of slaves by inheritance they set them free. My father emancipated the last of them, being one of the younger of the fourteen children of James and Ann (Paul) Taylor.

My mother's maiden name was Hickman. She was of English descent. The Hickmans settled in Delaware about one hundred and forty years ago. Roger Hickman's marriage did not please the aristocratic pride of his parents, as we learn from family tradition, and, they bearing down on him a little too severely, Roger struck for liberty, and with his wife went to what was then the "far West," and bought land and slaves and settled on Back Creek, in Bath County, Virginia, and there brought up a large, industrious family in the Presbyterian faith. Their son William married a daughter of Captain James Elliott, also a Revolutionary soldier, and they brought up a large, well-to-do family : my mother was their firstborn.

Stuart Taylor and Martha E. Hickman were united in marriage in 1819, and settled in Rockbridge County. They each had a sound, powerful constitution of body and mind. Their English school education was quite equal to the average of their day. Their practical common sense and energy were largely above the average. My mother was mistress of the manufacture of all kinds of cloth known in her early life, plain and ornamental, and every department of the process, and knew how to develop men and women to stand the wear and tear of life for the probable average of three quarters of a century. My father was by trade "a tanner and currier," but had been brought up a farmer. He was a mechanical genius, utilising wood, iron, and leather for all the purposes of his own farms and tanyard and the demands of the market. With his endowment of common sense he combined great sympathy for men, beasts, and birds ; these, with sound judgment, made him a popular leader of men within the radius of his activity.

My parents, soon after their marriage, joined the Presbyterian Church, and tried, in their way, for thirteen years, to live up to the standard of doctrine and moral rectitude of that Christian body. They had the form of godliness, and tried to be good and to teach their children to be good, but they lacked soul-converting power. Our preacher, Rev. Andrew Davidson, was an earnest, impressive speaker, often causing his congregation to weep aloud on account of their shortcomings, and all the people of that region held me preacher in affectionate reverence. Our place of worship was a " Union church," built largely by an old Methodist named Lambert ; but up to my twelfth year I never saw a Methodist or heard of their " preaching around." But about that time Joseph Spriggs, of the Baltimore Conference, announced that he would preach at Lambert's church on Thursday afternoon of every alternate week.

The Methodists were " a sect everywhere spoken against " in that region, so that our family were careful not to be seen in such company. One day my father, on horseback, was passing the church as Spriggs's congregation were assembling, filling the grove with their horses, the same as for the regular preaching on the Sabbath. His curiosity was excited, and a desire enkindled to venture in to see what could attract so great a crowd on a week day. He dismounted, and, going to the door, found the church so crowded that with difficulty he got a seat against the wall near the door. Spriggs's text that day was, "Except a man be born again, he cannot see the kingdom of God." He was a Gospel sharpshooter. The truth commended itself to my father's judgment, and was applied to his heart by the awakening Spirit of God. He was convinced of the truth of what he heard and convicted of sin, and so drawn to the preacher that he thought if he could induce him to go home with him salvation would come to his house that day. So he pressed his way through the crowded aisle and met the preacher as he descended the pulpit stairs, and begged him to become his guest. Spriggs expressed his willingness, but declined to go with him on account of previous engagements.

For two weeks father's mind seemed to be in an utterly bewildered state, and he was in such agony of soul he could scarcely take food sufficient to sustain life. Under the pretence of "going a-hunting" he spent much of his time in the mountains, gun in hand, when he scarcely thought of shooting anything but himself, seriously contemplating suicide. I went with him on his hunt one day, and he spent most of his time at the root of a large chestnut tree, with his face in his hands, groaning and weeping. He only needed some Philip to lead him to Jesus.

Two weeks after my father was "struck," under that first Methodist sermon he ever heard, a Methodist camp meeting was commenced at Cold Sulphur Springs, about ten miles from our home. That was in August, 1832. Father felt strong drawings toward the camp meeting, but his pride and prejudice would not allow him to go avowedly to such a place; but wishing to drive a herd of his cattle into the "mountain range," six or seven miles in the direction of the camp, he said to me and one of his farm hands, "We'll drive the cattle into the mountains, and then we'll slip over and see what's going on at the camp meeting."

The first Methodist preaching I ever heard was at that camp meeting. The preachers impressed me as being a superior race of human beings. I revered them as I would have revered angels, but kept well out of their way, for I feared them. Eight or ten of the "God-men" occupied the stand during the preaching, then they all came down into the altar to labour with the mourners. The altar was a square inclosure to accommodate from one hundred to two hundred persons, specially for the use of seekers of salvation, and the ministers and laymen and women who went in to instruct and pray for them.

For about three days my father heard the preaching, but as soon as an invitation was given to seekers to come forward to the mourners' bench he hurried off to the Springs and strolled round among the giddy crowds of the outer circles. On the last night of the meeting a sermon preached on the story of the prodigal son, by John V. Rigden, brought him to a decision to mortify his pride and have salvation at any cost. When the call was given for seekers, my father said to John Buchanan, a well-to-do neighbour of ours, who was also a nominal member of a Christian Church, "John, let us go into that Methodist altar." "Agreed," replied John. Only two vacant sittings remained in the altar, and just inside the gate. John led and took the seat nearest the entrance, and father had to pass him to get to the next seat. They both soon after dropped on their knees as seekers of pardon.

My father at once with flowing tears cried, "God have mercy on me a poor sinner! O God, for Christ's sake, have mercy on me a poor sinner!" In fifteen minutes, to use his own simple expression, he piled up his short prayers till they reached to heaven, and God responded, "Son, thy sins are all forgiven thee." He was filled with the Holy Spirit and carried away in raptures of joy. He thought he heard the rejoicing of angels and the shouts of his mother, who some years before had gone to join the hosts of the blood-washed on the other side.

Next day, on our return home, he said to me, "William, I am converted." Then he laughed and cried and shouted hallelujah. "Yes, William, I am converted to God; converted among the Methodists. God bless the Methodists! I hated and dreaded them, but God has wonderfully saved me at a Methodist camp meeting. God bless the Methodists! How I do love them, and shall always love them, I am sure; but I shall not leave my own Church, for I think God can use me as a witness among them and do them good."

As soon as we reached home my dear mother came out to meet us. Father embraced and kissed her and said, "Honey, I'm converted. God has saved me from my sins." He shouted hallelujah, and my mother wept. Then he called all the family and servants together, read a lesson from "the family Bible that lay on the stand," and kneeled down and gave thanks to God for salvation, and prayed earnestly for mother and for the children and servants by name.

Some years before, in his desire to be good, my father bought a book of prayers, with the purpose of trying to have family worship by reading a prayer; but it seemed like mockery to him. So he never attempted to have family worship till the day I have just described.

Next morning, after family worship and breakfast, he mounted a horse and rode at large through the neighbourhood, and called on all the elders of the Church and other leading members, and told them his wonderful experience, and asked them when they were "born again," and why they had not told him about it long ago. Father was not censorious—never was; but he was sublimely in earnest, and, filled with love and sympathy, he hoped to get them all into the same happy experience which so thrilled his heart and life. None of them attempted to argue with him, because they knew he was too much for any of them on that line before he went to the camp meeting; but now his utterances filled them with silent amazement. They would say nothing in his presence, but they reported that Stuart Taylor "had gone crazy, and scandalised himself and his Church at the Methodist camp meeting."

Stuart Taylor was not crazy. He was a level-headed man in his day, and clearly perceived that he could get no help and do but little good in the Church of his early choice, as it was at that day. So he deliberately made up his mind to join the Methodist Episcopal Church.

A fortnight after the day he came home with the good news, he and his family were encamped in their own tent at Shaw's Camp Ground, seven miles distant from where we lived. At that camp meeting my mother was saved, and father, mother, and myself joined the Methodist Episcopal Church and helped to form "the society" at Lambert's meeting house, which was attached to the Lexington Circuit. William B. Edwards, the preacher in charge, received us into the Church.

My father was naturally a leader of men, and soon became so in the Church of his newborn life. From the first and through his long life in the work his ruling passion was to get people saved. He became an ordained local preacher, but for over forty years his ministerial services, far and near, were more itinerant than local. He was in easy circumstances, and devoted a large portion of his time to special evangelistic services. His only reward—for he refused pay—was the joy of soul-saving success. He assisted me in protracted meetings on four different circuits in which I was a minister. He was the most willing and the most welcome helper I could get. He was a great singer, a powerful exhorter, and as for knee-work among seekers of salvation, there seemed to be no limit to his zeal and power of endurance, always first in the fight and the last to retire from the field. His confidence in man and his grand possibilities were second only to his confidence in God and in free and full salvation in Jesus.

Designing men sometimes took advantage of his confidence, and would contract debts which they never paid and probably never intended to pay. But his faith in the many was never shaken by the deceptive hypocrisy of the few.

The civil war swept like a tornado over the State of Virginia. The valley was in possession alternately of the Union and of the Confederate army. The trimmers knew not which side to shout for. But everybody who was acquainted with Stuart Taylor knew which side he was on; indeed, he was recklessly bold in declaring his unflinching fidelity to the Union cause. A conspiracy was planned for his arrest and execution in Castle Thunder, but the Lord was so careful of him that he moved General Johnston, commander of that division, to issue an order that Stuart Taylor should not be molested; and he was not.

In the midst of the war troubles the society of Lambert's meeting house, all except my father, left the Methodist Episcopal

Church and joined in a body the Methodist Episcopal Church, South. As he stood alone they all tried to persuade him to go with them. "No," said he; "if I should turn my back upon my Church and my nation, especially in this the day of their sorrow, I should say the Lord would serve me right to turn me out of heaven and bar the doors against me." He then applied to the Baltimore Conference for a minister to be sent to his house, and he would support him and his family. This request was granted; a minister was sent, and remained with him till the war was over. A new place of worship, meantime, was built in the neighbourhood, and a new society of the Methodist Episcopal Church was formed.

My father's house was always a welcome home for God's ambassadors, and both father and mother loved them and were never more delighted than to have them in their home and minister to them. They were Methodists in heart, life, and profession, but welcomed to their hospitality ministers of other Churches.

Father and mother enjoyed an unwaning honeymoon, which shone on their happy married life through its whole period of about fifty-four years. I have no remembrance of ever hearing an unkind word pass between them.

Father wrote me when I was labouring in Ceylon, saying: "Our old friends wanted us to have a golden wedding and allow them to honour us with their gifts. I respectfully declined, saying, 'We have got on so well with the old contract for fifty years that I prefer it for another fifty years, or as long as the Lord shall be pleased to spare us.'" In the same letter he added: "When mother and I were surrounded by our growing family we often spoke with sadness of the coming time when they would scatter abroad and leave us in lonely desolation. The dreaded time has come. They are all married, except Rebecca and John, who are in heaven; the nine who survive have comfortable homes of their own, and we are left alone, but not lonely. Indeed, we never were so free from care and so really happy before. God has blessed us in our children. They are all healthy, all religious, all Methodists, all industrious, all peaceable and peacemakers, and three of them Gospel ministers. We are happy thus to know that our great lifework is done. Our sun is setting, and not a cloud in the west. We are waiting cheerfully on the bank of the river for the boatman to come to take us home."

My birthday was the 2nd of May, 1821—the beginning of a family of five sons and six daughters. In the latter part of my third year I spent a few months at Grandfather Hickman's, and there learned some useful lessons, one of which I will mention. Seeing a large cluster of bees hanging down from the front of the hive, I said, "Ah, my sweeties, I'll fix you." So I got an empty horn of a cow and filled it with water and dashed it on the bees. They resented it and speared me most unmercifully. The lesson I learned was to attend to my own business and not meddle with the affairs of other folks.

About a year later I went with Aunt Nancy Thomas, one of father's sisters, riding for twenty miles behind her on the same horse, to spend a few months with Grandmother Taylor. During the few months of sojourn with my dear grandmother she advanced me rapidly in the difficult art of English orthography, and, better still, she explained to me my filial relation to God, under the covenant of grace, so that I walked in the daily sunshine of His love, till forfeited by sin. It occurred on this wise: In the early part of my sixth year I saw a little old knife, not worth two cents, lying on the floor of a verandah. I knew it belonged to another little boy, but I coveted it and put it into my pocket. Then came on me for the first time that awful seasickish sensation of guilt and remorse which indicated the forfeiture of my infantile justified relation to God. The thing was all the more grievous to my conscience because it occurred many miles away, and I could not get back to replace the knife; so I threw it away in utter disgust.

I learned to read the New Testament before I had seen seven summers. I read in the Book about repentance, and mourned alone in sorrow that I did not know how to repent, and thought I must perish in my ignorance and sin. My parents took great interest in teaching me; but neither of them then knew the Lord; so I had no one to show me the way. I read of the love of Jesus and how kind He was to the little children, but that was long ago, and He had left this world, and I knew of no possibility of speaking to Him. I read about His life and death, and that He had gone back to heaven, and thought, " Oh, if I had lived in those days when Jesus dwelt with men, then certainly I would have gone to Him like the little children I read about ; but He has gone away, and I have no Saviour."

But it came to pass in those days of my darkness that I heard a coloured servant-girl tell what she heard a black collier say. It was to me a wonderful story of dreams and visions ; but the sum of it was that the poor negro found Jesus and had got all his sins forgiven and washed away. I had " the Word of God," but lacked " the testimony for Jesus." That lack, second hand, was now in a small measure supplied. I said to myself, " If this black man has found Jesus and got his sins forgiven, then, somehow, Jesus isn't so far away after all. If this poor sinner has found Him why can't I find Him ?" Still, I did not know how to proceed. But soon after, as I sat one night by the kitchen fire, the Spirit of the Lord came on me and I found myself suddenly weeping aloud and confessing my sins to God in detail, as I could recall them, and begged Him for Jesus' sake to forgive them, with all I could not remember ; and I found myself trusting in Jesus that it would all be so, and in a few minutes my heart was filled with peace and love, not the shadow of a doubt remaining.

I was fully conscious at that early, far-away time of having been forgiven, and of having received " a new heart and a right spirit." Then I went and kneeled down by my trundle-bed and said, " Our

Father which art in Heaven," and realised sweetly that He was my reconciled Father. Every word of that prayer that I had so often repeated from memory without realising its meaning was as precious manna to my spirit. I can never forget the heavenly rest that filled my soul that night. For many weeks I walked in the light without a bedimning cloud, and often wondered that I had groped in the dark so long when the way was indeed so plain. I daily sang with sweet emotions of joy the hymns my mother had taught me. All the blessed experiences of those days were to me facts as clear and vivid as the play of the lightning and of the beautiful lines of light in the rainbow; but I could no more describe my experience within than I could describe these phenomena of the heavens, and had no one to speak to me nor to whom I could speak of these spiritual things.

I cannot say how many weeks or months I lived in this blessed union with God, but in course of time, when one bright day I was in my father's cornfield, Satan came to me as an invisible person and opened a conversation with my inner consciousness. I did not know Satan then, and was quite ignorant of his devices. It had never struck me that he lived in this world, though I had read of his deeds of darkness in the olden time. So he said to me, " What was that you were reading about this morning ? "

" I was reading about the believers in Jerusalem who sold their possessions and brought the price and laid it down at the apostles' feet."

" Yes, you read it, did you ? "

" I did read it this very morning."

" Well, have you done that ? You see, you never can own anything if you go on in this way. You must sell everything you have and give the money away; and if anything should ever come to you you can't keep it for yourself, but must give it up as soon as you get it."

" All right, I am the Lord's, and I'll do whatever He wants me to do."

" But have you done it ? "

I replied, " No, I haven't yet, but I will."

" You will, hey ! Then why don't you do it ? "

So, in a hasty stock-taking of what I had, I could not recall an item of anything that had any money value in it except some skins in my father's tanyard, which would not be turned for weeks to come nor tanned in as many months; so I said, " I have nothing but the skins."

" Well, you must get them out of the tan vats to-day, and sell them, and give the money away, or lose your peace."

" I am willing, I am willing; but I can't get them out of the tan vats now."

" Then God commands you to do something you can't do."

" Well, I want to do it, and would if I could."

" Yes; but you can't, and you know you can't; so God requires you to do what you can't do."

I was cornered, and in great confusion of mind assented to the devil's lie, that God required of me the performance of an impossibility, and immediately the light that was within me became darkness; and oh, how great was that darkness! The old deceiver thus drew a weapon from the armoury of God, and with it slew me, and set on his victim with a grin of satisfaction and scowl of contempt. When I think of the dreadful fall of Lucifer and the eternal wreck and ruin it brought on him I often pity him; but I never had any respect for him since the day he took such a mean advantage of the ignorance of a poor little boy. Like the eunuch of Ethiopia, I needed a Philip to come along and explain to me that the extraordinary beneficence of Barnabas and others, who sold their possessions and laid down the price at the feet of the apostles, was not a law requiring believers at large thus to dispose of their property, but was a genuine expression of Christian sympathy to meet an emergency. Thousands of pilgrims who had come from all parts of the Roman world to attend the feast of Pentecost had been detained by their acceptance of the Christ and the work He required. Their own limited supplies exhausted, they would have come to grief by starvation and pestilence but for the extraordinary liberality of Barnabas and many others of the same spirit. So in all the ages, to the present day, the spontaneity of Christian love and sympathy to meet emergencies has been the same. The tithe, or tenth, of net income of every producer in the world belongs to God, in a financial sense, and any one withholding it "robs God." Having discharged his debt to the owner of the world, if he has the means to spare and a liberal heart to bestow charity, God accepts his free-will offerings and gives him due credit on the score of beneficence. The case of persons possessing nothing, or nothing available, as in my case, is covered by what is written: "If there be first a willing mind, it is accepted, according to what a man hath, and not according to what he hath not." But no Philip came along in my hour of need; and in my ignorance, instead of fleeing at once to Jesus and taking shelter in His bosom, I stood in the open field and tried to reason with the old sophist who through the centuries has been deceiving the nations. I got into the castle of Giant Despair and lost the key.

Instead of bright sunshine in my spirit it was dense darkness; instead of joy and gladness in blessed union with Jesus I had unrest and wretchedness. I wished most earnestly that the blessed life of love and peace would return to me, but I seemed to have lost all knowledge of the way back to God. I then vainly tried to fill the aching void with worldly entertainments, but it was like a hungry child feeding on sawdust and shavings.

It was almost five years after my defeat that my father was saved at the Cold Sulphur Spring camp meeting, and two weeks later, at "Shaw's Camp Meeting," my mother was converted to God. At that camp meeting I went forward as a seeker at every call for two days and nights. I was trying to pray my way in, and

knew not how to surrender to God and receive and trust Jesus.
I was praying for the blessing instead of receiving the Blesser.
One night near the close of the camp meeting, when at the
"mourners' bench" praying and crying at the top of my voice,
"Jimmie Clark" took me in his arms and soothed me down somewhat, and said: "Now, William, I am sure you do repent, and
that you do believe. 'Believe on the Lord Jesus Christ, and thou
shalt be saved.' Now you do believe on the Lord Jesus Christ;
therefore you are saved."

I replied, "Unless I feel that He saves me, I can't say that I am
saved."

"But you are looking at the dark side all the time, and can't hear
His gentle voice of mercy, nor feel the touch of His loving hand.
Now look at the bright side; thank God for giving Jesus to die for
you; praise Him for salvation in Jesus. Just say it and you will
soon feel it. 'Glory to God for salvation in Jesus!'" So I did
as he told me, hoping to feel the saving power within, as he assured
me I should. But I had only uttered the words, "Glory to God for
salvation," when he shouted, "Hallelujah! William is saved." My
father came running and embraced me, and exulted, and others
joined in the general rejoicing over my conversion. I had ventured
on an experiment, under the advice of a well-meaning brother, and
hoped to feel the assuring witness and renewing work of the Holy
Spirit in my heart.

When, after the excitement and confusion of the moment, I could
inquire within, I felt utterly blank, dark, and desolate, and my old
enemy, getting a grip on my timidity, said: "It has gone all over
the camp that you are converted. If you say now that you are
not converted you will grieve your father, and the people will say
you have been playing the hypocrite. The meeting will close
to-morrow, and you can quietly go home and there cry to God and
find the joy."

As far as possible I avoided a profession, for I had a horror of
hypocrisy, but was so deficient in moral courage as not to be able
to contradict the statement that had gone abroad, and was hence
utterly wretched. On returning home I cried and prayed by the
hour; but the heavens were as brass to me, for I was in a false
position. I joined the Methodist Episcopal Church at the camp
meeting with father and mother, and regularly attended prayer and
class meetings, and tried to be good.

About a year after I was deeply awakened by the Holy Spirit
one night at a series of revival services at Lambert's meeting house.
It seemed to me as plain as daylight that if I would go forward
as a seeker among the mourners I should find salvation in a few
minutes. The Spirit said, "Go, go now," but Satan said, "Don't
go, unless you have your father with you to explain your case." I
looked for my father. He was usually at the front and easily seen;
but on this occasion I spent over half an hour hunting for him, and
when I found him in the gallery instructing a poor sinner my call

was slighted, and my heart was utterly destitute of the tender emotion and sorrow for sin I had so sensibly felt an hour before. Then Satan told me that I had rejected God's last offer of mercy to me and that the Holy Spirit had left me for ever, and the nightmare of despair settled down on my soul. Some weeks later I went forward as a seeker, but felt no tender emotion or sorrow for sin, and could not for a moment break the dark cloud of despair that enveloped my spirit.

About two years after I joined the Church I was one night at a Presbyterian prayer meeting, and the leader called on me to pray. I put my head under the bench at which I was kneeling and tried to hide myself from view; but after a little delay he called on me again to lead in prayer. So I was caught, and could see no way out but to obey orders. With some sense and a great deal of sound I made what was reported to be a startling success, which was noised abroad. The Methodists had not called on me to pray, because I was telling them in class meeting that I was not at all clear in my experience; but now they began to call on me regularly to lead in prayer, which I never refused to do. My father took me to his revival meetings to help him, and depended very much on my praying up the rousements. So my life, for years, was a series of long struggles to be good; praying in private and in public prayer meetings, with sad lapses into secret sins, maintaining an outward life of reputed consistency as a member of the Church, yet in heart utterly destitute of hope in God. I knew too well, I thought, when the Holy Spirit gave me His last call and departed to return no more.

At about the age of fourteen I had what was called "the slow fever," a sort of typhoid, I think. It was thought I must die at that time. Father used to sit over me and inquire, with flowing tears, if I had peace with God. I felt that I had no hope beyond the grave, but determined not to grieve father and mother, so evaded the point of their inquiry. The Lord in mercy raised me up and spared my very unhappy and unpromising life.

In my twentieth year I rode twenty miles on horseback one day in company with John Middleton, a pious Methodist blacksmith residing in Lexington, Va., to a revival meeting in progress at Rapp's meeting house, on Buffalo Creek. John was a sympathising, loving Christian, and told me much of his early experience in trying to be good, and it so corresponded with mine that a ray of hope pierced the depths of my darkness; and at that revival I went forward again as a seeker. William H. Enos, our preacher in charge, said, "That is not your place, William," and called on me to lead in prayer. I obeyed the order, and prayed for all the rest of them, and said, "Amen," and remained among the seekers praying for myself. I got a little light and a few rays of hope at that meeting.

A fortnight later I went to a camp meeting at Panther Gap, ten miles from home. James Gamble, the preacher in charge on that circuit, was an earnest and successful Gospel minister in the old Baltimore Conference. Soon after my arrival at the camp I was called on to pray, which was a hindrance to my going forward as a seeker of salvation. I, however, prayed as usual; but when seekers were called I went forward, and when the meeting for that night was closed and the congregation retired I remained on the floor under the benches. William Forbes and his son, two humble colliers, remained with me and sang softly and said a few words occasionally; and as I lay there in silence I realised the presence of an invisible Person, seemingly but a few feet distant from me, and it came to my mind, "Jesus has come"; and in a moment I received Him, and trusted Him to take me in hand and do the best He could for one utterly abandoned and lost; and I sweetly realised in my soul, "Oh, He loves me; He saves me! I do love God, I do love the brethren, I have indeed passed from death unto life. Glory to God!"

"Satan came in like a flood," injecting into my mind vulgar and profane thoughts, and then insinuated, "Ah, you see you can't be a child of God and feel that way;" but I rested on the bosom of Jesus, and He lifted up a standard against the enemy of my soul and kept me in safety. I was thus restored to my standing in the kingdom and family of God about 10 P.M. of the 28th day of August, 1841. There I have dwelt, in "the secret place of the Most High, and under the shadow of the Almighty" from that day to the present.

For six dreary years before I was restored I groped in the darkness of despair, believing that the Holy Spirit had abandoned me for ever. So, to find out that I was mistaken, and to realise that I was saved, gave me joy that was unspeakable. But I was greatly troubled with "wandering thoughts" and the vile suggestions of Satan, and had an awful dread of falling, which, combined with love and sympathy for unsaved people, led me to work for God with quenchless zeal; yet I was naturally so extremely bashful that nothing short of my fear of offending God could have kept me up to the line of my opportunities.

During the remaining days of that camp meeting I was as keen on the scent for souls as a setter after the game. The order of the day was for one man to preach, and another to follow with an exhortation and a call for seekers to come forward for instruction and for the prayers of good people. As soon as this call was made I went out into the congregation to persuade sinners to be reconciled to God. When I found a young man under awakening, but refusing to come forward to the mourners' bench, I would invite him to walk and talk with me in the adjacent forest, and usually after the talk and a season of prayer together "in secret," he would return and accompany me to the altar of prayer.

The day the camp meeting closed, as we were departing for our homes, I stopped in the road in front of a dry goods and provision store, and exhorted the merchant and a group of his customers to make their peace with God at once, reminding them that the camp meeting "harvest was past, and the summer ended."

That was the beginning of my "street preaching," a most unnatural thing for me, and always a heavy cross, but a means of grace to me and of the salvation of many souls. My fear of neglect and condemnation led me to approach all sorts of hard cases, and I was admonished by my good father to discriminate more closely, and not to lock horns with men who were far in advance of me in age and intelligence.

On our way from this camp meeting Satan laid a snare for my soul. We had to pass through a tollgate requiring, for horse and rider, the payment of eighteen cents. My father, doing a great deal of business over that road, paid a stipulated amount for himself and family by the year.

A very respectable lady and a member of the Church, for whose accommodation I would have run a mile any day, came to me, saying she had a request to make of me. I said, "All right, sister; I am at your service."

"I want you to give me your place in the waggon and to ride my horse, so that I won't have to pay toll."

I exclaimed, "Oh, my good woman, that would involve my conscience, for God could not pass it as a straight transaction!"

Soon after I went, by invitation, to lead a prayer meeting at the house of Brother and Sister Hill, at the forge in the gap of the North Mountain, near where I was born. The Lord gave me one soul at that meeting, a black man, who became a steadfast Christian.

Satan took advantage of my very sensitive and overscrupulous conscience and gave me a great deal of trouble, but the Lord was very patient with me, and often defeated him. One day, passing on horseback, I saw the county poorhouse, about two hundred yards distant across a field. I said to myself, "There's the home of a great many poor people, poor old men and women, who will in the near future go to their graves, and many of them probably are unsaved. I ought to go and tell them of Jesus, and that, as He saves me from my sins, so He will be glad to save them if they will consent. But they are all strangers to me, and will think I am a self-conceited intermeddler, wanting to pass myself off for somebody and acquire notoriety. I am in a hurry, and must accomplish my business errand and hasten home. Yes, but this is my first, and will probably be my last, chance to speak a word for God to those poor old people, and my testimony for Jesus may be the means of saving some of them."

So I dismounted and climbed a high fence, and made a straight cut across the fields to the poorhouse. At the corner of the nearest house to me I saw an old man sitting on a stool. I hastened my approach and kneeled down before him, saying, "My dear old father, I have come to tell you about the love of Jesus, who died for us, and who has taken away all my sins." I testified and exhorted, and the Holy Spirit gave me unction and utterance, which drew the people around me in large numbers, so that, after speaking personally to about half a dozen, I invited them all to assemble in a large room, where we could all worship God together. We then had a very interesting meeting—singing, Scripture reading, exposition, testimony, and exhortation. It was indeed an occasion never to be forgotten, though I made no mention of it to any one, as my conscience censured me severely for my cowardly hesitation about it.

In my penitential struggle at the camp meeting these words of Jesus rang in my ears like the voice of God: "When thou art converted"—or returned from thy flight—"strengthen thy brethren." Acting promptly on that responsibility, I did not lose an hour by delay, but proceeded at once to soul-saving work, as the Lord opened my way. I made no profession of a call to preach the Gospel, and never asked, then nor since, for any office in the gift of the Church; but I was so burdened on account of the peril of unsaved sinners that I became very unhappy and cried to God to pity me, and lead me in the way of His own choosing. So He gave me instruction through a dream. In pouring out "His Spirit upon all flesh," children, heathen, and all others not sufficiently advanced in His school to have their minds directly opened to understand the Scriptures, are taught of the Spirit by means of "dreams and visions." So the Spirit said to me in a dream: "My child, you are needlessly disturbing your mind about the work God has for you to do. You must tarry at Jerusalem till 'endued with power from on high'; then God will call you as He did Jonah, when He said distinctly, 'Arise, go to Nineveh, that great city.'" The prophetic unction of Jonah, by anticipation, so filled me that I sprang up and the peace of God pervaded my spirit, so that I gave myself no further trouble on the subject of preaching, but left it all with God.

Soon after this I was helped on to an advance line of work by means of another dream. In my dream I was listening to an earnest preacher of the Gospel. At the close, when he dismissed the congregation, he remained standing in the pulpit and sang a solo while the crowd passed out; many meantime quietly remained in their seats. After singing a few verses the preacher, looking steadfastly at me, said: "William, God has a special work for you to do. If you will follow His Spirit, confer not with flesh and blood, turn neither to the right nor to the left, your wisdom will be like the continual dropping into a bucket." In addition to the words, a vision of the whole thing was distinctly presented to my view, including a large empty bucket, with the rapid dropping of the purest water. When I awoke I was assured that I was walking after the Spirit according to the best light I had, but knew not the interpretation nor special design of the vision.

The following Sabbath I heard William H. Enos preach in Lambert's meeting house, and at the close, when he dismissed the congregation, he remained standing in the pulpit and sang a solo as the crowd passed out. About thirty persons, including myself, quietly remained for the class meeting. When Brother Enos reached the conclusion of his solo he came directly to me and said, "William, I want you to go out." His penetrating gaze and emphatic words frightened me; so I promptly left the house and cut for home by the shortest path across the fields and through the woods, wondering why I should be ordered out of the church in the presence of the whole class.

On the return of my dear parents, father said, "William, what became of you to-day? Brother Enos sent me to call you in, and I could not find you anywhere."

"When Brother Enos ordered me out of the house I thought it was time for me to leave."

"Well, you had nothing to get scared about. As soon as you retired Brother Enos said to the society, 'I have had my eye on William Taylor for some time past, and I believe God has a special work for him to do, and I wish to submit his name to the Church as a suitable person to receive an official license to exhort.' So the nomination was put and carried unanimously, and I was sent out to call you, and had to return answer that you were not to be found."

Then I seriously pondered the whole matter, and saw the beginning of a life realisation of my dreams. I said to myself, "I have but little knowledge, but with a perpetual dropping of divine wisdom into my bucket God will put me through on the line of obedience."

Soon after Brother Enos presented me with a license to exhort, written in beautiful German letters by Sister Enos, and signed by the plain hand of the preacher in charge. I was led on so fast that my license to exhort never "came up for renewal."

During that fall—1841—I laboured in several protracted meetings in different parts of our circuit, and spent the ensuing winter at school in Lexington, and conducted the regular prayer meeting every Wednesday night, and held meetings on Sabbath days in different parts of the adjacent country. During the summer of 1842 I taught school at Rapp's schoolhouse, on the south branch of Buffalo Creek, near where I had lived with my grandmother when I was five years of age. Sixteen years had passed. Grandmother, who first taught me to pray, had died and gone to heaven. My schoolhouse was the house of worship also for that region of country, with a week day appointment on the circuit plan every alternate week; but more than half the appointments were disappointments, on account of the failure of the "circuit preachers" in coming to time. Good, faithful ministers they were, but they had a large circuit, rough roads, and occasional illness, and the fact that I was on the ground and would be sure to take the meeting fully accounted for their absence.

One day, when a young preacher came and preached, he had

occasion to reprove a young man for disturbing the congregation. The fellow rushed out, threatening he would thrash the preacher as soon as he should come out of the house.   The minister was a small man, and was evidently badly scared.   But as soon as he was ready to start I said to him, " Take my arm, brother, and I will see you safely on your horse."   And so I did.   Forty years after that the same minister, aged and honoured in the work of the ministry, said to me, " I shall never forget the day, Brother Taylor, when, at Rapp's schoolhouse, you saved me from a thrashing by the hands of a big ruffian."

I began my work as a teacher on the 30th of May, 1842.   Near the close of my three months' term I gave a few days' vacation, in which myself, and one or two more young fellows walked fifteen miles to attend a camp meeting on Fincastle Circuit, in Botetourt County, and had a good time.   Our Presiding Elder of Rockingham District, N. J. B. Morgan, was in charge of the camp meeting. He was a tall, commanding, fine-looking man, a pulpit Boanerges in his day, a general in administration, and could not be satisfied with less than two thousand converts per year in his district.   He was as a nursing father to me.

At this camp meeting he called me to him in the preachers' tent. He stroked my hair softly and drew me near to his loving heart and said, " Brother William, I want to send you as junior preacher with Francis A. Harding, on Monroe Circuit."

"Why, Brother Morgan, I never preached in my life.   I can't preach."

He caressed me kindly and said, " God has called you to preach, and I know you can do it, and God will bless you and give you success."

I was awed and amazed, moved and melted, and hardly knew what to say.   After a pause I ventured to ask, " What books should I take with me from which I may learn to preach ? "

" Take the Bible and the Methodist Hymn Book."

" But I can't complete my school engagement in less than three weeks."

" All right ; finish up as quickly as you can, and I will have everything arranged for you."

So I returned to my school, and, in addition to the work it involved, I had a series of revival services and seven powerful conversions to God.

CHAPTER II

It was the 8th of October, 1842, when I was sent to my first circuit under appointment of the presiding elder. In the current chapter I will recount the story of my first years in the regular ministry. The period extends, in time, from 1842 to 1849, when I was sent by Bishop Waugh to California.

It may not be considered out of place here for me to give the uninitiated a peep into the symmetrical adjustment and practical working of the wonderful system called Methodism.

Our bishops are constituted by an election by the General Conference, and the "laying on of hands of the presbytery," according to the New Testament and the formula prescribed in our Discipline. No law guarantees the life tenure of the office, but thus far it has gone for life, except in one case of resignation. Any bishop is at liberty to resign; every bishop is liable to arrest, trial, and expulsion if he does not behave himself. No bishop in the history of Methodism thus far has dishonoured his office, all of them being God-given men. Every bishop has his work assigned to him by the authority of the General Conference. In regard to the home Board of Bishops, its appointing power is delegated to it by the General Conference; and the Board, at its semi-annual meetings, assigns to each bishop the field of episcopal jurisdiction, as per "plan of episcopal visitation," made and published every six months; all being itinerant and not diocesan bishops.

There is no difference in the functions or in the official standing of our bishops and missionary bishops, the only difference being in the fact that the General Conference, instead of delegating its appointing power, exercises it in relation to missionary bishops by a direct appointment to a definite foreign field for an indefinite period of time, they being, in common with the home Board of Bishops, responsible to the General Conference for their conduct.

The General Conference, the legislative body and high appellate court of the Methodist Episcopal Church, meets the first day of May every four years, and is constituted of one ministerial delegate for every forty-six ministers, and two lay delegates from each Annual Conference, in home and foreign countries alike. Young

2

Conferences, not measuring up to this numerical standard, are each entitled to elect and send one ministerial and one lay delegate to General Conference.

An Annual Conference is composed only of regular travelling ministers and accepted candidates for the ministry.

A Quarterly Conference is constituted of the travelling and local preachers, exhorters, class leaders, stewards, trustees, and superintendents of the Sunday schools. In large stations there is a "stewards' and leaders' meeting," the preacher in charge presiding and receiving reports from all the departments of work represented, or " of any who are sick, or any who walk disorderly," requiring the immediate attention of the pastors—a wonderful and most effective piece of ecclesiastical machinery.

The presiding elders come next to the bishops, and are sometimes, as in official records, designated by the initial letters P. E.

The office of an American presiding elder corresponds with that of a " chairman of a district " in English Methodism, each having supervision of about a dozen circuits or stations, with their ministers and official members. Every circuit and station must be embodied in one of the districts of an Annual Conference. The office of a chairman of a district differs, however, from that of a presiding elder in the fact that he has at the same time the pastoral charge of a circuit, and has only co-ordinate authority with the superintendent pastors in his district, except when invited by their courtesy to preside at their Quarterly Conferences, or is called by some exigency specially requiring his attention.

A presiding elder is practically a sub-bishop, and is appointed to his office annually by a bishop, or sent back into the ordinary pastorship by a bishop.

A presiding elder devotes his whole time to the supervision of his district. At the Annual Conference sessions the presiding elders are officially the advisers of the presiding bishop in making the appointments of all the ministers of the Conference for the ensuing year. The presiding elders are expected to hold all the Quarterly Meetings, four on each circuit or station per year, and to inspect carefully the written reports presented from every department of Church work.

All candidates for license to preach or to exhort must be examined and elected by a Quarterly or District Conference, and all candidates for admission in an Annual Conference must be examined and recommended by the same. The written certification in each case must bear the name of the presiding elder.

Class leaders are appointed, changed, or suspended by the preacher in charge of a circuit or station.

In Wesleyan Methodism a preacher in charge is styled " the superintendent " of a circuit.

The class leaders are subpastors, each having charge of a dozen or more of the members of the Church, each one of whom he is expected to see weekly.

The difference between a circuit and a station is simply in the fact that a circuit embraces in one pastoral charge a number of small villages or country preaching places. In large towns and cities, where a pastorate is limited to one principal church, with its mission outshoots, it is denominated a station; but the organic functions of both are the same. In England they are all called "circuits."

As before stated, my presiding elder, N. J. B. Morgan, appointed me to Monroe Circuit with Francis A. Harding. He was the same Brother Harding who, two years later, was suspended from the ministry by the Baltimore Annual Conference for refusing to manumit his slaves, and whose appeal to the General Conference of 1844 became the entering wedge that split in twain the Methodist Episcopal Church. While preparing to go to my appointment I received a letter from my presiding elder to this effect:

"MY DEAR BROTHER WILLIAM,—I want you to go to Franklin Circuit instead of Monroe. The junior preacher of Franklin Circuit spends so much of his time sparking round among the young ladies, and so little of his time in the work he was sent to do, that the stewards insist on his removal from the circuit. So I will send him to New Castle Circuit and give him a chance for his life, and send you to take his place on Franklin Circuit. Thomas H. Busey is preacher in charge. He is a good preacher, a powerful exhorter, a man of noble bearing every way. He will be a patient, kind, loving father to you. I am very glad to send you with Busey instead of Harding. But before you go to your appointment I want you to preach one round on Lexington Circuit. The preacher in charge will be absent a few weeks on other duties, and I want you to supply for him till he shall return to his circuit. 'Be of good courage; God is with you.'"

"A prophet is not without honour, save in his own country and in his own house." That is certainly the rule, but there are exceptional cases. Honour or no honour, the first circuit round of my itinerant ministry was in my native county, among the companions of my youth and my kindred, one of the appointments which I filled being at Lambert's meeting house, where I had held my membership in the Church from my boyhood, and another at Lexington, the county seat, among my schoolfellows. I had become quite accustomed to exhorting in the altar of our church there, at week-night prayer meetings, but had never entered the pulpit. So when I entered the sacred desk and faced a Sunday morning crowded audience I became as giddy-headed as a fresh sailor boy at the masthead and as blind as a bat on facing the sun. I shut my eyes and opened my mouth, and in my heart cried to God, and He filled me with divine light and love, gave me ready utterance, and we had a good time. The few weeks thus spent on my native circuit were an assuring preparation for the field of labour to which I had been appointed, which was a four-week circuit, seventy-five miles in extent.

My father gave me a good outfit—horse, saddle, bridle, and the indispensable saddle-bags of the itinerants of those days, well filled with clothing and books. Thus equipped, about the 1st of October, 1842, I kissed father and mother, brothers and sisters, good-bye, all of us weeping, and started out on an itinerant ministerial career that has already run through a period of about fifty-three years without a break, except a week or two that I was confined to my bed with the measles, over fifty years ago.

The first night I spent on Franklin Circuit was at the house of Esquire Jones, near Cowpasture River. He received me with genuine Virginia hospitality, and tried by the introduction of many topics to draw me out into some line of conversation; but I was too bashful and slow of speech to sustain a conversation with him on any subject, and misinterpreted his well-meant endeavour to interest me and thought he was quizzing me, and wished myself a hundred miles away.

Next day the squire and his family accompanied me to the church near by, where it had been duly announced that the young preacher was to preach his first sermon on the circuit. The house was crowded. I hoped to overcome the nightmare of embarrassment that choked me almost to strangulation by the preliminary exercises, but did not succeed. I announced a beautiful text from Isaiah, "Let the wicked forsake his way, and the unrighteous man his thoughts: and let him return unto the Lord, and He will have mercy upon him; and to our God, for He will abundantly pardon." I never in my life in trying to preach made a flat failure, but that day came the nearest to it of any effort I ever made. I called for my horse and got away from Jones's as quickly as possible. Mounted on my horse and off at good speed, my first impulse was to push on to regions unknown and engage in some employment to which I was better adapted; but I soon dismissed that as a temptation of the devil.

I was suffering from dyspepsia, and was as lean as a pelican in the wilderness. I had an over-scrupulous conscience, which hedged and hampered the narrow way, rendering it impassable for angels or men, and which upbraided me continually for not keeping in the path when I was in a perpetual struggle to do my very best. Despite my timid slowness of speech I was obliged to witness for Jesus to every man, woman, and child with whom I was brought in contact, even for a few minutes, and to beseech them to be reconciled to God. It was a good way to spend the passing moments and to make the most of my opportunities, and the Lord often helped me; but sometimes I missed it nearly as far as the pious barber who felt it his duty to talk to every man about his soul who came to be shaved. In many cases it worked very well; but one day, when a very highly cultured gentleman came in to be shaved, the barber's courage failed him. He spent a long time in applying the lather to the gentleman's face, and then strapped his razor to sharpen his courage till the lather on the man's face was nearly dry; then turning suddenly toward the gentleman, razor in hand, the barber said, "Are you prepared to die, sir?" The man sprang to his feet and ran away in great alarm, thinking the barber had gone crazy and was going to cut his throat. "He that winneth souls is wise."

Well, to return to our narrative, I may add that the embarrassments to which I have referred, and the burden of the work to which I was called and my conscious unfitness for it, rendered me of all men the most miserable during most of my waking hours; but I knew that I had been saved by the merits and might of Jesus, and that I had been moved by the Holy Spirit to preach the Gospel, and that I had not knowingly departed from God nor shunned to declare the whole counsel of God, and had great freedom of utterance in the pulpit, though not out of it; so I held on firmly to Jesus, and He led me by a way that I knew not, and I found out later that God and His people had a much higher appreciation of me than I had of myself.

From the hospitable home of Squire Jones I went to "Doe Hill," and got on better in my attempt to preach, having no big squire in the congregation to frighten me.

My next appointment was Crabbottom, which in numbers, intelligence and wealth was the heart of the circuit, Franklin being the head. Squire Amiss, an official member at Crabbottom, was a man of superior intelligence, very tall, well built, fine-looking, and a legislator of the State. I learned before my arrival at Crabbottom that Squire Amiss was a very attentive hearer and a good judge of preaching ability, and that his judgment had great weight throughout that community, and, indeed, through all the circuit, and that I would find out his opinion of me and of my preaching in fifteen minutes from the announcement of my text. When a new preacher arrived Amiss always took his seat in the altar with his back toward the pulpit, leaning forward, covering his face with his hands. If the preacher did not please him he never raised his face from his hands during the whole discourse. He was a gentleman, and would entertain the preachers with royal hospitality whether he liked their preaching or not. If a new preacher's discourse pleased him he would remove from his seat in the altar and take a sitting in a front pew, head up, and with a pleasant expression face the preacher. My great ambition was to please God rather than man, but I felt the importance also of pleasing men in hope of doing them good, and could not be indifferent as to how I would strike the squire.

So as I entered the pulpit on a bright Sabbath morning there sat Squire Amiss, his back against the pulpit, with his face in his hands, in a devotional attitude. The Holy Spirit helped that morning, as He did always when I tried properly to help myself and trusted Him. When I had preached about ten minutes Squire Amiss took his position in a front side pew, where preacher and people could see his glowing face. So I went on with all sails set before a good breeze, and followed the preaching with a good old-time Sunday morning class meeting, attended by all the members in from the country.

From Crabbottom I went to North Fork, a country appointment, where Father Patterson and Brother Houck, of the United Brethren Church, were holding a protracted meeting. I filled my appointment and helped them a couple of days. Brother Houck had been often to my father's house and felt a great interest in me on account of my father, and asked me many questions that he might be the better able to give me good advice. When he learned I was suffering from dyspepsia and was regularly taking medicine he said, "Oh, Brother William, don't take any more medicine as long as you live. I suffered in the same way when I entered the ministry, and made an apothecary's shop of my stomach, and it broke down my constitution and drove me prematurely into the impotency of old age. Oh, Brother William, don't take any more." I laid his impressive warning to heart, and was a total abstainer from physic for fourteen years, till, in California, I had a breaking out of nettle rash, and my wife, feeling uneasy, begged me to take a dose of pills.

More than twenty years elapsed after that before I took another dose, and I seldom ever took anything more than simple domestic remedies, till four years ago, on coming to Africa, to relieve the fears of my friends I took quinine, which, as a vegetable tonic, I have found to be of use occasionally. Brother Houck's good advice, I believe, was the means of adding many years to my life. It had nothing to do with the extreme view of faith healing, but led me to checkmate the bad effects of a chronic ailment, which I would not dignify by the name of sickness. By diligent attention to the laws of health, and being very careful about the quality and quantity of my diet, I have preserved my body from the effects of surfeiting and undue stimulants, and thus added length and strength to my life.

From North Fork I crossed the mountain to Franklin, and was introduced for the first time to my colleague, Thomas H. Busey, and his lovely Presbyterian wife. Oh, they were so kind to me! They melted my heart and won my ardent affections; there was neither undue familiarity nor reserve.

Having spent a few days in and about Franklin, Brother Busey and I set out on horseback to go to quarterly meeting at Rehobeth. We put in two days on the way, and commenced, as usual, on Saturday morning. We preached turn about, and Busey impressed me as an able preacher and powerful exhorter. We had a great "quarterly love feast" Sabbath morning at nine o'clock. Among our early converts at that meeting was James McCourt. He was a Scotchman by descent, but had been in America for nearly one hundred years. At the time he was "born again" he lacked three months of being ninety-nine years old. We will meet the old man again on my next circuit.

Well, from the quarterly meeting at Rehobeth I went down Back Creek to preach at Charlie Hamilton's, and arranged to spend the night preceding at Grandfather Hickman's. Grandmother had died but a week before, and went to heaven, where all good Presbyterians go when they die.

I was confidentially informed that grandfather had said, "If Will Taylor comes here pretending to preach I will send him home to his mother."

Grandfather was a mechanical genius. He owned a good farm and built on it a water-power mill with his own hands. He made guns and steel traps for catching bears and wolves, he made dulcimers and could play on them beautifully; he made also an abundance of hard cider from his extensive apple orchard, and often drank of it to excess and talked to himself. Dear old man, he tried to be good. His youngest son, Roger, with his wife Martha, occupied with him the old homestead.

Uncle Roger and Aunt Martha received me most cordially, but grandfather most coolly. He barely half shook my hand, and inquired, "How is your mother?"

"Very well, I thank you, grandfather, when I parted with her three weeks ago." He took a seat in a remote corner of the reception room as far from me as he could get.

I gave him special attention, and knew well his vulnerable points. So I said, "Grandfather, how is your mill working now?"

"Like a charm; she never did better work than she is doing now."

"Ah, she was put up right; she always did good work. Did you kill many deer last hunting season?"

"Not so many as when I was younger and could get over the mountains easier; but I killed some fine ones."

"How did you get on trapping for bears and wolves?"

Every question drew him several feet nearer to me, and soon he was seated close to me, and in a great glee of talk shook hands as heartily as though I had just arrived from home.

In the evening by invitation I conducted the family worship. Next morning, when I mounted to proceed down the creek to my appointment, grandfather, Uncle Roger, and Aunt Martha mounted their horses without a word of inquiry about the preaching or who was to preach. We had a good crowd and a blessed manifestation of the Holy Spirit at Hamilton's that day. I returned and spent the night at grandfather's. The old man could but talk of the sermon and of the strange things which were coming to pass, and with tears said, "My son William is a minister, my grandson William is now a minister too. All my children are members of the Church, and will, I trust, meet their mother in heaven. As for me, I want to be good, I try to be good. Oh, William, I want you to pray for me and preach in my house every time you come round. Preach at Hamilton's at your regular time in the day and preach here at night." I did as he desired. My father visited me later on and preached for me at Hamilton's and also at grandfather's. Aunt Martha was going into consumption, and I believe received a clear experience of salvation before I left the circuit. Grandfather wept much when I bade them farewell, and I trust gave himself to God and received Jesus. Both he and Aunt Martha died soon after.

The Conference year ended with the month of February, so I served but five months on that circuit. We had a good work of salvation all round. At a quarterly meeting held at Crabbottom I was duly examined and recommended to the Baltimore Annual Conference as a suitable person for admission into the travelling ministry.

About the 1st of April, 1843, I received a letter from my presiding elder informing me that I had been received on trial in the Baltimore Annual Conference, and had been appointed as the junior of Rev. Zane Bland, on the Deerfield Circuit. One of my appointments was but ten miles from my father's house. The circuit embraced the mountainous regions of Augusta, Rockbridge, Bath, and Pendleton Counties—poor farming districts and no towns, but a loving, plain, kind, appreciative class of mountaineers.

I made a full round on my circuit before my colleague arrived. The first place I struck was the house of Mr. E. Joseph. He was a harmless, easy-going Methodist brother who never would set the world on fire, but his wife Mary did in many places. Their two sons, Jim and Zeek, and their daughter Prudence, all Methodists, partook of the quiet nature of the father and much of the persuasive working power of their mother; a most estimable, loving family whose acquaintance I made at Panther Gap camp meeting, where I was saved a year and a half before. This dear family had settled in a new home about a fortnight before I rode up to their door and informed them that I was the junior preacher of their circuit. They received me joyfully, and said, "Our house must be one of your regular preaching appointments. We have no members in this neighbourhood outside of our own family. We are in the midst of a notoriously wicked people. The sheriff of this county is afraid to travel this road alone, and perhaps the Lord has sent us to settle down here to help you get some of them saved."

"All right," I replied, "I think we had better begin to-night. Let Brother Jim and Brother Zeek mount their horses and go through the neighbourhood and tell the people to come to-night to your house and hear the Gospel preached."

The old man sat down in the corner and laughed. The old woman shouted, "Hallelujah! Glory! Glory! Glory!" Prudie cried, and Jim and Zeek ran for their horses. I did some earnest crying to God to lead us, by His infinite wisdom and love, in our stupendous undertaking. The two principal rooms in the house would hold about forty persons, and that night we had them pretty well filled. We interested the people greatly with our singing, and I had liberty in proclaiming to them plain Gospel tidings. At the close I announced, "To-morrow, the Lord willing, I will preach to you here at 11 a.m. and at early candlelight in the evening. Tell all your people to come, and come yourselves." I and the Josephs kept the fire burning meantime, and next day, at 11 a.m., we had a house full of hearers. After preaching I said, "Now we will have a class meeting. But few of you know what sort of a meeting that is, but all of you may stay, and I'll show you what we call a class meeting." So they all, with one accord, stayed to "see the show." We had some lively singing, and got some of them to help us. I told a little of my own experience of the saving grace of God, and then took the roughs one by one. The first one I tackled was a burly-looking fellow with reddish sandy whiskers, clad in homespun, homewoven, and homemade woollen, dyed brown in ooze of walnut bark. I shook hands with him and said, "How are you?"

"Very well, I thank you. How does it go with yourself?"

"First-rate, thank the Lord! I am well, soul and body, and I am glad to make your acquaintance. Will you kindly give me your name?"

"Yes, sir; my name is Radcliffe."

"You are a farmer, I presume?"

"Yes, sir; I own a little farm about a mile from here."

"Well stocked, I hope, and under good cultivation."

"Yes, sir; I have cattle, horses, pigs, and sheep, and am putting in a pretty large crop of corn. My wheat and rye last year were above the average for this country."

"And your family?"

"Yes, sir; I have a wife and four children."

"All enjoying good health?"

"Yes, sir; no reason to complain."

"Every blessing we receive is a gift from our gracious God and Father. I am glad, Mr. Radcliffe, He thinks so much of you, and of your wife and children, as to bestow all these mercies on you. I hope you take off your hat to Him sometimes and say, 'Thank you.'"

"Well, sir; I am sorry to say I forgot that."

"What a pity! When we receive a gift from anybody, we always have the good manners that mother taught us to say, 'Thank you'; and yet you say for all God's gifts you have never said, 'Thank you.'"

"I am very sorry that I have been so forgetful, but I hope from this day I will think more of these things and learn to say 'Thank you' to God."

I prayed earnestly for the dear man, and he was in tears when I left him, and approached the next man in a similar way. So I went round and "class led" every man and woman in the house in a style that they all could understand, and yet in a spirit of loving earnestness that the Holy Spirit alone can inspire. At night the crowd and the interest were at the flood. Next day I preached again at 11 a.m. and at night. In the four days we had eight or ine of those desperate people saved, and a class organised. We never had a set series of "special services" at Joseph's, but on every round my colleague and I preached a few times at their house. We organised a Church of about fifty of the new converts of that neighbourhood.

Zane Bland was an unmarried man, about four years older in the ministry than myself—one of the blandest men socially I ever knew, full of eccentric wit that would, it was said, make a horse laugh. He was one of a family of twenty-four Blands, brought up on the "North Fork" of the Potomac.

Zane weighed over two hundred pounds, very strong, and was swift in a foot race. We often, after preaching and labouring with seekers of salvation till 10 p.m., got something to eat, and then for healthy exercise tried our strength in a wrestle or our speed in a foot race. He was fleshy, and I was lean as a greyhound. In a short race or wrestle he had the advantage. I took the measure of his wind, and always arranged to give myself time to run or to wrestle him out of breath and surpass him. He was a brave man. Once when holding a revival meeting at Floyd Court House, West Virginia, a big bully of a fellow tried to break up the meeting. Zane politely requested him to desist, but he became furious and made a pass at Bland to knock him down. The preacher parried the stroke, caught him by the collar, and threw him on his back in the aisle; then three or four of the brethren seized him and led him out of doors. It was a cold winter night, and he was minus his hat. Brother Bland went on singing and working away with the penitents as though nothing had happened; but the ruffian outside was storming and swearing and daring Bland to put his nose outside of the house, and was thus from without seriously disturbing the meeting. So Bland gave the work in charge of a brother and slipped out, and as the desperado was calling for Bland he stepped up close to him and responded, "What do you want with me, sir?"

"Oh, Mr. Bland, is that you, sir?"

"Yes, sir; what do you want with me?"

"Nothing, Mr. Bland, only that you will please to pass my hat out to me."

On my first visit to Red Holes, I rode up to the country chapel, hitched my horse, and walked in, and there sat two old ladies. I introduced myself, and they said, "No one expects the new preachers so soon; having to make two hundred miles from Conference on horseback, they can't be here for a fortnight yet."

"Well, sisters, I am one of them, and I am here. Where are all your people?"

"All our men are engaged at a logrolling a quarter of a mile west of here. Some of the women are helping to prepare the supper for the logrollers, and the rest are at home."

"Well, sisters, I can't come all the way here to Red Holes for nothing, so I'll tell you what we will do; you go round and tell all the women of this neighbourhood that the young preacher of the circuit, sent by the bishop, will preach here to-night at ' early candle-lighting,' and let everybody come and hear his message. Meantime I will go to the logrolling and tell all the men, and we'll have a crowd here to-night and a good time." The dear old sisters waked up to the subject and spread the news widely.

A logrolling is a free thing, requiring strength of muscle, but no ceremony of etiquette. In that country timber had no marketable value. When a farmer cleared a forest the great trees were cut into logs about fifteen feet long, and when the chopping was all done and all the brush piled in heaps and burned, then the men for many miles came by invitation and rolled the logs into great heaps so that they could be burned. So I rode up to the edge of the clearing, hitched my horse, and climbed the high " staked and ridered fence," and as I advanced to the front I picked up a handspike and went to work and exhibited my strength and superior skill in putting the big logs where they were wanted. I saw the mountaineers eying me and talking to each other in undertones, expressing great wonder who the stranger might be. I let them guess and wonder while I worked away till the big job was nearly completed and the men began to draw together within range of my voice. Then I announced: "The young preacher sent to your circuit by the bishop will preach in the chapel to-night. Get through with your supper as quickly as you can and all come come and hear the young preacher. He is two weeks in advance of time, but he is one of that sort, always trying to take time by the forelock."

"Are you sure the preacher has come ? "

" Oh yes, indeed ; there is no doubt on that subject."

"Wonder if a great logroller like you can be the preacher ? "

" Come and see."

In that afternoon I got a grip on that people more than equivalent to six months' hard preaching and pastoral work. We had a crowded house then and every time I preached at Red Holes ; also a big revival and many saved.

One day when preaching at Red Holes I saw in my congregation James McCourt, who was saved a year before at our quarterly meeting at Rehobeth, on Franklin Circuit, at the age of ninety-eight years and nine months. So now he was one hundred years old less three months. At the close he ran up and shook hands with me.

" You are abiding in Jesus, Father McCourt ? "

"Oh yes, Brother Taylor, and He is becoming more and more precious to me every day."

" How wonderful that He has spared you so many years and in such vigour ! "

" Yes, I never had the headache in my life, and no serious illness of any sort. I walked across four mountains to-day to hear you preach once more before you leave your circuit."

Meantime he tripped along by my side in a glee of talk like a boy.

"If the Lord spares me three months longer I will complete my hundredth year. Dr. Ruckner says he is going to have a celebration on my birthday, completing a century, and have me run, to see how fast a man of my years can get over the ground."

I was wonderfully interested in the dear little man, one of my first early converts, but I saw him no more. About thirty-five years after I met Brother Bevens and wife in Chicago. Sister Bevens was a daughter of Charlie Hamilton, at whose house I preached on Back Creek. They were well acquainted with James McCourt.

"Well, Brother Bevens, tell me about him."

He replied: "I was at the celebration Dr. Ruckner got up on the centenary of James McCourt. The old man was in perfect health, happy in God, and cheerful as a lark. The friends made up a purse of one hundred dollars to give him as a token of their love and respect for him, but they said, 'We want to see you run, and if you run one hundred yards in five minutes we will give you a present of one hundred dollars.' The distance was measured carefully, the signal for starting sounded, and the old man ran the hundred yards in three minutes instead of five. When the dear old man was one hundred and three years old he came out to Queen Anne County, north-west of Chicago, to visit some of his grandchildren— a good old Christian man, who had the happy art of cheerfulness that made everybody about him cheerful. After a visit of several months, when he wanted to return to Virginia, the railway company were so pleased with his spirit and bearing that they gave him a free pass back to his home. He lived four years after that, and died in the Lord at the age of one hundred and seven years."

Brother Bland and I wrought hard and had a good soul-saving advance at every appointment. The people were very kind to us, but were not able to give us much money.

When Zane Bland and I closed our work on Deerfield Circuit I went with him to visit his people on "North Fork." Then Zane and I travelled together on horseback to the city of Winchester, and there took stage for Washington city. The Conference held its session that year in the old mother station in that city, known as "The Foundry." It was my first visit to a large city, except the city of Richmond in boyhood, when I steered a boat for my father down James River to that city. Nearly everything that I saw at the capital struck me as exceedingly grand, especially the great department buildings.

At that Conference I became acquainted with Rev. Adam Miller, now of Chicago. He was a young German itinerant, and about as green as I was myself. At the Conference missionary meeting, held in the Foundry Church, Adam was put up to make one of the principal addresses of the occasion. He was tall and lean. His coat had been worn to the thread, and the ladies, he said, had reorganised it, turning the inside out, so that it looked like a new coat. He stood before the vast assembly and hesitated and stammered and balked, till they set up a great laughing all over the house. Then Adam said: "Friends, you must have patience with me. I'll get into the subject pretty soon now. You see, I am an awkward Dutchman, and I am dreadfully scared." With that and an approving laugh he got loose, and really made the master speech of the evening.

The Baltimore Conference, with three hundred ministers, was in those days the largest, and in revival power the most effective, Conference in American Methodism. Its annual sessions usually covered two or three weeks. On the great occasion of reading out the appointments of such a body of ministers this was my first experience of such a sight. I was greatly interested in reading the features of the men who were in dread of a *dis*appointment; a feeling I never shared, for any circuit was good enough for me, and I had no anxiety on the subject. When Fincastle Circuit was named the bishop read out distinctly, "B. N. Brown, William Taylor." It was a good appointment in Botetourt County, and next adjoining my native circuit.

I had several blessed ingatherings of newly converted souls on Fincastle Circuit, among whom was the young lady who subsequently became my wife; also her brother and three sisters, all of whom remain steadfast in the faith to this day.

CHAPTER III

ON THE SWEET SPRINGS CIRCUIT

My colleague and I closed our term of service on Fincastle Circuit about the 1st of February, 1845. Conference came annually, early in March, and it was a hard time for itinerant preachers' horses. The roads were often deep in mud one day and hard frozen the next. We had that year over two hundred miles to travel to Baltimore city, where the Conference was held.

I had a good roan-coloured young horse, brought up on my father's farm, and, in company with several other young preachers, the trip to Conference, though laborious, was quite enjoyable. We spent our nights on the way in the homes of our people, who were always glad to entertain the preachers and feed their horses as they journeyed to and from Conference.

The Conference was held in Exeter Street Church.

I now began to make the acquaintance of the distinguished men of the Conference, but in my very humble opinion of myself I would not presume to approach one of them personally, unless on an errand of duty; however, they all seemed to know me and shook hands with me on every opportunity. I could not account for it, but indirectly learned that when Brown Morgan, my presiding elder, presented my name two years before as a candidate for admission into their ranks, he made a speech which impressed the Conference greatly in my favour; so, while I felt myself to be " little and unknown," I maintained an elevation of six feet in their midst, and was well known. I was told Morgan closed his speech on my case by saying, " He is a young man whom the sun never finds in bed." As he sat down Bishop Soule—presiding—arose and said, " Mark my words, brethren, you will hear from that young man again."

I was at my father's house, two hundred miles away at that time, and this incident did not come to my ears till years afterwards, when it helped to account for the special interest the old men of the Conference took in me.

When the appointments of preachers for the ensuing year were read, the name of a new circuit on the Rockingham District was announced, " Sweet Springs Circuit." The tag ends of two old circuits were cut off and added to Sweet Springs Valley, Dutch

Corner, Irish Corner, and a few other neglected corners not included in any circuit, and organised into the new circuit.

When the bishop announced the new name, "Sweet Springs Circuit," there was a flutter among some of the mountain boys, who were in dread of an appointment to it, knowing it to be a very hard, and perhaps hopeless, undertaking. The appointments were read out slowly, so that all who wished could write them down in his own memorandum book. One brother sat on the pulpit stairs in a very conspicuous place, and was engaged in writing down the whole list, but when his own name was announced in connection with a place he dreaded, he uttered one emphatic word of dissent and dropped his pen to the floor and never picked it up. I had nothing to mar my enjoyment of the scene, for I did not care a feather where they sent me, knowing that in every place there were sinners to be called to repentance. When asked where I would like to be sent my reply was, "Not to a fat, flourishing circuit, but to one where there are plenty of sinners." So on this occasion the announcement came exactly to my liking, "Sweet Springs Circuit, William Taylor."

It was whispered round, " Poor Brother Taylor will starve on the so-called Sweet Springs Circuit. The people live there principally on blackberries, and they have no money."

The only chapel I found on the circuit was at Gap Mills, and that a " Union Church." A man there had a flour mill, sawmill, distillery, and store of dry goods and groceries. That was the nearest approach to a town within my bounds.

Sweet Springs was a notable watering-place and summer resort for pleasure, and for health-seekers from all parts, and hence large buildings for their accommodation; but out of the season there was scarcely anybody to be found there but the keeper of the hotel. Sweet Springs Valley was about ten miles long and three miles wide, between two ranges of mountains, and was occupied by small farmers, who lived for the most part by the roadside, their farms lying in the rear of their residences. They had learned much from the refined summer pleasure-seekers which was not refining nor elevating to them. They were noted for frivolity, dancing, and drinking. There was one Roman Catholic residing in the valley, and one woman and her daughter who had somewhere joined the Methodists as seekers of salvation; all the rest of the population of the valley were "outsiders" not connected with any Church. We had but about a dozen members at Gap Mills, embracing an excellent family by the name of Carpenter. Jake Weekline and wife lived on the backbone of the Alleghany range between Gap Mills and Sweet Springs Valley. They were Methodists, and their house became a preaching place. I found a few more at Second Creek. There we had William Smith and Aleck Carson, both local preachers. Smith was a good, modest, quiet man and consistent Christian.

Carson was equally pious, a man of great originality and native mental power. He was a cooper by trade, and had been reputed the most profane swearer in all that region of profanity. But he went to a Methodist revival a few years before I met him and was awakened and saved. He at once went to the preacher, and in presence of the congregation said, "Will you allow me to join the Church?"

"Certainly, brother; I'll put your name down now."

"Oh, I am so glad. I have been so bad I was afraid you would not allow me to join; I do want to be a good man, and I need all the help I can get."

So he returned home rejoicing, established family worship, and was getting on nicely, till one day, when setting up a barrel, the brace hoop slipped, and down went his staves into a heap, and before he could collect his thoughts he uttered an oath.

He threw himself on the ground and rolled and groaned, and cried for mercy till the compassionate Friend of sinners healed and restored him. He never slipped again. He said nobody ever spoke to him about his soul till he went to the mourners' bench at the Methodist meeting; but as soon as it was noised abroad that Aleck Carson had joined the Methodists, "scarce a day passed that some Baptist or seceder from the Scotch Kirk did not come into my shop to debate with me on disputed points of doctrine."

He said to each one, "You see, my friend, I am only a babe, but I want to learn all I can; so you will please state your point plainly and your proof texts, and I will write them down in my memorandum book and give them due consideration; but as I am a young learner you must give me time." So he got Watson's *Institutes*, and carefully studied every point with their proof texts and their plain interpretation. He was so mild and teachable that each party seemed to think they had captured him. He mastered the arguments on every question raised before he attempted a reply; then as a master in theology he mowed down his opponents as he would grass in a hayfield: not one of them ever faced him a second time.

One day a reverend Calvinistic minister, a very learned and able man, rode to his shop door and said, "Mr. Carson, I have come five miles to have a theological debate with you." "All right, your reverence; wait till I tighten the hoops of this barrel, and I'll go with you to the house." So he got his barrel set up, laid aside his apron, put on his coat, and conducted the preacher to his humble home. In two hours Carson logically and scripturally took the ground from under the Calvinist, and the learned divine held up his hands in astonishment and said, "Oh, Mr. Carson, I've never met your like before; you must be the greatest man in the Methodist Church."

"Oh no, sir. There are plenty of niggers in the Methodist Church who know much more than I do. The trouble is not in the strength of my argument, but in the utter weakness of your cause."

After that no man dared to ask him any more questions.

I do not remember the aggregate number of members I found on Sweet Springs Circuit; I think somewhere between thirty and forty, all of moderate attainments and limited means, but most confiding and kind.

As soon as I preached around at all the old appointments on Sweet Springs Circuit I began to acquaint myself with the possibilities of extension.

I said, " Where can I find a preaching place in Sweet Springs Valley ? "

One replied, " The only place is the dining hall of the hotel at the Springs. A Methodist preacher tried it there a few times many years ago."

" Ah, indeed ; and did he get many people converted there ? "

" None that we ever heard of."

" Then that is not the place for me. I must go where I can at least have a fair chance to get somebody saved."

I mounted my roan and rode through the valley to find the largest farmhouse, and asked permission to preach in it. The largest house I could find was on a crossroad, nearly half a mile back from the main road. I sat on my horse and called out the man of the house and told him who I was and what was the object of my call.

He replied, " I am no Christian, but would not object to your preaching here if my wife was well, but she is very sickly, and could not bear to have company about the house." He did not invite me to dismount; but I thanked him for his kind expressions and bade him good-bye.

I returned to the main road and called at the house of Dan Weekline. Dan was not religious, but was a brother to Jake Weekline, before named. Mrs. Weekline said her husband was not at home that day, but invited me to put up and feed my horse and stay for dinner, which I did cheerfully. During the dinner hour I got from her all the information I could in regard to the people residing in the valley, and asked permission to preach in her house.

She replied, " I have no objections, and will speak to my husband on his return and let you know."

" Very good ; then please send me word to my appointment at Jake Weekline's next Sabbath afternoon, and if your husband consents give notice to all the people in this region that I will, the Lord willing, preach in your house next Wednesday, at eleven o'clock."

Receiving a cordial invitation from Dan and his wife to have a regular appointment at that house, I went on Wednesday, as had been announced, and found two rooms of the house crowded.

The interest was so great that I announced a Sabbath afternoon appointment there for every alternate week, " beginning with next Sabbath week at three o'clock."

On the first Sunday afternoon there I found the crowd so great that not half of them could get into the house, so I preached in the shade of a sugar maple grove near by. A gracious influence attended the preaching. I announced that " at 3 p.m., two weeks from to-day, I will, God willing, preach again under these trees, and you who have families and who want to dedicate yourselves and your little children to God may bring your children, and I will baptise them." In two weeks I had still a larger crowd, and baptised seventeen children. I then announced, " When I come again I will preach to you morning and evening on both Saturday and Sabbath, and thus each day for a week. All of you come and bring your friends."

I said to the Weeklines and a few others at tea that evening, " God is going to give us an ingathering of souls, and I will organise here the biggest class on the circuit and appoint Joe Carson the class leader for it." My words created a great laugh. Joe Carson was brother to Aleck, a six-footer of enormous proportions, an avowed bitter opposer of the Methodists, and reputed to be the most profane swearer in the valley. I was aware of all these things by common rumour, but I knew he had a combination of the best natural qualities of any man in the valley for that position, and would therefore be the man whom the Lord would save and call to that responsible leadership. It was not a prophecy but a calculation with me.

When I returned to commence my series of special services, Father Perkins and two young ladies, one of whom was a New England schoolmarm, teaching in Monroe County, came to help me for a few days. The ladies visited from house to house and did us good service. The schoolmarm also gave me a few copies of *The Guide to Holiness* then published in Cornhill, Boston, which were of great service to me personally. Saturday we had a large attendance and a deep awakening. Sunday forenoon, after preaching, I called for seekers to bow at a row of benches set for their convenience, and eleven sought with cries and tears, and about half of them received Jesus and testified to an experience of salvation.

When I came to preach that Sabbath evening I found the people in great commotion. A Mrs. Carlisle had gone forward at the morning meeting and obtained peace with God. When John, her husband, heard of it he came in a great rage and wanted to whip somebody—anybody who dared to meddle with him or his wife. His wife, he said, had already disgraced herself by mixing with the accursed Methodists. He couldn't and wouldn't stand it. " If my wife persists in this thing I'll leave her; I won't live with such a woman." Some of my friends wanted to take hold of John and lead him away, but I said, "Oh no; let the dear fellow alone. He will come to himself before the week is out "

On Tuesday night John was rolling and screaming in despair. He said, " I have committed the fatal blasphemy against the Holy Ghost, and will certainly be in hell very soon."

We assured him, " Jesus loves you and is now bending over you in sympathy and will take you into His arms as He did the little children—put His saving hands on you, pray for you, reconcile you to God. He will take you into His kingdom and family and bless you with joy unspeakable; and He will do it all to-night." John received and trusted Him, and was saved that night. He and his happy wife and about thirty others who were saved during that week joined our Church.

That gave me already the biggest class on the circuit, but no one tall enough above the rest to be a leader. Joe Carson came about three times and went away in bad temper, and came no more during the series.

Next in order was a series of services at Jake Weekline's, on the mountain, where but few people lived. We had, if I remember accurately, seven converted, one of them a black boy living with the Weeklines, who became an exemplary Christian. Joe Carson came two or three times to that series of meetings and was affected by the preaching, but ran home to wear off his convictions.

My next series of meetings was at a schoolhouse down the creek a few miles below Gap Mills. I forget the name of the place. I preached twice on Saturday. Sabbath morning we had a great crowd, not a third of whom could get into the house; so I preached in the shade of a large spruce pine-tree. I mounted a box with my back to the huge forester and laid my Bible on a small dead limb projecting from its trunk. Looking over my audience, I saw, to my agreeable surprise, Joe Carson and his wife. They had come ten miles on horseback that morning to attend my meetings; so I thanked God, and in my heart prayed earnestly for them. After preaching there in the open air that forenoon I invited seekers to come forward for instruction and the prayers of those who knew God, and kneel at a row of benches set for the purpose. About a dozen came promptly, and among them was Mrs. Carson. Joe saw her down, and sprang to his feet and ran to the woods like a wounded deer. He ran about one hundred yards and fell prostrate on the ground. A brother saw him tumble, and went to him and found him crying and begging God not to kill him, but spare him and give him another chance.

Three or four professed conversion that morning, but the odds against us appeared to be very great. We had the sheriff of Monroe County, a Mr. C——, son of the richest man, it was said, in the country, and Mr. C—— busied himself in going through the congregation urging the people "not to be humbugged by this babbler."

At night, not having so great a crowd, we had our meeting in the schoolhouse, which would seat about one hundred persons. When I called for seekers at the close of the preaching Joe Carson walked across the rear end of the house and took his wife by the arm, and side by side they came and knelt at the penitent form. Mrs. Carson and a few others were sweetly saved that night, and testified to an experience of the saving power of Jesus.

That forenoon, after preaching, when I invited seekers, Carson and a half dozen others came promptly forward. As we were in the act of kneeling to pray I saw the sheriff, who had been moving round to dissuade persons from going forward, coming in a rage to the front, and I said : " Hold on, brethren ; don't kneel down yet." By that time the sheriff seized a young woman who was kneeling as a seeker by the arm, and I said, " Mr. C——, is that lady your wife ?"

" No."

" Is she your sister or daughter ?"

" No."

" Then what have you to do with her ?"

" She is my cousin, and I'm going to have her away from here. This is no fit place for her to be, and I will have her out of this. I don't believe in this thing of forcing people."

" Oh no, Mr. C—— ; I don't believe in trying to force anybody to renounce his sins and seek forgiveness from God. Ask her if she was forced, and if she says ' Yes,' then take her away at once."

He did not put the question, but a lady near by did, and she replied, " I came freely, of my own accord, and I must be allowed to seek the forgiveness of my sins."

" She is too young," shouted the sheriff, " to act for herself in such matters."

" Oh, you see she is not a child, but a young woman, well understanding what she is about ; but if you take the responsibility, Mr. C——, of standing for her, will you stand for her in the day of judgment ?"

" No ; but I'll have her away from here."

" Now, Mr. C——, take your seat beside the young lady, and see all that is done, and hear all that may be said to her, and see that she has fair play. Here is a good seat, Mr. C——." But he let the lady go and returned to the rear. As he passed me I said, " Mr. C——, the young lady wants to be saved, and as you need salvation as well as the rest of us we will pray that you too may seek and find the pearl of great price."

" I need it, Mr. Taylor, as badly as anybody else."

Then I said, " Let us pray."

The powers of darkness gave way, and the work of God went on in full tide. Mr. C—— was well acquainted with Joe Carson, and witnessed his awful struggles that day as he seemed to be possessed of " many devils, which threw him down and tore him." For half an hour or more he lay prostrate on the floor and groaned and frothed at the mouth like a man with hydrophobia, but finally gave up and accepted Jesus as a present, all-powerful Saviour, and then arose and plainly testified to a sweet deliverance from the power of devils and sin.

The young lady that Mr. C—— tried to turn back testified also for Jesus as her Saviour.

When I pronounced the benediction that day Mr. C—— came up and took me by the hand and said, " Mr. Taylor, I want you to go home with me."

" Certainly, Mr. C—— ; I'll go with pleasure." The devil whispered to me, "He wants to seek private revenge." I replied in my mind, "If he does he will not find it."

Mr. C—— talked all the way home and after our arrival, telling me how he had been brought up to hate the Methodists, and how for years he had made it his business to oppose them.

"I now see that I was in the dark and doing the work of the devil. I see my folly, and whether I shall join them or not, I certainly shall defend them henceforth, for I see they are right."

I afterwards baptised his wife and children, but unhappily Mr. C—— did not fully surrender himself to God, at least not while I remained on the circuit; but he never missed a meeting which I held in his neighbourhood.

Mrs. Carson told me afterwards how she and Joe were induced to ride ten miles on that memorable Sunday morning to attend my meetings. During the night she dreamed that she, her husband and children, were lost in a desert and famishing for want of water. They searched for water till they had become utterly exhausted and sank into hopeless despair; then all of a sudden they heard a shout of a familiar voice. "Oh, that is the voice of Mr. Taylor; how strange that he should be away out in this desert! Hear what he says: '"Ho, every one that thirsteth, come ye to the waters!"' And as I looked," said Mrs. Carson, "with longing hope in the direction whence came the voice I beheld a flowing stream of the most transparent water that I had ever seen, and said, 'We shall go and drink and live, and not die in this desert;' and in my joy I awoke and awakened my husband and told him my dream and the interpretation thereof. If we stop in the desert of sin in which we have lived so long we shall utterly and for ever perish and lead our children to destruction. We must go and let Mr. Taylor lead us to the 'river of pure water of life, clear as crystal.' So we hastened to get ready, and mounted our horses and went to the meeting, where we drank freely and were led out of the desert of sin and death."

Our next series of special services was held at the house of old Father Perkins.

At the close of my week of special services in Sheriff C——'s neighbourhood I was announced to commence a series at the Perkins appointment; but on account of the number of bright conversions to God that week, and the deep awakening in the community at large, and the subordinate consideration that I had promised to celebrate a marriage there on Thursday of the week ensuing, I concluded that the Perkins people would accept for the present a four-days' meeting, and allow me to follow, as it seemed to me, the manifest leading of the Spirit, and resume work in C——'s neighbourhood on Wednesday night, attend to the marriage celebration on Thursday, and go on with the meetings as long as the Lord would give us signal success there. So I adjourned that series on Friday night, to be resumed on Wednesday night of the following week. Next day I went on and preached at the house of Father Perkins, according to appointment. After preaching I gave them an account of the blessed work of God in C——'s neighbourhood and the liberty I had taken in shortening the time of their series at present, to be resumed as quickly as the Lord would permit, and then be protracted indefinitely.

Father Perkins was a plain, blunt, but good man of the old school, a local preacher in our Church, who in summer heat would take off his coat and preach in his shirt sleeves. He took the floor, and in the most earnest and emphatic manner entered his protest against any change of the plan.

I could make no defence, but said, "I thought you would be so glad to hear of the opening work of God in a hitherto fruitless field that you would, after a series of four days, cheerfully consent to let me follow what seems to me to be a manifest leading of the Spirit of God; but as you hold me to the original agreement, as before announced, I must fulfil it to the letter."

I was cornered, and, being young and inexperienced, Satan took occasion to torment me. I was grieved to hazard the possibilities of the progressing work in the other neighbourhood, and was committed, by public announcement, for preaching on the same day and hour at two places twenty miles apart, and no opportunity of recalling the one ignored by Daddy Perkins. So I cried to the Lord in my trouble, and He heard my cry. It was a greater grief to me to be unable to fulfil a promise made to a man or to a congregation of men and women than many are prepared to appreciate. So I cried to the Lord, and He gave me deliverance far exceeding the immediate occasion of my distress.

From the day of my restoration to filial union with God, four years before, I earnestly sought holiness of heart—perfect love to God. I saw that by the redemptive covenant and provision in Jesus Christ, by commands and promises, by invitations and admonitions, by the recorded experiences and testimonies of holy men of old, it was plainly taught in the Bible as the common privilege and duty of all believers. I carefully read Wesley's "Plain Account" and the like narrative of Adam Clarke, John Fletcher, and a host of credible witnesses, and was greatly enlightened and encouraged. I heard the subject preached by many of our ministers, and saw Rev. William Prettyman and a few others invite believers to come forward as seekers just as sinners were invited to do in seeking pardon, and I always responded to such calls and went forward for entire sanctification, but without success. For my own information, and as a preparatory qualification for the intelligible instruction of others in similar complications, I had to suffer a while.

Peter, by the inspiration of the divine Teacher, says, "The God of all grace, who hath called us unto His eternal glory by Christ Jesus, after that ye have suffered a while, make you perfect, stablish, strengthen, settle you." So I was in this intermediate school. I had been pardoned and regenerated and was being preserved by the power of Jesus from sinning, without one voluntary departure from Him during the four years of my renewed allegiance; but I was tormented by an over scrupulous conscience and other involuntary disabilities, and deprived of settled peace.

The principle of obedience was wrought in me by the Holy Spirit amid frequent struggles and painful apprehension on account of the evil of inherent depravity. It was sincere and unreserved from the beginning, but I needed light to apply and strength to fulfil it.

I had to learn the difference between essential human nature and the carnal mind. The one, according to God's design in His original creation of man and in His new creation by the Holy Spirit, is to be developed and utilised for its legitimate purposes; the other, an extraneous diabolical thing, to be destroyed by the might of the Almighty and separated from us for ever. Yet the carnal mind, though foreign, has so diffused itself through our whole being and so identified itself with every part of it, that it requires special divine enlightenment to enable us to discriminate clearly between these two opposite things. The human body has five senses. They are a part of God's creative ideal; hence, essential and legitimate. It has three appetites, with the affections which connect them with our mental and moral constitution.

We have, also, mental appetencies, with their affections—the mental appetency for knowledge, the sinful lust of which would manifest itself in self-conceit, pedantry, and pride; the mental appetency for property, the lust of which is covetousness and its train of abuses; the mental appetency for power, which in lustful excess results in tyranny and oppression; and so on through a long list of this class, together with another class adapted to the relations we sustain to society, to the state, to the family, to our neighbours in general.

Our mental and moral constitution is specially endowed with higher attributes essential to our relations to God and to eternity. All these belonged legitimately to the constitution of man before "sin entered," and will be retained in our sanctified being when "cleansed from all filthiness of the flesh and spirit."

The carnal mind is that diabolical infusion which permeates all these appetites, appetencies, attributes, and affections, and fills them with enmity to God and leads the unsaved into all manner of misapplications, lustful excesses, and abuses, dishonouring to God and destructive to man. Hence, one leading characteristic of holiness is light—divine light—to enable us to perceive clearly what the Holy Sanctifier has come to do for us; what to destroy and remove, what to retain, purify, and adjust to their legitimate purposes, so that we may receive and trust the Lord Jesus for all that He came to do for us, and no more.

The principle of obedience must not only be enlightened, but must be in proportion to the enlightenment, enlarged to the measure of full concurrence in practical obedience to all perceivable duties in the field of enlarged vision, and must, moreover, be perfected so as to accept at all times the behests of God, covering all possibilities in His will; not those only which come within the radius of an enlarged vision, but those in the immeasurable margin beyond; not only our legal obligations to God and man as defined by the decalogue, but the broadest application of the new commandment as exemplified in the life and death of Jesus Christ.

On the eve of His departure from the world, in a solemn charge to His disciples He said, "A new commandment give I unto you, that ye love one another as I have loved you." What was the measure of His love for us? Love up to the legal lines of the Ten Commandments? On those legal principles He would have stood on His rights and would have executed judgment upon us according to the law. He would have retained His glory and stayed in His own happy home in the bosom of His eternal Father, and sent us to the place prepared for the devil and for all his followers. But under the new commandment, which does not antagonise our legal rights and duties, He voluntarily and gladly gave up His rights, and, under the weight of our wrong-doing, became obedient unto death, even the death of the cross

To discriminate clearly between temptation and sin was another lesson I had to learn in the school of Christ under the tuition of the Holy Spirit. Christ "was in all points tempted like as we are, yet without sin." It is not sin in us to be tempted in all points like as He was, but in yielding to temptation, which always entails sin and condemnation.

I tried the theory of a gradual growth out of sin into holiness, but found from sad experience it was not in the nature of sin to grow out, but to grow in and grow on, and bring forth fruit unto death, and that it had to be restrained till totally extirpated by the Holy Sanctifier.

A sincere spirit of legalism, more than anything else, trammelled my faith and prevented the Holy Spirit from perfecting that which was lacking in my faith. It was not theoretical but practical legalism. I did not for a moment trust to anything I had done, but, under cover of vows and covenants to be holy, I was really trusting to what I was going to do. To the best of my knowledge I presented my body, my whole being, on God's altar, and worked myself nearly to death trying to be holy. I was often blessed and comforted, and hoped at the moment that I had found the pearl of perfect love, but soon perceived I was mistaken. I had been justified by faith, kept in a justified relation to God by faith; my ministry from its commencement had been attended by the soul-saving power of Jesus, and why I failed to cross over into the promised land of perfect love was a profound puzzle to me; but I was getting light and gathering strength in the struggle.

In the month of August, 1845, I attended a camp meeting on Fincastle Circuit, the old camp where my presiding elder, three years before, appointed me to the work of an itinerant minister. On my way to the camp meeting I saw that in connection with an entire consecration of my whole being to God, which I had been sincerely trying to gain from the beginning, I should pay no particular attention to my emotional sensibilities nor to their changes, nor to the great blessings I was daily receiving in answer to prayer, but should simply accept the Bible record of God's provisions and promises as an adequate basis of faith, and on the evidences contained in these divine credentials receive and trust the divine Saviour for all that He had come to do for me, and nothing less. I was then and there enabled to establish two essential facts: (1) To be true to Jesus Christ; (2) to receive and trust Him to be true to me. So there, on my horse in the road, I began to say more emphatically than ever before, "I belong to God. Every fibre of my being I consecrate to Him. I consent to perfect obedience. I have no power to do anything toward saving myself, but in utter helplessness I receive and trust Jesus for full salvation."

Then the tempter said, "Take care; don't go too fast; there may be reservations in your consecration you don't think of."

I replied, "I surrender everything I can think of and everything I can't think of. I accept a *principle* of obedience that covers all possibilities in the will of God."

"But you don't feel anything different from your ordinary experience?"

"The Word of God is sure. On the evidence it contains I receive and trust the Blesser without any stipulation as to the blessing or the joyful feeling it may bring."

I went on to the camp meeting maintaining my two facts as the Lord gave me power to do, without the aid of joyous emotional sensibility or feeling.

My dear father was there as an earnest worker. I was delighted to be with him, for besides being a kind father he was in Jesus a brother to me. I met many old friends at that meeting, for it was on the circuit I served the year preceding, and found many sources of real pleasure; but my struggle within was so severe that I had but little enjoyment of any sort.

In conversation one evening at that meeting with Aunt Eleanor Goodwin, a saintly woman, I said: "In the years of my unbelief and apostasy I acquired such a habit of doubting that I have never yet been able fully to conquer it."

Instantly the taunt of the temper rang with an echo through the domain of my spirit nature: "Can't, can't; you can't do it."

I saw that I had inadvertently made a concession which Satan was using to defeat my faith, and I said: "Aunt Eleanor, in saying that I have not been able to conquer my old habit of doubting I see I have made a mistake. God commands us to believe and be saved. He does not command impossibilities; so in regard to believing——receiving Christ—for all that He has engaged to do for me, I have said 'I can't believe' for the last time. I can do whatsoever He commands; for He hath said, 'My grace is sufficient for thee.'" So I at once revised my spiritual vocabulary and ignored all the "can'ts," "ifs, and "buts," as used by doubters in regard to the grand possibilities of the grace of God. That was a victory for my faith, but I felt no special cleansing power within.

At the close of the camp meeting I returned to my circuit, steadily maintaining my facts. Through the series of my special services in Sweet Springs Valley, at Dan Weekline's, where we had the blessed work before described, and the series at Jake Weekline's on the mountain, and in the series of Sheriff C——'s neighbourhood, I stood by my two facts, as Abraham stood by his offered sacrifice, in spite of smothering darkness and devouring fowls, but I felt no assurance of the Holy Spirit that I was sanctified wholly. I was not; my consecration, so far as I know, was complete, but the point of self-conscious utter impotency where faith ceases to struggle and reposes calmly on the bosom of Jesus I had not quite reached.

One sleepless night during my week of services with Daddy Perkins I said to myself, "What shall I do? A blank disappointment at C——'s next Wednesday night will be damaging to my reputation for judicious management and fidelity to truth, and preclude the possible achievement of greater soul-saving victories there! To preach at the two places twenty miles apart is impossible!" In a moment the oft-repeated fact went through me like an electric shock, "With God all things are possible." I nestled on the bosom of Jesus and rested my weary head and heart near to the throbbing heart of infinite love and sympathy. I laughed and cried, and said, "Yes, all things are possible with God. He can arrange for two appointments at the same hour twenty miles apart. I don't know how. He may have a dozen ways of doing it, and I will let Him do it in any way He may choose. Yes, and I will let Him do anything else He has engaged to do for me." I was not praying specially for holiness that night, but I rested my weary soul on the bosom of Jesus and saw spread out before me an ocean of available soul-saving resources in God, and overheard the whispers of the Holy Spirit saying, "Jesus saves you. He saves you now. Hallelujah!"

Satan was listening, and said, "Maybe He doesn't."

"But He does, and it is the easiest thing in the world for Him to save me from all sin, wash my spirit clean, and make me a full partaker 'of the divine nature.' I can't do any of it. He can do it all, and I will henceforth let Him attend to His own work in His own way." Instead of receiving a great blessing I received the great Blesser as the bridegroom of my soul. I was fully united to Him in the bonds of mutual fidelity, confidence, and love. I have from that day to this dwelt with Jesus and verified the truth of "the record of God concerning His Son." Through the mistakes of my eyes, ears, judgment, and memory, I have given Him trouble enough, and myself too; but He has wonderfully preserved me from sin and led me to victory in a thousand battles for the rescue of perishing sinners in many climes; and, strange as it may seem, the greatest Gospel achievements of my life have resulted from His overruling some of my greatest mistakes.

I claim no exemption from the infirmities, temptations, trials, and tribulations to which the children of God have been subjected through all the ages of the past, and cheerfully concur in God's providential adjustment of them for the correction, discipline, and development of Christian character. To be sure, I have thus far been exempt from serious bodily illness ever since I was a lad of about fourteen years, and in nearly one hundred voyages, long and short, at sea have never been detained an hour by shipwreck or quarantine. I thankfully accepted these providential mercies; but did not receive them in answer to prayer. I am not indifferent to such things; but I know not what is best for me, and my Father does; so I prefer to leave all such things to the manifestation of His own pleasure, and appreciate them the more highly in that I had not teased and begged and bothered Him about such things. Moreover, I don't want any exemption from, or mitigation of, any hard discipline that God sees needful in character building for eternity.

Paul was true to God, yet subject to the most severe discipline. He prayed for exemption, and God answered his prayer by saying, " My grace is sufficient for thee ;" and Paul replied, " Most gladly, therefore, will I suffer." From that time on he "gloried in tribulation," even though at one time it killed him and threw his mangled body to the Lystrian dogs ; that gave his soul an opportunity to sweep up through the midst of the spheres to the heaven of God and glorified souls and take in visions of glory utterly indescribable, which fixed his residence henceforth more in heaven than on earth. He simply stayed on the earth after that on the principle of self-sacrifice, that he might be used in saving sinners and in building up the Church of God among men, and that he might furnish an example of patient sufferings, which, in his person, were in number, variety, and depth an aggregate equivalent of all the possible sufferings of all God's children, for a purpose outside of personal development, which he thus states : "That in me first Jesus Christ might show forth all long-suffering, for a pattern to them which should hereafter believe on Him to life everlasting." One pattern of that sort was enough. One chart drawn from such an experience was sufficient for the safe navigation of the stormy sea of life from that day till the judgment day. Therefore, while no loyal servant of God, as was Paul, is ever required to endure all, or a hundredth part, of what Paul suffered, yet every one is liable to any number or variety of Paul's aggregate of sufferings, as God may appoint as the portion of each one.

When the Church in Thessalonica was passing through great tribulations Paul wrote them, saying, "I send Timotheus, our brother, and minister of God, and our fellow-labourer in the Gospel of Christ, to establish you, and to comfort you concerning your faith ; that no man should be moved by these afflictions : for yourselves know that we are appointed thereunto. For verily, when we were with you, we told you before that we should suffer tribulation ; even as it came to pass, and ye know." God does not afflict willingly, nor grieve the children of men, but for our profit. To be forewarned is to be forearmed. When tribulation comes crashing down on us, to know that we are appointed thereunto prepares us to endure meekly and prove the sufficiency of the grace of God, and the wisdom and kindness of God when it "yieldeth the peaceable fruit of righteousness unto them which are exercised thereby."

The theory of a Pullman car passage to heaven with the great Physician aboard to exempt us or immediately relieve us from all diseases is a poor preparation for the stern realities of disciplinary sufferings on the Pauline line; and its counterpart, that the suffering of protracted sickness is proof that the sufferer has entailed it by a sinful departure from God, puts a club into the hands of the "accuser of the brethren," with which he beats them to death.

So I don't pray for exemption from any afflictions or tribulations to which God may appoint me. My one concern, requiring continual watchfulness and prayer, is to maintain intact the two essential facts before stated, to be at all times true to Jesus and to receive and trust Him at all times to be true to me.

As for the tribulations to which I may be appointed, I ask no less and desire no more than may come exactly within the range of God's will. We may, indeed, in what may appear to us as unbearable anguish, cry with the suffering Son of God, "Now is my soul troubled; and what shall I say?" Shall I say, "Father, save me from this hour?" But there is a purpose in all this; for "for this cause came I unto this hour." "Father, glorify Thy name."

So if we are true to God and trust Jesus, we have nothing to fear from without, and should not allow the innumerable changes in our emotional sensibilities to infringe the immutable principles of our covenant with God.

I grew in grace and in the knowledge of God before I was purged from all iniquity, but much more rapidly afterward. When the obstructions to growth were removed and my union with the infinite sap sources of the living vine was completed, then why should I not "grow up into Him in all things"? Holiness, therefore, does not fix a limit to growth, but adjusts the conditions essential to a continuous "growing in grace and in the knowledge of our Lord and Saviour Jesus Christ," which is limitless and eternal.

Well, when I went to my preaching appointment next day Father Perkins met me and said, "Brother Taylor, we can arrange for Wednesday night here, and you can go Wednesday and fill your appointment as announced, celebrate the marriage on Thursday, and return to us by Thursday night."

"All right, Father Perkins; let it be so written."

So from a very small beginning God has been leading me along the high lines of human impossibilities from that day to the present moment.

We had good meetings, but not many saved, at the house of Father Perkins.

So far as I was concerned I made things satisfactory at the other place and held our ground, but, failing to take the tide at the flood, we lost our opportunity of achieving greater victories.

At the Irish Corner we fitted up an unoccupied dwelling house for our special services. My dear father came on horseback about seventy miles, and gave grand assistance for a few days. When soul-saving success became manifest Satan became alarmed; for he claimed exclusive rights in the Irish Corner. So he sent a lot of his faithful servants who tore the roof off our house and threw off the logs of the upper story, it being an old-fashioned log house. We quietly repaired it and went on with our meetings.

A farmer by the name of Armstrong heard of "the great doings at the Methodist meetings," and came one night to see and hear for himself, and went away in a great rage of anger, saying: "Some meddlesome fellow has told the preacher all about me, and he exposed me before the whole congregation. I'll find out who the villain is who has taken on himself the trouble to tell on me, and give him a thrashing that will teach him a lesson; and I will keep away from the meetings and not give that preacher another chance to put me to the blush."

By the evening of the next day he changed his mind. He wanted to learn more about the strange things that were coming to pass at the meetings, but to avoid another possible exposure he went in advance of any one else and concealed himself behind the door. He stated afterward: "As soon as the preacher read his text he began at once, as it appeared to me, to expose me before all the people. He did not repeat the things he told last night, but opened up a new chapter of worse things that I feared he would let out against me last night; but he reserved them and fastened them all on me to-night, and all my neighbours will know that he means me. I got awfully angry there behind the door, but I was cornered, and could do nothing but bite my lips and swear to myself; but after a long cogitation in my anger I began to get another view of the case, and said to myself: 'I must be mistaken. It was not at all probable the preacher knew anything personally about me last night, and certainly he don't know I am here to-night. He said last night that nearly all the people here were strangers to him, but that he held the Gospel glass before them, and they could see themselves and all their meanness more distinctly than he could tell them. I now see the truth of what he says. God is in this mystery. His Spirit has found me out, and my own guilty conscience tells me who I am and what I have done as a rebel against God. I can't carry this hell in my bosom any longer. I'll make a clean breast of it at once.'" So out he rushed from behind the door and kneeled at the mourners' bench and sought and found the Lord. I afterward visited him in his own house and heard his testimony to these facts.

To the few scattered members I found, we added about one hundred probationers, and organised the Sweet Springs Circuit, the thing I was sent to do—a circuit of such proportions and resources that a man and his wife were appointed to it in the ensuing year.

Before I left I appointed Joe Carson leader of our class at Dan Weekline's, and was afterward informed that he became the best leader on the circuit.

The Sweet Springs Circuit was the fourth and last country circuit I ever travelled, all my subseqnent appointments being in large cities (which, though substantially the same as circuits, are in America called " stations ") and in evangelistic and foreign missionary work. I have ever desired to visit those fields of my early ministry, to see how my beloved people do, and cheer them on in their heavenward pilgrimage, but have never had the opportunity, except to meet a few of them at camp meetings remote from their homes.

A few years ago I met a minister in a Western Conference who was born and brought up in the bounds of the Sweet Springs Circuit. He informed me that nearly all who were saved there under my ministry were abiding in Jesus and doing well ; some of the leading men had suffered decline during the war but had in the main recovered. He said the class books in which I wrote the names of all the members and probationers composing the Church of our new circuit in 1845, with the dates showing, by " P " for present and "A" for absent, without a good excuse, the weekly class meeting attendance of each member, were in a good state of preservation ; but instead of being laid aside with old books and newspapers were still taken to the class meetings as the first book in a series of added books of the same kind. When one is filled a new one is stitched on and the whole carefully preserved.

CHAPTER IV

To get from Sweet Springs Circuit to the seat of the Conference in Baltimore city in March, 1846, required me to travel on horseback two hundred and seventy miles through the deep mud of the breaking winter, with a nightly freezing surface not hard enough to bear up a horse and his rider, but very hard on the horse's legs; but I had the company of my dear friend, Rev. C. A Reid, and a few other mountain itinerant young preachers, so that it was more a pleasure trip than one of hard service. Having written in a book which I carried in my pocket a synopsis of the books in the course of study on which I was to be examined at the Conference, I redeemed the time of travelling by carefully reviewing what I had written, so that without the burden of the books I had the gist of their contents in my pocket and in my memory, ready for use on short notice. As a schoolboy my ambition to "stand head" in the spelling classes led me to study my lessons well. So, combined with a thirst for useful knowledge, my ambition to excel in the examinations was very much like that of my boyhood.

Having nothing to do with the debates in Conference but to listen that I might cast my vote aright, which, with the swaying arguments and eloquence of the advocates, I found to be a difficult task, I was modestly trying to interest my young brethren in the ministry more fully in the doctrine and experience of holiness. I had ordered and received from Boston a good supply of back numbers of *The Guide to Holiness*.

One day a venerable D.D. saw me distributing these as tracts among the preachers, and said, "Brother Taylor, what have you got there?".

"It is a monthly magazine, called *The Guide to Holiness*."

"Oh, indeed! The Bible is my guide to holiness."

"True, my brother, that is the divinely inspired book to define our needs and our obligations, and to reveal to us God's provisions in Christ for our pardon, and our cleansing from all sin, and His promises covering the demands of every case, and the recorded testimony of 'a cloud of witnesses,' who have verified and attested the truth of Bible teaching, and the charge of Jesus to all His saved

47

ones, 'Ye shall be witnesses unto Me unto the uttermost parts of the earth.' The fathers are dead, and new witnesses have to be raised up through all the ages, and to 'the uttermost parts of the earth,' to bear witness for Jesus by mouth, pen, and press, to prove that Jesus is alive, is still accessible, and still 'able to save to the uttermost all who come unto God by Him,' according to the teachings of the Bible; so this monthly, *The Guide to Holiness*, is a testimony record according to the eternal purpose of God." The dear old brother bowed assent, smiled, and passed on his way.

In presenting the truth of God, especially on the subject of holiness, I always tried to avoid ambiguity, make every point as clear as possible, keep within the lines of admitted truth, and avoid debate.

I preached holiness as a Bible doctrine from the time I entered the ministry; and when I experienced its full cleansing power I added my testimony to confirm the truth of what I taught, and have continued ever since, through dry seasons and wet seasons, proving from the Bible that it was the duty of every living man, woman, and child under the sun, and the possible attainment of all who will " walk after the Spirit, and not after the flesh."

Not being unduly censorious, nor suspicious, nor a debater, and preaching holiness on the line of practical common sense and personal experience, I never encountered much opposition to it, either from preachers or people. The truth of this statement is not limited to Methodist pulpits and people.

For example, about twenty-six years ago I conducted a ten-days' series of special services in Great Queen Street, Edinburgh, in the church of Rev. Moody Stuart, a minister in the Free Church of Scotland, in which many persons received the Saviour. I preached one Sabbath from the text, " God is love; and he that dwelleth in love dwelleth in God, and God in him. Herein is our love made perfect, that we may have boldness in the day of judgment."

The pastor called to see me next day and said: " When you announced your text, I feared you would antagonise the prejudices of my people and mar the good work so manifest in our midst, and I hid my face, unwilling to see the faces of my people; but I was soon relieved of all apprehension and became profoundly interested in your clear statements and illustrations of the truth of God. My elders and a number of my people called at my study this morning to tell me how greatly they were pleased and benefited by the discourse of yesterday morning." He perceived that preaching scriptural holiness would not disintegrate his congregation.

Later, in the vestibule of the church, he said to me one evening, " I can almost realise fully the experience of holiness as you explain it, but sometimes I am overcome by my quick temper. In five minutes I pull up and pray to God and get forgiveness."

" Then, my dear brother, there is a difference of five minutes in our time. If you will set your timepiece forward five minutes, and, on the principle that 'an ounce of prevention is better than a pound of cure,' watch, and the moment the temptation strikes, receive and trust the ever-present and all-sufficient, preserving Saviour, then by His might you will be the victor, and not the victim."

He grasped my hand and said, "We agree exactly." I could have dug down into the tenets of his theology and raised points of disagreement, and gone into a debate that would have devastated the work of the Holy Spirit by which He was healing and uniting so many hearts in love. The debatable questions were entirely irrelevant to the business in hand.

To return now to the closing day of that Conference session of 1846.

It was quite presumable in those days that of the three hundred ministers present not one of them, outside the bishop's cabinet, knew where he would be appointed for the ensuing year. After the closing prayer the bishop presiding explained the delicacy and great difficulty of appointing so many men with their families, and tried to prepare many of them for their disappointment; that was the occasion when crowds of sympathising friends filled the house to overflowing. Then the bishop solemnly and slowly read the appointments, followed by the farewells, accompanied by the congratulations of the many and the condolements of the few, who generally found out within a few months that their appointments were, after all, very good.

I was in no trouble about my appointment, wheresoever it should be, but I readily presumed that I should be read out as the junior of N. J. B. Morgan; but his name was announced as pastor of the "Foundry," in Washington city. I said to myself, "All right; if I don't go with Brother Morgan I'll go somewhere else." The next announcement was, "Georgetown, Henry Tarring, William Taylor."

Brother Morgan explained to me afterward that when he found that he could not have a colleague, he had me stationed next door to himself, and that he would expect me to dine with him every Saturday, which invitation I honoured as frequently as the duties of my charge would allow. I never had a truer friend than was he, and his friendship never waned. Oh dear me, the fathers whom I revered and loved are nearly all dead! I must be getting old. Yes, I am marching along through my seventy-fifth year. Thank God, I feel in every bone and muscle of my body the health and vigour of my early manhood, and my spirit is full of the life and the native wit and fun that bubbled in the springtide of my boyhood, and all these blending with perfect loyalty to God, perfect faith in Him, perfect love for Him; and as I march through the mountains of Africa I sing:

> "I'm happy, I'm happy, O wondrous account !
> My joys are immortal, I stand on the mount;
> I gaze on my treasure, and long to be there,
> With Jesus, my Saviour, His kingdom to share.
> Oh, who is like Jesus? He's Salem's bright King;
> He smiles, and He loves me; He taught me to sing.
> I'll praise Him, I'll praise Him, and bow to His will,
> While rivers of pleasure my spirit do fill!"

Pardon my digression.

I promptly made my appearance at my post in Georgetown. I never tried to put on appearances or to sugar-coat the truth of God to adapt it to carnal tastes. Apart from the grace of God in my heart it was not in my nature, or that of my parents, to be discourteous on any occasion, but to be courteous and kind at all times. It was not a matter of study with me to popularise myself with the folks. I went to them in simplicity and sincerity as a messenger from God, and made no apologies and asked no favours, and was most kindly received by the Georgetown people.

Soon after my arrival in Georgetown a wealthy Methodist lady of that city, who took pleasure in preparing sumptuous dinners and late suppers for the preachers and for her upper-class friends, sent me a cordial invitation to one of her banquets. It seemed to me a jolly time for all the guests except myself. I saw no opportunity of getting any sinners converted or believers purified that night, and wished myself at a prayer meeting.

It was a habit of my life to retire to rest often earlier but not later than ten o'clock, and to be up and out by five in the morning. The sumptuous dinners served at different hours of the first half of the night, course after course of cakes, sweetmeats, coffee, and tea, with fruit and nuts following each other, broke in on me. As an unfortunate dyspeptic I could not indulge in such varieties and such quantities of good things. I was quite at home in the pulpit, but so embarrassed on such a nice social occasion as to be unable to excuse myself and retire; so I dragged through the dreary hours so full of hilarity to others and got to my bedroom as the clock struck twelve.

I fell on my knees and told my Father that He knew that I meant no harm in going to the Methodist banquet, and how I was detained and exceeded my hour for retirement, and that I felt sorry and was very much ashamed of myself, but had learned enough of high life of that sort to last me for twenty years to come.

I spent two years in the Georgetown Station, the limit allowed by the Discipline at that time, but never had another evening to devote to any such entertainment. What with the regular prayer and class meetings of the two churches, white and coloured, a weekly meeting at Father Hardy's in Upper Georgetown, which I opened, and which has since grown into a separate self-supporting station, together with other extra appointments, I had no time to spare for social chitchat and feasting, though useful in their way. I often took tea with our people and went to my appointments without delay. I arranged for an evening to go with my good friend Brown Morgan to hear J. B. Gough lecture on temperance in a great hall in Washington, and was greatly pleased and profited by the marvellous charm of his simple eloquence.

Henry Tarring, my preacher in charge, was a humble, holy, loving brother and an earnest, effective preacher. He was called the "weeping prophet," from the fact that he seldom preached without tears, sobs, and half-choked utterances, which also caused many of his hearers to weep. It was his way to win, and all right for him, and an element of power; but I was not favoured with a special talent of that sort. I could wield with precision a Gospel sledge hammer which often broke the rock in pieces, but couldn't cry, except alone at the feet of Jesus under a profound sense of His presence with me and His love for one so unworthy. Of late I weep when I meet my heroic missionaries in their trenches at the front.

I never collided with my preacher in charge. So far as I know I always pleased him, not by trying to, but by going ahead on every line of duty and by bringing things to pass.

Soon after my arrival in Georgetown I felt called to preach the Gospel to the outside masses. As "a fisher of men" I felt it my duty to look out for the shifting shoals of fish, and cast my Gospel net wherever I saw a chance for a good haul. So I proposed to preach on the afternoon of each Sabbath in the Georgetown Market. But few encouraged me, for it seemed to be an unpromising venture; none opposed me, for they knew I would do just what I thought the Lord wanted me to do, whether anybody opposed me or not. I was not naturally reckless, nor daring, nor desirous to be odd, but just the opposite. A conviction of duty with me was paramount to every other consideration.

So, early in April, 1846, I opened my commission in the market house between Bridge Street and the canal. My loud singing soon drew a crowd of all sorts and sizes. The congregation was very orderly and well behaved, and gave attention to the word preached, and the Lord manifestly set His seal on the movement from the commencement. During my two years in that city, weather permitting, I never missed a market house appointment. When I was to be away on other duties I so announced in advance, and no appointments were made in those exceptional cases. Sometimes our congregations were dispersed from the market by a cry of fire. Generally my advice was, "Run and quench the fire, and come back and bring the fire-fighting crowd with you, and you will find me here." Sometimes I sat down and waited; at other times the people remaining joined me in singing hymns. In either case we never failed to gather a larger and, if possible, more attentive congregation than the one that had been dispersed by the fire alarm.

In the month of October, 1846, I was, by Rev. B. N. Brown, my old colleague on Fincastle Circuit, united in marriage with Miss Anne Kimberlin, at the home of her grandmother Richie, on a bluff overlooking the James River, in Botetourt County, Va. Forty-nine years have passed since the occurrence of that important event, and the conclusion of the whole matter is that the Lord made the selection for me and did His best. She has braved the storms of life which have since swept over us with the spirit and courage of a true heroine, sharing in full measure my fortunes and my misfortunes. She began life four years and a half later than I did, but at the time of our marriage she looked much younger and I much older than we really were. When walking the avenues of Washington the remark was often dropped by passing observers, "There goes that beautiful young lady and her father."

Brother Tarring and I had a pleasant and prosperous year in our joint pastorate, and had a good report to make at its close to the Conference of 1847, which was held in Washington city.

In the examination of character in the Conference, when my name was called my presiding elder said, "No objections to Brother Taylor." Then, according to custom, it was in order for me to retire till the Conference should hear the report of my presiding elder as to my labours for the preceding year and the report of the chairman of the Committee of Examination on the Course of Study. But instead of promptly retiring I addressed the chair and asked and received permission to speak. I said, "Mr. Chairman, since the session of Conference last year the Lord has given me a wife. My wife is an heir to an undivided estate in which there are about a dozen slaves. She is anxious to manumit her portion of them, but they will not come into her possession, nor hence be at her disposal in any way, till the youngest heir reaches her majority by age or marriage. As we shall have much to do with the training of her coheirs—her young brother and two young sisters—we hope, by the will of God and the concurrence of all concerned, to manumit the whole of the slaves together, and thus avoid the separation of families. If the Conference desire a pledge for the emancipation of all that may come to my wife, we will give it."

The bishop replied, "If F. A. Harding had made a manly speech of that sort at the Conference of 1844 it might have prevented a split that rent our Church in twain. We want no better pledge, Brother Taylor, than what you have just given."

I thus foreclosed all surmises and discussions about my connection with slavery.

The issue in regard to the freedom of the slaves resulted just as I predicted. Within four years from that time the youngest heir was married, and on the night of her marriage a deed of manumission was executed, signed by all the claimant heirs, and from my own pocket I gave them one thousand dollars in gold, and my father engaged their passage and put them aboard a ship bound for Liberia, where they arrived safely in due time.

At that session of the Baltimore Conference two able representatives of the Free Church of Scotland, which had but recently struck for liberty, self-support, and independence, were introduced to the Conference. They gave us a history of the State Church and of the new organisation; they also preached during the session of the Conference several able sermons and received a voluntary contribution of funds from the preachers and people for their cause.

At the close of that Conference Henry Tarring was appointed Presiding Elder of the Winchester District, so I unexpectedly lost my beloved colleague. Rev. Thomas Sewall was appointed preacher in charge of Georgetown Station, and I was appointed to the pastorate of my preceding year. I was glad to believe that association with such a colleague as Thomas Sewall would polish me up and increase my power of usefulness. But he was troubled with a bad cough and was threatened with consumption of the lungs, and before the year was half out he went, under medical advice, to Montgomery, Ala., where he spent the remainder of the year.

The pastoral work of the double charge then devolved on me. My preaching work occupied all the hours for preaching, so that I could not in person fill his appointments, but had to provide for them. It became, therefore, a part of my work every week to hunt up competent men to supply the pulpit of my absent colleague. I pressed into the business some able Methodist ministers who were members of Congress, some also who were employed in different departments of the general government of the nation, and sometimes an eloquent beggar from the West seeking assistance in the erection of churches and colleges. With all this I kept up my market-house preaching and the routine work of both charges, but could not command much time for special revival services.

During my first year in Georgetown I was so closely confined to my work that I saw but little of Washington or the great men of the nation, but in my weekly hunt for preachers to supply for Brother Sewall I was brought into contact with many great and good men whom personally I never should have known otherwise. I thus found opportunity also to visit the Senate and House of Representatives and witness their proceedings. I heard Daniel Webster and Henry Clay in their eloquent pleading before the United States Supreme Court.

The war with Mexico was waged in that year, so that I heard many of the big war guns in Washington, and saw most of the distinguished men of the nation at that period ; was introduced also to the President of the United States and his lady, and preached to them in one of our city churches. Such opportunities improved were compensative for my extra losses and labours occasioned by the illness of my preacher in charge.

The Conference for 1848 was held in Baltimore. During the session of the Conference I preached in Monument Street Methodist Episcopal Church by order of the Committee on Public Worship, one Sabbath evening. Some one said to me, "That was 'a trial sermon.'" I did not know exactly what he meant. I knew that I tried to do my best, as I always do, but I learned that Sterling Thomas, called the Bishop of North Baltimore, was on the lookout for a junior preacher for North Baltimore Station and had me appointed to preach that evening to see whether I would fill the bill. I was glad I had nothing to do with such arrangements and knew nothing about them ; otherwise I could not have preached with much freedom. Brother Thomas was a butcher, a large, rotund man, with red face, powerful voice, very imperative as a commander, carried great influence in the community for good, a powerful worker in the Church, and had a large family, some of whom were saved when I went there (for that proved to be my next appointment), and more before I left.

North Baltimore Station at the time of my appointment had a Church membership of about eighteen hundred. Soon as the spring birds began to sing I commenced open-air meetings for every Sunday afternoon in Bellaire market. Neither of my colleagues ever offered to take any part, but they never made the slightest objection to my going ahead in any advance movement.

We drew immense crowds at the market, and Father Darling, the sexton at Monument Street Church, expressed his surprise again and again at the great inflow of strangers into the church every Sabbath evening. Later he found out that they were non-churchgoers till attracted to my preaching in the market, and came thence to the church. Many of such were saved there during the fall revival services.

In all varieties of pastoral work and preaching, indoors and out, my great ambition was to let the Lord make of me all He could for the salvation of the people. In reading of the preaching of Benjamin Abbott, and of the multitudes who fell under the power of his words like men slain in battle, and sometimes lay in a state of insensibility for hours, I became greatly exercised on the subject, and prayed earnestly to God that if He could use me in that way more effectively than the way in which He had led me, so to use me. So while this struggle was going on in my mind I was preaching in Monument Street Church one Sabbath forenoon on the parable of the barren fig tree, when, near the close of the discourse, a man fell down in a state of insensibility. Some strong men carried him out.

His wife followed, wringing her hands, weeping, and saying, "Oh, my poor husband is dead; not a Christian, not prepared to die. Oh, what shall I do? My poor husband is lost!" They got a hack and hauled him home and sent for a doctor. The physician came quickly, and had the man covered up in bed with a large mustard plaster over the region of the thorax and stomach, and set men to rubbing his limbs to promote circulation. He was nearly as cold as death, and his limbs were as stiff as a poker. After half-an-hour or more of this heroic treatment the "dead" man began again to live, and, putting his hands over the mustard plaster, he inquired, "What is this?"

"It is a mustard plaster. You have been very sick, and the doctor has been here to see you, and the mustard plaster was put on to make you better."

"Why, there is nothing ails me but sin. A mustard plaster won't take it out. Send for Mr. Taylor."

So the messenger came in haste and conducted me to the place. I went in, and there was Curry, still in bed, and the men were rubbing him. I instructed him somewhat as to the nature of his ailment, and that it was a very bad case. I informed him that the only Physician who could be of any use to him had come, and was now ready to undertake his case.

"You have only to submit your case to Him, consent to His treatment, and receive and trust Him for a cure. 'As many as received Him, to them gave He power to become the sons of God.' Receive Him, receive Him now!"

In about fifteen minutes, as I talked to him and prayed for him, he surrendered to God and received Jesus Christ. He trusted Him, obtained pardon and peace, and sprang out of bed rejoicing.

I said to myself, "Well, thank the Lord, my prayer is answered. That is a regular knock-down case, such as I have been reading about."

That afternoon, when preaching to a crowd in the market, I gave an account of the case of dear Curry, illustrative of the saving power of Jesus as a present Saviour and added, "If the brother is here he had better come forward and bear his testimony to the healing power of the great Physician." Sure enough, he was standing but a few feet behind me, and at once mounted the meat-block on which I stood and told the people what a great sinner he had been up to that morning, and what a great Saviour he had found, confirming all I had said about him. Then I exhorted the people to submit to God and receive Jesus at once.

Away in the street in front of where I stood and on the outer boundary of the congregation stood a man, a grocer, by the name of Shilling, a man not in the habit of going to any church. Shilling and his wife had been out for a walk, and, hearing the singing, they came close enough to hear the preaching, and he was so deeply awakened by the Spirit that he left his wife standing in the street, pressed his way through the crowd, and dropped on his knees on the brick pavement just in front of the block on which I stood. I and a number of earnest workers gathered around him. We sang and I instructed him. In about twenty minutes he intelligently submitted to treatment and received Jesus and was saved. Then he stood on his feet and gave a clear testimony to his experience of God's pardoning mercy, shook hands with many of the brethren, and went back for his wife, and they returned to their home.

Then I put the two things side by side. First, the case of "knock down and carry out"; and the second, like the poor leper, who came and, kneeling down to Him, said, "Lord, if Thou wilt, Thou canst make me clean." He felt his deep need beyond the power of human remedies or skill. He believed that Jesus had the power, but was in doubt whether He was willing to heal him—an intelligent reasoning process. Jesus said, "I will; be thou clean;" and immediately the leprosy departed from him and he was healed.

So I said to myself, I will watch these two cases and see which will pan out the better.

Brother Curry joined the Church, was an easy-going brother, did not backslide, so far as I could learn; but I never heard of any fruit resulting from his testimony or work.

Brother Shilling joined the Church, and in a short time had his wife saved, his mother-in-law and others of his household saved, and in the Church at large became a very useful man. I met Brother Shilling last summer at a camp meeting, still working and witnessing for Jesus.

So if the Lord can't get a certain class of sinners down in any other way we shall be glad to have Him knock them down, as He did Saul of Tarsus and the man Curry; but to receive the truth, count the cost, and deliberately say, like the prodigal, "I will arise and go to my father," and do it, is the rule; the other, the exception.

In the month of August, 1848, I and my wife attended the Shrewsbury camp meeting, Lowe's camp ground, north of Baltimore.

After two or three days of service had passed I preached one night on holiness. The Holy Sanctifier shed forth light on the subject with great effulgence, and in the altar services that followed a widely known and wonderful worker, Mrs. Phebe Palmer, appeared unheralded. It was her first appearance in that region, and the sight of her was an inspiration; but her wonderful talks that night and daily afterwards, till the close of camp meeting, were full of divine light and power, and gave a great impetus to the spread of Scriptural holiness through that region of country.

That was my first acquaintance with that prophetess of God, and my last was in Liverpool, England, in the winter of 1863, as she and Dr. Palmer were closing their long and successful campaign of Gospel work in the United Kingdom, and I was on my way to Australia. Our next meeting will be in the home country of our King, "where the wicked cease from troubling, and the weary are at rest."

The weekly preachers' meeting of Baltimore, held at old Light Street Church, was a great institution, in which I was simply a close observer and quiet learner, always seen there, but seldom heard.

One morning about the end of September, 1848, as I was on my way with rapid strides to the preachers' meeting, and nearly at the turning from Baltimore Street into Light Street I heard my name called, in almost a screaming voice, in the rear. So, stopping suddenly and looking round, I saw Christian Keener, an old saint, well known and loved in that city. He ran up nearly out of breath, and, taking my hand, simply said, "Bishop Waugh wants to see you immediately in the bookstore of Armstrong & Berry."

As I walked back with Brother Keener I was querying in my mind, "What on earth can a bishop want with me? I've not been doing any censurable thing."

"Brother Keener, what does the bishop want with me?"

"I don't know; he saw you passing and sent me to call you, and I had to run to overtake you, and asked him no questions."

So in the back office there sat the venerable bishop. He arose and shook my hand cordially, and asked me to be seated. So as I took my seat I thought, "Now it is coming, what I know not; but, trusting in Jesus, I am prepared for anything that He may appoint or allow. Nothing outside of those lines can come to me, so I am safe enough."

Then the bishop said: "Brother Taylor, the General Conference at its session last May, as you may know, made provision for founding a mission in California, and authorised the appointment of two missionaries for that distant field, which is attracting so much attention just now on account of the reported discovery of gold there. The selection and appointment of the two missionaries devolve on me. I have for some months been looking about to find the men every way suitable. It will require men of great physical force and courage, men of pure hearts and clean hands, and clear exponents of Methodism in doctrine, experience, and practical life. I have appointed Rev. Isaac Owen, of the Indiana Conference, as one, and want one more. From what I have learned and seen of you I think you are the man for that difficult work, and I have called you in to inquire if you will accept the appointment."

I replied: "Well, Bishop Waugh, I can only say, when I was admitted into the Conference the question was put to each member of our class, 'Are you willing to be appointed to foreign missionary work in case your services shall be needed in a foreign field?' Most of the class put in qualifying words and conditions, and some said emphatically, 'No!' but I said, 'Yes.' I had not thought of such a possibility, and had no thought of offering myself for that or any other specific work, but I was called to preach the Gospel by the Holy Spirit, under the old commission, 'Go ye into all the world and preach the Gospel to every creature,' and I suppose that includes California. I never volunteered for any field or asked for an appointment to any particular place, but have always been ready, and am now, to accept as a 'regular in the service' an appointment under the appointing authority of our Church to any place covered by the great commission. It is not for me to say I am the man suitable for California, but leaving myself entirely at His disposal, giving you wisdom to express His will concerning me, I will cheerfully accept your decision and abide by it."

The bishop simply replied, "Go home and consult your wife about it, and let me know by next Wednesday at my house."

The bishop shook my hand with a grip expressive of great emotion, and I went on my way. I had not had time to think about my wife's part in the business, and saw at first glance toward California some apparently insurmountable obstructions in our way: First, Anne's condition of health; second, her young sister just entering her teens, adopted into our family; third, her elder widowed sister lying ill at our house, over two hundred miles from her home, and unable to travel.

I said to myself: How precipitant in me to consent to go away to California without a moment's reflection, hemmed in as I am by unpassable barriers! To this I mentally replied: I did not seek the appointment, never sought one, but never declined an appointment coming from the legitimate authority of the Church. This is a test of principles which I have maintained thus far in my itinerant ministry, while preachers all around me, old and young, were fretting about the secret work of wire-pullers, and the danger of being sent where they did not want to go. I always said to such, I am sure to be suited in my appointment, for I will get it from

God. I don't know anything about wire-pullers, or the work of deputations to the bishop's council, and have no fear of any of them. I commit my person and family wholly to God and trust Him to send us to just the place He shall select. There is but one individual in the universe who can defeat His purpose. I will see to it that he shall not in any way interfere with it. I am, in the order of God's providence, under the authority of our Methodist Episcopacy, and shall, therefore, get my appointment from God, through the bishop presiding. It don't matter who pulls the wires if there are any wires to pull, nor what intermediate agency may enlighten, prejudice, or in any way influence the bishop's mind, or whether by his farseeing wisdom or shortsighted blunders he will appoint me to the place selected for me by infinite wisdom. If I should personally meddle with it I should most likely defeat God's purpose and have a miserable *dis*appointment. Called by an authorised bishop to go to California, I can only say, Lord, here am I. If You want me and mine for Your work in California You know how to put us there; if not, You know how to reverse the choice of the bishop and release us from the responsibility, which I am entirely willing to bear or not, as Thou shalt appoint. We shall reach the right conclusion on the *à priori* principle under a special providential leading.

So I went to our parsonage. Anne met me at the door, and I said, "Bishop Waugh wants to send us as missionaries to California. What do you think of that?" She made no reply then, but ran upstairs to her room, and in a few minutes, while I still remained standing, she came running down the stairs smiling and said, "Yes, I'll go with you to California."

"How did you settle the question so quickly?"

"I went upstairs and kneeled down and said, 'Lord, Bishop Waugh wants to send us to California. Thou knowest, Lord, that I don't want to go, and can see no possible way of getting there; but all things are possible with Thee, and if it is Thy will to send us to California, give me the desire to go.' In a second or two He filled and thrilled my whole being with a desire to go to California." The question was settled.

Forty-seven years have passed over our heads since that day, but neither of us ever entertained a doubt that God called us, and no mention was made about the difficulties in our way.

At the time appointed I called on Bishop Waugh and said, "Anne is exactly of the same mind with myself, and both are subject to your order."

We then had a long talk about California. "The gold was discovered while digging General Sutter's mill race, in January last, 1848. The treaty ceding California by purchase to the United States, at the city of Mexico, was not signed until May. Yet before the news of the gold discovery had reached the contracting parties, and in the same month, our General Conference ordered the founding of a mission there, knowing nothing of the gold. There will be a great rush of emigration from this time on, indefinitely, so we must lose no time in establishing the mission."

I said, "I can start on short notice."

The venerable man of God kneeled down with me and commended me and mine to God, and then he gave me my commission for California and said he would let me know when to get ready to sail, meantime to proceed with my work in North Baltimore Station.

California was then so far away, and transit so difficult and so expensive, that in accepting an appointment as missionaries to those remote ends of the earth we never thought that we should again see Baltimore or our friends in the East this side of the resurrection of the dead. We hoped to be off promptly, while dear Anne was strong and able to travel, but in that we were disappointed. The news spread like lightning that we had been appointed to California, and our official men, led by Sterling Thomas, got after the bishop with a long stick, metaphorically, and so belaboured him for removing their young preacher in the middle of his first year that for the sake of peace he had to say that I should remain and complete my Conference year there.

Brother Tippett's mind was prepared for my being sent away by a dream which I told him some weeks before Bishop Waugh sent for me. I dreamed that Brother Tippett and I were pastorally visiting the people, and I had in hand a bundle of tracts, when two large copper-coloured men, darker than Indians of the East, stopped me in an alley and said, "You must leave this place, and come with us and show our people the way to God." I immediately ran and overtook Brother Tippett in a wide street, and told him that God, by some of His swarthy, neglected children, had called me to go with them. They are waiting for me and I must go; so I gave him my bundle of tracts and bade him good-bye, and as I met my guides again I woke. So when Tippett heard of my sudden appointment to California, he said, "I expected something of that sort, it is all right."

I went on with my work, but in the meantime bought and forwarded supplies of provisions by ship around Cape Horn, expecting after Conference to go to California *via* the Isthmus of Panama.

My friends in Baltimore framed and furnished a chapel 24 × 36 feet, and prepared for it a tin roof all ready for putting up on our arrival. I spent a short apprenticeship with Brother Day in putting on tin roofing, so that, in the absence of a tinsmith, I could put on the roof myself.

In March, 1849, the Baltimore Conference held its session in Staunton, Va. It was arranged that we should go by steamer from New York to Aspinwall, leaving about the middle of March. So Anne and I and our little son, Morgan Stuart, made a hasty visit to my friends in Rockbridge County and to hers in Botetourt County, and said, "Good-bye, till we meet in heaven."

We purposed to spend one day at Conference and hasten on to take ship at New York. But on reaching the seat of Conference I received a letter from our missionary secretaries in New York saying that they had heard of such sickness and detention on the Isthmus of Panama that they did not think it advisable for us to go there at present, and that they had not therefore bought our tickets, and that all the tickets for passage up to July had been taken. So there we were at sea before the time! The secretaries made no suggestions as to how or when we should go to California. So I remained at Conference to its close and held a holiness meeting in the afternoon of each day for the edification of our young ministers.

At the close of Conference we returned to Baltimore, not knowing when or by what means we should get to California. I at once searched the advertisements and the piers for a ship bound for San Francisco, and found one, but the agent said there was not a vacant bunk left in the ship. They had ten first-class passengers and about one hundred steerage, and could not take another one. So I said, " All right ; the God of the seas will show us the way to our work."

Next day I received a note from the agent saying that a family booked as first-class passengers had backed out and would not go. So I went and engaged the space thus vacated on the ship *Andalusia*, Captain Wilson, a Baltimore clipper of about one thousand tons, much superior to the average of sailing ships of that day.

Our insurmountable difficulties were not mentioned except to the Lord, and having committed them to Him we seldom ever mentioned them to Him again. In buying our tickets I arranged with the agent that a good physician should go as surgeon of the ship. The Missionary Society had booked self, wife, and two children, I having written them of our little sister. The widowed sister was still unprovided for, and too ill to travel to her home ; but her physician said a sea voyage was the best thing he could recommend for her. So at the last day of grace I bought a ticket for her passage to San Francisco, and she recovered on the voyage. She afterward married Dr. Bateman, of Stockton, California, and has since brought up a family. The little sister grew up with us, married a merchant in the same city, and has brought up a family.

On the 3rd of June, 1849, off Cape Horn, our little daughter Oceana was born. She stayed with us till she was fourteen months old, and then left us for the city of the great King.

Our only stop on the voyage was at Valparaiso, where we got the latest news from California, the first of which was that Governor Mason had been deposed from office by a mob, and that the only preacher who had put in an appearance there was killed by the miners, and headed up in a barrel and marked "beef"! This news, which I did not then know to be for the most part false, made me think of certain evil prophecies that some of the friends had uttered, to the effect that I was taking my family away to perish among barbarians.

If Satan meant to terrify us by such lies he did not succeed. Judging from the blizzard he blew on poor old Job we may conclude that so far as the Divine Ruler of the world may give him tether he still makes a great stir in the elements in which we live. We had in our ship's company more than one hundred passengers, among whom was Rev. Robert Kellan, who joined us in Valparaiso. For three days out from that port, with a good breeze, all sails set and glistening in the cloudless light of a full moon, we were quite undisturbed by Satan's California lies; but he seemed to get into a rage of anger and swooped down on us in a white squall, which snapped our main and mizzen topmasts and all the upper masts and spars, and piled them in a confused mass on the deck. Still nobody was scared, but with an aft breeze and foresails all set we made two hundred miles per day, and, having spare timbers and ship carpenters aboard, all repairs were made without detention. We anchored in the harbour of San Francisco in good health and cheer, in September, 1849, after a voyage from Baltimore of one hundred and fifty-five days, including three days' detention at the port mentioned.

PART SECOND

PLANTING THE CROSS IN CALIFORNIA

CHAPTER V

FIRST VIEWS OF THE FIELD

THUS I found myself in California. It was at sunset on the autumnal equinox of 1849 that we anchored off the north beach of San Francisco harbour. All of us being strangers in a strange land, no one ventured to go ashore that night, though very hungry for news. Soon a brother of one of our passengers boarded our ship. So we crowded around our visitor, and in answer to our inquiries he informed us there was no war in the country, but peace and prosperity. Fortunes awaited all who could work or gamble ; clerks were paid two hundred dollars a month ; cooks, three hundred dollars. Card-playing, however, was the most profitable, hence the most respectable, business in the country.

I inquired, "Are there any Gospel ministers or Christian churches in California ?"

Our newsman said, "We had one preacher, but preaching don't pay here ; so he quit preaching and went to gambling. There was a church in town, but it has been converted into a gaol."

Then some one whispered to him that I was a minister, and had the materials for a church aboard.

" I advise you," said he, "to sell the church, for you can make nothing out of it as a church, but you can sell the materials for ten thousand dollars."

I replied, " My church is not for sale, sir."

These are some of the pills I had to take the first night. I learned later that his assertions in regard to wages were true, and those in regard to gamblers closely approximated the truth ; his ecclesiastical history was false, except that a small rude frame building on the plaza which had been used as a place for the preaching of the Gospel was later used as a gaol.

Next morning, Saturday, September 22nd, I accompanied Captain Wilson, the master of our ship, the *Andalusia*, on his first trip ashore.

We ascended the hill above Clark's Point and got our first view of the city of San Francisco. Not a brick house in the place, and but few of wood—and they were constructed mainly of lumber from goods boxes—and three or four single-story adobe houses; not a pier or wharf in the harbour, but a vast encampment in tents of about twenty thousand men and about ten women. I felt oppressed with an uninvited apprehension that under the influence of the gold attraction of the mountains I might wake up in the morning to find the tents struck and the inhabitants of the city of tents gone to parts unknown.

I inquired of many if they had heard of Rev. Isaac Owen, who, with his family, had started with waggons across the plains before I sailed from Baltimore. None had heard of him.

I made diligent inquiry whether there were any Methodists in the city. Hearing the name of J. H. Merrill, I remembered I had read a published letter from Rev. William Roberts, giving an account of his having organised a little Sunday-school in San Francisco in 1847, as he was on his way as a Methodist missionary to Oregon, and that he appointed J. H. Merrill as its superintendent. So I sought and found J. H. Merrill, and learned from him that he was indeed the Merrill appointed by William Roberts as superintendent of the first Sunday-school in California. He informed me that he was not a Methodist, but knew a number of them in the city, and pointing to the frame of a little church not yet covered, which was being built on a neighbouring hill, he said, "Yonder is their new church." And, pointing to a house near us, added, "There is a Methodist family residing in that adobe house. Mr. Finley, the head of the family, is sick, and will be glad to see you."

"Will you kindly introduce me to the sick man?"

"Certainly; with pleasure."

So in a few minutes I was introduced to my first Methodist family. Brother and Sister Finley seemed surprised and rejoiced to see me, and gave me much information in regard to the country and resident Methodists. I enjoyed their company and had a good season of prayer with them—my first pastoral visit in California; and then they informed me that they were not Methodists, but Campbellites; but we were soon united in Christian friendship and love, which continued during my pastorate of seven years in that city.

As I was taking my leave of these my first Methodist acquaintances, I was met at the door by a plain man of very pleasant features, to whom Sister Finley introduced me. "This is Brother Troubody. He is a Methodist;" and I ever found him to be a quiet, humble, true man of God. He introduced me to Brother White, a local preacher from Illinois, but more recently from Oregon. He had a large family, all Western pioneers, all sociable and kind, and earnest Methodists of the shouting kind. They lived in a small rough board house covered with blue cotton cloth. Brother White's house, called "the shanty with the blue cover," was the Methodist place of worship for the city.

In my continued search that first afternoon I could get no tidings concerning the whereabouts of Brother Owen, but Brother White handed me a letter from Rev. William Roberts, the Superintendent of the Oregon and California Mission Conference, informing me that he had appointed me preacher in charge of San Francisco Station, and Rev. Isaac Owen to the charge of Sacramento city and Stockton.

That was an afternoon of thrilling interest to me, and contrasted hopefully with the unfruitful search of the forenoon of my first day in San Francisco.

On Sabbath morning, September 23rd, I preached from "What think ye of Christ?" The Spirit of the Lord was manifestly present with us. At 3 p.m. of that memorable Sabbath day I met the class in "the shanty with the blue cover," which was packed inside with earnest worshippers, and many stood outside the door. Their experiences were characterised by originality, freshness, and thrilling interest.

Some of them had crossed the plains; others were just from a voyage round Cape Horn; some had, on their passage across the isthmus, seen scores of their friends swept away by the malignant fevers of Panama. All had seen sights, encountered dangers, made hairbreadth escapes from death, and could all sing, "Out of all the Lord hath brought us by His love." That was a class meeting never to be forgotten.

We spent the following week in learning California prices and modes of life and in trying to secure a house in which to live.

Captain Wilson kindly invited us to remain aboard ship till we could make arrangements for housekeeping, and allowed us the free use of his boat in passing to and from the land. This was quite an item, for the lowest price of boat hire for the shortest distance was one dollar for each passenger. Potatoes were fifty cents a pound; South American apples, fifty cents apiece; fresh beef, fifty cents a pound; dried apples, seventy-five cents a pound; Oregon butter, two dollars and fifty cents a pound; flour, fifty dollars a barrel; and so on for provisions of every kind at about the same rate.

As for house rent, there were but few in the city to be had at any price. Near to our chapel was a rough, one-story board shanty, about twelve feet square, with a slab shed roof. On inquiry I learned that the rent was forty dollars per month, which I was willing to pay, but an Episcopal minister had secured it.

I then spoke of building a small house, but learned that lumber was sold at the rate of from three to four hundred dollars per thousand feet.

At the close of our class meeting in the afternoon of my second Sabbath the question was raised, "How shall our preacher get a house to live in?"

It was decided that the only way was to build one; and then an effort was made in the class to see how much could be raised toward that desirable end. But the sojourners were "strapped," and the resident brethren had subscribed all they felt able to give toward the chapel, and could do but little for the parsonage; so the effort resulted in a subscription of twenty-seven dollars—perhaps enough to buy the nails and hinges. But I never was haunted with the ghost of a doubt that God called me to California, nor, hence, a doubt that He would provide for me and mine. So I had my household goods and provisions, which we had brought with us from Baltimore, landed; and paid ten dollars per dray load to have them hauled up the hill and piled up near the chapel; there they lay in the open air for a fortnight.

In this emergency Captain Otis Webb sent me word that he was building a good two-story house near to our chapel, which would be finished and ready for use in a week, and that we were welcome to the use of it, rent free, for a month, he reserving but one room of the five contained in the house for his own use. So, after remaining a fortnight as the guests of Captain Wilson, aboard our good ship *Andalusia*, we moved into Captain Webb's new house. We highly appreciated his generosity and enjoyed the high order of his gentlemanly bearing—a friend in need and a friend indeed. Few persons in San Francisco were so comfortably settled as we, by the good will of our dear friend Captain Otis Webb—rent free for a month.

Messrs. Collins & Cushman presented us with a new cooking stove worth a hundred dollars in the market. We had brought with us from Baltimore a year's supply of provisions, so that in our great dependence we were pretty independent.

The question pending was, What shall we do at the end of the month?

Some persons, believing more in dependence than independence, said, "You were sent here by the Missionary Society, and they are bound to support you."

I replied, "The Missionary Society never did and never can support a missionary and family at California rates of expense. House rent alone would amount to five thousand dollars a year; but I will never draw on the Society for a dollar additional to the appropriation—750 dollars—already made. If I can do no better I will take my axe and wedges, and go across the bay to the Red Woods and get out lumber for a house and build it myself."

" Are you a carpenter and builder ? "

" No, but I am a Methodist preacher of the old school."

A brother who had located from the travelling ministry to seek a fortune in California said, "Poor Brother Taylor will work himself sick, and that will end the matter. It had been better for him to come to California on his own hook, as I did."

He was the "poor brother" who licked the dust in pining sickness through many weary weeks while I gathered strength in the struggle for missionary efficiency and self-support; and by the might of body and mind with which God had invested me, and the guiding hand of His providence, by which He daily led me, I was exempt from sickness and my labours were crowned with success.

Brother Asa White and his two sons-in-law, and his two youngest

5

sons, had a shanty in the Red Woods, where they spent much of their time getting out lumber and hauling it to the *embarcadero* at San Antonio—a big name, but no town. So it was arranged that I should go to the woods and get out lumber on my own account and "ranch" with Brother White. Brother A. Hatler kindly proposed to go with me and assist.

So on October 10th, 1849, we crossed the bay in a whaleboat to San Antonio, and, carrying our blankets, provisions, and working tools, we walked up the mountain five miles to Brother White's shanty. Brother Hatler and I put our provisions into the mess and were admitted as guests, with the privilege of wrapping ourselves in our own blankets and sleeping on the ground under the common shelter.

After supper we were entertained by Brother White's historic reminiscences of earlier days spent in Illinois and westward. The following is a specimen:

Joe Flower was a bricklayer, and boasted that he was proof against all religious agency or influence. Brother White induced him to go to a camp meeting, and talked to him very seriously about the peril of his soul while at enmity with God. Joe baffled him with light, foolish remarks, and finally said, "I will go among the seekers and hold down my head an hour for twenty-five cents."

Brother White, "Here is the money, Joe." So Joe was committed, and went and did as he proposed. White went and kneeled down beside him and prayed with increasing power, in the midst of which an awful thunderstorm broke on them. The thunder and lightning were terrific, but White prayed on till Joe dropped on his knees and cried to God for mercy, and received Christ and salvation before he arose to his feet. Next day they made a collection for missions, and Joe put in the twenty-five cents he won the day before, and told his experience of peace with God.

We were thus entertained with Brother White's stirring stories till bedtime, and then after a hallelujah season of family worship retired to rest.

During the early part of one afternoon I went to a woodman's tent to sharpen my draw-knife, and found there a sick man by the name of Haley. As soon as I mentioned the subject of salvation to him he cried like a child, and said, "I once enjoyed peace with God and was a member of the Baptist Church, but in these Western wilds I got off the track and lost my religion."

I prayed with him, and he promised that from that hour he would devote himself to God and accept Christ. Soon after he received the great Physician and said, "Oh, I am so glad that you called to see me; I had thought of sending for you, but I felt so guilty that I could not muster courage to do so. Now I feel that God, for the sake of Jesus, has pardoned all my sins. My soul is happy. I am not afraid to die now."

Three years after that, at the close of a preaching service in San Francisco, a man introduced himself to me and said, "Do you remember praying for a man given up to die in the Red Woods, in 1849?"

"Yes, sir ; I remember him well ; his name is Haley, but I never learned whether he recovered or not, but he found peace with God and rejoiced in prospect of an early departure for heaven."

" I am that man, and my soul is still happy in God."

So far as I know he was the first man saved through my agency in California.

We wrought till Friday afternoon, the 12th of October, but spent our strength for naught in trying to split some unsplittable timber, and returned that afternoon to San Antonio landing. We there lay on the ground to sleep, but spent most of the night in looking at the stars, listening to the weird howlings of the coyotes and the gabble of thousands of wild geese, all apparently exulting over their pre-emptive rights to all the vast plains now covered by the city of Oakland and its adjacent villages.

Sabbath, October 14th, was my fourth Sabbath in the city and second in our new chapel, which was crowded with attentive hearers, and the class meeting in the afternoon was an extraordinary season of refreshing.

I returned to the Red Woods on Monday, the 15th, but Brother Hatler could not leave his business to return with me ; so I had to depend on my own unaided mind and muscle, led by the good providence of Him who had called me to meet such emergencies. I provided for my pulpit the Sabbath following, so as to give me two unbroken weeks in the Red Wood Forest, and on the Sabbath I preached under the shade of a large red-wood tree to twenty-five woodsmen. One of my hearers, a man of forty-five years, heard preaching that day for the last time ; then apparently in good health, but, being taken suddenly ill, he died a few days later.

During this trip to the woods, covering a period of nearly two weeks, I procured the lumber needed for my house. My scantling, which I bought in the rough, split out like large fence rails, I hewed to the square with my broad-axe. I made three thousand shingles, and exchanged them with a pit sawyer for twenty-four joists each seventeen feet long. I bought rough clapboards six feet long and shaved them about as regularly and as smoothly with my drawknife as if with a plane. These were for the weather-boarding. I used similar boards, slightly shaven, for roofing, which were waterproof and very enduring. I bought the doors from a friend at the " reduced price " of eleven dollars per door ; the windows for one dollar per light, twelve dollars for each window. Hauling my stuff from the Red Woods to the San Antonio landing cost me twenty-five dollars per thousand feet. The regular price for transport thence to San Francisco was forty dollars per thousand feet, but by hiring a boat and working with my own hands I got the work done for less than half that price.

I bought a lot on the north side of Jackson Street, above Powell, for twelve hundred and fifty dollars, kindly lent me without interest by Brother Hatler, which I paid back in due time.

Brother Hatler, being a carpenter, gave me instruction in the business of house building. I hired a few carpenters for twelve dollars each per day till I got the house under roof and then dismissed them, and did the rest of the work with my own hands, except that now and then a passing brother would give me a few hours on the building. But I wrought daily from dawn till dark till the house was finished, a desirable, comfortable, two-story house 16 × 26 feet.

The total cash cost of my house was fourteen hundred and ninety-one dollars and twenty-five cents.

In six weeks from the time we moved from the ship *Andalusia* to Captain Webb's house we moved into our own mission house, and thus avoided the payment of one cent of rent. I had two rooms upstairs to let to help pay for the building, and had another fitted up for strangers, and especially for preachers, if we should ever be favoured with such angel visits. By the time we got the room ready Rev. J. Doane and his wife, missionaries for Oregon, arrived, and were as much surprised as we were rejoiced that such a home for preachers was found in San Francisco. But we had to wait more than a year for the first recruits of missionaries for California.

In addition to the timber and lumber for our house I brought from the woods enough to fence the back part of our lot for a garden, which I put under cultivation by the commencement of the wet season, so that in a few weeks we had an abundant supply of radishes, turnips, greens, and lettuce. Ours was the second garden ever planted in this city, and was to all passers-by an object of surprise and ground of hope for the future of this country of supposed sterility.

A restaurant keeper passing by our garden one day said to Mrs. Taylor, " I would like to buy some of your greens, madam ; what do you ask for them ? "

" We have not offered any for sale, but as we have more than we need you can have some at your own price."

He replied, " I will give you ten dollars for a water-pailful."

He gathered a pailful and paid the money. A few days after he returned for another pail of greens, and, filling his pail, Mrs. Taylor asked him how he could afford to pay such prices.

" Well," said he, " I boil the greens slightly with a little bacon, and get for them fifty cents a fork. I make a very good profit on them."

Mrs. Taylor thought our little home would be more homelike if we could have a few chickens, and applied to a neighbour who had some.

The lady replied that she would be glad to accommodate her, and as she was a missionary would let her have some at a reduced rate.

" How much, Mrs. C——, will you charge me for a rooster and two hens ? "

" You can have the three, madam, for eighteen dollars."

So the money was paid and the fowls were promptly delivered. I built a house for their accommodation and put on a lock for their protection ; but it didn't protect them, for a few nights after some foxy fellow pulled a board off the back of the house and carried away the cock and one of the hens, and we saw them no more.

Having to buy milk for our little Oceana, we got a supply daily from a neighbour at the "low rate" of one dollar per quart. Our milkwoman did business also in the egg line, and offered us six dollars per dozen for all we could spare. She gave us but six dollars per dozen because she bought to sell for nine dollars. So when it was not convenient for us to pay money for milk we found our eggs, at fifty cents apiece, a convenient currency.

In the course of human events in this eventful country our milk-woman moved away, and we bought, for milk, some kind of chalk mixture that made our little girl sick. So I went to Sacramento city, where, it was said, good cows could be bought at a very low price ; I bought one for two hundred dollars, and milked her myself, and didn't water it ; so we had plenty of good milk of our own. Such are historical glimpses of California life in 1849.

As for hardships and sufferings, I had none. My hard work in house-building was a good acclimatising process, much cheaper and better than a fever and a bundle of doctor's bills, and it prepared me the more effectually to endure the ministerial toil to which I was called, and I thus secured a comfortable, healthful home, while the great mass of our city folks lived in very inferior shanties and tents, many of which were laid waste by the merciless blasts of the un-usually severe rain-storms of 1849 and 1850. Moreover, I never drew a dollar from the Missionary Society above the amount of the first and only appropriation for my support. So that my mania for self-support, which many pronounce excessive and incurable, is no modern dream with me. If God will inoculate a few thousand efficient missionaries for Africa with the same mania they will lead its millions to God in a comparatively short time and at a cost relatively small.

Rev. Isaac Owen commenced his pastoral work in Sacramento city about three weeks after my arrival in San Francisco. His missionary party consisted of himself, wife, and five children, and Rev. James Corwin, who had left the Indiana Conference to accompany his old friend, and to devote himself to our itinerant work in California, to which he did devote himself through the many remaining years of his life. He had a humble, loving, and lovable spirit, and was very successful as a pastor.

Brother Owen, not knowing anything about his appointment by Rev. William Roberts to Sacramento city, made no stop at that city, but crossed the Sacramento River and drove on to Benicia, *en route* for San Francisco ; but learning at Benicia that Sacramento city was his station, and that I, under appointment, was hard at work in San Francisco, he returned to Sacramento. However, owing to the exhausted condition of his faithful oxen, that had just made the long pull of two thousand miles from Indiana to the Pacific coast, he shipped most of his goods on a schooner bound up

the river, and rapidly drove his waggons back, with less than half
freight, so as to be on hand to receive the cargo from the schooner;
but the wayworn missionaries had to wait many days for the arrival
of their needed goods. The delay was occasioned by rough weather.
The schooner was capsized, and all the mission goods—clothing,
beds, books, etc.—had to be fished up from the river. These things
were essential to their settlement in a country so new, where every
needful thing had been brought so far and at so great a cost that to
supply the loss by purchase was out of the question; but I never heard
a murmur from the lips of any of the sufferers. They were utter
strangers to discontent or discouragement.

Meantime, I shipped my Baltimore-California Chapel to Sacramento for Brother Owen. He immediately secured a church lot,
and in a few weeks was preaching to crowds of adventurers in our
chapel, which was the first house of worship built in that city.

There was, at that early date, daily steam communication between
San Francisco and Sacramento city; the estimated distance there
by water was one hundred and twenty miles; by the shortest railway cut it is eighty-three miles.

The steamer route was across the San Francisco and San Pablo
Bay, thirty-three miles to Benicia, opposite the Strait of Carquinez,
a mile in width, through which the Sacramento and San Joaquin
Rivers run into San Pablo Bay, passing through the strait. A large
class of steamers ascended the Sacramento River to the vast
encampment of tents and rude cabins called Sacramento city. A
smaller class of steamers went up the San Joaquin to Stockton.
The former was then the commercial emporium for the Northern
mines and the latter for the Southern mines.

Brother Owen and I were thus in frequent communication with
each other by comers and goers and by letter, but did not see each
other till nearly the end of that most eventful year in the memory of
old Californians – 1849.

About the 22nd of December of that year I took passage on the
steamer *Senator* for Sacramento to visit Brother Owen and party,
fare thirty dollars; but Mr. Charles Minturn, agent and part owner
of the Sacramento Steamship Company, gave me a free passage.
She was a substantial, capacious river boat, and on her up-river
trips densely crowded with adventurers bound for the Northern
mines. She was on that line for years, and it was currently reported
that she took in gold enough as fares to load her. We had to pass
at least one night aboard, but used all the daylight we had in the
novel sight-seeing so enchanting to the view of all newcomers.
Among other sights on that, my first trip North, was a herd of elk
with the huge antlers of its bucks. They seemed to be trying their
original powers of locomotion against the steam power of our boat,
running up the west bank of the river opposite to us for the distance
of a good race, and then struck off at a tangent and were soon out
of sight. Arrriving in Sacramento city, I was cordially received and
entertained during my stay by Rev. Grove W. Deal, M.D., and William

Prettyman, who occupied the same little house. They were old friends from Baltimore city.

Brother and Sister Owen had not fully recovered from the wear and tear of their long journey across the plains and their sad reverse after their arrival; yet in the short time they had been there they had put up, besides the Baltimore-California Chapel, a good parsonage which cost five thousand dollars. We walked and talked together for several days, and laid the foundation of a mutual friendship that never was marred.

In addition to educational plans for the future we agreed that we should immediately extend the sphere of our evangelistic and pastoral work, he to include with Sacramento city, Stockton, Benicia, and the region generally north of the bay, while I, in addition to San Francisco, should occupy San José and Santa Cruz.

January 10th, 1850, I was again in San Francisco, accompanied by Brother Corwin, who was on his way to Stockton, where he organised a Methodist Episcopal Church and built a chapel and parsonage partly by subscription and in part by his own hands, he, like the great Prophet of Nazareth, being a carpenter as well as a preacher.

On the 17th of January, 1850, Brother Owen and family, whose church had been carried from its foundations by the flood and their dwelling house rendered untenantable, arrived in San Francisco on their way to San José Valley.

I engaged him to fill my pulpit while I should go and prospect San José and Santa Cruz, requiring an absence of two or three weeks. Mrs. Taylor being overworked with the care of her babes and household duties, I sought diligently for some person to assist her during my absence.

Sister Merchant, an old maiden lady, had arrived a few weeks before, having put in the dreary days and nights of a tedious voyage round Cape Horn in composing poetry. She uttered many sensible sayings, yet it seemed that somewhere in her mental constitution there was a screw loose ; but she was, nevertheless, regarded as a reliable helper in a family. She affirmed that she could do house-work of every sort from garret to cellar. She was the only female servant in the city, and I was in luck to get such a helper during my absence. The California preachers and their wives in those days had to serve each other and the people. So, with Brother Owen to take my pulpit and pastoral work, and Sister Merchant to assist my wife, I was prepared to itinerate and extend our work. Sister Merchant was delighted with the opening into a preacher's family. She said she " always loved the preachers and their wives, and would gladly take all the work off Mrs. Taylor, and nurse the baby too."

Brother J. Bennett, an exhorter in our Church, was passing through the city at that time from Coloma gold diggings—"a lucky miner "—to his home in Santa Cruz, and I arranged to accompany him. On Saturday, January 19th, 1850, we took passage on a little steamer for San José, distant forty-two miles by steamer and eight miles by land travel.

We paid twenty-five dollars each for a steamer fare, and landed at the *embarcadero* at 5 p.m. It was my second trip inland; every scene was new, the distant mountains east and west, the grassy valleys extending to the water's edge beautified with flowers of the brightest colours, the waters teeming with fish, and the air vocal with the screeching notes of countless thousands of wild ducks, geese, and pelicans—altogether a scene indescribable, yet indelibly photographed on the memory of a stranger.

Leaving the steamer, Brother Bennett and I waded the eight remaining miles of our journey to San José, through mud and water, in some places knee deep. It took us three hours. We got supper and lodging half a mile north of the town at the house of Widow White.

Soon after breakfast, Sabbath morning, January 20th, we went into the town and arranged for preaching services at the house of Mr. Young. At 11 a.m, I preached from "Fear not, for they that be with us are more than they that be with them."

Our first preaching service was an occasion of joy and rejoicing; the class meeting that followed the preaching was one of the old-time melting meetings,

> "When heaven came down our souls to greet,
> And glory crowned the mercy seat."

That night I preached at Mr. Young's again, and the little flock had a great time of tearful rejoicing that the long-desired day had come when they could hear a regular minister, be gathered into the fold, and receive the ordinances of the Lord's house.

Brother Bennett and I had still before us a journey of thirty miles by mule trail across the rugged coast range of mountains. We could have walked it without much trouble, but he had a heavy miner's pack, which we carried alternately in our tramp of the Saturday before, and concluded that horse power would greatly relieve our burden-bearing and help us across the streams that were too deep for comfortable wading.

So on Monday morning we searched the horse market and found that the hire of a horse would be eight dollars a day. As I expected to spend a week in the visit to Santa Cruz, including travelling time, I soon gave up the idea of hiring horses. The next thing was to buy a horse, but we learned that all the horses of any value were running at large on the plains, and were not obtainable in time for our purposes. Finally, in the afternoon, we learned that our host had one on his premises which he had not shown us, because not at all suitable. We requested to see him. He was a sight to behold—a small young, red horse, very lean, his hair all turned the wrong way, his mane nearly all torn out by the roots, with a scabby rope mark round his neck. He looked as though he had been hung up in the teeth of a hurricane.

"I say, Mr. Young, where did he come from?"

"I had him tied to a mule which ran away with him and dragged him by the neck for half a mile."

" My, he must have good stuff in him to stand all that and live! What is your lowest cash price for him ?"

" Eighty dollars."

"You will throw in saddle and bridle ?"

"Yes, sir; the whole rig."

" Here's your money." The first Methodist horse of California.

About an hour before sunset we started on our journey, to spend the night a few miles on our way at the house of Brother Campbell. When we came to Pueblo Creek, which was at full flood on account of recent heavy rains, we presumed that for so short a distance across our horse could carry us both, as he seemed firm and steady under my weight and that of the miner's pack, so Brother Bennett mounted behind the saddle, and " Bony Red" proceeded till he reached the middle of the stream, when down he fell and would have drowned without a struggle if we had not helped him up. We hauled him on and got him over, and thence led him on to Brother Campbell's, reaching there at dusk. An appointment was immediately sent out and a congregation of three families and six travellers assembled to whom I preached that night, and we had a good season of refreshing. After preaching we spent the night with Asa and family. They were extremely kind, and gave us an early breakfast of fried chicken and eggs, good coffee and biscuits.

We travelled a few miles over the flooded plains, and came to an overflowing creek. I forded it on "Bony Red," and dismounting sent him back for Brother Bennett, and he did his work so well that we dismissed the temptation to think that we had been sold in the purchase of the horse.

The mountain scenery of that day's travel was beautiful and grand beyond description—a grove of redwood trees of immense size, then vast fields of wild oats cut in every direction by trails of deer and grizzly bears.

Crossing the westerly foothills, we passed a large herd of sheep guarded by a shepherd's dog. He had the sole charge of the flock. He kept between us and his sheep, and warned us by his growl not to meddle with him or his charge. Such dogs were very common in California in those days, and very faithful to their trust.

From the top of the mountain range we saw spread out the great valley of San José, adorned with countless acres of rich pasturage and dotted over with herds of cattle, horses, mules, and flocks of sheep. Looking westward, over the mountain peaks, foothills, and valleys, a distance of about twelve miles, there lay the Pacific Ocean in measureless placid grandeur.

Night overtook us—a moonless night—before we cleared the foothills of the mountains, and we had a deep, swollen creek to cross. Brother Bennett, knowing the ford, went over first, and " Bony Red" came back for me, and we got over safely and reached the home of my fellow-traveller at a late hour. It was a joyful meeting of the old gold miner and his family.

I found at Santa Cruz a class of about twenty members, also

a number of Spanish families. The American portion of the population was composed principally of families who had settled there before the discovery of California gold, and had their children growing up around them; hence the place was more homelike than any other I had seen in the territory. They had also the best school and largest Sunday school in the country.

In the organised class of twenty were four local preachers. One of them, a young man of considerable ability, was employed to teach the village school at a salary of two thousand dollars a year, and at the request of the society had become their preacher and pastor till a regular missionary should be sent them.

On Saturday, at 11 a.m., I preached in the house of Brother Anthony, from "Therefore, leaving the principles of the doctrine of Christ, let us go on to perfection." The Holy Spirit gave unction to the truth. I preached again Saturday night.

At 9.30 a.m., Sunday, we held a love feast, and a joyful feast it was. Those old pioneers who had crossed the plains in 1846 and carried their religion in their hearts, and who had been for years as shepherdless sheep in the wilderness, now found themselves in the glory of an old-fashioned home love feast; they wept like children and praised God from hearts filled with gratitude and love.

At 11 a.m. I preached in the schoolhouse from "What think ye of Christ?" The place was crowded, and I was pleased to see in my audience several Spanish families who seemed interested in the Word.

After the sermon I administered the sacraments of baptism and of the Lord's Supper. About twenty persons partook of the emblems of the broken body and shed blood of their blessed Lord for the first time in California, and by tears, sobs, and shouts of glory to God expressed the gladness of their hearts.

After preaching that night two of Brother Bennett's daughters presented themselves as seekers for salvation, the first women penitents I had, up to that time, seen in California.

I made a plan of preaching appointments for our local preachers, and left the work in their hands till I should return in the ensuing spring. Santa Cruz was then but a small village—now a flourishing town of probably ten thousand. It is a delightful place, on the north side of Monterey Bay, in the midst of one of the most fertile spots in the country, swept daily by moderate sea breezes.

I have been a pioneer most of my life, but never carried any weapons of defence. Brother Anthony asked me to carry and deliver in San Francisco a quantity of gold dust, in payment for goods, he being a merchant. I did not covet such a responsibility, but there being no express conveyance in the country I could not refuse to accommodate the good brother. So he put it in two equal parts into a pair of holster cases, and laid it across the horn of my saddle. It presented a formidable appearance of self-defence, but really contained nothing but gold dust.

On Tuesday, January 29th, I retraced my steps alone over the mountains to San José Valley. It rained the whole day, and during the forenoon the fog was so dense I could not tell certainly whether I was going east or west. The mountain path was in many places steep, slippery, and dangerous. In one such place my "Bony Red" fell down; and finding he was on the eve of a roll down the mountain, I sprang off on the upper side and saved him from a roll and slide which would probably have killed him, though he had learned to endure hardness and was very tough. He was soon on his legs again and ready for service.

I met two rough-looking Spaniards on horseback on the mountain. They wanted me to stop and talk. One came up close and asked for a match to light his cigar. When I told him I had no matches, and when they saw my big holster cases, they lost no time in getting out of my sight. Getting down to foothills and hollows, I stopped at the house of a Mr. Jones, who had a sawmill and lived there in the forest with his family. They were very kind in providing me food and a good fire for drying my clothes; thus refreshed I resumed my journey. By the time I got through the mountains and foothills night overtook me—a moonless, starless night—and the valley being a vast sea of water and mud I lost my way. I was trying to get to Brother Finley's, where I knew a welcome was awaiting me. As I was urging "Bony Red" through the waters I saw a light in the distance, which I supposed to be the point for which I was steering; but as I approached I was attacked by some huge dogs. My shouting brought out the denizens of the hut, whom I perceived were Indians. We could not speak a common language, but the kindly fellows silenced the dogs and I paddled on through the dense darkness. In an hour I reached the mission of Santa Clara, which later has become a flourishing town and has been for years the seat of the University of the Pacific.

One of the old adobe houses of the deserted mission was at the time of my untimely visit bearing the name of Reynold's Hotel. After seeing that "Bony Red" was well fed I was conducted into the bar-room, where a jolly lot of gamblers were employed in card-playing. By the time I got thawed out and refreshed by a good supper they got through with their game and gathered around the fire, which was kept blazing in an oldtime chimney-place. I took a seat in their midst and led in a conversation about the varieties of life in San Francisco, which led on to a description of the sick men in the hospitals there and of their varied experiences, living and dying.

None of my bar-room associates knew me, but listened with close attention to my facts illustrative of the real life of California adventurers.

Finally, one said, "Come, boys, let us go to bed."

Another replied, "Yes; but we must have another nip before we turn in."

I said, "Gentlemen, if you have no objections, I propose we have a word of prayer together before we retire."

They looked at each other and at me in manifest surprise, and

I looked at the bar-keeper, who was standing ready to sell a " nip " of brandy to each one at twenty-five cents apiece. After a little pause the bar-keeper replied, " I suppose there's no objection, sir."

" Thank you, sir. Come, boys, let us all kneel down as we used to do with the old folks at home and ask the God of our fathers and mothers to have mercy on us."

They all kneeled down as humbly as children, and I prayed for them and for their kindred and loved ones at home, but now so far away, with dreaded possibilities of never meeting again in the flesh. I prayed earnestly that these adventurous young men, and their fathers, mothers, sisters, and brothers far away, might all surrender wholly to God and receive Jesus Christ and be saved and be prepared for happy reunions on earth or in heaven.

They took no more " nips " that night, but slipped off to bed without a word. I said nothing to them directly about their gambling and drinking, but took the inside track of them. I met one of them next day in San José, and he seemed as glad to see me as if I had been his old kinsman.

Next morning I rode out on the plains to see my friends. I determined to save up my returning steamer fare on the price of my horse and ride back; but as the whole country was flooded and much of the rich soil in miry solution I feared " Bony Red " would stick fast in the mud, so I exchanged him at Brother Campbell's for a well-conditioned, substantial iron-grey horse and gave thirty dollars to boot. I afterward learned that " Bony Red " developed into a very strong and serviceable animal. I was glad to hear it, for I got a good bargain in the exchange.

I visited our people in San José, and preached again at the Youngs' on Wednesday night. We had a good audience and a blessed season of refreshing by the manifest presence of the Lord.

On Thursday morning, January 31st, I started through the deep mud and water on a fifty-mile journey to San Francisco. I knew not where I should spend the night; nowhere on the road, if my grey could get through to San Francisco by next morning. Being an entire stranger in that strange country, I pulled through several miles in the wrong path, but happily met a Spaniard who kindly showed me the right way.

About nine o'clock at night I reached San Francisquito Creek, which was booming with a roaring and dashing that frightened my horse. The night was so densely dark that I could not see the opposite bank, and tried in vain to get Grey into the stream, and had to give it up for that night and return to the highest ground I could find. I thought if there was an Indian's wigwam or human habitation of any sort I might, in a visual sweep of the darkened horizon, catch a glimmer of light. Happily, thus, I saw a light up the east bank of the creek, not far distant. Riding up, I found it was the camp-fire of three hunters, two of whom were very drunk. They said I might warm myself by their fire, and they would lend me a blanket for the night. I " staked out " my horse to graze, for though the valley was covered with water the new grass was about eight inches high, and very tender and nutritious.

As I returned to the fire the drunker man of the two met me and said, " I want to have a word with you," and staggering round behind the tent, he said, " Stranger, you mustn't mind anything that this man may say to you. He's a clever fellow, but he's pretty drunk to-night. Stranger, you mustn't mind him."

After I seated myself by the fire the three fellows got into a loquacious glee, and each gave a yarn of his personal adventures and experiences—details too horrible to be repeated.

When they reached a pause, they said : " Now, stranger, it is your turn to give us a little of your experiences."

So I gave them an account of my foolish rebellion against God, and how I proved that the way of transgressors is hard, but, like the prodigal son we read about, I returned to my Father in penitential grief and sorrow. God was very merciful to me ; I submitted wholly to Him, received and trusted Jesus Christ for salvation from sin and Satan's power, and obtained it.

They stared at me in great surprise, and finally one of them said, " You're a preacher, ain't you ? "

" Yes ; I pass for one where I am known."

" Golly, boys," said one, " didn't he catch us ! "

Another said : " Where did you come from ? We never dreamed that there was a preacher in this country. You must excuse our vulgar ways, for we didn't know you were not one of our kind."

They showed me extra attention and kindness, and gave me a good early breakfast next morning, for which I felt grateful to God and to His prodigal wanderers. The creek had ebbed to safe lines, and I proceeded homeward with yearning heart to see my dear wife and our darling children—Stuart and Oceana.

CHAPTER VI

TRIALS AND TRIUMPHS OF 1850

SAN FRANCISCO was then a city of tents. The winter, or wet season, of that year was unusually severe, both in the volume of the rainfall and the fury of the gales. Often, during the darkness of the night, many tents were swept to the ground, exposing their dwellers to the blasts of the merciless tempests.

I could thank the Lord I was not homeless, as other men were. I had a good house of my own and room to spare. We had more applicants for our spare room than we could accommodate; however, as we were working out the problem of self-support, and had our house and lot to pay for, we admitted a few excellent men, who gladly shared our home, with all we could provide, and rendered a fair compensation.

Owing to hardships from long sea voyages and the wear and waste of an exhausting tramp across the plains, and the poor accommodations of the dwellers in tents and the poorer food supplies on which they were trying to subsist, there was a great deal of sickness and dreadful mortality among the masses that were crowding daily into the city. Hundreds died from a consumption of the bowels. Outward symptoms, except the consumptive cough, were very similar to those of consumption of the lungs, and, unless promptly taken in hand, it was as certainly fatal. Many died in their tents, but the city, before it was really able, provided hospital accommodations for hundreds.

I spent much of my time with the poor fellows so sick and so far from home and friends. I helped many to let go every other hope and let the loving Lord Jesus take them on His bosom, as He did the little children of the olden time, and pray for them, and put His saving hands on them, and bless them with pardon, peace, purity, and a blessed entrance into His own fine country, "where there shall be no more death, neither sorrow, nor crying, neither shall there be any more pain." The triumphant death scenes delineated in my book, entitled "Seven Years' Street Preaching in San Francisco," tell the story in its matchless details, which my present limited space will not allow.

In the latter end of that year of desolation and death the darkness was deepened by a visitation of Asiatic cholera, which, according to the death roll published, carried off two hundred and fifty men in San Francisco and eight hundred in Sacramento city.

In those days there came a man to that coast who seemed to belong to the old prophetic age. He was a friend indeed to all in need. He had nothing but the clothes he wore; he was a hard worker, but worked for nothing, yet he lacked nothing, and nothing was really needed, of human resources, by any sufferer in the city that he was not ready promptly to supply.

As quickly as a vulture could scent a carcass that strange man would find every sick person in town and minister to his needs, whether of soul or body. If he needed a blanket the stranger, who was soon known to everybody, went at once to some merchant who had blankets to sell and procured the gift of one for the needy man; so for the need of any article of clothing; or even a bowl of soup, he would bring it hot from the gallery of some soup-maker. He was soon known as a direct express almoner, working most efficiently along the straight lines of human demand and supply.

His appearance deeply impressed me at first sight. One Sabbath morning after preaching in my little church in Powell Street I was met at the door by a tall man wearing a well-worn suit of grey jeans and a slouch white wool hat with broad brim. He was lean and bony; he was sallow from exposure to the sun, and his features were strikingly expressive of love, sympathy, patience, and cheerfulness. He grasped my hand and held it, and wept as though he had met a long-absent brother.

I took him home with me and heard his story. He was a native of central New York State. He was then about thirty-five years old, and had been devoted to the work of God among the poor, quietly, unofficially, and without pay, from his youth. He had spent many years instructing the Indians in the far West, and was recognised and honoured as a chief among them. Once, when his tribe was overwhelmed and driven from their homes by a more powerful war tribe, the white chief refused to run, but hastened to meet the advancing warriors, commanded a hearing, and dissuaded them from the further execution of their murderous purpose.

He had great sympathy for the suffering slaves of the South, and cried to God for the overthrow of slavery. He had spent much of his time for the relief of the blacks in our large cities. When overworked in sick-rooms he would plant and cultivate a field of corn, and thus recover strength and acquire independent means of subsistence.

During the year 1849 and the beginning of 1850 he was labouring among the sick and needy people, white and coloured, of Washington. One night while thus engaged at the capital the Lord, in a vision, showed him San Francisco. The city of tents was mapped before him in minute detail. He noted its topography, its few houses and many tents, and saw the hundreds of sick men as they lay in their tents and in the hospital, and saw a tall young man busily engaged in ministering to them ; and the Lord said, " Alfred, arise, go to San Francisco, and help that man in his work."

" Next morning I arose and went by early train to New York and took passage for San Francisco. I spent," said he, " many weeks among the sick and dying at the Isthmus of Panama, and thence got passage in a Pacific steamer which anchored in the harbour of San Francisco. From the deck of the ship I recognised the city just as I saw it in vision thousands of miles away. I knew that my man, from his appearance, was a Gospel minister, and set out at once as soon as I got ashore to find him in some pulpit in the city. I went to four chapels before I reached yours, and waited till the minister of each came in, and I said of each as he entered his pulpit, ' No, he is not the man I seek.' It was late when I reached your chapel. You were well on in your discourse. The house being crowded, I stood at the door, and said, ' That is the man whom God showed me in vision away in Washington city.' This is my apology for the unceremonious, hearty greeting I gave you as you came out of the door at the close of the service."

That was my friend Alfred Roberts, the most unselfish man I ever knew. Day and night he ministered to the sick and dying of that city for many months as he only could do.

Then he went to Sacramento city and devoted many months, extending into the spring of 1851, doing everything he could for the relief of the cholera patients.

In that campaign Roberts broke in his health, and returned to San Francisco a helpless wreck of his former noble manhood. I gave him shelter and all the help he was willing to receive, and nursed him till he was able to walk around at will. Then he said, " My work in California is done." So two members of my Church bought for him a first-class passage to New York for three hundred dollars, and he bade us a final farewell.

After his departure I heard nothing from him for nearly three years, when I received a letter from his own hand written in Jerusalem, Palestine. In that letter he gave me an outline of his labours during the intervening years. He said he returned to his old field of labour in Washington, but, suffering the disability of poor health, he devoted some months to manual labour on a farm in his native state and recovered the health and strength of former years.

Then he went to England and spent a few months in London among the sick and destitute folk. He then went to Italy, and besides the bodily relief he gave to many he distributed among the common people a thousand Italian Bibles and Testaments. As such labours were not tolerated there in those days he was pursued and greatly annoyed by the police ; but the Lord was with him and delivered him from the hands of his oppressors. Then he went to Jerusalem to labour among the Turks.

When I visited Jerusalem in the spring of 1863 I made the acquaintance of Bishop Gobat, resident bishop there under the joint auspices of England and Prussia. He was a genial, communicative man of God, and had a son-in-law then, the Protestant missionary of Nazareth, whose service one bright Sabbath morning I attended in that renowned city of Mary, Joseph, and Jesus.

Bishop Gobat gave me a detailed account of the labours of "that remarkable man," Alfred Roberts, in Jerusalem. Besides relieving the sick he spent much of his time in the instruction of Mohammedan pilgrims.

The bishop said: "Roberts knew no language outside of his mother tongue, but he came frequently to our book depository and got us to select the most interesting and instructive portions of the Arabic Bible and other books, and mark the pages with the beginning and ending of each stirring portion, and went with these tracts for distribution. He knew the import of every tract. He had such a remarkable insight into the character of men by a glance of his eye that in a crowd of a thousand Turkish pilgrims he would select his orator for the occasion, and enlist him and show him what to read and proclaim to the people, and so day by day he had great crowds of attentive listeners to the Word of God. He finally worked himself down, and it was clearly manifest that his constitution was broken and that his work was done. We all loved him as a brother in Christ, and I fitted up for him a comfortable room in our college building on Mount Zion, and my own daughters waited on him daily in cheerful sympathy for him during a lingering illness of two years, when he died in peace, and we buried him on Mount Zion but a few yards from the tomb of King David."

I wept over his grave amid the crowding memories of the past, and thought of the coming resurrection glory when Alfred Roberts and King David will both respond to the same call of the Son of man, and together ascend from the heights of Mount Zion to meet the Lord in the air, and each alike receive a crown of glory.

On my return from Santa Cruz I learned that Sister Merchant, instead of being a servant in my family, assumed to be mistress, and had both my wife and a neighbouring family also to wait on her.

The day after I left she became deranged in mind, and said, "The Lord's children are kings and priests, and I am one of them sure, and it don't become kings and priests to be doing housework."

She refused to leave, saying: "This house is the Lord's, and I am the Lord's, and I have a right to stay as long as I please. I am astonished that Mrs. Taylor should have the audacity to speak to me about leaving the house of my heavenly Father. Mr. Taylor wouldn't do such a thing. He is more sanctified than Mrs. Taylor. He'll settle the question of my rights as soon as he gets home; he will."   .

She took possession of an upper room in my house which I had just let for a rental of fifty dollars a month, on which I was depending to help me to pay for it. She refused to yield possession to the man who rented it, but remained in it day and night and demanded her meals regularly and other attentions needful for her comfort, and kept Mrs. Taylor and her children awake much of each night with her weird songs and loud prayers. Poor thing! Her

6

heart was nearer right than her head. Having no home and no friends in that wild country, Mrs. Taylor would not have her turned out of doors, but patiently did her bidding. It was some time after my return before we could procure comfortable quarters for her elsewhere. Soon after, however, she recovered her equilibrium, made money, and after a year or two returned East with funds in hand. This was our first experience with servants in California.

At that time we had no asylum in California for the insane, while many in the race for riches went mad, and their condition was deplorable indeed. Some were sent to the hospital, some to the " prison brig," and some were confined in private outhouses.

I saw one in the hospital who was always on the bright side, always cheerful, and was as polite as a French dancing master. He said, " I am Daniel Webster's private secretary."

He received me graciously, saying, " Good morning, Commodore Perry, I am very happy to see you, though most unexpectedly. Walk in, walk in, Commodore ; give me your cap and be seated ; I'll call Mr. Webster ; I'm sure he'll be delighted to see you. He was speaking of you at the breakfast table this morning. I was just reading, Commodore, as you came in, one of your despatches from the seat of war. That was a dreadful fight you had with the Philistines ! The American navy never had such a contest before, and never before achieved so great a victory. All glory to the American navy ! All honour to Commodore Perry ! Let the stars and stripes float for ever, I say."

Another of the desperate sort, a ship-master, was confined in a stable near where I lived. At all hours we could hear his stentorian voice giving utterance to imprecations and threats, and to complaints of bad treatment. He tore off his clothes and suffered greatly from cold.

Our good neighbour, Mrs. Arington, got permission from the doctor in charge to visit the captain. She provided regular meals of good food for him, and treated him kindly. He ceased his mad ravings and spent much of his time in lauding the dear woman who became his friend when he had none ; and she had the compensating pleasure of seeing him restored to health of body and mind.

Having added a horse to the number of my family cares, I took some new lessons in California prices. For a sack of barley, one hundred and fifty pounds, I paid fifteen dollars. For a hundred pounds of hay—miserable stuff it was, too—I paid fifteen dollars, and carried it home on my horse in one load. But having pastoral charge of our infant Churches at San José and Santa Cruz, requiring frequent visits, I found it cheaper to keep a horse even at those rates than to pay the enormous fare of the public conveyances.

February 10th, 1850, Brother Owen and I, assisted by a few brethren, dug the foundation and commenced the erection of a small Book Room adjoining our church on Powell Street. Carpenters' wages were twelve dollars a day, so, being unable to pay such prices, we did the work with our own hands, and did not consider it a hardship.

While Brother Owen's family still occupied Father White's shanty in San Francisco, their little daughter, two years old, took croup and died on February 13th. She was a beautiful child, and they having carried her across the plains she became an early partner in their toils and sufferings and had greatly endeared herself to all the family. The weather-beaten missionary and his quiet, patient wife joined hands and bowed together over the corpse of their lovely babe, and kissed a final farewell till the resurrection. It was a scene that caused me to weep then, and to weep now when I recall it. The good brother bowed his head and received the shock like a veteran in the army of God, inured to "hardness as a good soldier"; but Sister Owen, dear woman, had been so worn down by hardship and toil, and her nervous system was so shattered, that the lightning seemed to strike through her whole being. She never fully recovered from the effects of that bereavement.

Brother Hatler and I dug the grave on the north-west corner of the Powell Street Church lot, and we buried there the little jewel of Jesus, the first member of our first California corps of missionaries to pass on to the celestial glory.

Soon after Brother Owen removed his family to San José. He built a small house half a mile east of the town, in which he settled Sister Owen, with his daughter and three sons. On March 2nd Brother Owen returned alone to his pastoral charge in Sacramento city. The waters having assuaged, he had his church, which had been washed from its foundations, brought back to its moorings, and proceeded in his work with his characteristic push and energy.

On March 2nd, 1850, while I was at work in the Book Room, Brother Tronbody and a good-looking stranger came in, and I was introduced for the first time to Rev. William Roberts, Superintendent of the Oregon and California Missions. I was delighted to meet him, and to have him as my guest; and was led more and more to appreciate him as one of the Lord's noblemen.

Death in California in those days, without any of the mitigating circumstances attending the death scenes of old settled Christian communities, was clothed with extraordinary terrors. A little boy was crying in a street of San Francisco one rainy morning in the winter of 1849 and 1850, and a man said, "Little boy, what's the matter with you?"

"Daddy's dead, and I don't know what to do with him."

The lad conducted the man into a small tent, and there lay his dead father all alone. We learned that he owned a farm in Missouri, and had plenty of friends at home, but lingered and· died unknown to any one but his little boy.

April 6th I was called to see Dr. G. He lay in a small shanty on a sand hill. The doctor had received a religious training and had a pious wife at home, but there he lay, a stranger among strangers, reduced to penury, far gone in chronic diarrhœa, utterly dispirited, no hope in this life, and, worse than all, no hope beyond the grave.

He said to me, " I have always known it was my duty to serve

God, and have had numerous offers of mercy in Jesus Christ, but, though outwardly a moral man, I have indeed lived a great sinner against God all my life, and now I am caught! I'm caught at last! God is about to call me to judgment without mercy."

I urged him to try to submit to God, and receive Jesus Christ as his atoning Saviour.

"Too late now," said he; "I have been so presumptuous and wicked there's no hope for me. I sometimes catch at a glimmer of hope, but lose my hold, and all is darkness. There appears to be a thick veil between my soul and God, a bar that I cannot get over. I feel that when I shall leave this world I shall have no home and no employment. I wish I never had been born. For what purpose have I had an existence? The world could have done without me; I've done no good in it. I might have been saved, but I refused every offer of salvation; now I must be the embodiment of everything that is despicable and wretched and mean for ever."

I talked and sang and prayed, and did my best to persuade him to submit to the treatment of the great Physician, and receive and trust Him, but could not stimulate a hope or stir him to an effort.

Later when I called to see him he said, "I have been trying since you were here to seek Jesus, but I cannot find Him."

When I represented to him the mercy of God in Christ he replied, "God has given me commandments to keep, but I have been breaking them all my life. I have often felt guilt and sorrow on account of my sins, but did the same things again, and now God has gone from me."

I said, "The trouble is, you have gone away from God, but His voice of mercy is, 'Turn ye, turn ye, for why will ye die?' and Jesus says to you, 'Ask, and ye shall receive; seek, and ye shall find; knock'—importunately knock—'and it shall be opened unto you.'"

"I fain would ask, but when I try I talk to vacancy; I find not the ear of God; I know not how to seek; and I cannot find the place to knock."

In deepest sympathy I said, "Oh, my dear brother, you must not give way to despair."

"It has come on me, it covers my soul with the pall of death and overwhelms me in darkness without hope."

Soon after this interview death struck him and he imploringly begged, saying, "Help me up! Oh, do help me up! Set me down on the floor." Poor fellow, he wanted to flee from death. There is no reprieve in that war. He was helped out of bed by those present but died before they could get him back. What suicidal madness to postpone the great business of life till time and strength are gone for ever!

On the Sunday of our quarterly meeting Rev. J. Doane, on his way to Oregon, by appointment of our Missionary Society in New York, preached for us at 11 a.m. I announced that morning I would preach at 3 p.m. on the plaza, in the open air, to the gamblers and all outdoor people who might wish to hear.

It was a startling announcement, causing fear and anxiety to most of my people. Most of the gamblers were located on the north and east side of the plaza, or public square. They occupied the largest and best tents, followed by the best houses in the city. Every saloon had its bar and a band of music, and they were in full blast every day and night of every week, and Sunday was the greatest of the seven. Their tables were loaded with piles of gold dust and coin, surrounded by crowds of gamblers and sight-seers.

The gamblers were so numerous, and commanded so much money and influence, they were above all law, except the law of sin and death.

It was no new thing for a man to be shot and carried out and buried like a dog, but no arrests followed. There was not a gaol in California then, nor for two years after, and no administration of government at all adequate to the demands of justice or the protection of life.

The country had just been bought from Mexico and was still under the forms of Mexican law, with an *alcalde* to preside over the city of San Francisco. So when I announced that I would preach on the plaza and throw Gospel hot shot right through the masses of every saloon, it was feared that the gamblers would take it as an insult and shoot me. There was no legal protection or redress. It would only be said next day, " The gamblers killed a Methodist preacher yesterday. He very imprudently went down to preach on the plaza, and before he got fairly at it they shot him."

At the time appointed, in company with my heroic young wife, I walked down to the plaza, and a few of my people followed. Seating my wife on a chair, I mounted a carpenter's workbench which stood in front of the largest saloon. Mrs. Taylor had a voice of peculiar melting melody and of marvellous compass, and my baritone could be heard by nearly half the city; so as soon as I mounted the workbench I opened up on the—

ROYAL PROCLAMATION.

Hear the royal proclamation,
The glad tidings of salvation,
Publishing to every creature,
To the ruined sons of nature—

Jesus reigns, He reigns victorious,
Over heaven and earth most glorious,
Jesus reigns !

Hear, ye sons of wrath and ruin,
Who have wrought your own undoing ;
Here is life, and free salvation,
Offered to the whole creation.

'Twas for you that Jesus died,
For you He was crucified,
Conquered death, and rose to heaven ;
Life eternal's through Him given.

Restless hundreds of excitable men came running from every direction to see what new wonder under the sun had appeared. The gambling houses were nearly vacated. The crowd surrounded me nearly a hundred deep on all sides. I was in for it. I had to arrest them or they would arrest me. I had crossed the rubicon; the tug of war was imminent.

I shouted, "Gentlemen, if our friends in the Eastern States had heard there was to be preaching this afternoon in Portsmouth Square in San Francisco they would have predicted disorder, confusion, and riot; but we who are here have no thought of any such thing. One thing is certain, there is no man who loves to see those stars and stripes floating on the breeze [pointing to the flag], and loves the institutions fostered under them—in a word, there is no true American who may not be depended on to observe order under the preaching of God's Word anywhere, and maintain it if need be. We shall have order, gentlemen!

"Your favourite rule in arithmetic is the rule of loss and gain. In your tedious voyage around Cape Horn, or your wearisome journey across the plains, or hurried and perilous passage across the Isthmus of Panama, and during your few months of sojourn in California, you have been figuring the rule of loss and gain.

"Now I wish most respectfully to submit you a question under your favourite rule and have you work it out. The question I submit may be found in the twenty-sixth verse of the sixteenth chapter of the gospel of our Lord by Matthew. Shall I announce it? 'What is a man profited, if he shall gain the whole world, and lose his own soul?'"

Perfect order was observed and profound attention given to every sentence of the sermon that followed.

That was our first assault on the enemy in the open field in San Francisco, and the commencement of a seven-years' campaign outdoors, some details of which will appear as side lights of my story.

In the evening of that day I preached in our chapel, which was crowded, and four men presented themselves as seekers of salvation.

Up to that time the idea of getting anybody saved in California, except such as were sick unto death, seemed preposterous even to good people. In the wild rush for gold no one seemed to have time to seek the Lord, but I continually held my people to the "now-salvation" doctrine of the Gospel, suited alike, in all countries, to all kinds of men.

I preached every night through that week, and three men received Jesus and gave a clear testimony to an experience of His saving power.

That was the first revival in California. Our little society was greatly refreshed by the demonstration of the power of Jesus to save sinners even in California. Our class meetings were largely attended by Christian travellers as well as by our own members, among whom we had not a few substantial men of God. I will name a few of them. L. F. Budd was a remarkably inoffensive, conscientious brother, of generous disposition, refined feelings, and stern integrity. He had spent some years in Costa Rica, Central America, as a commercial agent for a firm in the East, and while there led a wealthy coffee planter to the Saviour, who wrote cheering letters to Brother Budd, which he used to read to me in California, expressing his great desire that a pure Gospel might be preached to his Spanish people in Central America. Brother Budd became the owner of a good house and lot in San Francisco, which he refused to let to any man who sold rum.

A man applying for his house said to him, "Budd, I don't see why you should be so squeamish here in California; why, you are worse than the old fogies at home. The people will have liquor; somebody will supply the demand at a great profit, and I may as well do it and make money as anybody else. I will give you three hundred dollars per month for your house, which is now empty and yielding you not a cent. I will take care of it, and what does it matter to you what I use it for if I return it to you in good order?"

Budd replied, "My dear sir, the curse of God is hanging over this rum traffic and all who are concerned in it, and my policy is to stand from under."

William H. Codington, from Sing Sing, N. Y., had the appearance of a ruddy-faced, beardless boy, but opened a butcher shop on his own account in Kearney Street.

Sabbath breaking was almost universal throughout the land, but young Codington hung up in front of his shop, in large letters,

THIS MARKET CLOSED ON SUNDAYS.

I knew many Sabbath-breaking butchers there who were considered wealthy, but their fortunes came to an untimely end in the insolvent court; but Codington prospered in business, married a good young lady, and both were valuable workers in the Church.

Robert Beeching, from New York, had a hard time crossing the plains, and arrived without funds, with clothes worn nearly into rags. He came to class on his first Sabbath in San Francisco, and, apologising for his rough appearance, told us of his sufferings and privations by the way.

He said, "I have been accustomed to wear decent clothes in New York, and I am ashamed to come into church looking as I do; yet I love Jesus and want to be with His people."

He was a tall, well-proportioned, fine-looking gentleman. I fell in love with him on sight, and took his hand and led him to the highest seat in the synagogue. He was a fine musician, and was offered thirty dollars a night to play the violin in a gambling saloon. It was a well-circumstanced temptation, for he was out of money and could find no employment; but he did not parley for a moment. At our next class meeting he said: "'Truly God is good to Israel, even to such as are of a clean heart. But as for me, my feet were almost gone; my steps had well-nigh slipped. For I was envious at the foolish, when I saw the prosperity of the wicked.' 'Surely they stand in slippery places, and shall be brought to desolation and utterly consumed with terrors. But Thou, O my God, art my portion for ever.' 'Whom have I in heaven but Thee? and there is none upon earth that I desire besides Thee.'"

In the utterance of these experiences his tall, manly form, flowing tears, sweet, commanding voice, all combined to produce an effect in the class room never to be forgotten. He then sang a solo of triumphant sentiment which thrilled the heart of every one present. Now, after more than forty years, I feel the thrill of that occasion.

On New Year's Eve, at the end of 1849, we held our first watch night meeting in San Francisco. I preached from the text, "What shall I render unto the Lord for all His benefits toward me? I will take the cup of salvation, and call upon the name of the Lord. I will pay my vows unto the Lord now in the presence of all His people." After preaching, a majority of those present spoke of the benefits they had received from God during the past year, and their deliverances from the dangers of the deep and of the desert.

Then on our knees we sang the covenant hymn:

> "Come, let us use the grace divine,
>   And all, with one accord,
> In a perpetual covenant join
>   Ourselves to Christ the Lord."

CHAPTER VII

OLD CALIFORNIA SOCIETY

I WILL now say something of society such as it was in California in those days. Of course there were human beings there mixed together, but they had not yet coalesced on any line that belongs to a true social life. California was indeed a vast social Sahara. The element of social life, to be sure, is inherent in our being, and has, perhaps, a more prominent and varied manifestation in human life than any other principle essential to humanity. Its most appropriate sphere of manifestation is in the well-ordered family. It gives vitality and felicity to connubial, paternal, maternal, and filial relationships. It constitutes the integral bond which unites the family together, the severance of which is as the lightning bolt entering a man's soul. The man or woman in whom this principle is dead is a misanthrope, and abides in darkness, uncheered by one ray of light or hope; loves neither father, nor mother, nor brother, nor sister, nor son, nor daughter; a miserable being, all alone in the world. The man who has no appropriate object on which to exercise his social affections is a Selkirk, standing on his lonely island surrounded by an ocean waste, fit emblem of the deep, dark void of his own restless soul.

Look, for example, even at Father Adam in Eden, with a brand-new creation all beaming in untarnished glory, and by the Creator Himself pronounced good, spread out before him. But among the teeming millions of animated nature, all moving in their pristine strength and beauty, there was not found a helpmeet for poor Adam, though he sought one diligently. The Lord saw that he was in a bad state of single wretchedness, and said, "It is not good that the man should be alone; I will make him a helpmeet for him." When Adam awoke from a deep sleep and set his eyes on an object worthy of his love, the most beautiful creature he ever saw in his life, part of himself, for himself, and all his own, loving him, and waiting to be loved by him, his paradise was complete; and Father Adam had ten thousand sons in California in 1850, any one of whom would have been most happy to sleep such a sleep as that, and to have *two* ribs taken out, if need be, to wake up in possession of a helpmeet. Alas! poor fellows, they often slept a deep sleep, and dreamed about extracted ribs, and waked but to stare out on their own isolated wretchedness.

The tearful adieux of fathers and sons and brothers as they departed for California told of the deep-gushing fountains of social sympathy and affection which swelled in their hearts. For weeks afterward they gazed daily, with tearful interest, at mementoes from loved ones already painfully distant; but they had launched out on unexplored seas of wealth-seeking adventure and must look ahead. Many were without moral quadrant, compass, or chart, but all had the telescope of manifest destiny through which they could see in the distance the auriferous mountains. Dark clouds sometimes intercepted their vision, but their edges were so beautifully fringed with the sunshine of hope that they only added grandeur to the scene. Each one felt as certain of getting there and of making his pile as did the prophet Balaam when trotting over to Mount Peor; but, poor fellows, how many of them, like the prophet, were driven to the wall!

Having reached the land of gold, and the flurry and surprises of the arrival over, then came the initiation of the "greenhorns" into the mysteries of California life, which was a very interesting, and in many cases a very serious, affair. Many arrived destitute of both friends and funds. Home reflections and associations brought painful contrasts to view and led to gloomy forebodings, and had to be dismissed from their minds. Those who put up at the hotel at thirty dollars per week found no soft beds in rosewood, with downy pillows, but occupied bunks made of rough boards on the side of the wall, shelving one above another as in emigrant ships. I have seen not only the walls of hotel lofts thus lined with bunks, but large cribs of them extending up to the roof of the house, covering the entire floor, except narrow passages giving access to them. Sheets were a superfluity not indulged in; pillows were of straw; mattresses, where they had any, were of the same; but in many cases the sleeper lay on the board which held him up off his fellow-sleeper beneath. I tried one night to sleep in one, which, unfortunately for me, was covered with cross slats, evidently designed for a mattress; but the last mentioned very important article, in such a case, was not there. Turning and rolling on these slats, I longed for morning. The soft side of a board, compared with them, would have been a luxury.

To the foregoing sleeping arrangements, if you add a few coarse grey blankets, you will have an original California lodging house, furnished. I heard it positively asserted by many who had been made tremblingly sensible of the fact, that in some houses a few pairs of blankets supplied a houseful of lodgers. As the weary fellows turned in one after another, they were comfortably covered till they would fall into a sound sleep, and then the blankets were removed to cover new recruits, and thus they were passed around for the accommodation of the whole company.

By way of variety, the adventurous lodgers in those pioneer hotels were visited frequently by the third plague of Egypt, accompanied by a liliputian host of the flea tribe—a sharp and restless race. Any man who is not proof against fleas, or who cannot effect a good insurance on his skin, had better keep away from old Spanish towns and Indian villages. When I was at Valparaiso I preached for the Rev. Dr. Trumbull, spent an evening in his company, and heard him relate a little of his experience with fleas. Said he: " When I first came to this place I feared the fleas would worry the life out of me. I could neither eat nor sleep, nor stay awake with any comfort. But after a few weeks I got used to them, and now I pay no attention to them. The biting of a dozen at once doesn't cause me to wince, nor lift my pen from my paper."

Others, not willing to pay much for the mere name of boarding at the hotel, formed mess companies, pitched their own tent, bought a skillet and coffee-pot, and kept bachelor's hall. This mode of life is familiarly known in California as ranching. Their tent or cabin is called the ranch, from *rancho*, the Spanish name for a farm. Ranchers usually cook by turns, sleep in bunks furnished with a pair of blankets and a few old clothes. A pair of trousers rolled up with an old coat makes a pretty good pillow.

Wash day among the ranchers came but seldom and was never welcome; for there were no wives or daughters or Bridgets to do the washing. Even in the city of San Francisco, in 1849-50, there was but little washing done. Men had not yet learned how, and to have it done cost from six to nine dollars a dozen; so it was generally found cheaper to give their check shirts a good wearing (white was out of the question) and then shed them off into the street and put on new ones. I have seen dozens of shirts lying around in the streets and vacant lots, which had thus been worn and never washed.

There were yet other fortune-seekers who, instead of ranching in companies, went alone. How they lived I know not; but they slept, each in a home-made cot, at each end of which there was a fork driven into the ground, in which lay a ridgepole, with just enough of canvas stretched over it to cover the cot. The cot, tent and all, were but about four feet high. There was one of this kind during the winter of 1849-50 near where I lived in Jackson Street. In the morning I could see the fellow crawl out of his cot from under his little tent, sometimes headforemost; at other times his feet would first appear. While I have seen large tents carried before the blast, ridgepole, rigging and all, this little tent, which looked like a covered grave, stood the storms of winter without moving a pin.

The various classes thus described are not made up of isolated cases, but represent the great mass of the early denizens of the golden land—men who wore checked shirts and grey or red flannel instead of coats, trousers fastened up by a leather girdle, such as was worn by John the Baptist, and planted down to their knees in the coarsest boots the market afforded. These were the men who, but a few months before, were known among their friends at home as doctors, lawyers, judges, and mechanics, clothed in broad-cloth and fine linen, each as a centre of social light and life, around which daily revolved the beautiful and gay, fair daughters, sisters, and wives.

How did these men so soon become rustics in California ? What became of their polish ? I will tell you. A large class of California adventurers thought about home and mourned their absence from loved ones till gloom and despair settled down on their souls. Hope died, energy and effort were paralysed, and they became helpless and worthless. Some of this class moved around like spectres a few months and then managed to beg or otherwise secure their passage home to friends. Whether social life ever had a sound revival in them I know not.

There was one of this class with whom I was acquainted who took a shipment of bonnets to California in 1849. There were very few American ladies in the country ; the Spanish ladies wore no bonnets, so my friend P—— found no sale for his goods. He had some money also, but knew not what to do with it. Once or twice a week he came to consult me as to what he should do.

Said I, " My dear fellow, you must go to work ; you cannot long bear California expenses unless you draw upon California resources. Moreover, if you continue to mope about the streets you will take the blues so badly that you'll die ; you must do something. If you can't open a large store, open a stand on the streets till you can do better ; if you can't do that, go to work in the streets ; roll a wheelbarrow at four dollars per day."

" I can't work in the streets," said he ; " I've always been accustomed to merchandising, and can't do manual labour ; but I must go into business."

" Very well," said I, " seek an opening to-day and go at it."

Some time after this, as I passed down Commercial Street, I saw Mr. P—— striding diagonally across the street to me. His face seemed much elongated, and I expected to hear a sad tale. Approaching me, he said, " Mr. Taylor, what shall I do ? " He was choking with an agony of emotion.

" What's the matter now, Mr. P—— ? "

" Oh," said he, " I loaned my money to my messmate. He said he wanted it but a few days, but now he's got it and gone, and I shall never see it again."

" Well, Mr. P——," I replied, " I'm very sorry for you ; but it's no use to mourn over lost money any more than over spilt milk. There's Captain Wooley, whom I know well ; he made one thousand dollars, and one day last week, as he was leaving his ship, he put his purse containing one thousand dollars in gold dust into his pocket ; but, poor fellow, he had no wife with him to sew up the holes in his pocket, so as he was descending his ship's ladder his purse, gold and all, slipped through a hole in his pocket into the bay. Well, sir, the captain said he never looked back nor lost one moment grieving over it. He knew it was gone, and just went to work, with great purpose of heart, to make another thousand.

"Yesterday as I walked in Montgomery Street a man called me by name: 'Mr. Taylor, look here. I made five thousand dollars, and had it hid away in my shanty here, and last night some rascal came and stole every dollar of it; so I'm just where I started. But never mind,' continued he, 'I'll go to work and make five thousand dollars more, and will try and put it where the rogues can't get hold of it.' And Mr. E——, a friend of mine who boarded up town, went down one morning to his auction store, which he had just filled with goods on his own account, but lo! the store, goods and all, were gone! While he slept the whole was consumed by fire. Did he stop to mourn over his losses? No, sir; he got another place and went into business before the setting of that day's sun. And here are hundreds of men who had made a fortune, and had it all invested in their storehouses and the goods that filled them, and in a single night the dreadful fires we have had laid them all in ashes. Well, sir, in the midst of smoke and ruins a new store, phœnix-like, springs right up, and is filled with goods by the time the smoke of the former fortunes have cleared away. So you see, Mr. P——, if you would get along in California, you must pick up courage and go to work, and stick to it till success crowns your patient toil."

Mr. P—— soon afterwards returned home, where he should have stayed in the first place.

Another of this class came often to me to know what he must do to be saved from starvation. So I said to him one day, "Mr. L——, a wag was once asked, 'How many dog days are there?' His prompt reply was, 'Every dog has his day.' Now, Mr. L——, if you'll go to work and be patient I think you'll have your day in California as well as others."

He afterwards succeeded much better, and attributed his success mainly to that little piece of advice. But a great many of this class in their despondency gave up, and sought comfort in the intoxicating bowl and went down to infamy and death. As I walked over the Sand Hills back of San Francisco I found Simon S—— lying under a scrub oak in rags, reduced by drunkenness and disease to the verge of the grave. As I exhorted him to give up strong drink, seek salvation, go to work, and become a man, oh, how bitterly he wept! But, poor fellow, energy was gone, hope had fled, nothing left to stimulate an effort.

H—— S——, a fine business man with an interesting wife and child in the city of B——, was taken from the gutter by his friends again and again. They knew him at home and loved him and greatly desired to save him; but finally, during one of those dreadful nights of storm and tempest in San Francisco in the winter of 1849, he was picked up by the police and put into a station house out of the rain; and in the morning when they went to wake him up they found him cold in death. I have seen such cases by hundreds by the wayside and in hospitals. Their name is legion.

There was another large class of California adventurers who, retaining their social life and hope and energy, tried to substitute objects of social affection for the wives, sisters, and daughters they could not see. These substitutes consisted of pet dogs, cats, etc. A company of men ranching near where I lived in Jackson Street had at one time a couple of grizzly bears with which they spent their social hours. A pet coon made a pretty good companion for some; others preferred a caged wildcat or California lion. One man whom I used to see often had a large family which accompanied him wherever he went. His family consisted of a bay horse, two dogs, two sheep, and two goats. Whenever I met one of that circle (and they were often seen in the streets) I saw them all together, and they seemed to be a very harmonious family indeed. Now, these animals seemed to be very mean substitutes for families at home; but, poor fellows, what better could they do?

About this time the Methodist Company, in the ship *Arkansas*, Captain Shepherd, arrived. According to their advertisement in New York the company was to be composed entirely of Methodists, and many joined it with that understanding, thinking it the rarest chance that ever was to get to California without being brought into contact with the wicked rabble that mixed in with promiscuous companies. But when they got out to sea and gathered the flock together they soon found that the goats outnumbered the sheep. The voyage, socially and morally, was by no means a pleasant one; and I have no doubt that many of them adopted St. Paul's conclusion that to be freed altogether from fornicators, covetous, extortioners, or idolaters, then must ye needs go out of the world. On the night of their arrival in the port of San Francisco, before they could land, a heavy gale caught their ship, which dragged her anchors and was carried by the violence of the storm till she struck Bird Island. There they were in midnight darkness, thumping among the breakers; and for a time they thought the whole ship's company must perish right there in their destined port; but by cutting away the masts they finally succeeded in saving the hull, cargo, and passengers.

The captain was subsequently known in San Francisco as Judge Shepherd. He brought a few very mean men to California; but also some as noble and good, perhaps, as ever landed in that port; such men, for example, as Calvin Lathrop, who for seven years was favourably known in California in the various relations of minister of the Gospel, Bible-class leader, gold digger, and clerk, and who filled so efficiently and satisfactorily for years the office of publishing agent of the *California Christian Advocate*. He returned to his family in New York, but remained a thorough Californian.

Self-support in California at times required more economy and harder work than in Africa at the present time. Wood in the market was forty dollars per cord, and very poor stuff at that. I couldn't afford to burn wood at those rates.

The Sand Hills back of where I lived had been thickly covered with evergreen scrub oaks, but they had been all cut off clean as a newly mown meadow. I, however, took my axe and went to work on a stump, and soon found, to my agreeable surprise, that more than half the tree was under ground; that the great roots spread out horizontally just under the surface; so I had a good supply of wood at the simple cost of cutting and loading it on my wheelbarrow and rolling it home. I had made a rare discovery, but, like the negro who first struck the rich gold lead in "Negro Hill," I soon had plenty of men to share my fortune.

The said coloured man, I am told, went into the mines to dig some gold for himself, and, thinking the diggings all free for everybody, he struck into the first good-looking place he came to. Presently along came a rough-looking miner, who said angrily, "What are you doing there in my claim, you black rascal?"

"Oh, massa, I didn't know dis are your claim!"

He then went off a little way and saw a hole in which he thought he might find gold, so he jumped into it and went to work; but immediately a man came running at him in a rage, and shouted, "Get out o' my hole, you lazy nigger, or I'll knock your head off!"

"Lor'sa, massa, me didn't know dis are your hole! Good Lor'sa, massa, where must I go?"

"Go up on the top of that hill and dig," replied the miner, not dreaming that there was gold there, for as yet the value of hill diggings had not been found out.

But the poor old coloured man went on the hill and sank a shaft (just like digging a well), and wrought there several months, when it was discovered that he had struck a rich lead, and was taking out the big lumps. He then soon had plenty of company to share in his rich discoveries. The hill was afterwards known as "Negro Hill," and yielded hundreds of thousands of dollars.

Steamship and stagecoach companies in the early days of California became noted for their generosity to Gospel ministers. Captain Gelson, as one of the owners of the steamer *M'Kim*, that plied between two cities, offered a free passage to all regular ministers—those sent out as missionaries, or those having pastoral charges. I believe in that way the precedent was established; at any rate, it became a custom with the owners and agents of steamboats running on the Sacramento and San Joaquin Rivers to give to all regular ministers a free ticket; and when the California Steamboat Navigation Company was organised they adopted that as an item in one of their by-laws. They subsequently thought that the privilege was abused; that preachers multiplied too fast for the wants of the country; in other words, that many who were not pastors, and possibly not preachers at all, took advantage of it.

It was said, for example, that a man took passage on a Sacramento boat for himself and a lot of mules. When the captain demanded his fare he replied, "Oh, I'm a preacher, sir." "Indeed!" said the captain, and, pointing to the mules, inquired, "and are these preachers, too?" The fellow had to walk up to the captain's office and settle. In consequence of these abuses the company passed a resolution making it necessary for all ministers wishing to travel on their boats to apply to the president of the company, who would, on the evidence that they were ministers, give them a free ticket.

Upon the whole, the liberality of California steamboat companies towards ministers of the Gospel stands unrivalled in the history of steamboat navigation, and saved to the preachers (all of them poor enough in regard to means) an expense in travelling amounting to an aggregate of thousands of dollars. Stage proprietors in California also showed a commendable liberality in the same way.

In the early days of California, Gospel ministers and their wives had to do their own housework. The idea of a regular servant in a preacher's family, when servants got larger salaries than preachers, was out of the question. The preachers and their wives had to serve each other, and both together serve the children and the people. I knew a California presiding elder who used to roll up his sleeves and spend a day over the washtub as regularly as he went to quarterly meeting. I have turned out many a washing of clothes, and baked many a batch of bread, and think I understand the details of kitchen work better than I do bookmaking. There were, however, preachers in California who would not hazard their ministerial dignity in the kitchen or over the washtub, but were contented to let their wives struggle through all such drudgery alone at whatever hazard.

As soon as California pioneers made up their minds to settle permanently in the country their conduct underwent a great change for the better. They began earnestly to manifest interest in the establishment of schools and churches, the regular preaching of the Gospel, the better observance of the Sabbath, and whatever they thought would contribute to improve the social condition of society. Some who could leave their business went in person for their families; but many more, not being able to leave without too great a sacrifice of time or money, sent for their families. Single men, also, from similar considerations, came to similar conclusions in regard to permanent settlement. Some, having matrimonial engagements at home, began to arrange for their consummation with reference to a home in California. Others determined to live in California at any rate, and trust to getting a wife to share their fortunes, either from home or by good fortune from among the arrivals of fair ones, or from the divorcement or death of some fellow who had a wife in California. A great many young men modestly but seriously requested my observation to find out and my mediation to try and secure for each of them a good wife. I once received a letter from a stranger whom I had never seen, living in Bodega Valley, to this effect :—

"DEAR SIR,—You will please pardon the liberty I take in addressing to you this note, and especially for introducing the subject it contains. I am a young man twenty-nine years old, five feet ten inches high, possessing a sound constitution and good health. I have a good farm, well stocked, well improved, and all paid for. I want to make this my home. I am a single man, living alone; but I find it not good to be alone, and I want a wife. I thought, as you always take an interest in every good work, and as you live in that great port of entry, you might be kind enough to recommend to me some lady who would make me a good wife. I would like to have one possessing common sense, good disposition, and one who understands how to attend to household duties. I think I could make such a woman happy, and should not expect her to work beyond her own inclination. I am not very particular about beauty, nor whether she has a cent of money. If you can render me any service in this matter I shall be exceedingly obliged, and will, besides, remunerate you handsomely for your trouble. Please write me at your earliest convenience."

His proper signature and address were added; but, poor fellow, the demand was so great among my intimate acquaintances, and the supply so limited, that I could do nothing for him. If it had been practicable for a man to open an intelligence office, with a good supply of wives instead of servants, he would have had a run.

Mr. S——, a friend of mine, in the city of Sonora, negotiated for a wife through a very respectable married lady in that city, to whom he was well and favourably known. The said lady had a niece in the East who she thought would suit, and be well suited in my friend, Mr. S——. So it was agreed that Mr. S—— should write the said young lady, proposing marriage and the offer of money to pay her passage to California, and accompany the letter with his photograph, and that the aunt should also write, giving all necessary information, etc. The young lady was requested to answer at her earliest convenience, and, if she acceded to the proposition, to accompany her acceptance with her photograph. It seemed that the young lady had been desiring to go to California to see her aunt, and on receiving such news from a far country made up her mind to go without delay.

The next mail carried back her consent and the likeness of her smiling face, and as soon as the passage money could be sent from her unseen lover she embarked for California. The two lovers were introduced to each other and united in the holy bonds in the house of the aunt. I learned that they were perfectly delighted with each other!

There were in California, according to the State census returns in 1856, in a total aggregate population of five hundred and seven thousand and sixty-seven, but seventy thousand white women all told; while there were one hundred and seventy-five thousand men of war, men liable to military duty, between the ages of eighteen and forty-five.

Now, in view of the foregoing facts, it is not difficult to conceive the thrilling social effects of a semi-monthly arrival in San Francisco of wives, families, and charming, virtuous Marys. An

7

observer could tell a month in advance when a man was expecting the arrival of his real or intended wife ; the old slouch hat, check shirt, and coarse outer garments disappeared, and the gentleman could be seen on Sunday going to church, newly rigged from head to foot, with fine beaver or silk hat, white linen nice and clean, good broad-cloth coat, velvet vest, patent leather boots, his long beard shaven or neatly shorn ; he looked like a new man. As the time drew near many of his hours were spent near the wharves or on Telegraph Hill, looking for the signal to announce the coming steamer. If, owing to some breakage or wreck there was a delay of a week or two, then the suspense was awful beyond description. I remember how my good friend, Hon. D. O. Shattuck, Judge of the Superior Court of San Francisco, who was waiting the arrival of his family on the steamer *North America*, was agonised when he heard of the wreck of the steamer sixty miles below Acapulco. After much delay and suffering, however, they arrived in safety.

When the signal flag on Telegraph Hill, announcing the arrival of a steamer, was thrown to the breeze there was a general rush, and before the arrival gun was fired the wharf was crowded with such men as we have described, and by those who sympathised socially with them, to the number sometimes of from three to five thousand.

The two steamship companies had to put up a gate at the head of each of their wharves to prevent the assemblage of crowds, and gave strict orders to let none pass in unless they had families or friends aboard. But even after that enough had families, or wives in anticipation, or particular friends aboard, to crowd the wharves still. Men by hundreds assembled through social sympathy to witness the happy greeting of men and their wives who had not seen each other for years, accompanied by dancing and shouting for joy, embracing, kissing, laughing, and crying. The disappointment of some was almost like a thundershock. I knew a man well who boarded a steamer expecting to meet his wife, and the disappointment threw him into a spell of sickness, from which he did not recover for nearly a fortnight.

I knew another who came from the mines to meet his wife, waited several days in San Francisco for the arrival of the steamer, and then, instead of meeting his wife, received a letter from her stating that she feared to make the voyage, and had indefinitely postponed it unless he would come home to accompany her. The poor man was almost deranged, now weeping with grief, now enraged, saying: "I'll never send for her again, and I'll never go home as long as I live ! If she can get along without me I can get along without her. I'll go back to the mines and live and die a hermit." Then after a pause he would add, " But there are my children ; I can't bear to give them up ! "

I took the poor fellow to my house and reasoned with him on the subject until I succeeded in reconciling him somewhat to his disappointment. After a few months his family arrived.

My friend Brown, from Baltimore, had two disappointments before his wife arrived. At the time he expected her he boarded the steamer and learned to his sorrow that she was not aboard. He then thought the next steamer would bring her without a doubt. Two dreary weeks went by, but he was a good fellow and waited patiently; and when the steamer got in he was on hand in good time, you may be sure. Rushing aboard, he inquired, " Is Mrs. Brown aboard ? Is Mrs. Brown aboard ? "

"Oh yes," replied one who seemed to know; "she is in her state-room, No. —."

He hastily took the circuit of the state-rooms to find the number. Mrs. Brown heard in the meantime that her beloved husband was aboard, and was filled with ecstasies. Finally Brown found her state-room, and sprang in to embrace his wife, when oh! shocking to their hopes, they found it was neither of them; he was not the man and she was not the woman! Soon after his wife and family arrived.

I had another Baltimore friend who was a widower. Having at home two very interesting daughters, and a second wife engaged, he sent for the three to come together to California. At the wharf he was met by his youngest daughter, who alone was left to tell the sad tale that the other two had suddenly sickened and died and found a grave in the coral depths of the Pacific.

Another friend of mine had his family coming out in the splendid *Queen of the Seas*. When she was due he prepared a great feast and invited about two hundred guests to celebrate his wife's arrival. When he boarded the ship his little daughter met him and pointed him to a box which lay in a boat on the hurricane deck, securely folded in tarpaulin, and said to him, " There's mother ! "

CHAPTER VIII

MY HOSPITAL MINISTRY

In the fall of 1849, as I walked down Clay Street one day, my eye rested on a sign in large red letters, "City Hospital." I stopped and gazed at it till my soul was thrilled with horror. The letters looked as if they were written with blood, and I said to myself, "Ah, that is the depot of death, where the fast adventurers of California, young men in manhood's strength stricken down by the hand of disease, are cast out of the train and left to perish. There all their bright hopes and visions of future wealth and weal expire and are buried for ever. There are husbands and sons and brothers thousands of miles from sympathising kindred and friends dying in destitution and despair. Shall I not be a brother to the sick stranger in California, and tell him of that heavenly Friend 'that sticketh closer than a brother?'" The cross of intruding myself into strange hospitals and offering my services to the promiscuous masses of the sick and dying of all nations and creeds was, to my unobtrusive nature, very heavy, but I there resolved to take it up ; a decision which I have never regretted. I went immediately to the said hospital and inquired for the physician who had it in charge; introduced myself to him and told him the object of my call; to which he replied, "I can readily appreciate your motives, but then you must know, sir, that we have very sick men in every room, who could not bear any noise. Anything like singing or praying might greatly excite them and make them worse. I prefer you would not visit the wards unless some particular man wishes to see you."

"Well, Doctor," I replied, "I certainly would not wish to do anything that would be injurious to any patient, but I have been accustomed to visit the sick, and think I so understand my business as to talk and sing and pray, or do whatever may seem appropriate, not only without injury to any one, but in a manner that will even contribute to the improvement of their physical condition. By diverting their minds from the dark realities of their own condition and unhappy surroundings, and by interesting them in some new associations and themes of thought, I may impart to their minds vigour and hope, which unite with gathering strength and make successful resistance against disease. Those who are hopelessly diseased cannot receive much injury from my visits, while I may be instrumental in benefiting their departing souls. If you please, Doctor," I continued, "you can go with me or send a man to point out the men to whom you do not wish me to speak, and to see that I do no injury to any one."

Said the doctor, "I have no time to go with you, and nobody to send."

Another doctor present then added, "It is not proper that he should go through the hospital."

At that moment an old man, who had been sitting in the office listening to our conversation, said, "Doctor, there are many sick men in the hospital who I know would be very glad to receive a visit from this gentleman ; and if you will allow me, sir, I will conduct him through the rooms."

The doctor replied, "Very well, take him upstairs first, and then down to the lower wards."

" Aye, aye, sir," said the old tar, as he beckoned me to follow him upstairs. He introduced me to every patient in the house, and made a greater ado over my arrival at the hospital than if the *alcalde* had visited them. I was first conducted through the pay rooms, the department of those who, in whole or in part, paid for their keeping. Many small rooms had but from two to four men in them. Others, larger, had as many as twelve. I spoke to each patient, inquiring after their condition in health and the state of their soul. I then addressed a few words of sympathy and religious instruction to all in the room collectively, sang a few verses in a soft strain, and prayed in an audible but subdued tone, adapting the petition, as nearly as possible, to the wants of their individual cases as I had learned them, and so passed on, performing similar services in each room.

After going through the pay rooms I was next conducted across a yard to a separate one-story building about thirty or forty feet in size, divided into two wards, each containing from forty to fifty sick men. Here the city patients proper were confined together as closely as possible to allow room between their cots for one person to pass. I thought the upstairs rooms were filthy enough to kill any well man who would there confine himself for a short period ; but I now saw that, in comparison with the others, they were entitled to be called choice rooms, for the privilege of dying in which a man who had money might well afford to pay high rates. But these lower wards were so offensive to the eye, and especially to the olfactories, that it was with great difficulty I could remain long enough to do the singing, praying, and talking, I deemed my duty.

The ordinary comforts, and even the necessaries of life, in California in those days were very rare and costly, and to the patients were things to be remembered in the experience of the past only to add, by contrast, a keener edge to their present sorrows.

The nurses were generally men devoid of sympathy, careless, rude in their care of the sick, and exceedingly vulgar and profane. One hundred dollars per month was about as low as anything in the shape of a man could be hired, and hence hospital nurses were not only the most worthless of men, but insufficient in number to attend adequately to their duties.

I remember a poor fellow, by the name of Switzer, dying in one of these wards, who told me that he lay whole nights suffering, in addition to the pains of mortal disease, the ragings of thirst, without a drop of water to wet his lips. A cup of tea was set in the evening upon a shelf over his head, but his strength was gone, and he had no more power to reach it than a man on a gibbet. He was a Christian, too, a member of the Congregational Church, and I have no doubt went from there to heaven. When he got to that country in which "there is no more death, neither sorrow nor crying," and looked back to the place where he left his corruptible body, the contrast must have filled him with unutterable surprise.

The most prevalent and fatal disease in California at that time was chronic diarrhœa and dysentery, a consumption of the bowels very similar in its debilitating effect on the constitution to consumption of the lungs. Men afflicted with this disease have been seen moping about the streets, looking like the personification of death and despair, for weeks, till strength and money and friends were gone, and then, as a last resort, they were carried to the hospital to pass a few miserable weeks more in one of those filthy wards, where they often died in the night without any one knowing the time of their departure. In the morning when the nurses passed round they found and reported the dead. A plain coffin was immediately brought, for a supply was kept on hand, and laid beside the cot of the deceased, and he was lifted from the cot just as he died, laid in the coffin, and carried out to the dead cart, the driver of which was seen daily plodding through the mud to the graveyard near North Beach, with from one to three corpses at a load.

It turned out that the old man who piloted me through the hospital on my first visit was an old shipmaster, Captain A. Welch. He introduced me that day to his friend, Captain Lock, who died soon after, having after my visit professed to find peace through Jesus and a preparation for heaven. Captain Welch told me that, seeing his friend neglected, he said to the doctor, "Captain Lock has had no attention for forty-eight hours, and is dying from sheer neglect."

"Well," replied the doctor, "let him die; the sooner the better. The world can well spare him, and the community will be relieved when he is gone." He died that night. Before his death he gave his clothing to his friend, Captain Welch, but the captain told him he would not touch a thing he had while he was alive; but as soon as he was gone the nurse relieved the captain of any trouble with the effects of the deceased man.

The doctor fell out with Captain Welch because he spoke his mind so freely, and threatened to turn him out of the hospital.

"Yes," said Captain Welch in reply, "I saw Captain —— pay you for the ten days he had been here eighty-six dollars, and after his death you collected the same bill from his friends. Now, sir, if you want me to show you up, just turn me out."

The doctor then took his cot from him, and the captain said, "Doctor, where shall I sleep?"

"Sleep there on the floor," replied the doctor, pointing to a corner where they laid out the dead when it was too late in the evening or the weather too bad to remove them directly from their cot of death to the dead cart.

The captain said he lay there one night with four corpses around him, and could hardly get his breath. I have heard patients complain of very foul play toward those who had money, but sick men are apt to be sensitive and suspicious, especially in such a place as that, and I always hoped that the facts were not so bad as represented; but from what I saw I had my fears for the safety of any man's life who had money in the hospital at the time of which I speak.

The hospital changed hands several times, however, within a few months, and one or two good physicians, and I believe honest and kind-hearted men, had for a short time the care of the sick, and were really working a reform in the old hospital, before the whole care of the city patients was, in 1850, transferred to Dr. Peter Smith, in a new hospital near the corner of Clay and Powell Streets, where the sick had better accommodation and more attention shown them.

Old Captain Welch was in the old hospital over a year, and would doubtless have died if he had been confined to his room, but he was out where he could get pure air most of his time. He had a very sore leg, and the doctor told him that it was mortifying and would have to be amputated. Finally several doctors came into his room with a table and a lot of surgical instruments and said to him, "Come, captain, we want to lash you to this table and take off that bad leg of yours."

"I won't have my leg taken off," replied the captain.

"If you don't," said the doctor, "you are a dead man, or as good as dead, for that leg is mortified now."

"Well," said the captain, "if I die I'll die with both legs on me."

The doctor became enraged, and said to him, "If you don't obey orders immediately and submit to the rules of this house you shall leave it this day."

"Very well," rejoined the captain. "And that very day," said the captain to me afterward, "I took up my sore leg and walked off with it, and have not been back since."

John Purseglove, a good Methodist brother who had just arrived in the city, sick and destitute, was sent to the hospital; but, finding that he was sinking daily and would soon die if he remained there, he prayed to the Lord to give him strength to get off his bed and walk away. He said he believed the Lord would help him, and according to his faith so was his effort, for he immediately crawled out, and without saying a word to doctor or nurse or anybody, he scrambled away by the aid of a couple of sticks, determined, if he must die, to die somewhere else. Some of the brethren soon found him and fitted up a room for him and supplied his wants till he recovered. He always believed that by leaving the hospital he slipped right out of the clutches of death.

I have no recollection of more than three Methodists who died in the San Francisco hospital, and they were sick on their arrival and had never been reported to the Church. Indeed, there were but very few hospital patients connected with any Church. I met with many backsliders there who had once been Church members, but were not then.

To transcribe in detail the hospital scenes which have been daguerreotyped on the tablets of my memory during a period of seven years in San Francisco would make a volume. My purpose, therefore, in these reminiscences is simply to present a few specimen scenes and individual cases of hope and despair occurring at different periods in the history of that city.

My usual mode of visitation was to speak personally to as many as possible; inquire into their condition and wants, bodily, spiritual, and otherwise; act as amanuensis for the sick and dying, recording last messages to friends at home; get letters out of the post office and convey them to the sick; carry messages to friends in the city; and in very early days, when waiters were scarce, I often ministered to the bodily wants of the sick, dressed blisters, turned or raised patients, fixed their beds, gave them drink, and sometimes comforted the convalescing with a little of Mrs. Taylor's good home-made bread, and gave them such advice as I thought might be useful to them.

As a spiritual adviser in my hospital visits I generally addressed them personally and tried to lead them to seek an acquaintance with the sinner's Friend. I then usually sang in each ward in a soft tone, one, two, or three appropriate pieces, and prayed for them collectively and personally, so far as I had been able to learn their personal condition and wants, and frequently, either before or after prayer, made some remarks in the form of an exhortation to be reconciled to God. I usually introduced religious exercises by saying, "If my brethren in affliction have no objections, we will sing a few verses and have a word of prayer together." I do not remember of ever hearing an objection made but once, and that was by a poor man who became very much ashamed of his conduct before the exercises were over. Many, to be sure, seemed careless and indifferent, read novels while I prayed, and never seemed to profit by what I said; but a large majority seemed to appreciate very highly my efforts for their good. Even foreigners who could not understand my language seemed greatly interested, especially in my singing.

I was once travelling in San José Valley, and, passing in sight of a company of Spaniards who had stopped at a spring of water to refresh themselves, one of them came running to me and grasped my hand as though I had been a brother he had not seen for a dozen years. For a moment I could not tell how to interpret his conduct; but I immediately recognised him as a man I had often seen in the hospital. He had been a great sufferer, and I had many times bent over him and inquired after his welfare, and it seemed that my attentions to him, or the singing or something else, had made a deep impression on him.

In my book on "Street Preaching" there is a chapter of triumphant death scenes, in which are given a number of cases of hopeful conversion to God among hospital patients; those, alas! are but the exceptions and not the rule.

I remember after pleading with a dying man to give his heart to God he said, "Oh, it's not worth while now; I'm getting better; I'll soon be well. I feel no pain at all, and nothing ails me now but want of breath. I can't breathe easy; but I'll soon be relieved."

Poor man! I could then hear distinctly the death-rattle in his throat, and yet he would not believe that there was any danger. In a few hours he was a corpse.

I remember a fine-looking young man from New York whom I tried hard to lead to Christ; and after talking and singing and praying with him, and doing everything I could to induce him to try and seek Jesus, I said to him, "Now, my dear brother, when will you begin to pray and try to give your heart to God?"

"Well," said he, "I think I will make a commencement in about three weeks."

The poor fellow, though he would not believe it, was dying then, and I knew it, and hence I continued to press the subject of a preparation on his attention till he drew the cover over his head to escape my appeals. A few hours afterwards he was covered with the pall of death.

Young C—— M—— was accidentally shot, and immediately sent for me in such haste that the messenger stopped me in the midst of a street sermon, and entreated me to go at once and try to relieve the mind of the dying man. When I presented myself beside his bloody bed he said, "Father Taylor, I'm glad you've come; but, oh, I'm in such pain I can't talk or pray now! Please call again in an hour; perhaps by that time I'll feel better." I prayed with him, and called again, but found him gasping in his last struggle.

Without noting a hundred such cases, as I might, which have come under my own observation, I will, for the further illustration of the subject, add but one other case.

He was a very genteel-looking man who died of cholera in the hospital during the fall of 1850. He was in a collapsed state when I found him. I said to him, "My dear brother, have you made your peace with God?"

"No, sir," said he; "I can't say that I have."

"Do you not pray to the Lord sometimes to have mercy on you, and for the sake of Jesus to pardon your sins?"

"No, sir."

"Have you never prayed?"

"No, sir, never in my life."

"You believe in the divine reality of religion and that we may have our sins all forgiven and enjoy the conscious evidence of pardon, do you not?"

"Yes, sir; I believe in religion, and think it a very good thing to have."

He was calm and composed ; his dreadful paroxysms had passed, and the fatal work was done. He was then poised on an eddying wave of death's dark tide, which on its next swell would whirl him out of the bounds of time into the breakers of eternal seas beyond. I saw his peril, and pulled with all my might to bring the lifeboat of mercy by his side. I got very near to him, and entreated him to try to get into it and save his soul, but I could not prevail on him to make an effort ; under the force of the ruling habit of his life he coolly said, " Well, I'll think about it."

I have seen hundreds of poor fellows sleeping away their lives without any apparent consciousness of danger, and I have heard men call this peaceful dying !

A great many, however, of those whom I have seen in the death struggle shook off the apathy I have described and awoke to the keenest sensibilities of conscience and the most dreadful forebodings of future ill ; but a large majority of such wrapped themselves in the mantle of despair, so dark and impervious that no ray of hope could reach their souls.

A gentleman from Boston, very near his end, said to me: "My friends are nearly all religious ; I have passed through a great many revivals, and have had a great many pressing invitations and opportunities to seek religion. How easy it would then have been for me to have given my heart to God ! What a fool I was ! Why did I not embrace religion and be a happy man ? But, alas ! I did not when I might, and now I cannot."

When Mr. R——, from Baltimore, was seized with cholera he sent for me to come and see him, and said to me when I entered his room, " My wife, who is a Christian woman, has been writing me ever since I came here to make your acquaintance and attend your church, but I have not done it ; and, what is worse, I am about to leave the world without a preparation to meet God." He was as noble-looking a man as could be found in a thousand, and, knowing many of his friends in Baltimore, I felt the greatest possible sympathy for him. After labouring with him about an hour, in urging him to try and fix his mind on some precious promise of the Bible, he said : " There is but one passage in the Bible that I can call to mind, and that haunts me. I can think of nothing else, for it exactly suits my case : 'He, that being often reproved hardeneth his heart, shall suddenly be destroyed, and that without remedy.' Mr. Taylor," continued he, "it's no use to talk to me or to try to do anything further ; I am that man, and my doom is fixed."

The next day when I entered his room he said to a couple of young men present, "Go out, boys ; I want to talk to Mr. Taylor." Then he said : " I have no hope, my doom is fixed, but, for the warning of others, I want to tell you something that occurred a few months ago. I was then in health and doing a good business, and a man said to me, ' Dick, how would you like to have a clerkship ?'

I replied, 'I wouldn't have a clerkship under Jesus Christ.' Now, sir, that is the way I treated Christ when I thought I did not need Him; and now when I'm dying, and can do no better for this life, it's presumption to offer myself to Him. It is no use; He won't have me."

Nothing that I could say seemed to have any effect toward changing his mind. A few hours afterwards, when he felt the icy grasp of death upon his heart, he cried, " Boys, help me out of this place!"

" Oh no, Dick, you're too sick; we cannot help you up."

" Oh do help me up; I can't lie here."

" Oh, Dick, don't exert yourself so; you'll hasten your death."

" Boys," said the poor fellow, "if you don't help me up, I'll cry murder!" and with that he cried at the top of his voice, which was yet strong and clear, " Murder! murder! murder!" till life's tide ebbed out and his voice was hushed in death.

CHAPTER IX

AMONG THE MINERS AND MERCHANTS

THESE brief reminiscences of early days in California would not be complete without mention of life among the miners. As an illustration of the miner's hope, faith, patience, and endurance, I will instance the Live Yankee Company, of Forest City. I was informed when there that, as an experiment, they commenced a drift into the mountain between that city and Smith's Flat. The mountain was so high that it was impossible to prospect it by sinking a shaft to the bed rock, the nearest way to the heart of the mountain being in a line from the base.

They soon encountered a stratum of solid rock, nearly as hard as pig metal. The company, having no capital outside of their muscular power and dauntless energy, had to get their provisions on credit, and worked in that drift, boring, blasting, and digging for three years before they got the colour, but struck it at last, and were amply repaid for all their toil. They took out a simple lump while I was there worth seven hundred dollars.

Miners were not all successful, but they nearly all abounded in hope and energy. I seldom ever met with one who had not a good prospect. No matter what his past disappointments and losses had been, he was going to do first-rate as soon as he could get his claim open or his pay dirt washed out. Even the little boys of the country partook of this spirit. A lucky miner, determined to take his family back to the Atlantic side, came on as far as San Francisco, and, while stopping at Hillman's Hotel, awaiting the day of embarkation, went out one night and fell among thieves, who robbed and murdered him. His body, three days afterwards, was found in the bay. His poor widow was almost heart-broken, and their little miner boy, only four years old, when he heard that his papa was dead, went to her and said, "Ma, don't cry! *don't cry!* We'll dit along. You won't have to beg, ma! Dist wait till I get a little bigger, and I'll do up and dig a hole wight down in the mountain and det out the dold for you. Ma, don't cry! You won't have to beg!"

A Baltimorean made five thousand dollars in the mines, and started to go home to his family, but was induced to go into a fluming operation and spend a summer in the river. He concluded that it was no use to go home with only five thousand dollars, when, by staying a few months longer, he could double that amount. The operation in the river was unsuccessful, and the poor man lost not only every dollar of his money, but, by working in the water so much, lost his health and never got farther homeward than to San Francisco. I found him there in the charity hospital, just as he was sinking into the grave.

The prospectors constituted a very large and useful class of miners. They were always dreaming of immense treasures of undiscovered wealth. No matter how well they were doing, when they got a few hundred dollars ahead they must be off with pick and pan and miner's pack, and seldom ever stopped till their money was all gone, and then they set to work in one place again till they could make another raise.

They were constantly discovering new diggings and opening immense treasures for others to gather and enjoy, while they continued to toil and go, and toil and go again, enduring the greatest hardship and labour and poverty, living on hope, but dying in despair. They were very much like their hardy pioneer brothers who led the van of Western emigration, lived in log cabins, supplied their families with plenty of game and pounded cake, slept on their arms, and defended the outposts of civilisation against savages and wild beasts; an honest, generous, noble set of men, who deserved much but got nothing more than a plain subsistence, and usually died in poverty.

As a specimen of California prospecting, I will mention the case of my friend C——. He arrived in San Francisco in 1850, and obtained employment at Mission Dolores in the brick-making business, which was his trade, at seven dollars per day, with the promise of steady work by the year. After making a few hundred dollars he became dissatisfied. Said he, " I've not seen my mother for several years, and I can't stay more than a year or two in California, and I see plainly that in that time seven dollars per day won't make such a pile as I want."

So he gave up his situation and went to the mines, where he knew he could do better with even ordinary success, and, besides, stand a chance of making some big strikes. I met with him a couple of years afterward, and said, " Well, Friend C——, how do you get along?"

"Oh, pretty well," replied he; "I opened a first-rate claim in Mariposa County last year, but just as I got it in working condition the water failed, so I had to let it lie over. When the time came that I could have worked it I happened to be away up near Downieville, and, having a good claim there, I didn't go back to Mariposa. I have taken out a good deal of gold, but in prospecting from place to place I have spent it all; but I have some good claims which will pay big by-and-by."

Three years after that I met friend C—— in American Valley. "Hallo, my old friend; how do you get along?"

"Oh, pretty well, but I'm not ready to go home yet "

"I presume your dear old mother would be glad to see you by this time."

"Yes, indeed; and I would be glad to see her; but I can't go home till I make something."

"Well, how near are you ready?"

"I don't know. I have made money, but in travelling from place to place I have spent it all. I have been up to Oregon since I saw you, and had a chance to get a first-rate farm there if I could have stayed; but I had some rich claims in Mariposa, and thought I ought to come down and look after them; but when I got there I found that some fellows had jumped my claim, and I could not get them off without a great deal of trouble, so I came away and left them. I afterward opened a good claim near Yreka, but my partner was a disagreeable, quarrelsome fellow, so I sold out for a mere song and came away. I have a good prospect near Elizabethtown which, I think, will pay well when I get it opened."

Another with whom I was acquainted, who had not seen his family for six years, said to me one day, "For five years I have set a time to go home about every six months; but every six months has found me either dead broke or doing so well I could not leave."

But few of this adventurous class of prospectors would submit to the mortification of returning to their friends without money, and but few of them ever had enough money at one time to pay their passage home, while nearly all of them, with their mining skill, might have made a fortune had they remained in one place and saved their earnings.

The moral condition of the miners was by no means what it should have been. But very few of them were particularly anxious to go to heaven. I preached to a large assembly of miners one Sunday afternoon in the streets of Placerville, then a flourishing mining city of six thousand inhabitants. In front of my goods-box pulpit stood a stagecoach, which was crowded to its utmost capacity with as many of my auditors as were fortunate enough to secure so good a seat.

I endeavoured to show the multitude before me their unfitness for heaven in their unregenerate state, their utter want of sympathy with God or adaptation to the immunities of heaven. To illustrate the truth of my position I said: "If God should despatch a railway train to the city of Placerville this afternoon, to convey passengers direct to heaven, the conductor might shout 'All aboard' till the setting of the sun and not get one passenger. Heaven has no attraction for you. It is a place to which you don't want to go. Why, if the flaming steeds of Elijah's chariot of fire were hitched on to that stagecoach, and the driver cracked his whip for the heavenly country, every fellow in it would jump out;" and in a moment the coach was cleared. Every man in it leaped for the street in apparent fright from the apprehension that, perhaps, Elijah's horses might be hitched to the coach and they be taken off to glory, a place to which they did not wish to go.

Sunday in the mines was remembered only as a day for trading, recreation, spreeing, business meetings, and preparation for the business of the ensuing week. It was very common to see large cards hung up in boarding houses and business places like this:

"ALL BILLS PAID UP HERE ON SUNDAY."

That was the day for miners to get their blacksmith work done and lay in their supply of provisions for the week; the day for holding public meetings for the enactment of miners' laws or other municipal business. Under a general statute each mining district enacted its own laws by the voice of the majority, regulating all the mining claims of the district. Under these laws they could sue and be sued, and everybody had to conform to them. Mining companies and water companies also did collectively a great deal of their business on that day, and promiscuous masses of all sorts assembled at the hotels and drinking saloons to drink and spree without restraint. What was worse, the standard of moral law was thrown down and its authority denied. When we remember what a large majority of those men were educated in Christian countries, and that many had been professors of religion, it is easy to see how quickly even a Christian people will relapse into heathenism if deprived of the wholesome restraints and elevating influences of the Gospel.

In a preaching tour I made through the mines as late as 1855 I travelled nearly a week without the privilege of any Christian association, and I longed for the opportunity of taking a Christian by the hand and of feeling the warming sympathy of a heart that loved Jesus. On entering a mining town I inquired at the hotel whether there were any professors of religion in that town.

"Yes," answered the landlord; there is one. Mr. J——, our blacksmith, is a good Christian man." And different boarders added, "Yes, Mr. J—— is a good man if ever there was one. He has his family here and everybody looks up to him."

So at my earliest convenience I hastened to see Brother J——. He received me very cordially and introduced me to his family, all of whom looked very neat and respectable, and I rejoiced in the privilege of meeting a Christian family away in those wild woods.

As soon as I accepted the offered chair I inquired of Brother J—— how he was prospering in religious life.

"Well," replied he, "I think I am getting along pretty well considering all the circumstances; but not so well as I did in Illinois, where I enjoyed the public means of grace. My greatest drawbacks here are my having no religious meetings to go to and my having to work on Sunday. I support my family by blacksmithing, and the miners must have most of their work done on Sunday; and, to tell you the truth, I have worked here in my shop every Sunday except two for five years. One Sunday I was sick and could not work, and one Sunday I went to hear the only sermon that was ever preached on this creek, which was delivered by Brother Merchant."

"Oh," thought I, "if this is the best man in these mountains the Lord pity the worst."

I travelled nearly a week before I found another Christian. He was an old shipmaster, a good old Methodist from Boston. I invited him to go to Long Bar, on the north fork of Feather River, to hear me preach on the following Sunday.

At the appointed hour Sunday morning I had a large audience to preach to under the shade of an ancient pine tree. The sound of the Gospel had never echoed through those hills before. Looking over my audience, I discovered the old captain, and felt glad to think that I had at least one praying heart who could sympathise with my mission and my message of mercy. After the meeting I asked the old captain to take a walk with me up into the mountain to pray. I felt that I needed the warming influence of a little prayer meeting, and supposed that he did also. Finding a suitable place, I sang a few verses and prayed; I then sang again, and, thinking I had got the good brother thawed out and that he in turn would contribute to the fire of my own heart, I called on him to lead in prayer. But I couldn't get a grunt out of him. Thought I, " Poor old captain, he is dried up."

I announced an afternoon appointment for preaching in the same place, and thought from the size of the morning audience and the apparent good effect of the preaching upon them that I should have a much larger congregation and a better time at the second appointment. But to my surprise I did not have more than twenty hearers ; and when I cast about to know the cause I learned that, according to custom, nearly the whole population of the neighbourhood had by that hour of the day become too drunk to attend preaching. Such a variety of antics as they displayed beat anything I had ever witnessed. Next morning I found most of them sober and ready for work ; and to show their appreciation of my ministerial services they gave me a donation for my Bethel cause of nearly one hundred dollars.

The cases here given are to illustrate the general character of the miners in those regions. I found in nearly every place I visited honourable exceptions—sober, serious men who deeply deplored the prevailing wickedness of the miners; and everywhere I went there was a general expression of desire for the regular preaching of the Gospel and the establishment of its institutions among them, and a liberal support for a preacher and his family was pledged. I found a few merchants, too, who would not sell goods on the Sabbath. A man of my acquaintance, who passed for a minister of the Gospel before he went to California, opened a provision store in the southern mines. He commenced business with the determination not to sell liquor or break the Sabbath. He had a moderate degree of success on that principle, but nothing to compare with the success of his business competitors who sold liquor and kept open on Sunday. His pecuniary sense became shocked a great deal more by what he considered his losses than his moral sense was comforted by his spiritual conquests. So, having mining friends to call and see him on Sunday, he was induced to leave his back door ajar so that any who desired might be accommodated with a pair of boots or a week's provision. That paid so well that he was induced next to leave his front door ajar. He then in a short time, in accordance with that dangerous but popular maxim, "May as well be hung for stealing a sheep as a lamb," set his door wide open and added liquor to his stock. He felt that it was all wrong, but pleaded necessity, and thought that as soon as he could make a certain sum of money he would quit the business, go home, and do good with his money. For a season he had extraordinary success, and employed thirty yoke of oxen—all his own—on the road from Stockton to his place of business. He besides had several hundred head of valuable cattle.

Finally there came a night in which he was surprised by the Indians, who stampeded his cattle, burned up his store, goods and all, and the ex-reverend gentleman fled for his life, and begged his way down to Stockton as poor as Lazarus. He regarded his reverses as a judgement for his apostasy and repented his fall. When I made his acquaintance he was in the honourable business of milling, making flour to supply his neighbours with bread, and was bringing forth fruits meet for repentance. I heard him in a public meeting give a tearful narrative of the facts above stated.

Brother H——, a friend of mine, opened a provision store in the northern mines. The first Sunday after opening a company of miners came to get a supply of provisions at the new store; but to their surprise they found the door closed, and going to the rear they found the new merchant in his tent.

"Halloo, old man! We've come to buy provisions from you. We are glad you have opened a store in these diggings; it's what we have wanted here for a long time."

"Well, boys," Brother H—— replied, "I have opened a store here and intend to keep a good supply of everything; but I want you to understand from the start that I will never sell you any liquor, and will never sell you goods of any kind on Sunday."

"Well, old man, you may just as well pack up your duds and go home, for you can do nothing here on those terms."

"You have a right to your opinion, boys," replied Brother H——; "but I intend to do right, whether I make anything or not. If I can't make a living without poisoning my neighbour by selling rum, and offending God by breaking His holy day, I'll starve or beg my way home; but I intend to give it a fair trial before I abandon the effort."

"Old man," rejoined the miners, "we are hungry; we ate the last of our provisions last evening, and have come to get something to cook for our breakfast. Let us have enough for to-day, and we will come to-morrow and lay in a supply for the week."

"Boys, you can fast and pray to-day," replied the merchant; "and you'll learn next time to make timely provision for the wants of the Sabbath."

8

With that the miners got angry, swore a little at the old fool, and left; but everywhere they went they told about an old fogey who had "come up into the mountains to teach us all how to keep Sunday."

They thus advertised him all through those mountains, and thinking men at once came to the conclusion that a man maintaining such a position must be an honest man. "We can depend upon the word of such a man as that. Rely upon it, he won't cheat us." The result was that the better class of miners poured in upon him for supplies at such a rate that in a few months he made his pile and returned East to his family.

Wicked as were the mass of California miners, they always displayed some good qualities. They had all encountered hardships and sufferings, and most of them had hearts to sympathise with the unfortunate. Though appeals to their charity were of almost daily occurrence, yet no man in real need that I ever heard of ever made a fruitless call on the miners for help. They were magnanimous, too, in their liberality; but they had an utter abhorrence of little, mean things. For example, there was a fellow at Smith's Flat who, to gratify some secret, brutal passion of his own, tied a chicken and put it alive on the fire and cooked it for his dinner. The thing was made known in the town, and the miners immediately called a meeting and unanimously passed a resolution to the effect that the chicken roaster's presence was no longer desired in that camp, and that fifteen minutes be given him, after due notice from the committee appointed for that purpose, for his disappearance from those diggings, never more to return. Several months had elapsed up to the time of my visit there, but he had not been seen in those parts after the expiration of the ominous fifteen minutes.

Notorious thieves were often expelled from a mining town in that way, while notorious murderers were hanged by the neck. Judge Lynch transacted a great deal of business in California in those days. However much may be said in condemnation of his court, this could be said in favour of the denizens of California, that riots, and a promiscuous shooting into the masses, killing the innocent with the guilty, such as has been enacted in some of our Eastern cities, was never known in California; such, for example, as I saw in Washington in May, 1857, when to quell an election riot one hundred and ten hired soldiers, with muskets loaded with ball and buckshot, fired upon an unsuspecting crowd of citizens, instantly killing eight unoffending men, besides wounding many others. This I witnessed—if, to be sure, getting up from my dinner table just across the street and standing behind a brick wall to avoid being shot myself may be called witnessing it.

Such riots and such promiscuous killing I never heard of in California. In the administration of California lynch law, the thunderbolt of public fury, always fell only on the head of the guilty man who, by the enormity and palpable character of his crime, excited it, and then not till his guilt was proved to the satisfaction of the masses comprising the court.

For example, a stranger called late one evening at the cabin of a miner who had his wife with him, and begged for lodgings, saying he was a poor traveller, had been unfortunate in business, etc. The miner and his wife pitied the poor stranger, took him in and gave him the best they had. Next morning the miner had occasion to go away a few miles. When he was out of sight the accommodated stranger murdered the woman and proceeded to rob the house. Before he got through with his nefarious work, however, the miner returned, saw what was done, and raised the alarm.

The murderer was caught and tried. A meeting of miners was called, a judge was appointed to try the case; witnesses were examined and the guilt of the criminal proved, upon which the judge stated the case to the mass composing his court, who unanimously voted guilty and death by hanging. The judge decided that the criminal should have fifteen minutes in which to prepare for death. He was then hung by the neck to a tree.

I give this fact without comment, simply to illustrate the character of Judge Lynch's proceedings in the days when he held office in California.

It is a fact, which I believe is generally admitted, that just in pro- portion as the law acquired power in California for the protection of her citizens, in that proportion lynch law was dispensed with, and when the legal authority of the State attained to a degree of honour- able dignity and strength sufficient for the accomplishment of its glorious ends throughout that State, then Judge Lynch resigned his office, and for ever declined re-election.

Ministers of the Gospel, in California's worst days, were permitted to preach in bar-rooms, gambling saloons, public thoroughfares, or wherever they wished without hindrance or disturbance. For ex- ample, I went into the city of Sonora at nine o'clock one Saturday night, not knowing a man in the place; and finding the streets crowded with miners, who had gathered in from all parts of the surrounding mountains, I felt a desire to tell them about Jesus and preach the Gospel to them; so I asked a brother whom I chanced to meet to roll a dry-goods box into the street nearly in front of a large crowded gambling house; and taking my stand I threw out upon the gentle zephyrs of that mild April night one of Zion's sweetest songs, which echoed among the hills and settled down on the astonished multitudes like the charms of Orpheus. My congre- gation packed the street from side to side. Profound attention prevailed while the truth, in the most uncompromising terms, was being proclaimed. At the close of the exercise many, strangers to me, who had heard me preach in the streets of San Francisco, gave me a hearty greeting, among them a notorious gambler, who shook my hand and welcomed me to the mountains.

CHAPTER X

MISSIONARY LIFE THEORETICAL AND PRACTICAL

My pastoral and evangelising work in San Francisco, indoors and out, covered, without a break, a period of seven years. During the first two I was pastor of Powell Street Church, the first Methodist pastorate in California. Meantime the California Conference was organised by Bishop Ames, and Rev. S. D. Simons was sent to Powell Street, and I was appointed to open and develop a Seamen's Bethel enterprise in that city, to which, in connection with the general hospital work and outdoor preaching in which I had been engaged from the beginning, in 1849, I devoted about five years, extending to the session of the Conference in San José in September, 1856.

God in His Word and in His providences has revealed and established two leading modes of spreading the tidings of salvation to perishing sinners of distant lands. The first is to send the Gospel to heathen lands by His ambassadors, and the second is to send the heathen to hear the Gospel in Christian lands.

The divine authority of the first mode is found in the great commission, " Go ye into all the world, and preach the Gospel to every creature." But the apostles receiving it were to tarry at Jerusalem until endowed with power from on high. By the time the power descended upon them, God in His providence developed the second mode.

When the apostles came down from that celebrated upper room, from that extraordinary protracted prayer meeting, with hearts of love and tongues of fire, lo! right at the door were assembled representative dwellers of at least fifteen different nations. These listened to Peter's great Pentecostal sermon, and not only heard and saw the wonderful works of God, but felt in their hearts that very day the power of pardoning grace, and went back to their homes, declaring everywhere the great things which had come to pass in the Holy City, and holding forth, in the experience and conduct of a new life, the torch of redeeming love in the darkest and most remote portions of the earth, long before the preachers had even planted one foreign mission on the plan of their appointments. God was beforehand with them then, as He has been ever since.

The fact is, their views in regard to foreign missionary work and the redemption of the race were as yet so contracted that they would not preach the Gospel to any but Jews, until, by the exhibition of the "great sheet" with its animals of every kind, the apostle Peter's shackles were loosed and he was compelled by the direct command of God to go and preach to the house of Cornelius.

St. Paul was the first foreign missionary to go abroad and establish missions among the heathen and make a practical demonstration of the first mode referred to; but in nearly every place he visited he found scattered abroad the Pentecostal seeds of truth, which had been borne, as it were, on the wings of the wind by the efficient workings of the second mode. The planting and sustaining of our Christian missions among the heathen and semi-heathen nations of Europe, Asia, Africa, and Oceania are in strict accordance with the first mode.

Foreign missionary work is Scriptural in its authority, and must be sustained. Foreign missions are worth more than the cost of sustaining them for the influence they exert on commercial adventurers and seamen of all nations. Many a prodigal son has been arrested and brought to Christ in foreign lands by Christian missionaries who might not have been otherwise reached.

A. M. Brown, a sailor of my acquaintance, was extremely wicked and profane, an avowed enemy of Christ and His Church, and especially of missionaries in foreign fields. He openly opposed the missionaries at the Sandwich Islands, Navigator's, and other islands of the Pacific, and did all he could to place obstructions in their way. From California he shipped to Constantinople, and a few days after arrival there was seized with cholera and fell helpless and alone in the street. I heard him say, "While I lay there dying, as I believed, I thought of my past life, and awoke to a sense of my dreadful condition as a sinner, and felt that I should soon be in hell. Despair, with all its horror, seized my soul, and thinking that it was then too late to pray I said to myself, 'Why did I not attend to that before? Why did not some one warn me of my danger? I had a father who once made a profession of religion, but he never told me what a dreadful thing it is to die in sin and go to hell. Why didn't some preacher or some Christian friend tell me of all this? No man has cared for my soul; and now I'm dying in the streets of a foreign city and going to hell.' And," said he, "in an agony of despair I cursed the day of my birth; cursed my father for his neglect; cursed the preachers and cursed the Church; and then my paroxysms of pain would come on, and I writhed under the scorching rays of the sun till life was almost gone; and when I had a little respite I thought of my mother and wept and said, 'Oh, if I had a mother's care, or if I had some one who could understand my language, and could tell them what to do for me, I might yet live!' The Turks would stop and look at me, jabber to each other, and pass on. When all hope had gone from me a man came and looked at me, and I thought, 'Oh that he would speak to me in a language

I could understand !' He spoke, but, alas! it was in the Turkish tongue. Seeing I did not understand him, he addressed me in my own mother tongue. Such music never filled my soul before. He spoke such words of kindness and sympathy as never before fell on my guilty ears. He had me taken to his own house, and under his skilful treatment and care I was relieved in a few hours.

"That good Samaritan was an American missionary; he saved my life, and, more than that, led me to Christ. Three days after my recovery, while still at his house under instruction, God, for Christ's sake, forgave my sins and healed my soul."

From that day Brown became a steadfast, zealous Christian, and later was a local preacher in my charge in San Francisco, and one of the most efficient workmen I had; and when I received a request from the Hawaiian Tract Society to send them a colporteur for Honolulu, Sandwich Islands, I sent them A. M. Brown, who successfully preached the Gospel in the port where he once so wickedly opposed it.

I preached one night in the summer of 1855 in McGinnis's provision storeroom at Twelve Mile Bar, on the east branch of the north fork of Feather River. A large part of my congregation were Chinamen, who listened with great attention. A tall, intelligent-looking fellow called "Chippee" took out his pencil and noted down such thoughts as he understood on a piece of wrapping paper as gravely as a New York reporter. The next morning the clerk at the store asked him to translate his notes into English. Said Chippee, "What you call him talk las' night?"

"That was Mr. Taylor, of San Francisco."

He noted the name in his book, and, looking and pointing upward, said, "What you call Him, *Him*—Fader, big Fader, up there—what you call *Him*?"

"We call Him God," said the clerk.

He put that also in his journal. He then gave a translation of his notes, now in my possession: "Tell all men no gamble; tell all men no steal 'em gold; tell all men no steal 'em cargo; tell all men no talk 'em lies; tell all men to be good men."

That was the first sermon Chippee ever heard, and those were the ideas he gathered.

What Peter saw in visions on the housetop of Simon the tanner was exhibited in fact in California, and none of them common or unclean nor excluded from the covenant of mercy and redeeming love. It has been my lot to preach the Gospel many times, if not to every creature, to at least specimen representatives of all the creatures of human kind in this lower world.

I think I never felt a greater thrill of pleasure in proclaiming a free Gospel to the human varieties of California than I did one Sunday morning on Long Wharf, San Francisco. I sang together a vast crowd of such variety of human kind as was seldom seen except in California. Peter's congregation on the day of Pentecost for variety was a small affair compared to it. When the song ended I said:

"Good-morning, gentlemen; I am glad to see you this bright Sabbath of the Lord. What's the news? Thank the Lord, I have good news for you this morning—'Behold, I bring you good tidings of great joy which shall be to all people.'"

I then addressed them as individual representatives of the different nations, thus: "My French brother, look here!" He looked with earnest eye and ear while I told him what Jesus had done for him and his people. "Brother Spaniard, I have tidings for you, *señor*," and told him the news. "My Hawaiian brother, don't you want to hear the news this morning? I have glad tidings of great joy for you." I then told him the news, and that his island should wait for the law of Jesus. "John Chinaman, you, John, there by that post, look here, my good fellow; I've got something to tell you." Thus I travelled over all creation, calling by name all the different nations I could think of with their representatives before me, and I felt unspeakably happy in the fact that throughout creation's vast realm I could not find a rebel to whom I could not extend the hand of Christian sympathy and say, "I have good news for you, my brother, 'glad tidings of great joy which shall be to all people.'"

When I had got around, as I thought, an Irishman in the crowd spoke out, and said, "And may it plase your riverence, and have-ye nothing for a poor Irishman?"

"I ask your pardon, my dear Irish brother, I did not mean to pass you by. I have good news for you. Jesus Christ, by the grace of God, tasted death for every Irishman on the Emerald Isle; and let me tell you, my brother, that if you will this morning renounce all your sins and submit to the will of God He will grant you a free pardon and clean all the sins and devils out of your heart as effectually as your people say St. Patrick cleaned the toads and snakes out of Ireland."

"Thank you, sir," he said; "I raly belave ivery word you say, and I'll thry and be a bitter man."

An intelligent Italian came to me to know where he could get an Italian Bible. He wanted to read to his companions. He was one of a party of twelve Italian refugees who took part in the revolution of 1848 and had to flee for their lives. He and his party had been in California eighteen months and had often heard me preach, and were anxious to learn about our Bible and religion.

A company of Maltese lived near me for several years. I gave them a Testament and told them about St. Paul's shipwreck and sojourn on their native island. They seemed as delighted with the book as if it were the family records of their fathers.

One Sunday as I was preaching in Washington Street I observed in the congregation an old Italian weeping. At the close of the service he grasped my hand and said, "Oh! dat what I like; tell all the people about Jesus. When you preach again?"

"On the Plaza at three o'clock."

"I'll be dere; I likes it."

A Prussian arose at one of our meetings and said, "I come to

Galifornia to git golt; now I don't come for golt, I vant to find dat Jesus you all talk about. I vant to find Him. His handt been heavy on me since I be in Galifornia. He shake me; He shake me now. I dream I was dying and a big schnake had me, and Brodder Taylor come and knock de schnake away. De schnake is de debbil. All you pray for me to get away from de debbil and find Jesus."

One Sunday afternoon, preaching on the Long Wharf in San Francisco, and wishing to illustrate the distinction between a decent, well-behaved sinner, outwardly, and a violent, outbreaking sinner, I remarked, after stating the point, "Gentlemen, I stand on what I suppose to be a cask of brandy. Keep it tightly bunged and spiled and it is entirely harmless, and answers some very good purposes; it even makes a very good pulpit. But draw that spile and fifty men will lie down here and drink up its spirit and then wallow in the gutter, and before ten o'clock to-night will carry sorrow and desolation to the hearts of fifty families. See that man there trying to urge his horse through the audience" (all eyes turned from the cask to the man). "If he had kept his mouth shut we might have supposed him a very decent fellow; but finding the street blocked up with this living mass of humanity, he drew the spile, and out gurgled the most profane oaths and curses. But, while there is as much difference now between outwardly moral and outbreaking sinners as between a tightly bunged and an open cask of brandy, I would invite your attention to a time when there will be no material difference between them.

" Should you attempt to get this harmless cask of brandy through the custom house in Portland, Maine, the inspector would pay no regard to the outside appearance or separate value of the cask. He would extract the bung, let down his phial, draw out and smell its contents; then shake his head, and mark it 'Contraband.' My friends, God has a great custom house through which every man has to pass for inspection before he can be admitted into His kingdom. When you are entered for examination do you imagine that the great omniscient Inspector will pay any regard to your outside appearance or conduct? Nay, my dear sirs, He will sound the inner depths of your souls. All who are filled with the Spirit of Christ will be passed and treasured up as meet for the Master's use; but all who have not the love of God shed abroad in their hearts will be pronounced 'contraband,' and branded eternally with, 'Depart, ye cursed, into everlasting fire, prepared for the devil and his angels.'"

One Sunday morning as I was preaching in Davis Street, a fellow came close to the barrel on which I stood, and looking up into my face, said, "The apostle David says, 'It is hard for thee to kick against the pricks.'"

"See here, my friend," said I, "when did you arrive, sir?"

"I came from the old country," said he, "about six years ago."

"But I want to know when you came to California?"

"Oh, a good while ago," said he.

"How many days since?" said I

He hesitated, and looked for an opening through the crowd by which he might escape, and then replied, "About two weeks ago, sir."

"I knew," said I, "by your conduct that you had recently arrived and had not learned how to behave yourself here yet. You seem to imagine that we are all a set of heathen here in California, and that you can 'cut up' and do as you please. Now as you are a stranger in these parts, I will inform you that the order of the day in California is for all classes of society to respect the preaching of the Gospel and never to disturb a preacher in the discharge of his duty, and the fellow who dares persist in it may expect that even the gamblers will give him a licking."

I have often caused men when trying to make a disturbance to run and hide themselves by offering an apology for their conduct— "Don't hurt that poor fellow, friends: we must make great allowance for his bad conduct. It is fair to presume that he has just arrived from some barbarous island in the Pacific and has not learned how to behave himself." To turn the eyes of an audience, sparkling with good-natured contempt, upon a fellow, will move him as suddenly almost as a charge of bayonets. I have, however, always run such fellows off the track so good-humouredly that I have never yet had an after difficulty with one of them.

Once in early summer I had an appointment to preach one week night in a large bar-room on Moor's Flat, in the mountains. The congregation assembled early and spent an hour in playing ball. When the bell rang for preaching the mass of the audience assembled in the porch and cracked jokes and sang lewd songs with the design, I thought, of intimidating the preacher. After letting them conduct the exercises in that way for a few minutes, I said, "Hold on, boys, and let me sing you a song."

They gave audience, and I sang. Nothing could be more calm than the salubrious atmosphere on that occasion, and the surrounding mountain heights and deep canyons and giant trees of the dense forest all combined to render the scene impressively grand and solemn. The echoes of the song came back from the neighbouring mountains, and the trees seemed to be praising God in the melody of song. The singing ended, I said, "Now, boys, walk in here; I have something to tell you." They all slipped in as quietly as possible, and I had a blessed season in pressing home upon their hearts the word of life.

I spent the first Sabbath of October, 1850, in Sacramento city, and had the privilege of preaching three times in our Baltimore-California Chapel, so called because our kind Baltimore friends framed it and paid for it and sent it to California. I selected a goods box on the levee for a pulpit and opened my commission for the first time in the streets of that city. While singing the "Royal Proclamation" two men rode up to where I stood. I never learned their names, but for convenience will call them Bacchus and Fairplay. Bacchus was pretty drunk, and began to yell and make a great ado. Judge W—— and a few others took hold of his mule's bridle and tried to lead the disturbers away. "Let that alone," cried Bacchus. "Let go his bridle," said Fairplay. "This is a public street, and you have no business to interfere with him. Let him go, I tell you. If you don't let go I'll see that you pay dearly for it." And many other hard threats were uttered by Mr. Fairplay.

The singing, which had been continued without interruption, together with the strife and hallooing of the drunken man, attracted an immense crowd. When the opening hymn was ended Judge W—— and his companion had got Bacchus off to a distance of about thirty yards, and had about equally divided the crowd. At that moment I called to the judge and his company, saying, "If you please, gentlemen, let him go and I'll take care of him." But they had become so zealous in the matter that they seemed determined to drag him away, and would not let him go. By the time I had sung another song of Zion they had gone but a few feet further off, and had half the audience, who appeared to be more interested in the fate of the drunken man than in the songs of the preacher. I then called to them again, and said: "Gentlemen, you had better take my advice. If you will let that man go, I will send him away in one minute. I am suprised at you Sacramento folks. Come down to San Francisco and attend preaching on the Plaza next Sunday afternoon at three o'clock, and I'll show you how all classes there behave themselves. Men naturally run after an excited crowd, but you have all seen the great attraction, a drunken man on a mule. Now, let me manage that fellow, and all of you come up here."

With that they let Bacchus's mule go. I then addressed his threatening, storming companion, Fairplay, and said, "I deliver that man up to you, sir; I want you to take charge of him and lead him away. Take good care of him, if you please."

"Yes, sir," said he, "I will," tipping his hat as he made his best bow, and immediately led him away.

The audience so blocked the street sometimes from side to side with a living mass of humanity that it was difficult for a man to get through. A waggon or dray would therefore be subjected to considerable delay in making a passage through, and I frequently took advantage of the opportunity and gave them a little grape as they passed. Once, when a lean-looking man, driving a poor horse, was trying to urge his way through the crowd, I said, "Look at that poor man! Working seven days in the week is bringing him rapidly down to his grave. A man cannot break the law of the Sabbath without violating a law of his own constitution. Look at his sunken, sallow cheeks and his dim eyes! How the sin of Sabbath-breaking is telling on him! He'll die soon if he don't reform. Look at his poor old horse! The Lord ordained the Sabbath for that horse, but his merciless master is cheating him out of it. See there, how he beats him! After all, I had rather be the horse than the man, if he dies as he lives."

On another occasion a wag, thinking to have a little sport, tried to ride through the crowd on one of the smallest of that small species of animals, the jack. His animal refusing to go through, I said, "See there; that animal, like Balaam's of the same kind, has more respect for the worship of God than his master, who only lacks the ears of being the greater ass of the two."

The man, in great confusion, beat his animal out of sight in double-quick time. The reader may wonder how I managed to restore the equilibrium of the audience after such a scene. I always tried to anticipate that difficulty, and would follow such scenes by the most solemn appeal the subject in hand would allow. The sudden surprise of such appeals sometimes produces a thrilling effect for good. An important end is accomplished when a sleepy congregation is by any legitimate means fairly waked up. First melt and then mould the metal

One Sunday morning I stood on the deck of the steamer *Webber*, at Long Wharf, and announced as my text, "In that very night was Belshazzar, king of the Chaldeans, slain." Nearly opposite to where I stood, on the other side of the wharf, lay the steamer *Empire*, which had been chartered to convey a company of California legislators on that day to Vallejo, the seat of the Legislature of the State at that time. The *Empire* was steaming up for her Sunday excursion, while I was trying to raise the steam on the *Webber* against Sunday excursions. My song drew to the side of our boat a large crowd, while the embarkation of the honourable legislators drew an equally large crowd to their boat; but I had the whole of both parties within the compass of my voice, and I preached to the *Empire* party more especially. As I doubted whether many of them ever went to church, I thought it a rare opportunity of giving them a little Gospel truth.

I illustrated, by the life of Belshazzar, that a Sabbath-breaking, licentious, carousing, drunken man was utterly unfit for any official position in the gift of any respectable nation, and to elect men to make our laws whose brains were addled with brandy, and who showed so little respect for one of the highest laws and most venerable institutions of God, the holy Sabbath, was a wicked absurdity and a burning shame to the American people. I did not design, by these reflections, to implicate the whole of the California Legislature, for it contained some very good men, but I thought them peculiarly applicable to the party addressed on that occasion. I illustrated, further, the end of such a course of procedure by the Mene, Tekel, Upharsin—the numbering, weighing, and dividing of the Chaldean kingdom, and the slaying of her wicked king.

A number of months after this occasion a stranger called on me, and requested a private interview. Said he to me, "Do you remember preaching from the deck of a steamboat at Long Wharf nine months ago from a text concerning the destruction of Babylon and the death of Belshazzar?"

"I preach there every Sunday morning. Oh yes," I replied, "I do remember it now, by the Sunday excursion which started that morning from the opposite side of the wharf."

"That was the time to which I allude," said he, and then related the following facts concerning himself: "I was up to that morning a confirmed Universalist, and was withal a very wicked sinner. As I was walking leisurely down the wharf that morning I heard you singing, and went into the crowd through curiosity to hear what was to be said on the occasion. While you were preaching a strange fearfulness which I cannot describe came over me. I felt a smothering sensation at my heart and thought I was dying. My Universalism all vanished like smoke, and I felt that if I died then I should certainly go to hell. For some time I knew not what to do. I came very near crying out, but something seemed to say to me, ' Pray, pray to God in the name of Jesus Christ for pardon. So I began earnestly to pray. For three weeks I suffered a constant fearfulness and trembling. I felt every moment as though some dreadful calamity or judgment was about to befall me. I was afraid to go to sleep at night lest I should wake up in hell, and every day there seemed to be literally a heavy mist before my eyes, which made everthing look dark and dreary. But all these three dreadful weeks I continued to pray, and suddenly, while I was praying and trying to trust in Jesus Christ, it appeared to me that a stream of light shone right down from heaven into my heart, and in a moment I realised that my burden of sin was gone, and instead of fearfulness and a nervous tremor I felt all the vigour of renewed youth. The mist of my eyes gave way to the brightness of morning. I praise God for His pardoning mercy. I have been up in the mountains ever since. I have had but few public religious privileges, but have had my private prayers, and have been recommending religion to all my associates. Jesus has been very precious to my soul all the time. To-morrow I expect to sail for home, and I want to see you before leaving and get some tracts and religious books for distribution aboard ship. I feel as though I ought to do all I can in the cause of Christ."

He did not expect soon, if ever, to return to California. So we closed our interview with a final farewell, and a mutual pledge to each other to live for God and meet again on the other side of the river.

On one occasion after the benediction a stranger spoke out saying : " Gentlemen, you all know how laboriously and successfully Father Taylor labours here on the Plaza from Sabbath to Sabbath. Now I move that we take up a collection. I will not urge you to give ; I know you are all ready."

"Pass along the hat," said one.

"Let it come this way," said another.

"Stop, stop," said I. " Gentlemen, I am much obliged for your kind feelings, but I never allow a collection to be taken up outdoors for my benefit. I preach every Sabbath twice in the church in Powell Street, and all who are so disposed can give there ; but you will please do nothing of the kind there. I cannot have my street preaching trammelled by collections."

I preached about six hundred times in these streets ; occasionally took up collections for poor men and for building the Seamen's

Bethel (I collected four hundred dollars at one time on the Plaza for the Bethel), but never took up one collection for my benefit, though often in need. My reason is that in the streets I proclaim a free Gospel, the royal proclamation to heathen and Christians, to Jews and Gentiles, to Catholics and Protestants, to inhabitants of every nation, and I am unwilling to furnish ground for any of these to impugn my motives or to say, " He can afford to sing and preach in the streets when he gets a good collection every time."

At eleven o'clock in the night of Saturday, May 3rd, 1851, a fire broke out in our city, which raged till nine o'clock in the forenoon of Sunday, the 4th. It was the most destructive fire by which the city had yet been visited. The loss was variously estimated at from twelve to twenty millions of dollars. Several hundred passengers had just arrived on the steamship *New Orleans* on the evening the fire occurred, and the city was filled with strangers besides, so that it was impossible to tell how many persons perished in the conflagration.

Many of the streets were planked, and on each side were wooden sewers, which served as flues to conduct the fire, and greatly facilitated its destructive progress through the city. Our Old Adobe escaped, and at the appointed hour for preaching I stood in my place in the porch. It appeared to be a very unpropitious time for collecting an audience. The people were running to and fro under a high pressure of confused excitement, and many were busy in collecting together their little savings from the fire, many tons of which were scattered in tangled confusion all over the Plaza. I, however, threw out amid the smoke and dust and noise of the vast field of desolation which was spread out before me one of Zion's sweetest songs, and drew together about one thousand men. My text on this occasion was, " Except the Lord build the house, they labour in vain that build it ; except the Lord keep the city, the watchman waketh but in vain."

CHAPTER XI

In the spring of 1852, as I was on the Long Wharf one Sunday morning discoursing to a large audience on the " one thing needful," I proceeded first to show what it was that was needful to the well-being of the bodies of men ; that true religion, as a regulator of the appetites and passions, preserved men from a great variety of excesses which were destructive to health and happiness. Illustrating this, I said to the crowd, " Go with me, if you please, through the hospitals of our city. Ask the hundreds of sufferers to whom I will introduce you the cause of their afflictions, and, while you will see some good men brought down by unavoidable diseases, you will find that a large majority of those miserable beings have been there imprisoned for the violation of physical laws from which this needful thing would have saved them."

" That's true, Father Taylor ; that's true, every word of it," cried an old man in the audience.

" Yes, sir," said I, in reply ; " you know it by sad experience. There, friends," I continued, " you have a living illustration of the truth of my position. That old man, lacking this needful thing, indulged his appetite for strong drink, and, as a consequence, I found him two years ago in the hospital. He lay there for many months, suffering everything but death. The physician succeeded at last in doctoring up his old carcass, and if he had given his heart to the Lord and obtained the healthful, preserving influence of His grace he might have continued a well man. But he went out still destitute of the one thing needful, and in a short time he again took the cup of death, for which he had to serve another long term in the hospital. With naturally a good constitution, if he had been possessed of vital godliness the probability is he would not have lost a day from sickness in California. He is a shipmaster, and capable of doing well for himself and his family ; and he came here, too, at a time when he had a good opportunity to make a fortune, and but for the want of this one needful thing he might to-day be reclining on his well-earned California fortune by his own happy fireside, surrounded by the wife of his youth and the lovely children the Lord has given them.

" But here he is, a wreck of manly strength, foundering on the

126

leeshore of the dreadful sea of inebriety, his wife clad in the habiliments of mourning blacker than widow's weeds, and his beautiful daughters disgraced, poverty-stricken, and broken-hearted. I fear he will never see them again, and if he does he is unfit for the relations, duties, and associations of the head of such a family." The poor old captain was now weeping and crying audibly, as a boy that was being castigated. " I would not, my friend, unnecessarily hurt the feelings of the poor old man. He knows I am one of the best friends he has in this land, and that I have often entreated him as a brother and prayed at his side, and have done everything to keep him from self-destruction and to induce him to seek the one thing needful."

In the next place I went on to show, by a variety of proofs and illustrations, the value of religion to the soul.

The darkest chapter in the history of California is that which records the disruption of family ties and connubial relationships, occasioned, primarily, by the rage and rush of thousands of heads of families to her mines of gold. Many families of children were thus neglected when they most needed a father's watchful care and counsels. Many a wife pined with a broken heart on account of the absence of her husband, and the husband a desolate, isolated wanderer in a strange land. In many cases these husbands were unsuccessful, and often unable even to raise money enough to carry them to their poor, dependent families at home. Very many of both husbands and wives died without the longed-for meeting again. The mails, surcharged with death shocks, for years passed back and forth, from ocean to ocean, and ever and anon, suddenly and unexpectedly as a thunderbolt from a clear sky, the lightning leaped from the train and struck the widow's heart, and hope departed. Still more dark and dreadful is the record of connubial infidelity which hopelessly sundered and desolated hundreds of once happy families.

In the midst of all these dangers the meeting of true and faithful husbands and wives after weary years of separation was an occasion of thrilling interest, and often furnished scenes which baffled the painter's skill. Such scenes occurred at our wharves on the arrival of each ocean steamer. A few incidents characterising them are contained in the following extract from my journal :

"Tuesday, February 3rd, 1852.—I boarded the steamer *Panama* upon her arrival this afternoon to see if there were any missionaries aboard. Her trip had extended three days beyond her time, and much solicitude was felt for the safety of her precious freight of five hundred passengers.

"About four thousand persons crowded down Long Wharf to witness her arrival. Quite a company of anxious wives who had come to join their husbands stood on deck looking out to catch in the distance the joyful recognitions of those they loved. One simple-hearted, beautiful little woman, getting a glimpse of her husband in the crowd, clapped her hands and danced for very gladness. One man rushed on deck and threw his arms around his wife as though he would run right away with her, and then, with arms around each other, they walked abaft in the greatest glee, not seeming to be conscious that anybody was in sight of them. Nearly all that met embraced and kissed each other, some laughing and some weeping, amid the cheering of the multitude. A Mrs. Gardner, who had less of youthful fire than many, but I should say not less of genuine affection, was quietly seated on deck waiting the arrival of her husband. The old gentleman took off his hat when he got within a few feet of her, and with his venerable bald head bared approached her with an air of dignified affection which I cannot describe."

But a sad case I saw, and it was one of many of the same kind. A man hastened aboard with joyous heart to meet his wife, and was told that three days out from Panama she had suddenly sickened and died, and had found a grave in the deep blue sea. He was taken to her state-room, and there were her things just as her own hands had left them.

On July 4th, 1852, I preached a temperance sermon on the Plaza. I drew a picture of the aggressive marches of the enemy and the horrible havoc he was making of American flesh and blood and property and tenderest ties and dearest hopes, and asked them what they would do if any foreign potentate or power should invade our territory and commit such outrages with the bayonet. Shades of Patrick Henry! Wouldn't Uncle Sam's boys rally and run to the rescue? "Come forward to-day like John Hancock and his invincible compatriots, and sign this 'Declaration of Independence.'" About forty persons came forward and signed the temperance pledge.

While I was discoursing an old woman who kept a grog shop close by where I stood came out and cried, "Don't listen to him. He's an impostor. He's preaching for money—telling lies." "Dry up, old woman," replied some of the outsiders; "dry up! We know what's the matter with you. Your craft is in danger. He is taking away your customers. We know Father Taylor. He is a good man, and he's telling the truth." The woman immediately disappeared. Just as I closed my remarks a man tried to get the attention of the audience, and said, "This man is an impostor hallooing around here to get people's money." "Stop, stranger," said one; "what is your business here in the city?" "Why, sir," replied the fellow, after being closely pressed for an answer, "I am a gambler, and I did a first-rate business and made money here till these preachers came to the city. But this fellow is hallooing at the people every Sunday, and has broken up my business. I can't get a decent living." "Good! good!" said one and another. "Hearken, friends," said I; "this gambler has paid me a high compliment. He says I have broken up his business." "Good! good!" responded the people. The gambler "vamoosed," and I have not laid eyes on him since.

In January, 1853, an article appeared in the *Alta California*, a popular daily of the city, over the signature of "Merchant," against the Sabbath as a day of religious observance. He attempted to prove from the Hebrew Bible that nothing more was contemplated in the institution of the Sabbath than a day of recreation, feasting, and dancing. He announced that that was the first of a series of articles on the same subject. The Sabbath following, January 30th, I had a large audience on Long Wharf, and took my text from "Merchant's" article in the newspaper, and preached on the origin and design of the Sabbath. The merchant, unhappily for himself, had chosen Nehemiah as his favourite author; so we sent Nehemiah after him to deal with him as he did with the "merchants and sellers of all kinds of ware" which he expelled from the city of Jerusalem for doing as these Long Wharf merchants do here every Sunday. How successful I was in presenting the truth and in showing up the fallacy of "Merchant's" positions could perhaps be better decided by the congregation in attendance. But the rest of "Merchant's" series on the same subject never appeared.

On Sunday afternoon, June 26th, 1853, I found a man in my Bible-class who seemed to be in distress. I spoke to him and he said, in answer to my inquiries :

"I was educated in my youth for a Universalist preacher, but I could not believe the doctrine, and instead of preaching I went to sea. I believe in the doctrine of fore-ordination and reprobation. I have been in great distress of mind for fourteen years. My soul is all over diseased. I have had no peace except what I got by drinking. I drank rum to relieve my distress. I have been hoping that God would have pity on me and bring me in, but I fear He never will do it. I fear I am a reprobate, and that there is no hope for me."

"But, my brother," replied I, "God has declared, in the most solemn and unequivocal manner, 'As I live, saith the Lord God, I have no pleasure in the death of the wicked ; but that the wicked turn from his way and live : turn ye, turn ye from your evil ways ; for why will ye die?' Again, it is a declaration of inspired truth that Jesus Christ, 'by the grace of God, hath tasted death for every man.' What for? Did He make a mock provision for such as were reprobated to eternal death?",

"Ah, but we are told," said he, "that though many are called, but few are chosen."

"Truly ; but does God call the many, and proclaim to them the tidings of salvation deceitfully, to mock their fears and aggravate their bondage under chains of inexorable fate? Surely the righteous God is sincere in His offers of mercy to all sinners. Christ answers the question why so few are chosen of the many called : 'Ye will not come unto Me, that ye might have life.' Now, my brother, God has been very desirous to save you for a long time ; but you would not let Him. He has been calling you for fourteen years, and you would not come. Instead of hearkening to the voice divine and obeying your Lord you ran off to a grog shop and got drunk. Do you ever pray to God for mercy?"

"What!" said he, "I pray! I pray! Why, it would be blasphemy

9

for such a wretch as I am to pray. The prayers of the wicked are abomination to the Lord."

I replied, "Solomon says, 'The sacrifice of the wicked is abomination;' but it is nowhere said in the Bible that the prayers of a penitent sinner are abomination; but it is said, 'Let the wicked forsake his way, and the unrighteous man his thoughts: and let him return unto the Lord, and He will have mercy upon him; and to our God, for He will abundantly pardon.' The poor publican felt as guilty as you do, and 'would not lift up so much as his eyes unto heaven, but smote upon his breast, saying, God be merciful to me a sinner. I tell you, this man went down to his house justified,' pardoned in answer to a sinner's prayer."

"Oh, but," said he, "they were not nearly so bad as I am. The iniquities of my fathers for four generations seem to be visited upon me."

"Oh, you know," said I, "that the proverb, 'The fathers have eaten sour grapes, and the children's teeth are set on edge,' has passed away long ago, so far as answering for the sins of our fathers is concerned. Within the last fortnight more than half a dozen sinners equally as bad as you, some of them the worst men in the city, have, in this Bethel, called upon God and obtained mercy, and they are happy in His love to-day."

As soon as the Sunday-school and Bible-class closed he was taken into the shipkeeper's room, where, surrounded by some warm-hearted sailors, he cried to God, in the name of Jesus, and in an hour experienced redemption through the blood of the Lamb, even the forgiveness of his sins. He soon afterward went to sea. The Lord kept him steadfast.

CHAPTER XII

On Sunday, January 8th, 1854, after preaching on the Plaza from the text, "If our heart condemn us, God is greater than our hearts, for He knoweth all things," a stranger spoke to me, saying, "There is a man by the name of S——, from B——, lying at the point of death in that house, the third door from here" (pointing to the door). He also intimated to me something of S——'s notorious character as a wicked man; and said he, "S—— did not send for you, but his parents were religious, and perhaps you may do him some good."

I went in and found him attended by four or five men, who appeared to receive me very kindly. He lay pale and ghastly, evidently very near the grave. I said to him, "Friend S——, do you suffer much pain?"

"No," replied he, very abruptly.

I then turned away and exchanged a little conversation with his companions, and in about five minutes I approached him again, and, in the mildest and most hopeful manner I could, said, "Friend S——, do you not feel as though you might rally and recover?" hoping to gain access to his heart.

He replied, "When I want anybody to talk to me, I'll send for him."

"I have called in," said I, "as a friend feeling the greatest sympathy for you, and am ready to do anything for your comfort in my power."

"I'd thank Mr. H——," said he, upbraiding the man whom he suspected of asking me in, "to attend to his own business." And then addressing me he continued, "Before you came in here I had some peace, but you have knocked me all into a kink, and if you will just go away I think I can die in peace."

He lived close to where I preached on the Plaza, and he had probably heard me preach a hundred times; and thus my presence, without the utterance of a word in regard to the condition of his soul, brought to his mind, doubtless, a thousand Gospel associations which seemed to throw him into unutterable tortures. His only peace depended on his banishing from his mind all thoughts of the past and future. Poor fellow! how sorry I felt for him! If the presence of a poor street preacher clogged with mortality "knocked him all into a kink," to use his own language, how could he bear the presence of the holy angels and of the great multitude of the redeemed in glory were he admitted to heaven? How could he bear the presence of the awful God whom he had insulted and defied all his life? How preposterous the idea of any man's being received into the kingdom of glory without an education adapting him to heavenly enjoyments, a moral fitness for such a place! Heaven would be the most unbearable of all hells to such a man as poor S——. He left the world a few hours after I saw him.

I remember receiving the following letter concerning a duellist's funeral :—

"SAN FRANCISCO, *November 9th*, 1854.

"REV. MR. TAYLOR.—DEAR SIR,—Colonel Woodlief, a gentleman from Texas, with whom you probably had some acquaintance, was killed yesterday in a duel with Mr. Kewen. Previous to the duel in the morning he expressed a desire that, in case of his death, you should be requested to perform the appropriate ceremonies over his body. If you will be kind enough to do so, sir, you will confer a favour upon the many friends of Colonel Woodlief, and particularly upon his lady. The funeral will take place at two o'clock this afternoon, from the Tehama House.

"Very respectfully your obedient servant,
"RICHARD W. ALLEN."

Colonel Woodlief's untimely death was sincerely regretted by the large assembly of his friends who attended his funeral. It is not an easy task for a minister, in the presence of such an auditory and a weeping widow, to do justice to the cause of truth and the feelings of his hearers. I once heard a minister preach at the funeral of an alderman in San Francisco, and though the man was known to be a notorious drunkard, and it was believed he had killed himself by hard drinking, he was held up by the minister in the presence of the mayor, councilmen, and a vast assemblage of citizens as a paragon of moral excellence. The impression was conveyed that he had without doubt been admitted to glory because he was an honourable alderman of the city of San Francisco. My moral sensibilities were shocked. I would not unnecessarily hurt the feelings of bereaved friends. But thus to obliterate moral distinctions in character and indorse such men, without repentance, as suitable subjects for the kingdom of heaven, gives the lie to God's Holy Word and encourages sin. My fears for the effect of that sermon on the community were such that I was led, on the following Sabbath, to preach to a large audience on the Plaza from this text: " In hell he lifted up his eyes, being in torment."

On the occasion of Colonel Woodlief's funeral I said : " My dear friends, you are doubtless all acquainted with the person and character of Colonel Woodlief and the melancholy circumstances of his death. He was, by birth, a fellow-Virginian with myself, and was always, I believe, regarded by those who knew him as a high-minded, honourable gentleman, and I exceedingly regret that I cannot add a Christtian. He was one of my regular hearers on the Plaza, and was often deeply affected by the word of truth. Some months ago, just after a sermon there one Sunday afternoon, I said to him, 'Colonel, allow me to introduce you to Captain McDonald.' Taking him by the hand, the colonel said, 'I know the captain very well; we fought side by side on the fields of Mexico.' 'Ah, indeed! and did you know,' I replied, 'that the captain has embraced religion since he came to California?' 'Oh yes,' said he; 'I know that too. He told me all about it.' 'Well,' said I, 'do you see what a great change it has wrought in him?' 'Yes,' said he, 'I see it, I see it.' His eyes filled with tears and his utterances were choked by strong emotion. When he could speak he said, 'Don't talk to me on that subject; I cannot stand it.'

"That was a gracious moment for Colonel Woodlief. The Holy Spirit was touching the tender chords of his soul, and wooing him towards the cross of Jesus. Oh, how sorry I am to-day that he did not yield to His blessed influence and become a Christian. Religion would have made him a happy and useful man, and we should have been spared the mournful duty we are called upon to perform to-day. For, had he possessed the love of God in his heart, the probability is he would not have been challenged; and had he been, he would have acted under a higher code than that adopted by chivalrous though erring men. He would have exhibited a moral heroism, in standing for his duty to God, himself, his wife, and to society, that would have put to shame the moral coward that would engage him in mortal combat. Oh that he had obeyed the calls of God's Holy Spirit! Then, had he died in the order of Providence, we should stand around his corpse with very different feelings. We could then, indeed, mix a sweet solace into the bitter cup of the weeping widow. Beware, my friends, of grieving the Holy Spirit! Seek, while you may, God's pardoning mercy. Place yourself under His parental protection, as obedient children, that you may be saved from, or prepared for, the dangers and death incident to mortal life. Jesus Christ, your best friend, is waiting now at the door of your hearts for an answer. He is very desirous to save every one of you from your sins, and only asks your consent."

During seven years—from September, 1849, to October, 1856—my regular street preaching, fifty-two Sabbaths per year, was kept up without a break wherever I chanced to be, but almost wholly in San Francisco, where I served in a pastorate of two years in First Methodist Episcopal Church, and five years in the seamen's work of that port. Though troubled with dyspepsia, I was not at any time laid up on account of illness. I had the bereavement of losing our dear Oceana, born off Cape Horn in 1849, who went away with the angels at the age of fourteen months. Later we had to give up our precious Willie at our Father's call. But the great tribulation of my life was occasioned by the wreck and ruin of our Seamen's Bethel enterprise. By the liberality of my friends in San Francisco we built and paid for a commodious Bethel for seamen, sojourners, and citizens, which became the spiritual birthplace of many souls ; but the great want of the port to provide protection for seamen against the shoals of sharks which lay in wait for them was a capacious home for sailors.   I bought a lot on the water front of the city at an early period with my own money, which so appreciated in value that I refused for it an offer of twenty thousand dollars, and made a gift of it as a site for our seamen's home.   Having no money with which to put up the buildings required for such an enterprise, we were led to entertain a proposal of a responsible man to the effect that if we would build on said lot a house according to plans which he submitted, he would rent it from us to be used by him for a temperance hotel till we could pay for it by the rent he would give us, at the rate of one thousand dollars per month, and then turn it over for the sole purpose of a home for seamen.   The current rate of interest on money in California in those days was three per cent per month, payable monthly in advance, but the rents being proportionately high the success of the venture was worked out by figures to a demonstration.   The house was built, the hotel was opened, but soon the gathering financial storm of 1855-56 became a cyclone that swept the Pacific first, and, gathering impetus by the force of its own movement, tore its way through the United States and shook the nations of Europe to their foundations.

In the midst of this great panic a fire broke out on the city front and reduced our new building and all its contents to ashes.   Rents stopped ; interest on money went on.   Values depreciated from two to five hundred per cent.   Those who held mortgages took the property at its depreciated rate, and those who had no mortgages took my word for it, though all was lost as by a storm at sea when a captain's ship sinks from under his feet into the ocean, and, bereft of all but life, he is happy even with that to reach the shore.

At the session of the California Conference, at San José, in 1856, my accounts were carefully investigated by my Conference, and I was acquitted of all blame, and resolutions of confidence and sympathy on my behalf were unanimously passed.   That was well enough in its way, but would not pay my bills in the bank.

Meantime I wrote my first book, entitled " Seven Years' Street Preaching in San Francisco," and got as I believe an intimation from the Lord that I should return to the Atlantic States, labour as an evangelist, print and circulate my book, and raise and refund the money sunk in our lost cause.   The Bethel itself, built by the gift of our people, was saved, and used as a Bethel for years, then sold by order of our Church authorities, and the money used to build Bush Street Methodist Episcopal Church, which lives and grows and exhibits a large new church edifice.

Many of my friends advised me to repudiate the whole thing, as I was not responsible for the disasters that had befallen our cause any more than a captain whose ship goes down in a storm at sea ; but I did not entertain that suggestion for a moment, feeling that the honour of God and His cause was involved.   But I settled two principles of procedure: first, that I would not ask or receive gifts of money for my lost cause, but depend solely, entirely on the profit of my book sales; and, second, that in every case I would do my best by preaching and altar service for seekers of salvation *before* I would mention books or my need of funds; and I stuck to those principles to the end of the chapter. My Conference asked the bishop presiding, Bishop Scott, to give me leave of absence, as they could not help me, that I might have a chance to help myself; which the bishop did as an exceptional case, but requested me to supply at Marysville and Yuba City for a few weeks till the arrival of the Rev. J. A. Bruner, then on his way from the Eastern States.

I and my family became the guests of Captain and Mrs. Webb, residents of Yuba City, and were most hospitably entertained. I filled all the regular appointments of the station, and preached to the masses in the public streets besides.

Near the close of my engagement for service at Marysville, Captain Webb and I planned a deer hunt in the Coast Range mountains. I was greatly overworked, and Mrs. Webb and her two little children needed an outing. So we set off on a journey of ninety miles across the wild plains of the Upper Sacramento Valley and over the near mountain ranges. Captain and Mrs. Webb and their two little children were in a covered two-horse spring waggon, while I rode on horseback and led a second. We encamped by a small mountain stream of water between the mountain ranges east and west, on Friday evening. On Saturday the captain killed a fawn, which gave us a supply of fresh venison. The Sabbath dawned brightly upon us, but I hardly knew what to do with myself, so I proposed to preach to the captain and his wife, and they cheerfully concurred. I felt at once that I had assumed a delicate and difficult task. I had had no acquaintance with them till I went by invitation to sojourn at their house just a few weeks before.

I learned from others who knew them that, though liberal supporters of our Church, they were not members, though they had been members and truly loyal ones in early life, but had removed from Virginia to Missouri, and thence across the plains and over the Rocky Mountains to California, and had lost their standing in the Church and their peace with God; so to speak plainly to them and avoid objectionable personality was a difficult thing indeed, but I trusted the good Spirit of the Lord to help me.

So I gave out my hymn in the regular order of worship; we sang, and I read the lessons. Then I announced as my text, "When for the time ye ought to be teachers, ye have need that one teach you again which be the first principles of the oracles of God."

I said: "I am in the habit of adapting my subject and the treatment of it to my audience, and wish to give this text a personal application to my hearers. I learn that the captain allied himself with God in his early life and was blessedly saved and gave promise of usefulness. He ran well for a season, but, moving from one region of the country to another, he became so absorbed by new scenes and associations that he lost his hold on God. Had he remained unswervingly true to God and kept up vital union with Jesus, the true Vine, long ago he would have become a teacher in the Gospel ministry, and would ere this have gathered a harvest of precious souls into the granary of the Lord.

"Sister Webb, I learn, was also saved in early life, and, led by the Holy Spirit, might, by her quiet, winning way, have won many souls for Christ; but she, alas! has gone astray, like her husband, so that now 'when ye ought to be teachers, ye have need that one teach you again the first principles of the oracles of God '—need to turn back and begin with the alphabet, the A B C of the religion of Christ. Worse still, ye have to unlearn a great many bad things that ye have learned in Satan's school.

"The captain, for example, speaks unadvisedly sometimes to his children. I heard him shout at that little boy the other day, 'Willie, if you don't come away from there I'll knock your head off.' What sort of talk is that to a sweet little boy? I know that little boy, and I know that he has brains in his head and logic in his brains, and will draw one of two conclusions from those premises—either, first, that he is an awful brute of a man to knock his dear little boy's head off, or, second, that he does not mean what he says, and is, therefore, not truthful. I want so to walk and so to talk in my daily intercourse with my children that they will respect my memory when I am dead.

"Moreover, the captain is in the habit of swearing sometimes. I don't mean to say that he is guilty of the vulgar, profane oaths which foul the air along our streets. There is a variety of oaths of different shades of turpitude. Some swear by God, some by heaven, some by Pharaoh, some by the devil, some by Jupiter, some by George, and some by Jemeny. The captain swears by Jemeny. But Jesus says in regard to all such oaths, 'Swear not at all.' Sister Webb is quiet and amiable; I have not seen or heard of an objectionable word or deed that I can call in question; but the safe course for either of you is to come back to the first principles, and in penitential grief surrender your all to God and receive Jesus as a present almighty Saviour, and trust in Him to save now." We concluded the service in the regular way, by singing, prayer, and the benediction. As soon as the congregation was dismissed the captain grasped my hand heartily and said, "Dear sir, I thank you for your candour and kindness."

He then named a number of our good ministers, saying, "They have been welcome guests at my house for years, and must have seen my faultiness the same as you have, but never did me the kindness of calling my attention to my naughty sayings. You will never catch me again."

I soon perceived that the awakening Spirit had directed the arrows of truth, and that the captain was under deep conviction of sin. His whole nervous system became so shaken that though a famous old hunter he could not hit a deer broadside sixty yards distant. I saw him try. He afterwards tried to put a bullet into a large tree on short range and could not do it. After two days we planned to leave the good sister and the children and two of our horses in camp, while I and the captain would go ten or fifteen miles westward to high Coast Range Mountains, and sleep, and get the advantage of an early morning hunt on better ground. We kindled our camp fire on the top of a high mountain, from which a sweep of vision in the clear atmosphere took in a panoramic view of the inland valleys to the east and the broad Pacific, and I waked up in the night and saw the moon peeping over the horizon far in the distance below, and quoted Charles Wesley's words, "My soul mounted higher in a chariot of fire, and the moon, it was under my feet."

On the second Sabbath of our sojourn in the Coast Range Mountains of California I preached again to Captain Webb and his good wife in the spirit of tenderest Christian sympathy and love. Monday ensuing was our set time to start homeward, but the captain said that he could not get the consent of his own mind to return to his home and his business associations till he should recover his lost standing in the knowledge of God.

The time was at hand when I had arranged to take steamer with my family for New York. So I bade captain and wife and little boys good-bye, and left them in the mountains. I brought back the two horses I took out, and two pairs of the venison hams I had taken, one pair as a present to my friend Captain Haven, of San Francisco, who generously presented me with tickets for self, wife, and children by Pacific Mail Steamship Company's line from San Francisco to New York.

Early in the month of October, 1856, we embarked in the *Golden Gate*, bound to Panama. We then had three living children, Morgan Stuart, Charles Reid, and Osman Baker, the eldest about nine—Oceana and Willie had gone to heaven, the first about fourteen months and Willie about one year old.

Passing out through the Golden Gate, we encountered heavy seas, and the whole crowd of passengers, without any visible exceptions, became seasick. Poor little Charlie had a feast of pears that day, and between his heaving paroxysms he cried out, "Mamma, I don't like pears. I don't want any more pears." On each Sabbath, by invitation of people and captain, I preached to the crowd on deck. All were orderly and attentive. Poor fellows! I presume they are nearly all dead. I am comforted by the fact that, for more than fifty years of my Gospel ministry, on every occasion I stood near the strait gate that opens into the kingdom of God, and tried by the help of the Holy Spirit to show poor sinners the way in. A gatekeeper don't aim to get off fine speeches, but keeps repeating, "This is the way, gentlemen and ladies. Walk in."

On the voyage to Panama one dear fellow from Baltimore, who had lost his property in the great panic, and lost his mental equilibrium on account of it, jumped overboard. The cry of "Man overboard" brought the ship to a standstill. A lifeboat was lowered and its crew of brave boys pulled back in search of the drowning Baltimorean. After half an hour of suspense the lost was found and rescued, and by the care of his friends got back to his home and recovered his mental equilibrium.

Coming up Panama Bay through a shoal of porpoises, a passenger shot one of them. It bled profusely, and at sight of the blood the whole herd of its kind pursued it to its death. It often leaped high above the surface of the water in its vain attempt to save itself from its friends and relatives. We had all seen attempts of that sort during the great financial panic in California!

Our little boys had never seen a railroad, and, getting into a car at Panama and moving off to Aspinwall, Charlie shouted in surprise, "Pa, where are the horses?" Coming to a curve bringing the engine into full view, I said, "Charlie, look. See the big horse that pulls the waggon. See how he snorts."

Gazing in astonishment, he said, "Where did they get him?"

At Aspinwall we took passage for New York on the steamship *George Law*. She took us through all right, but a few months afterwards, loaded with homeward-bound Californians, she foundered in a storm and went down in the depths in the dead of the night. Before morning dawn a sail ship hailed them, and in the true spirit of American gallantry all the women and children were lowered into the lifeboats and taken aboard the sailer, with a request from the captain of the steamer to stand by till morning. Not a woman or child was lost, not a man saved except a few picked up from the open sea.

A lucky miner who had made his pile offered ten thousand dollars for a passage in the boat which had conveyed the women and children to the sail ship, and the officer of the deck shouted in response, "Jump overboard." His life was in that jump, but he said, "Wait till I run below and get my gold dust;" but before he could return to the deck the boat was far out on the stormy sea, and soon after the steamer sank and the vast crowd of rich and poor went down together.

Many of them were my personal friends, one a leading member of my Church in San Francisco. He had written his wife in Boston, whom he had not seen for years, to meet him in New York on the day set for the arrival of his steamer. She waited long, but in vain. Later she met one of the survivors of the ship, who said, "I saw your husband after the ship had disappeared, and he called me by name and said, 'I am pulling through. In half an hour I shall be in heaven. Say good-bye to my wife.'"

PART THIRD

IN THE OLD STATES AND CANADA

CHAPTER XIII

PREACHING IN EASTERN CITIES

On our arrival in New York, it being my first visit to that city, I went without money to the Methodist Book Concern to get my first book, "Seven Years' Street Preaching" put into marketable shape. Dr. Abel Stevens was Editor of the *Christian Advocate and Journal*, and Dr. Strickland assistant. I knew nothing about proof reading, or putting through the press, so I applied to Dr. Stevens to edit my book. He said his time was so fully occupied that he could not possibly undertake it, but that Dr. Strickland, who had edited Peter Cartwright's autobiography, was just the man for me; so I employed him. He read my proof sheets, and made a few brief alterations, which he said did not alter the sense, but improved the style. I replied that I always appeared in public with my own clothes on, and that it was my style, and not his, which I wished my book to represent; so I corrected the doctor's corrections, and clothed all my facts in my own homespun attire.

The Annual Meeting of the Missionary Committee was opened in New York a few days after my arrival. One of the principal preachers announced for the Sabbath of the meeting was absent, and I was appointed to take his place both in morning and night, and the Lord gave me words of wisdom for the occasion. The burden of China lay heavily on the hearts of the committee at that time. About ten years had been spent there by our missionaries in levelling down mountains and hills, and filling up valleys, and preparing "the way of the Lord," but "the glory of the Lord" had not been revealed up to that time in the salvation of a single Chinaman. The committee did not show the least hesitancy in going on with the work, but I think Dr. Nathan Bangs expressed the general feeling of the committee when he vehemently exclaimed, "Oh, if we could get one Chinaman soundly converted to God, it would inspire the whole Church with hope and zeal for this work." Well, they held on firmly, and during the ten years next ensuing their China missionaries reported more than a thousand Chinamen converted to God ; and in latter years "the glory of the Lord" is being revealed through all parts of the Chinese empire.

My friends Ross and Falconer had a leading agency in building a Seventeenth Street Methodist Episcopal Church, and were members of it, so for a commencement I gave their church a week of special services, resulting in the quickening of Christian workers and the conversion of a few sinners.

At that early period of my work in New York I renewed my acquaintance with Mrs. Phœbe Palmer, to whom I was first introduced at Baltimore camp meeting on "Low's Ground" in 1848. On my arrival in New York in 1856, I soon became identified with the Tuesday holiness meeting, which was initiated by Mrs. Sarah Lankford, Phœbe's sister ; but Dr. Palmer and his wife were more widely known as its leaders. It has been regularly kept up for more than half a century, and eternity alone can reveal the extent of the work wrought in the hearts of countless thousands by the Holy Sanctifier at those meetings.

Soon after our arrival in New York in 1856 we were struck by our third family bereavement. We had buried in California our dear ocean-born girl and our dear bright-eyed Willie, and now our little Osman, of two summers, was taken away from us by a Father's hand. Our hearts and eyes gave forth their fountains of grief ; yet we did not murmur, but rejoiced that our dear babes had gone to their home in heaven.

During the winter I preached in many New York and Brooklyn churches.

In the spring of 1857 I attended a session of the old Baltimore Conference, of which I had been a member. I was most cordially received and invited to address the Conference, and gave that venerable body an account of my feats and defeats in California.

At the close of this series I took my dear Anne and our two surviving children, Morgan Stuart and Charles Reid, to my old home to visit father, mother, brothers, and sisters. We had not seen them for eight years. When I bade them adieu to go to California I never expected to see them again. I spent a few days with these loved ones, and left my family with them during the ensuing summer, while I made the tour of the camp meetings of New Jersey, Delaware, and the Eastern Shore of Maryland.

From Titusville camp I went home with the Rev. George Hughes, then stationed in Trenton, and preached for him Sunday morning and evening, and that day heard the sad news of the mutiny and great war in India, jeopardising the lives of our missionaries there. At my next New Jersey camp I heard a leading layman relate this experience :

"I was not brought up in Methodist lines, but about twenty years ago I attended some of their revival meetings and became deeply convicted of sin. I cried day and night for mercy, till one day I got my sins forgiven, and shouted glory to God. My parents thought something dreadful had come upon me, and that I should certainly die, so they sent a man ten miles for Dr. Henry to come in haste; meantime they locked me up in a room of their house, and I passed the time of my confinement in praising God for the peace and joy that filled and thrilled my soul. In due time Dr. Henry came. He felt my pulse and looked at my tongue, and said, 'William, I must shave your head and apply a plaster to it.' I said, 'Doctor, the trouble was not in my head, but in my heart; but the Lord Jesus undertook my case. He took away my sins and gave me a new heart; so now I am all right, and do not need any other medical treatment.' He replied, 'William, you are my patient, and you must submit to my treatment.'

"So I submitted in Christian meekness, and he shaved my head and blistered it and tortured me for three days. Then a Methodist who had heard of my case came with the doctor and asked me, in the doctor's presence, how I felt. I said, 'Under the treatment of the doctor here I have got a very sore head, but under the treatment of the great Physician my heart has been healed, and I am very happy.' Then my friend said, 'Doctor, you have entirely mis-apprehended this case. Nothing in the world ails this young man except that he has got his sins forgiven. This is the Methodist religion that he has got.'"

The doctor gave up the case. Methodist religion has spread so widely since, and so diffused itself into all the older Churches of America, that medical doctors are not required to diagnose or treat those who are afflicted by it.

I held services in 1857 also at Eutaw and Charles Street Churches. The latter was noted as being the only pewed church in Methodism south of Mason and Dixon's line. Rev. Ben Brook was preacher in charge. The church was composed largely of rich merchants and bankers, who had combined and built up a church suited to their standing and taste. It was usually designated by outsiders as the seat of Methodist aristocracy and pride. Twelve years had elapsed since their organisation as a Church, during which period they never had what was considered there as a revival. On this occasion of my visit to Baltimore Rev. Ben Brook, the pastor, begged me to assist him in a series of revival services. I replied, "I cannot help you without the concurrence of the leading members of the Church."

"Well," said he, "I will announce for you to preach in our church next Thursday night; they will come out to hear you, and after preaching I will consult them."

I went on Thursday night, according to appointment, and found a good congregation assembled. After preaching he introduced the subject of a series of special services. About half a dozen of his official members promptly responded one by one, and all concurred in the statement that such a thing was utterly impracticable at that season of the year. They said in effect, "Most of us are merchants. The month of April is passing away. We are in the midst of our spring trade, and cannot leave our counting houses before midnight six nights in the week. We have never be able to succeed in a revival here at a suitable season of the year, and to attempt such a thing at this most unsuitable season is out of the question." One of the trustees said, "It is a settled thing I cannot be here, and I cannot consent to the opening of the church in my absence."

Rev. Ben Brook sat quietly until they were through, and then arose, trembling with emotion, and gave them a detail of their history for the past twelve years, and their fruitless attempts to have what could be called in Baltimore a revival, and added, "I have been working here for over a year, and have seen but little success in soul saving. You are all very kind to me; there is no better station in the city, but I cannot stand this sort of work any longer. I must see something done or quit. Brother Taylor is with us and can help us. He cannot be with us in the fall, the usual time for revivals; so my feeling is that if you won't concur in this proposal I shall have to put on my hat and bid you good-bye."

After a little pause the leading church officials said in effect, "Well, Brother Brook, we have expressed our minds plainly, and have not changed our view of the case; but if you and Brother Taylor are willing to face the failure and disgrace of an abortive attempt, then go ahead; we will not stand in your way." So the meeting was dismissed.

I then said to Brook, "I don't feel exactly free to work under such discouragements, so you had better excuse me." But in a spirit of apparent desperation he seized my hand and said, "Oh, Brother Taylor, don't leave me! Let us proceed in the name of the Lord, and He will help us." So I said, "All right." Then we settled on a plan of work:

"1. We will light up the main audience room every night and invite the Lord and the people to the best accommodation we have, instead of trying it in the basement, as heretofore.

"2. We will have a meeting at 11 o'clock A. M. every day in the week, and do the hand-to-hand work which may open to us by the daily request for prayers at our forenoon meeting. We will call for information from those present, giving us the names and addresses of persons under an awakening of the Spirit.

"3. We will employ all our available time in visiting from house to house, inquiring specially for such as may be commended to our notice at the morning meetings, and do what we can for them by personal effort.

"4. The pastor must examine personally every one professing conversion to God at our meeting, and satisfy himself, as far as it is possible, of the saving character of the work in each case, and keep a record of the facts, name, and address of each one.

"5. The pastor must preach to his people every Sunday morning, and I will take all the other preaching appointments each week."

So we went to work systematically on that line.

The first Sunday the church was crowded, as usual, and Ben

Brook preached a powerful sermon suited to the occasion. I talked that morning to the people in the Penitentiary, and at night to the aristocrats in Charles Street, preaching the same Gospel to the two extreme classes of that city.   There was great interest and apparent awakening, but no person responded to the call for seekers.

Uninspired prophets had predicted that we could not, at that season of the year, get a hearing on week days, noon or night; but to our agreeable surprise we had at our Monday forenoon meeting more than half a hundred ladies and a few men.   We invited all persons present who had any knowledge of persons under awakening whom they desired to mention as special subjects for prayer to announce their names and addresses.   For these we prayed specially and visited them personally in the afternoon.   I was delighted to find among those high-toned aristocratic people, especially their ladies, many humble, earnest Christians, among whom was Mrs. Theobold, who was a widow and the daughter of the celebrated surgeon of that city, Dr. Smith.   She said in the forenoon meeting that she had a sister, Mrs. M., in whose salvation she was especially interested, but could scarcely command faith sufficient to present her name as a subject of prayer, because her sister was a very devout Roman Catholic, exemplary in her life, but was, she believed, resting in a form of godliness without the power; however, she begged us to pray for her sister.

Monday night we had, what exceeded all expectation, a crowded house; profound attention, but no one came out as a seeker. Tuesday morning meeting was about as large as that of Monday, with an increase of divine unction.   Tuesday night a slight improvement on the night preceding, both in numbers and interest. Wednesday morning it rained, and we had but few out.   Wednesday evening we had a good congregation, and a number came to the altar, surrendered to God, received Christ, and publicly testified to an experience of salvation.   The news spread rapidly that there was a revival in Charles Street.

So the work went on increasing daily.   The second week the large basement hall was crowded at the forenoon week-day meetings. Merchants and others seemed to have plenty of time; many became earnest workers who had never taken part at the front before.   In the second week Mrs. Theobold invited her sister, Mrs. M——, to go with her to the meeting.   She replied, "Your preacher will denounce the Roman Catholics and hurt my feelings, so I cannot go to such a place;" whereupon Mrs. Theobold assured her that though the preacher proclaimed plain Gospel truth he never gave unnecessary offence to any one.

So Mrs. M—— accepted her invitation and came to the meeting. On her way home she expressed a great desire to be saved.   She came with her sister the next forenoon, and was seated on a front form which was used for the seekers.   Ben Brook approached her and said, "Please, madam, take a seat back further."   She promptly obeyed.   Then he said, "All persons under awakening who desire to seek salvation will please come to these front forms, that we may pray for you and instruct you." Mrs. M—— returned at once and knelt down at the penitent form and submitted herself to God and accepted Christ.

Old Major Dryden, one of the rich old members, whose voice had never been heard in prayer, was resurrected, and one night prayed about as follows :—

"O Lord, twelve years ago we built this house. We poured out our money freely and constructed this beautiful edifice. These fine pews have been sepulchres to the dead, and these fine cushions the habiliments of our graves. We have had good preaching, but we awoke not. O Lord, Thou knowest how helpless and hopeless was our deplorable state. But during these meetings, blessed be Thy holy name, the voice of the Son of God has awakened the dead, and they have come forth a great army, and are on the march for the conquest of souls for Thee. Now we are glad that we put our money into this beautiful building, and that at last Thou hast accepted this our offering, and we will trust Thee henceforth to make this the house of Thine abode, for Christ's sake. Amen!"

The work went on, and in the course of three weeks over two hundred of the newly converted people were added to the Charles Street Church.

At one of the camp meetings of that season a man of mature age and commanding presence followed me from the stand where I had been preaching that morning into the preacher's tent and sat down beside me ; next to me on the other side sat Rev. Brother Willis, an able young minister. The stranger unceremoniously commenced a bitter tirade against Christianity and the Bible, and talked flippantly about the immutability of law ; hence the impossibility of miracles. I sat quietly without a word of reply till he was through. He had raised more than a dozen debatable issues. Brother Willis was in a fidget, and said to me afterwards, "I did not see how you could sit quietly and hear such a slanderous misrepresentation of God and His Gospel."

Willis was a gentleman, and would not interrupt the prater, as his address was directed entirely to me.

"Well, you see how I fixed him ? " said I.

"I do, indeed, and I see that was just the thing to do."

When the fellow had fired his last gun and silence ensued I said, "Well, my friend, there is one point on which we can agree."

In apparent surprise he inquired, "What point is that ?"

"We mutually concede the fact that there is a standard of right, a law of righteousness, by which the conduct of human beings, both in their relations to God and to each other, should be regulated. We may not agree as to the precise lines of its application, nor the source whence nor the medium through which it comes to us, but we do mutually agree that such a law exists, and that we are amenable to it."

"Oh yes, I agree with you on that point."

"Then allow me to ask whether with undeviating fidelity through all the vicissitudes of your past life you have kept that law?"

He coloured and coughed and tried to evade my point, but I looked straight into his eyes and said, "Have you?"

Then after a pause of a few moments he replied, "Well, sir, to tell you the truth, I must admit that I have not."

"Then what are you going to do about it? You have been most positively asserting the immutability of law, and now you admit that you have been a habitual breaker of an immutable law. What can the law do for a law-breaker?"

I proceeded to show him that all human attempts to repair the breach by reformation or penance or compensation were entirely inadequate and irrelevant, and that if the Bible did not, through the incarnation, death, resurrection, and mediation of the Son of God reveal a ransom and a remedy adequate to the demands of the case there was none. No human court can righteously acquit a guilty criminal, but, however incomprehensible the mystery, the fact is clearly revealed in the Bible that God can be just, and the justifier of him that believeth in Jesus, and will freely forgive and acquit every poor sinner who will confess and forsake his sins, and receive and trust Jesus Christ as an all-sufficient Saviour. "As many as received Him, to them gave He power to become the sons of God." This free gift implies a divine act of acquittal at the bar of justice, a divine communication of the fact to the spirit of the penitent believer, and a divine inward renewal of the heart.

The man sat quietly while I kindly opened up these facts verified in human experience. He finally said, "I have never experienced any such thing, and therefore can't believe that there is any such experience possible."

"You have no experience of life in California," I replied. "You have not been there, and conclude, therefore, that there is no such country in the world. I have spent over seven years in California, and testify to what I have experienced and know to be facts. Would you go before this great camp meeting congregation and contradict my statement of facts on the ground that you had never seen California and knew nothing about it?"

Just then the bell rang announcing the hour for the afternoon public service, and I bade my man a good-bye and took my seat on the preachers' stand.

About half an hour afterward I felt a gentle jerk of my coat skirt, and looking round I saw my man close in the rear of the stand. The public service had opened, so there was not a word uttered by either of us, but he handed me a letter and turned away, and being but a passing stranger in that region I never saw him again. The letter read substantially as follows:—

"REV. TAYLOR.—DEAR SIR,—Your convincing arguments have covered all my points, and your kindly spirit has quite overcome my foolish prejudice against God's truths. My wretched infidelity! I am ashamed of it, and do and shall for ever abandon it."

10

I spent about three months of the summer of 1857 in Philadelphia, and preached in all the Methodist churches of any note in that city. Soon after my arrival in that city the Preachers' Meeting appointed a committee to wait on his excellency the mayor and get his consent to my preaching in the open air. The committee reported at the next meeting that the mayor respectfully declined to grant the request, on the ground that there was a city ordinance prohibiting outdoor preaching. A few weeks later, however, I opened preaching services in Eleventh Street Market. I wrote and printed a series of tracts on street preaching, distributing a new tract after preaching in the market each Sabbath. We had crowds of hearers of all sorts and sizes, and we sowed Gospel seed broadcast, and a great and growing interest was awakened on behalf of the outsiders.

At the request of the ministers I opened market-house preaching at other centres also, with a promise that they would keep the little stone rolling after my departure. After I had been preaching many weeks in the markets a dear Presbyterian minister said to me : " My conscience has long been troubled on account of the neglected masses who never go to church, and I applied to the mayor for permission to preach in the markets, and he forbade me to do so. I am curious to know how you, as a stranger, got so readily into this work."

" Well, sir, I got in as I suppose Paul got in at Athens. I walked in, and proclaimed the Word of the Lord under the authority of the great commission, ' Go ye into all the world, and preach the Gospel to every creature.' I have no wish to set the municipal authorities at defiance at all. I simply obey the order of the King, and consent to take the consequences."

It was during the fall of the year 1857 that for the first time I visited New England and attended New Market Camp Meeting, in New Hampshire. It was at that meeting I saw and heard for the first time the old hero of a thousand battles and world-renowned friend of the sailors, Father Taylor, of Boston. At that meeting I became acquainted also with my abiding friend and fellow-worker in the cause of industrial and self-supporting missions, Rev. William McDonald, and heard him preach on his favourite theme, perfect love.

I was most cordially received at that camp meeting by preachers and people, and had freedom in preaching the Gospel to them.

After the close of the camp meeting I spent about a fortnight in Boston and preached for Father Taylor; also in Hanover Street Methodist Episcopal Church, and in Bromfield Street Church. I preached in the forenoon and attended a general fellowship meeting at night in the last-named grand old hive.

Brother Hawley, one of the official members, in the course of the evening related some of his experiences in California. He said, in effect :

" Soon after I arrived in San Francisco in the year 1850 I was taken ill. Nearly all the people there were sojourning in tents, and there was not a hotel in the place ; but I got shelter in the upper room of a rustic storehouse. With my illness, poor accommodations, and utter loneliness I feared that I should die. I felt a great longing for fellowship with some one who loved the Lord, but feared that I should have to go to heaven to find one. Sabbath came, and thoughts of home and Church and Christian friends, but the loneliness of my situation was like a horrible nightmare that I could not shake off. Then, all of a sudden, I heard a powerful voice singing in strains of enchanting melody:

> " ' Hear the royal proclamation,
>   The glad tidings of salvation,
> Publishing to every creature,
>   To the ruined sons of nature,
>   Jesus reigns.'

" I could hear but few words of the preaching that followed. I was too feeble to get out, but was comforted to know that there was at least one preacher in that vast encampment. I could hardly call it a city, except a city of tents, with a few houses like the one I occupied, made up largely of the lumber of goods boxes.

" To my great surprise and joy, an hour later, by some singular leading of Providence, the preacher came into my room and inquired about my condition and needs, and sang and prayed, and by the help of God drew me up from the slough of despond, and from that hour I began to recover. But for that man of God I think I should have died. I now have the honour and pleasure of entertaining my friend in need as my guest. His name is William Taylor."

During my sojourn with Brother Hawley, in Boston, he gave me the following experience of a Christian woman of his acquaintance, then residing in South Boston:

" On a dark, stormy night a ship was passing slowly down the English Channel. The man at the lookout shouted that he heard the voice of a woman on the dark waters. A boat was immediately lowered and manned by a crew of brave sailors, who, as they approached nearer the object of their search, heard a woman sing:

> " ' Jesus, Lover of my soul,
>   Let me to Thy bosom fly,
> While the nearer waters roll,
>   While the tempest still is high !
> Hide me, O my Saviour, hide,
>   Till the storm of life is past ;
> Safe into the haven guide,
>   O receive my soul at last ! '

" The singer proved to be a woman clinging with one arm to a fragment of a ship that had just been wrecked, and with her other arm pressing to her bosom her infant child. Being a Christian, and expecting to be drowned and to go to heaven that night, she was giving expression to her triumphant faith in those wonderful words of sacred song."

Dear Anne and her two little boys spent the summer and fall of 1857 with my dear father and mother at their home in Rockbridge County, Virginia. Our dear Ross was born there in September of that year. I visited my parents and all the dear ones again late in the fall, and took my family soon after to Newark, New Jersey. We rented for the winter a comfortable, well-furnished house in a very accessible and said to be a very healthy location in that city. This did not mean any cessation of my widespread and constant labours abroad, but comfortable quarters for Anne and our three boys, giving me a few hours with them one day in each week.

It turned out, however, that I had to spend more time with them than I expected. In a few weeks after we were comfortably settled our little Charlie and Ross were struck down with smallpox, and then, when it was too late, we found out that we were in the midst of that plague concealed from public view; so I shut myself in with my sick boys for a month. Charlie, then of about four and a half years, had the confluent form of that horrible disease. A kind homeopathic physician from Elizabeth city treated them very skilfully, so that they got through without any relapse. Meanwhile Stuart put up this sign on a tree in the yard: "Smallpox! Walk in and catch it!" We sat at a window overlooking the street and watched the men and women as they came along to see them read and run.

Poor Charlie suffered most during the stage of recovery. I had to watch him through the dreary nights to prevent his little fingers from tearing the skin off his face. I would say, "Charlie, don't scratch your face; you will spoil it, and you can't be our pretty little boy any more."

"I won't scratch it any more, papa."

Soon after I would have to caution him again and again, till finally he said, "I can't help it. Won't you tie my hands, papa, so that I can't scratch?"

I did not tie his hands, but watched and gently restrained them. One night he said, "Papa, won't you ask the Lord please to make me well?"

"Yes, dear Charlie, I will."

I then wept before the Lord, and begged Him to pity and heal my boy.

Then said Charlie, "Papa, do you think the Lord will make me well?"

"Yes, I think He will."

"When do you think He will?"

"In about two weeks."

Then he silently measured up the time in his mind, and said, "I do wish He would make haste."

Later he said one night, "Papa, please tell me how to pray."

From the time he was able to lisp the name of Jesus he had been accustomed to pray, but now he felt the pressure of a deeper need, bordering as he was on the lines of personal moral responsibility; so I explained to him the Saviour's object lesson of the fathers and mothers bringing their little children to Jesus that He might put His hands upon them and pray. When they got close to Jesus they let go the hands of father and mother and came to

Jesus, and Jesus took them up in His arms, and with His own hands took all the bad out of their hearts, and prayed to His own Father for them that their names should be written down in His book as His dear, obedient, loving children, to be filled every day with truth and love and all good things that God's own dear children need, living or dying, on earth or in heaven. When Jesus was in the world, so that the children could see Him with their eyes, they came to Him, but ever since He went to heaven He is too far off to be seen with our eyes; but in His Spirit, which our eyes can't see, He comes right into the little children—"that which may be known of God is manifest in them, for God hath shown it unto them." I was persuaded that "the invisible things of God"—spiritual things that pertain to the needs and supply of the soul at this point of transit from the vale of infantile innocency to the plane of personal moral responsibility—are clearly seen, "even His eternal power and divinity" (R. V.). At this stage the child has only to yield itself wholly to Jesus, receive and trust Him to take it in hand and have His way with it. The end of repentance is submission to the will of God, and the act of saving faith is the act of receiving Jesus. Under the leading of the ever-present Holy Spirit all that is easy for a little child, and adult sinners cannot get into the kingdom of God with anything less."

So Charlie prayed, and I cried. Next night he called to me in gleeful tones, "Papa, ain't you glad that Jesus died for sinners?"

"Yes, Charlie, I'm very glad."

"Papa, I'm glad too, for Jesus died for me. He has gone to heaven out of sight, but in His Spirit He comes into me and makes me so glad. Oh, how I do love Him!"

I don't believe my dear Charlie had forfeited the justified relation secured to him by the free gift which was unto justification of life, through the righteousness "of the Lamb slain from the foundation of the world," but that he entered into the high form of the acquitted relation of a responsible subject of the kingdom of God—justification by faith with its concomitants, the regenerating "grace and peace of our Lord Jesus Christ." That is what Charlie received by faith while under the smallpox *tribulum*, and he manifested the fruits of it daily till the day of his death.

Ross was the baby, and suffered less than his brother Charlie, and gained less by what he suffered. The rest of us escaped the scourge.

During this confinement in Newark I redeemed the time of those evil days and wrote my third book, entitled "California Life Illustrated," which had a circulation of over thirty-five thousand copies; also a small book, entitled "Address to Young America and a Word to the Old Folks," on my favourite theme of abiding in the kingdom of God. This little work had a circulation of twenty-five thousand copies.

CHAPTER XIV

DURING the years 1858-60, six days and nights of each week I preached in most of the cities and towns in Ohio, Indiana, and Illinois. My uniform method, even for every single night service, was to preach, exhort, invite awakened seekers of pardon or purity to come to the altar, where we instructed them and prayed for them, and heard the testimony of those who obtained pardon and peace, occupying the time to about half-past nine p.m. The keeping power of Jesus is just as adequate and just as available as His converting power, and uniformly the entire congregation, with exceptions scarcely perceptible, remained till the benediction was pronounced, about ten p.m. We held them by announcing the programme at the opening of each service, the last point of interest being a talk about California. This applies specially to the week-night meetings. My Sabbaths were devoted wholly to Gospel services, with a promise to give them a talk on California on Monday night.

Brother John M. Phillips, of book agency renown, once said to me : " Soon after Brother B——'s return from his episcopal tour in India he was announced to preach in Cincinnati. The church was packed from the top to the bottom with an anxious throng, all hungry for a feast of the latest news from India. The bishop preached to them a very good old sermon that they had heard him deliver from the same pulpit but a few years before, and he made no allusion to what he saw or heard or did in the far East, and the people went away hopping mad."

I replied, " Oh, they just wanted to hear some lion stories."

" Well, he should have told them some."

When an old dame of the culinary art was asked how to cook a hare, she replied, " The first thing to do is to catch him." The first thing for a speaker to do in addressing an individual or an audience is to arrest attention. Metal has to be melted before it can be moulded.

I gave a few weeks of the fall of 1858 to Rev. D. P. Mitchell, Presiding Elder of the Alleghany District, Pittsburg Conference. It was a hard field, preoccupied by United Presbyterians and Campbellites, good people in their way, but in those days full of the spirit of controversy. They would publicly challenge the Methodist preachers for public debate, and crow over their refusal as proof of

a bad cause or inability to defend it.   Mitchell was a powerful West
Virginian, both in bodily and intellectual force.   He was a native-
born logician, possessing great piety and perfect equilibrium of
temper.   As soon as possible after his appointment to that district
he made a careful survey of his whole field, then but very partially
supplied with houses of worship, and noted the populous centres,
in each of which he secretly determined in his own mind to build a
church, no matter whether there were any Methodists living in the
neighbourhood or not.   When he was about ready to commence
operations in a place selected he flaunted a red rag, and would at
once receive a challenge for debate from one or other of the parties
named.   He always accepted the challenge, and immediately all
preliminaries were settled with the time and place for the debate—
usually in some grove where a stand and seats were provided in
good style—the debate to occupy at least three days, with competent
judges appointed.   The whole programme was extensively advertised
in all the papers available and by great placards posted up in all
public places.   Soon the whole country fizzed with a glow of fervent
heat, so that the great crowds came trooping in to see the fight.

Mitchell was master of the situation.   He managed to extend the
discussion to its limit of three days, and then by a conversation of
unanswerable logic and laughable sarcasm he swept the field.   His
antagonist usually left abruptly without waiting to hear the decision
of the judges.

He had a three-days' hitch with a noted Campbellite who made
the assertion that every mention of water in the Scriptures was
literal, and was never used to represent spirit or spiritual operation.

Mitchell in reply asked the gentleman a few questions which led
to a colloquy to this effect:

" ' Ho, every one that thirsteth, come ye to the waters.'   Is that
' literal ? ' "

"Yes, most assuredly."

" ' Whosoever will, let him take of the water of life freely.'   Is
that ' literal ? ' "

" Yes, certainly ; any child can see that."

" ' Whosoever drinketh of this water shall thirst again : but
whosoever drinketh of the water that I shall give him shall never
thirst ; but the water that I shall give him shall be in him a well
of water springing up into everlasting life.'   Is that ' literal ? ' "

" Yes, yes, all literal."

" ' He that believeth on Me, out of his belly shall flow rivers of
living water.'   Is that ' literal ? ' "

" All literal, all literal."

" Well, then, I have only to say that in western Kansas, where
water is so scarce, such a man would be a great blessing to that
country as a mill seat and water supply ! "

The mill-seat man seized his hat and ran !

Then Mitchell, without a smile, announced that he would preach
there that night, and continue a series of preaching and soul-saving

prayer-meeting services for a week or ten days. In that series he would enroll from twenty to a hundred newborn souls, organise them into a Church, circulate a subscription paper, and raise funds to erect a chapel in that neighbourhood, and let out the contract, buy the lumber and other material, and set his carpenters to work before he retired from the spot. Meantime he would be quietly planning to move in a similar way at some other point, usually remote from the scene of his last success. His methods were varied to meet peculiar emergencies. He kept his own counsel and his movements could not be anticipated.

He had two poor families living in Butler. The church of the United Presbyterians was about a mile out of town, but they held a preëmptive claim on Butler and all the region round about. Mitchell wrote to one of his members residing in Butler to arrange for a preaching appointment on a Sabbath named, and to have it stated that the presiding elder would preach. As per announcement, the elder was on hand in due time. It was a dark, rainy day, and no assembly and no preaching place available. The agent reported that he tried in vain to get the use of a house or a barn, but could find no open door for a Methodist minister in that section of the soil. Mitchell preached in the cabin of one of his families. The roof was bad, and the rain poured in plentifully on preacher and people.

Mitchell then announced that on a certain day he would commence a camp meeting in a well-known grove of timber near the town of Butler. He had his men stick up huge posters in all places accessible, advertising the camp meeting. He had meantime negotiated for the use of the grove with the owner, a sceptical old sinner who was not allied with any Church. Mitchell's camp meeting became at once the ridiculous theme and standing joke of all classes of the people. " A corncrib would hold all the people of Mitchell's camp meeting, with pews taken," they said.

As Mitchell passed around his district he engaged a large number of his well-to-do families to come to his camp meeting at Butler and be sure to get their tents up and be ready the day before the opening of the meeting. He also drafted a corps of his most able preachers to be there in time for the opening service. The whole plan was carried out with military precision. The day before the announced time the roads were thronged with waggons, teams, and crowds of people on foot, and before night a town of tents was built, laid out like a great encampment of soldiers.

It was in every way the greatest surprise of the age for that country. The meeting was carried on with marvellous effect for a week. Nearly a hundred new converts were enrolled, a Methodist Church in Butler was organised, and a subscription raised near the close of the camp meeting for building a church in Butler, and the contract for its erection made and signed before the closing doxology of the camp meeting was sung.

I assisted Brother Mitchell in the dedication of his Butler church in due time. Most of the funds required had been previously paid in. The balance was raised at the dedication. Some of the United Presbyterians, who had been strong in their opposition, generously joined hands to help the Methodists to pay the amount required to present the house to the Lord free from debt.

Most of my time, six days per week, during the year 1858 was devoted to evangelising work in western Pennsylvania and Ohio, attending camp meetings and conferences, and occasionally holding a week or two of special services in a single church. I had a goodly heritage—incessant hard work six days per week, always surrounded by good, loving, Christian friends, and blessed with conscious peace with God and all the time with saving power among my hearers. And yet, though grateful to my merciful Father in heaven for these innumerable blessings, I suffered daily a painful sense of loss like a great bereavement on account of my isolation from home and family.

From 1858 to the spring of 1861 I preached in nearly all the towns of any note in Ohio, Indiana, Illinois, and in some in Iowa.

I had much difficulty in most places to induce the people to admit a sufficiency of fresh air into their preaching halls and churches to keep their bodies and minds in a healthful and receptive condition. For example, I had an appointment to preach one night in a new church in Lena, Illinois. The windows were paint-locked and could not be opened. The door was the only breathing hole in the house, and that was so crowded by the people occupying all the standing room that but little air could get in.

At the beginning of the service I explained, as usual, the necessity of fresh air. I said, "In fifteen minutes you will use the vitalising power of all the oxygen in this audience room, and emit from the lungs and from the countless millions of pores of each mortal body in this assembly poisonous gases which will stupefy body and mind and defeat the purpose for which we have assembled." With such words I scarcely restrained the people from spending their time in poisoning each other. I assured them that fresh air was one of the essential conditions to a receptive state of mind and body, and said, "If you can get a window or two open, we can have many people converted to God here to-night. If not we shall have a poisoned, sleepy congregation, and you will go home and tell what a miserably poor preacher you had." Some of the trustees tried the windows, but could not open them. Then I saw one of them wrapping a handkerchief around his right hand, and with it he knocked out a pane of glass about twenty inches square and gave us a good breathing hole. That saved us from defeat. At the close of the sermon a crowd of seekers pressed their way to the altar, and a number of them were converted to God, among whom was a Roman Catholic woman, who told her experience in beautiful simplicity. Years afterwards as I passed through that region I was informed that she developed into a very steadfast, consistent Christian.

The State prohibition movement at that period, commencing in Maine, rolled westward. The State of Indiana fell into line and passed a prohibitory law which was in force about three months.

During that period it is said that not a drunken man was seen in that State, and the good people thought the morning of millennial glory was dawning upon them. Then one of the judges of the Supreme Court came along with his legal lever under a cry of "unconstitutionality," and reopened the floodgates of intoxicating drink.

I spent a night in Kokomo, a country seat, and learned that after months of universal total abstinence in the town a man was seen staggering in the street more than half drunk. The people called a mass meeting of inquiry to find out where the man got the whisky; they discussed the subject and appointed a committee which they called the "Smelling Committee," to smell out the man who dared to sell drink in that town. Said committee found a barrel of the deadly stuff that had been secreted in the town; the owner was "smelled out," and was being tried before Judge Lindsay the day I left there for violation of the "nuisance law."

In another town, Williamsburg, further south, there were seven grogshops. The ladies had a meeting and considered the perilous situation, and served a notice on all the rumsellers in town to close by a certain day named, or they would be forced to the extreme necessity of destroying all their intoxicating drinks. The moral suasion of the ladies did not move them, so on the day appointed nearly a hundred women appeared in line in the street, each with a hatchet in hand; a deep snow was thawing, and the streets were flooded with streams of water. A minister stationed there at the time told me that when they first appeared in the street they picked their way carefully along the sidewalks to keep their feet dry, but when they had cleaned out three or four of the grogshops, knocking in the heads of barrels and pouring out the liquor in streams, they just trudged along in the middle of the street, wading through the slush and never stopping until they cleared the town of grogshops. I received these facts on the ground on which they occurred, and from witnesses of the scenes described. I make no comment on the facts stated, except to say that they indicate the deep sense of cruelty, injustice, and woe brought upon women by the destruction of their husbands and brothers through the liquor traffic, and the desperation and daring to which it may yet lead. That was long before the modern crusades of Ohio. This indicates the character of the crusade in Indiana. The Ohio crusaders depended mainly on praying in front of the rumshops. The Hoosiers depended mainly on the effective use of their hatchets. The crusade, in still another form, is becoming world-wide through the Women's National Temperance Union, and if men fail to do their work righteously at the ballot box and on the field the women will take it up.

In Ohio, Indiana, and Illinois I shook hands with some of the surviving pioneer heroes of the West, among whom were Jimmy Havens, Peter Cartwright, and Wilson Pitner. Father Havens was a short, thickset, muscular man, specially endowed with the rare gift of good common sense and with great power of endurance; he was a man of intelligent, earnest, Christian character, and an indefatigable worker as an early founder of Methodism in that State. For a time he travelled a circuit that comprised almost the entire State of Indiana. He told me it took him so long to go around his big circuit that his own dogs didn't know him when he got home.

He displayed his muscular Christianity at a camp meeting he held once in the neighbourhood of Indianapolis. One evening during the meeting he learned that a mob of desperadoes had been organised in Indianapolis to break up the camp meeting. Their plan was to go out in force and put out the camp lights, and knock down or kill all who might dare to oppose them and have their own way with the rest. So Father Havens organised a special police force to protect the camp. Soon after dark his policemen were driven in from the surrounding woods by the great mob, which seemed to strike terror into the hearts of all the people. The police were afraid to touch them or to stand for the defence of the encampment. Havens on inquiry found out the locality of the principal leaders, and told some of his police to follow him, but to keep back in the dark, so as not to be seen, and he would go himself and speak to the leaders of the mob. He went straight to the rendezvous of which he had heard, and found six desperate fellows together. He remonstrated with them, and declared that he was conducting an orderly meeting under the protection of the law, and did not wish to be disturbed, and begged them to go away and let them alone. They swore that they were going to have things their own way. Havens replied, "Now, boys, I will give you five minutes to get off this ground or take the consequences." They laughed and mocked him, and wanted to know what he could do. He said, "If you don't leave these premises in five minutes you will find out." They just stood and jeered him. "Three minutes have gone; you have only two minutes more." They stared in astonishment and called him an old fool. He said, "I give you notice, boys, that your time is nearly up!"

At the end of the five minutes, before they knew what he was going to do, as they were attempting to rush upon him, he struck them one by one and felled the whole of them to the earth. His men in the rear seized three or four of them, and the rest, with their followers, ran away. When Havens got back to the camp he found the people in a great fright and the preacher who was to preach that night begged to be excused; so Havens took the pulpit and preached himself. Subsequently the rowdies brought suit against the preacher for assault. He appeared in court and defended his cause by a simple statement of the facts in the case. The judge gave the fellows a severe scolding for their bad behaviour and dismissed the suit.

While I was with Peter Cartwright I studied him closely. He was an extraordinary man in his day. The children of both of those great men grew up for God; some were ministers, and all useful members of the Church of their fathers. Their fathers were live men, and made common cause with their children and won their hearts for Jesus.

Wilson Pitner was not so widely known abroad as was Cartwright. As a specimen of his simplicity as a speaker and an illustration of the spirit of self-sacrifice which conquered the West for Methodism, and which, if carried out, would conquer the world, I note the following narrative of facts which I received from eyewitnesses. At a session of the Illinois Conference in the early days Pitner was called on for a missionary speech. He stepped on the platform and said :—

"Mr. President, ladies and gentlemen, my heart is in this missionary work, but silver and gold have I none. I travel a poor circuit in northern Illinois. It is a rich country, but settlements are new and have not yet realised sufficient returns for their industry to buy their salt or to pay the preacher. They have plenty of corn, and they live on corn bread without butter. They furnish corn to feed me and my family and horse, and I am thankful for that, but they have no money. I could not get money to buy a suit of clothes to wear to Conference. The elbows and knees of my clothes are patched, as you see. My old hat wore out months ago, but I took my trap and wended my way across the prairies of Illinois, and ascended a bluff near the Iowa line overlooking the Mississippi.

"There I kneeled down at the root of a friendly oak that crowned the bluff and put up a prayer. I said in my prayer, 'O Lord, Thou knowest what a poor circuit Thy servant has to travel. My people are kind-hearted, but they have no money. I have no money, Thou knowest, to buy clothes to wear to Conference. But, blessed Father, I think I can scuff through with this suit for another year ; but there is my old hat, that is a scandal to the profession ; but, Lord, Thou hast plenty of beavers running round here, doing no good to the world, so far as I know. I want to go down to this great river of Thine and set my trap for a beaver, and if Thou wilt be so kind as to send along one of Thy big beavers to-night into my trap I will be very much obliged, and remember Thy kindness as long as I live.' I put up my prayer in faith, and did some watching and work as well. I went down and searched the river bank diligently till I found a beaver slide, where the animals were in the habit of sliding down the bank into the river for their personal entertainment ; and I set my trap at the bottom of the slide, just under water, and went home meditating. Next morning, just as the light of the day began to streak the eastern horizon, I was well on my way to the Mississippi to see what the Lord had done for me in answer to my prayer. Just as the great orb of day began to roll his mellow light across the bosom of the great father of waters, I was descending the bank, and when I reached the bottom I saw that sure enough the Lord had sent me one of the biggest beavers He had. I knocked him on the head and took off his rind, and carried it up on the bluff and laid it down at the root of that friendly oak, where I had put up my prayer, and kneeled down upon it, and with tearful eyes returned sincere thanks to God, as I had promised to do. I dressed the skin until it became as soft as silk, and converted it into a beaver cap to wear to Conference. There is no other such cap at this Conference as the cap the Lord gave me in answer to my prayer, and I praise it highly, I can assure you. My heart is in this missionary work, and I have nothing else that represents money value, so I give my cap for the missionary cause." And suiting his action to his words he tossed his cap into the collection basket.

Wilson Pitner made a visit to Nauvoo and spent a night there with Joe Smith, the founder of Mormonism. He pleaded with Joe all night to give up what he knew to be an imposture, and reminded him that he knew well that the book he pretended to have produced was written by a Presbyterian minister in Washington County, Pennsylvania, by the name of Spaulding, written only as a romance. Plenty of people still living knew Spaulding and his manuscript. He was well-known as the pastor of Lindsey's Church, in Washington County, near the Virginian State line. After Spaulding's death it was thought that his manuscript, printed as a romance, would help to support his widow, and for that purpose it was put into the hands of Neisbitt & Co., in Pittsburg. They promised to examine the manuscript and report, but when the widow's friends made inquiry about it the manuscript could not be found. Sidney Rigden was a printer in that office, and Rigden and Joe Smith knew well what became of Spaulding's manuscript. "And you know, Joe Smith," continued Pitner, "that you are deceiving the people, and that if you do not give up your iniquitous course the judgment of God will fall upon you." According to Pitner's statement to me, "Joe sat and listened, but every now and then he would spring to his feet and invoke all the curses of Mormonism upon me. I sat there quietly and replied, 'Joe Smith, do you think I am afraid of you? With the love of God swelling this jacket of mine I could swim the fiery gulf and shout, Glory to God!' We had it up and down the whole night, and just as the morning dawned I left him; but as I said good-day I added, 'Joe, you know I would not harm a hair on your head, but I tell you if you don't repent of your sins and quit deceiving the people you will be dead and in a perdition before many weeks.'" It so turned out that within a few weeks Nauvoo was taken by storm, and Joe Smith was killed.

I was working in Illinois when the gathering storm of the civil war broke upon the nation. Two of my own brothers went into the Federal army, one of whom, through exposure and severity of the weather during the siege of Fort Donelson, was struck down with typhoid fever and died.

My work was hindered by the war excitement through the West, and the wildcat currency, familiarly known as "stumptail," required us to examine the bank reports daily to see how short the tail had become, and often we found no tail at all. So I concluded that I could serve the cause of God better by a visit to my friends in Canada. Accordingly I spent a year, from the spring of 1861 to the spring of 1862, in the Upper and Lower Canada, preaching as an evangelist in all the towns of any size. I had a most cordial reception by the Wesleyan Methodist Conference at its sessions at Brantford in 1861, and its ministers opened wide to me the doors of all their churches; so with the hearty co-operation of preachers and people I put in six days per week, including nine camp meetings that year. The work extended over a wide range of territory, and under the blessing of Providence reached thousands of souls.

PART FOURTH

MY WORK IN AUSTRALIA

CHAPTER XV

TO PALESTINE BY WAY OF EUROPE

I NOW arrive at my first passage of the Atlantic. Providence led me forth by way of England into Australia. My principle of world-wide evangelisation took the helm of my life, and pointed the way to the remote island empire of the South Pacific. These are the circumstances of my going:

In February, 1862, while labouring in Peterboro, Canada, I was the guest of James Brown, M.D. Dr. Brown had spent some years in Australia, and gave me a glowing account of those rising colonies, but stated that they greatly needed just such evangelising help as I could give them. "They have cleared the forests," said he; "they have ploughed the fallow ground and sowed the seed, but they are not successful like you in gathering the harvest; so that in a short time you could render them a service immeasurable in breadth and in its ingathering of innumerable precious souls." The doctor thus spent days on me, and made an impression upon my mind that I could not dispose of except by taking it to the Lord in prayer. So I went out into a wild forest, kneeled down in the snow, and prayed until I was certified by the Holy Spirit that the Lord wanted me in Australia. My family returned to our old home in California, and on May 1st, 1862, I took passage for Liverpool on the steamship *Kangaroo*, *en route* for Australia.

After a voyage of fourteen days we anchored in the Mersey River, at Liverpool. On the first Sabbath morning after arrival I found my way to Brunswick Wesleyan Chapel, and was introduced to the pastor as a minister just from the United States. The pastor promptly retorted, " The dis-United States ? "

" No, sir; the temporary disruption of my nation will not alter its name or its united nationality."

He was an able minister, and I was greatly interested in his sermon, but was surprised to see that he stood up to pray and that the whole congregation remained seated. I kneeled as usual.

With as little delay as possible I went directly from Liverpool to the Wesleyan Conference, then in session at Camborne, Cornwall, and put up at a hotel. I had letters of introduction from ministers in Canada to William Arthur, Dr. Prest, and many other distinguished members of the Wesleyan Conference. So I was cordially received. I was surprised to find that their Conference business was conducted in a social, conversational way, instead of by parliamentary usage, to which I was accustomed in our own Conferences in America. I was more surprised to see the free use of wine by the ministers at the dinner table. On being invited on all such occasions to take a little for my stomach's sake I respectfully declined, and gave my reasons, in which I embodied a speech on total abstinence.

At that Conference I heard Mr. Punshon for the first time. I also heard Mr. Rattenbury preach in Gwennap Pit to a vast crowd filling the pit from bottom to top and all around the edges, just such a crowd as Mr. Wesley describes in the days when that was one of his regular preaching places. I was permitted to preach thrice in their chapels during Conference, also once in the street, and once a thousand feet down in Dalcoath Mine, then under the management of Captain Charles Thomas. His son, Captain Josiah Thomas, conducted me down the shafts to a depth of seventeen hundred feet. At the depth of one thousand feet I sang and collected a large number of miners, to whom I preached, and to which many responded in loud amens and hallelujahs. I was informed that there were fifty miles of cuttings in that famous tin mine. Coming up from that horrible pit, I was invited to dinner at the home of my friend Captain Thomas, and had occasion to deliver my temperance talk at the dinner table.

From the Conference I accompanied Rev. William Crook to Drogheda, Ireland. I preached a week in his church in that town, and a goodly number of his people entered into the liberty of the children of God. I conducted special services, usually for a week, but in some places for two or three weeks, in each church, in Dublin, Belfast, Portadown, Armagh, Enniskillen, Sligo, Bandon, Cork, and other places of less note, covering a period of about four months.

In Armagh, the ancient home of my Scotch-Irish ancestors, I found plenty of folks ready to claim kin with me, although more than one hundred years had passed since my ancestors emigrated to America, so that I found it impossible to trace reliable lines of relationship. But I loved the Irish, and highly appreciated their great kindness to me and my opportunity of ministering to them and of witnessing the salvation of many sinners in their churches.

Meantime I had to take part at their dinner-table discussions on the pros and cons of the civil war in America, then in progress. The rank and file of Great Britain stood naturally in sympathetic attitude toward the Federal nation, but the London *Times* espoused the cause of the Southern Confederacy, and created such a fog in that murky atmosphere that the common people could not see their way out.

In the beginning of 1863 I wrote and published in London a royal octavo pamphlet entitled " Cause and Probable Results of the Civil

War in America—Facts for the People of Great Britain." I wrote as I always do, over my own signature, and, being familiar with the leading facts of the case and the measure of them from Maine to California, I came to the stand as a witness. I felt that something had to be done quickly at that end of the line. One cruiser had already gone out from England; the *Alabama* and others were contracted for; so, to prevent the nation from being misled and the disturbance of friendly relations between Great Britain and the United States, I came to the front and said what I had to say as a witness. I did not stop to sell my pamphlet, but secured a long list of names of lords, ladies, ministers, and people of all classes, and sent out for free distribution eleven thousand copies.

I loved and pitied the Southern people, and always expressed kind words in praise of their good qualities, but deplored and abhorred their fierce attempts to rend in twain the North and South, whom God had joined together.

The English press noticed my pamphlet, but none of them attempted to challenge my facts. Some of the leading papers in the opposition raised the inquiry, "Who is this man Taylor? What business has he here?" Others said, "This man Taylor used to be a street preacher in California. We don't know what he is doing here."

My pamphlet was one of the text-books used by the Rev. Newman Hall, who delivered lectures in the principal centres of England in the interest of our Federal nation. Leading Quaker Friends in Manchester circulated them extensively among their people, and I had the happiness to know that some good resulted from my humble effort to render service to my country.

I heard President Hayes, years afterwards, express his belief that my pamphlet, circulated in England at that time, was worth more to our cause than a regiment of soldiers at the front. That pamphlet, which was then prophetic, would serve well as a history of the cause and results of the civil war in America.

I spent seven months in England and Ireland on this my first Australian trip as an evangelist. I was most kindly received by the people to whom I ministered, and whom I loved sincerely; but my call was to Australia, taking a look at Palestine on my way out. I never went abroad to see, but saw as I went.

While in London a young man who heard me deliver a lecture in St. James's Hall called to see me, and expressed a great desire to accompany me to Palestine. I respectfully declined to take charge of him, as he had never been away from home; but he was so anxious to go with me that he brought his mother to intercede for him. She was a widow, and this young man was her only son. He was called James, but I pleased him by calling him "Jimmy." She had given him a good education, and he was preparing to enter the ministry in the Baptist Church. He was a young man about six feet in height. He evidently had ability in him, but no facility to bring it out. His mother was a woman of means, and cheerfully furnished money for his expenses.

11

CHAPTER XVI

IN THE LORD'S LAND

EARLY in the spring of 1863 I and my young man took passage for
Paris, and spent a week in looking at the wonders of that wonderful
city and its environments; then went on to Marseilles and took
passage to Beyroot in Syria. We touched at Palermo, in Sicily.
We proceeded through the Grecian Isles in the Ægean Sea and
spent a few days in Smyrna. There I met a number of the missionaries of the American Board, and received from them a great
deal of very interesting and valuable information in regard to their
missions in Turkey, east and west. Leaving Smyrna, we touched
at Pompeiopolis, and explored its wonderful ruins, and went on to
Alexandretta, at the north-east angle of the Mediterranean Sea.
There we struck the old war-path of Alexander the Great and his
armies, and the old apostolic line of travel between Antioch and
Cilicia. We saw at Alexandretta a caravansary of great antiquity,
where Barnabas passed a night on his way to Tarsus to seek Saul.
From Alexandretta we proceeded down the coast of Syria, and
landed at Beyroot, where I made the acquaintance of Dr. Thomson,
the author of "The Land and the Book," that most interesting history
of Palestine. There I made arrangements for a tour of observation
through the Holy Land. Dr. Thomson kindly wrote out for me a
plan of travel, naming definitely every place that I wished to visit
and the length of time to be given to each. Of course I had to
employ a dragoman and enter into articles of agreement with him
and acknowledge them before the American consul, covering all
the arrangements for the journey.

On Monday morning early my dragoman came with the saddle
horses, one for himself and one for me and another for Jim; also
five donkeys to carry the tent, cooking utensils, and food for the
journey of a month. One of the horses was ordinary, and the
other was a poor one; so I gave Jim the choice, and he was sharp
enough to choose the better one. He had never mounted a horse
in his life, and had a great time in getting astride the animal.
Finally he succeeded, and put his feet as far through the stirrups
as he could, and without taking hold of the reins held on to the
mane with both hands.

We set out to go twenty miles south next day to Sidon, and passing out through the southern suburbs of Beyroot we came to the cross-roads, and Jim's horse, concluding to go to Damascus, set out on the Damascus road as hard as he could run, the dragoman in pursuit. So we had a horse race to start with. The dragoman ran him down and led the horse back, and we made another start. After we had gone a few miles Jim's horse would not leave the party, but whenever we came to a patch of grass he stopped and grazed until we were nearly out of sight; then he would come after us as hard as he could run. Once, when halfway up to us, Jim's hat was blown off, and on he came, his hair streaming in the wind like that of John Gilpin. When the horse overtook the company he slowed up, and Jim jumped off and ran back to get his hat. He was next seen pursuing his horse, trying to catch him. The horse seemed to enjoy the fun, and ran across the path zigzag; finally Jim seized him by the tail and held on and managed to get hold on the bridle, and after many unsuccessful attempts succeeded in mounting. This young man was just from the city, and never seemed to learn how to manage a horse, as similar ridiculous things were repeated nearly every day for a month.

After leaving Sidon the dragoman showed us where Jonah landed from his whaling voyage, and also showed us where he was buried. The cenotaph had been recently covered with new red velvet, and conveyed the idea that Jonah had been dead but a few days. So I turned my face to the inner walls of Jonah's mausoleum and laughed until I cried at the ridiculous nonsense of such traditions, and made up my mind that I would not listen to such again, but give my attention to well-attested geographical and historical facts, which were quite sufficient to occupy all the time I had at command.

We spent a night at Sidon, which is thought to be the oldest city in the world, bearing the name of Sidon, the great-grandson of Noah. It is a walled city with narrow streets. I spent a pleasant evening in visiting missionaries of the American Board stationed there, but slept in my tent outside the walls. Next day we took our lunch near the ruins of the old city Sarepta, and proceeded on our way to Tyre. We spent some time exploring that region, and proceeded to Acre and ascended Mount Carmel, and thence to Nazareth, and spent the Sabbath and a few days ensuing traversing the paths pressed by the feet of the dear child Jesus, and witnessed the Easter celebration of the Greek Church.

Our tent was pitched in an olive grove near to the fountain, the only water supply of the town, where Mary used to come with a pitcher on her head to draw water. The Easter celebration and festivities drew together in the olive orchard where we were tented a vast crowd of men, women, and children, dressed in their Oriental costume, the women especially displaying a vast amount of jewellery —rings on their fingers and pendants in their ears and noses.

The little girls spent the day mainly in swinging and singing. Nearly every olive tree had one or two swings attached to its limbs, and the whole orchard was vocal with the songs of the little girls from morning until night. The little boys dressed, put on airs of great dignity, would not sing, and would not even assist in swinging the girls.

From Nazareth we went to the top of Mount Tabor, a conical truncated mountain of nearly a thousand feet elevation, covered with shrubbery. From Mount Tabor we passed on to what is believed to be Cana of Galilee, and on to Tiberias, on the west coast of the Sea of Galilee. When we arrived the surface of the sea was as smooth as a sea of glass, but about nine o'clock at night we had a tornado which carried the spray over the walls of Tiberias and to a considerable distance into the town. The sea is five hundred feet below the level of the Mediterranean, surrounded by hills and mountains. The rarefaction of the atmosphere creates a vast vacuum, which draws from the higher strata of the snow-capped region of Mount Hermon a cyclone of cold air to fill the vacuum, the same phenomenon arising from the same cause as in the days of old.

At Tiberias we met a party of Englishmen and Americans, among whom was a minister of the Gospel from Boston. The minister said that he had made an arrangement for an excursion on the lake the next day, which was the Sabbath, and invited me to stop and go with them. I informed him that in all my journeyings I rested on the Sabbath day and preached when I had an opportunity, the same in Palestine as in America, feeling it my duty and privilege to remember the Sabbath day, to keep it holy. He replied, "That is the right thing to do; but I am travelling with a company made up largely of English gentlemen, and they have the management of affairs, and I have to go with the crowd." I informed him that I was master of my own expedition, as usual.

We went swimming in the Sea of Galilee and visited the Hot Springs a little south of Tiberias, and returned and spent the Sabbath in Nazareth; thence we proceeded by the usual path to Nain and to Dothan, and then on to the great mound-shaped hill on which the city of Samaria stood, and thence on to Shechem. We ascended Mount Gerizim, explored the ruins of the old city of the Samaritans, and their temple walls, covering over two hundred feet square, and their ruins, of from five to ten feet high, remaining.

I asked a Samaritan, "What is the name of this ancient town?" and he said, "Sychar." I asked an Arab, separately, what that town was called, and he said, "Sychar." I counted as many as eight cisterns which had once been used for collecting water from the clouds. When they ran short the nearest permanent supply of water was Jacob's Well, at the south-east base of the mountain, about one thousand five hundred feet down from the summit. So we descended from the mount to the well of Jacob. At the mouth of the well was an excavation six feet deep and eight feet wide, walled up to afford a shade and a resting-place for travellers. The well was covered with a large flat stone, with a hole in the centre in which a large stone key was inserted. We were wearied in our journey and thirsty, and had nothing to draw with and the well was deep. So we called an Arab labourer, who was at work a little distance from us, to come with his pitcher and well-rope and draw for us. He removed the key and opened the well and let down his rope, but it was too short. It would not reach the water, so we got two or three silk sashes from the Arabs and tied them to the rope and drew a pitcher of water, beautifully transparent and deliciously sweet, from Jacob's Well.

The distance from the surface to the water was about eighty feet. The water was probably ten or fifteen feet deep in the well. I subsequently read the adventures of a traveller through that region who stated emphatically that he visited the spot and there was no well there. It had possibly been closed up, and he did not find it. It was there nevertheless.

On our way thence to Jerusalem we camped and slept, as nearly as can be ascertained, on the spot where Jacob slept and dreamed and saw a ladder extending from earth to heaven, the angels of God ascending and descending upon it.

We proceeded thence to the Holy City, and pitched our tent outside the walls a little north of the city. Next morning, the day after our arrival, we went to the American consulate. The consul was absent, but the vice-consul, who was a native of Jerusalem, received us courteously. Jim took occasion to go at once to the bank on which he had a letter of credit, and drew his money. Not wishing to carry money, I had a letter of credit on Beyroot which was sufficient to pay my part of the expenses through to Alexandria, and was depending on Jim's draft on Jerusalem to pay his half through. The consul arranged to spend the day with us, so we walked about Jerusalem and "marked well her bulwarks."

The city is surrounded by a wall from twenty to eighty feet high, about ten feet thick. The extent of the wall, inclosing the city in rhomboid shape, is two and one-eighth miles, built by Sultan Solyman in A.D. 1542. We visited all the points of special interest, including the sepulchre of the kings and the great quarry of Mount Moriah, whence it is supposed a large part of the building stone of the ancient temple of Solomon had been quarried and elevated through a huge shaft up to the spot now covered by the Temple El Aksa. The solid rock of the quarry is soft yellow limestone, which hardens and whitens by exposure. We discovered why there was no sound of hammer in laying the stone. We saw great blocks of stone quarried and left standing, from which we could clearly see how it was done. Blocks were still attached to the original solid mountain of rock. The blocks were about eight feet by two by two in dimensions, standing in perpendicular position. The two outer or exposed surfaces of each block had been quarried and dressed with an iron-handled chisel.

We visited the Mosque of Omar in Jerusalem. It is an octagonal structure; each angle is sixty-seven feet. The diameter of the interior is one hundred and forty-eight feet. It would require a volume to describe all the wonderful scenes and associations there brought to view. Many books have been written on the subject, and I shall not attempt it. We also ascended the Mount of Olives and saw the Garden of Gethsemane, and there, seated under an ancient olive tree, Jim and I read the entire gospel by Mark, and called to mind the places we had seen where most of the scenes described had occurred, many having transpired in sight of the spot we then occupied.

We kneeled under the ancient olive and prayed, and the very same Jesus of whom we read manifested Himself to us in the blessed realisation of His saving power.

We spent several days on that first visit to Jerusalem, seeing all the sights of particular interest. On the evening of the first day, when we returned to our tent, I saw my travelling companion fumbling through his pockets as though he had lost something. I said, " Jim, what is the matter ?　Have you lost anything ? "

" Yes," said he.　" My pocket-book is gone."

" All your money in it ? "

" Yes ; I drew it all from the bank this morning and put it into my pocket-book, and I don't know what has become of it. I cannot find it."

I had paid out all my money for my half of the expenses through, and was depending on the half that Jim was to furnish for the final settlement with our dragoman. So I found myself in straitened circumstances. The next morning after breakfast we went to the office of the American consul. We could hardly hope to get track of the money, but soon after we entered the consulate the consul inquired if either of us had lost a pocket-book. I said, " Yes ; my friend Jim here has lost his."

" Well," said he, " my janitor, who is a Mohammedan, found a pocket-book lying open on the settee there. He swore by Mohammed that he had not taken any of the money out, but passed it to me open as he found it."

I told Jim to count his money and see if it was all there. He carefully counted it and stuffed it into his pocket without saying a word. I said to him, " Is your money all there ? "

" Yas."

I made him haul it out and give the Mohammedan a dollar. Then I said to him, " I will borrow your money and settle with you before we separate, at the Pyramids of Egypt." So I took charge of his money.

From Jerusalem we made the usual trip to Jericho, the Jordan, and the Dead Sea. We learned that a short time before a British lord, and five noblemen with him, went down from Jerusalem to Jericho and fell among thieves. They were not left by the roadside half dead, like the poor fellow we read about, but they were stripped of all their belongings except the clothes they had on their backs,

We met a number of exploring parties in different parts of Palestine, and they were all armed, and had an escort of soldiers to protect them against the Bedouin Arabs. My policy was to take nothing with me worth stealing, move along quietly, and attend to my own business, treat men and dogs with common civility, and sleep in an open tent with no guards except the guardian angels whom God sends to look after those who trust in Him. I was sorry when my camp was contiguous to that of those protected parties with sentinels keeping watch through the night, for they kept up a shouting one to another and disturbed my rest. So I always preferred to camp in some quiet spot where no travellers were within half a mile of my tent.

But on our trip from Jerusalem to Jericho we fell in with a party of English and Americans with their mounted native guards on Arab steeds. Coming to an open field, the Arab horsemen engaged in horse racing and sword exercise, performing some wonderful feats of agility, and Jim's horse caught the spirit of the race, and with no restraining hand upon him he dashed into the crowd of racing horses and went back and forth. Jim's hat was blown off, and his long hair was streaming in the wind, which made him the most laughable sight to be seen on the journey. He managed by hanging on to the mane of his horse with both hands to retain his place and came out all right. He was a very remarkable young man!

We always had our prayers and regular Scripture reading aboard the ships in which we travelled, in the hotels where we stopped, and in our tent every night and morning. I found him to be a very pious young man, a beautiful reader, and he prayed in charming simplicity. He was a teetotaler, and in all respects conducted himself with great propriety. But if he ever had any emotion in his soul he succeeded most thoroughly in concealing it. He never betrayed in the whole journey, mixing up often with troops of Bedouin, the slightest emotion of fear or pleasure or surprise. He never expressed admiration or wonder at anything he saw. One day a flock of gazelles swept across the plain in full view, and I shouted, "Look, Jim! look, look!" I saw his head turn slowly on its axis, but his countenance never changed. I said, "Did you see the gazelles?"

"Yas."

Passing through the mountains on the way from Jerusalem to Jericho we visited, at the base of the mountain, on the edge of the Jericho plains, a large flowing spring supposed to be the same whose waters were healed by the prophet Elisha, and which still sends forth its healing streams through the plain. Naught remains of the once famous city of Jericho except a few native huts.

We passed on to Jordan and bathed in its waters. I struck out into the current, which excited the alarm of an Arab, and he pursued me, saying, "A man was drowned there but a few weeks ago, and it was very perilous to go into the swift current." I told him not to distress himself. I understood the situation perfectly and did not need any help. It is a very crooked and rapid stream. Its fall in sixty-six miles from the Sea of Tiberias to the Dead Sea is one thousand feet. The stream circles around a distance of nearly two hundred miles to make a straight line of sixty-six miles. At its Dead

Sea mouth it is one hundred and eighty yards wide. At the place of the crossing and baptism of Jesus it is about one hundred feet wide and twelve feet deep.

The Dead Sea was also visited, and some of our party bathed in it. I found that its waters, though transparent, were unpleasantly sticky; so I preferred not to go into it. I accidentally got a pair of kid gloves saturated with it, and when they were dry they broke to pieces as though they had been boiled.

From the Dead Sea we went to Masada, an impregnable Greek fortress in the mountains. We went thence to Bethlehem, and saw on adjacent hills the shepherds keeping watch over their flocks, and saw the sights in that ancient town representing historic memories most sacred.

We also visited Hebron and the burying place of Abraham, Isaac, and Jacob. From Hebron we returned to Jerusalem, visiting the pools of Solomon by the way, and had an additional exploration of the Holy City. I took occasion to call on Bishop Gobat, who had charge of an Episcopal mission which was under the joint jurisdiction of England and Prussia. The Bishop received me very cordially and gave me an account of the labours of my old California friend, Alfred Roberts, who died in peace and was buried on Mount Zion, but a few rods distant from the tomb of King David.

I visited his grave close to that of the singer of Israel. I had been warned by the consul, also by Dr. Thomson, not to attempt to enter the mausoleum of King David, as it was constantly guarded by most fanatical Mohammedans, and no tourist's life was safe inside its walls. But after we had seen everything else of special interest in the city I said to Jim, "Let us go to the tomb of David at a venture." So we walked straight up to the entrance, and several of the fanatical guards rushed out to meet us. I gave them the salutation common in that country, and approached them and shook hands and smiled. They gathered around me and stroked my beard. I could not speak their language, but I smiled on them again and made inquiry by signs what I should pay to go through the mausoleum and see the tomb of David. They stated the price, which was not large. I paid the money and they conducted us through. I don't know on what ground they excused themselves for so doing, but, from the length of my beard and the influence of my presence upon them, I concluded, upon reflection, that they probably thought that I was a Mohammedan sheik, and the beardless youth my son, from some remote province, and they treated us accordingly.

While at Jerusalem my dragoman said, "I am afraid the government will seize my animals under the impressment law," and wanted me, if possible, to secure protection for his animals. I took him to the American consul, who heard his cause and replied that while he and his animals were in my employ he, as consul, could, under my rights as an American citizen, protect his property, but when discharged from my service he could not protect him against the claims of his own government. He was not disturbed in Jerusalem, but when we reached Joppa and I discharged him from service, the poor fellow came to me with a very sorrowful expression on his countenance, and said that the government had seized his three horses and five donkeys and driven them off to the government stables.

In Joppa we engaged passage, by a French steamer, for Alexandria, in Egypt. The ship lay out more than a mile in the offing, and three hours before the time for sailing Jim and I hired a boat to take us to the steamer; but before we had made half the distance we were struck suddenly by a tornado, kindred to the one that struck poor Jonah's ship in the olden time. We had to "about ship" and pull for the shore, and came very near being swamped and swallowed up. I was vividly reminded of the sad experience of Jonah, but was comforted by the assurance that I had never taken a ticket for Tarshish nor disobeyed my heavenly calling. By the extraordinary pulling of our men and the good providence of God we safely reached the land.

The steamer, under the pressure of the gale, weighed anchor and put out to sea two hours before her time for sailing, and we had to remain at Joppa for a week longer. We visited the "house of Simon the tanner," and saw a tanyard hard by the sea, suggestive, at least, of the sights and scenes of the olden times there.

We got a refund of our passage money, and bought tickets by a Russian steamer and proceeded on our way to Alexandria, where we spent some days examining the wonders of that wonderful city. Thence we took our way to Cairo, one hundred and ninety miles, and interested ourselves with the strange sights and scenes of that old city. Planning to visit the Pyramids, it was desirable to cross the Nile and get out to them before sunrise.

So we made an agreement with the donkey boys to bring us two donkeys and call us by four o'clock in the morning. We were waked up in due time, and I was up and washed and dressed and down from the third story of the hotel in less than ten minutes, and found the donkeys, with their drivers, ready to start. I waited for Jim, waited and waited, until the dawn of the morning. Then I ran upstairs to see what ailed him, and found him undressed bending over the washbowl scrubbing his neck and ears with a soapy woollen cloth, making preparation to climb the Pyramids. I urged him to hurry up and not to waste our valuable time. He took no offence at my plain talk, but I could not perceive the slightest quickening of his movements. The result was that the sun was about an hour high before we reached the Pyramids. We climbed the Great Pyramid, explored its great interior chamber, examined the Sphinx, and returned to Cairo in the evening of the same day.

The next morning Jim bought a third-class ticket back to Alexandria, *en route* to the home of his mother in London. He travelled out with me as a first-class passenger, but said that he would economise on his return trip; hence bought a third-class railway ticket and climbed into a car surrounded by a kind of fence without doors, and, there being no seats of any sort, the passengers were crowded in with Mohammedans all squatted on the floor, and Jim, seeing no space on the floor, sat down on the shoulder of a Mohammedan.

The poor fellow squirmed and complained, but Jim was unmoved. Soon after the car whistled and rolled off, and that was the last I saw of my friend. I had taken care of him as I would of a child, and now I had to leave him to his own resources. He wrote me afterwards that he got home safely, but lost everything he had except the clothes he had on. He said, "I gave my things to a man to carry, and he carried them, and I have never seen them since."

I embarked in the early spring of 1863 at Suez on the steamer *Mooltan*, of the Peninsula and Oriental line of steamers. My ticket from Suez to Melbourne, Australia, cost me one hundred and twenty pounds, including a liberal supply of wine and whisky. I said to the ticket agent in London, "You charge me on my ticket to Australia twenty pounds for drinks. I am a total abstainer, and protest against paying such a sum for no value received."

"We have our rates, and I am not at liberty to change them. You are at liberty to drink or not, as you like."

A few years later the company sold the tickets at reduced rates, and sold the drinks to such as wished to spend their money in that way.

The *Mooltan* was a ship of about four thousand tons, with good accommodation, though crowded with passengers, most of whom were bound for India. At Point de Galle, Ceylon, the passengers for Australia were transferred to a smaller steamer, the *Mooltan* being bound for Calcutta. I had no opportunity of preaching on the *Mooltan*, but joined in the Church of England service on each Sabbath morning. On our Australian steamer we had a British nobleman and some officers of the army, who expressed a wish to hear me preach the Gospel. They had consultation among themselves and deputed one of their number to confer with me and get permission from the master of the ship. I, of course, gave cheerful consent, but the captain positively refused to allow it on his ship. Then followed an altercation between the committee and the captain that rose to such a height that the captain kept to the bridge and his room, and to the end of the voyage was not seen to walk the deck or sit at the table for his meals. I had nothing to do with it, and was very sorry to be even the innocent occasion of the trouble.

My first peep at Australia was at Albany, at the south-western extremity of the continent, where our ship anchored for eight or ten hours. Captain A——, a genial fellow-passenger, and I spent most of the day in the bush of scrub timber, and among the wild flowers of every colour and tint, and birds in great variety, such as we had never seen before. I drew many of the feathery tribe into the trees near to us by whistling notes new and attractive to them.

On inquiry we learned that there was a small chapel in the town and a minister of the Church of England. We also found a man and his wife who were Wesleyans. They had no minister, but were building a Wesleyan chapel with the hope of getting a minister sent to them. It was a frame building about 24 × 34 feet, inclosed and under roof. Captain A—— gave one pound. I had paid out so much *backsheesh* in Palestine that I had but two dollars and fifty cents left; but I borrowed five dollars from Captain A—— and gave it to the new chapel fund.

Our next port was Melbourne. Amid the crowd passing from our ship to the shore I lost sight of Captain A——. There I was, a stranger in a strange land, with two dollars and fifty cents in my pocket and no letter of credit on anybody. On inquiry I was told Scott's Hotel was the best in the city, so I selected a room in Scott's Hotel in which I put my trunk.

I had a letter of introduction from my friend, Mr. McArthur, of London, to his house of commercial business in Melbourne; so I proceeded at once to the house of McArthur & Co. Mr. Finlay, head man of the premises, a most genial brother, received me most cordially. I drew another letter of introduction out of my pocket from Rev. T. N. Hull of the Irish Conference, for whom I preached a week in Belfast, to his brother-in-law, James Copeland. So I said to Brother Finlay, "Are you acquainted with Mr. James Copeland?"

"Oh, yes; he is connected with our firm, and is at his desk in the next office."

So I entered his office and presented myself and my letter. He did not stop to read it, but seized me with both hands, saying, "We have received several letters from Mr. Hull in regard to your coming, and have been on the look-out for you for several months. We give you an Irish *Caed mile faltha* (a hundred thousand welcomes). Come with me; I want to introduce you to the Chairman of Melbourne District and Superintendent of Melbourne First Circuit, Rev. Daniel J. Draper."

So we went, and I was introduced to Rev. Mr. and Mrs. Draper, who gave me a cordial welcome to their home and to the colony, saying, "We have read and re-read of your California experiences as recorded in your California books." Mr. Draper proceeded to say, "I want to engage you at once to preach for us in Wesley Church, next Sabbath, morning and evening,"—an edifice that cost two hundred thousand dollars, with sittings for over two thousand persons.

I replied, "The habit of my life as an evangelist is to preach in the same pulpit Sabbath morning to the church members, at 3 p.m. to the children, and in the evening to the masses of unconverted sinners, and continue nightly up to Friday night."

"That is a good programme, but you are just off a long voyage and need rest. Preach for me next Sabbath and take next week for rest, and commence your week of special services on the following Sabbath. I am now in the midst of my quarterly visitation of the classes. Next week I can finish that work and duly advertise your coming services."

"This being Thursday, I will have a good rest before Sabbath, and my time is so precious, so far from wife and children, and so much work before me, that I cannot on any account consent to lose a week; but, to avoid any disturbance of your plan of pastoral work,

I can arrange to give next week to Melbourne Second Circuit, and give you the week following."

"Oh, no; I must have you for all the services of Wesley Church next Sabbath."

"Very well, I will give you all of next Sabbath, and if the Lord does not give us a clear intimation that we should proceed at once according to my proposal, I will accept yours." We then kneeled down and submitted the case to God.

Just then Rev. J. Waugh, the Chairman of the Ballarat District, came in and gave me an Irish welcome and a pressing invitation to labour in his circuit and all the circuits of his district. I was a few minutes later introduced to Rev. Brother Simmons, Editor of *The Wesleyan Chronicle*, the Methodist weekly paper of the colony of Victoria. So within an hour the main body of the Australian continent was opened for my work. I had accepted Brother Copeland's invitation to put up with him. His home was in a suburban village named Hawthorn, five miles out, but with his good horse and carriage it was but a pleasure trip. So my host ordered my trunk from Scott's Hotel to his Hawthorn home, and I had my two and a half dollars in my pocket. The Copeland family consisted of James and Hugh, bachelors, and their maiden sister, Eliza, and Brother Finlay and wife lived next door; so that my home and its belongings were all that I could desire.

As we drove out to Hawthorn, Brother Copeland said, "I am very sorry that you have arranged to commence your great work at Lonsdale Street Church. It is the high place of Methodist pride and formalism. The Church of England service is read and chanted every Sunday afternoon, and while they have many earnest, humble Christians, the obstructions are so formidable that you can't make the success that would establish a commanding precedent which would give you the flood tide that you will need in your tour of the colonies. Brunswick Street Church is large and commodious, and is crowded with the common people who will hear you gladly, and you could be sure of a grand success there which would arouse the city, and then you would be able to succeed among the aristocrats of Lonsdale Street."

I replied, "You know, dear brother, that I am not the author of the present arrangement, but it is exactly according to my mind. By the power of God we will storm Sebastopol, and then the smaller forts will run up the white flag."

We had most cheering Christian fellowship at Hawthorn. On Saturday we drove into the city to note the progress of advertisement and preparation for a week of special services at Wesley Church. We found Brother and Sister Draper on the wing of preparation for the coming campaign of next week in their church, and they pressed me kindly to make their house my home while at work for them. This was early in the month of May, 1863. At 10.30 a.m. of a lovely Sabbath day of that charming climate the main body and galleries of Wesley Church were packed with expectant hearers.

CHAPTER XVII

MELBOURNE EVANGELISATION

In a short time the tide of salvation was at the flood and soon extended to St. Kilda and all the other Melbourne circuits.

The government made liberal offers of building sites for houses of worship to all denominations of Christians who would erect a chapel on each lot selected within a given period of time ; also for educational purposes. Those Wesleyan pioneers selected about a dozen sites, and erected a chapel on each one within the time specified. They came very near losing the last one, and were finally notified that if the chapel was not built upon it within ten days it would revert to the government.

It was thought to be impossible for them to come to time on it, but it was a valuable site in a suitable centre, and they could not afford to lose it. So, on the last day of grace, I dedicated their new chapel, a plain but commodious, comfortable house of worship, all seated, ready to accommodate about five hundred persons. They also secured, under the same liberal offer of the government, ten acres of land within the city limits for a Wesleyan college. Walter Powell offered ten thousand pounds if the colony of Victoria would raise ten thousand pounds for the erection of buildings, as an outfit and partial endowment for the college. During my stay in that colony a great convention of the friends of education was called, and I had the honour of staking Walter Powell's ten thousand pounds against the liberality of all the Wesleyans and their friends of Victoria for the establishment of Wesley College. They accepted the challenge and paid down the cash, and the college was built and named.

Next to my ambassadorship in soul saving in Australia the raising of money to pay for their newly-built churches was a speciality in which the Lord gave great success. I refused throughout the whole campaign to receive gifts of money for my own cause, and was, therefore, the more welcome in every field in which I laboured. The people themselves were so appreciative and so anxious to reciprocate that before I had spent a week in any new field it came to my knowledge that the people were contriving to make up a purse to give me, often arranging for a great "tea meeting" for collecting

a large fund to present to me. But I invariably got the superintendent of the circuit to announce to the people that California Taylor
refuses to receive any money in the form of a gift, but he will tell
them before he leaves what they can do for him. So the meeting
in each place would progress without any side issue of any sort till
the last day of my service. Then I explained to them the facts in
regard to my Seamen's Bethel embarrassment and my method of
relieving it, and that my business was, with the co-operation of
ministers and their working forces, to extend the kingdom of Christ
far and wide through the medium of the pulpit and the press; that
all my evangelistic labours were given gratuitously, and that by
means of the press I paid my own travelling expenses and supported
my family, and turned over the surplus profit to liquidate the debts
involved by fire and flood in California ; and announced that all who
wished to lend a hand could find my books at the store of some
merchant whom I named in each case. So that in that line they
patronised me liberally.

Next to my preaching, the Lord used the books in rendering the
work continuous, permanent, and fruitful.

My mission to Australia was in fulfilment of an unmistakable providential programme and the accomplishment of a great providential
purpose. All Christian Churches, Roman Catholic and Protestant,
had been early planted and were taking root in the virgin soil in
those vast colonial countries already known as the Southern World.

Besides the South Sea Islands, New Zealand, and Tasmania,
Australia is a continent about two thousand miles in extent, both
north and south, east and west. My work extended through all the
inhabited portions of these vast regions, countries that Mr. Wesley
had never dreamed of when he said, "The world is my parish."
Wesley personally compassed but a very small portion of what he
claimed as his parish, but Wesleyan Methodism is extending to
its utmost limits.

The Wesleyan ministers in the United Kingdom of Great Britain
and her colonies are noted for their plain preaching of the Gospel
according to the standards indicated by Wesley, Fletcher, Watson,
and others, and their faithful adherence to their rules in carrying out
all the details of early Methodist pastoral work. So the pioneer
Methodist ministers of Australia had laid a broad and solid foundation,
and had strong and growing Church organisations in all the important
centres of this great field. They had levelled down mountains and
hills and filled up the valleys, made crooked places straight and rough
places plain, and had prepared the way of the Lord on a broad scale,
and the time had come for the glory of the Lord to be revealed, so
that all the people of those vast colonies could see it. America is
in debt, to an incalculable extent, to English Methodism.

Under a great compensative law of providence I was sent across
the waters under a divine commission as a Gospel engineer to help
those faithful track layers to get their engines and trains on the
track, and to get the steam applied so as to secure the purpose for

which all this heavy outlay of time, toil, and talent had been expended, and thus pay an instalment on our indebtedness to British Methodism.

During my labours in those colonies, covering a period of nearly three years, on my first tour they reported a net increase in the Church membership to the Australasian Conference of over eleven thousand members. Then, by a steady growth through a period of three years in my absence, to which I added another evangelising trip through those colonies of fourteen months, ten thousand more were added. So that during those six or seven years the official Minutes of the Conference reported a net increase of twenty-one thousand members, many of whom became ministers. So that the work was manifestly of God, and hence permanent and progressive to this day. My quotation of aggregate results was taken from the official reports of ministers and their Conference Minutes. I kept no records of names or the numbers of the thousands of persons, old and young, who received Christ and salvation at the meetings I conducted.

My method of work in every place was to preach the Gospel, and at the close of every sermon to invite all unsaved people who were convinced of the truth of God as proclaimed, and convicted of sin, and desired to be reconciled to God, to come forward and kneel at the communion rail and other convenient places, so that I might personally grapple with their difficulties and show them the way into the kingdom of God. We did not make their coming forward an essential condition of salvation. We urged them to surrender to God in their pews, or by the wayside, or at their own homes, and if they had not succeeded in finding salvation in secret places, or in a way unobserved by others, we advised them, as they had been public rebels against God, it was but fair to Him and His cause, like Zaccheus and another publican we read about, that they should make an open confession and a public renunciation of their evil deeds. "He that covereth his sins shall not prosper, but whoso confesseth and forsaketh his sins shall find mercy."

Our altars were usually crowded on every occasion with awakened sinners; and as fast as they surrendered and accepted Christ, and obtained the witness and experienced the regenerating work of the Holy Spirit, all who were so prompted arose and testified to the facts in their case. "With the heart man believeth unto righteousness; and with the mouth confession is made unto salvation." Then they were conducted by class leaders and introduced to the superintendent of the circuit in the vestry adjoining the church in the rear. It was his business, according to our instructions, kindly but thoroughly to investigate each case and satisfy himself as to the genuineness of the work in each heart; and that every one who could not give a satisfactory testimony from a conscious experience of pardon and peace with God should be kindly advised to return and continue as a seeker until he should obtain a clear experience of salvation.

Of each one whose testimony was clear and satisfactory we took the name and the address and made inquiry of the Church relationship or preference of each one. If they were already members of any other Church, or preferred to become members of any other than the Wesleyan Church, they were so entered on the book of records, and advised to go and report as quickly as convenient to their own ministers. All who expressed a wish to connect themselves with the Wesleyan Methodist Church gave their names at once, and were assigned to a class that night. A list of their names was passed to their respective leaders before they left the place of worship, with instructions that the leader should visit them in their homes and get them to class meeting without delay. In order to train all such in the way they should go from the start, I announced publicly that no class meeting should be suspended during any week of the special services, but should meet half an hour earlier than usual, and get into church by the close of the preliminary service in time to hear the text and get the benefit of the preaching.

Thus the revival tide did not cut its way through all the embankments, submerging all the different branches of ordinary Church work, but flowed out through all the dykes and refreshed all the gardens, to give new vitality and growth to all the trees growing by the rivers of water, that their leaves should not wither, and that they should bring forth their fruit in their season.

We usually spent one week in a church, but two or three weeks in a few large centres, and only a day or two in many of the smaller ones. Our regular order of service was to preach on Sabbath morning to the church, the body of believers; in the afternoon to children, and at night aimed directly at the awakening and salvation of sinners. With those preliminaries we counted on a crowded altar of seekers and the salvation of a good portion of them on the first night, and worked specially on that line till Tuesday or Wednesday night. On Thursday night I preached to the Church specially on the doctrine and experience of entire sanctification to God, and invited all believers present who were not living in that experience to come to the altar, where they were in the habit of renewing their oaths of allegiance to God, and under the clear light then shining upon them to make their consecration complete, and receive and trust the Lord Jesus for full salvation. Many thus had their loyalty, faith, and love perfected.

In addition to the believers who were sanctified wholly, we usually had also on the same night a number of sinners saved. On Friday night we had a grand rally along the line to complete the harvest for the week. Saturday was a day for rest and for travelling to another field of service. It was quite common to take up one day in the week for our tea meeeting and a special effort to raise funds to pay off their church debts. I took opportunity on all such occasions to speak concerning God's law of the tithe. Having established human rights to time, he set apart six days in which his human subjects were commanded to do all their work, and reserved the seventh of time for the purpose of rest for mankind and all beasts of burden, and a day for special religious meditation and the collective worship of God. He enforced the order by the precedent of His own use of time as an object lesson and an example for them to follow; for in six days the Lord made the heavens and the earth and all things therein, and rested the seventh day and hallowed it. It is a matter of no moment whether there were cycles of time called days, represented by days of twenty-four hours each, suited to man on earth, or twenty-four millions of years, each reckoned in the eternity of God. The proportion in either case is the same—six days for labour, one day for rest.

So when God established human rights to property He reserved the tenth of all our net profits or earnings. "All the tithe of the land, whether of the seed of the land, or of the fruit of the tree, is the Lord's: it is holy unto the Lord." "And concerning the tithe of the herd, or of the flock, even of whatsoever passeth under the rod, the tenth shall be holy unto the Lord." It may be said that our person and property and everything we have belong to the Lord. In the broad sense, as subjects of His government and children of His household, that is true. But God has been pleased to enter into a business co-partnership with His subjects and His children, unto whom He is kind and liberal, allowing us to have and to hold in our own right nine-tenths of all that we make, and reserving as His share of the business one-tenth, and that is to be distributed to His poor subjects who cannot make anything. So, if we want to have God's blessing on the fruit of our hands, we must deal honestly and fairly with Him. God makes complaint of many, saying, "Ye have robbed Me," and they reply, "Wherein have we robbed Thee?" And He answers, "In tithes and offerings."

What is the result? "Ye are cursed with a curse." It doesn't pay to rob God. What is His order? "Bring ye all the tithes into the storehouse, . . . and prove Me now herewith, saith the Lord of hosts, if I will not open you the windows of heaven, and pour you out a blessing, that there shall not be room enough to receive it." He does not command you to bring the free-will offering; He will honour and reward all who do so, but the free-will offering must be entirely voluntary; while to pay the tithe is a legal obligation, and to withhold the tithe is to rob God. To encourage us to obedience He adds, "I will rebuke the devourer for your sakes, and he shall not destroy the fruits of your ground; neither shall your vine cast her fruit before the time in the field, saith the Lord of hosts. And all the nations shall call you blessed: for ye shall be a delightsome land, saith the Lord of hosts." The term "devourer" is a generic term representing all the destructive things, as the locust, caterpillar, grasshopper, chintz bug, the army worm, the potato bug, cyclones, and untimely frost, and all other pestilential things that destroy the fruits of the ground and constitute the curse entailed by robbing God. Such teaching should not be left to the meetings for raising money, but should have its place in the education and will of our people, especially our young converts in God's financial economy.

Daniel J. Draper was a broad, thickset, rotund man; a good preacher, an able administrator, a social, kind-hearted gentleman, with a keen sense of the ludicrous, and always enjoyed a good laugh on suitable occasions. The dear man and his good wife some years after my acquaintance with them spent some time in England on a visit, and on their return passage for Australia, aboard the steamship *London*, which was swamped in the Bay of Biscay under the pressure of a furious gale, they, with more than one hundred others, were drowned. Out of the whole ship's company only twenty-one escaped. The twenty-second, who had a chance, was a young lady. She got position for a leap into the lifeboat on the crest of the last wave of hope, but through fear she failed to jump and perished. The report of the survivors was that most of the ship's company, seeing no hope of escape, fell on their knees in prayer, and Rev. Mr. Draper and his wife were labouring among them the same as at the penitent altar, talking to them and praying for them and urging them to receive Jesus, till preacher and people went down into the depths of the Atlantic together.

James Bickford was also a good preacher, and a very wise counsellor in anything pertaining to important business. He got his early training as a missionary in the West Indies. At one time while there he got out of patience with his people on account of their many wants and complaints, and said to a crowd of them one day, "I can't stand this any longer; I shall have to put on my hat and leave you."

An old coloured sister responded, "Massa Bickford, don't go yet; one ounce of sugar will ketch more flies than a gallon of vinegar." So he hung up his hat and stayed and learned wisdom of the coloured people.

On a certain occasion he took passage in a small schooner bound from Georgetown, Demerara, to Essequibo. In weighing anchor and getting out into the stream it collided with another schooner and tore away its bowsprit, but went on its way without stopping to apologise for the damage that had been done. After they had gone six or eight miles they saw a boat with six powerful oarsmen in hot pursuit and shouting to Bickford's captain, "Heave to!"

The captain of the vessel they had injured was in hot pursuit. The captain of the retreating vessel said to a boy, "Go below and load full pipes, and bring them here to me."

The boy ran and brought the pipes. By that time the other boat came sweeping alongside, her captain shouting, "Heave a line!"

The rope was cast and tied to the boat of the injured vessel, and the captain climbed up the side of Bickford's schooner in a dreadful rage, swearing at an awful rate and threatening vengeance. "You tore out the bowsprit of my vessel, and I will have you arrested and brought before the magistrate. I will make you pay dearly for such carelessness."

The other captain sat quietly and listened till he got through; then he said, "Captain, I am very sorry we injured your vessel, but we had scarcely sufficient room for getting out from our moorings, and the wind caught our sails suddenly and we were borne down upon the prow of your vessel and couldn't help ourselves. I knew you to be a gentleman, and deferred explanation till I could see you on our return trip. Such men as we are have no business before a petty magistrate; we can settle our own affairs. If you can wait until I get back I shall be glad to put a new bowsprit into your vessel and charge you nothing; but if I can find a suitable stick of timber aboard you can put it in yourself and I will do as much for you the first chance I get."

With that he shouted, "Boy, go down into the hold and see if you can find a good piece of timber for the captain."

"Aye, aye, sir;" and away ran the boy to get the timber.

He said to another boy, "Bring a couple of pipes and a match;" and in a few moments the two captains were seen seated side by side enjoying a friendly smoke. Meantime the boy below was fumbling around in search for a piece of timber suitable for a bowsprit, when in fact there wasn't a stick of timber there. So he came back and reported that he couldn't find any timber suitable.

The captain said to his friend, "Well, captain, you can get a stick on your return, and repair your vessel and charge it to my account."

He replied, "All right, captain; good-day, good-day."

The young minister was listening and learning how to deal with men, leaving out the falsehood of the captain's successful scheme.

I have it to say that I highly appreciated and dearly loved and honoured all the preachers and their wives among whom I laboured through the years that I spent in Australia, New Zealand, and Tasmania, but my time and space will only allow a brief illustrative reference to a few of them.

After my campaign in the circuits of Melbourne I went to Geelong, forty-eight miles west of Melbourne by rail. We had there a blessed work of God, both in the edification of believers and the awakening and salvation of many sinners. My home there was with an Irish merchant tailor by the name of Burke. He was a quiet, lovely, and loving man, with a wife of the same sort; both intelligent, earnest Christian workers. Sister Burke and her little sister, on a voyage from Ireland to Australia, came very near finding a watery grave. Their ship was borne down by a furious storm, and for two or three days they expected her to be swallowed up. When they thought their ship was engulfed in the ocean depths the two sisters embraced each other, consigning themselves to God in joyful hope of an entrance into heaven; but the little sister clinging tightly said, "You must hold me tight, and don't let the sharks eat me till I get drowned." Happily, however, the storm abated, and the sharks didn't get the Lord's little girl.

From Geelong I went to Castlemaine, about one hundred miles north-west of Melbourne by rail. It is a large mining town, surrounded by extensive gold fields.

The superintendent of the circuit was Rev. William Hill. He had spent a number of years as a Wesleyan missionary in Ceylon. When he had been there a few years as a young man his betrothed, a young lady, came out from England to be united with him in marriage. On her arrival she found him down with what appeared to be a fatal form of fever, and near the gates of death. One of her fellow-passengers, reputed to be a wealthy merchant, made proposals of marriage to her on the voyage. She told him that she was engaged, and was on her way to join her intended husband. When the said merchant saw the condition of the missionary he renewed his suit, but she scorned the proposal, telling the man never to speak to her again, and took charge of the sick missionary and nursed him through his illness. After his recovery they were united in marriage.

Brother Hill was subsequently stationed in Melbourne, and there met with a tragic termination of his life. There was a movement by means of public conventions and speeches throughout the colonies against capital punishment. It was gaining popular influence every day, seriously affecting the administration of justice by the courts. A dreadful man convicted of murder in the first degree was, under the influence of this popular excitement, sentenced to life imprisonment.

William Hill was in the habit of regularly visiting the stockade, or prison, in which the said murderer was incarcerated. Mr. Hill's services were all gratuitous, through sympathy and interest in the prisoners. He was well known and beloved by the officials and by the criminals. By mutual arrangement the warder opened the prison cell of each prisoner in turn to admit Mr. Hill, and then turned the key on him for ten or fifteen minutes, giving him time to talk privately to the prisoners and to pray for them. Thus one by one he would go through the whole stockade. So one day he was locked up with the murderer referred to, and talked to him kindly about his soul, then kneeled down and prayed; and while praying, with his eyes shut, the murderer quietly drew an iron bar from his cot and smashed the preacher's brains out. The telegraph lines spread the news with lightning speed through all the colonies, and the verdict of every colonist was that he ought to be hung.

That put a stop to the agitation against capital punishment in the Australian colonies, and so far as I know it has never been revived since. The man was tried for the murder of the preacher and he was sentenced to be hung. Wesleyan ministers and others visited him and prayed with him. He professed to find peace with God, and they entertained the hope that he was saved. Under the sentence of life imprisonment he remained an impenitent murderer, but under the sentence of death, according to the original law, "Whoso sheddeth man's blood, by man his blood shall be shed," he was brought to repentance. The Lord hath no pleasure in the death of a sinner, either temporal or spiritual, but a murderer is such a dangerous being in society God hath given an order to put him where he cannot do any more harm.

From Castlemaine we proceeded to Sandhurst, about twenty miles north. Sandhurst and Golden Square are also mining towns in the midst of a rich mining region. In these and other mining towns, extending to Echuca, on the south bank of the Murray River, we had a blessed work of God among the miners. I subsequently made a tour to Kyneton, Kilmore, and away on to Beechworth, to the north-east, and to Albury on the dividing line between the colonies of Victoria and New South Wales. Many miners and traders in those wild regions were also brought to God by our services.

The long trip of over two hundred miles to Beechworth and Albury I made by stage-coach. Returning, I proceeded to Ballarat, ninety-eight miles north-west from Melbourne. Ballarat was next in population to Melbourne, in the midst of a rich mining district.

My home was at the house of Brother J. A. Doane. His name is seen in connection with some of the popular tunes of our own day as a composer of music. He was a prominent leader in the church, and was superintendent of a large Sunday-school. The first series of services there extended over a period of three weeks. About five hundred persons of all sorts and sizes, each examined by the pastor, were reported converted to God. Two theatres of the town were closed up for want of patronage. The larger one of the two was sold to a temperance organisation and used as a temperance hall—a higher class of entertainment in the facts and forces of personal salvation than in the fiction and farces of theatrical sensation.

From Ballarat I went to Creswick, a few miles north of Ballarat, a flourishing mining town. There we had a blessed work of God during a week of special services. I became acquainted there with an old California miner whose Christian name was Tom. He was a pugilist and a desperado in his way. But he was induced to come to meeting. A short time before my visit there he was awakened, and sought and found the Lord. On being invited to join the Wesleyan Church he said, "I can't join the Church till I read the New Testament and see whether I can live up to it."

So they gave him a New Testament, and he read it carefully through. Then said he, "I accept everything I have read in the Testament as the truth of God, and I consent to obedience to the best of the ability that God shall give me. But I read in one place that if a man shall strike me on one cheek I must not strike him back, but must turn the other cheek and let him strike it. I have been a pugilist for many years, and I think my habit of striking back is so fixed that I shall not be able to keep that command, and I will have to wait a little bit longer."

Soon after a fellow-miner by the name of Bob came into Tom's tent in a terrible rage, and swore at Tom and threatened to thrash him. Tom silently prayed to God for help and kept his mouth shut. As Bob increased more and more in the violence of his threatening gesticulations Tom said to his partner, "Come, let us go to work."

Bob followed after them, storming and threatening. Bob had a big dog with him, and hissed his dog on Tom. Just as the dog was going to seize his leg Tom brought his miner's pick around with a sweep and knocked the dog into the miner's prospecting hole, which was four or five feet deep. Bob had to stop to get his dog out, then he came running after them as hard as he could run and, rushing up, struck Tom with his fist on one cheek, and Tom turned the other cheek, saying, "There is another cheek, Bob; fire away."

Bob turned suddenly about and hastened away. He came again that night and begged Tom not to sue him for assault. He inferred from Tom's refusal to retaliate with his fist that he meant to sue him through the law. Tom shook hands with him and assured him that he wasn't going to sue him. All he wanted for him was that he should seek Jesus. Bob began to come to meeting with Tom from that time. When I saw them Bob had not yet professed to experience salvation, but he was seeking it.

So Tom said to the minister, "I am ready now to join your Church. I have read the rules, and I have proved the sufficiency of the grace of God to enable me to keep them."

And he was keeping them conscientiously and successfully then, and will, no doubt, to the end.

We held a series of meetings also at Clunes. One of the men converted to God at Clunes soon after wrote to a merchant in Ballarat confessing to have cheated him out of one hundred and fifty dollars and of injuring his reputation, asking pardon for both, and promised to refund the money within a given time. Quite a number of satisfactory cases of restitution occurred in connection with this movement in different parts of Australia.

When I was labouring at Ballarat the Rev. W. Woodall was the preacher in charge at Scarsdale, a new mining town. Four months prior to that the Wesleyans commenced to organise a Church there, but had no chapel or suitable place of worship; but the preacher said if I would agree, after filling a line of appointments occupying a couple of months, to give him a week at Scarsdale he would go to work meantime and have a church built.

So I promised to give them a week at the time appointed, and came to time, but the minister met me with a sad tale of discouragement. He had the frame of his church up and under roof, and the floor laid, and three parts weatherboarded. One side had been left open, extending the sitting accommodation through a large tent, giving an accommodation in the chapel and the tent together for fifteen hundred persons. But a reverend gentleman claiming to be in the direct line of succession to the apostles, living in Smythesdale, two miles off, had procured a hall in Scarsdale, and had, according to previous announcement, delivered a lecture the night before against revivals and American revivalists. The house was crowded. "He didn't mention your name," said Woodall, "but described your height and appearance, and your methods of work, ridiculed your preaching and especially your singing, and seemed to carry the sympathies of the crowd, so that I fear we shall not be able to stand the tide of opposition that he has raised against us."

The next forenoon we had the chapel and tent packed, and during that day and three days ensuing, including preaching one day at Linden, eight miles distant, we had over forty souls converted to God, and a big tea meeting, which resulted in raising a large part of the funds requisite to complete the church. When the reverend gentleman saw what a victory we achieved he put an article in the paper, called the *Greenville Advertiser*, complaining that a local preacher had the impudence, at the close of his lecture, to call in question the truth of his statement in regard to the revivalist; then went on to say that he hadn't told the half he could have told.

That article was answered in the next issue of said paper by a Baptist gentleman who attended our meetings; he called the public attention to three points : First, the bad taste of this man coming the night before the opening of these special services to lecture against revivals and American revivalists. Secondly, the ridiculous conceit of the reverend gentleman in presuming to tackle such a man as California Taylor. Thirdly, he should have taken the advice of an old philosophic Pharisee, "If this work be of men, it will come to naught : but if it be of God, ye cannot overthrow it."

The said minister replied to that in an article in the next issue of the paper, stating that "the meeting was most disorderly, reminding him of a stockyard, with the squealing of hogs and the bellowing of bulls." There were fifteen hundred witnesses in that neighbourhood who knew that charge to be untrue. Our meetings, indeed, were of a most orderly character there as elsewhere. So that the community at large, including his own people, brought such a pressure to bear upon him that within two weeks his bishop removed him to the far interior.

My next appointment on leaving Scarsdale was at Hamilton, eighty miles west through the open prairie.

Hamilton is in the midst of a vast sheep-growing country. Most of the available land of all those colonies had been monopolised by the sheep growers. Owing to the light character of the soil and the shortness of the grass it was estimated that every sheep required an acre of ground, so that the land was let out under a twenty years' lease by the government at a very small rental, in large tracts from ten thousand to one hundred thousand acres in each sheep run.

Thus Australia became the most famous of all wool-producing countries, so that the wool growers and the bankers were considered the rulers of the Southern World. It was almost impossible for a farmer to get the title to a small piece of land for cultivation. The government, being anxious to encourage immigration from Great Britain, refused to renew leases to wool growers, and advertised to sell the land at auction in blocks or sections of six hundred and forty acres, depriving every bidder of the right to buy more than one section.

We had a good work in Hamilton. I went from there fifty miles to Portland, a town of two thousand in population, near the coast.

After Portland we took in Belfast, Warnambool, and other towns on the south coast. We had streams of blessing all along the line, compassing a vast region of the country, sparsely settled, covered with sheep by the million, interspersed with countless flocks of emus and kangaroos.

I was told that a short time before my arrival in that region the sheep growers became so disgusted with the kangaroos for their fondness for the kangaroo grass, which the squatters wanted for their sheep, that they ran two lines of wire fencing each more than a mile in length in the form of the letter V, and the men turned out on their fleet horses, each with heavily loaded whips, and, forming a great circle with their dogs, they drove countless numbers of kangaroos into the vortex and clubbed a thousand of them to death. They did not skin them nor make any use of them—just killed them to get rid of them and let them rot to enrich the ground.

I always took great interest in seeing what they called the old man kangaroo getting over the ground as but few other animals can do. I have seen the old mother kangaroo wait for a half dozen baby kangs and hide them away in her jacket pockets and hop away with her precious cargo as gracefully, if not quite so fast, as the old man. I didn't think much of the gallantry of the old man in going off and leaving her in charge of all the children.

A Scotch coach driver, with whom I travelled on a long journey in that country, told me that once on a fleet horse he pursued an old man kangaroo and brought him to bay, and attempted to knock him on the head with his loaded whip. The kangaroo dodged the stroke, pulled the Scotchman off his horse, and with his forearms around him got one of his hind feet up and ripped his clothes off from chin to thigh; and, he added, "But for the mercy of God that I fell near to a fallen tree and lay close up to its trunk he would have torn my insides out. Meantime a friend of mine galloped up and knocked him on the head."

The second colony I visited was Tasmania. I first held a series of services for three weeks in Launceston, a beautiful city of ten or twelve thousand inhabitants. The Wesleyans there had a fine large church. For many years Launceston was the home and place of business of my friend Henry Reed. He was a merchant there for a number of years.

He was a man of great intellectual power and force and business tact. His principle was to buy and sell for cash, and he made a fortune on that plan. While still a young man he made a business trip to England by a sailing ship around Cape Horn. Off the Cape his ship was caught in a heavy gale, and sprang a leak which the captain said would swamp the ship in three hours if not stopped. It was impossible to remove the freight and stop it from the inside in that time. But the brave sailors, with extraordinary management, succeeded in drawing a sail under the bows of the ship and back sufficiently to cover the leak, which gave them time to remove the freight and close it up from the inside; and Henry Reed, when he realised the wonderful escape he had made from death, wept with gratitude to God, and solemnly vowed that from that moment to the end of his life he would be a Christian. He brought out his brandy bottle and pack of cards and threw them into the sea, and made a public declaration that henceforth he would live for God. He exerted all his will power, depending on his own strength of purpose, and did his best. But he soon found that sin was deeply seated in his inner being and held him in bondage, so that the good that he would do he could not; the evil that he would not was just the thing he did. He kept at it, however, with Pharisaic zeal. He thought it would be of great assistance to him to have a good wife; so he married an estimable lady, with whose brother I made my home part of the time of my sojourn in Launceston.

Mr. Reed was happy in his marriage, but it brought no relief to his imprisoned spirit; so, accompanied by his wife, he took ship again to Tasmania and resumed his business, carried it forward with his usual success, but fasted and prayed till his wife became alarmed and employed a doctor to look after him.

The doctor tried to drive him off his knees and compel him to take more food, but Henry continued to have his own way in spite of the devil and the doctor. But after a couple of years or more he made up his mind to go back to England, thinking he would have a better chance to be good there than in Tasmania; but he did not like to expose himself to the temptations of a passenger ship. So he determined to charter a ship on his own account with a good religious captain and crew, and thus protect himself from evil communications.

He advertised for a ship and crew according to his own ideal. In a short time he procured a good ship, fitted her out, shipped a good religious captain and crew, and said, "Sail for London."

He had not been long on his voyage before he found that his captain was utterly incompetent, and had let his chronometer run down; so Henry took charge of the ship himself and navigated her to London; but he couldn't give up the idea of having some religion on board. So he announced to his crew that he would have a service every Sunday, and told them that he would not compel them to attend service, but if they would come and behave themselves properly the steward would give each of them an extra ration of grog as they passed out of the meeting. So they all attended the service and behaved themselves very properly and got their extra grog. His service consisted in reading a psalm and a chapter of a book entitled "The Whole Duty of Man."

On his arrival in London, having plenty of money, he devoted himself largely to visiting hospitals, and made liberal distributions of his money to the sick and suffering. He made it a point to go and hear all the celebrated ministers that were in his reach, and try to find a remedy for his sin-sick soul. After spending about two years in that way he concluded that after all he could serve God better in Tasmania than in England; so he returned to Tasmania.

During his absence on that trip the Rev. Nathaniel Turner, who for many years had been a missionary in New Zealand and the Friendly Islands, but was now a member of the Australasian Conference, had been appointed to Launceston. He was a grand old missionary. Under his ministry in Launceston, Tasmania, during Reed's absence, a great work of God had been manifested. A Christian merchant from Liverpool had settled there who was a great worker in the Church. During the revival under Mr. Turner a large number of persons had been converted to God. Among the converts in that revival were the Hon. Mr. Gleadow and the Hon. Isaac Sherwin, members of the Legislative Council of Tasmania, and old friends of Henry Reed. Soon after Mr. Reed's return Mr. Gleadow prepared a banquet of welcome in honour of him inviting a large number of his friends.

At the table Mr. Reed chanced to sit next to the Liverpool merchant, and in conversation soon became deeply interested in him, and begged the merchant to accompany him to his own home that night after the banquet, that he might cultivate his acquaintance. The merchant respectfully declined the invitation, saying, " To-night is the night for my class meeting. '

Mr. Reed said, "What do you mean by a class meeting? I never heard of a meeting of that sort before."

" Oh," said he, "it is a social religious meeting where the people assemble and talk one to another on religious subjects, tell of their religious trials and triumphs, and edify one another and pray for one another."

"Well, my dear sir, that is just the kind of meeting I would like to attend ; won't you let me go with you to your class meeting ?"

"Oh yes, Mr. Reed, if you will go I shall be glad to have your company."

But soon after he got up unceremoniously, and as he was passing out through the door Mr. Reed shouted after him, "Hold on, Mr. —— ; I thought you were going to take me to class with you !"

"Well, I concluded that it was too much to expect of you to leave your friends and to go to a class meeting."

" I told you that was just the kind of a meeting I wanted to go to ; and I insist on going with you. Friends, please excuse me, I am going to class meeting."

So he went, and sat down in a company of eighteen or twenty plain-looking men and women. One after another they told their experience, their struggles with their old bad nature and vain efforts to try to be good, and that when they had given up all hope in self and all works of righteousness, and surrendered to God and accepted Christ, God pardoned their sins, sent His Holy Spirit into their hearts, and changed their vile nature. They told how the conflict went on—of their victory every day through faith in Jesus.

Though Mr. Reed had been brought up in the Church, accustomed from childhood to read or hear prayers, he had never in his life up to that time heard a witness testify to a personal deliverance from sin and Satan and a real change in heart and life. The words of those witnesses were accompanied by an unction from the Holy Spirit which applied the truth to his heart, and he said, " Friends, this wonderful thing you have got is the thing I need ; " and he dropped on his knees right there.

They gathered around him and prayed for him, and soon after he let go self and sin, and in utter helplessness accepted the Lord Jesus Christ as his Saviour, and Jesus in that hour saved him.

Soon after Mr. Reed joined the Wesleyan Methodist Church and became a local preacher. While he pursued his business with unabated success he became, I think, without any doubt or question the most successful soul winner in that colony. He made a regular daily business of it.

When he was riding along the road and came to a company of convict road-makers he would dismount, hitch his horse, collect them together, read the Bible and explain it to them, kneel down on the gravelly road and pray for them. He also held special services for soul-saving. The plain people came from a radius of ten or fifteen miles to attend his meetings; so that he soon had a large class of people brought to God through his own agency.

We had three weeks of special services in Launceston, with marvellous soul-saving results.

My principal home during the period of my special services in Launceston was with the Hon. Isaac Sherwin. He and his wife and daughter were all filled with loyalty and love to God, quietly but eminently useful in Church work, hospitable and affectionate in the highest degree, yet without ostentation. They lived in the sunshine of prosperity, yet in part beclouded by a sad bereavement.

As I turned over the photograph album that lay on their centre table, and called the attention of Sister Sherwin to the photo of a very interesting-looking young man, I inquired, "Whom does this represent?"

I saw the tears gathering in her eyes as she replied in utterances broken by emotions of grief, "That is the photo of young Mr. B——, of Hobart Town, who killed our son Henry."

"What! Is that the way you cherish the memory of men-killers in this country?"

"Yes; Mr. B—— is a fine young man. He was a fellow-student with Henry at Horton College, and came home with Henry to spend his vacation with us. The two young men went out gunning one day, and Henry was brought home dead; young B—— accidentally shot him."

Then she showed me a letter of condolence written by the young man who had killed her son.

If it had been in evidence that young B——'s will had taken action against the life of his fellow he would have been hung up by the neck and filled a felon's grave. But it was manifest to all that he had no such purpose in his heart, hence did not even forfeit the confidence of the friends whom he thus bereaved.

I proceeded from Launceston, one hundred and twenty miles south, by coach to Hobart Town. Hobart Town was the largest town in Tasmania, and Launceston second. The former is now called simply Hobart. The population of Launceston has now increased to over seventeen thousand, and that of Hobart to fully twenty-five thousand souls. There are also many smaller towns in Tasmania, in all of which

I laboured. So that swollen streams of salvation flowed through the island from end to end.

The Tasmanians are a teachable, confiding, loving, and lovely people; but few traces of old convictism were anywhere to be seen. The "old hands," sent ostensibly for their country's good, were nearly all dead. Many of them were very good people, and died in the Lord, and left a good inheritance for their children. One of the survivors with whom I became acquainted was a Wesleyan local preacher. He chanced to be passing from his work to his home, in one of the northern towns of England, when a mob was being arrested for breaking up wheat-threshing machines, the introduction of which was thought to interfere with the labour market in England, and occasioned mob violations which led to the transportation of the rioters. My friend John was found thus with bad company and was hurried off with the rest on the convict ship to Van Diemen's Land.

John's wife was left behind, but he had his Saviour with him; so he consoled himself with the belief that as these poor fellows had no chaplain the Lord had permitted him to be arrested and convicted, and thus to become their chaplain; and he devoted himself assiduously and successfully to the work of his ministry. He served out his term of ten years and subsequently made money, brought out his wife, and, though not wealthy, had a comfortable home of his own when I had the honour of an introduction to him. He was an old man then.

I said, "Well, Brother John, how do you prosper?"

He replied, "Oh, Brother Taylor, I don't think I have that perfect love that you were preaching about to-day; I have been trying to serve God ever since the days of my youth. I have had a hard pull of it; the Lord has been very patient with me, very kind, but I have not been made perfect in love, and I feel very sad about it. I fear the mainspring is broken."

I had previously heard of the consistency of his life as a Christian and of the success of his humble ministry, so I said to him, "Oh no, Brother John, the mainspring is not broken, it is run down; it just needs to be wound up, and it will tick on all right;" and he very feelingly said, "O Lord, wind me up;" and I said "Amen." He repeated, "O Lord, do wind me up now."

Said I, "A timekeeper to be wound up has to lie quietly in the hand of the winder; if you will submit yourself wholly to God, and let Him take you in hand, He will wind you up all right."

He responded, "Blessed Lord, I do submit; I put my life, soul, and body into Your hands. I want You to have Your own way with me, and wind me up to-day." Then he said, "Why, bless God, He is winding me up; oh, hallelujah! He has wound me up snug. Now I have got it, I have got the perfect love of God, and I expect to keep on all right now to the end of my life."

And so he did; he lived but a few years longer, and left a shining record of past usefulness.

At Longford, twelve miles south-west of Launceston, I spent two nights in special services. I became acquainted with a prominent citizen of that town who had been brought up a Unitarian. A few days after I left Launceston for Hobart this Unitarian gentleman was passing a bookstore in Launceston, and saw in the window a large portrait painting. After looking at it intently a few moments he inquired of the bookseller, "Whom does this striking picture represent?"

The bookseller replied, "That is Mr. Taylor, from California."

"Well, it is very strange I never heard of that man before, but that is the man who appeared to me in a dream two nights ago. I dreamed that I went to a meeting. The house was crowded with people and this man was in the pulpit preaching to them, and he revolutionised all my ideas of God and salvation; that is the man. I recognise him as distinctly as if I had known him in person, and I must hear that man if I have to go to Hobart Town to do it."

"Well," said the bookseller, "you need not go to Hobart Town to hear him; he is visiting all the towns, and in due time you can hear him in Longford, for he will soon be in this locality."

So he was on the look-out for his man, and was one of the first to welcome me to Longford. Though my time there was so short he took in the teaching with great avidity, and I had reason to believe, as his dream indicated, that his ideas were not only revolutionised, but his heart was changed.

Returning from Tasmania, I rendered some additional service to the work in Melbourne.

I proceeded thence to Sydney, the great commercial emporium of New South Wales, a city at that time of about two hundred thousand population. I spent many months in that city and its suburbs, giving at least a week of special services to each chapel. The work was mainly among Wesleyan Methodists; but other Churches were also quickened and enlarged. Rev. Dr. Steele, a Scotch Presbyterian minister, a man of lovely catholic spirit, took quite an interest in our meetings.

It was observed that a family belonging to his church by the name of McDonald, especially the mother and her two daughters, were seen at the first meeting I held in York Street, and they, with other members of their family, were seen at every meeting I held in or near that city for months; and it was a matter of some surprise to those who knew them that while many were waiting to see the outcome of the movement before identifying themselves with it, those Presbyterians entered into the work from its commencement.. The McDonalds were godly people of high repute. Three of the sons were bankers, all fine-looking men, each with a heavy black beard. The mother had an old-time prejudice against beards, and often begged her boys to shave, which they respectfully declined to do. But for months before my arrival she ceased to remonstrate with her sons against wearing beards. The key to the whole thing came out in a statement she made one day in my presence at her dinner table. Addressing me, she said, "Three months before your arrival in Sydney I was led by the good Spirit into a great struggle of prayer and fasting on behalf of the Churches of this city and colony. Iniquity was abounding, and the Churches were so formal and dead they seemed utterly unable to stand the opposing tide of wickedness, much less to move aggressively for the salvation of the people. This burden upon my heart so increased that I was unable to take sufficient sleep and food to keep me up, so that my health was sadly impaired. I was led to pray specially that the Lord would send some one through whom He could stir the hearts of the people of this city and colony, and so bring them into harmony with Him, so that He could use them effectively for the accomplishment of their work.

"I was finally relieved one night by a vision through a dream. I saw a beautiful chariot without any horses or any visible power of locomotion, moving slowly over the city just above the housetops, and I saw standing in it a messenger from God, a tall, straight man with a long beard, and he was sowing seed broadcast, and proclaiming in the name of the Lord. In my dream I wept for joy, and said, 'That is the man the Lord is sending in answer to my prayer.'

"In my dream I gazed with tearful eyes at the man's face and figure till an impression was made on my memory as clearly defined as a photograph, and I thought, 'If I ever see that man I shall certainly know that he is the man that God sent.' I awoke and my weight of anxiety was gone from my heart. My prayer was answered, and I said, 'That man will surely come.' At that time I had never heard of you, and knew not that there was such a man in the world, but from that time on I was on the look-out. Three months afterwards I saw it announced that Rev. William Taylor, from California, was to commence a series of special revival services in York Street Wesleyan Church. I hastened to the first service announced, and as soon as I entered the door and saw you standing by the pulpit, I recognised you at a glance as the man I had seen in the Gospel chariot three months ago.

"I needed no other certification as to whom this stranger might be. But from the first meeting I, with as many of my family and friends as could possibly arrange it, never failed to be present at your meetings in or near the city."

Among the suburban churches in which I conducted revival meetings was a beautiful new Gothic structure at Newtown. Rev. Joseph Oram was the pastor. He made a careful record and reported one hundred souls converted during the week, one of whom was W. J. F., a nephew of the Duke of Wellington, a celebrated barrister and crown prosecutor for the colony of New South Wales. He was nominally a Christian before, but came forward and kneeled down with other seekers, and sought and found reconciliation with God and a new heart, and from that night became and continued a most efficient Christian worker.

He rendered effective service at a number of my meetings in different parts of the colony, and mainly through his agency a number of lawyers, with others, were converted to God. He remained a member of the Colonial Church of England, on the broadest principle of catholicity and co-operation with all Churches.

After we thus spent three months in Sydney churches there was a great desire expressed by many that we should, if possible, procure a hall that would accommodate the outside masses, for whom there was no room in the churches. My friend Ebenezer Vickery offered to pay the rent required, to the extent of fifteen hundred dollars. A committee was appointed to search for a suitable hall. The largest auditorium they could find was the Prince of Wales Theatre, that would seat about two thousand persons; so they built and seated a preaching stand, to accommodate about twenty preachers, in Hyde Park. No seats were provided for the audience. They were to stand on their feet. As the meetings were to be at night we laid on gas, which emitted, through two great stars some six feet in diameter, two hundred jets of gaslight. This profusion of light was reflected upon the audience by a framework above the front of the stand, leaving the preacher in the shade. I preached there in the afternoon on two Sabbaths and ten week nights to a vast crowd of people, estimated variously at different times to be numbered from ten to seventeen thousand hearers. At the close of each preaching service all persons who were awakened under the preaching and desired salvation were invited to go promptly to York Street Church, where a working force was in readiness to instruct them in the way of righteousness and lead them to the Saviour. Very many were saved during that series of services. Among them was a tall, commanding man, a Scotchman by blood, but born in Australia. He had never known the fear of men or devils.

Once when two belligerent tribes of Australian natives were set in battle array and were about to commence a fight with their spears, war clubs, and boomerangs, this man rushed in between the two barbarian armies and commanded the peace. The men of both armies were his friends, and shouted to him not to go in there, that he would be killed. He held his ground between the two parties, passing along the line back and forth, shouting to them to desist, and finally they obeyed his orders, repaired to their camps, and dropped the contention.

This man lived at Mudgee, one hundred miles in the interior; but he attended my meetings in the park in Sydney. The lightning of God's awakening Spirit struck him, and he was so frightened at the discovery of the perilous condition of his soul, on account of his rebellion against God, that, as he stated afterwards, he could not wait to walk from the park to York Street, but ran like a poor manslayer to the city of refuge; and when he entered the church he didn't sit down, but moved rapidly and kneeled down at the altar of prayer. My remembrance of that scene is as fresh as yesterday, though that was twenty-eight years ago. His name was William Blackman. He joined the Wesleyan Church, and became an extraordinary Christian worker.

We took in most of the towns of New South Wales, ministers and people co-operating with a will.

Brother Joseph Wearne, the owner of flour mills in Sydney, an earnest Christian worker, drove me in his carriage across the mountains one hundred miles to Bathurst. On our way we became acquainted with a Brother Scott, a generous-hearted Irishman, on the banks of Fish River. I said to him at the breakfast table, "Well, Scott, are you engaged in raising cattle?"

"No; unfortunately I am growing horses."

"How many horses have you?"

"At the last count I had two thousand, most of them as wild as kangaroos. Some time ago I offered a man half of all that he could make to lasso a few hundred of them and take them to Sydney market and sell them. He broke in several herds, and they brought in Sydney market from one pound to seven pounds each. But the expense of putting them into the market swallowed up the profit, so it didn't pay. The price of a horse here, as he runs with the herd, is a shilling. The pick of a herd would be two-and-sixpence."

Four or five years afterwards, on my second tour through those colonies, I met Brother Scott, and asked him what he had done with his horses. He said that he had boiled down a lot of them and sent the oil and the bones to Sydney market; but the expenses of preparation and transport were such that the business didn't pay, and he gave it up. "I gave no further attention to the horses; there are a couple of a thousand running somewhere; if anybody wants a horse he has my consent to go and catch him."

We had a blessed work of God at Bathurst. One minister there of another denomination felt it his duty, in anticipation of my coming, to warn his people against going to hear "that California man." That turned out to be a good advertisement for our work. A number that came were converted to God. They said "We should not have heard of the meetings, and should have known nothing about them, but for the announcement of our minister." So, unwittingly, he did them a good service.

I went from Bathurst forty or fifty miles across the continent to Mudgee, the home of my friend William Blackman.

The Wesleyan Methodists had but recently completed a new church edifice there. Their pastor was Rev. Brother Turner. He had an earnest Christian working corps, but they had drained their money resources in building their church, and were then about three thousand pounds, or fifteen thousand dollars, in debt.

I got acquainted with one dear fellow in that church whom they had picked up in the gutter some three years before and got him saved. He was then a poor, penniless, abandoned drunkard; but they clothed and fed and fostered him, and in a few weeks he looked like a new man, as he was in fact. They gave him some money to buy a basket of oranges to start the orange peddling business, so he was known as "the orange peddler of Mudgee." He sold oranges and talked salvation. People believed in him and encouraged his trade, and after a few weeks he bought a handcart and enlarged his business operations.

Two or three years afterwards the new church was completed, and the trustees had a breakfast meeting. It is a common thing among English Methodists in raising money to have a breakfast meeting and to invite all their moneyed friends to breakfast. You should never ask an Englishman for money when he is hungry. Take him when he has eaten a good breakfast. If he has the money, and you have a cause worthy of his attention, he will give his money freely.

After this breakfast in Mudgee the patrons were invited to walk up and lay their offerings on the table in front of the pulpit. Many responded, some paying five pounds, some ten, some twenty, some of the merchants paying as high as fifty pounds. By-and-by the orange pedlar walked up. Nobody seemed to suppose he had made more than a living. He walked up and faced the audience, and told his experience, giving the date and circumstances of his conversion to God, and added, "I was a poor, ragged drunkard, an abandoned sinner. These kind Wesleyan people drew me up out of the horrible pit of drunkenness and led me to Jesus, and He saved me from my sins. These people bore with me and kindly led me, showed me Christian sympathy and love, and started me in business. God has prospered me, and to-day I want to put down on this table all my earnings in the orange trade, above expenses, as a thank offering to God and to these people for their kindness to me."

He had a bag in his hand supposed to be filled with copper pennies. At the close of his speech he emptied the contents of his bag on to the table, and the clerk counted and reported two hundred and fifty sovereigns in gold. So they said, "It pays to gather up drunkards and take care of them."

During the progress of my week of service there at Mudgee I went by invitation to dine with a wealthy wool grower, eighteen miles distant. The floods were out and the rivers were booming. William Blackman, in his carriage drawn by a span of splendid horses, forded the river at the peril of being carried away, and took me through in a little over two hours. Brother Turner accompanied us on horseback. We saw the process of wool-washing before it was shorn from the sheep. The sheep were washed in warm water, and then they swam in the running creek within t hecircle of a secure railing and came out perfectly white and clean; after that they were shorn. It was just in the shearing season, and the owner had about eighty hired shepherds and shearers, so he had me to preach on the verandah of his spacious house to his shepherds, shearers and family, aggregating about one hundred persons. After preaching we sat down to dinner. Before he commenced his dinner he made a speech to this effect:

"I belong to the Church of England; that was the Church of my fathers. I expect to live and die in it. But I have been closely observing the Church work being done by the Wesleyans in these colonies, and I believe that they are doing more work and better work than in any other organisation of the kind in this country. They have put up a good chapel at Mudgee, but I learn that they have a debt of about three thousand pounds, and from my knowledge of the men and the amount they have already contributed this is a burden more than they are able to bear, and I make this proposition : If they will go to work and raise within one year two thousand pounds I will give them one thousand pounds cash and their Church will be free from debt."

We then proceeded to take our dinner. So we went back to Mudgee that afternoon. Brother Turner called on the trustees and other men of means and said, "If you will raise a thousand pounds I will raise the same amount from my friends in other parts of the colony."

So they made an effort the next night, and the money came in freely. The stage-coach called at the door for me at ten o'clock at night for a drive through to Sydney, one hundred miles. I left in the midst of a shower of banknotes, and did not know the final result till my return to Australia some years later, when Brother Turner informed me that the two thousand pounds were raised and that the wool grower paid his thousand pounds, and the Church was clear of debt, " and was relieved most opportunely," he added, " because we have had a financial panic since that which would have swamped us."

I was informed that just back of the mountains, fifteen miles from Mudgee, there were over fifteen hundred head of wild cattle without any owner, ranging through the mountains at will. Just a little before my visit there the wild bulls got into the habit of coming down to the plains and frightening the people. So the men turned out on horse-back with their rifles and shot thirty of them in one day, simply to abate the nuisance, without using the hides or flesh of any of them.

Soon after my visit the country round about Mudgee was thrown into a panic on account of a " bushranger "—the Australian name for a highway robber—who made it a business to rob individual travellers and "stick up" stagecoaches and rob the mails and passengers. The people appealed to the government for protection, but months of peril passed without relief.

So Brother Blackman said to a brave Wesleyan brother named Woods, "I fear, Brother Woods, that the government will not relieve this community of this terrible peril and panic, so I think we had better pursue this robber and arrest him."

" All right," said Woods, " I will go with you."

The two men mounted their fleet horses, with their blankets and provisions, and went on a hunt for the bushranger. They were two weeks tracking him. They travelled through the day and camped wherever night overtook them. They learned, among other things, the size and shape of his horse's shoe, so that they could recognise his tracks. On the last night, having taken his bearings, they travelled all night, but a few hours behind him, and at nine o'clock in the morning they sighted his camp fire, and, approaching softly, found that he was asleep, his two horses hitched near to him.   Our two men took their positions from two different standpoints, so as to cover him with their rifles, and Blackman shouted to him to get up. That aroused him from his sleep, and Blackman shouted, "Discharge your pistols in the air above you, and break the butts off."

He responded, "Who are you?"

Then Woods shouted, "Obey the order at once, or you will find out who he is."

They both stood with their rifles levelled on him.   So, seeing there was no chance for escape, he discharged his pistols in the air and broke off the butts, and they closed upon him and ordered him to mount his horse.   They did not bind him, but rode, one in front, the other in the rear, and kept an eye on him and brought him to town and delivered him up to the authorities.   He was tried and sentenced to the penitentiary for fifteen years.   Blackman visited him in the prison regularly, furnished him with books to read, and was hoping to get him saved, and if clearly "transformed by the renewing of his mind" he hoped after a few years to get him reprieved. Blackman's cool courage was equalled only by his sympathetic kindness of heart.   The government tendered Blackman a vote of thanks and presented Woods with a gold watch.

We had a blessed work at Kiama and at other points down the coast and south of Sydney, and also at Newcastle and Maitland and other circuits north of Sydney.

Brother W. J. F——, crown prosecutor, rendered me grand assistance at Maitland, a town of three or four thousand population.   Through his agency two lawyers publicly sought and professed to obtain reconciliation with God at that series of meetings.   One of them, Mr. M——, was a man of note in many respects.   He kept an open sideboard with choice liquors free to any of his friends at any time they might choose to walk in and help themselves.   He spent money freely on horse racing.   He was an able lawyer and a jolly fellow in high circles of social life.   Through the crown prosecutor's influence he was induced to come to my meetings.   After he had been to hear me a couple of times he was called on to preside at a public dinner to be given in honour of a distinguished citizen who was about to leave for England.   At the dinner table a minister who didn't believe in revival work related a damaging story about the California evangelist.   Mr. M——, addressing the preacher, said, "I have heard California Taylor preach, and I am prepared to say, without implicating your honour, sir, that you are peddling lies against Taylor.   I think things have come to a poor pass when one preacher has no better business than to peddle lies against another preacher."

Mr. M—— was relating this encounter to the crown prosecutor, and he said, "If I hear any more of these people around here retailing lies against Taylor I will knock them down."

His friend said, "Oh, they can't hurt Taylor; that is not the way to seek redress.   You come to the meeting and see what good you can get, and never mind the talk of the people."

Mr. M—— was already converted to me, but not to God. He came to the meeting the next night and became deeply awakened. The night following, when I invited seekers, he took his wife by the arm, and side by side they walked up and kneeled at the altar of prayer. We exhorted them to surrender to God and accept Christ. They did so, and testified distinctly to a personal experience of justification by faith and peace with God.

The news of their conversion produced a great sensation throughout the town of Maitland.

The next day he was passing the hotel, and a lot of his old bar-room companions and the hotel keeper shouted in derision, "Here comes a saint;" and as he approached them they said, "Hello, Mr. M——, we heard that you had been to the bull ring of that American preacher."

Mr. M—— walked in and said, "Hold on, boys, I will tell you all about it. It is true that I was at the Wesleyan Church last night and heard that California man preach, and God's Spirit shone into me and showed me what a miserable sinner I was, and I surrendered to God and accepted Christ and obtained remission of sins and a new heart; and that is the thing you all need. Take my advice and go likewise and seek the salvation of your souls."

Then addressing the hotel keeper he said, "You know that I have spent hundreds of pounds at your bar, but I have taken my last drink, so it will be a great loss to you; but if you will follow my example and accept Christ and get saved you will be a great gainer."

He boldly witnessed for Christ on all suitable occasions, public and private, so that in a short time there was not a dog in town that would use his tongue in the presence of Mr. M——.

The man who claimed to be his minister called to see him and said, "Mr. M——, I hear that you have been to the meetings of that foreigner, and that you have been mixed up with these despised Methodists. I hope it is not so."

"'Yes, it is, and I am glad of it," said Mr. M——. "And allow me to say, ever since I came to this town, many years ago, you have had free access to my house and to my sideboard, to help yourself to whatever you wanted; you have laughed with me and joked with me and drunk whisky with me through all these years, but never hinted to me in all this time that I had a soul to be saved. And now that God has had mercy on me through the agency of Mr. Taylor I think you ought to be glad and to rejoice with me."

"Then, Mr. M——, will you promise me that you won't leave your mother Church?"

"No, sir; my mother Church never gave me any motherly attention; so I shall hold myself free to join the Church in which I can get and do the most good."

The fourth colony to which I extended my services was Queensland. We went by steam five hundred miles from Sydney to Brisbane. There we had an outpouring of the Spirit during nearly two weeks of services, with a good average success.

From Brisbane I went by steamer five hundred miles north, to Rockhampton. On the way up our steamer ascended Mary River to Maryborough, an important timber mart, where I preached once to the people during the few hours that our ship lay at anchor. On the way up Mary River quite a number of Australian natives boarded our ship. A rope attached to the stern of the vessel was drawn along in the water for a distance of twenty or thirty yards, and they, one by one, swam out into the stream away above us, and as the ship passed them they watched their chance, to seize the rope. The advanced movement of the ship at the rate of six or seven knots per hour drew the black fellows under the water, so that they had to pull themselves one by one against the current with their heads under the water. It was a most difficult achievement. About half of them failed to get aboard. Those who pulled themselves hand over hand up under the stern of the ship then readily climbed to the top and got aboard. They came aboard stark naked, but were at once presented with a gunny bag for each one, and, cutting a hole through the bottom, they passed their heads through and were thus rigged out in full costume in a few minutes. They were very graceful in their movements, very polite, seemed quite jolly, and were very grateful for small favours. The little presents they received they tied on to their heads and jumped overboard, and were soon out of sight.

We saw vast flocks of red ibises along that river; beautiful birds, both in their plumage and in their towering, circular flight.

Having to return south by the same steamer on which I went up, I had but three or four days in Rockhampton. Our meetings were well attended, and we had a good quickening of believers and some souls brought to Jesus.

Returning to Sydney, I took ship immediately for New Zealand, and preached a week at the beautiful town of Nelson; then went by another steamer through Cook Strait to Wellington, the new capital, where we had an excellent series of meetings, at which several distinguished citizens were converted to God.

The war was raging at that time between the Maoris and the English soldiers. Nearly all the Marois of New Zealand live on the Northern Island, and are supposed to number about twenty thousand. The men are tall, brave and powerful. They had waged war off and on against the English soldiers for about a quarter of a century. They would fight until their ammunition was exhausted and then retire to the inaccessible mountains, grow potatoes, make gunpowder, and get ready for another battle. They were extraordinary engineers in their way. In a night or two they would construct a *pa* or fortress, that would resist English guns for a fortnight, and when the place was taken by storm there was not a rat or rag to be found in it.

A part of the plan was to construct a tunnel by which they could escape in their extremity and come out on the other side of the hill, while the English soldiers were hunting for them, and then go off to some other hill and construct another *pa* and float their flag of defiance.

Their method of constructing a fortress was to dig a deep trench to the extent of the enclosure they wished to use as a fort, and set about three lines of heavy logs in a trench, on end, about three deep, and ram them around solid with clay and stones, so that cannon balls spent their force before they got half through. They would never go out into an open field, but always fought from behind their own intrenchments, and in their last extremity pop into their tunnel and leave the premises without two cents of value to grace the victory of their besiegers.

Colonists were sometimes killed who were associated with the red-coated soldiers. The Maoris never seemed to show a disposition to kill the colonists; but flaunting a red rag to a mad bull could no more surely excite the fight in him than the sight of a British red-coat would infuriate a Maori.

The British soldiers were finally nearly all withdrawn from New Zealand, and the settlement of their war difficulties was left to the colonists and friendly natives. Since that time their troubles gradually abated till of late years I have heard nothing more about them.

I went by steamer from Wellington to Dunedin, the southern extremity of the Middle Island. The settlement of Dunedin was primarily composed of Presbyterian Scotch immigrants, for the purpose of establishing a class settlement composed of the elect only. There were two strong Scotch Presbyterian churches and one Wesleyan there at the time of my visit. I preached in all of them, and my message was received with appreciative cordiality.

In due course I took ship from Dunedin to Lyttelton, a port town of the province of Canterbury, the capital of which bears the name of Christchurch. Lyttelton was founded by Lord Lyttelton and a company composed of select members of the Church of England. It was a class settlement. The port town was called after his lordship. Christchurch is a few miles inland, or underland, for it is reached by a railroad tunnel through a mountain, not quite finished when I was there, so that I had to climb the mountain. It is a beautiful city on the bank of a river flowing through a broad, fertile valley between rugged mountains.

I crossed the Altantic Ocean twice in company with Lord Lyttelton, and found him a genialChristian gentleman. On one of those voyages our High Church captain said he would not allow a Dissenter to preach aboard, not even in the second-class passengers' saloon; but his lordship Lyttelton and others obliged the captain to give his consent, and his lordship came to my preaching on each Sabbath that we were aboard; so he was a liberal Churchman.

One of the largest and most costly churches in the Christchurch class settlement was a Wesleyan Methodist church, in which I preached for a week with blessed success among a most lovely and loving people.

I took steamer at Lyttelton for Sydney, a voyage of about one thousand two hundred miles, touching at Wellington on the way. I spent a few weeks in New South Wales and a few weeks also in

Victoria, and had a very encouraging review of the work and a favourable opportunity for the edification of young believers.

I proceeded from Melbourne to South Australia, the sixth and last colony in which I laboured in the Southern World. It was announced that I should commence special services in Pierie Street Wesleyan Church, in the city of Adelaide, on a certain Sabbath. I expected to arrive on Friday, but owing to stormy weather our steamer did not arrive till Sunday noon; but I got there in time to preach that afternoon and night.

I had in South Australia the same hearty reception and co-operation by ministers and people that I had in the five colonies in which I had laboured two a half years. We had a wonderful work at Pierie Street, and, indeed, in all the four circuits of that city.

Mr. Ironside, the superintending minister of Kent Town Church in that city, begged me to give his people a week of special services, saying, " If you will come and preach a week in our new unfinished chapel we shall get Thomas Waterhouse converted to God and he will help us to pay the debt on our church, and will build us a college. His wife is a Methodist and a good worker in the church. Mr. Waterhouse is very kind, but holds so tightly to his money that we can get but very little help from him." It was my great pleasure to get such a man saved, not for the sake of his money, but of love for his soul and his growing young family. So when I got through at Pierie Street I proceeded to Kent Town. By pre-arrangement with the minister I made my home at the house of our friend Waterhouse. Though he was a millionaire he was an unobtrusive, humble, kind, hard-working man.

I had family worship with them morning and night, and my host and his good wife went with me to every meeting I held there, and exhibited increasing interest in the work. I improved every opportunity to pour the truth into the mind and heart of my host, but made no direct assault upon him. Toward the latter part of the week of special services there he invited me to take a drive with him in his carriage, saying he wanted to converse with me personally. So on that drive he gave me a brief history of his life.

He said he had been brought up in the Church of England, but had married a Methodist lady. Since that, when he went to church at all he went with his wife to the Wesleyan Methodist church. He was not, however, a regular churchgoer at all. Said he: "The trouble is, when I go to church and hear a stirring sermon I get into great trouble in regard to my relations to God and eternity, but when I try to make up my mind to become a true Christian I am headed off and defeated by the theological dogma of God's foreknowledge. It comes to me in this way: If God foreknew that I would be saved and in due time get to heaven, I need not trouble myself about it. If He foreknew as a certainty that I should die in my sins and go to hell, what can I do to alter an immutable certainty? So, to relieve the distressing perplexity involved in my mind, I stay away from the house of God."

I asked him to give me the chapter and verse where any such dogmas were taught in the Word of God. "Oh," said he, "I have heard them preached for years, and I take for granted that they are taught in the Scriptures."

"I take it upon me to say that you may search the Bible through and you will find no such teaching in it. You will find frequent reference to God's foreknowledge, but no such extreme issues as you have stated. God knows perfectly all existing things in all worlds. He knows the possibilities along the lines of cause and effect of all existing things; and His governmental administration covers all the certainties and all the contingencies that can possibly come to pass in the future ages, and perfectly provides for all such possible events; so that He can never be surprised or embarrassed in His administrative provision to meet any and all such contingencies. Thus, His prophetic announcements, reaching a thousand years into the future, were uttered in full knowledge of the possibilities of their fulfilment; He himself adjusted all the varieties of agency or other conditions employed by Him to bring to pass the fulfilment of His own prophetic utterances. So He knows the possibilities of the individual subjects of His government contingent on the freedom of the human will. But contingencies can't be known in advance as certainties. If they were certain they wouldn't be contingent. There may be, to be sure, and usually is, a certainty hinging on a contingency, but until the certainty actually supersedes the contingency, and thus becomes certainty, it cannot be known as a certainty.

"To say it is impossible for God to lie or to do undoable things is no more a reflection on His attribute of omnipotence than to say that He cannot know an unknowable thing is a reflection upon His attribute of omniscience. So your salvation, or damnation, hinging on the contingency of your moral freedom, remains an open question with God and men till settled by the final decisions of your will, which remain unknowable things till they become certainties in fact."

The countenance of my friend lighted up as he exclaimed, "Oh, that is wonderful! That lets me out of the snare of the devil and the theologians!"

On his return to his house he told his wife that he saw the gates of the kingdom of God ajar, and that he was going in; he had made up his mind that he would go forward as a seeker to get further instruction that night. However, I was disappointed in seeing him remain in his pew during the prayer meeting and not present himself as a seeker, and that was our last meeting of that series.

The next morning he said, "I suppose you were disappointed last night that I did not go forward with others to seek the Lord. I was just in the act of going forward when the preacher came to me and said, 'It is not necessary for you to go forward and kneel down there with that motley crowd; seek the Lord in your pew, and I will come around to your house to see you and we will have a talk.' So I took his advice, and I am feeling as wretched as any poor rebel against God is likely to feel in this life."

"Well," said I, "you know it is not far to where I commence a new series of meetings in the Second Adelaide Church, and I will continue to share your hospitality through next week, and shall be glad to have you attend those services also. You don't need to wait, however; if you can surrender yourself to God and receive Christ here in your own room, all right. But it is very appropriate and often necessary for public rebels against God to make a public renunciation of their rebellion and a public avowal of their loyalty."

He and his wife went with me, and at the meeting on Sabbath night he came and knelt down with the publicans and sinners, humbled his pride, and surrendered to God, received Christ, and was saved. Naturally a quiet man, he made no loud profession, but distinctly testified to his experience of pardon and peace from God. Then he applied to the pastor of the said Second Wesleyan Church of Adelaide for admission into his church as a member. The pastor replied, " You live within the bounds of the Kent Town Circuit, and we pastors have an agreement among ourselves that we will not encroach upon the territorial bounds of each other's circuits."

Mr. Waterhouse replied, " I like my preacher very well, but my confidence in him as a guide to the narrow path that leads to heaven has been broken. When I was on the eve last Friday night of going and kneeling with other seekers he said to me that it was not necessary that I should go forward ; so that, while he required the common herd of sinners to publicly confess and renounce their sins, because I happened to have a little money he said that I had no need to go and kneel down with those folks ; that I could find the Lord as well in my own private pew. So I can't trust myself in the hands of such a shepherd. And as for your agreement with other pastors of the city with regard to your territorial limits, it may be all well enough in its way, but I can't allow it to infringe my moral freedom to choose to join whatever church I like. If I should choose to join the Presbyterian, or any other church, it is my own business ; who has any right to say what church I shall join, or who has any right to shut the door of their church against me ? "

The minister replied, " Very well, I will see the pastor of Kent Town Circuit and explain it to him, so that he will not feel hurt with me, and enter your name on my church register."

Subsequently Brother and Sister Waterhouse attended nearly all my special services in the city and most of the towns adjacent, and manifestly increased in the knowledge and love of God.

Wherever I spent a week for special soul-saving services, one evening was devoted to a tea meeting to help to meet the financial demands of the circuit. The order was first a plain tea, followed by a public meeting crowding the church, at which addresses were delivered and the offerings of the people received. At every such meeting I delivered a speech on God's law of the tithe and free-will offerings, the first under a divine legal requirement, the second a voluntary thank offering.

After some months of services in the different churches Brother

Waterhouse said to me, "I never knew what I was worth financially, nor the extent of my yearly income, till I heard your lecture a few times on systematic giving, both under the law of the tithe and the higher law of liberal free-will offerings. Your lectures have led me to take stock of all that I have to see how much I owe the Lord— to see how much I owe on old account, and how much I should pay on running account."

I did not ask him nor did he show me his exhibit, but just as Mr. Ironside had predicted he helped Kent Town Circuit to finish paying for their new church, bought twenty-three acres of ground in the city of Adelaide and with some help from the people built and endowed a Wesleyan Methodist college, known as Prince Albert College.

Michael Kingsborough, one of very many of my dear friends in that city, gave me the following illustration of the change wrought in the heart of Mr. Waterhouse :

"A few weeks before you arrived I went into his office and begged him to contribute on a scale worthy of his ability to a very needy cause which I presented, and he offered me three pounds. I declined to take it, and arose abruptly to leave his office ; he called me back and said, ' I will give you five pounds.' That is all I could squeeze out of him, and I wanted at least a hundred. A few weeks after his conversion I went into his office to enlist his interest in a cause not half so important as the one I previously submitted to him ; when I mentioned the subject, before I had time to present any argument, he said, 'All right, Mr. Kingsborough, I will give you a cheque for two hundred pounds, and if you need more call again.' The iceberg had melted and from it flowed the living waters.

I extended my evangelising labours through all the towns of any note of South Australia, preaching the sound, simple Gospel which, through the Holy Spirit, was made the power of God unto the salvation of multitudes of those very interesting people.

The three annual sessions of the Australasian Conference, held during the period of my labours within its bounds, covering a period of nearly three years, reported a net increase in their Churches of over eleven thousand members. Of course this was the outcome of long preparatory work, and a hearty co-operation everywhere of ministers and people in conjunction with my leadership on the lines of special evangelising effort.

I made a great gain by amending, through the teaching of the Holy Spirit, our old orthodox definition of saving faith. By the old formula we said to a seeking sinner, "Do you renounce your sins, consent to part with whatever is wrong and do right ? to avow your allegiance to God without reserve ? If so, then you have only to believe and be saved. Believe that Jesus died for you and rose again. Believe that He is able to save to the uttermost all that come to God by Him. Believe that He is able to save you. Believe that He is willing to save you. Believe that He is willing to save you now. Take one step more, and believe that He saves you ;

not that He has saved you, not that He will save you, but that He saves you now." This was our old Methodist formula from the days of Wesley down, and countless thousands have been saved by faith through its presentation.

Every line of it is simple and sound except the last. When we say to a penitent soul, "Believe that He saves you now," suppose in point of fact He doesn't; then he is told to believe what is not true. When a poor sinner reaches the *now* when God saves him, God notifies him of His pardon by His Holy Spirit, and the Holy Spirit regenerates him, and his salvation becomes a matter of fact; not a matter of belief, but a matter of experience which he knows, and to which, as a witness, he bears testimony. The redeeming feature of our old method of teaching was in the fact that it insisted on a continuance of the struggle on the part of the penitent, until he received the direct witness of the Spirit, and consciously realised His renewing work in his heart. It is, therefore, as a whole, incalculably superior to a more modern yet popular way of teaching penitents the way of faith—saying, for example, to a sinner, "'He that believeth on the Son hath everlasting life.' Don't you believe on the Son ?"

"Yes, of course I do; everybody who is not an infidel believes on the Son."

"Then if you believe on the Son you have everlasting life."

The sinner replies, "I am a poor hardened sinner; I have no evidence that I have been accepted of God; I certainly feel no change in my heart."

"Oh, it is not a matter of feeling at all, it is a matter of faith. 'He that believeth on the Son hath everlasting life;' you believe on the Son, therefore, you have everlasting life. Just take your Bible and go into Christian work and show others this way of faith."

Suppose such a teacher should present the documentary credentials of a great physician to a man groaning under an attack of cholera, and read the papers to the poor fellow, and say, "Do you believe that ?"

"Yes, I have heard of that doctor before; I believe that."

"Then you are cured."

"Oh, these cramps are getting worse; they will kill me if I don't get relief."

"Now hold on, just read this again; I will read it over to you."

"Yes."

"Now you read it over yourself."

"Yes."

"You firmly believe that ?"

"Why, yes, certainly I believe that."

"Then you are cured."

"I don't feel that I am cured."

"Oh, it is not a matter of feeling at all, it is a matter of faith."

That is an illustrative parallel case.

In the analysis of saving faith we have, first, the natural functions of faith; second, the spiritual power of faith through the operation of the Holy Ghost; third, the basis of faith, documentary and verbal —the documentary credentials of the doctor, corroborated by the testimony of witnesses who have been cured under his treatment; fourth, the act of faith, which is the act of submitting to treatment and receiving the doctor. That act of faith necessarily precedes the cure. We feel our need, we examine the facts and evidences; we thus get confidence in the doctor, consent to the treatment, and accept him as our physician. Then if the doctor has the skill adequate, by the blessing of God, he effects a cure, and the cure becomes a matter of permanent consciousness, and the ground of testimony to the facts of the case. Thus the act of saving faith on the part of the penitent sinner is the act of receiving Christ.

"As many as received Him, to them gave He power to become the sons of God, even to them that believe on His name." Believing on His name implies a perception of what His name imports, derived from His credentials, documentary and verbal, leading to a surrender to Him and an acceptance of Him.

The end or object of repentance, therefore, is unreserved submission to the will of God, abandoning self and all hope in self, and the act of faith is the act of receiving Christ. But that is a thing of the heart as well as of the head.

"With the heart man believeth unto righteousness," but "the heart is deceitful above all things, and desperately wicked: who can know it?" God knoweth the hearts and trieth the reins of the children of men. God alone is competent to know when a poor sinner submits and receives Christ. The moment He sees any poor sinner thus surrender, abandon hope in everything else, and receive Christ, no matter whether by ten years' or ten minutes' repentance, that moment the eternal Father, through the merit and mediation of Jesus Christ, acquits the believing penitent; as a judge He acquits him at the bar of justice; as a Father He forgives him. That part of the transaction is called justification by faith. That transpires at the mediatorial throne, hard by the throne of immutable justice. In this wonderful transaction mercy and truth meet together, righteousness and peace kiss each other. That changes the relation of the poor sinner from that of a condemned criminal to citizenship in the kingdom of God, and from that of a poor prodigal outcast to restored filial union with God. Then, "because he is a son, God sends forth the Spirit of His Son into his heart, crying, Abba, Father." "The Spirit Himself beareth witness with our spirit, that we are the children of God." The Spirit Himself, not by proxy, angelic or human, notifies him of the wonderful transaction that has just transpired before the throne, and, simultaneously with this notification, he throttles the lusts of the flesh and purges them out—"adultery, fornication, uncleanness, lasciviousness, idolatry, witchcraft, hatred, variance, emulations, wrath, strife, seditions, heresies, envyings, murders, drunkenness, revellings, and such like"—plenty more of the same sort—and sluices and renews the premises by "the washing of regeneration and renewing of the Holy Ghost," which is followed immediately by the fruits of the Spirit—"love, joy, peace, long-suffering, gentleness, goodness, faith, meekness, temperance,"—working by love, purifying the heart, manifesting itself appropriately in words and deeds.

During my twenty-three years as a minister of the Gospel, up to that date, I used the old orthodox formula, " Believe that He is able to save you, believe that He is willing to save you, believe that He is willing to save you now, take one step more and believe that He saves you ; " it is all sound and reliable except the last clause. All through those years I was puzzled and perplexed at that point ; I kept the poor fellows on their knees for days or weeks or months till they obtained the witness of the Spirit of their pardon. I had such a dread of heterodoxy that I never called in question, in all that time, the soundness right through of this definition of faith. I was led by the Spirit in the beginning of my work in Australia to appreciate the value of the word "accept," and later accompanied with it the word "receive," in their highest and best use. "As many as received Him, to them gave He power to become the sons of God;" and "as ye have therefore received Christ Jesus the Lord, so walk ye in Him." Of course I had seen these words before in our hymns ; I saw them when a boy in the Catechism of the Presbyterian Church and in the Scriptures ; but the place where they belonged, with all their vital force and effectiveness, is preoccupied by a fallacy, "Believe that He saves you now ;" and they thus become practically obsolete.

So I at once, for my own use, amended the formula, and the rapidity with which thousands received Christ and testified to the facts of their conscious pardon and regeneration through the Spirit, and the exemplification of it in their lives, and the permanency of the work, led me to shout, "Eureka!" and a part of my mission ever since has been to spread through all English-speaking countries of any note in the world, and far into heathenism, this simple, sound, practical definition of saving faith.

My evangelistic services in South Australia extended to all the towns in the colony of any note, and were attended with the demonstration of the Holy Spirit to the salvation of multitudes of her lovable people.

I had for some time been in correspondence with my wife and children in regard to their joining me in Australia. The matter was favourably considered at both ends of the line, but their coming was postponed from time to time till it became a question of doubt whether or not they would come at all.

I became acquainted in Victoria with a Baptist missionary from India by the name of Smith, who interested me in the stupendous work to be wrought in that empire, and in the possibility of reaching housands of them through the English language, especially through the agency of the Eurasians, who had learned the English language from their fathers and also the native language of their mothers, and were, therefore, a valuable go-between class, bridging the gulf between a stranger and the native masses. So I made up my mind that, completing my work in the Australian colonies, I would take India on my route home to California and see what the Lord would do through my agency in India.

So I wrote my family that by a given date I would be off for India. If they should come in time I would take them with me. If they should come after my departure they could follow on and find me at Bombay or Calcutta, or some other centre of that great country.

When nearly through with my engagements in South Australia I received a telegram from Sydney, New South Wales, informing me that my wife and three sons, Stuart, Ross, and Edward, had arrived in that city, and were comfortably settled in the family of my friend Dr. Moffitt, all in good health and cheer. They had come from California to Sydney in a sailing vessel loaded with wheat.

They had some adventures and some perils by the way. Their captain and crew picked up a man, so nearly dead as to be insensible, from the wreck of a ship that had foundered at sea. He was restored to health, but one of their own passengers was taken ill and died and was buried at sea.

I responded by telegram, that by a given date I would complete my work in South Australia and would meet them in Sydney. A few days later I received a telegram announcing that Stuart, our eldest son, was very low with fever. So I wept and cried to God and hastened my departure from the scene of my recent labours. I had just written, in connection with my daily work, my book entitled " Reconciliation ; or, How to be Saved," and on my voyage from South Australia of a thousand miles to Sydney I wrote my book " Infancy and Manhood of Christian Life."

The steamer from Melbourne to Sydney was packed from stem to stern with a crowd of fast men who were on their way to Sydney to a shooting match. They spent their evenings largely around the dining table playing cards, smoking cigars, drinking brandy, and cracking jokes. So my book on holiness, which has had a circula tion of about thirty thousand copies, was mainly written in the midst of that crowd by the same light in which they were playing cards with oaths from the unlucky losers.

I had not seen my family for over four years. I kissed my wife and wept. Ross had grown out of my knowledge ; I took him into my arms and kissed him and said, " Ross, do you know me ? "

He said, " Yes, papa."

" How did you come to know me ? "

" My mother told me it was you."

So he received me by faith based on his mother's testimony.

Then Edward, who was only two years old when I left him, came in. I took him into my arms and kissed him and said, " Do you know me ? "

" Yes, papa."

" How did you come to know me ? "

"Oh, I remember you very well."

He probably remembered me by my photo, with which he was familiar. Our poor son Stuart was suspended in a doubtful scale between life and death. Dr. Moffitt, an eminent physician, in consultation with another, were doing the best they could. Ross, Edward, and I went into a retired place in the suburbs of the city and had a prayer meeting for their brother. I prayed with all the earnestness of a broken heart; Ross prayed, and Edward prayed, and the three of us wept together. Soon Stuart began to show signs of recovery. We were then on the eve of the hot season in Australia. Dr. Moffitt said that Stuart would certainly die if he remained in Australia during the hot season. To go to India would be no better. He said the only ground of hope he could see was to take him to South Africa. "Go," said he, "by a sailing ship, and spend the hottest part of the year in the Southern Hemisphere at sea, and arrive in Cape Town at the close of the hot season."

So within a fortnight Stuart was able to be carried aboard the steamer and we proceeded to Melbourne, and, after a few days of rest there, we went on to South Australia. From there we got passage on a clipper sailing ship, *St. Vincent*, to Cape Town, South Africa.

God had a most important mission for me to fulfil in South Africa.

PART FIFTH

MISSION TO SOUTH AFRICA

CHAPTER XVIII

THE BEGINNING AT CAPE COLONY

I HAVE now narrated the providential circumstances that first carried me to Africa. It was the southern part of the continent to which I was born by the ship *St. Vincent*, and anchored in Table Bay, Cape of Good Hope, at sunset, March 30th, 1866.

This colony, like Australia and Canada, is ruled by a governor (appointed by the home government), assisted by an executive council, as well as by upper and lower houses of Parliament, respectively named the Legislative Council and the House of Assembly. The council contains fifteen members, eight of whom are elected by the votes in the western districts, and seven by those in the eastern province, while the assembly comprises forty-six members, elected by the various constituencies throughout the colony. The judicial establishment comprises the Supreme Court, of four judges, who hold sessions in Cape Town, and circuit courts in the country districts ; also an eastern province high court of judicature. The numerous courts of resident magistrates, in all the larger villages, exercise limited jurisdiction in all civil and criminal cases.

Cape Town, the capital of the colony, is located at the base of Table Mountain, which rises very precipitously to an elevation of about four thousand feet, and is nearly as flat as a table on the top and often covered with a light, fleecy mist, gently dropping over the edge like a tablecloth. The mountain constitutes a grand background for the city, and contrasts beautifully with the splendid flower gardens and groves of oak and Scotch firs which abound at its base, in and around the city. Cape Town has a population of 28,547 (1866), of which 15,118 are whites, about 12,500 Malays, and 1000 Hottentots and Kaffirs.

There are three large Dutch Reformed churches in Cape Town, containing an aggregate of three thousand members. Rev. Andrew Murray, Jr., pastor of one of them, a liberal and thoroughly evangelical man, was Moderator of the Synod. His father, Rev. Andrew Murray, an old pioneer minister in the Dutch Reformed Church in South Africa, has given three highly accomplished and pious sons to her ministry. There are three Protestant Episcopal churches in the city, one Presbyterian, one Independent, one Evangelical Lutheran, and two Wesleyan—one for English and one for coloured Dutch.

My friend, Henry Reed, in one of his voyages to Australia stopped, in the year 1840, in company with his family, at Cape Town. Rev. Mr. Hodgson, who had been labouring for some years as a Wesleyan missionary among the natives in the Orange River country, was then Superintendent of the Cape Town Circuit, and greatly interested Mr. Reed with a narrative of his adventures in the interior, and introduced to him a Christian native man who had just come with a waggon from Orange River to Cape Town.

This native man was a Christian hero, as the following facts related by Mr. Hodgson to Mr. Reed will show. The lions in the Orange River country, when they get old and too stiff or too lazy to follow their trade of catching bucks and other active animals, sometimes crouch about the kraals and pounce upon a man ; and when they begin that kind of work they soon acquire such cannibal proclivities as to become very troublesome customers.

An old lion had been making some such unwelcome visits to the kraal to which this Christian native belonged, and one day he and two others took each a gun and went out in search of him, hoping to make a final settlement with him. A few miles distant from the kraal, passing over the brow of a ridge into a little vale, they suddenly surprised a large lion feeding on the remains of an animal carcass. The lion, preferring fresh meat, seemed glad to see them, and without ceremony advanced to give them a greeting. The men, in their sudden fright, declined the interview and ran for life. The Christian man quite outran his two heathen compatriots ; but as he was making away with himself as fast as he could the thought struck him : " One of those men will be killed ; neither is prepared to die ! I am prepared, thank God ! I had better die, and give them time for repentance ! " He instantly stopped and faced about ; the two men passed him, and before he could transfer his thoughts from his heroic consent to die for his heathen neighbour to a purpose of self-defence with his gun the lion was upon him. With the force of a mighty bound the lion struck him on the breast with his paw and tore off the skin and flesh to the bone. Then with his forefeet upon the body of his victim he took one of his arms in his mouth and crunched and mangled it. Then he got the stock of the gun between his teeth and ground it to splinters. Meantime the others, seeing their friend down, returned near enough for a sure shot ; both fired, and the lion dropped dead beside his bleeding victim.

Brother Reed examined the deep scars left by the paws of the lion, which the noble fellow would carry to his grave. " Scarcely for a righteous man will one die : yet peradventure for a good man some would even dare to die. But God commendeth His love toward us, in that, while we were yet sinners, Christ died for us." And here was one of Africa's sable sons so imbued with the self-sacrificing spirit of Jesus that even for a bad man he was willing to die.

On my first Sabbath in Cape Town—1st of April—I preached at two Wesleyan chapels. The limited capacity of the chapels and the smallness of the congregations contrasted unfavourably with the fine churches and packed audiences of Australia.

In the afternoon of the 7th of April I attended the anniversary meeting of the Wesleyan Sunday-schools and delivered an address on the Gospel doctrine of having all the children converted and trained for God. Rev. Andrew Murray gave an exhortation.

Brother Filmer, one of the superintendents, in his speech said: " Seventeen years ago we had a revival in this town ; about fifty souls were soundly converted to God ; some of them have become missionaries, and others remain useful members of the Church. Then five years ago we had another revival, principally among the Sunday-school children. About forty professed to find peace with God. Some of them have fallen away, but the most of them have remained steadfast, and I find some of them among our Sunday-school teachers now, and others are useful members of the Church. I am now feeling, hoping, and believing that we are on the eve of another outpouring of the Holy Spirit."

I thought, " Well, such revivals during a period of seventeen years are much better than nothing, but fall very far short of God's purpose and provisions in Christ and the spiritual demands of nearly thirty thousand sinners."

On Sabbath, April 8th, I commenced a series of special services in Burg Street Wesleyan Chapel, which were kept up for nine days. A few seekers came forward the first night, ten and upward each night of the series till the last, when the altar was crowded with about thirty seekers ; but our congregations were not large, and the whole machinery of church agency seemed very weak.

The members of the church seemed very willing to do what they could, and I believe they were much strengthened, and twenty-one souls were reported by Brother Hardey as giving satisfactory testimony to the fact of their conversion to God.

We had so many seekers the last night in Cape Town that I felt rather sorry to leave, but I had to go then or wait probably a month for the next regular steamer. So on Wednesday, April 18th, I took passage on the steamer *Natal*, a clean, comfortable little boat of four hundred tons, for Port Elizabeth. We expected to reach Algoa Bay on Friday, but in consequence of head winds and rough weather we did not arrive till Saturday afternoon.

REV. JOHN RICHARDS, the Superintendent of Port Elizabeth Circuit, met me at the wharf and kindly conducted me to his house.

I spent two weeks in Port Elizabeth, preached sixteen sermons, and lectured one night on " Reminiscences of Palestine." We had from ten to twenty seekers forward every night, and conversions to God on each occasion, but how many were saved I know not, as the minister said he knew them and did not, so far as I know, keep a record of their names. I had a preaching service on Saturday night for the natives—Kaffirs and Fingoes. The chapel, seating about three hundred and fifty persons, was filled. William Barnabas, a good man, local preacher and native teacher, was my interpreter. I felt very awkward in preaching through an interpreter, and being very weary from excessive labours through the week, I did not enjoy the service, and saw but little indication of good from the effort.

On the second Sabbath, besides the regular morning and evening preaching for the whites, I preached in the afternoon from the court house steps. A little shower of rain at the time of assembling kept many away, but we had out about six hundred persons, and it was a profitable service. I thus preached the Gospel to two or three hundred who would not otherwise have heard it from me. During preaching a funeral procession passed close by. The subject suiting the occasion, I illustrated it by the dead returning to dust.

On the evening of my arrival in Port Elizabeth Brother Richards introduced me to the first Kaffir I had ever seen. He stood before me six feet four inches, with finely developed form, good head, very pleasant countenance, and a superior display of ivory. " This man," said Brother Richards, " is one of our local preachers, Joseph Tale, from the Annshaw Circuit, about one hundred and fifty miles in the interior." Through William Barnabas I asked him many questions about the work of God among his people. He gave a very encouraging account of the number and steadfastness of their people on the Annshaw Mission. I told him that when my boxes were opened I would give him some books. He said his children could read English, and they would read them to him. I felt great sympathy with the native work, and deep regret that I could not preach to them. I had no faith in successful preaching through an interpreter.

Brother Richards made me a plan for a two months' tour, embracing Graham's Town, King William's Town, Queenstown, Cradock, and Somerset, each appointment about eighty miles from the next. I should have two weeks for Graham's Town, and a week for each of the other places, and a week at Port Elizabeth, on my return, in waiting for a steamer to take me on to Natal. He accordingly informed the ministers of my arrival, and they all wrote me a cordial invitation to visit them, and with them came pressing invitations from Salem, Bathurst, Fort Beaufort, and Uitenhage Circuits. The last two I added to my plan. I made no provision for preaching to the natives, for not knowing their language I did not hope to be able to work successfully among them.

On the 5th of May I went from Port Elizabeth to the beautiful town of Uitenhage. At Port Elizabeth I had been sojourning a few days at the house of Mr. W. Jones, a somewhat eccentric but very genial Welshman and a local preacher in the Wesleyan Church.

Brother Jones gave me the use of his carriage and two horses and his son Philip to drive me to Uitenhage. We took with us Mrs. John Richards and Miss Jessie Jones. Sister Richards was in such a poor state of health when I arrived that she feared she would not be able to attend many of my meetings, but as she entered into the work her health improved, and after two weeks' special services at home was now going to help me a week among her friends in Uitenhage, among whom she was blessed in doing a work for God. During our journey that day she took occasion to say that she had been greatly edified by my Gospel ministrations, and was much pleased with me in everything she had seen except my beard, in regard to which she put me on my defence.

I said, "Sister Richards, when I was in Belfast a Primitive minister waited on me to say, ' There are some good people in this city who are greatly prejudiced against a beard, and I think you could be more useful among them if you will go to a barber and get shaved.' In reply I said, 'I would not do anything which would be damaging to any person following my example; for instance, I don't use tobacco in any form, I don't use wine or spirits, except sacrament-ally or medicinally. I have been a total abstainer from my youth, for the good of others, as well as for myself. As to the beard, while in the genial climate of California with youthful vigour on my side, I did not feel the need of it, and wasted much precious time in cutting it off; but having returned from California to the Eastern States of America my thin jaws were exposed to the north-west blasts of New York, Wisconsin and Iowa, which gave me neuralgia, and I suffered what appeared to be almost the pains of death. So I found that I was obliged to seek protection for my face, and instead of bundling up in a sheepskin and an artificial respirator, the constant readjustment of which would consume time and give trouble, I just threw aside that barbarous instrument, the razor, to see what the God of providence would do for me; and this flowing beard was the result, and it answered the purpose exactly. I soon got well of neuralgia, and have never had it since. I have found it a good comforter, a good respirator, a good shield against the reflecting rays of the summer sun, which used always to blister my face and crack my lips till I could neither laugh nor sing without the shedding of blood. Moreover, it was a protection against gnats and flies. By a deep inspiration in preaching, which is essential, I used sometimes to take down one of those pestiferous little fellows into my throat, and then followed a sudden change in the exercises. I have suffered from none of these things since I submitted to the Lord's arrangement, planting the beard where it was needed. I have found it of great service to my vocal organs, and hence necessary to my work of preaching the Gospel, and to cut it off is to impair my working effectiveness, and so far a sin against God.' With that the Irish brother said, 'I suppose it is not worth while to say anything more about it.' 'No, my dear brother, I cannot do a wrong thing on any account, and I also like to help to break down an unreasonable prejudice in this matter, under the influence of which many a poor Irishman is daily shedding tears through the operations of an old dull razor.' The good people of Belfast soon got over their prejudice against my beard, and we had a blessed work of God during my stay among the sinners of that city."

Uitenhage is an old Dutch town located on the slope of a beautiful valley near the banks of Zwartkops River.

The number of converts during our brief series in Uitenhage was not reported to me; but there was manifestly a deep and general awakening in the town, and among the converts were some influential persons, who made valuable members of the Church, I doubt not.

On Friday we returned to Port Elizabeth, where I delivered a lecture on "St. Paul and his Times;" and at 5 a.m., Saturday, my kind host, Brother Sydney Hill, saw me safely into the post cart, a rough conveyance on two wheels, drawn by four horses, and that day, while I was resting, I was jolted over a rough road to Graham's Town.

After a hard ride in the post cart ninety miles from Port Elizabeth I arrived in Graham's Town at 6 p.m. My home was with Mr. W. A. Richards, one of the proprietors of the *Journal*, a large triweekly, having the greatest circulation of any paper in the colony. He was a stepson of the founder and senior member of the firm, the Hon. R. Godlonton, who was a colonist of forty-six years' standing, and an old Wesleyan as well, and for many years a member of the Legislative Council, or upper house of the Colonial Parliament; yet he was really a spiritually-minded, useful member and active worker in the Church.

On Sabbath, May 13th, we had Commemoration Chapel crowded three times with a superior-looking class of people, with a sprinkling of redcoats (English soldiers) among them. In the morning I preached from the last words of Jesus, "But ye shall receive power, after that the Holy Ghost is come upon you: and ye shall be witnesses unto Me both in Jerusalem, and in all Judæa, and in

Samaria, and unto the uttermost part of the earth." In commencing a series of special services I always preach first to believers on a subject embracing the personality, immediate presence, and special mission of the Holy Ghost and the adjustment of human agents to His gracious arrangements as essential to success.

At 3 p.m. I preached to the children, with as many adults as could crowd into the church. At night I preached specially to sinners. At the opening of the prayer meeting which followed I invited seekers of pardon to present themselves at the altar of prayer, but not one came. I knew that the awakening Spirit had thrust His piercing sword into the hearts of many sinners, but did not press them to come forward. Many believers were greatly disappointed in not seeing some go forward, but thought it was the pleasure of the Holy Spirit thus to set the Church more fully back to their home work of self-examination and more thorough preparation for the coming struggle for the rescue of perishing souls.

On Monday many leading brethren called to bid me welcome; but all expressed their disappointment at the results of the labours of the day previous and their great sorrow that the Church was in such a low spiritual state. They spoke gratefully of a work of God in 1822 at Salem, twenty miles distant, and a second revival in 1830, in Graham's Town, which extended to some of the country circuits. Their third and great revival was in 1837, when about three hundred souls were saved. A fourth revival, less extensive, but really a very good work, especially among the young people, took place in 1857; but now they felt a painful sense of coldness and ineffectiveness. I assured them that as soon as they were ready for an advance movement the Holy Spirit would lead them on to victory. I reminded them of the carnal obstructions to the work of God in the Church, which must be sought out and removed by individual repentance and reformation, through faith; and that there was at least one serious physical difficulty in the way. "Your beautiful church is not by one half sufficiently ventilated for a large audience. The immense amount of carbonic acid gas thrown out from the lungs of fourteen hundred persons, and the porous discharge of matter from their bodies must on each occasion poison the atmosphere in the church in a very short time. This poison, being inhaled, corrupts the blood, blunts the nervous sensibilities of the people, and hence precludes vigorous mental action, produces headache and drowsiness, and sadly injures their health; and when it comes to that, the best thing is to quit and go home as quickly as possible. We can't afford to spend our precious evenings there in poisoning each other, for that is the very kind of stuff that killed the British soldiers in the Black Hole of Calcutta. It is out of the question to have a great work of salvation without a good supply of oxygen."

They could not readily realise that their really splendid church could be so defective in anything, but expressed a willingness to make such changes as might be found to be necessary.

We had to go thoroughly into the subject of ventilating the chapel.

I begged them to employ a competent mechanic to put ventilating apertures in the windows above and below. They had two such on each side of the chapel in the windows below, but none above. But to make any permanent change a meeting of the trustees must be called, and perhaps much time consumed in the preliminaries before the work could be effected. So, to close the debate and secure the end by a short method, Brother Atwell, one of the trustees, who was allowed to do daring things without being called to account, because all who knew him felt sure that under all circumstances he would do what he conscientiously believed to be the right thing, went into the gallery, hammer in hand, and knocked a pane of glass out of each window on both sides, which afforded a good supply of fresh air for our crowded audiences, and thus removed a physical barrier to our success and gave us a wide-awake people to preach to.

On Monday night we had the church well filled above and below. Nearly enough remained for the prayer meeting to fill the main audience room of the church. Over thirty seekers came promptly forward, and about a dozen of them were justified by faith, and obtained "peace with God, through our Lord Jesus Christ."

Volumes might be filled with the details of what was said and done in connection with our series of meetings in Graham's Town, but I will simply give a few specimen illustrative facts of a work which in extent, numerically, was limited compared with the numbers saved during a series of the same length in any of the Australian cities. But the work in Graham's Town was of vast importance, not only in its local effect, but in its far-reaching influence on the extensive mission field among the surrounding African tribes.

On Thursday, the 24th of May, out on the hills overlooking Graham's Town, in the mimosa scrub, we had a Wesleyan celebration of the Queen's birthday. It was a delightful social entertainment, where I had an opportunity of speaking to many friends, and among them many of the young converts. Mr. H——, a tall man with a heavy beard, came to me as soon as I alighted from Brother Richards's carriage in the grove, and said : " Mr. Taylor, I have come to ask your pardon for what I have been thinking about you. I felt so badly under your preaching that I went forward to the altar last Thursday night, but I felt worse and worse. Just beside me was a woman who was in such an agony of distress that I soon began to neglect my own case in my sympathy for her. I wondered that you did not come at once and do something for her, and while I was looking and hoping that you would come I saw you walk past her. Now, I am telling you this that I may ask your pardon for what I had been thinking about you. When I saw that woman's flowing tears and saw you pass without seeming to notice her, I got angry and wanted to pull your beard. Knowing that such a proceeding would not be suitable to the occasion, I got up and went away.

" Last Sabbath, when you preached in the Market Square, I stood so near to you that I could see into your eyes, and saw there such a flood of sympathy for sinners that I was fully convinced that I had done you great injustice in my mind, and felt ashamed that I had allowed such feelings so to influence my conduct. Then I began again in earnest to seek the Lord. Last night, during the prayer meeting, I surrendered my soul to God and accepted Jesus Christ as my Saviour, and immediately I was filled with unspeakable joy. Now I see that you were right all the time, and that you understood the woman's case and that I did not ; that she had to feel her own utter helplessness and surrender herself to God."

On the second Sabbath night of our series I saw an interesting-looking man at the altar of prayer in an agony of soul on account of sin. Several good brethren stood near him, and said to me, as I was about to speak to the penitent, "This is one of our best members," pointing to the man at the altar. "He is not simply a nominal member, but an active worker, reproving sin and trying to do good daily, and also the superintendent of one of our Sabbath schools. He is subject to seasons of great darkness, and is now under a cloud : but it is all the result of severe temptations."

At the close of the following week the said seeker came to see me and related his experience, in substance as follows :

He was first awakened when twelve years old, but, having no one to instruct him, gradually lost his convictions of sin. Then, twenty years ago, he was greatly awakened, and resolved to be a servant of God, and joined the Wesleyan Church. "For several years I strove hard to live right, and attended all the means of grace within my reach. Then I became acquainted with a very bad man, who was the means of leading me astray, and for a short time I was out of the Church; but I was very wretched, and made a sincere and humble confession, and was again admitted to the Wesleyan Church. I then doubled my diligence in trying to work out my salvation with fear and trembling. I often fasted from Wednesday till Friday.

"Once during my fast I received an order to perform a hazardous duty as a sergeant in the army. Some of my fellow-soldiers begged me to break my fast, or I could not accomplish my work ; but I kept to my fast, and though in a very weak state fulfilled my duty. I have spent many days in prayer in the kloofs and caves of the mountains, and often wished that by laying down my life I could get relief for my soul. I once resolved to die on my knees or get relief. I got some relief, but did not get salvation. I have for some time been teaching school, and have been trying to do good in the Sunday-school, but got no rest for my soul. During the first week of your preaching I was thoroughly waked up, but I felt very bitter against you. By last Sabbath I felt so badly, so guilty before God, that I could not show my face, but spent the day alone in the hills, trying to pray. But on Sabbath night I went again to hear you preach, and when you appealed to murmurers against God, and asked them if they would be willing to have their miserable existence terminated by annihilation, I responded in my heart, 'Yes, I would hail such an opportunity with gladness.' I then went forward, but found no peace.

"But the next night, in your sermon on believing, you unravelled every knot of unbelief by which I have been held down all these years. Your account of that man in Mudgee, New South Wales, who said, 'I can't believe, oh, I can't believe,' suited my case exactly, and I said, 'I'll never use that fatal expression again. I do submit myself to God, living or dying, to do with me just as He likes. I do believe His record concerning His Son. I do have confidence in Jesus as an all-sufficient Saviour of the very chief of sinners. I do accept Him as my Saviour now.' I began then at once to get hold on Christ by faith, and while they were singing, 'Oh, the bleeding Lamb! He was found worthy,' I clearly realised, what I had always admitted in theory, that though I should give all my goods to feed the poor, and my body to be burned, it would profit me nothing; but the Lamb of God, slain for sinners, was indeed a sufficient sacrifice for my sins, and I did accept Him then as my Saviour. I returned home quietly resting on Christ as my Saviour. About one o'clock that night, while steadily clinging to Jesus, the Holy Spirit so manifested the pardoning love of God to my heart that I could not restrain my joyous emotions, but went and waked up Mr. G—— and told him that I was saved, and we praised God together. If a legion of angels had told me that all my sins were forgiven I could not have had a clearer evidence than I had within my heart through God's witnessing Spirit."

It must not be supposed that such a work can be wrought in any place without strongly exciting the antagonistic forces of carnal nature and Satanic power in the hearts of many worldly men and women, and not unfrequently we find some misguided good people who will forbid any person "to cast out devils" who will not follow them.

Many false things and many hard things were said in Graham's Town during the progress of our work by the wicked, and much opposition was manifested in certain quarters where we had a right to expect better things; but as I seldom ever read or listen to such things I will not burden my pages with them.

An extract from a letter written by "mine host," Mr. A. Richards, a month after my departure, may serve to illustrate the continued progress of the work of God in Graham's Town:

"Everything is going on very satisfactorily here. The work of God is widening, extending, deepening. Many are seeking the higher spiritual blessing of holiness of heart. Our house has reason to be thankful and to praise God. We have a prayer meeting in our dining-room every Monday evening. Last night seventy were present. At the mid-day prayer meeting there were one hundred to-day, and a gracious influence was at work." Then after speaking of a number by name who had recently been saved, he adds: "The number of seekers is daily increasing. I should think the devil must feel rather bad at seeing so many of his soldiers returning to

God. He can't say they are rebels against him, for they all belong to God. The work is going on here, too, among the natives. About one hundred are converted, twenty in each of the last three nights."

That was the beginning of a work among the natives there after I left. I did not work among them except to preach one sermon through an interpreter, and found it a very slow business.

The Kaffirs there were blessed with the ministry of my friend, Rev. W. J. Davis, who needed no interpreter, and reported several hundreds of them saved after I was there.

After my lecture on Friday night, the 1st of June, I gave my last words of counsel and exhortation to my dear brethren and sisters in Graham's Town. It was a solemn occasion, for though I never preach farewell sermons, or encourage any ado on the occasion of my final departure from any place, still I am always reminded that Christian love and sympathy, so beautifully illustrated at Miletus, is the same in all ages and among all people.

I had a rough journey of eighty miles before me and my work in King William's Town the following Sabbath. At 4 a.m. of Saturday, June 2nd, Mr. D. Penn called with his cart and two, and we commenced our long day's journey. Brother Penn had a pair of fine travellers, which took us thirty miles to breakfast. Then we got a pair of fresh horses, which he had sent on two days before, and they made the rest of the journey of fifty miles just as the sun sank from view in the western horizon. Brother Penn was an old colonist ; had been in the Kaffir wars ; had had a great variety of experience, and entertained me all the way with marvellous narratives, illustrating colonial life. While I enjoyed them very much I was too weary to note them.

Arriving at King William's Town I was kindly entertained by the superintendent of the circuit, Rev. J. Fish, and his excellent wife.

CHAPTER XX

KING WILLIAM'S TOWN, located on the banks of the Buffalo River, in the midst of a fertile grassy country, was commenced by the establishment of a military post there in 1835. It was subsequently abandoned by the authority of the home government, but re-established in 1848, and became the capital of British Kaffraria, a large tract of country extending from the old eastern boundary of Cape Colony to the Great Kei River. It was settled by an enterprising class of people, and became a flourishing province. The people prayed earnestly for a colonial government of their own ; that being denied them, British Kaffraria was in April, 1866, annexed to Cape Colony. On Wednesday, June 6th, in the midst of our series of services in King William's Town, a Kaffir came running with the message that four missionaries were in the path and would arrive—pointing where the sun would be—a little after noon. In due time we saw in the distance four Englishmen on foot coming into the town, accompanied by a few Kaffirs. Their appearance suggested the sacred historic scene of the Master and His rustic-looking fishermen whom He was teaching to be fishers of men, walking into the city of Capernaum. These brethren had walked from Annshaw mission station, twenty-five miles distant. We watched them with peculiar interest as they approached. One of them I recognised at once as Rev. John Scott, from Graham's Town, and I was introduced to Revs. Lamplough, Hillier, and Sawtell.

Rev. Robert Lamplough had for nearly six years been, and then was, the Wesleyan missionary to King Kama's tribe of Kaffirs, the residence of the king and head of the mission circuit bearing the name of Rev. William Shaw's missionary wife, " Annshaw." I had heard much of Brother Lamplough's faithful ministrations in Graham's Town, where he had laboured before his appointment to the Kaffir work. I had learned also that though he was not much acquainted with the Kaffir language he was preaching successfully through an interpreter. I was therefore very glad to meet him, but could not anticipate the glorious results of our acquaintance with each other.

Brother Lamplough introduced to me his two native candidates for the ministry, whom he had been training for several years. One was William Shaw, son of Kama; the other was Charles Pamla, who belongs to a family of Amazulu chiefs. These, with two others, were the first South African natives proposed for the ministry among the Wesleyans. The Free Church of Scotland had one educated Kaffir minister, Rev. Tio Soga.

William Shaw Kama had given up the prospect of becoming the successor of his father in the chieftainship of his tribe that he might be a missionary to the heathen, and desired to be sent far hence, among those who had not the Gospel. Charles Pamla had sold his farm and good house that he might devote his undivided time and energies to the one work of saving sinners by leading them to the only Saviour. He was about six feet high, muscular, well-proportioned but lean; quite black, with a fine display of ivory; good craniological development, regular features, very pleasant expression, logical cast of mind, and sonorous, powerful voice. He was the man whom God appointed to open for me an effectual door of utterance to the heathen.

Brother Lamplough, Hillier, and Sawtell gave us valuable assistance in our prayer meetings in King William's Town; their Kaffir candidates for the ministry and companions in the local ranks looked on, listened, and learned what they afterward turned to good account. I spent much time with these missionaries and our kind host in conversation on the best methods of missionary enterprise.

On Thursday morning, the 14th of June, Mr. Joseph Walker sent his carriage to take me to Annshaw. We were soon on our way across the Buffalo, a beautiful stream, and up a long range of hills to their summits. There we had a beautiful view of the town we had left, and in every direction a measureless extent of grassy hills and valleys, interspersed with occasional groves of the mimosa and wild aloes and patches of jungle of a great variety of shrubbery and intertwining vines.

About 2 p.m. we saw the silvery serpentine flow of the Keiskamma, and the mission village of Annshaw on its banks. The natives were assembling from all directions and standing round in groups, waiting the arrival of the strange *umfundisi*, and as we descended the hills they came running to meet us and bid us welcome, among whom was King Kama.

King Kama was about six feet in height, well-proportioned, and corpulent. He had a large head, a broad face, very benevolent expression, with the usual, not black, but dark copper colour of the royal line of Kaffir chiefs. He was altogether a noble-looking old man. The colonial government allowed him a small pension. About twelve thousand of his tribe were settled about him and were under his rule, subordinate to the English government in the colony. It is a sad fact, but may be said to illustrate the uphill work of the missionaries among such people, that Kama was the only paramount chief or king in Southern Africa who was connected with any Christian Church. Rev. William Sargent, who established the Annshaw mission station, and hence knew Kama well, told me he heard him, in a missionary address, tell his experience, in which he said: " When I became a Christian my fellow-chiefs and many of my people laughed at me ; said I was a fool, and that I never should become a ruling chief; that my people would throw me away ; that I should become a scabby goat and a vagabond on the earth, without home or friends ; but just the reverse of all that has come to pass. I was then young, and had no people ; my older brothers had a great people, but they rejected Christ, and lost their people and everything they had, and I remain the only ruling chief of my tribe." Kama ever remained true to the Wesleyan Church.

The paramount chief of the Amatembu tribe, from which nearly all the ruling chiefs get their "great wives" (the mothers of the ruling line of paramount chiefs), sent, by a deputation of his counsellors, with all the ceremony due to such an occasion, a young woman to Kama, to become his "great wife." In the olden time a refusal on Kama's part would have furnished an occasion for war. When this party arrived near Kama's "great place" they sat down, according to the ceremony to be observed in approaching a chief, to wait his pleasure. Kama refused to see them, but sent them a bullock that they might slay and eat, and then go about their business. They tarried but a night, and left unceremoniously in the morning.

Kama at this time was poor, and Mr. Shaw advised him to buy a waggon, telling him that it would help him very much. When Kama told his people that he was going to buy a waggon they were afraid, and tried to hinder him in every possible way. But Kama would not listen to them, and so he gave Mr. Shaw ten fat oxen that he might buy a waggon for him in Graham's Town. That waggon made Kama rich, so that in time he had three kraals full of cattle.

Chief Kama lived in a good, substantial house of English style, about three hundred yards from the chapel. The mission house was a large one-story cottage, with verandah extending all along the front. The chapel was a wood building, plain but neat, and seated about six hundred persons. These, with a few square native houses, stood out as the prominent buildings of the place ; next to these, and more interesting to a stranger, were the humble dwellings of the natives. These were, for the most part, round huts.

At the time of my arrival at Annshaw there were in the circuit a Wesleyan membership of six hundred, most of whom were Kama's Kaffirs ; the rest were Fingoes. Charles Pamla, an Amazulu Fingo, had been labouring, principally among Kama's tribe, as an unpaid evangelist for several years.

Brother Lamplough gave me Charles Pamla to interpret for me. Before the service I took him alone and preached my sermon to him, filling his head and heart full of it. After he had heard me preach in King William's Town I asked him if he could put my sermon into Kaffir.

" No, Mr. Taylor, I think I could not. I understood the most of it, but I can only interpret low English, and you speak high English."

I at once determined to study low English. And now when I was preaching to him alone I told him to stop me at every word he could not perfectly understand. I was fully committed to make one more effort at the second-hand mode of preaching through a spokesman. Having gone through with the discourse, I gave my man a talk on naturalness.

"But," said he, "I must speak loudly sometimes."

I then saw that by naturalness he thought I meant simply the conversational style.

"Oh yes," I replied, "as loudly as you like at the right time. The scream of a mother on seeing her child fall into a well is as natural as her lullaby in the nursery. God has given us every variety of vocal power and intonation adapted to express every variety of the soul's emotions, from the softest whispers, like the mellow murmurs of the rippling rill, up to the thundering, crashing voices of the cataract."

I, however, put it into "low" English, so that he understood me perfectly.

At 4 p.m. of Thursday, June 14th, we commenced our first service. I stood in the small pulpit and Charles on the top step by my side. In front we see the crowded audience of natives packed into every square foot of space, including the aisles. The mission station people—men and women—are all clothed in European dress, the headdress of the women consisting of a handkerchief, usually red, turbaned round with some display of taste. The heathens are painted red with ochre, the men wrapped in a blanket, the women wearing a skirt of dressed leather, with headdress, similar to the fashion of the station women.

To our left, in the corner, sat Sister Sawtell, Sister Lamplough, and her children; in the altar below us were the two circuit ministers; on our right, next the wall, were King Kama and the Fingo chief Hlambisa, from Amatola Basin, fifteen miles distant, who ruled a tribe of fifteen thousand Fingoes in the Amatola Mountains. He was Brother Pamla's uncle, but a hardened old heathen with about a dozen wives. We announced as the text the last words of Jesus: "Ye shall receive power, after that the Holy Ghost is come upon you: and ye shall be witnesses unto Me both in Jerusalem, and in all Judæa, and in Samaria, and unto the uttermost part of the earth."

The sermon was entirely to believers. I believe Charles gave every idea and shade of thought as naturally and as definitely as if they had originated in his own brain. Indeed, black as he was, he seemed a transparent medium through which my Gospel thoughts, rendered luminous and mighty by the Holy Spirit's unction, shone brightly through the soul windows—the eyes and ears of my sable hearers—down into the depths of their hearts.

All through the discourse of one hour and a quarter there was a profound silence throughout the assembly, rendered awful in solemnity by the deep consciousness that every one seemed to feel the presence of a power which, like a slumbering earthquake, would soon break forth in manifest grandeur.

After a season of silent prayer at the close of the discourse, silent for a time but slightly interrupted by the uncontrollable emotions of the people, we dismissed the assembly to give a little time for refreshment and reflection before the evening service.

After a hasty tea I went alone with Charles and gave him in detail the sermon for the evening, and we again stood before the people at 8 p.m., and preached to sinners from the text, " As I live, saith the Lord God, I have no pleasure in the death of the wicked ; but that the wicked turn from his way and live : turn ye, turn ye from your evil ways ; for why will ye die ? "

We had about the same congregation, in the same order as in the afternoon.   During the preaching of over an hour the beaming faces of believers, the distorted features of sinners, the tearful eyes of both, all in solemn silence before the Lord, and the voices of His prophets, presented altogether a scene which neither painter nor poet can describe, and yet to be felt and witnessed was to receive an impression never to be effaced while memory endures.

At the close of the discourse I said, " Charles, I will sing a hymn suitable to the subject, but I only know it by memory to the time of the tune and can't line it for you, but I will sing a line at a time and you will put it into Kaffir."   I then sang line by line, leaving time for the translation into another language :—

> " Sinners, hastening down to ruin,
>   Why will ye die?
> Jesus is your soul pursuing ;
>   Why will ye die?" etc.

Charles not only put every line into Kaffir, but after the first verse he gave them the tune as well, though he had never heard it before. When spoken to about it the next day he said that he was not aware of the fact that he had sung it, as he only meant to give the words.

The ministers present seemed to think it the result of an extraordinary inspiration of the Holy Spirit, which was true in a very glorious sense, but I believe the Spirit's work on the whole occasion was perfectly adjusted to the human conditions employed, and did not miraculously rise above or suspend any physical law.   The fact was, I had a very apt scholar for my interpreter.

He had so thoroughly digested my lectures on "naturalness" that, though he had a voice for variety, pathos, and volume so grandly superior that he could not be an ape, yet in his own natural voice he gave every intonation of mine, running through at least two octaves during the discourse ; so when he commenced to render the lines which I was singing he seemed at first a little confused, for he had lost the keynote of my intonations, but soon his voice mounted up into the regions of song, and echoed perfectly as a keyed instrument my singing tones, just as he had before echoed my speaking tones.

Through all the preaching service, addressed mainly to the intellect, conscience, and will, there was the keen piercing of the Spirit's sword, and deep awakening, but profound silence.

Before the prayer meeting commenced I explained the simple

plan of salvation by faith to the seekers collectively just as I would to each one personally. Then we invited all who had intelligently and determinedly decided to surrender themselves to God and accept Christ as their Saviour to come forward to the front forms. They came at once as fast as they could press their way. Beginning at the front forms, they filled form after form with seekers, till at least two hundred penitents were down on their knees. There was no loud screaming of any one above the rest, but their pent-up emotions now found vent in audible prayers, sighs, groans, and floods of tears.

When the prayer meeting had thus progressed for about fifteen minutes, Brother L—— said, "Had we not better dismiss them and let them go off alone and seek by the river? The old missionaries have told me that it will not do to let them give way to their feelings, lest they run into wild extravagance. They will go off to the river and pray all night."

"Why, my dear brother," I replied, "this is not a rush of blind emotional excitement. The most of these people have been under your teaching for years, and we have just explained the way of salvation to them, so that under the enlightening power of the Spirit every child here of ten years can understand it. They are now intelligently coming to Jesus. The Holy Spirit is leading them. Why interrupt them at this most important juncture and send them off to the river to battle with Satan alone, and take a bad cold as well? They are emotional beings, to be sure, and have not the same control of their feelings as the mass of Europeans; but all the noise of this occasion is in beautiful harmony with all the facts in their case. This is unquestionably the work of God. We will just keep our hands off the ark of God, and let the Holy Ghost attend to His own business in His own way."

Upon reflection Brother Lamplough heartily concurred and entered most earnestly into the work. It was not long before they began to enter into the liberty of the children of God. As fast as they found peace the new converts were separated from the seekers and seated apart on the other side of the chapel. They were then quiet as the Gadarene "sitting at the feet of Jesus, clothed and in his right mind." All were personally examined as to their experience, and the names of those who gave a satisfactory testimony to their having obtained peace with God, through an acceptance of Jesus Christ, were written down, that the pastor might the more readily find them and get them at once into the visible fold of the Church. At the close of the prayer meeting it was found that seventy souls had professed to find remission of their sins that night. To me it was the harmony of heaven. I felt an indescribable joy, not simply on account of the great work of God in the salvation of the Kaffirs, which was an occasion of joy to the angels of God, but especially because the spell that bound me within the lines of my native language was broken. I could now preach effectively through an interpreter, and the heathen world seemed suddenly opened to my personal enterprise as an ambassador for Christ.

Friday, the 15th of June, at 10 a.m., we preached again to about the same crowd we had the preceding day, and continued the prayer-meeting service till 2 p.m. During the three services one hundred and fifteen persons professed to obtain pardon of their sins.

After a hasty dinner Mr. Harper took me over the hills thirteen miles to his house in Alice, also called Lovedale. One of the industrial schools, established under the patronage of Governor Grey, was located in that lovely dale. It was under the direction of the Scotch Presbyterian missions, and was being carried on, I was informed, with a good degree of success. Getting in late, and leaving next morning, I could not give myself the pleasure of visiting the institution. The Wesleyans had a comfortable chapel there, small, but large enough for the demands of the village. I preached there that night to a full chapel. Most of them were very serious and attentive, but one man, well-dressed and apparently influential, kept up a sort of incredulous scoffing, grinning all the time. In extraordinary contrast with the results of the preceding night not one seeker responded to the call so far as to say, " What must I do to be saved?" Many, I believe, however, were awakened, who followed us to Fort Beaufort, thirteen miles distant, and afterward, there and at Heald Town, embraced Christ. A good work in Alice followed, and a healthy young society was organised there.

At Fort Beaufort, twenty-five miles from Annshaw, I received a letter from Brother Lamplough, dated June 19th, which indicates the progress of the work in Kama's tribe.

" My dear Brother,—Never was such a work seen among the natives of Kama's tribe before, and I question whether there has ever been such a work for power and rapidity in this country before. To have about three hundred souls brought to God in less than five days is indeed a glorious thing, especially when we consider that no more than a thousand people have been brought within the sphere of the influence."

Charles Pamla gave me the following incident :

An old heathen who lived eight miles from the station was waked up by songs in the night, sung by some of his converted grandchildren returning from the meeting where they had found Jesus. The old man, hearing the wonderful story these young witnesses had to tell, took up his sticks and hobbled off straightway to Annshaw, arriving about the break of day. Hearing the voice of praise in the chapel at the morning prayer meeting, he went in and heard the prayers and prophesyings of God's people. "The secrets of his heart were made manifest, and, falling down on his face, he worshipped God," and was enabled that morning "to report that God was in them of a truth," from a blessed experience of salvation in his own heart. When he reported himself among the young converts of that meeting he asked the minister what he should do about his two wives.

" You will have to give one of them up."

"Well," replied the old man, "one is a young woman, and I love her; the other is an old woman, the wife of my youth. She is old, and can't work much, but she is my true wife, and she has always been kind to me, and I will keep her and give up my young wife. But I am not angry with her, and I don't know how to tell her to go away. I will bring them both here to-morrow and let you explain it to them."

"Very well," replied the missionary, "that will do."

So the next day the old man was seen in the distance, hobbling along on his two sticks, close after him his old woman, and next, in single file, his young woman and her three children. It was a painfully interesting and yet pleasing sight.

The old man brought his two wives into the chapel and marched straight to the missionary. Brother Lamplough went into an explanation of the whole matter to the astonished women, who, it appears, did not know what was to be done. When the minister's decision was announced the old woman cried out, "I am glad of that. I always loved my dear old man, and did not want him to give half of his heart away to another woman. Oh, I am so glad to get him back to me, and now he is all my own!"

The younger woman stood weeping, and all naturally thought that to be "thrown away," as the Kaffirs would term it, in that style, was an occasion of great grief, which would lead to an unpleasant scene; but when her turn came to speak she said, "I thank God for this. I am not angry with the old man, but I have been living in sin, and now I want to find Jesus Christ too;" and, as she wept and commenced tearing off and throwing away her heathen charms and trinkets, she said, "What is to be done with my children? May I take them with me? I will go home to my people and serve Jesus Christ, but I want to take my children with me; I want to take my children with me, I want my children."

The old man, under Kaffir law, could have held the children, but he promptly said, "Yes, take the children, and teach them to love Jesus Christ."

"Our last stroke is being levelled against Kaffir beer," said Brother Lamplough. "I do not know a single leader or local preacher who touches beer now in this circuit. This is a grand thing, and the result of five years' hard fighting."

CHAPTER XXI

FORT BEAUFORT, HEALD TOWN, AND SOMERSET EAST

FORT BEAUFORT, situated on the lower part of the Kat River, was first established as a military post soon after the Kaffir war of 1835, and has gradually developed into a good average African town.

My home was at the house of the superintendent of the circuit, Rev. John Wilson, a man of an excellent spirit and an earnest minister, who, with his truly missionary wife, had been in the South African work for many years. Two of their daughters, who had long been seeking, were saved during our series of services. I was agreeably surprised to meet a large force of my Graham's Town workers and friends who had come forty-seven miles to Fort Beaufort to attend our services.

During our brief service sixty-five whites professed to find peace with God. Some of them gave promise of great usefulness to the Church.

Mr. E——, who had been forward several times as a seeker, exclaimed with tearful eyes as he entered into liberty, "Talk about sacrificing all for Christ! What had I to sacrifice but my sins and all my wicked abominations? A sacrifice indeed! Why, it's a glorious riddance! And in return I have received in Christ the priceless gift of eternal life. Glory to God!"

While I was working at Graham's Town, Mr. Alfred White, one of the oldest pioneers in the country, who lived on the Umzimvubu River, in Kaffraria, nearly four hundred miles east of Graham's Town, persuaded me to go overland through Kaffraria to Natal, instead of by sea, as I had contemplated. I did not then hope to be able to do much good, but I wanted to see the practical working of the mission stations among the heathen in their own country and learn what I could.

When I was at Annshaw I made arrangements with Brother Lamplough, to have Charles Pamla go with me through Kaffirland as my interpreter.

Heald Town, called in honour of James Heald, Esq., treasurer of the Wesleyan Missionary Society, is a large Fingo settlement and mission station, six miles distant from Fort Beaufort. This is the site of the largest industrial school established under the patronage of Sir George Grey.

Rev. William Sargent, the missionary at the time of my visit, was brought up in the colony, and having been in the mission work for many years was quite at home in the native language, manners, and customs; he was a true friend to the natives and an earnest missionary. He removed his whole family to Fort Beaufort so that they all might enjoy the benefit of our week of special services there. He had written me requesting a visit to his natives in Heald Town, but, not having the natives in my plan of appointments, and having engaged to labour with the whites for weeks ahead, I could not promise, but at our first interview I arranged to give them a week-day service.

So on Tuesday, June 19th, Brother Sargent took me up with his cart and pair, and set off for Heald Town. When we arrived, a little before the hour appointed, the chapel, with sittings for about eight hundred, was packed with about one thousand natives and twenty whites.

The head teacher, Mr. T. Templer, met us, and said: " We have Barnabas here, from Graham's Town ; he is a splendid interpreter, and we'll get him to interpret. He says he would rather not, as he's here on business, in his working clothes, but I'm sure he'll consent if we press it."

"Give me anybody else," I replied. "I tried him in Graham's Town, and he got his voice up an octave too high at the start, and sang out the whole sermon in two or three monotonous tones that did not suit me at all. He is a good fellow, and we must not hurt his feelings, but if you are not committed to him, and can give me any other Kaffir who can talk English, don't engage Barnabas."

" We are not committed to him, but consider him the best we can get. We have a Kaffir boy, my assistant teacher, who understands English, but he is not a professional interpreter."

" He's my boy; send him to me quickly, as our time is nearly up and the people are waiting."

Brother Sargent immediately sent for him and brought him into a private room in the institution, a real black boy, about twenty years old, five feet six inches in height, prominent forehead, good eye, pleasant countenance, a quiet, unobtrusive youth, a good singer, can write music and play on the harmonium, but rather a feeble voice for addressing a large assembly—Siko Radas.

Brother Sargent said he had to celebrate a marriage either before or after preaching. We at once arranged that Brother Sargent should open the service in the usual way and attend to the marriage, and allow me that time for drilling my young interpreter.

I preached my sermon to Siko and gave him a lecture on naturalness. We entered the church before the marriage ceremony was over. The bridal party were all black, but well-dressed, and presented a very genteel appearance, and signed their names to the marriage records with self-possession and neatness of execution. The bride was covered from head to foot with a fine white veil.

The bridal party sat in the front form, just before us. I did not occupy the little pulpit, but stood beside my interpreter in the altar. Siko put my sentences into Kaffir very rapidly, but distinctly, and, as I learned, correctly. There was evidently an extraordinary power of the Holy Spirit resting on the audience during the preaching, but silence reigned, except the slight murmur of suppressed sobbing and tears. At the close of the preaching we dismissed the assembly, giving all who wished an opportunity to retire. The bridal party and a few others left.

Before we proceeded further with the prayer-meeting I explained in Gospel simplicity the way of salvation by faith, so that the seekers might intelligently come to Christ without further personal instruction. We then invited the seekers to come forward and occupy the forms from the front, as far back as might be necessary. They rushed forward with that violence which the kingdom of heaven suffereth, and many of the violent took it by force that day At least three hundred seekers were down on their knees within a few minutes. They were all praying audibly, the floor was wet with tears, yet none seemed to be screaming louder than his neighbour. Brother Sargent seemed for a few moments fearful, thinking it might lead to confusion; but I reminded him of the undeniable evidences that God the Holy Spirit was moving in the matter, and however much of human dross and infirmity might be mixed into such a mass of superstition and sin the people had been well instructed, and the Holy Spirit was fully competent directly, and through the agencies available, to manage the business, and we should work with Him, not interfere with His work.

Brother Sargent at once and heartily acquiesced in my views, which were supported so thoroughly by Scripture teaching and precedent, and by the logic of facts before our eyes, that we could do but little else than stand still and see the salvation of God. We had Brothers Janion, Atwell, Webb, Roberts, and other Graham's Town brethren present. They seemed a little confused at the first shock; for my meetings at Graham's Town, as in every other place among the whites, were conducted in quietness; but in a few minutes they were reassured by their faith in God and the power of His Gospel, and entered into the work with their characteristic earnestness. In the recess there were fourteen whites down on their knees as seekers; so that the brethren who could not speak Kaffir found ample employment among them.

As fast as the seekers entered into liberty they were conducted to seats, first in the right wing of the chapel and then in the left, and then in front, where they gave their testimony to their minister, who wrote down their names in his pastoral book. The services closed at 4 p.m., having extended through five hours. Seven whites reported themselves among the converts, having, during the service, embraced Christ and found salvation in Him. Six of them were one whole family, a grandmother, her daughter, son-in-law, and three children. It was a touching scene to see the poor old woman in the centre and her children and grandchildren embracing her with flowing tears, praising God, telling her how happy they were in the love of Jesus.

Of the natives, Brother Sargent recorded the names of one hundred and thirty-nine who professed to find peace with God during our service of five hours. We then hastened back to Fort Beaufort, where I preached, and had a glorious work among the whites that night.

On Thursday morning, the 21st of June, Brother Sargent drove me again to Heald Town, according to the announcement made the preceding Tuesday.

We went before our crowded audience fully equipped, trusting to the immediate presence and saving power of the Holy Spirit. The prayer meeting was conducted as on the first day. Among the seekers were many aged persons. The awful presence and melting power of the Holy Spirit on this occasion surpassed anything I had ever witnessed before.

I realised by faith on that occasion what I never can explain. If the dispensation of the Spirit is to extend to "that great and notable day of the Lord when He shall judge the quick and the dead," and if the everabiding Spirit is as available now, and as willing to fulfil His mighty mission now, as He was on the day of Pentecost, why is the world not saved? I wept over the defective faith and ineffective methods of the Church, and thought how the Holy Spirit is grieved in not having suitable agents for the successful prosecution and consummation of His work, according to God's purpose and adequate provisions in Christ. As I saw dead souls by the score stand up by the power of the Spirit, till they became like an army around us, and heard them witnessing to the saving mercy of Jesus in their hearts, I felt the keen retort of the South Australian black fellow at Lake Alexandrina. A man whom this native had known for twenty years was warning him for the first time against the danger of losing his soul, and the sable son of nature said with vehement indignation, "If you know all this time that black fellow going to hell, why you no tell black fellow till now?"

A majority of those before me, to be sure, had been born and brought up under Gospel teaching; their old friend Ayliff, who led them out of Kaffir bondage, had lived and died among them at that very spot; in the chapel before us was a slab to his memory, on which it was stated that the last prayer he ever offered, just as he was stepping into death's dark river, was that God would bless and save his "dear Fingoes." His prayer was now being answered among the ones to whom he last preached; but I thought of the millions beyond, who have not to this day heard of Jesus. Oh, I felt that, dearly as I loved my country, my Conference, my home, and, above all, my dear family, if it were the Lord's will to adjust my relations satisfactorily in regard to those sacred interests, and call me to this work, I would hail it as a privilege to lead a band of black native evangelists through the African continent till Ethiopa would not only stretch out her hands, but embrace Christ, through the power of the Holy Ghost, from the Cape of Good Hope to the Mediterranean!

At the close of this second service at Heald Town, Brother Sargent reported the names of one hundred and sixty-seven native and three European converts during the service of five hours, making an aggregate for the two services of three hundred and six natives and ten whites saved "by the washing of regeneration and renewing of the Holy Ghost, shed forth abundantly upon us, through Jesus Christ our Lord." These, added to the sixty-five Europeans at Fort Beaufort, made a total of three hundred and eighty-one souls brought to God and justified freely by His grace during our brief ministry of only five days.

An extract from a letter I received from Brother Sargent, dated July 17th, nearly a month after I left, may serve to illustrate the continued progress of this work in Heald Town:

"I am thankful to say that the good work of the Lord is still progressing favourably at Heald Town. About sixty more have found peace since you left, and I have no doubt but that there would have been a much larger number but for the fact that I have had to be away so often that the penitent meetings have not been held so frequently as I could wish. There is much earnestness manifested among the people, both old and young. You would be amazed and delighted to hear their cries of a night till after nine or ten o'clock, and in some cases till daylight in the morning, pleading for the pardon of their sins. The valleys and rocks below the mission house are literally vocal with the cries of penitents, morning, noon, and night. You will be glad to be informed that last Saturday, in our local preachers' meeting, the local brethren, in receiving several new candidates on the local preachers' plan, passed a resolution that no one using Kaffir beer or any other strong drink shall be allowed to exercise the office of local preacher among them. Next Saturday the class leaders intend passing the resolution respecting themselves, not allowing any to exercise the office of class leader in Heald Town who will not give up the drinking of Kaffir beer and all other intoxicating drinks."

As we returned from Heald Town to Fort Beaufort, accompanied by a large number of Europeans on horseback and many natives on foot, though we drove rapidly, to be in time for the evening appointment, some of the black fellows, happy in the Lord and light on foot as Elijah before the chariot of Ahab, ran so fast as to keep up with us most of the distance of six miles.

Mrs. Thomas Guard witnessed all the scenes of that day, and, possessing a very refined taste, a nice sense of propriety, and not favourable to noisy religious exercises, I was a little surprised to find her enthusiastic in her expressions of admiration of all she had seen and heard. I had observed that she looked on and wept and smiled alternately during most of the service, and as we drove along she said, "I have seen most of the crowned heads of Europe, was at the opening of the great exhibition in 1851, have witnessed and felt the thrilling effects of the most imposing pageants of royalty, but I never saw anything for sublimity and soul-stirring effect to compare with the scenes of this day. I would not have missed the meeting of to-day for anything that could be offered."

On Friday morning, the 22nd of June, Brother Sargent, in company with his son and daughter, drove me twenty miles with his cart and pair to the village of Adelaide, on my way to Somerset, which is about eighty miles distant from Fort Beaufort. At 2.30 p.m. I preached at Adelaide in the Presbyterian church, Rev. Peter Davidson, pastor. Mr. Francis King sent his cart and pair and driver to convey me that afternoon to Bedford, twenty miles further on my way, Brother Sargent and Davidson accompanying.

The Kings were of the Graham's Town stock of Wesleyans, where their good old father then lived. They were sheep and cattle farmers. Being native-born Africanders, as the native Europeans are called, they had had many adventures both in times of war and peace. Francis King said he and another young man were once travelling together to Namaqua Land to explore the copper mines (three hundred and fifty miles west of Cape Town). They were on horseback, but were unarmed. Away in the wilds two hundred miles west of Cape Town they were suddenly surrounded by a dozen bushmen, who seized the bridles of their horses and stopped them.

"I knew," said King, "from their general character and their movements that they designed to rob us, and perhaps kill us too; but fearing that we had concealed weapons they offered no violence except to hold us fast.

"My companion was greatly alarmed and said, 'We're sure to be killed.' But I said, 'Jim, don't show the least fear, keep perfectly cool, and we may providentially find a way of escape.' After we had waited some time a square, burly-looking fellow came up having six toes on each foot, and joined the rest in holding on to our bridles and stirrup leathers. I soon found that this six-toed fellow could speak a little Dutch, so I said to him, 'Take us to the water, we want to drink.' They immediately set off with us, holding our bridles on each side, and took us a mile or two to a spring. We dismounted, and holding our horses with one hand managed to get a little water, for we were nearly famished. I talked to them familiarly all the time, as though I of course thought they were our friends. I told them I wanted to buy ostrich feathers, and I wanted them to go and get me some. Two of them ran away, and after an absence of nearly an hour came back with a few feathers. I paid for them and said, 'This is not half enough; I want you all to go and bring me all the feathers you can get, and I'll pay you a good price for them.' So they all started off under the impulse of the moment to get feathers.

"As soon as they got out of sight we mounted and rode off for life. That was in the after part of the day. We travelled all that night and till late in the afternoon of the next day before we stopped

long enough to make a cup of tea. That afternoon as we passed
along I discovered a bees' nest in the rocks. Near sunset, over
forty miles from where we left the bushmen, we encamped for
the night. We had just taken a cup of tea and were talking of
our narrow escape, when lo! the six-toed fellow and his party
were upon us. They came and seated themselves in a circle
around us without saying a word. I talked Dutch to Sixtoes, but
he made no reply. I laughed and talked as though nothing had
happened, or was likely to happen, while I was trying to invent
a method of escape. I knew if we showed fear, or if they should
find out that we were unarmed, it would be all up with us. All
at once I thought of the bees' nest, and I said to Sixtoes, 'Wouldn't
you like me to show you a bees' nest? You all must be
hungry after your journey, and I'm sure a little honey will do you
good.' Then he began to talk a little, but in a very surly spirit.
I said, 'Come with me and I'll show you a bees' nest, and you can
get a good feed of honey.' I got up and started, and they followed.
Jim said, 'Frank, you are not going to trust yourself alone with
those savages, I hope.'

"I replied, 'Get the horses ready and take them to the other side
of the ridge beyond the bees' nest, and wait there till I come.' I
took the bushmen to the nest, and they all at once began in great
haste to work their way into the rocks to get the honey; finally one
of them drew out a fine piece of comb, full of honey, and I ran up
and snatched it and began to eat. They looked at me and began
to mutter; but said I, 'Dig away, you'll find plenty of honey in
there.' So they went to work with greater eagerness than ever,
while I began to walk backwards and forwards eating a little honey
and humming a tune, watching my opportunity.

"While their attention was taken in their scramble, each trying to
get his full share of the honey, I got out of sight and ran for life.
The horses were ready and we put them up to their best speed for
about thirty miles. In almost utter exhaustion we then off-saddled
and knee-haltered our horses, and half buried ourselves in the sand
and soon fell asleep.

"We had not been long asleep, as I afterwards found, when I was
awakened by something cold touching my toe. It was a bright,
moonlight night, and I instantly recognised the dog of those bushmen
smelling my feet, but was glad to see him trot away without barking
at us.

"I shook Jim and whispered to him to keep a sharp lookout but
not to move a muscle unless attacked. In a few minutes I heard
our pursuers run past but a few rods distant from us. They lost
their scent, we took another direction, and saw them no more."

Rev. John Edwards, Superintendent of Somerset Circuit, met me
at Bedford and drove me thence nearly forty miles in his cart and
four, to his own house in Somerset.

The Wesleyan Chapel for the whites had recently been enlarged
to double its former size by the addition of a transept as large as the

old chapel; altogether it would then seat over three hundred and fifty. The native chapel was about the same size.

A number of persons had come fifty and others seventy miles to attend the meetings. Among them was a Mr. Nash, from Ebenezer, fifty miles distant. He was a good farmer, a kind-hearted man with an interesting family; but I was told that he was given to drink, so that his life and all that he had were in jeopardy. He called to see me on Saturday evening soon after my arrival. Said he, " I never would have thought of coming to this meeting but for Hon. Mr. Burch, of Uitenhage. He used to be my neighbour before his removal to Uitenhage, and recently he was in our neighbourhood and was telling myself and others about your preaching in Uitenhage, and what suprised us most was that he said that he had found the pardon of all his sins at your meeting."

Nash attended all the services, but did not yield till Wednesday, when he surrendered to God, accepted Christ, and was saved. Nearly all those who came so far, through the testimony of Mr. Burch, went home happy in God.

At each native service the chapel was crowded. I was greatly favoured in having Siko Radas, from Heald Town, to interpret for me. He was having a holiday during his vacation, and spent it in riding nearly eighty miles on his own hired horse to help me at Somerset, and thence eighty miles to Cradock to help me there. We had not such a mass of people to preach to in these towns as at Heald Town, but, in proportion to the population, we had a blessed harvest of souls.

CHAPTER XXII

CRADOCK AND QUEENSTOWN

On Friday, the 29th of June, Mr. Sargent drove me, from Somerset, forty miles on my way toward Cradock. We spent the night and preached at the house of Mr. John Trollip. Rev. W. Chapman, Superintendent of Cradock Circuit, met me at Mr. John Trollip's and drove me in his cart and pair, through a gale of wind and blinding clouds of dust, a distance of about forty miles to Cradock.

I commenced my work in Cradock on Sabbath morning the 30th of June. My first service was to preach to the Kaffirs, through Siko Radas, at 7 a.m. About one half the natives of Cradock speak Kaffir and the other half Dutch, making it necessary to have two native chapels and separate services in each language. Mr. H. Parks, a discharged old soldier and Dutch interpreter in the magistrate's court there, was my interpreter. The language is not nearly so euphonious as the Kaffir, but I was interested in marking its near relationship to the English.

It was arranged that I should preach to the natives on Thursday, but their new chapel, which will seat between four and five hundred, was not ready, and it was finally announced that I should preach to the natives and whites together in the court, behind the mission house.

At 11 a.m. the heterogeneous mass nearly filled the court. We take our stand on the back verandah of the mission house. The court is bounded on our left by a wall, in front by a carriage house and the garden fence, on the right by the stables and a wall, altogether affording almost as good protection from outside intrusion, if the danger of such had existed, as the sacred precincts of a church. The central group of our audience is composed of Kaffirs and Hottentots of every colour and of every variety of native costume. They have brought their sleeping mats, each about three feet wide and six in length, and have spread them out to sit and kneel on. Many of them are seated on benches provided for them, but many more are down on their mats. Next, in a massed circle and in scattered groups, we see all classes of the whites. Brother Park stands ready to put my sermon into the Dutch language, but we see so many Kaffirs in the audience, who know neither English nor

Dutch, that we say, " Poor souls, can't we have another interpreter ? I wish we had Siko Radas here, but he has gone back to his school."

"There's a Kaffir here just up from Port Elizabeth, called Jack, who can speak English," said Brother Chapman, " but I don't know whether he can interpret."

" Jack, come here, my man," said I ; and up came a black Kaffir, about five feet eight, very plainly dressed, wearing an old straw hat. " Brother Jack," said I, " can you put my words into Kaffir ? "

" Yes, sir," replied Jack.

" Brother Park will put them into Dutch, and you will follow him, and put each sentence into Kaffir, just as you would talk to them about shearing sheep."

I had no time, under this extemporised arrangement, to give Jack my sermon privately, as I was in the habit of doing for my interpreters, but proceeded at once to business. The three of us stood side by side, Park close to my right, and Jack next. I gave every sentence in a clear but condensed form, and for over an hour the piercing light and melting power of the Gospel flowed out through the medium of three languges at once without the break of a moment's hesitation. Men, women, and children wept, and I doubt not angels gazed and rejoiced. At the close of the preaching we invited all who wished to surrender to God and accept Christ to kneel before the Lord at once. Scores of the Kaffirs knelt down on their mats, with cries and streaming tears. The whites, with no such provision, went down on their knees in the dust, bench after bench was crowded with them, and, ah, what a scene ensued !

While I was without, pointing these struggling souls to Jesus, Brother Chapman came to me, saying, " Brother Taylor, will you please come into the house and speak to a woman in despair ? She is a very clever, influential woman, and will make a noble Christian if she is saved ; but she says her day of grace is gone, and that nothing remains for her but the blackness of darkness for ever." I went and found her in a sad state of mind, to be sure ; but after some time we got her composed so as to converse and reason on the subject and convince her that this dreadful discovery of extreme heart wickedness is the result of the Holy Spirit's awakening mercy. " Though you can see no way of escape, my dear sister, God sees the way of salvation open for you, and the proof of that is the fact that He has sent His Spirit to show you your bondage and lead you to Jesus. Now, if you consent to surrender yourself to God, consent that He take your case in hand and do with you as He wishes, take from you all your sins, impose on you whatever is right, you may at once accept Christ as your Saviour. God hath sent Him into the world to save sinners, even the chief of sinners. That was His business when manifest in the flesh ; that is His business through His invisible Spirit now as really as then. God offers Him to you in His Gospel as your Saviour, the Holy Spirit presents Him at the door of your heart as your Saviour. He is knocking at the door. Now, you will accept Him and be saved by Him, or reject Him and perish.

Accept Him now by faith. It is not presumption, but confidence in God's most reliable record concerning His Son. If what God says about Him is true, then Christ is worthy of your confidence, and if so why not receive Him now? You cannot improve your case by anything you ever can do, and you cannot add anything to God's ransom and remedy. Then, on the faith of God's testimony, receive Jesus now as your Saviour from sin. You must say, 'I accept Him; I accept Him on His own terms, I accept Him on God's recommendation, I accept Him now, I accept Him;' say it till your heart says it, and in that moment God will justify you freely by His grace, and His Holy Spirit will bear witness with your spirit to the fact and fill your heart with His pardoning love."

Finally she began to say, "I accept Christ, I accept Him;" and in a few moments she received the witness of forgiveness and was filled with joy unspeakable, and oh, how she wept and talked of the amazing love of God!

My Dutch interpreter's wife and daughter were saved that day, and a large number of whites, Dutch, and Kaffirs. I have given but an inadequate glance at the scenes of that day. The pastor reported one hundred and fifty whites and one hundred and sixty coloured justified by faith, besides a number wholly sanctified to the Lord.

At early dawn on Friday morning, the 5th of July, I was seated beside Brother Tucker, my host, in his splendid carriage, behind his two fine grey Arab steeds, *en route* for Queenstown, over eighty miles distant. Brother Tucker accompanied me thirty miles on my way, where we dined at the house of his brother, and I bade my dear friend adieu. Mr. Hines was in waiting, and drove me that afternoon twenty miles in his cart and four to his own house in the village of Tarkisstaat. The Wesleyans had a small chapel there, but no society. The Dutch Reformed Church being a little more central, and having been kindly offered for our use, I preached in it that night. We did not hold a prayer meeting, but a respectable citizen of the town, Mr. J. F——, called next morning to inform me that, after the preaching the night before, he went home and wrestled in importunate prayer, till he was enabled to submit to God and accept Christ, and was made happy in the assurance of pardon.

On Saturday, Mr. Hines drove me thirty-five miles to Queenstown, where I put up at the house of the Resident Wesleyan minister, Rev. H. H. Duginore.

We had a number of visitors at our services from different parts of the colony. Messrs. Shaw, Barnes, Elliott, and others recently converted to God at Fort Beaufort, were there and rendered us good service. Mr. Elliott was a hotel keeper who gave up his canteen. We had a few from Graham's Town, and Mr. Jakins from Salem Circuit, one hundred and twenty miles distant.

At our Graham's Town series two of Brother Jakins's daughters and a son-in-law were saved, and now he had come one hundred and twenty miles to attend my Queenstown meeting with the hope of seeing his two sons, who were farmers in that district, brought to

God. He did us good service at our meetings, and had the happiness of seeing his sons happy in Jesus before he returned.

Some whole families were saved at our Queenstown series, and many sweet surprises and affecting scenes were witnessed. A dear mother in Israel, named Turvey, had two grown-up sons, both unconverted; but one was so wild in his career of sin that she almost despaired of ever having him brought back to God. The mother had brought up a large family of children in affliction and darkness, for she was blind and had not seen the light of the sun for many years. She was a real daughter of sorrow, but a patient Christian. The great grief of her heart was her prodigal son.

One night during our series a brother went to her and said, "Mrs. Turvey, your son is at the altar of prayer among the seekers, and wants you to come and talk to him."

Her gushing tears were the index to the unutterable emotions of joy and grief which thrilled her heart as she exclaimed, "Oh, I thank God that my dear George is coming to Jesus; but my poor prodigal! I'm afraid he'll never be saved!"

She was then conducted to the place, and feeling her way down to her penitent son she cried, "Oh, George, my dear son, I'm glad to find you here; but poor Edward! Would to God he were here too!"

"Mother," exclaimed the young man, "you are quite mistaken; it is not George; I am indeed your prodigal son, and I want you to forgive me and to pray that God will forgive me."

The prodigal returned that night and was admitted into the royal household of faith. George, who had always been a comfort to his mother, was not saved till the following week, at Kamastone. When the mother got the joyful news she rode twenty miles to Kamastone to greet her dear son and rejoice with him in thanksgiving to the God of the orphan and the widow.

Our services at Queenstown extended through five days, from the 8th to the 12th of July. During this series of services about one hundred Europeans were reported by the minister as new witnesses for Christ.

While at Queenstown, Charles Pamla joined me.

James Roberts, with a light gig which he had made to order, and four draught horses, to convey me through Kaffraria, seven hundred miles to Natal, joined me at Queenstown. He was accompanied by my son Stuart, from Cape Town, where his mother and two little brothers, Edward and Ross, were sojourning.

CHAPTER XXIII

KAMASTONE, LESSEYTON, AND WARNER'S

HAVING closed our week of services in Queenstown on Saturday, the 14th of July, Mr. William Trollip, who, with his wife, found peace with God a couple of days before, took me and my son Stuart up into his carriage and pair, with his good wife, and drove us twenty miles to Kamastone mission station. We were cordially received and kindly entertained by the missionary, Rev. William Shepstone, who had been actively engaged in the missionary work through a period of more than forty years.

After a good tea and a social hour with Brother and Sister Shepstone I strolled through the mission grounds by the light of the moon with my son Stuart, a youth of nineteen years. Owing to his absence from me at school a couple of years before I left America and my absence abroad for several years, and his recent illness so prostrating him as to preclude a searching conversation, though the son of my youth, my first-born whom I had carried on my heart to the mercy seat every day of his life, he was almost a stranger to me. I knew he had joined our Church when a child, and at the age of eleven years professed to receive the regenerating grace of God, and that his teachers and his mother had always given a good report of him; yet the details of his inner life had been a sealed book to me, but in our walk that night he unbosomed his heart and gave me the history of his life.

It was an event in my life never to be forgotten. He had suffered great religious depression, had encountered great trials, but had held his ground all through from the time of his conversion. In the exhilaration of his returning health he had said and done many boyish things which led some to misjudge and misrepresent him and cause anxious solicitude on the part of his parents; but his afflictions had been sanctified to his good, and he was now cleaving to the Lord and happy in the love of Jesus. As I listened to the narration of his experience I shed grateful tears and praised God on his behalf. During my long providential separation from my family, labouring for the salvation of strangers and their children, I had maintained an unwavering faith that God certainly would not allow my children to perish, but would, through the agency of their dear, godly mother, fully supply the lack of service occasioned by my absence. Now I received a practical support to my faith, which greatly cheered me in my work.

On Sabbath, the 14th of July, at 10 a.m., we commenced our work at Kamastone. Every square foot of space in the chapel is crowded. The space right and left, from the pulpit and altar back to the side walls, is filled with the white colonial farmers from a radius of twenty miles. Next to them, on the right and front from the pulpit, are nearly one hundred bastard Hottentots. Opposite to them on the left and through the whole body of the chapel, back to the door and round the doors and windows outside, are all the varieties of Fingoes and Kaffirs.

The preliminary service is conducted by the venerable superintendent ; then he is seated in the altar, while I and Brother Pamla take the pulpit. While we explain to them God's provision of salvation, the personality and abiding presence of the Holy Spirit, and His methods of saving sinners through human agency, you feel and see the indications of a rising, swelling tide of the Spirit's power, and you wonder that, under the pressure of such pent-up mental and emotional action, there is not a single audible response—all faces upturned, smiles, tears, distorted features, trembling limbs, but not a murmur. Lo! there's a man back near the door who cannot longer restrain his feelings, but with one burst of half-smothered emotions see him try to rush for the door, to take himself away and not disturb the *umfundisi* or his hearers. In his attempt he falls down, but keeps moving on hands and knees through the packed masses in the aisle ; out at the door he rushes, and away where he can roar till his overcharged soul is relieved. All this we see from the pulpit ; but nobody is disturbed ; all remain quiet and catch every sentence and drink in the Spirit as the thirsty land drinks the rain. We close the service with singing and prayer by Brother Pamla.

At 2 p.m. we again stand before a packed audience in the same order as in the morning. In the morning the preaching was to the believers ; now we open a Gospel battery upon the ungodly, and the shafts of truth directed by the Spirit's unerring aim pierce the hearts of hundreds. At the close of the sermon we proceed with a prayer meeting. We invite the white seekers to kneel at the altar rail and the Kaffirs to commence with the front forms and kneel at every alternate form back to the door, thus leaving space for their instructors to pass through them and get access to every seeker. Soon the altar is crowded with whites, and about two hundred natives are down as seekers of pardon. Now their pent-up feelings get vent, and amid floods of tears, sighs, and groans they are all audibly pleading with God in the name of Jesus Christ for the pardon of their sins. No one voice is raised much above the rest, so that it seems to create no confusion.

Charles is a general in conducting a prayer meeting, judiciously arranging everything, rightly employing every worker under his command, and setting all an example by working most effectively himself. A large number embrace Christ and find salvation at this service. Giving a little time for refreshment, we commenced another preaching service at 7 and continued the prayer meeting till 11 p.m. It was a day never to be forgotten by any who witnessed its scenes and felt the power of the Spirit as manifested at the three services.

On Monday, at 11 a.m., the chapel was again greatly crowded. Brother Shepstone, as usual, conducted the opening service. As I always preached my sermon to my interpreter alone, and as most of our time was occupied in public, we often took the time of the opening service for our preparation for the pulpit. At the Monday prayer meeting the crowd of seekers seemed almost as great as it was the day before, though several scores had been saved. Many whom we saw yesterday in their penitential struggle, apparently suffering the agony of death, weeping and piteously pleading for release from Satan and the death penalty of the law, are now with shining faces singing and witnessing for Jesus.

My son Stuart was greatly blessed, and for hours we see him labouring with a party of young men, several of whom he won to Christ.

See the altar crowded with whites; one after another they receive Christ and are filled with unspeakable joy! Fathers and mothers embrace their saved prodigal sons and daughters in their arms, kiss them and weep tears of gratitude and praise God.

There's a heathen doctor among the seekers decorated with strings of beads, shells, and all sorts of trinkets and charms. He feels that these things are hindering his approach to Christ, and now he scatters them. Nothing has been said about these things in the preaching or personally to the seekers. These are not simply the ornaments of their half-naked bodies, which might justly claim a little covering, even of beads in the absence of something better; they were the badges of their heathenism, their gods and charms, in which they trusted for health, good crops, good luck in hunting, deliverance from their enemies, and all those demands of human nature which God only can supply. Hence in accepting Christ they violently tear these idols off and cast them away.

We see women tearing open the brass bands on their arms and throwing them down. They were great treasures before, but now they hate them. Many of those who an hour ago were roaring in the disquietude of their souls are now sitting quietly at the feet of Jesus with tearful eyes and smiling faces. Many, however, exercise their first new life in witnessing for Christ.

See that Kaffir Boanerges; how he talks! I wish we could understand his language. "Charles, what is that man saying?"

"Oh, he says, 'I never knew that I was such a sinner till the Holy Ghost shined into me; then I saw that I was one of the worst sinners in the world. Oh, I cried to God, gave my wicked heart to Him, and received Christ. Glory to Jesus! He has pardoned all my sins!'"

We'll look after the white seekers. There's an old man who has had a hard struggle. He was at it all yesterday; but now he has accepted Christ and rejoices in the love of God. There is a little boy who was forward yesterday, but his countenance is bright; we'll see what he has found.

"My little brother, have you given your heart to God?"

"Yes, I have."

"Have you received Jesus as your Saviour?"

"Oh yes, and He has forgiven me all my sins."

"How did you feel when you came forward?"

"Oh, I felt nasty."

"How do you feel now?"

"Oh, I feel nice."

A few feet from this boy we see a large, fine-looking Kaffir woman, well dressed in English costume, wearing a large scarlet shawl. We saw her bow down calmly as a seeker; with flowing tears and subdued utterances she gave herself to God and received Christ, and obtained salvation in less than fifteen minutes. Now her countenance is beaming with joy unspeakable.

"Charles, ask that woman where she belongs?" With what marvellous grace and eloquence she talks! "What does she say, Charles?"

"She says she walked from Heald Town, forty-six miles, to get to this meeting. She could not get to your meetings in Heald Town, but heard of the great work of God there, and has come here to get you to tell her how to come to Jesus. She says she believed what her friends at Heald Town told her about the great salvation, but now she has found it herself and says the half had not been told her."

There's a grand pantomime! We don't know what that Kaffir man is saying, but really his action is most earnest and graceful. "Charles, what is he saying?"

"He says, 'I was going on in my sins, and did not know that I was in any danger till to-day. But to-day the Holy Ghost shined upon my path. I saw hell open just close before me, and I was rushing into it; but I turned to God and laid hold on Christ, and He has saved my soul from hell.'"

See that old Kaffir woman supporting her withered frame on sticks as she moves up and down the aisle in a regular Kaffir dance, and talking so earnestly. A more comical-looking old creature I never saw. "Brother Shepstone, what's the matter with that old woman?"

"I don't know; she looks like a crazy person. I'll go and hear what she's saying."

Down the aisle amid the struggling masses of the seekers and the saved the old missionary goes to hear the talk of the old woman. Returning with a smile, he says: "She's not crazy at all, but has just come to her right mind. She has obtained salvation, and is exhorting the people to go on and tell everybody about Jesus. She is in a transport of joy. I know her now. I have seen her at a heathen kraal in the neighbourhood, but I never saw her in the chapel before."

" Her age must date back a long way toward the flood."

" I don't know how old she is," replied the old missionary ; " but her son, whom I know, is seventy-five years old."

I look again at the old creature and laugh and weep. She seems to be related to the antediluvians ; whether this seventy-five year old lad was her oldest or youngest son I did not learn, and yet she is but to-day born again and has become a babe in Christ !

These are mere bird's-eye glances into a scene that cannot be described. We had a grand service on Monday night. On Tuesday, at 11 a.m., we preached on Christian perfection, went into the philosophy of the subject and of the Spirit's gracious adjustment to the instincts, appetites, and passions, and explained clearly God's purpose as to their existence, proper discipline, and appropriate exercise. The whole thing was simplified, so that every believing Kaffir could see it. Brother Shepstone said he never supposed before that the Kaffir language could be used to convey so perfectly the whole Gospel, and had never conceived it possible for an interpreter to put such a variety of English words and ideas into Kaffir. He expressed his surprise repeatedly that Charles not only put my ideas into Kaffir in their nicest shades of meaning, but did it with such masterly facility. The fact is, though I gave him every statement of truth and illustrative fact in a sermon, just as I would give them in preaching directly to an English audience, yet I had always gone through each subject of discourse beforehand with him alone.

If he did not understand a word I at once ignored it and substituted one that was familiar to him ; but he was so thirsty for knowledge himself that, if possible, he always preferred to learn the meaning of my words and to select new Kaffir words to fit them and the exact meaning of a foreign illustration he would give through a corresponding figure familiar to the Kaffir mind. For example : " An ivy crawled out from between the roots of a beautiful sapling and entwined itself around the trunk of the young tree. It gradually absorbed the strength of the soil and moisture that the tree needed for its life, and tightened its many-folded girth till it obstructed the sap vessels of the tree. The tree had grown tall and mighty, but the deceitful ivy did its deadly work. The noble tree declined, lingered long, but finally died. When I stood by the grand old tree it was dead, and all the dews of heaven, and the fruitful supplies of the earth, and all the skill of all the gardeners could not cause that tree to bud. It was dead. Application : the deceitful ivy of sin in the souls of all sinners."

There is no ivy in South Africa ; therefore the literal base of that figure would be utterly lost on a Kaffir, but the milkwood of South Africa furnishes a figure quite as forcible. It entwines itself around a tree as gently as the ivy, its hundreds of delicate tendril feeders encircle the tree, mat together, and then unite in solid wood, until it completely envelops the grand old tree. The foreign thing at first simply seemed to hang on as a loose, ornamental foliage, but in process of time the tree within its folds is choked to death, and its gradual decay supplies nourishing food for its destroyer for generations to come.

I have often seen noble trees of different kinds in all stages of this deadly process, and could not restrain a thrill of sympathetic horror of being thus hugged to death and devoured piecemeal.

When I first introduced my ivy illustration to Charles he said, " The Kaffirs don't know what you mean by ivy."

"Very well," said I, "we'll not use it."

"No," said he, "it is too good an illustration to lose; since you have explained it to me I understand it well, and if you will give it as the ivy I will give it exactly by the milkwood, which every Kaffir knows."

We closed our special series of services at Kamastone at 3 p.m. on Tuesday, the 17th of July. Just before we closed Charles gave them an account of the great work of God at Annshaw, and told them how they had battled for years to put away all heathen customs from among them, especially the drinking of Kaffir beer, with all its attendant abominations, and that the work of God never prospered among them till they had put away all these things and come out fully on the Lord's side, and then the Holy Spirit came among them and saved hundreds of their friends and of wild heathens. That was the beginning of the total abstinence movement in South Africa. At present (according to reports of 1893), "there are over thirty thousand members in the Wesleyan missions in South Africa, and they are all professed abstainers from intoxicating liquors." While Charles was speaking Brother Shepstone became so interested in his narrative that he got up from his seat and stood before the pulpit, looking up at my man, and finally, seeming to forget himself, he shouted out, "Hear! hear! hear!"

During our series of two days and a half, in which we preached six sermons and held twelve prayer meetings, Brother Shepstone took the names of two hundred natives and twenty whites, who professed, at those services, to find the pardon of their sins through an acceptance of Christ.

An eyewitness to the baptismal service, admitting one hundred and forty adult heathens to the Church, as above stated, writing to a local journal in Queenstown and quoted by the *Wesleyan Missionary Notices*, says: "Many of the candidates for baptism were grey-headed men and women. In one instance we saw an aged man and his wife, tottering on the verge of the grave, who, a few months ago, were walking in the paths of sin, but now clothed and in their right mind. Women who, a short time ago, were found at the dance, besmeared with red clay, and indulging all the licentiousness of those abominable scenes, now were clothed in decent European apparel, not only being baptised themselves, but bringing their infants also. The large church was crowded with attentive observers, and no one could view the scene unmoved or without feelings of deep gratitude to the great Head of the Church. In several instances these converts have suffered considerable persecution from their heathen relations; some have been driven from their homes, some have been severely beaten, others have been tied fast to the pole of the house and watched, that they might not go out and pray to the Great Spirit. Yet in almost every case persecution has only produced the same effects it did in days of old, to make the objects of it more determined than ever to serve God rather than man."

Charles and Stuart were not quite ready when Brother Trollip and I left Kamastone for Lesseyton, and our hope that they would soon overtake us was not realised.

When the darkness of a moonless night settled down upon us we had about six miles yet to drive to reach Lesseyton. In working our way through the mimosa scrub we could not from the carriage see the road, and had to get out and walk. When we arrived the chapel was crowded, but Charles had not come, and there was not a man who could interpret for me. I knew Charles would certainly come if he could find his way, but as he was a stranger in those parts that seemed very improbable. We waited anxiously for him for about an hour, when I heard the rattle of horses' hoofs in a neighbouring scrub, and hailed and got a response from his familiar voice. Some one had recommended him to come by a more direct path, in taking which he lost his way. We commenced preaching about half-past eight and continued the prayer meeting till 11 p.m.

The Spirit of the Lord was present and wrought wondrously. About one hundred and fifty seekers of pardon came forward, and about twenty of them professed to obtain it that night, but the mass of them were slow to accept Christ. Brother Bambana, the Tembookie headman of the station, at the close of the service conducted us to his house. Brother Trollip, being a merchant, and having always been greatly prejudiced against the blacks, would not have consented a week before, on any account, to lodge at the house of a coloured man; but now he and his wife had the humility and simplicity of little children. They had entered into the kingdom of heaven and were fellow-citizens with the saints and the household of God, to which fraternity our sable host had belonged for many years, and it was their privilege to enjoy his simple, genuine hospitality. He gave us good food, good beds, and good cheer. Mrs. Bambana would command respect among any class of sensible, discriminating people as a person of good common sense and great kindness of heart. She was a class leader, I was told, of rare excellence. They had two adult sons, who had received a fair education and could speak English sufficiently to enable us to converse with them a little. They were both seekers of pardon that night. Brother Bambana was greatly interested in the account I gave him through my interpreter of the four millions of Africans whom God had delivered from slavery in America, and of the efforts being made by their friends for their education and salvation.

The next day, Wednesday, the 18th of July, at 10 a.m., we were again in the chapel with a crowded audience. Besides Brother and Sister Trollip, and one white man, who followed us from Kamastone, there were no other whites present except a Dutch family, and they could not understand anything that was said; but the truth went home to the consciences of the Kaffirs, and nearly two hundred came forward as seekers.

There we see them down in every alternate seat back to the front door. The struggle is long and hard; now they begin to get into the liberty of the sons of God. How the new converts do talk and exhort! They are unusually demonstrative. See them with up-lifted hands and streaming eyes telling the wonders of the Holy Spirit's work in their hearts. There is a Kaffir woman, with painted face, covered with heathen ornaments, but oh, how she talks! "Charles, what is that woman saying?"

"She says she has been a very great sinner, but she has got all her sins forgiven; she says Jesus has saved her soul, and she don't know what to tell Him to let Him know how thankful she is for His kindness. She wants all her friends to come to God. They are heathens; not one of them knows Jesus, and she never knew Him till now. She says she knows her friends will persecute her and try to make her give up Jesus, but she is going to cleave to Him till she dies. She is begging all her Christian brothers and sisters to pray for her, that she may not only stand firmly, but lead all her kindred to Christ."

Many of the converts, as soon as they get pardon, come up the aisle, telling me and Charles what God has done for them. A young Kaffir man who came up and told us that God had saved him then fell down and, swinging by the altar rail, wept for an hour. "Charles, what's the matter with that poor fellow? He don't look as if he was saved."

Charles questions him, and replies, "He used to belong to the school here for two years, and was taught to read God's Word; but he says he was a scabby goat and was turned out of the flock and became a heathen. He says he has received pardon for all his sins, but has been so wicked and ungrateful he cannot forgive himself."

There are Bambana's two sons down, pleading for pardon. They were there last night. Now one of them enters into liberty, runs and kisses his mother, and the father and mother embrace him and weep and thank God. Now the other accepts Christ and joins in the family bundle of grateful embraces.

See an old man away at the lower end of the chapel. He has just found Jesus. He mounts a form and talks to the people. Now he comes up the aisle, weeping and talking. Brother Bambana has seated himself at the end of a form near the altar. The weeping old man suddenly seizes Bambana's foot and, nearly jerking the old man off his seat, kisses the bottom of his boot. We have heard of washing the disciples' feet and of kissing the pope's toe, but to kiss the sole of a Kaffir's boot is a new idea. On inquiry we learn that this old man, just converted, is Bambana's shepherd, and because his master was so faithful and kind as often to talk to him about his soul he was very angry with his master; but now that he has found salvation he sees that his master was the best earthly friend he had, and he has taken that method of expressing his humiliation and gratitude.

These are but glimpses of the indescribable scenes of that day. The trouble was that, having to preach at 3 p.m. to the natives in Queenstown, eight miles distant, and conduct a fellowship meeting for the whites at night, our time in Lesseyton was too short. During our two services there, however, the names of fifty-eight new converts had been recorded, and about one hundred seekers left. Many of the young converts were aged persons.

We bade adieu to our dear friends at Lesseyton and hastened on to our appointment in Queenstown. That was my last night in Queenstown. The next night I expected to preach at Warner's, fifty miles distant on our route through Kaffraria.

We had completed our arrangements and were ready for an early start next morning. Our party consisted of my friend, Mr. James Roberts, and myself in the cart, Charles Pamla on a bay pony which had carried him over one hundred miles from Annshaw, and my son Stuart on a sorrel tripling Kaffir pony I bought for him at Kamastone.

It was hard to part with such dear friends as Brother and Sister Dugmore. Two of their daughters and a son had been saved at our series, and three other sons were among the seekers. Up to that time twenty-three sons and daughters of our missionaries, in different parts of the colony, had found peace at our meetings. At our final farewell Brother Dugmore, a man who gives to God all the glory for his work, but a dear lover of the brethren, hung round my neck and wept, and said, "God bless you, my dear brother; you have brought salvation to my house."

On Wednesday, July 18th, we left Queenstown to travel fifty miles that day to Warner's. The residence of J. C. Warner, Esq., known by the name of Woodhouse Forests, is the head of a new mission, embracing a portion of Tembookie territory and a part of Fingoland, under the superintendence of a very active, promising young missionary, Rev. E. J. Barrett.

Brother Warner is British Resident for Kaffraria and the representative of the English government to all the tribes living between Cape Colony and Natal, and being a Wesleyan preacher he is in a position of great responsibility and usefulness.

From Queenstown we travelled that day over a hilly, rough road forty-six miles, and had yet four miles of our day's journey to make in the darkness of a moonless night.

Rev. E. J. Barrett came to meet us and to be our guide. We had a pair of horses that had been sent on thirty miles the day before, and they were fresh and fiery, and not so manageable as they became a couple of hundred miles further along. Descending what appeared to be a smooth bit of road at the rate of about eight knots, a sudden jolt sent us both over the larboard, head foremost down the hill. We thought the thing had upset, but, relieved of our weight, it righted up, and when we got our bearings we heard the rattle of the horses' hoofs and the cart wheels away in the distance.

Brother Barret, who was a few rods ahead of us, came rushing back, crying out, "Are ye killed?"

"Not dead yet; pursue the horses as fast as you can."

Away he galloped in pursuit.

We gathered ourselves up and found that, though our clothing was torn and we were scratched and bruised considerably, there were no bones broken; so we picked up a load of rugs and coats cast out of the cart and worked our way in the dark to Mr. Warner's. About an hour later Mr. Barrett arrived, telling how many miles he had travelled in different directions, but could get no tidings of the runaway horses and cart. A company of Kaffirs were then sent out in all directions. Different parties up to midnight reported no success. We had comfortable lodgings in Mr. Barret's Kaffir hut, built by himself. It was eighteen feet in diameter, seven-foot walls, with an elevation at the apex of about fifteen feet. The British resident and his family lived in a larger but more rustic Kaffir hut near by. At the dawn of next morning Brothers Warner, Roberts, and Barret went to the place of disaster and saw where the upper cart wheel had struck a large ant-hill, causing out ejectment; hence tracing the spoor, they found that the horses had run down the hill a distance of a quarter of a mile and turned at a right angle away from the road. Further along the cart spoor was within three inches of a precipice, overhanging a little lake deep enough to have drowned the horses had the cart gone over and drawn them in. About a mile from the road, in the veldt, they found the horses standing still, attached to the cart as when we were driving them, everything right; even the whip stood erect in its place. I was thankful, though not surprised, for I had said the night before that as we were doing work for God, and could not replace our conveyance nearer than Queenstown, and as our engagements demanded haste, I did not doubt that He who takes care even of the sparrows cared much more for the souls we might be instrumental in saving in Kaffraria, and would see to it that our animals and conveyance would be preserved from harm and that we should pursue our journey in safety.

On Friday morning, the 20th of July, I selected a suitable place for our preaching and prayer meeting in a beautiful grassy vale about four hundred yards from our hut. I took some healthy muscular exercise in rolling a large boulder to a suitable spot for a pulpit or platform from which to preach.

The population of this region was rather sparse, and the notice of our coming was very short, so that we did not see the crowds we had been accustomed to see in older communities. At 11 a.m. our service commences. Circling in front of us, seated on the grass, are first the women and children, and next the men; on the outer edge of the circle, to our left, are a lot of painted heathens, with their red blankets thrown loosely round their naked bodies,

The congregation numbers about two hundred persons. Our first sermon is to the believers, unfolding to them God's provisions and plans for the salvation of the world, administered by the personal Holy Ghost, who employs believers as His visible agents. We close by singing and prayer, and advise them to think much and pray much alone, take some refreshment, and come again at 3 p.m. At the close of the afternoon sermon we invite the seekers of pardon to kneel down on the grass. About one hundred and forty bow before the Lord and enter into a penitential struggle, with a general wailing of lamentation and tears, which cease not for three hours, only as they enter into liberty. We see among them several of the red heathens.

"Do you see that tall, well-dressed Kaffir down on his knees as a seeker?"

"Yes."

"That is Matanzima, a Tembookie chief, a brother of Ngangelizwe, the paramount chief of the Tembookie nation."

We see Charles bending over the chief for half an hour, trying to lead him to Jesus. Poor fellow! he seems to be an earnest seeker. Near the close of the meeting Charles brings the chief to me, and I explain to him the way of salvation by faith, and beg him to surrender himself to God and accept Christ as his Saviour now. He seems very teachable and anxious to know God. Among a number of questions I put to him, that I might ascertain the obstructions in his way and help him to consent to their removal, I said, "Matanzima, how many wives have you got?"

"Two," said he.

"How many children have you by them?"

"Two children by one wife, and one by the other."

"The laws of Jesus Christ will allow you to have but one wife. Are you willing to retain your first as your lawful wife and give the other one up?"

"Yes," he replied promptly; "but what shall I do with her?"

"You must explain to her that you do not put her away in anger, but because you have consented to obey the laws of Christ, which allow a man but one wife; you must not send her away in poverty, but give her whatever she needs for herself and the support of her child, and let her go home to her own people."

"Well," said he, "I will bring her to Mr. Warner and let him settle it."

"Yes," said I, "that will be the best way. Now, having settled that matter in your mind, and consenting to give up all your sins, you need not delay your coming to Jesus Christ, but embrace Him as your Saviour now."

But, instead of a present surrender and a present acceptance of Christ, I saw from his face that he was considering the wife question and wavering in his purpose to give up the sin of polygamy, and soon began to put on his gloves, for he was a fine-looking, well-dressed man, and said, "Now, I must go home."

He did not tell me that he could not consent to Gospel terms, yet I felt but little doubt that, like the rich young man who came to Jesus, and hearing what he should "do to inherit eternal life," he declined and went away sorrowful in his'sins. I was very sorry to believe, and to say to the brethren, that the chief wavered, and would not long remain a seeker.

I mention this case to illustrate one of the most serious difficulties to be encountered in bringing the Kaffirs to God—their ancient system of polygamy.

Meantime, about sixty persons of all ages professed to obtain the pardon of their sins. As fast as they got the witness of forgiveness they were conducted to a place to our left hand to be examined by the missionary.

"Now, Brother Barrett," said I, "you will please to hear the experience of these new converts and get their names and addresses, so that you may know where to find them, and get them into class and under good pastoral training for God. If any are not clear in their testimony to the fact of conscious pardon through the Holy Spirit's witness with theirs, kindly advise them to go back among the seekers and seek till they get it."

It was too cold to preach out that night, so we had a fellowship meeting in Brother Warner's stable specially for the young converts. Over thirty of them arose voluntarily and promptly, one after another, and in great simplicity told what God had done for their souls. The experience of every one was clear except one man, who told about some great light that he had seen some months before and heard a voice telling him that he would be saved. Brother Barrett challenged his experience and asked him several close questions. Charles also questioned him to draw out of him a testimony to a genuine experience of salvation, if he was in possession of it; but his tale was ignored and the people warned against seeking to see sights and to hear audible voices, for the Spirit itself beareth witness with our spirits —not to our eyes or ears, but to our spirits—that we are the children of God. It was a very profitable service for mutual edification.

In a subsequent letter Brother Barrett confirmed my fears in regard to the chief:

"I am sorry to say that Matanzima, the Tembookie chief of the right-hand house, has not retained the religious impressions produced on his mind by your preaching, and has not even permitted me to hold service at his place." (Herod heard John gladly, and did many things, but did not give up his stolen wife, and soon after cut the preacher's head off.) "How can he be a Christian when his powerful counsellors are heathens? I think the chiefs will have to be moved by the nation, and not the nation by the chiefs. A Kaffir chief possesses power only for evil, to fight, to eat up and destroy, but not to improve the condition of his people."

I felt very sorry to leave Woodhouse Forests so soon. We had seen a good work indeed during our one day's services, but if we could have spent a week among them a great work might have been wrought; but my limited time and pre-announced appointments forbade. On Saturday morning, the 21st of July, we bade adieu to this new and interesting mission station and commenced a journey of fifty miles that day to Butterworth.

Brother Warner furnished us a pair of horses to take our conveyance twenty miles, to the Tsoma River, and accompanied us on horseback several miles. At the Tsoma we overtook our horsemen, who had gone on early with the horses, so as to give them a little rest while Brother Warner's pair was doing the work for us. There is an old military station at the Tsoma, and at that time a small detachment of British soldiers, under Colonel Barker, who received us into his hut with a cordial greeting, and entertained us with genuine English hospitality. Rev. John Longden, the missionary at Butterworth, had been there a few days before and prepared the way for us and provided a relay of fresh horses at the Tsoma, which, however, we did not need and respectfully declined to use.

The Tsoma, which is a fine African river, is deep, rocky, and dangerous for travellers, but the water being low we crossed without difficulty. On we go, over high hills and across deep valleys, through a country abounding with grass from one to two feet high, ripened and dried into a rich orange colour. This wavy ocean of grass, which stretches out in every direction into the immeasurable distance, is interspersed with occasional groves of timber and island-looking rocky hill peaks and cliffs. About fifteen miles from the Tsoma we met a Kaffir boy, who said, "Mr. Longden has sent a pair of horses to Captain Cobb's for you," pointing across the hills toward the captain's house, nearly a mile off the main road. So we out-spanned our horses and walked over. The captain, a dashing but generous pioneer Englishman, gave us a cordial welcome. He was a magistrate, under Mr. Warner, over a portion of her Majesty's Fingo subjects.

The last eight miles of our long day's journey were made after the day had departed. The road was rough and dangerous, but our trusty guide rode before and shouted, "To the right," and "To the left," alternately, turning us away from rocks and gullies which might have cost us an upset, at the peril of our necks.

By the mercy of our Master we reached Butterworth about 8 p.m., and were welcomed and kindly entertained by Rev. John Longden and his excellent missionary wife.

CHAPTER XXIV

BUTTERWORTH, CLARKEBURY, AND MORLEY

The Butterworth mission station was established in 1827 under the superintendence of Rev. W. Shaw, by Rev. Mr. Shrewsbury, assisted by Rev. W. Shepstone. The great chief Hintza, of the Amagealeka tribe, had not given his consent for the establishment of the mission in his country, but had not refused, so Mr. Shrewsbury proceeded in the work by faith. "But a few months after," says Mr. Shaw, "with great Kaffir ceremony he sent to the station one of his brothers and a company of his counsellors, mostly old men (counsellors of Kauta, his father), with the following remarkable message: 'Hintza sends to you these men, that you may know them; they are now your friends, for to-day Hintza adopts you into the same family and makes the mission the head of that house. If any one does you wrong, apply to them for redress. If in anything you need help, ask them for assistance;' and as a confirmation of the whole, pointing to a fat ox they had brought, 'There is a cake of bread from the house of Kauta.'"

The mission, thus placed under the protection of law, by the blessing of God and the fostering care of several successive missionaries, grew and prospered for six years, when its harmonious relations were disturbed by the Kaffir war of 1833-34. Hintza joined in the war against the colonists, "behaved treacherously toward certain European traders, who were at the time in his country: and it was believed, also, that he contemplated the murder of his missionary," Rev. John Ayliff, and the destruction of the station.

The mission was re-established after the war, but was destroyed again in the war of 1846-47.

Krielie, the son and successor of Hintza, was anxious for the rebuilding of the mission house and chapel, and gave for the purpose as many cattle as, when sold, were necessary to cover most of the expense of erecting the mission buildings and compensate for the personal losses of the missionary.

At one time, when Rev. W. J. Davis was stationed there, the country was dried up, the cattle were dying, and there was a general apprehension of famine. The chief Krielie assembled a large body of rain-makers near to the mission premises, and with a great gathering of the people they went on with their incantations and vain repetitions daily for a week.

Brother Davis kept himself advised, through his agents, of all their proceedings. Finally, the rain-makers said they could not get any rain, and had found out the reason why and the cause of the drought. When the attention of the people was fully arrested by such an announcement they told their anxious auditors that the missionaries were the cause of the drought, and that there would be no rain while we were allowed to remain in the country.

That brought matters to a very serious crisis, for the rain-makers are generally very influential, usually being doctors and priests as well. When the chief wants rain he sends some cattle to the rain-makers to offer in sacrifice to Imishologu, the spirits of their dead, who are presumed to have great power with Tixo (or God), who will send rain. If they do not succeed the rain-maker returns answer that the cattle were not of the right colour, that cattle of certain peculiar spots were necessary. The details of these spots and shades of colour are so numerous that the rain-maker can not only drive a good trade in the beef line, but stave off the issue till, in the natural order, a copious rain descends, for which he claims the credit, and it is known all over the country as such, a rain-maker's rain. Thus they maintain their influence, and when a number of such men combine against a missionary it becomes a very serious matter.

So when brother Davis heard of the grave charge brought against the missionaries, and specially against himself and family, as they were the only missionaries there, he saw that he must act in self-defence at once. So the next morning, which was Thursday, he rode into their camp while they were in the midst of their ceremonies, and demanded a hearing. They stopped their noise and confusion to hear what he had to say, and he proceeded as follows :

I shall give you a very short talk. Your rain-makers say that the missionaries are the cause of the drought. I say that the rain-makers and the sins of the people are the cause of the drought. The missionaries are as anxious for rain as you are, and our God would give us rain but for your wickedness and rebellion against Him. Now I propose that we test the matter between your rain-makers and the missionaries. They have been trying here for one whole week to bring rain, and have not brought one drop. Look at the heavens, there is not even the sign of a cloud. Now stop all this nonsense and come to chapel next Sabbath, and we will pray to God, who made the heavens and the earth, to give us rain, and we will see who is the true God and who are His true servants and your best friends."

Then Nomsa, the " great wife " of Hintza, who had interposed to save the life of Brother Ayliff a few years before, and the great chief Krielie her son , and their *amapakati*, held a consultation, and decided to dismiss the rain-makers at once, and accept the issue proposed by Brother Davis.

The next day was observed by this missionary Elijah and his

Christian natives as a day of fasting and prayer. On the Sabbath morning the sun, as for many months past, poured his burning rays upon the crisp Kaffrarian hills and valleys, with their famishing flocks, without the shadow of an intervening cloud. At the hour for service the usual congregation assembled, and besides them the great chief and his mother, and many of the heathen people from their "great place." There was a motley crowd of half-clad mission natives, a lot of naked heathens, the great chief in his royal robe, consisting of a huge tiger skin, his queen mother, with beaded skirt of dressed cowskin and ornamental brass wristlets, armlets, and head trinkets, and there, at their feet, the missionary and his family—a grand representation of Church and State, all sweltering with heat, all uneasy, all anxious to see a little cloud arise ; but not one, even of the size of a man's hand, appeared when the service commenced.

After some preliminaries Brother Davis asked the people to kneel down and unite with him in prayer to the Lord God of Elijah to send them rain from heaven. The man of God pleaded his own cause and that of the people at the mercy seat, and importuned. No man was sent to look toward the sea ; but while they remained on their knees in solemn awe, in the presence of God, they heard the big rain drops begin to patter on the zinc roof of the chapel, and lo ! a copious rain, which continued all that afternoon and all night. The whole region was so saturated with water that the river near by became so swollen that the chief and his mother could not cross it that night, and hence had to remain at the mission station till the next day.

That seemed to produce a great impression on the minds of the chief, his mother, and the heathen party in favour of God and His missionaries, and Brother Davis got the name of a great rain-maker ; but signs, wonders, and even miracles will not change the hearts of sinners, for Nomsa lived and died a heathen, and her royal son remained an increasingly dark and wicked heathen.

The Butterworth mission station was destroyed the third time during the Kaffir war of 1851-52, and lay waste about ten years. The mission was established the fourth time, and promised to be more flourishing than ever before, under Rev. John Longden, who commenced operations there about 1862.

We were comfortably quartered in the mission house, and Brother and Sister Longden, with good fare and good cheer, rendered our sojourn with them very pleasant. On Sabbath morning, the 22nd of July, I walked round about their little Zion to find the most suitable place for open air preaching, as we anticipated that the chapel accommodation for about four hundred would be inadequate. We selected a beautiful spot, a quarter of a mile distant, on the bank of the river, richly carpeted with grass.

My labours with the heathen that day caused me to feel keenly my inability to penetrate their heathenish darkness and grapple successfully with their prejudices and superstitions, from my want of an acquaintance with Kaffir life [and customs ; so I determined, by the help of the Lord, with the best sources available, that though I should

not have time during my brief sojourn to master the Kaffir language,
I would master the Kaffir mind. I at once enlisted Charles in the
work of studying native Kaffirism. At suitable times he got the
oldest men together and questioned them about the customs and
faith of their heathen fathers, and wrote down their statements; by
this means, and by what we could learn from the missionaries and
from "Kaffir Laws and Customs," a book compiled from the experience and testimony of several of the oldest missionaries, specially for
the benefit of the government, we made progress in the acquisition of
useful knowledge, which could not be obtained in any college in
Europe, and knowledge that we both turned to good account by the
help of the Holy Spirit.

We had preaching that night in the chapel and a glorious harvest
of souls. On Monday, Tuesday, and Wednesday we preached in
the forenoon by the river, and at night in the chapel. On Thursday
and Thursday night there was a great marriage feast in the neighbourhood, which had been postponed several days on account of our
meetings; so we took that day and night as a season of greatly
needed rest. We resumed again on Friday, and closed our special
series Friday night.

We shook hands with a distinguished old heathen at Butterworth.
His fame was based on two adventures of his life. One was, according to the account in Kaffraria, that on one occasion when Rev.
William Shaw was trying to cross a swollen river the current was
too strong, and carried him down the stream, greatly imperilling his
life; this heathen man plunged in and assisted the *umfundisi* in
getting safely to land. The other was, that in his early life he killed
a boa constrictor. That will give undying fame to any heathen Kaffir,
as one of the greatest men in the nation; indeed, so great, that his
skull is, above all others, selected as the medicine-pot of the great
chief. If such a distinguished individual, however, is allowed to die
a natural death the charm is lost, and his skull is unfitted for such
distinguished royal purposes. But the great snake killer, on the
other hand, must not be surprised and murdered. He must yield
himself a willing sacrifice, and abide in quietness for ten preparatory
days, and then be murdered decently, according to royal decree.
Many, I was told, had thus given themselves up to die and be
canonised among the most honourable Imishologu. This old fellow,
however, was not as yet sufficiently patriotic or ambitious of glory
for that, but chose rather to retain his skull for his own personal use,
and let old Krielie, his master, get on in his medical arrangements
as best he could, and hence took good care to keep himself beyond
Krielie's dominions.

We were introduced to a much more remarkable character at
Butterworth than the killer of the boa constrictor.

Brother Longden gave us in substance the following history of
Umaduna. He said that some months before, in visiting some
heathen kraals, he inquired at each one if there were any Christians
among them. Coming to a kraal containing about three hundred souls,

he put his question to many in different parts of the kraal, and received from all the reply, "Yes, there is one Christian in this kraal. He's a little one, but he is a wonderful man. He has been persecuted, many times beaten, and threatened with death if he did not quit praying to Christ ; but he prays and sings all the more."

Mr. Longden was greatly surprised and pleased to learn that such a martyr spirit was shining so brightly in a region so dark, and sought diligently till he found the wonderful man of whom he had heard such things, and to his astonishment the great man turned out to be a naked boy, about twelve years old. Upon an acquaintance with him, and the further testimony of his heathen neighbours, he found that all he had heard about him, and much more, was true. Hearing these things, we sought an interview with Umaduna, for that was his name. He had attended our meetings from the first, and I had often seen him among the naked Kaffir children in my audiences, but did not know that I was preaching to such a heroic soldier of Jesus till the last day of our series. That day we sent for the lad to come into the mission house, that we might see and learn of him how to suffer for Christ. He hesitated, but after some persuasion consented and came. He was small for a boy of twelve years, and had no clothing except an old sheepskin over his shoulders ; quite black, a serious but pleasant face ; very unassuming, not disposed to talk, but he gave, in modest and firm tones of voice, prompt, intelligent answers to all our questions. The following is the substance of what we elicited from him, simply corroborating the facts narrated before by the missionary :

I said to him, through my interpreter, " Umaduna, how long have you been acquainted with Jesus ?"

"About three years."

"How did you learn about Him and know how to come to Him ?"

"I went to preaching at Heald Town, and learned about Jesus, and that He wanted the little children to come to Him. Then I took Jesus for my Saviour, and got all my sins forgiven and my heart filled with the love of God."

He was not long at Heald Town, but returned to his people, and had since emigrated with them to Fingoland.

"Was your father willing that you should be a servant of Jesus Christ ?"

"Nay ; he told me that I should not pray to God any more, and that I must give Jesus up, or he would beat me."

"What did you say to your father about it ?"

"I didn't say much ; I wouldn't give up Jesus. I prayed to God more and more."

"What did your father do then ?"

"He beat me a great many times."

"Well, when he found he could not beat Jesus out of you what did he do next ?"

"He got a great many boys to come and dance round me and laugh at me and try to get me to dance."

" And wouldn't you dance ? "

" No, I just sat down and would not say anything."

" What did your father do then ? "

" He fastened me up in the hut, and said I must give up Jesus or he would kill me. He left me in the hut all day."

" And what did you do in there ? "

" I kept praying and sticking to Jesus."

" Did you think your father would kill you ? "

" Yes, if God would let him. He fastened me in the hut many times and said he would kill me."

" Umaduna, are you sure you would be willing to die for Jesus ? "

" Oh yes, if He wants me to."

" Are you not afraid to die ? "

" No, I should be glad to die for Jesus, if He wants me to."

Brother Roberts gave him a copy of the New Testament in Kaffir for his use after he should have learned to read, and said he had intended to speak some words of encouragement to the boy, but on hearing him talk he found the rustic little Christian so far in advance of himself that he could not say anything to him.

On Saturday, the 28th of July, we travelled nearly fifty miles from Butterworth to Clarkebury, our next field of labour.

This mission station was called Clarkebury in honour of Dr. Adam Clarke.

The only Europeans killed by natives in connection with our Kaffrarian missions lost their lives in connection with this station. The first was Mr. Rawlins, an assistant, who was killed by a horde of marauders, not far from the station. The other was the Rev. J. S. Thomas, a thorough Kaffir scholar and an energetic, brave missionary. It should be said to the credit of the Amatembu nation, that they as a people had nothing to do with the assassination of these good men, but deeply regretted their fall, which was by the murderous hands of a band of robbers. The missionaries, however, have suffered endless petty annoyances from the heathen chiefs and people. The following story, told me by Rev. W. J. Davis, may serve as an illustration of this:

" When I was stationed at Clarkebury, in 1832, the Tembookie or Amatembu chief Vadana coveted a pot we daily used in our cooking. He came and begged me every day for that pot for a long time. I gave him many presents, but could not spare the pot, and positively refused to give it up.

" Finally the chief said, ' Davis, I'll have that pot ! '

" The next day Vadana came with thirty of his warriors, all armed with assegais, a kind of javelin, their principal war weapon.

" They stood in defiant array before me, and the chief said, ' Davis, we have come for that pot.'

" ' We need the pot,' I replied, ' for cooking our food, and, as I told you before, I won't give it to you.'

" ' You must give it to us, or we'll take it.

" ' With thirty armed warriors against one unarmed missionary you

17

have the power to take it, but if that is the way you are going to treat your missionary just give me a safe passage out of your country and I'll leave you.'

"'Davis, are you not afraid of us?' demanded the chief sharply.

"'No, I'm not afraid of you. I know you can kill me, but if I had been afraid to die I never would have come among such a set of savages as you are.'

"'Davis,' replied the chief sternly, 'are you not afraid to die?'

"'No! if you kill me I have a home in heaven, where the wicked cease from troubling and the weary are at rest.'

"Then, turning to his men, the chief said, 'Well, this is a strange thing. Here's a man who is not afraid to die, and we shall have to let him keep his pot.'

"When the chief was turning to go away he said, 'Davis, I love you less now than I did before, but I fear you more.'

The chief never gave his missionary any further trouble about his pot, but showed greater respect to him than ever before.

My purpose was to remain at Clarkebury only till Wednesday morning, but Brother Hargraves said that he had sent a messenger to Ngangelizwe, the great chief of the Tembookie nation, inviting him and his counsellors to attend our services, and that the chief had returned answer that they could not be with us at the commencement, but would come on Wednesday. So we consented to stay at any rate till after Wednesday. On Sabbath morning, the 29th of July, we had the chapel crowded, and had about one hundred and fifty penitents forward that first night, and many souls were saved during our series of services.

On Thursday morning, the day appointed for the chief to come with his counsellors to our services, a messenger arrived, according to Kaffir custom, to announce that "Ngangelizwe is in the path." He had but fifteen miles to travel from "great place" to Clarkebury, and we thought he might arrive by midday.

About 3 p.m. his vanguard appeared on the high hill half a mile east of the station and took their stand. Half an hour later another party came in sight and halted in like manner. It was then nearly an hour before the great chief, with the main body of the royal *cortège*, appeared. The cavalry of the train, consisting of about forty counsellors, fell into line single file, the chief being about the middle, and all came down the hill at a full gallop. Arriving, they at once dismounted, but all remained outside the mission yard with the horses except the chief and his brother Usiqukati, who came directly in. Brother Hargraves met and shook hands with them at the gate and introduced them to me and my party. All the ceremony required on our part, I learned, was simply to pronounce the name of the chief and shake hands, and so with his brother.

The name Ngangelizwe means "Big-as-the-World."

He had a very extensive, rich, grassy, well-watered, undulating, beautiful country. His tribe numbered about one hundred thousand souls, of whom fifteen or twenty thousand were warriors. The chief was nearly six feet in height, straight, well-proportioned, of the copper Kaffir complexion instead of black, a smooth, pleasant countenance, a sweet, charming voice. The two chiefs took tea with us in the mission house, while the *amapakati* (his counsellors) and their attendants went to the huts provided for them.

The chiefs were well-dressed, in English costume, but their men had each simply a kaross of dressed skin or a red blanket.

Soon we are all in the chapel for the evening service. Charles and I stand side by side in the altar; to our right and left sit the missionaries; in the front seats before the altar railings sit the king and his brother, and on the same seats in front about a dozen Europeans, including several British soldiers from Fingoland. Then we see next the body of the chapel halfway down filled with these heathen counsellors and attendants and a lot of red heathen from Fingoland, making, perhaps, one hundred and fifty of this class; then in the rear, and at all the doors and windows outside, are the regular worshippers to whom we have been preaching twice a day for four days.

We close the preaching service and dismiss the congregation, to give an opportunity for all to leave who do not prefer to remain for the after service. No one stirs to get out. We call for the seekers to kneel before God, surrender to Him, and accept Christ. Many of our former hearers fall down on their faces and worship God, and soon report from a blessed experience of pardon that God is in them of a truth.

The chief and his people sit and gaze and wonder. During the prayer meeting Brother Henry B. Warner stands up near the window to my right, and by his commanding appearance, good voice, and eloquent, euphonious ring of the Kaffir language at once arrests the attention of the whole assembly, and, addressing the chief and his counsellors, tells them the story of his own conversion to God; they all knew him well from of old and knew what a sinner he had been, and now learned the details of God's saving mercy to him, demonstrating the truth of the Gospel news they heard that night, followed by an earnest exhortation to them to seek God without a moment's delay. Then we all kneel down in solemn silent prayer. Nothing is heard now but the suppressed sighs and sobs of wounded souls in the different parts of the house, pierced by the Spirit's two-edged sword.

The presence of God the Holy Spirit moving perceptibly among the prostrate mass of men before us becomes awfully sublime beyond description. The salvation of these heathens now hangs in the scales of a poised beam; many of us feel that the Spirit hath clearly offered to them the gift of eternal life in Christ. They are almost persuaded. They have reached a crisis. Let any one of these old counsellors avowedly take a decided stand for God, and the whole of them will follow his example. Unable to get beyond that point, we close the service at 11 p.m., and all silently retire from the field to come up to the work again in the morning.

Early the next day Brother Warner had a long talk with Ngangelizwe's counsellors. They admitted to him that what they had heard at the service the night before was true, and that they were conscious of an extraordinary influence on their minds, and that they believed their chief wanted to accept Christ; but, said they, "Ngangelizwe cannot act alone, for he is bound by solemn promise not to be a Christian; and none of us can act alone, because we exacted that promise from him, and we are bound in honour to stand to our own position. We cannot go and do ourselves what we have bound the chief not to do."

That day we had the chiefs and counsellors in chapel in the same order as the night before. We preached from St. Luke's abstract of St. Paul's preaching to a heathen audience on Mars Hill, on the Unknown God. We traced the parallel between the moral condition and superstitious worship of the literary heathen of Athens and the illiterate heathen Tembookies. We have clear indications in Kaffir traditions, sacrifices, and devotions of the struggle of their moral nature to feel after the unknown God, and to find a supply for the conscious woes and wants of their souls. Having dug down effectually into the regions of their beliefs and conscious experiences, and having brought out their admitted facts demonstrating the truth of Bible delineations of human corruption, guilt, and bondage, and their vain efforts, by their sacrifices and sufferings, to atone for their sins, or gain rest for their souls, we declared to them the unknown God and His glorious provision of mercy for them in Christ. We then pressed home the fact that God "now commandeth all men everywhere to repent." Illustrating the work of repentance wrought by the Holy Spirit in the hearts of sinners, resulting in their acceptance of Christ, I gave, among other examples, the cases of Thakombau, King of Fiji, and of George the Third, King of the Friendly Islands. I showed that their complications in the sin of polygamy, and all forms of heathenism, were quite as bad as anything in Kaffirland, but that yielding to the Spirit they had triumphed, and had become Christians.

We explain, in simplicity, the duty of repentance and an intelligent acceptance of Christ by faith in God's own record concerning Him, and the Spirit's witness and renewing work, demonstrating the truth of the Gospel and the saving power of Jesus. At the close of the sermon we proceed as usual with the prayer meeting. A large number of seekers came forward, and a similar struggle to that of last night, between the powers of light and darkness, ensues. Ngangelizwe shows great concern; his brother is evidently in an agony of awakening; some counsellors seem in great distress; others of them, by their looks and a scoffing display of their great teeth, are using their influence against the work. One fellow, with a large cowskin kaross over his shoulders, is a child of the devil, an enemy of all righteousness, as full of all subtlety and mischief as Elymas the sorcerer.

In the midst of the prayer meeting Charles rises from his knees and stands within an arm's length of the chief and his brother, and exhorts them personally for half an hour. You see at once that my

Zulu is master of the difficult situation. The natural gracefulness and perfection of his action, and the power of his logic, told manifestly on the trembling Felix before him. The missionaries and others who understood the Kaffir said afterwards that they had never heard such a display of Kaffir oratory in all their lives. He explained to Ngangelizwe that the powers that be are of God, and hence it was for God, and not a lot of wicked counsellors, to put down one ruler and set up another, and that a man who will reject the counsel of God and follow the counsel of wicked men shall certainly come to grief as that the righteous God rules in the heavens.

"Kobi and Pato," continued Charles, "were great chiefs. Kama, their brother, was a boy, and had no people. These three chiefs had the offer of Christ; Kama was the only one that accepted Him; Kobi and Pato rejected Christ and called Kama a fool, and said he would be a scabby goat and never have any people. Their wicked counsellors told them if they received Christ they would lose all their people, all their cattle, and have nothing, like poor Kama; but what was the result? God gave them up to follow their wicked counsellors, who advised them to go to war with the English. Kobi died a miserable refugee and had the burial of a dog. Pato had spent many miserable years a prisoner on Robbin Island. Kama remained true to God and kept out of the war against the English, and now all the people of the Amaxosa nation, once ruled by Kobi and Pato, belong to Kama, who is going down to his grave in honourable old age, in the midst of peace and plenty, full of a glorious hope of a blessed home in heaven. More than one thousand of his people have accepted Christ, and all of them abide in the peaceable possession of their homes, under the protection of the British government."

This but indicates the range of Charles's inimitable discourse to Ngangelizwe, and he appealed most solemnly to Usiqukati to submit to God and receive Christ, whatever the chief and his counsellors might do.

Our time for such a work was too short. I felt sure that they could not stand many such shocks of awakening truth, applied by the Spirit's power, as it was on the two occasions when we had them before us. Ngangelizwe afterwards shook hands with Charles, and they had a friendly private interview. The political league seemed to be the principal barrier.

Ngangelizwe said he would stay and hear us again that evening; but about sunset a man came dashing down the hill at full speed, his horse in a foam of perspiration and panting for breath, and announced that one of Ngangelizwe's children was dying, and that the chief must return to the great place at once. The chief said he was very sorry to leave, but that he was obliged to go.

I learned some weeks afterwards that Ngangelizwe invited one of the local preachers to preach at his "great place," and after he had preached told him to come every Sunday and preach to him, for he wanted to have preaching at his place, whatever the *amapakati* might say. The missionaries believed that all that ado about the dying child was a ruse got up by some of those wicked counsellors to hurry Ngangelizwe away for fear he would that night become a Christian.

Having thus lost the heathen portion of our audience, instead of preaching that night, as we intended, we had a fellowship meeting. Up to that period of our series of services one hundred and eighty-five persons, on a personal examination, had professed to have obtained the pardon of their sins. About seventy, principally the young converts, spoke at our fellowship meeting that night. I sat beside Brother William Davis, who interpreted their talk to me. It was marvellously interesting. I can give but a few specimens, and they are as weak as water compared with their native Kaffir originals, accompanied by graceful actions and tears and the peculiar idiomatic force of their language.

A man stood up and said, " I always hated the mission stations, and hated all the people who went to them. Often when I have seen them going to chapel I got so angry I wanted to kill them. But I heard that Isikunisivutayo was coming, and I came to see what was to be done. I stood outside the chapel last Sunday and laughed and mocked. On Monday night I came in and Isikunisivutayo set me on fire, and I felt that I was sinking into hell. I left as quick as I could and started home, but my sins were such a load on me I could not run, but fell down and thought I was going to die. The next morning I felt very glad that I was not in hell. I came to the meeting that day and received Jesus, and now my soul is full of glory."

Isikunisivutayo means a burning fire-stick or torch. In the fall the whole country is covered with a thick growth of brown grass from one to two feet in height. As spring approaches, to get the full benefit of the new crop for their cattle, they take their burning fire-sticks and soon set a thousand hills in a blaze, spreading and sweeping in every direction to prepare the way for the new harvest of grass. It is common with the Kaffirs to give every distinguished stranger some characteristic name, by which, instead of his real name, he is known among them.

I was told beforehand that I should get a new name, and there were not a few European conjectures as to what it would be. Some thought it would be Longbeard, which bears no comparison to the appreciative, poetic descriptive name which the Kaffirs gave me, The Burning Fire-stick, which the Lord was using to set the whole country in a blaze, burn up all their dead works, and prepare the way for spiritual life, verdure, and plenty. Among the converted heathen at that fellowship meeting, one old man arose, threw his kaross gracefully across his breast and over his left shoulder, and told a marvellous story about his heathenish prejudices against the mission stations and the missionaries. " My heart," said he, "was as tough as the hide of a rhinoceros, but last night the Spirit's sword cut right through it and let in the light of God. I received Jesus Christ and He gave me a tender heart filled with His love."

These are mere specimen illustrations of the experience of over sixty persons who spoke, and nearly all they said was repeated to me in English, sentence by sentence, by Brother Davis.

Our next station was Morley, thirty-six miles distant from Clarkebury; the missionary in charge was William Rayner. This station was named in honour of Rev. George Morley, Missionary Secretary in London. It was founded by Rev. William Shepstone in 1829.

Brother Rayner, with his own hands, assisted by his natives, had built a large, comfortable mission house and a pretty chapel which would seat about four hundred persons, and had built also a small chapel in a village five miles west of Morley.

On Sabbath morning, the 5th of August, I selected a small level plot of ground by a little stream at the foot of the high hill east of the chapel. Our audience contained four whites and about four hundred natives. We stood on the precipitous bank of the stream and cried, " The Spirit and the bride say, Come." About one hundred and fifty fell down on their faces and worshipped God, and many of them that day drank freely and were saved. That night we preached in the chapel and had a glorious work of the Spirit. On Monday Charles preached in the chapel. He preached once at Butterworth and once at Clarkebury, to the great astonishment of the missionaries.

On Monday night we preached again, and a great work was done. On Tuesday we had the chief of that part of Ngangelizwe's dominions, Ndunyela, twenty-five wives and women of his court, and about one hundred and twenty of his warriors. Ndunyela was a broad, thick-set man of about forty years, fine open face, not black, but a reddish bronze. Some of his copper-coloured ladies had a fine Jewish physiognomy, and all were well attired in native costume. His warriors were naked, except a blanket or kaross thrown loosely round their shoulders. Brother Rayner made them a present of a "cake of bread," namely, a bullock, which they slaughtered and devoured in the afternoon. They are very expert in butchering a beef with their assegais, and in cutting out all the fleshy parts into strips; these they broil on the fire till about half done, and the smoking strips of rare roast are passed among the long circle. One fellow seizes it and clinches one end of it with his teeth, and with his assegai cuts it off an inch or two from his mouth, just as much as he can get between his teeth, and passes it to the next, who follows his example. So on it goes round, strip after strip, a mouthful at a time, till nothing is left but the skin and bones of the beast. Every man has a right to a seat at such a feast. Whenever any Kaffir kills a beef all the men within several miles round will assemble as promptly as birds of prey, and any one of them will eat as much as the owner. If a man should refuse to make it a free thing he would be branded as a man too stingy and mean to live among them, and would be in danger of being smelled out as a witch. It is not easy for such people to appreciate English economy. To see a missionary kill a beef, and carefully cut it up and carry it into his house, and keep it to be eaten by himself and his own family, along at different times, as may suit his convenience, why, to a lot of hungry Kaffirs it is the most shocking piece of business imaginable! Hence, if they want to berate a mean fellow, after exhausting their old stock of opprobrious epithets, they cap the whole by adding, "Why, you are as stingy as a missionary."

Brother Rayner gave the chief Ndunyela his choice, to take his people home in the afternoon, after they had eaten their "cake of bread," or to stay for the evening service. We were anxious for them to stay, but wished them to act with entire freedom of will. He sent his women home, but he and all his men remained. They occupied the front seats in the chapel; we gave them the Gospel message in all plainness, and they seemed deeply impressed, but did not yield.

During the prayer meeting Charles had a close talk with the chief. He admitted that what he had heard during that day and evening had convinced him that he was a poor sinner, that Jesus Christ was the only Saviour of sinners, and that he and his people ought to receive Him, and when Charles urged him to surrender to God and accept Christ he replied, "I made Ngangelizwe promise that he would not be a Christian, and I am in honour bound to stand by our old customs, having compelled him to do so."

After the prayer meeting we had a fellowship meeting, and those heathen heard the distinct testimony of more than thirty witnesses to the saving power of Jesus in their own hearts. The pastor reported that one hundred and fifty were converted to God during our three days' meeting.

On Wednesday morning we set out for Buntingville, thirty-six miles from Morley Station. This mission belongs to Damasi, son of the great chief Faku, who, though legally the king of the whole Amapondo nation, has for many years allowed Damasi the sovereign rule of all the Pondos west of the Umzimvubu River, and the two governments are so distinct that each can make war or peace with other tribes without involving the other. Damasi had furnished most of the funds by the sale of cattle for the erection of the new mission house at Buntingville, and paid a large proportion of the funds necessary for the erection of the new chapel they were preparing to build.

We reached the "great place" of King Damasi about 4 p.m. Our horsemen had been there some time before us, and had a hut arranged for our accommodation. Brother Hunter introduced me to Damasi as Isikunisivutayo, a new *umfundisi* from the other side of the great waters. The chief was over six feet in height, large and corpulent, of a copper complexion, a generous, open countenance, and altogether a fine specimen of a heathen chief. He took us into his palace, which was a round hut about thirty feet in diameter, the wall about six feet high, made of clay, with a round roof of thatch, about twelve feet high at the apex. He introduced us to his "great wife" and some of his daughters, and showed us his fine store of firewood neatly piled up to the left as we enter, and his great earthen jars, cooking utensils, milksack, his royal robes or tiger skins, and his tiger tails. If any Kaffir kills a tiger he must at once inform the chief, to whom all the tigers are supposed to belong, who has the skin taken off with great ceremony, and dressed for himself.

None but a royal Kaffir is allowed to own or wear a tiger's skin. A tiger's tail stretched over the top of a stick about five feet in length is a formidable sight before the hut of any Kaffir. When the chief wishes to call a man to answer for any offence, especially when a fine is to be imposed or his property confiscated, he sends one of his *imisila*, or sheriffs, to set up a tiger's tail in front of the offender's hut. When the poor fellow comes out in the morning and sees the dreadful summons—for it is usually served when the man is asleep—he is filled with consternation and must go at once and reckon with his master, who has the power to take his property or his life.

All the documentary details and process necessary to arrest and arraign a civilised man are here accomplished at once by the magic spell of a tiger's tail.

The chief pointed to a high perpendicular cliff, half a mile from his hut, and informed us that he threw his bad fellows over that precipice and dashed them to pieces. Many a poor wretch, no doubt, has found a quick passage out of the world from that cliff, and yet Damasi's appearance was not that of a tyrant, but of a kind-hearted, generous man, and he was free from that mean spirit which most chiefs evince, of begging a blanket of every stranger who may visit them. When we subsequently sent word to the great chief Faku that we expected to visit him he replied to the messenger, "Is Isikunisivutayo travelling with blankets?"

His more noble son, Damasi, supplied us with new, clean blankets for our use, and everything we needed for our comfort during our sojourn with him, and scorned even a hint at pay in return. I was told of a clergyman who visited a neighbouring chief, who at once asked the *umfundisi* if he had brought him any blankets? "No," said he, "but I have brought you something better. I have come to tell you the good news about the great God, who made the heavens above us, and who made the earth, who made us, who gave you all your lands, your mealies, Kaffir corn, and pumpkins, and who gave you your cattle, goats, and sheep. He is our Father and——"

The chief, interrupting him, said, "Is He your Father?"

"Yes," replied the missionary; He is my Father, and has sent me to tell you good news."

"Well," said the chief with a grin, "if your Father is so kind as to give us all these good things for nothing, and if you are a true son of His, can't you give me one blanket?"

After Damasi had shown us the things in his house, his bloody cliff, and his great cattle kraal, said to be a thousand yards in circumference, and the largest one in Kaffraria, he said, "I am glad to see you, but the most of my people are gone. I will call all who are near to come to-morrow, but we are only a few now;" and then went on to tell us that, owing to the drought the preceding year, their stores of food were nearly used up, and that a large number of his people had gone to the Umzimvubu to get supplies of food, and that last night Umhlonhlo's people had attacked his son's kraal and driven away a large number of cattle and horses, and that the war cry had called a large number of his warriors away in pursuit.

While we stood talking to Damasi we saw a lot of young Kaffirs in pursuit of a bullock. Down the hill they came at full speed, and halted in front of us.

"There," said the chief, pointing to the panting bullock, "is a cake of bread for you." It was driven to the back of our hut, assegaied, skinned, and quartered with great despatch. The whole of the beef was hung up by quarters in our hut and the skin laid in a roll near the door. According to custom, the whole belonged to the strange *umfundisi*, who is expected to make a present of the hide to the chief, and also to send a forequarter to the chief's "great wife," and take the chief as his guest during his sojourn, all of which we performed with due ceremony. We had brought with us a supply of bread, coffee, and sugar; so with the beef broiled on the end of a stick we entertained his royal highness in good style.

On Sabbath morning, the 12th of August, our congregation assembled behind a hut near the chief's mansion, consisting of Damasi, his eight wives, and thirty or forty children (Damasi said he did not know how many children he had), and about one hundred warriors, armed with their assegais and shields, ready for war emergencies. Damasi came out in state. Instead of the red blanket he had worn the day before he had a large tiger skin over his shoulders, which constituted his entire dress, except a pair of rustic slippers on his feet. They all listened with great attention, but no decisive result was reached. Preaching to heathen, beginning with first principles, and leading them on to a living Saviour required at least an hour and a half, but we seldom failed to reach the salvation of souls on every such occasion. However, some of our friends thought we preached too long; so on this occasion we agreed to try a new plan, which was to preach half an hour, and then have a little talk with them personally and draw them out, and after a brief recess resume the thread of discourse and go on for another half hour, and so on.

We got into the subject very satisfactorily. They appeared to understand it, and nearly all seemed to agree that our words were true, but we had not reached the vital point of convincing them of their lost condition and of offering a present Saviour when the time came for recess. We then asked them to talk and ask any questions they wished on the subject of discourse. Some questions were asked and answered, when one of the counsellors said he "did not believe in a future state, or in Imishologu; that we all die like a pig, and there is no more of us." The chief replied to him, saying, "The man could not be such a fool as that, for all our fathers believed in Imishologu, and so do we, and our people."

The Kaffir infidel then got up and went away, and, seeing that they all were getting restless, we thought it best to dismiss them and have them assemble for another service in the afternoon. We felt that service to be very unsatisfactory. Charles seemed really dis-

couraged, the first and only time I found him so. I assured him
that the result was what we might have expected; having opened
our Gospel battery against such a stronghold of wild heathenism
we should have fired away till they should at least feel the weight
of our heaviest metal; but instead of that we had called a parley.
Charles cheered up, and we agreed that in preaching to the heathen,
no matter what others said, we would never stop short of giving
them the whole plan of salvation.

In the interval Damasi's counsellors gathered round him in a circle
and discussed the exciting topics of the day, especially the war with
Umhlonhlo, and when we assembled for a second service a number
of the warriors who were with us in the morning found it convenient
to be absent. The chief said their duties called them home. We
did the best we could to make up for our failure in the forenoon,
and at night we had a prayer meeting in our hut. We had as seekers
that night the three white traders, Mr. Straghan, son, and son-in-law,
two Kaffir men, one of Damasi's eight wives, and two of his daughters.
Mr. Straghan, his son-in-law, and a Kaffir man professed to obtain
peace with God. Next morning, before breakfast, we had a fellowship meeting, during which Damasi came into the hut. Chief Vava,
and two or three of his party, and the white men gave their testimony
to the saving grace of God. Then old Damasi said, " I and my
people are all Christians. We have all been Christians ever since
Mr. Wakeford came among us."

A hard old Christian, we thought, with eight wives; but he had
received the missionaries, and helped liberally to build a mission
house, and was engaged in building a chapel, and when Brother
Hunter's congregations fall off he has only to inform his great chief
to get a large audience of heathen; and why should he not have as
much claim to be a Christian as the formalists in Christian countries,
who do less for the cause of Christ ?

We felt very grateful for the old chief's kindness, and very sorry
that he did not so feel his need of Christ as to accept Him 'as a
Saviour from his sins. On Monday, about 10 a.m., we bade adieu
to Brother Hunter and his party, and to Damasi, and received his
" kuhle hamba," and under the conduct of our former guide, Brother
Morrison, pushed on in our journey toward Shawbury, distant about
thirty-six miles.

CHAPTER XXV

SHAWBURY AND OSBORN

SHAWBURY was named in honour of the old pioneer who planned and superintended the founding of the whole line of old Kaffrarian missions, the Rev. William Shaw. For picturesque scenery—hills, dales, mimosa groves, cataracts, deep gorges, and precipitous cliffs, overhanging the Tsitsa River, a bold and beautiful stream—the site of Shawbury surpasses all the rest.

This became the most populous, and was hence thought to be the most promising, of any of the Kaffrarian stations; but while it reached a population of three thousand souls its actual membership of professing Christians never much exceeded one hundred. At the time of our visit the number was about ninety-five, and the whole station involved in war complications jeopardising its existence. It is located within the lines of the Amapondumsi tribe, but the Tsitsa River near by is the boundary between that tribe and Damasi's Pondos, with whom they are at war; yet the most of the mission station people are Fingoes, and don't really belong to either of those tribes, and should not have been involved in the war at all, and would not if they had improved their opportunities and become Christians. As they did not belong really to either party they were under no legal obligation to fight, for both belligerent parties were bound by promise to the missionaries not to interfere with them; but those three thousand natives had their beautiful lines of huts on the mission station, their fields of corn, and cattle, enjoying the ministerial and magisterial care of the missionary, released from the iron rule of Kaffir law and the terror of the witch doctor, and yet, the mass of them refusing to submit to Christ, they "waxed fat and kicked," and God gave them a little leeway to themselves, and they soon got themselves into an awful complication of war troubles.

While I was labouring in Graham's Town I first heard of their sad state by a letter from their missionary, Rev. Mr. Gedye, to Rev. W. J. Davis, in which Brother Gedye stated that he had received notice from Damasi to leave the station, as he would not be responsible for his life or that of his family; for he meant to destroy Umhlonhlo and take his country, and the mission station was right in his warpath. But Umhlonhlo, on the other hand, had forbidden him to leave the

286

place, so he and his family were in jeopardy of life. Our sympathy was greatly enlisted for him and his family, and also for his native teacher, whom he was protecting in a locked room in the mission house against the threatened vengeance of Umhlonhlo, and earnest mention was made of them in our private and public prayers.

Some time after that Rev. Mr. Solomon, on his way to No Man's Land, spent a night near Shawbury, and, hearing of the position of Mr. Gedye, sent for Umhlonhlo to visit his camp next day, and thus obtaining an interview with the chief persuaded him to release his missionary and let him go away. Soon after Mr. Gedye took his family and went to Clarkebury, where I met him; his native teacher escaped also and went to Natal. Brother Hargraves, from Clarkebury, and Brother Rayner, from Morley, had gone to Shawbury, and had a council with Umhlonhlo and his leading men, to try to settle the difficulties between the chief and his missionary and prevent the total wreck of the station, which was hard aground in a place where two seas met; but I believe they considered their mission a failure, and brought away the impression that the mission people were so demoralised that there was but little hope for them politically or spiritually, for after their missionary left they had a Kaffir beer feast, had a great fight among themselves, battering and cutting each other, and had actually killed one man. This briefly, leaving out many details, was the state of the case so far as we had learned it before our visit to Shawbury; but we learned much more before we got through. On the last Friday preceding our visit Umhlonhlo's marauders had invaded Damasi's country and driven off a lot of horses and cattle, and on the Saturday night preceding the Shawbury mission people had rescued a lot of cattle which a band of Damasi's warriors were driving away from Umhlonhlo's dominions; so they were now in the midst of wars almost daily. There was but little danger to white travellers in the daytime, but at night it was not expected that warriors should readily distinguish the colour of a man's skin, and Umhlonhlo had issued an order that no one should travel within his lines after dark.

We left Damasi's "great place" on Monday, the 13th of August, and it being but thirty-six miles to Shawbury we hoped to reach there before night, not only on account of the chief's orders and the danger of travelling after dark, but also because of the very rough travelling near Shawbury and the dangerous ford of the Tsitsa; but unhappily we got a late start, so that five miles of fearfully steep, rough roads, and the rocky, diagonal ford of the river of about a hundred and fifty yards, had to be made in the darkness of a moonless night, through the lines of Umhlonhlo's armed sentinels.

We worked our way slowly along, and told all the warriors we met about the great preaching services to commence next day at the station, and to be sure and come and bring their friends. When we got to the drift it was so dark we could not see the line of the ford or where we should land on the other side; but we got a native guide, who piloted us through and on to the station. Our guide was not troubled to take off his clothes to wade across the river, for he had none on him, and had probably never been burdened with an article of clothing in his life. Neither he nor any of his compatriots have any laundry bills to pay.

To our agreeable surprise we found that Rev. Charles White, missionary from Osborn station, thirty-five miles beyond, had come to meet us, and was waiting to receive us at the mission house. There was a white trader still remaining on the station, a good man with a pious wife, who did what they could to supply all that we needed for ourselves and our horses. A kind native Christian woman did the honours of the kitchen for us, and with Brother White for our priest we were all right, unless we should be surprised by a night attack from the Pondos, which we felt assured would not be ordered by our friend Damasi while we were there.

On Tuesday, at 11 a.m., we had the chapel crowded with five or six hundred hearers. From our standpoint we preached to them plainly but kindly, illustrating from Jewish history the parallels of their own, and showed them that when the Jews were true to God they enjoyed the peace of God in their hearts and His protection against their enemies; but when they despised and abused their mercies they brought guilt and remorse upon their own souls, and God in such cases, after bearing long with them, and doing everything possible to bring them to repentance, delivered them over to their enemies and all the horrors of the most desolating wars, and their only remedy was a return to God. They sat in darkness and in the shadow of death, bound in affliction and iron, chained in dungeons, approaching death casting its dark shadow upon them, and why? "Because they rebelled against the words of God, and contemned the counsel of the Most High: therefore He brought down their heart with labour; they fell down, and there was none to help." Poor sinners! What did they do? "They cried unto the Lord in their trouble, and He saved them out of their distresses. He brought them out of darkness and the shadow of death, and brake their bands in sunder. Oh that men would praise the Lord for His goodness, and for His wonderful works to the children of men!" There was deliverance and a shout of victory and praise to God for His wonderful works.

"Now see how this fits the fact at Shawsbury. Here you have had the Gospel preached for thirty years. You have come to this beautiful spot from all parts, and have been living under the shade of God's missionaries. Besides a preached Gospel every week you have had schools for the education of your children, and many of you have been taught to read God's Book; the blessing of God has been upon your fields, your cattle, your children, your homes, even your dogs have been exempt from the curse of the witch doctors of the heathen! What have you done in return for all these mercies of God? Of three thousand souls on this station not quite one hundred of you are connected with the society at all—one hundred and six a year ago and now about ninety-five members on this whole station, and but a small proportion of them true disciples of Jesus ; and because ye have rebelled against the words of God and contemned the counsel of the Most High, therefore He is bringing down your hearts with labour, you are falling down, and there is no man to help you. We are not here to upbraid you, or mock you in your misery, but to pity you and beg you to consider your ways and turn away from your sins, and cry unto the Lord in your trouble, who may save you out of your distresses."

This is a mere illustration of the general drift of a discourse of an hour and half, which Charles sent home with the unmistakable ring of Kaffir periods which seldom missed their aim. We then called for penitents, and about fifty at once came out avowedly as seekers, and a small number were saved. We did not consider it safe to hold meetings at night, as they had to stand by their assegais to guard their homes ; but we announced for preaching again in the afternoon.

To our surprise at the next service our congregation did not exceed one hundred and fifty persons, and they seemed more dead than alive. We had about thirty seekers, and they were in a gloomy, unbelieving state, and but few accepted Christ. On Wednesday we preached twice, but only had out about one hundred and fifty, and it was a hard drag. An invitation had been sent to Umhlonhlo to attend the services, and on Wednesday he came to the trader's shop, but did not put in an appearance at the chapel, giving as a reason that Adam Kok, with eight waggons, and many of his men were passing through his country, and he had to go and meet them ; so he went to meet Captain Kok, and took with him the headman of the station, whom we hoped to lead in a different direction.

On Thursday we left Charles to do the forenoon preaching, and Brother Roberts, Stuart, and I set out for a visit to Tsitsa Falls, five miles distant. As we were passing the line huts eastward from the mission house we had an opportunity of seeing the Kaffir mode of storing away their corn. Gideon of old threshed wheat by the wine press to hide it from the Midianites ; so for a similar reason the Kaffirs hide their corn. They dig holes in their cattle kraals from eight to ten feet deep and from six to eight feet wide, lined with waterproof cement. The shape is that of the old Hebrew cisterns in Palestine, drawn in at the mouth to the diameter of about a foot, leaving space for a small Kaffir to descend to get out their hidden stores as they are needed. Their women carry the corn in large baskets on their heads. Kaffir corn grows like broom corn, with a seed of double the size ; and *mealies*, a staple with them, is simply maize or Indian corn.

We saw them, on this occasion, pouring in turn after turn, till the hole was nearly full of clean corn in good order. Those holes are thus filled and covered with a broad flat stone and then with the *débris* of the cattle kraal, and no stranger can tell from any outward indications whether there are any such deposits, or where hidden. During the wars the colonial soldiers used to thump over the cattle kraals with their ramrods sounding for corn.   If such a hole was partly empty it returned a hollow sound, but if full they were hard to find.

On our return we said, " Charles, how did you get on in the chapel to-day ? "

" We had out about the same number as yesterday, and I preached as well as I could."

" Did you have a prayer meeting ? "

" No, I thought we had better wait till you should get back."

Charles did not ordinarily wait for anybody where the Spirit led the way, but he felt the terrible repulsion which we all felt, but which as yet we could not understand.   That afternoon we preached again and had a few conversions.   We had a fellowship meeting.   About a dozen others spoke, professing to have obtained peace, but it was with trembling, and several who had professed did not speak at all ; so that in everything there seemed to be the presence of some diabolical spell.   Next morning, when we were preparing to leave with Brother White for his station, we learned that the official members of the society wanted to meet us in council, to which we readily consented without having the least hint of what was to be the subject of debate.   They soon gathered round us in the dining room, squatting down on all sides and in every corner, as sombre a looking set of natives as I had seen at any time.   I saw by their long pause that something solemn was pending, and soon perceived, by the direction of their eyes, who had been appointed to open the case and who was to plead their cause.   After a little time an old man whom they called Elijah arose, and with the gravity of a Roman senator said : " We want to know why the district meeting has thrown us away.   What great crime have we been guilty of that we should be driven off like scabby goats, to be devoured by the wild beasts ?   It is not common to punish men till they have been tried and found guilty ; even among the heathen a man is smelled out before he is eaten up, but here, in the midst of our dreadful punishment, we have come to ask you what is our crime ? "

I at once woke up to the subject, for I found that we were put upon our trial under a very grave charge, involving the issues of life and death.   A lawyer by the name of Job was sitting beside Elijah, biding his time, and from his flashing eyes and swelling jugulars I knew it was no child's play that we had to do.   So by a few questions in an undertone to Brother White I got an outline of the facts, and by this time Elijah was seated and Job was on his feet, and, passing his blanket round his otherwise naked body and throwing it gracefully over his left shoulder, proceeded in a subdued but masterly style of eloquence to say in effect : " What my brother has just said is true. The district meeting has thrown us away and we are being destroyed. We have always had confidence in our missionaries and in the district meeting, but our confidence has been betrayed and forfeited, and now we are ruined.   The most of these people on the station are Fingoes.   They have been brought up under the rule of the mis-

sionaries, and they came here into Umhlonhlo's country, not to serve
Umhlonhlo, but to live under the missionary, who was our father,
and we look to him for a father's care. These people have no right
to fight for Umhlonhlo any more than for Damasi, nor to be eaten
up by him. I am not a Fingo, I belong to Umhlonhlo, but the most
of these people do not; yet the district meeting has thrown them
away, delivered them to Umhlonhlo, who says they must all fight for
him against Damasi. Umhlonhlo himself has eaten many of them
up, and they are all in jeopardy of their lives every day, and he is
forcing old heathen customs upon them that they never were subject
to in their lives. All this has come upon the people here because
the district meeting abandoned us to the rule of a heathen chief.
We would gladly leave everything and go away, but the chief won't
allow us to leave; so here we are, and we want to know our crime
and why the district meeting has dealt with us so cruelly."

Then it came my turn to answer, and I arose and said: "Your
case is very deplorable, and we are sorry for you indeed, but now we
must find out the real facts in the case.

"Let us then look first at the action of the district meeting, which
you say is the cause of all your calamities. Whatever they did was
done in the fear of God, as your friends and pastors, and they did not
anticipate any of the evils which have befallen you; and but few of
the things you are suffering have come from their action, as I will
show you presently. It is not according to the Word of God that
ministers of His Gospel should be ruling magistrates over a great
community of all sorts of sinners such as are in this station.

"In establishing the Gospel first among the heathen in Kaffraria
the good men of God, in mercy to the people on their stations, whom
they gathered in from among the heathen to live with the missionary,
because they were Christian people, or earnestly seeking after God,
and wanted for themselves and their children a Christian education,
exercised all the authority which they considered consistent with
their own spiritual mission and the supreme authority of their paramount chiefs for the protection and proper training of their people in
everything necessary to qualify them to be good Christians, industrious workers, and good subjects of their chiefs, and also to furnish
to the chiefs themselves a model of Christian government. Their
one great work was to preach the Gospel and bring souls to Christ,
and the magisterial office they consented to bear for a time was an
incidental thing, to be given up in due time entirely to civil rulers,
whom God hath ordained separately for that work, just as ministers
are called separately for their work. If the rulers are unwise or
wicked because of the general wickedness of their subjects, then if
God's people cannot correct the bad government, nor readily escape
from the injustice they suffer, they must commit themselves to God
and endure patiently what God may permit for the trial of their faith,
who will, if they endure hardness as good soldiers, make all things
work together for their good

"St. Paul did not gather a lot of his converts and form a station

18

like this, and rule over two thousand nine hundred rebels against God for every one hundred believers in his fold. No such thing. He preached the glad tidings to poor sinners, and when he got them to accept Christ they would have been glad enough to have gone and lived with their *umfundisi*; but what did Paul say to them? 'Let every man abide in the same calling wherein he was called. Art thou called being a servant? care not for it: but if thou mayest be free, use it rather. . . . Brethren, let every man, wherein he is called, therein abide with God.' God will be with His people wherever they are, and if God be with them, and they remain true to Him, He will either deliver them from their tribulations or sustain them under them.

"That is God's way of spreading the Gospel in heathen countries, and in that way we shall not grow sickly, dwarfish Christians, that can't stand a blast of wind, but healthy, strong men, ready always to do or to die for God. In that way we shall not carry all the leaven and put it into a pot by itself, but shall have it distributed through the lump till the great mass of heathenism is leavened. This, you see, is God's way. The most of the missionaries who have established the mission stations and nourished the people at them so long are now anxious fully to adopt God's way. Here at Shawbury the missionary, being responsible to his chief for the conduct of three thousand people, and having to settle all your disputes, what time has he left to give to his one great work of leading the people to Christ?

"He felt it, and the district meeting felt it, and they in love to your souls thought it best to release him from that work, that he might devote his whole time to the work of teaching you and your children the way to heaven. There was no war then, and they could not anticipate any of the horrible things which have since come upon you.

"Now let us, in the second place, look at the real cause of your troubles. In the first place, the most of your people, under the name of being Christians, and enjoying all the privileges of a mission station, are notorious rebels against God, and have no right to expect special favours from God or His people. In the second place, you have not kept your treaty engagements with Damasi. At the beginning of this war Damasi, by a special messenger, asked you three questions: 1. Are you Umhlonhlo's people, or are you not? 2. Do you intend to join Umhlonhlo in fighting against me or not? 3. If you do not intend to fight me, give me a description of your boundaries, so that I may not pass over them with my armies. Was not that so?"

"Yes," replied the learned counsel on the other side, "that is true."

"Well, now, in reply you said: 1. 'We are not Umhlonhlo's people. We are mission people, but we live in Umhlonhlo's country, and are bound not to break his laws.' 2. 'We will not fight against you unless you cross our mission station lines.' 3. 'Our lines are so and so,' and you gave him your boundaries. Is not that true?"

"That is all true," said Job.

"So far the thing was all honourable and fair on both sides.

Now, if you had dealt honourably with Damasi he never would have interfered with one of you, and your missionary would not have been disturbed, and you would have had his influence all this time to shield you from the wicked excesses of your chief. But what did you do ? You got up a great sham fight for a lark, and though your missionary begged you not to go over the hill toward the river, in sight of Damasi's soldiers, you went in spite of him, and Damasi's soldiers, of course, thought you were going out to fight them and put themselves in battle array. Then Umhlonhlo, to help the devil to ensnare you, came along and ordered you to charge on Damasi's men, and when you refused you got his ill-will, and then he advanced and shot some of Damasi's men himself, and you got the credit of all that on Damasi's books. Though you did not design it, you thus did so break faith with Damasi as to put it beyond explanation to him, and then, having got yourselves into that mess, you gave up to Umhlonhlo and have since been regularly joined to him in array against Damasi, and have not only thus brought all this evil upon yourselves, but jeopardised the lives of your missionary and his wife and little children, and imposed upon him the greatest grief of his life, the necessity of leaving his work and fleeing away to a place of safety."

Then Elijah arose and said : "The words of the *umfundisi* are true words; but if the district meeting felt it their duty to make a change of such importance why did they not consult us first ? We are official members of the Church, and we are a party directly interested in such a change. Moreover, as the most of us have been all our lives on the mission stations and never felt the rule of a heathen chief, we should have been notified in time to prepare our minds for such a great change, so as to be able to bear it as good Christians."

Then Brother White replied, saying, "On my way home from the district meeting, some time before the matter was brought before Umhlonhlo, I told a number of your leading men what the district meeting had done, so that you might prepare your minds for it."

Meantime I saw, from the flash of Job's eyes, that he considered us his game after all. Up he sprang, excited, almost beyond self-control; but he poised himself very quickly, and with true Kaffir self-possession and dignity, yet with great spirit, retorted, "Yes, you told us what you had done at the district meeting as you went home. It was too late then for us to have any say in the matter. Why did you not tell us on our way *to* the meeting, so that we might decide what was best for us to do ? If we had known that you were going to give us away to a heathen chief we might have decided that it was better for us to pick up our assegais and blankets and go away to some other part ; but after we have been sold for nothing we are coolly told that the deed is done and that we belong to a heathen master."

It then came to my turn to deliver the closing speech, and I said : " I see now how the case stands. We, the district meeting, confess that we have made a great mistake in not giving you due notice of our intention and in not consulting you and fully preparing your minds for such a change, and I think I speak the sincere feelings of every member of that meeting when I say we are very sorry, and all we have to plead is what I have pleaded, our best intentions in doing a necessary thing to be done ; but we should have given you notice of our good intentions. The reason, I believe, you were not notified and consulted is that it was not till after the meeting had assembled, and the state of the work here made known, that it was felt necessary at that time to take such action.

"It was believed that the missionary was so burdened with magisterial duties in managing such a hard lot that the thing could not, in justice to your souls, be delayed, and there was then no opportunity of consulting any of you ; but now we see that we made a great mistake in not waiting to give ample time for consultation. But, while we confess to one great mistake, you will have to confess to two great sins, and then we must all humble ourselves before God, confess and forsake our sins, accept Christ as our Saviour, and ask God's gracious direction out of these dreadful tribulations. Your first great sin was to go, in spite of the wise counsel of your missionary, and break your solemn treaty with Damasi. Your second great sin is that, after bringing so many evils on yourselves, as we have shown, you have not only justified yourselves and blamed it all on the district meeting, but have gone on in greater excesses of sin, profaning this holy place with Kaffir beer feasts, quarrelling, fighting among yourselves, and have even murdered a man, and have not confessed your sins or repented. Even while we have been here, who had nothing to do with any of your matters, but came purely to help you in your distress by leading you to Jesus, you have kept up a quarrel in your hearts against us, and have thus prevented a great work of God, which with your agency He would have done for you, by us His servants, just as He has done at other stations we have visited. Now you must have done with Kaffir beer feasts and with beer drinking at home, surrender to God, accept Christ, and get right in your hearts and lives, and then we may hope that God, in some way, will give you relief and spare your lives that you may honour Him in the sight of the heathen. Meantime I have written to Mr. Shepstone, the chairman, and hope that he may be able to do something for you ; but his success depends on the mercy of God, and that depends on the course you take in regard to your sins."

Elijah said, "These words are true," and pledged himself to do the best he could to promote a real reformation. Job said the same, and the rest assented. Then we knelt down and submitted the whole matter to God, and the Comforter was graciously present to quicken and to heal. Our horses were then waiting at the door, and we rose from our knees and bade our penitent friends adieu.

I said to Brother White, as we passed out, "Ah, if we had had that council on the first day of our series here, instead of the last, we would have had a glorious work of God.'

This was the terrible incubus which had strangled all our efforts, and added to it was a great disappointment growing out of a mistaken apprehension that I was coming as their missionary to live among them ; and finding that I was only to be with them three days many left in disgust ; but if we had had the leading men with us we should have overcome that and had a grand victory.   We had with us at our services at Shawbury a native local preacher from Natal, who had come more than two hundred miles to visit his brother there, and when we left off he took up the work, and we learned that the following Sabbath he had the chapel crowded, and the Spirit of God was with him in power.   Soon after two of our missionaries went and gave them a helping hand, which Rev. William Shepstone, the chairman of the district, in a letter to me, describes as follows :

" My nephew found Shawbury so impressed on his mind that he could not rest ; so, like the honest Quakers of old, he yielded, and, taking Hunter's station in his route, Hunter readily accompanied him. They spent four days at Shawbury, holding services two or three times a day, and, to use Reyner's words, ' The Spirit of God came down upon the people,' and they left about one hundred souls who had, during their services, found peace with God and joined the classes. These, I believe, were all converts from among the heathen.   Last week I received a letter from Brother Gedye, who had returned thither, and is labouring with all his might, and he tells me that since his return about forty more have been brought in, and that David Cobus, the man who was the devil's own agent, and the principal cause of all the Shawbury troubles, is now, like Saul of earlier days, preaching the faith which once he destroyed, or tried to. Gedye says he is helping mightily in the work of the Lord.   That station is now in peace and quiet.   The belligerents fight around it, but the people are not disturbed, and not a soul moves from the station toward the battle ground.   I had written a letter to Damasi, on the subject of the neutrality of mission stations in war before your letter reached me, and obtained from him a promise that the missionary and all mission property should be respected.   Though Shawbury has been left without a missionary at a time it most needed one, God hath shown that nevertheless He can carry on His work in His own way.   Umhlonhlo has not been to Shawbury since Gedye's return, but has sent a message that they must pray, but does not say for what. Gedye thinks he means for rain, which is the most likely thing he would wish to see."

Our next field was Osborn, an offshoot from Shawbury.

The Osborn station belonged to the Amabaca tribe, but, like Shawbury, was situated near the borders of the great Amapondo nation, who were at war with the Amabaca, and it was therefore greatly exposed to the ravages of war.   But a few weeks before our arrival a large army of Faku's warriors came, variously estimated at from five thousand to eight thousand, under the command of Faku's son, Umgikela.   As this army penetrated the heart of the country the Bacas fled before them, and the warriors were busily employed in gathering up all the live stock within their reach, till they got near to the "great place" of the ruling chief, Makaula, who succeeded in rallying his surprised and scattered people, and in person led them to the charge against the invaders, and after a severe hand-to-hand fight with their assegais the Pondos began to give way, and soon in utter confusion and panic retreated. They had to run ten miles to get to the Umzimvubu River, the boundary of their own country. The Bacas, flushed with victory, pursued, and strewed the route for ten miles with the dead bodies of their foes. The mission station was in their path, and on the approach of the retreating army the mission people, in the excitement, fearing an attack on the station, turned out in a body, in spite of the remonstrance of their missionary, and poured a deadly volley in the front of the fleeing foe, which brought them for a little time to a stand, and the slaughter was fearful.

A Brother Lee had a trading station near, and the entrance to his house was blocked up with the bodies of the slain. One poor Pondo dashed himself through a window of the room occupied by Mrs. Lee with such violence as to cut an artery of his arm on the glass, and down he dropped beside the frightened lady, and without saying a word bled to death. A room of the mission house, with an outer entrance, which happened to be open, was packed with Pondos, and Brother White stood at the door to shield them from the assegais of the Bacas. The pursuers came on in the rage of their human slaughter and demanded access to the refugees in the room, but Mr. White said to them, "These men have placed their lives in my hands, and if you want them you will have to pass over my dead body." The Bacas seemed to think it hard that their own missionary should thus protect their enemies; but he taught them an example of forbearance and of justice to a fallen foe. That act, too, helped to mitigate the violation of the neutrality laws of the mission stations, of which his people were guilty. He gave sanctuary to his prisoners that night, and sent them home in peace the next morning. The army of the Pondos was pursued to the Umzimvubu, and many were slain in the river, but the Bacas did not pass over into Pondoland.

The Pondo army, to assist their flight, threw away nearly everything they had. Among the spoils were numerous shields and assegais and seven hundred guns, of which it appears they had made but little use. Between four and five hundred Pondos were killed. Though they fled for life, when caught they died like Stoics. For example, an old Pondo lay apparently dead, and a Baca exclaimed, "I killed him!"

"No," said another Baca, "I killed him."

With that the old Pondo opened his eyes and said, "You are both liars; neither of you killed me!"

Then the two merciless wretches took up stones and battered out his brains. Brother Lee, to clear his premises of dead Pondos, looped a reim—a rawhide rope—round their necks and dragged them away, and as he was about to put the reim round the neck of one of the dead men, the corpse, as he supposed, opened his eyes and said, "Do please let me lie still and die."

The Kaffirs never bury their dead who are slain in battle; the dogs, pigs, wild beasts, and birds of prey did what they could to prevent effluvia and pestilence by devouring their flesh, and the bones of their carcasses lay bleaching in the sun when we were there, a heart-sickening sight indeed. We had come as warriors, too—had come to conquer, not to spoil and destroy, but to proclaim a life-giving Deliverer to the dead souls of the savage warriors still alive.

At Osborn we determined to try a new plan for getting the heathen out to the preaching the first day. So on Saturday morning, the 18th of August, Charles, Roberts, Stuart, and myself, with Petros, Brother White's school-teacher, as a guide, set out on horseback and visited all the heathen kraals within a few miles of the station.

We rode up to a kraal and called to them, saying, "Bring out all your men, women, and children, and we will sing you a song about the country above."

We then dismounted, and standing in a line, holding the reins of our horses behind us, we sang in Kaffir "The Eden Above."

Then without adding a word we mounted and rode off leaving Charles to tell them that a new *umfundisi* from over the sea had just arrived, and had just come to pay them a visit and sing to them, and would preach at the station that day at noon, and "he wants all of you to come and hear the good news he has to tell you." Then riding on to another kraal the same was repeated, and so on till all within our reach were visited. In some places some of the men followed us to their neighbouring kraal, so that I could see at once that we were getting a hold on them. Sure enough, at noon we had the heathen to our meeting in force. The chapel would not hold the half of them, so we assembled them in the stable yard, which, with various buildings on four sides, was a large open court. The first sermon, therefore, instead of being to the church as usual, was to the heathen, from St. Paul's text about the Unknown God. Having given a very brief history of St. Paul's work among the people in the great city of Athens, we came directly to our work.

We did not simply proclaim the truths of the Gospel to them, for the work of an ambassador for Christ embraces much more than that, but followed St. Paul's method. He never begged the question. In preaching to the Jews he based his arguments on the clearly defined prophetic Scriptures, which his hearers admitted. In preaching to heathens he went directly down into the regions of their own experience, and brought to light, from their admitted facts, a conscious demand in their souls which they were vainly trying to meet, but which the Gospel only could supply.

During our short series of meetings at Osborn, Brother White, the pastor, examined one hundred and sixty persons, belonging mostly to heathen families, who gave good evidence of pardon and peace with God.

CHAPTER XXVI

EMFUNDISWENI

EMFUNDISWENI was our next field, including a few days at Palmerton, thirty miles distant. This was a new mission station : the minister's house was a one-story cottage, substantially built of brick, nearly one hundred feet in length, with verandahs front and rear, and contained nine rooms. The second preacher's house was on a pretty site across a hollow on a parallel ridge, occupied by Rev. Daniel Eva, a zealous young missionary sent out recently from England. Rev. Thomas Jenkins and wife were appointed to this station in 1838. He was a grand old pioneer missionary, and gave me so many stirring incidents that I cannot record them here, but refer my reader to my book entitled " Christian Adventures in South Africa."

The whole number of the converts at our Emfundisweni meetings, including those who were saved before I left for Palmerton, amounted to above one hundred and sixty-three persons, among whom were a doctor and five young chiefs.

On our return from Palmerton we arranged that while Roberts, Stuart, and myself, would go on and spend the Sabbath with Captain Kok's Griquas, at their request, and on Monday proceed on our way toward Natal, Charles should spend the Sabbath with Brother Jenkins and help on the glorious work among the Pondos, and on Monday night meet us at Ulbrichts.

So on Saturday, September 1st, we bade adieu to Emfundisweni and set out for Kok's camp. That was a day to be remembered, for by the time we got off the main beaten Natal track into the dreary hills and mountains of No Man's Land a cold drizzling rain set in, with a dense fog, which limited our field of vision to a radius of about fifty yards. Several times through the day we lost the trail, and much time was consumed in finding the spoor.

About 4 p.m. we heard the barking of dogs, the squealing of pigs, the bleating of sheep, and the lowing of cattle, and hoped we were nearing the camp. Coming to a pioneer's hut and stockyard, Mr. Roberts fought his way up through a pack of fierce dogs to the door to inquire where we were. He found nothing there but dogs and a few children whose parents were out. Stuart and his father and our weary horses stood shivering in the storm till Roberts came and told us that the Dutch-speaking children said that it was fifteen miles to Kok's camp, and that we had a high mountain to cross.

On and on we struggled over the mountain and down to a little river. It was now getting dark, and we knew not which way to go. We hoped we were near the Griqua camp, but we could see no lights and hear nothing but the hollow moaning of the wind in the mountains and the pattering rain upon us. When we got into places of great danger Brother Roberts, finding that I was a good driver, and not wishing to be responsible for my life, found it convenient to get out and walk. So when we crossed the river he gave me the reins and went circling round to try to find the path. I drove up a hollow, and away on to high ground, hoping to see Kok's city set on a hill, called the Bergliftig, but not a beacon glimmer shone out to cheer us. It was a moonless night, and with the clouds above and fog all round us, there was a darkness which we all felt. I waked the echoes of the mountains by shouts which I hoped might arouse the natives, but got no response.

I said, " Roberts, we have got into No Man's Land, sure. I have not seen a tree for many miles back, but I saw a few bushes on the cliffs near the river. If we can get back there over these dangerous gullies perhaps we can get wood enough to make a fire ; otherwise the severity of the cold and our wet clothes will finish the business for us."

Back we went to the river and outspanned. I felt my way among the cliffs to a bush about four inches through, which I cut down. It was green and wet, but by cutting wood off the seat of our carriage we at last succeeded in getting a fire. Thankful for a good cup of coffee and a supper savory enough for princes, we endeavoured to devise some plan for the preservation of life through the night. We spent hours trying to dry our clothes, but while we were drying one side the other was getting wet with the fast-falling rain. Stuart and I at last took a seat in the cart, which had a bonnet, which gave us some protection from the rain, and wrapping up as well as we could in our wet rugs we dozed and dreamed and shivered till morning. Roberts, meantime, dug a hole in the ground to get a dry place, and there, half buried, wrapped in his tiger-skin rug, he waited for the morning light.

The Lord graciously preserved us even from taking a cold, and in the morning, while Stuart was hunting the horses, and while Roberts was exploring the country to find somebody to tell us which way to go, I kindled a fire and prepared a good breakfast. Roberts found an English citizen of Captain Kok's kingdom, living not a mile distant from our camp, from whom we learned that we were quite out of our way, and there it was twelve miles distant to Kok's camp. He sent a young Hottentot to guide us. Amid rain, sleet, and snow, about noon we reached the town, where I had hoped to spend a quiet and profitable Sabbath. Captain Kok, who passed us in Umhlonhlo's country on his way to Cape Town, had not returned. His town had a population of about one thousand, built up of huts, with some pretty fair log and brick houses, and a fort with mud walls, about eight feet high, with piles of cannon balls and a few big guns with which to frighten the Kaffirs.

In the midst of the fort stood a good pioneer chapel, seating about four hundred persons. A plain house was given us in which to sojourn. We met a young English trader, who, as a Christian, was trying to do good to the rising community. A kind Griqua family cooked for us, and we got on well considering the state of the camp and the weather. At 3 p.m. we had the chapel crowded, and I preached the Gospel to them through a Dutch interpreter, a pious, intelligent man, the schoolmaster for the town, and yet totally blind.

At night I preached in English to about thirty persons in a private house. We had reason to hope that good was done, and yet no decisive results were manifest. On Monday the sun shone out, and though the roads were thought to be so slippery that we should not be able to cross the Zuurberg—the "sour mountain"—we could not afford to lose time, and so pushed on our journey. We passed a number of new, fertile, well-watered farms of the Griquas, and after crossing the Zuurberg came through a Griqua village, where they also have a chapel and regular worship among themselves. This village is near the lines of Alfredia, the newly annexed territory of Natal. Just across the line a mean white man has opened a shop for enticing the poor Griquas to destruction by the sale of brandy. Our route of travel left Alfredia to our right, and continued in Captain Kok's country some forty miles further to the Umzimvubu River, which is the old west boundary of Natal.

We reached Ulbrichts before night, took tea, and drove on three miles further to Mr. Blom's, where we spent the night. We waited on Tuesday for Charles till 11 a.m., and went on without him. In the afternoon of that day we reached Mr. Hulley's place, and preached in his large Kaffir-hut chapel, which will seat one hundred and fifty. Brother Hulley supports himself and his large family on a new farm in Kok's territory, on the west bank of the Umzimvubu, but is nevertheless a successful preacher among the Kaffirs, and has formed a society, and preaches to the heathen regularly in his own round native chapel. I was very sorry we could not command time to stay with him long enough for a grand advance among his people. We were very kindly entertained for the night, and next morning forded the river, which can be crossed only in a ferryboat, except in winter, and spent an hour with Mr. Hancock and family, who are Graham's Town Wesleyans, and very enterprising, useful people.

That day we travelled over forty miles through a beautiful and picturesque country of hill, dale, and mountain, but with few settlers, and much wild game. We saw more deer in greater variety that day than any other day of the whole journey, though we saw many beautiful herds of roebucks in Pondoland. We hoped to cross the Umkumas River before dark; but, though we sighted it from the mountain an hour before sunset, it was quite dark when we reached the ford, which we were told was deep, rough, and dangerous; yet our only stopping place was a public house on the other side. Near the river we met a native man, whom we found was from Indaleni, a mission station about twenty miles beyond. He had been out among the Kaffirs with two waggons, selling Indian corn and buying cattle in exchange. He was just the man of all Kaffiraria we most needed, to tell us about the ford, to supply us with corn, and to help us over a high mountain the next day, tying our cart to one of his waggons, and driving our horses along with his stock cattle.

We all got safely to the public house. The proprietor was absent, but had left his Kaffir servant to attend to the wants of the travelling public. His beds were passable, but he had nothing to eat except a few small potatoes and some bacon; but as we still had a supply of coffee, sugar, dried peaches, and bread, we fared well, and our "man of providence" brought us a bag of corn for our horses.

The next day we travelled to Indaleni, and were kindly entertained by the missionary, Rev. W. H. Milwood, and his good lady. I arranged with him to have Charles spend the Sabbath with him if he should come on all right. We had not heard from him since we left him at Emfundisweni. On the next day, Friday, the 7th of September, we journeyed on twenty-five miles to Pietermaritzburg, the capital of Natal. From the time we left Queenstown I had travelled six hundred and thirteen miles, while Roberts and Stuart had travelled fully seven hundred miles. Stuart's Kaffir tripler carried him through without giving in.

When Charles reported in Maritzburg the following Monday we found that he was only about half a day behind us all the way from Ulbrichts to Indaleni. He left Emfundisweni on Monday, according to agreement, but the roads were bad and the journey was too long. Finding that he could not reach Ulbrichts that day, he put up at a heathen kraal, near a chief's place. He got all the people together and preached to them that night, and again the next morning, and seventeen of them professed to renounce heathenism and accept Jesus Christ. He wrote back to Brother Jenkins, giving him their names and whereabouts. He also preached to the natives at Mr. Hancock's place, but had not time to follow up the effort.

He preached Friday night, Saturday, and Sabbath at Indaleni. An extract from a letter to me from Rev. W. H. Milwood will tell the story of that adventure:

"Under Charles Pamla's preaching here Friday, Saturday, and yesterday, many have been aroused to a sense of their danger through sin and have been led to seek forgiveness and holiness through the blood of Jesus. About seventy, young and old, profess to have gained the pearl of great price, and a few others are yet earnestly seeking. This is a matter of great joy to me, and will be to you, I am sure."

CHAPTER XXVII

IN THE COLONY OF NATAL

As I was straitened for time, and as the Natalians seemed to have but little appreciation of native stuff for the ministry—nay, strong prejudice against even the hope of raising up native ministers—and as my Zulu had become a workman that needed not to be ashamed, I thought it best to appoint him the general of the black legion, while I should bring up the smaller wing of the whites, and thus storm the citadel of infidelity and sin from two sides at the same time. So I commended my sable brother to the missionaries and bespoke for him an open field and a fair fight.

Bishop Colenso had just been booming away at an impregnable fortress of truth, the supreme divinity of Jesus Christ, and forbidding any to ask directly any favours from Christ, and ignored the very songs of Zion which contained prayers to the Son of God. The colonial papers had given the bishop all the aid and comfort they could, for his sensationalism was very edifying to the press financially; but at the time of our arrival that novelty had lost its power of charming, and some new strategic dash was needed to revive the flagging spirits of the bishop's troops; so on the first Sabbath night we spent in Maritzburg the bishop preached on "The Idolatry of the Bible," by which it appeared from his discourse, as reported to us by some who heard it, he meant an idolatrous reverence for the Bible. One of his illustrations was in substance as follows: A young man, a printer employed in setting the type of one of his (Colenso's) first books on the Pentateuch, became so affected by the doubts thus excited in his mind about the truth of the Bible that he went mad and committed suicide. The bereaved father of the poor printer wrote to Colenso, giving the facts about the dreadful end of his son, and charged the bishop with his death; to which the bishop replied that the father himself was the cause of the tragedy by teaching his son such an idolatrous love for the Bible that he could not bear to see the truth of its stories called in question, and hence his madness and self-destruction.

The two Sabbaths we spent in the capital Bishop Colenso and his thorn in the flesh, Dean Green, were booming away just across the street in a diagonal line from our chapel.

While in Maritzburg I delivered a lecture on "Reminiscences of

Palestine," and as I had occasion to join issue with one of Colenso's arguments, in which he tries to prove the physical impossibility of executing the command of Moses, as recorded in the twenty-seventh and twenty-eighth chapters of Deuteronomy, to proclaim the curses and blessings of the law from the two opposite mountains, Gerizim and Ebal, to the assembled hosts of Israel between, having myself personally, by measurement and vocal power, demonstrated the entire feasibility of the whole thing in the very place where Joshua, in the eighth chapter of his book, informs us that all that Moses commanded was done, I requested my committee to present the bishop with my compliments and send him a ticket to the lecture; but he did not put in an appearance. I afterwards learned that the bishop had left for D'Urban about the time the lecture was to come off, on a tour of episcopal visitation in that part of his diocese.

So when I went to D'Urban the bishop was at his post there. As I entered the town I saw the bills up announcing that the learned bishop was to preach next day, morning and evening, in the Anglican church.

At Verulam he preceded us a week. Rev. Mr. Elder there tried to blockade his pulpit against the bishop, and hence one of those scenes so common in his diocese, a violent removal of barriers and running the blockade.

The Sabbath I was in Verulam Colenso was back in D'Urban. The papers puffed him and eulogised his preaching, and a merchant of Maritzburg came to tea at the house of my host, Mr. J. H. Grant, in D'Urban, so drunk he could not walk erect, and spent an hour in berating Christians and Christian ministers, and was sure that the eloquent bishop, the most learned and reliable preacher in the world, would yet convert the whole of us. I happened to say, "Dr. Colenso," and he took offence that I should be so irreverent. "Bishop Colenso! Bishop Colenso!" he shouted, "the most learned and pious man in the world!"

There were some very respectable families, in a worldly sense, and of good outward moral deportment, who were identified with the bishop, but the majority of his followers were affirmed to be, by those who knew them well, such persons as have good reason to dread the threatened judgments of the Bible, and therefore hope the book is not from God. Colenso, too, gained influence with many by his genial, gentlemanly manners and Low Church liberality, in contrast with the stiff, Puseyitical, ritualistic character of the Bishop of Cape Town. Old Rev. Mr. Lloyd, Episcopal minister in D'Urban, in a friendly visit to my room, after talking to me for some time about the Bishop of Jerusalem and the Bishop of Sydney, whom I had the pleasure of meeting, spoke of Colenso, who had been in his pulpit the preceding Sabbath, and said, "Poor Colenso, I believe he is a well-meaning man, but has got wrong in his mind. I believe he will be in a lunatic asylum before many years go by."

Mr. Lloyd was a most kind-hearted old man, and would have been glad to draw that veil of charity over the learned prelate's theological idiosyncrasies. One of the D'Urban papers stated, as a proof that all the people had not lost confidence in the bishop, that in his recent episcopal tour he had baptised two children !

During those eventful five weeks in which the bishop made his episcopal tour and caused such a lively stir among the newspaper reporters, correspondents, and sensationalists of the church-breaking order, and doing wonders in his way, and baptised two babies, my Zulu and his black legion, and I with my palefaces, had marched steadily on against the armies of the aliens. The souls awakened by the Spirit, who surrendered to God, accepted Christ, and personally tested the truth of the Bible, and who got the demonstration of the supreme divinity of Jesus by the washing of regeneration and renewing of the Holy Ghost, publicly confessed that they had received redemption through his blood, even the forgiveness of their sins. They were also personally examined by their ministers, who, being satisfied with their testimony, wrote down their names and addresses, so as to get them under pastoral training. These new witnesses whom God thus raised up in refutation of the scepticism and infidelity of the times numbered over three hundred and twenty whites and over seven hundred natives, of all ages and stations in life, making an aggregate of more than one thousand persons. I only preached five sermons to Kaffirs during those five weeks, so that most of the success of that division of the army was under the leadership of my Zulu. I was glad of that, for it did more than volumes of argument could have done to break down a foolish caste and colour prejudice, and thus open the way for the employment of native agency, which God will mainly employ for the evangelisation of Africa.

When Brother Palma first went to D'Urban, Mr. Henry Cowey, a merchant, an excellent worker and local preacher, said to me. " There is a great deal of prejudice here against allowing a coloured man to come into the house of a colonist, but I have consented to take Charles to stop with me."

" You may think yourself very highly honoured, Brother Cowey, to have the privilege of entertaining such a messenger of God."

Brother Cowey afterwards reminded me of my remark, and said it was true, for he and his family had been entertained and benefited by Charles's sojourn with them.

Bishop Colenso's attempt to popularise the Gospel with the Kaffirs by his apology for polygamy did not take with the Kaffir polygamists at all, for they were sharp enough to see that if Christianity differed so little from Kaffir heathenism as that it was quite unnecessary to be at the trouble of a conversion from one to the other.

On our way to Pietermaritzburg, having crossed into the lines of Natal, Mr. H——, a very intelligent and influential man, gave Charles Palma a solemn warning against coming into contact with Bishop Colenso, which led in substance to the following conversation :

" He is a learned, shrewd, dangerous man," said Mr. H——, " and might shake your faith.

"Shake my faith in what?" inquired Charles.

"He might shake your faith in the truth of the Bible and in the divinity of Jesus Christ."

"I can't see how he could do that," replied Charles. "I proved the truth of the Bible and the divinity of Jesus Christ in my heart thirteen years ago. I was convinced of sin by the Holy Ghost according to the teachings of the Bible; I then walked after the Spirit according to the instructions of the Word of God, and He led me to Jesus Christ. I gave my guilty soul to Him and received Him as my Saviour, and got the forgiveness of all my sins through Him. None but God can forgive sins. It was on the truth of God's Word that I accepted Him as my Saviour, and then, according to the true promises of God, He saved me from my sins, a thing I know He never could do if He were not God. He not only saved me thirteen years ago, but He has saved me every day since, and saves me now. These are the facts that I know, and I can't see how any man's infidel speculations can shake God's facts revealed in my heart, which prove to me the truth of His Book."

"Ah! but the faith of many strong men has been shaken by Colenso," rejoined Mr. H——, "and you should be careful not to put yourself in his way; he might to you serious injury."

"Well, now, Mr. H——," said Charles, "will you please give me the strongest argument Colenso ever raised against the truth of the Bible?"

"No, I should be afraid it might do you damage."

But Charles insisted on knowing the strongest thing Mr. H—— could recall from Colenso's writings against God's Book, and finally Mr. H—— said, "Dr. Colenso shows, by an arithmetical calculation, that the Bible story about the ark breaks down; that it was impossible, according to the measurements given, for the ark to contain a pair of all the animals and seven of the clean animals, as stated in the story."

"Indeed," said Charles, "and that's it! Is that the strongest point the great man can make against the Word of God?"

"He makes a strong case out of that, and I can't remember a stronger in his writings," replied Mr. H——; and Charles showed his splendid rows of ivory in a broad, spontaneous laugh, peculiar to himself, and then said, "Well, now, seriously, Mr. H——, whatever may be our ignorance of ancient measurements, the fact is, if God should command me to build an ark, give me the pattern and dimensions, furnish plenty of timber of the right sort for such a ship, and plenty of shipbuilders, and one hundred and twenty years to fulfil my contract, I'll warrant you I would make it big enough; and I have no doubt that old Noah was as sharp as any Kaffir in Africa."

The fact is, taking the cubit at twenty-one inches, the measurements given in the narrative are adequate; but my Zulu took the bishop on his own ground. The Jews had a measure called a cubit, the Chaldeans had a very different measure called a cubit, just as we have different measurements bearing the same name now; for example, a mile in Ireland is about one third longer than a mile in

England, and an acre in England, Ireland, and Scotland represents in each country quite a different measurement of land. So Charles at a glance grasped the fundamental points in the story, those furnishing the clearest presumption of its truthfulness.

Mr. Pincent, of D'Urban, in Mr. George Cato's judgment, though not an eloquent pleader, was the best law counsellor in South Africa. After he had been forward with our seekers several times feeling after God his case, to his own mind, became desperate, and after giving me a statement of his rebellion against God, he inquired, "Now, do you think there is any chance for such a vile creature as I am to be saved?"

He was regarded as a moral, right-minded man, but now the Holy Spirit had revealed to him, what every sinner must see before he will consent to God's terms of salvation, the exceeding sinfulness of sin.

I assured him that it is a faithful saying, and worthy of all acceptation, that Christ Jesus came into the world to save sinners—even the very chief of sinners—and that if he would but surrender to God and accept Christ he would prove the truth of that glorious announcement straightway. We then went into the details of the struggle, and he was so sick of sin that I had but little difficulty in getting him to consent to a divorce from all sin and to accept God's will as the rule of his heart and life; but he stuck some time at the believing point. He wanted to pray on till God, for Christ's sake, would give him peace, and then he could believe. When I got him to see clearly that he must have confidence in a physician, and accept him before he could hope to be cured by him, he next stuck at the mystery involved in such a work. Realising his antagonism to God's immutable laws, and that a judgment had been given and recorded against him in heaven's court under the clearly revealed law, "The soul that sinneth, it shall die," "He that believeth not is condemned already," he could not see how it was possible for his legal relation to God's government to be adjusted so that he should be fully reconciled to God.

After fully explaining the Gospel plan of salvation by faith I finally got him down to the saving act of faith by the following illustration:

"Jesus Christ is our Advocate with the Father. Now, it is fair to presume that He understands His professional intricacies and difficulties. If He had not been perfectly qualified for that responsible position He would not have been admitted to the bar of heaven's court at all. Now suppose, Mr. Pincent, that one of your clients should elbow you round the corners of the street and keep insinuating, 'I can't see how you are to conduct my suit to a successful issue. I can't understand the complications of the case; it seems all dark to me, and I'm afraid you'll not succeed.' Then when the case comes on for trial in court, and your client insists on standing by you to tell you how to conduct the suit, and every few minutes gives you the benefit of his counsel, and dictates to you how you should attend to your own business, what would you do, sir? You would return him his brief straightway! Now, that illustrates your treatment of our Advocate with the Father, Jesus Christ the righteous. If a client understood the business he would not employ an advocate, and when he employs one he thus admits that he does not understand it, but that his advocate does, and he allows his advocate to conduct the suit in his own way, and is not concerned to know the intricacies involved, but only the successful issue."

This being the last point in the penitential struggle of my lawyer, he thus saw it clearly, and at once gave his case fully and unreservedly into the hands of His heavenly Advocate; and that very day he got his discharge from the death sentence of the law in the court divine, certified in his heart by the Holy Spirit. The moment God saw that, under the leading of the awakening Spirit, he fully surrendered himself and accepted Christ, at the instance of his Advocate the Father justified him freely. Brother Pincent became a witness and worker for God, and very useful in leading poor sinners to Christ.

It may be worthy of remark that near the close of our campaign Bishop Colenso called at the house of my host, Mr. J. H. Grant, in D'Urban, to see me, saying, "I wanted to see you and shake hands with you before you leave. God has given you your work to do, and you are doing it, and He has called me to another work, and I am doing my work. You don't suppose all who have been brought in at your meetings will stand, do you?"

I replied, "I certainly do suppose that the most of them will stand to the death; but few of them, owing to their very bad habits, bad associations, and the influence of bad examples, may relapse into sin."

Our interview being short, but little passed between us beyond the facts given. I could readily see how by his kind, gentlemanly manner he won the friendship of many persons, who said they received him as a gentleman without any reference to his ecclesiastical character and relations.

I arrived in Cape Town from my tour about the 20th of October, 1866. I found my youngest, Henry Reed, in his mother's arms, about two months old. We held a successful series of meetings at Simon's Bay, twenty miles west, and soon after, with my dear wife and three children, took the steamer *Norseman*, Union Line, for London. *En route* we visited at St. Helena the house in which Napoleon Bonaparte lived and the tomb in which he lay till removed to Paris.

PART SIXTH

ENGLAND AND THE INDIES WEST AND EAST

CHAPTER XXVIII

IN THE HOME OF METHODISM AND THE WEST INDIA ISLANDS

WE came by the *Norseman* from Cape Town to London, arriving a few days before Christmas, 1866. Myself and wife and four sons put up at a hotel facing St. Paul's Cathedral.

I entered without delay into evangelistic work in the leading Wesleyan chapels of that city. I laboured a fortnight in connection with the pastorship of Rev. Gervase Smith, at old City Road, and quite a score of souls were brought to God, and there was a manifest quickening of the Church. It was interesting to hear the songs and shouts of praise on the old battleground where John Wesley lived, laboured, and died. His grave and those of Richard Watson, Joseph Benson, Adam Clarke, and Sammy Bradburn, and other pioneer Methodist heroes, are in the cemetery adjoining the church.

The preacher's house, built by Mr. Wesley, is still in good repair, and occupied by the pastor of the Church. Mr. Wesley's clock, an old-fashioned German clock, stands in a little hall at the head of the stairs, from which we enter to the left Mr. Wesley's study, or proceed directly into the upstairs parlour. That clock has been keeping the time of the march of Methodism for more than one hundred years, and is still ticking the time of its widening way through all the zones of the globe.

Altogether I held special services from one to two weeks in sixteen different London circuits, including one series in a Presbyterian church in West End. We had usually from twenty to forty conversions in each place, but there was no swell of the tide communicating from one field of labour to another, so that we had to begin at the bottom at each place.

About midwinter, while thus engaged in London, I received a

letter from Henry Reed, requesting me to visit him at his home near
Tunbridge Wells. I had heard much about Henry Reed's successful
work in Tasmania, but had not met with him personally. I wrote
him in reply that my engagements in London would fully occupy
my time up to the 1st of May, 1867. He owned a farm about a mile
out of town, on which he had built a mansion which he named
Dunorlan.

I arrived at the appointed time, and was most cordially received
by Henry Reed and his noble wife. I was greatly impressed by
his magnificent stature and symmetry, his striking, manly features,
practical common sense, and cordial Christian spirit. He built his
mansion through the charity of employing mechanics during a hard
financial pressure, when they could not get work sufficient for the
support of their families.

His first wife had died and gone to heaven some years before,
and he had but recently been united in marriage to an Irish lady,
tall in stature, commanding in personal appearance, refined and
intelligent, and an earnest Christian worker, and withal an able
preacher of the Gospel.

Our week of special services was attended with blessed spiritual
results. Among my helpers at the penitent altar was Mrs. General
Booth, a woman of superior intelligence and education, comely in
person, probably equal to William in most points, and superior in
some. William Booth was then just commencing to organise his
Salvation Army among the poverty-stricken masses.

When I had been but a day or two at Mr. Reed's mansion he
handed me a little paper, and on opening it I found it was a cheque
for a hundred pounds, which he wished me to accept as a present.
I thanked him for his kindness, but informed him it was a principle
with me not to receive presents from anybody, and passed it back to
him. He stood silent for a few moments in apparent surprise.

"But you sell books, do you not?" said he.

"Yes; I have two methods of extending the kingdom of Christ
among men, the pulpit and the press. I depend on the press, by
means of my books, to pay a big church indebtedness, support my
family, and meet my travelling expenses, all on the principle of
business equivalents, and decline to receive gifts."

"Well," said he, "will you give me an open order on your binder
for all the books I want to buy?"

"Yes, sir; that is business on my line."

So I gave him an order on my binder for all the books he might
require on my account. I never learned how many books he ordered.
He circulated them extensively, and whenever he wanted to give me
a lift he sent me a cheque on book account.

He was the only man who got a chance to help me found the self-
supporting churches in India, out of which four Annual Conferences
are being developed. I never asked him for anything; never hinted
to him that I was in need of money; but in assisting to build houses
of worship for our Indian churches I seldom ever felt the pressure

of need that I did not receive a cheque from Brother Reed "on book account."

I went across with my family in the spring of 1867 from London to the great exposition in Paris. After two or three days of sight-seeing my wife and boys went to Lausanne, Switzerland, to spend the summer, and I returned to my evangelising work in England and Ireland. In the fall my wife left Stuart behind to study French, and she and the three little boys joined me in England. Our boys were growing up, and hence required to stop travelling to get their education, and their mother felt it her duty to stop with them and take care of them and bring them up for God. And so she insisted on taking the three little boys and returning to her home in California. I was not yet ready to return, and begged them not to leave me. I concurred with her judgment in relation to the education of the boys, but my great desire to be with my family rendered me quite unwilling to part with them ; but much of my grief grew out of sympathy with their loneliness in my absence. I was partly relieved of that source of trouble when I said to my little Eddie, "Don't you want to stop with papa, and travel in England ? "

"No," said he, " I want to go to California and see my dog."

So I consented to let them go.

Of course I knew they greatly felt their loss of a father's presence, but in the attractions of a home they would have so many other things to occupy their attention that it would not be so hard for them probably as for me. So in the fall of 1867 they took steamer from Liverpool to New York. I said to my wife, " The Lord has intimated to me that, though I can't go with you, He will go with you and give you smooth seas and pleasant weather."

Immediately on her arrival in New York she wrote me saying that all the way across the Atlantic the sea was so smooth there was hardly sufficient motion of the ship to make them sleep well.

When she went to the office of the Pacific Mail Steamship Company to get tickets to San Francisco and mentioned her name, the man in charge said to her : " I knew Mr. Taylor well in California in early days. I have heard him preach often in the streets of San Francisco, and it will be a pleasure to me to give you your tickets through."

As he represented a company he just gave her a cheque for the whole amount, to put her and the children and the servant-girl through to San Francisco. So the money I had given her to pay her passage she retained in her pocket for other uses. She had perhaps in that respect more sense than her husband in that she never refused money when it was offered to her !

Soon after her departure from England to California I took steamer for the West Indies. I had in the meantime worked out a line which I believed to be providential—to spend a year in the West Indies, and go thence by steamship from Panama to New Zealand, and thence to Australia ; and before leaving England for the West Indies I wrote to my friend Dr. Moffit that I would, the Lord willing, be in Sydney in one year from that date.

Our ship anchored about two miles out from Bridgetown, Barbadoes, about one o'clock in the night. The officer of the deck announced that they would tarry there but two hours. On our passenger list we had a wealthy sugar planter, a Mr. B——, and his two daughters. I became well acquainted with Mr. B—— on the voyage, and thought, as I was going there an entire stranger unheralded, that he might be of some advantage to me. Soon after we anchored two boats came from the shore for passengers. Mr. B—— engaged one and some British officers bound for Barbadoes engaged the other. They soon got their luggage into the boats. Mr. B—— and his daughters got into their boat, and I said to them, "Have you room for another passenger? I want to go ashore."

He said, "No, no; we have no room;" and they pulled off.

I went to the other side of the ship, where the officers were getting into their boat, and inquired, "Can you make room for another? I want to go ashore."

"No, sir; we are full up."

So I sat down and said, "If the Lord wants me here I guess He will put me ashore."

Both boats cleared and were gone. The time was short, but I soon heard a splash, and here came another boat, thoroughly manned, four big fellows with oars, a big black man at the stern, and he stepped aboard and said, "Do you want to go ashore, sir?"

"Yes, sir; there is my luggage;" and he had it in the boat in quick time. He gave me a good seat and pulled off. They were powerful oarsmen. We passed B—— and company and the officers before we got half way, and left them behind. I asked our captain, the big black fellow, where was the best hotel in which I could get good accommodation for the rest of the night.

He said, "We will take you right close to one, the best in town."

"Mr. B——, whom we passed in that boat, said that he was going to a hotel of another name."

"Oh yes; but it is not equal to the one I am going to; moreover, they have a ball there to-night, and no chance for sleep."

So we got ashore, and his men took my luggage and carried it up to the hotel.

I said, "What is your charge?"

"Five shillings;" and I paid it.

"Do you know Rev. Henry Hurd?"

"Oh yes; he be my preacher."

"Well, tell Mr. Hurd that you brought California Taylor ashore with you to-night, and that he is putting up at this hotel."

"Oh, bless de Lord! I be glad to see you. I be a Methodist; dis be de Methodist boat; dis be the boat what bring all de preachers ashore."

The hotel keeper said, "You are just in time, I have only one bed left. It is a good bed, and has a mosquito netting to protect you from the mosquitoes; they are swarming here like bees." So he took me up to bed and tucked the mosquito netting around me.

I had not been long in bed when Mr. B—— and his daughters and the officers arrived. They said they couldn't get lodgings at the hotel they went to; there was a ball there. They wanted lodgings. I heard the hotel keeper say, "The last vacant bed I had was taken a few minutes ago by a gentleman, and I have no place in which you can sleep."

The Lord was looking out for me. In the morning early, before I got up, Rev. Henry Hurd and another minister came inquiring for California Taylor; so I put on my clothing as quickly as I could and went down, and there were B—— and his two daughters and the soldiers, looking very forlorn; they had been fighting mosquitoes all the after part of the night.

Mr. B—— said, "What did your boatman charge you for bringing you ashore last night?"

"Five shillings."

"The miserable man who brought me and my daughters ashore charged us a pound."

He was an old settler in the island and knew how to get around. I was a stranger and was on the Lord's business, trusting in Him, and He looked out for me, as He always does.

I preached about three weeks in Barbadoes, indoors and out. We had a wonderful work of God. The island contains about one hundred thousand acres. It is a coral island, but thoroughly enriched with manure, and the whole of it cultivated like a garden, so that it is believed to support more people to the acre than any part of the world. There is a portion of that island which is so rocky and poor as not to yield adequate subsistence for the people. The town located there is called Speights Town, and there the Lord feeds the people with flying fish from the sea. They go out with seines elevated above the surface of the water, and carry lights on the opposite side, and the fish rise by the million and fly toward the light and drop into the seines. So that has become the principal industry of the people of that town and vicinity.

The Barbadoes people are exceedingly kind and appreciative. They think quite as highly of themselves as they ought to think. They call the island of Barbadoes "Little England." All claim to be English people, but most of them are black, and they are people that think aloud. When you walk along the streets you can hear what they are thinking about. I have walked the streets and could hear nearly everybody's opinion about the California preacher.

My next field was British Guiana, South America. John Greathead was preacher in charge of that circuit, and made me welcome. Then he said to me in confidence, " You have come in the nick of time; we have just opened our District Conference, and there is a terrible misunderstanding, and trouble brewing between the chairman of the district and myself and others. We came up square against it yesterday, and the fight is on to be renewed again to-morrow. So I see no remedy for this trouble except a big work of God such as you are accustomed to have where you go. So you are just the man for the emergency."

I said, "All right, Brother Greathead; we will go in and trust the Lord."

So I preached, as usual, that morning to the Church, in the afternoon to the children, and at night to the unsaved. When I invited seekers for pardon at night at the close of the preaching the altar and all the front seats were quickly crowded with weeping penitents. Between forty and fifty were forward, and many of them testified to a personal experience of salvation—preachers, chairman of the district, and all in it up to their ears. So Monday morning the District Conference resumed its business, and their wasn't a single allusion from any quarter to the brewing trouble of Saturday.

During our work in Georgetown the preacher reported five hundred persons converted to God. I also preached a number of times for a London missionary there, and many were converted in his Church.

I went by coach to the province of Berbice, and preached a few nights at a town—by the way, the greatest place for mosquitoes in creation, I think. They pursued the stagecoach like a swarm of bees. The moment the stage would stop they would pour in through the doors on both sides and cover the passengers and bite without mercy. Nearly every person we met was hard at work with a horse-tail brush or a bush fighting mosquitoes. When I was preaching in the pulpit I had to keep one hand hard at work with my handkerchief to knock off the mosquitoes.

We had a series of successful meetings in Berbice, then I returned to Georgetown and went by steamer easterly to Essequibo, and preached a week in that province. Returning to Georgetown, I received a letter stating that my son Stuart, who had been left in Lausanne, Switzerland, was dangerously ill with another attack of fever. So I immediately took ship for London. On my way across the Atlantic I wrote most of my book entitled "The Election of Grace," more than twenty thousand copies of which have gone out on their mission of mercy to multitudes who had been in bondage all their lifetime to the speculative dogmas on eternal election and reprobation.

I hastened on from London to Lausanne and found my boy convalescing. I brought him on to England, and took him to Great Malvern. He improved rapidly, and in five or six weeks seemed to be quite well. Meantime I conducted a week of special services in each of a number of towns adjacent, and then, to confirm the health of my son, I took him on a tour to the Highlands of Scotland.

Returning from the Highlands of Scotland to Liverpool, my son set sail for California, by way of New York, and I went to London and took ship to resume my work in the West Indies.

I held special services in the islands of St. Kitt's, St. Vincent, Nevis, Trinidad, Tobago, St. Thomas, Jamaica, and some other small islands. The Lord was wonderfully with us at every service. A small minority of the people of those islands are English, leading merchants, mechanics, and sugar planters, but the masses of common people are blacks and mixed. Their fathers and mothers, mainly, were the slaves emancipated long ago by the edict of the British government. Many of them were well-to-do, and all of them had a fair common school education.

They were so excitable and noisy in their religious meetings that their missionaries said to me that they were afraid to preach exciting truth to their people. When they did so in past years they would go wild, scream, and fall apparently dead, and jump and smash the benches. They had read about the wonderful work we had in South Africa, and were hoping that California Taylor would give them a call, and yet they were so much afraid that in such a work in the West Indies the people would go wild that not one of them invited me till after my arrival among them. But, to their surprise and joy, we had what they said was the greatest work that had ever been known in the West Indies, and yet the most orderly meetings they had ever seen there. There were flowing tears in abundance, earnest prayers, mourners in Zion, and clear, distinct testimonies given by the thousands who found peace with God, but no wild screaming and ranting at all ; yet I never told them not to make a noise.

I preached a few times in the island of St. Thomas, a Danish island. We had some very devoted Moravian missionaries there and a large church ; no Wesleyan organisation there at that time. There was a very great awakening. After the first service the ways to the church were so blocked I could hardly get in myself. The dear old minister in charge requested that we should not invite the people to come out publicly as seekers. So in the great awakening manifested by sobs and tears but very few were saved so far as we could learn. The pentecostal preaching of Peter in Jerusalem would have brought forth but little fruit but for the hand-to-hand work that immediately ensued. "Men and brethren, what shall we do?" In the after-meeting the awakened were told what to do, and three thousand believed and were baptised before the sun went down. That stands recorded in God's Book as an object lesson to show us how to "work together with God" on this line.

I closed my labours on that trip in the island of Jamaica. Subsequently Rev. William Boyce, Wesleyan Missionary Secretary in London, wrote me that their net increase of membership in the West Indies during the year of my labours among them aggregated more than five thousand new members.

Before I completed my campaign in the West India Islands the steamship company on whose steamer I expected to go from Panama to New Zealand had suspended their service, and I had to go back to London and take passage on the Peninsular and Oriental line of steamers, which cost me ten thousand miles extra travel and five hundred dollars extra expense above the route by which I had planned to go. But I reached Sydney within a week of the time I had stated in my letter to Dr. Moffit a year before. I had another blessed tour fourteen months of 1869 and 1870 in the Australian colonies and Tasmania, building up believers and widely extending the work. I found sixteen young ministers who had been converted to God during my former campaign in these colonies.

I left Australia in the latter part of 1870 by steamship from Melbourne to Ceylon. On the way out from London, nearly a year and a half before, one of my fellow-passengers was Miss Hardy, the daughter of a famous Ceylon missionary. She came out to be united in marriage to Rev. John Scott, the Chairman of South Ceylon District. The marriage took place soon after her arrival, and the ministers of the entire district, comprising three or four Englishmen and more than a dozen native ministers, had assembled at Point de Galle to attend the marriage. By a providential detention of my ship, which gave me four or five days for both public and personal preaching to them, they became deeply imbued with the spirit of direct soul-saving work.

Rev. George Baugh, Wesleyan missionary stationed at Kandy, far in the mountains of the interior, in a great coffee-growing region, said he would try my methods as soon as he could return to his station. Some months later he informed me by letter that soon after he went back to his station he preached an awakening sermon at the morning service and another at night, and then, instead of dismissing them as usual, he invited all who were convinced of their sins and of their need of a Saviour to come forward to the communion rail and surrender themselves to God and accept Christ. "His message to you is, ' He that cometh unto Me I will in no wise cast out.' Now all who want to become acquainted with Jesus and to be saved from your sins come and kneel down here, and we will pray for you." Nine came on the first call, and the meeting was protracted and many scores of Singhalese native people were grandly saved. Thence the work extended, and about a thousand natives were converted to God during my absence in Australia of about sixteen months.

During my first visit they pressed me to give them a few months of service on my return, which I did, according to promise; and, upon their showing, another thousand converts, during a campaign of three months, were added to their churches.

CHAPTER XXIX

LUCKNOW AND CAWNPORE

THE steamship *Malacca*, on which I came from Ceylon, cast anchor at 8.30 a.m. on Sabbath, the 20th of November, 1870, in the harbour of Bombay.

On deck stood Bishop Milman, of Calcutta, his chaplain, and two servants, besides a small cart load of luggage, waiting for the first boat to take them ashore. The bishop seeing me sitting quietly, book in hand, said, "Are you not going ashore?"

"Yes, bishop; but breakfast here will be ready in half an hour, and I don't think it advisable to leave a good breakfast behind and go hungry into a strange city."

He replied that he was in haste and could not wait, and soon after they descended the ship's ladder. Now two fair, tall, slender natives came abroad, wearing each a curious-looking flattened stove-pipe turban.

"Steward," said I, "what sort of fellows are these?"

"They are Parsees."

I was at once carried back to Cyrus, Zoroaster, and other wise men of the East, and was just beginning to live in the past ages, when one of them addressed me in good English and asked me to become his guest in the Byculla Hotel, adding, "We have a boat alongside, and a carriage waiting on shore."

I replied, "If you will wait till I get my breakfast I will go with you."

"All right; we'll wait; show us your baggage, and we will put it into the boat."

My small leather trunk and carpet-bag were soon passed down the ship's ladder. Braced up with a good breakfast and safely seated in the Parsees' boat, I said to one of them, "Are there any Methodists in the city?"

"Methodist! What is that? I never heard that word before."

They took me through a shoal of sharks—boatmen and 'long-shoremen—and I did not get a bite. As we drove off in our carriage and pair in good style we passed a clamorous crowd, and lo! in the midst of it, and its principal attraction, was a one-horse cab containing the bishop and his chaplain, brought to a standstill by an

298

extortionary lot of 'longshore coolies demanding pay! Any stranger not having run such a gauntlet can form but a very inadequate idea of the annoyance attending it. What a time the bishop must have had! I had no pleasure in his discomfort, for he was very genial and kind to me on the voyage; but I thanked God for His good providence in giving me a smooth sail into India.

Tuesday, 22nd. Just before breakfast a German sailor, who was then, he said, a city missionary, came with a message from Rev. C. Harding inviting me to stop with him. The sailor seemed full of love to God, but needing instruction. Feeling anxious to do him good and increase his power of usefulness, I talked to him till 11.30 a.m. The train for Lucknow was to leave at 1 p.m. Having to go three miles to the bank to get a bill of exchange on London, I took a cab and the German to show me the way, and went in haste. On our return we called for one minute at the Tract Society's building to see Rev. George Bowen. He was a long, lean brother. I had heard that he was the most devoted man of God in India, and lived very abstemiously, that he might have the more to give to those in need. If the Roman Catholics had had him they would have canonised him as a saint. He shook my hand and said, " Can I do anything for you? Will you have any money?"

I thanked him, and replied, " I am in need of nothing, my brother."

He expressed regret that I could not tarry a season in Bombay. I said, " Perhaps the Lord may bring me back," and bade him a hurried good-bye. By the help of the kind German I got back to the hotel in time to get my luggage on to the train. I took a second-class ticket for Allahabad—eight hundred and thirty miles. I have always been in the habit of travelling first-class as a matter of economy. My travelling time is my opportunity for rest. The recuperation of my overtaxed energies is more to be desired than money; but here in India I had to economise closely.

25th. I was met at Lucknow by Revs. Thoburn, Waugh, and Parker, and put up with Brother Thoburn, whom I knew years before, and who had written me to come to India.

26th. Was introduced to Joel, one of our first native preachers, and tried to drill him into the art of interpreting, but he was not quite well enough up in English.

Sabbath, 27th. Preached to a congregation of about one hundred and thirty natives, from Acts i. 8. Joel interpreted into Hindustani. He hesitated, and spoke very slowly; but I believe he gave the meaning pretty clearly.

At 6 p.m. we had a congregation of over a hundred English-speaking people, Europeans and Eurasians—Indo-Britons, or, as they are often called, East Indians. To these I preached in English, but it did not seem to affect them at all for good. Some stared at me as though I was there on exhibition, and others seemed disposed to have a jolly time among themselves. Our ministers commenced preaching here to the English-speaking people about ten years before; then after a few years they invited the Wesleyans to send a man to take up the English work, that they might devote all their time to the native work. For some years the Wesleyans occupied our place of worship, but more recently—they having built a chapel in the cantonments, two or three miles distant—Brother Thoburn resumed the English services, but had not as yet gone in to get them converted to God and utilised in our mission work. I took strong ground from the start in favour of getting these Europeans and East Indians saved and incorporated into our mission working force. In their present state the mass of them make a false appearance of Christianity, and are terribly obstructive to our great work of leading the heathen and Mohammedans to Jesus. Every one we get truly saved from sin will be a double gain to our cause—first, to remove a stumbling-block, and, secondly, to secure a living stone resting on the foundation of the apostles and prophets, and thus becoming an integral part of the spiritual house into which we hope to gather the perishing nations of this great empire. This will not draw us from the native work, but draw them to it as a co-operative and ever-augmenting force. The brethren had a consultation and consented to this change in their mission policy wherever a sufficient English population could be found contiguous to our native work.

29th. More natives out at 7 a.m. than we had yesterday. Brother Thoburn interpreted. Had a prayer meeting, and a native preacher prayed as they say he never prayed before.

At 6 p.m. we had about eighty hearers, text, Rom. viii. 3, 4. Called for witnesses and several gave their testimony for Christ. We then for the first time in the series called for seekers. Seven came forward, and five of them professed to obtain peace with God. All this produced a great flutter among the Pharisaic fashionables who came occasionally to our meetings.

30th. Over eighty persons at 7 a.m. meeting. Twelve seekers came forward, and ten of them professed to find the pardon of their sins and gave a clear testimony. There seems to be a great awakening. This is the first invitation to the natives to come out avowedly as seekers. I wanted first to get them well instructed and awakened.

Monday, December 5th. At 7 a.m. native service as usual. Brother Unis, a native school-teacher, interpreted. Half a dozen seekers of pardon, and two professed. About a dozen came forward as seekers of entire purity, the presiding elder among them, and he gave a beautiful testimony afterwards.

At 6 p.m. English congregation; eighteen seekers came forward; none examined, and no satisfactory result. A general feeling of distrust seems to have paralysed the workers. There may be some frogs in the net, I know not; but I do know that if there are any good fish among them we shall not get them into the boat in this way. I thought we had a good haul last night, and certainly the most of them looked well; but it seemed as though the lines were dropped at both ends, and the net was not hauled at all. I am not prepared to give a judgment in the case, not knowing the people; I only know that the Gospel I preach is adapted to all people, but with a doubting, hesitating Church it cannot succeed much with any. I am sure all my brethren and sisters here are anxious for a great work of God ; but some are not strong in aggressive faith, and some are very busy with other things, and think my meetings too long.

Tuesday, 6th. George Bailey received Christ this morning, told his experience, and exhorted the people in Hindustani, weeping as he talked. As we came out of the church Brother Waugh said, " I never but once or twice before heard such Hindustani as that—so clear, terse, and forcible."

One day last week, when Brother Thoburn returned home from a visiting tour, he said, " I was in a little hell to-day—the house of a widow and her two sons, nominally Roman Catholics, but practically worse than the heathen ; but George, the elder son, says he will come to the meeting."

That was George Bailey. His great-grandfather was a French Bourbon, but in some disturbance fled to the court of Persia, later to the court of Delhi, and became a general of the Emperor of Delhi. His grandfather was a general of the King of Oude, and his father a captain in the same service. Owing to English prejudice against the employment of French officers by the native rajahs their French name was dropped and the plain English name of Bailey given them instead. In the defence of Lucknow during the mutiny George was but a boy of sixteen years, but so distinguished himself as a soldier that the rank and pension of an ensign for life were given him. Now he has enlisted in the army of Jesus.

I was quite below par to-night with headache from loss of sleep, partly from the burden of this work on my soul. God is assuring me of His gracious designs, but our faith is being severely tested.

Wednesday, 7th. Called a council of war this morning, and I submitted two questions. First, Shall we open the doors of our church and gather up the fruits of our labour, or let them drift ? Secondly, Shall we continue the present order of special services ? Their reply to the first question was, " Open the doors." In regard to the second, Brother Thoburn said, " The work seems to be waning ; even you do not manifest the same confidence and incisiveness of effort as at the first."

He is a sharp brother, and could read me like a book. The fact is, so much was said about long sermons and long after-meeting, and the inability of people in this climate to stand such work, that I partially yielded to the judgment of others, and was also somewhat disconcerted by the general feeling of distrust which seemed to mildew the whole concern. They are all as kind and confiding as possible, and as I am but a novice in India I have been deferring to them perhaps more than was wise. I know what sort of effort is necessary to success in other countries, and I apprehend that India will require greater zeal and a more bold, aggressive faith than any other.

Thursday, 8th. Preached on Christian fellowship, and explained our policy and position as a Church, and invited candidates for membership. George Bailey was the first to present himself, which he did with characteristic promptness; seven others followed.

Friday, 9th. Fellowship meeting at noon. Isa Das, a native preacher, said, "I came to these meetings an unsaved man. I determined to seek salvation, but I thought to go forward as a seeker would disgrace me. One who has been preaching the Gospel for years to go forward as a seeker! I could not do it. It was too much for my pride. I went three miles out of town and kneeled down in the darkness of the night in a mango grove and prayed earnestly to God for the pardon of my sins, but got no relief. But last Wednesday morning I kneeled down there at that rail as a seeker, and received Christ as my Saviour, and got all my sins forgiven."

At the time he accepted Christ, Brother Thoburn said to me, "He is one of the most truthful, manly fellows in the mission, and there can be no mistake about his conversion."

Several others spoke to the point, but some were misty and vague. We had a general time of weeping over the low experience of some, and I was led to say, "Sisters and brothers, you know the difficulties peculiar to India—the paralysing influence of heathenism, formalism, and caste. It seems to saturate and mildew your very souls; and then you talk about the enervating effect of the climate. God made the climate, and God made the Gospel. If His Gospel is not adapted to this climate, then we will ask Him to change the climate to suit His soul-saving purpose and plan. I tell you God's Gospel is adapted to every climate and every variety and condition of human kind."

13th. Up to this time over one hundred persons have been forward as seekers, most of whom profess to have found remission of sins. Of these twenty-five have joined our Church; about thirty were members before, nominally; as many more are connected with the English Church, and others not organised in Lucknow. God is with us and doing the best thing possible under existing conditions.

14th. In the evening preached to the Church on witnessing and working for Christ. After the meeting I had a consultation with the missionaries in regard to Cawnpore.

It was urged that Cawnpore was outside of our Conference boundaries, and we had no right to go there; but that was met by the fact that Brother Thoburn had already preached there several times. One urged that if we should get converts there we had no money or employment for them. I said, "I never heard of the like before;" and it was finally agreed that if I would not commit the mission to any responsibility in regard to Cawnpore I might go and see what the Lord had for us to do there. I laid the whole matter before God, and had every lingering doubt against it removed.

They gave me George Myall, a native teacher and helper, who on Tuesday night last received Jesus and got an assurance of pardon, to accompany me as interpreter. He is a slow but trustworthy man, had for thirty years lived in Cawnpore and lost everything he had there in the mutiny, including nine hundred rupees in cash; but had been away from Cawnpore for the last five years.

Friday, 16th. Good meeting for believers at noon. At night two were saved, one of them a Roman Catholic. A Christian marriage in the city to-day. To celebrate the occasion they had a great dance in the Royal Park Hall, which lasted nearly all night. Except the dancing girls of India, who are the lowest of fallen women, the Mohammedan and Hindu women would not think of dancing with men. These great feasts to Bacchus, by people called Christians, are innovations on heathen morality, and scandalise the name of Christ.

17th. Left for Cawnpore at 1 p.m., arrived at 4 p.m., and was kindly received by Dr. Moffat.

Now I see a chain of providential pointers centring in Cawnpore. At the earnest request of my dear friend Dr. A. Moffitt, of Sydney, New South Wales, I promised to visit his nephew, Dr. Moffitt, at the Netley Hospital. I could not find time to fulfil that promise till my second return from the West Indies. Our ship, the *Tasmania*, arrived in Southampton early on Tuesday morning, the 16th of March, 1869; and I was to set sail again on Friday ensuing in the steamship *Syria* for Alexandria, *en route* to Australia. I had much to do in London, and time was very precious. I took a cab to go in haste five miles to Netley Hospital to see Dr. Moffitt. On arrival I was informed that the doctor had gone to his residence. I took his address, and the cabman said he would drive me " to the very spot." " Very well," said I, "go ahead; I'm in a great hurry."

When he drove to " the very spot " he found that it was not the spot where the doctor lived. After seeking in vain for half an hour I said, " I must be at the train for its next departure for London, and can't waste any more time."

Just then a man told us where Dr. Moffatt lived; so we drove to his door. Mrs. Moffatt received me with true Irish-lady hospitality, as I told her that I had a salutation for her husband from his uncle Dr. A. Moffitt, of Sydney. She said, " My husband is suffering from a severe cold and has lain down; but I will tell him that you are here."

She returned, saying, " My husband says he has no uncle in Sydney; but another Dr. Moffitt, our neighbour, who has just come in to see my husband, says that he has an uncle there."

So in the house I was not seeking I found the man I sought, and thus became know to the man I sought not, the Dr. Moffatt who subsequently came to India as surgeon of her Majesty's Fourteenth Regiment, and now had opened the way for our work in Cawnpore. I see more and more clearly that it is too late for me to begin to make plans for the Lord by which to work, when God has so long ago made plans for me. It is not mine to ask Him to indorse my plans and go with me, but by all available means to discern His plans and go with Him.

Sabbath, 18th. Preached in the Union Chapel, at 7 a.m., to a congregation of twenty-three soldiers and thirteen civilians. Went to the chapel at 2 p.m., and preached to twenty-three persons; then again, at 5.30 p.m., to a congregation of thirty soldiers and thirty civilians. Deep attention, but not ready for an advance, except to explain the situation and get the people to search the Scriptures and see if these things are so. It was arranged that our English services should be held in Dr. Moffatt's prayer room. During this week visited the colonel, the chaplain, and many soldiers' families, and preached every night; but with no decisive results in the way of conversions. When Christmas holidays set in the people were so taken up with excursions and home entertainments that we closed and never again resumed our special services at the Union Chapel and Dr. Moffatt's prayer room, but instead George Myall and I ran special services in the native city, in the houses of two East Indian families, about two miles apart, and preached daily also in the bazaars to the heathen and Mohammedans. At our outdoor services we had from two to four hundred hearers, and usually very attentive.

At our house No 1. I preached six nights before I invited any to come out avowedly as penitent sinners. I was waiting for them, to see them interpret and obey the leading of the Holy Spirit without human suggestion. On the seventh night, at the close of my sermon, a prominent East Indian midwife arose to her feet and said, "I feel that I am a great sinner, and I want to confess my sins."

"Confess your sins to God."

"Yes, but I have for many years been a public rebel against God, and common honesty and truth require a public confession and renunciation of wickedness."

With that she came and knelt down weeping near to where I stood; others followed. Within ten days after I organised a Church in that house, composed of fourteen of our new converts, born unto God there. The owner of it, our host, was a French Roman Catholic. At No 2. our noonday series gave us a new organisation of eight members.

January 5th. I said to-night to Dr. Moffat, who is a Low Church Episcopalian and son of an old deceased minister of the Episcopal Church in Ireland, "We now have twenty-two East Indian converts here, with two Hindus, Mrs. B—— and her adopted daughter, whom she took fifteen years ago from the breast of a dead Hindu mother on the banks of the Jumna. I have organised these converts into two bands, one at each of our preaching places, and they want to know what we are going to do for them in the way of pastoral care. They are all poor but self-supporting, and want no help in that way. I am pledged to the Lucknow brethren not to commit them for any responsibility. You have a leading agency in this work, and if it shall result in the establishment of a Methodist mission here it will be a feather in your cap."

"Yes, and a star in my crown."

"But you have already got yourself into disgrace in the eyes of your chaplain and others; so you had better count the cost before we proceed farther."

"Oh, my shoulders are broad; I don't care for any of them, except to do them good. They shall never hinder me from doing the work God may give me to do."

Next day, Friday, the 6th, I breakfasted with Mr. McLeavy, manager of the Bank of Upper India, and a friend of our work. I assured him of the possibility of securing an American Methodist missionary for Cawnpore if we proceeded to organise.

He promptly replied, "I hope they will send one to Cawnpore. The Presbyterians don't intend to establish a permanent mission here; Mr. W—— told me so. I have tried in vain to get my own church" (the Baptist) "to send a teacher here who could also hold religious services. There is no mission in this city of one hundred and fifty thousand population except that of the Propagation Society, and they are doing but little to meet the spiritual wants of this people. A Methodist mission would absorb all the interest that the Presbyterians and others now share among them as transient visitors. I will give all my influence to it, and I am sure others will do the same. If a school also could be established, with a competent teacher, it would realise three hundred rupees per month."

All this was spontaneous, and came in as another indication of Providence that we should plant a mission in Cawnpore.

Tuesday, 10th. This morning I drew up a rough draft of a petition addressed to the Indian Mission Conference, praying them to put Cawnpore on the list of their missions and appoint to it at their coming session a missionary. Mr. McLeavy copied it, and got the signatures of many of the leading men of the station, with a subscription of eighty rupees per month toward the support of the missionary, which he said could easily be increased to a hundred. With this petition and subscription, and the list of my candidates for membership organised into two classes—fourteen in one and eight in the other—on Thursday morning, the 12th of January, I returned to Lucknow.

The Indian Mission Conference assembled in Lucknow on Thursday, the 12th. On Friday the Cawnpore petition was presented and freely discussed. The Conference voted to put Cawnpore on the list and recommend the Missionary Board to confirm their action and appoint a missionary to it. On that night I preached, and we had the communion rail crowded with seekers of purity, and eight or nine penitents also. That night Dennis Osborne went up and got a baptism of the Spirit, and soon after joined our Church, and is now the most effective, soul-saving preacher, I believe, in the northwest.

Thursday, 19th. Preached at Bailey's at twelve o'clock to about eighty persons. I counted forty Hindus and Mohammedans. Brother Bailey interpreted, and did it well. After we had been preaching about half an hour a Mohammedan moulvy (a kind of priest) came in and sat down on a chair. Immediately seven of the best-looking, well-dressed Mohammedans got up abruptly and left the house.

I said to Bailey in an undertone, "What's the matter with those fellows?"

"The moulvy sat down on a chair above them;" and turning to him Bailey said, "Sit down there on the carpet;" and he did so.

Then, quick as a monkey, Bailey bolted downstairs and out into the street and overtook the deserters and brought them back, and demanded of them in the presence of the crowd an explanation of their conduct.

The oldest one of them replied, "We are all equals, and don't allow any of our people to take a higher seat than that of his brother."

Bailey pointed to the old moulvy on the floor, and they nodded assent. Then an East Indian gentleman and his sister got up to select a seat on the carpet; but the old Mohammedan took hold of their hands and begged them to sit down on their chairs, as that was their custom. We then proceeded with the discourse, and they all listened with great attention.

Friday, 20th. Preached again at Bailey's on the Prodigal Son. At the close the people seemed unwilling to leave, and Bailey overheard them saying one to another, "If that man would stop here he would win us all over to his side."

An old Hindu said to Bailey as he passed out, "I'll think no more about my own religion, but I'll think about the Lord Jesus."

The same old moulvy and his son, a well-educated young man, were here again to-day. They claim to be related to the late King of Oude. They and several other Mohammedans followed me to Dr. Waugh's, and again at night called on me at Brother Thoburn's. I told them my experience and preached to them for an hour. They expressed great regret that I was going to leave the city so soon.

Saturday, 21st. The Conference had no regular missionary for Cawnpore, but gave us Brother Mukurji, a converted Brahman, to labour in native work at Cawnpore. I went with him to-day to introduce him and smooth down the disappointment of my friends there in not getting a missionary. At the railway station I met the old moulvy and his friends, who came to see me off. I remained at Cawnpore till Tuesday, and put Brother Mukurji into the work as well as I could. He is an earnest, good brother; but the work at Cawnpore was not conserved as well as it could have been under more favourable conditions.

Brother Thoburn still went to Cawnpore occasionally and organised the English work; and Dr. J. Condon, one of the Lord's lay preachers, was appointed civil surgeon at Cawnpore soon after I left, and became a powerful worker.

A year later Brother Gladwin was appointed there as a missionary and developed the English work, and also regular native preaching and large schools in the city; and that station became the first self-supporting mission in the Conference, and also the seat of the Memorial High School. They appropriated missionary money there for buildings; but the preacher's salary was paid by the people from an early period of Brother Gladwin's appointment to Cawnpore.

Tuesday, 24th. On my return to Lucknow I found the old moulvy and his friends on the platform waiting for me; and they called again to see me that evening. It is all arranged for me to go to-morrow to Seetapore, on my tour through the mission. Brother Bailey is to go as my interpreter.

25th. We took the road in the dak-ghari (mail coach) at 8 a.m. The old moulvy and his son came to see me off, and were most anxious to know when I would return. I told the dear old man that I hoped to return in September.

" Oh, that is such a long time ; your words give me so much light and comfort. When you come again I will bring our nobles to see you."

Instead of returning in September, as I thought I should, I did not see Lucknow again for three years, and was sorry to learn then that my old moulvy was dead.

We drove fifty-two miles through a beautiful but poorly cultivated country, arriving in Seetapore at 5 p.m., and were welcomed by Rev. Brother Knowles, who had a tent pitched for us in the mission compound, or yard. (*Seeta* was the wife of Ram, and *pore* means city. This is the city of Ram's wife.)

Thursday, 26th. White frost covering the ground this morning. Preaching announced for the chapel at 8 a.m., but as the shivering natives had collected in the sunshine on the mission house verandah I preached to them there. Preached in the chapel at 11 a.m. Bailey interpreted and was master of the situation. We had to-day a general breakdown among the East Indians, and ten women and seven men came forward as seekers, and professed to receive Christ and peace with God.

CHAPTER XXX

CAMPAIGN FROM PANAHPORE TO BOMBAY

SATURDAY 28th. Our journey from Seetapore to Panahpore is about fifty miles. A little after dark we arrived in Panahpore (*Pana* means refuge). So we were welcomed by Brother and Sister Johnson and Brother Buck into the city of refuge.

Sabbath, 29th. Preached at 11 a.m. Good attention; but we did not invite seekers. Again at 5.30 p.m. At the prayer meeting following the preaching twenty-four men and six women came forward as seekers and professed to find peace. Some of them are servile, and not very reliable; but I felt a profound sympathy for them, and showed no distrust. Some of them spoke beautifully. One said, "A great light is shining into my heart." Another said, "My soul is filled with joy. It is like a spring bubbling up in my heart."

On Wednesday, February 1st, we struck our tents in Panahpore, five miles distant, and came to Shahjehanpore. *Shah* means king; *jehan*, the world; *pore*, city—called after Shahjehan, one of the Great Mogul kings of the country. We are quartered in Dr. Johnson's missionary bungalow.

The great missionary interest of this place is the Boys' Orphanage.

The orphanage contained one hundred and forty-seven resident boys and young men and about twenty day scholars. These were all instructed in the rudiments of the Hindi, Hindustani, and Persian languages; most of the larger boys also in the ordinary branches of English. They all learn a trade as well in the industrial department, farming, weaving, shoemaking, printing and press work, cabinet making, etc.

On the day of our arrival we preached in the orphanage chapel at twelve noon, and 6.30 p.m. All attentive and well-behaved.

Friday, February 3rd. Went out eight miles to Chandapore, to attend a monthly meeting of the fakirs and followers of Kabir.

We got a patient hearing to a sermon over an hour in length, and our testimony to a personal experience of salvation from sin by Jesus Christ, and a closing prayer that God would open their hearts and apply His truth.

Then the head fakir tried to checkmate our testimony by saying. "Oh, I drank of the river of life long ago, and got all that you say you have got. Kabir was the son of God, and through him all my sins were taken away."

I challenged him to produce Kabir's credentials.

"Where is the proof that he ever set up such a claim for himself? You say that your sins have all been pardoned and taken away, I must have the testimony of your neighbours on that point."

Then I appealed to the people: "Friends, you know this man. He says that his sins have been taken away. Is that true? Does he not cheat you, and oppress you, and tell you lies?"

The people cried out against him, saying, "He is one of the greatest sinners amongst us, and he is telling you lies now."

Then he changed his ground and said, "We are united to God; we are a part of God. We do nothing of ourselves; God does it all, and never imputes sin to us. We never sinned in our lives."

Bailey replied, "Then if I come and join your clan, and become a worshipper of Kabir, I may seduce your wife and take her away from you, and do all manner of wickedness, and you would say, 'Mr. Bailey—what a good man he is! True, he has given us a great deal of trouble, but, poor fellow! he is not responsible. It was God who did it all.'"

Many of the people cried out, calling the priest by name, "Shame, shame on you! You know well enough that we are all responsible for our conduct."

Thus we sowed the good seed among the people, silenced the batteries of the priests, and returned.

Preached in the orphanage chapel at 6 p.m. About seventy came forward as seekers, and twenty-five professed to find forgiveness of sins, and publicly testified for Jesus.

Saturday, 4th. My rest day; but while I was resting—at the earnest request of the leading English residents of the station, it being their only leisure day—I preached to them in our chapel at 4 p.m.

We continued special services on Sabbath and Monday. Over seventy during the series, mostly orphans, professed to obtain peace with God. The greater part of these, as I have heard from year to year, remained steadfast.

A journey of fifty miles brought us to Bareilly. We found a good and welcome home in the house of Rev. T. J. Scott, the Presiding Elder of Bareilly District.

The next house is the residence of Rev. D. W. Thomas, who, with his earnest, good wife, and Miss Fanny Sparks to assist him, has charge of the Girls' Orphanage a similar institution to the one for boys in Shahjehanpore. It contains one hundred and forty orphan girls, many of them now young women, well advanced in the rudiments of education, and in handiwork to fit them to fill their station in life.

Here we also found Miss C. Swain, M.D., at her post. She is a most successful medical practitioner, and gets access to the best families in the city. She has treated this year one thousand three hundred and thirty-five cases, and has in connection with this opened up an interesting zenana work.

Bareilly is a large native city and military station. On the evening of my arrival, at the request of our missionaries, I went with them to a temperance tea meeting for her Majesty's Twenty-fifth Regiment, and heard some good temperance talk and preached a little to the soldiers.

I preached in the orphanage chapel at noon to the one hundred and forty orphans—all old enough to sin, and hence old enough to be saved from sin. Bailey interpreted.

Preached in the bungalow used for regular native services at 6 p.m. Brother Bailey heard to-day that Justice Walker, whom he knew in Lucknow during the mutiny, was residing in Bareilly, and was a justice of the peace and treasurer of the city.

"I will take Brother Taylor to see Walker," said Bailey, "and we will get him converted to God."

The missionaries laughed at Bailey's newborn zeal, and said, "You can do nothing with Walker. His wife is a Mussulmani, and he has a lot of her Mohammedan kindred in his house. He never comes to preaching."

"Oh, I am sure we can get him saved," replied Bailey, and left abruptly, and went to call on his old friend. After reviewing their memories of the mutiny he said, "Mr. Walker, I want to introduce Mr. Taylor to you."

"No, Mr. Bailey; if you please, don't bring Mr. Taylor here. He'll be pitching into me about something or other, and I don't want to see him."

"Nay, nay, Mr. Walker; Mr. Taylor is a world-wide traveller and a kind gentleman. He will interest you on many subjects, and not pitch into you at all."

So Mr. Walker consented, and Bailey came in haste for me to go and get his friend saved.

We went to his office, and after a long talk on various topics, as I was about to leave, I said, "Mr. Walker, as I am stopping at Mr. Scott's, near by, and have but a few days to spend in your city, if agreeable to you I shall be glad to come some morning and conduct family worship for you."

"Thank you, Mr. Taylor; but I am a man of business, and have to go early to office, daily, and cannot possibly command the time."

"How about Sabbath morning?"

"Well, I have no particular engagement Sabbath morning."

"Suppose, then, you invite a few of your friends, and allow me to come to your house, and we will have family worship together?"

"Very well, Mr. Taylor; come next Sabbath, at 8 a.m."

A Mohammedan giant, who lives with Mr. Walker, whom we called "Goliath of Gath," was present at our meeting in the bungalow. Bailey recognised him as an old friend whom he knew in the mutiny. He seemed much pleased to see Bailey, and said to him, "You have found God. I wish I could find Him too!"

Friday, 10th. At the orphanage chapel Bailey interpreted well, as usual. The missionaries in different places often expressed surprise at his clear, terse translation of my Scripture quotations, so original and so forcible.

A grand meeting to-day among the oprhans. Sixty-seven of the elder girls came up as seekers, and twenty-six were saved.

At 7 p.m., in the bungalow, twenty-five men and fifteen women, native nominal Christians, came out as seekers, and professed to find Jesus. Goliath seemed under deep concern.

Sabbath, 12th. Had a service at Mr. Walker's at 8 a.m. Eighteen persons present, including his family. At the close, seeing that a good impression was made, I said, " Now, Mr. Walker, if you like I will come again to-morrow morning at seven o'clock and conduct your family worship. We can have a family service from seven to eight, and then you can have from eight to nine for breakfast and get to office in due time, at 10 a.m."

" All right, Mr. Taylor ; we shall be glad to see you again to-morrow morning."

At the orphanage chapel at noon we had about seventy seekers, and nineteen professed to find Jesus.

A young woman said, " I have received the forgiveness of my sins. No one has told me in my ear, but I feel the testimony of it in my mind, and I will always be true to Jesus."

Monday, 13th. Preached in orphanage chapel on the babes and sucklings, and the truth took hold on the smaller orphans. Some of them came forward, but more of the larger ones ; thirty-eight professed to find forgiveness of sins. At 6 p.m. I preached in the city schoolhouse to the English-speaking Hindus, Mohammedans, and Brahmos—the followers of Keshub Chunder Sen, of Calcutta. About one hundred present, crowding the room. I discoursed to them an hour. The Spirit of God was manifestly present to apply the truth. At the close Judge Bakhtawar Singh, a Hindu judge receiving a government salary of eight hundred rupees per month, arose and tendered his thanks and the thanks of the hearers for what they had heard.

If I had time to dispute daily with these people and pursue fully St. Paul's methods—having the same Gospel, the same Jesus, and the same Holy Spirit—I am sure we should see corresponding results.

Tuesday, 14th. Preached at Walker's at 7 a.m. About thirty present, and deep awakening. At the close Mr. Walker said, " Mr. Taylor, I hope you will come to-morrow morning, and every morning while you remain in the city."

" Thank you, Mr. Walker, I shall, the Lord willing, do so with much pleasure."

Preached at the orphanage chapel at twelve noon. Fifty seekers, and twenty-seven professed to find Jesus.

Wednesday, 15th. At Justice Walker's again at 7 a.m. Great awakening. All of them—about twenty souls—went down on their knees as avowed seekers of salvation.

Good service at twelve o'clock in the orphanage chapel. During preaching in the evening in the bungalow a cry of fire broke up our meeting for half an hour. About a dozen of the Walker family came out as seekers, and professed to receive Jesus.

Thursday, 16th. At Justice Walker's at 7 a.m. I preached, and

Mrs. Walker, the Mussulmani, came forward for Christian baptism. Brother Scott read the baptismal service in Hindustani, and we prayed for her and for Mr. Walker till they were filled with the Holy Spirit ; and then I baptised her with water.

I then read our General Rules and gave them an address on Church organisation and organised a Church in the house of Brother Walker, and appointed him to conduct a public service in his own house every Sabbath morning, assisted by the missionaries when they could command time.

At the noon meeting that day in the orphanage chapel Mrs. Walker publicly related her experience in her own language ; she could not speak English. At the close of the meeting Brother Scott said, " She has great command of the Hindustani language, and is most clear and emphatic in her testimony to the saving power of Christ."

I may simply add that Justice Walker kept up the meetings at his own house, and sometimes conducted meetings at the bungalow. Mrs. Walker was a large, fine-looking woman, apparently in the vigour of life and health ; but a few months after her conversion to God she was taken ill and died. Brother Scott wrote me that she remained true to Jesus and died in the Lord. After a year or two Brother Walker also died in the Lord, and the family moved away, I know not whither.

The giant passed through all this deeply awakened, and came to spend the evening with me at Brother Scott's the night of my departure ; admitted everything ; anxious to be saved, but hesitated. I know not what became of him.

Leaving Brother Scott's about 9 p.m. we travelled that night by dhuli dak forty miles to a camp meeting on the Budaon Circuit, Rev. R. Hoskins, missionary. We arrived at the camp just as the cheering rays of the morning sun began to stream through the mango groves.

At this camp meeting over thirty nominal Christian natives professed to find the pardon of their sins, and one Mohammedan was baptised by Brother Scott.

From the camp meeting we passed on to Chandousi. We made an itinerating tour of hard fighting and varied success at Chandousi, Babukhera, Joa, Sambhal, Bashta, Amroha, and Moradabad. Brother Parker, presiding elder, and his wife, a true helper, were with us during most of the campaign of six weeks.

Early in April we went to Meerut, a large native city and military station. Rev. Mr. McKay, church chaplain, and Rev. Mr. Gillau, Scotch Kirk chaplain, gave me an earnest invitation to work for them in English work. So Brother Bailey returned and took work under Brother Parker. He became a preacher in Hindustani and Hindi.

I preached daily in the kirk in Meerut for three weeks. I did not for a fortnight invite a seeker to come out avowedly on the Lord's side. Finally I invited them to come to the front, and seven came promptly forward, and we had a deep awakening among many who did not yield. I hoped for a great harvest of souls, but it struck the dear ministers as a novelty, because they had never seen the like before. They did not object publicly, but afterwards expressed their feelings, so that I did not consider it safe to repeat the call for seekers. I did not certainly believe that a single one was saved.

I went from Meerut to Delhi, and laboured three weeks with my old friend Rev. James Smith, the Baptist missionary whom I met in Australia eight years before. The weather was now so hot that we did not attempt to hold special services in his chapel beyond the regular Sabbath appointments, but we had preaching every week evening in verandahs and open courts, and prepared the soil and sowed the good seed, and in the following cool season Brother Smith, as his report states, gathered a good harvest. He was trying hard, and with a good degree of success, to place his mission on a purely self-supporting basis.

From Delhi I went to Ambala, and preached two Sabbaths for Rev. William Morrison, to her Majesty's Seventy-second Regiment, and in the week intervening we opened an English work in Sudder Bazaar.

I went thence to Bijnour, and wrought a few days for Rev. Henry Jackson, and had some souls saved; thence by dhuli dak, on a very wet night, forty miles to Moradabad; thence about forty more to the base of the mountains, *en route* for Naini Tal, and thence fifteen miles up the Himalaya Mountains, on Rev. Dr. J. L. Humphrey's pony.

The doctor was not only an indefatigable missionary, but a successful medical practitioner. From April to November of this year he treated one thousand eight hundred and thirty patients. He was also the founder of a medical school in Naini Tal. Colonel Ramsey, Commissioner of Gurhwal and Kumaon, was his ever-ready patron and a firm support to all our mission work in the Himalaya Mountains.

It was during this visit that Sister Humphrey and I compiled " Hymns New and Old," which have been so valuable to our rising Indian churches.

Spent a Sabbath at Rani Khet, and went on a week's journey through the mountains to Paori. This was my last work that year in our Mission Conference. A few hundreds of nominal native Christians professed to find peace at our meetings, and also a small number of Hindus and Mohammedans, and God gave a fresh divine impulse to the work, which thrills on with increasing power year by year. My work closed in Paori about the last of August. It was not considered safe to return to the plains earlier than October; so I set apart the month of September for a pilgrimage with the natives, to study them and learn what they did and suffered to get rest for their souls.

We reached Mussouri on the 5th of October. Spent a few days preaching for Rev. Mr. Woodside, American Presbyterian, in Dheradoon, and went thence to Lahore. At the call of the missionaries of the American Board of Commissioners for Foreign Missions to attend their annual meeting at Ahmednuggur I started for Bombay, about one thousand five hundred miles distant, on Wednesday, the 19th of October, 1871.

CHAPTER XXXI

THE city of Bombay was built on several small islands, which have been gradually united to each other by levelling down the hills and filling up the separating valleys. Thus the whole became one island, and that has been united to the mainland and firmly anchored to it by railway lines.

I travelled from Lahore to Bombay in the third class, first, because my funds were low, and, secondly, because I wanted to study native language and character. All were exceedingly kind and agreeable, except one old Hindu, who in all his waking hours was repeating his " Ram," " Ram," " Ram," and passing his beads along the string to keep the tally of his " Ave Marias." He seemed to be the most religious man, and certainly the greatest grumbler, of the whole crowd.

I arrived in Bombay at 11 a.m. on Saturday, the 22nd of October, put up again in the Byculla Hotel, and spent a quiet Sabbath. On Monday, at 11 a.m., I took a third-class ticket for Dhond, about one hundred and eighty miles south-east. The guards offered me a second-class, but I declined. The carriages were crowded ; but by a system of squeezing and packing there was room for a few more. There sits an old Brahman in the corner, behind a pile of his luggage, to preclude the possibility of contaminating touch by any ordinary mortal ; he raises his hands and screams at an intruder, and then draws himself up into the corner again in a great state of trepidation ; his caste may be broken and his soul lost. Now in comes an Irish guard, a regular packer, and, stuffing the Brahman's things under the bench, makes the Brahman the base of a layer of coolies. He smashes down the separating barriers which have stood the storms of ages, and indiscriminately packs away high castes and low castes together, like herrings in a barrel. Now, full up, we touch at another station. Here comes another old Brahman ; he looks into one carriage after another and sees the packed-in coolies and low castes. He is in a great state ; the bell is ringing the signal to start, and he stands hesitating at the door. Along comes the guard, and with the stentorian order, " Chuck him in there," we suddenly see the Brahman tumbling into the midst of the common herd.

I reached Dhond at 10 p.m. As I stepped on to the platform a thickset Scotchman introduced himself to me as a Baptist missionary from Bengal, the Rev. Mr. Ellis, also on his way to the annual meeting at Ahmednuggur.

"Here is a tonga waiting for us," said Brother Ellis, "and I have just received a letter from Rev. Mr. Bissell, saying that we can both come on in the same conveyance; but if you like I will get another and you can have this one to yourself."

"No, Brother Ellis; we will go together."

A "tonga" is a small two-horse cart, with two seats across, one facing toward the horses, on one of which the driver sits, with room for one passenger beside him, and the other for two passengers facing in the opposite direction, sitting back to back with the two in front.

I found Mr. Ellis a very genial, earnest Christian gentleman and missionary, and we passed the time very pleasantly and profitably together; but the wind blowing on our backs through that long chilly night gave us both a severe cold. We arrived in Ahmednuggur, the principal centre of the Maratti Mission, at the dawn of day. We were welcomed to the home of Rev. L. Bissell, D.D., and greatly enjoyed our sojourn in his charming family.

My first preaching service was on Thursday, the 26th. My interpreter was a converted Brahman, an able minister of the Gospel, and pastor of the Ahmednuggur church, Ram Krishna Punt.

On Friday evening we preached again, and also on Saturday at 8 a.m. There was a manifest awakening. Preached on the Sabbath at 9 a.m., when seven seekers came out avowedly, and two professed to find the Saviour.

Then I preached daily during the ensuing week. We had ten seekers on Monday, twelve on Tuesday, fourteen on Wednesday, eighteen on Thursday, and the same number on Friday. The attention of the people was much divided; those from a distance had the business of the meeting in its variety requiring their time; the residents were much occupied with their company; but God was with us and good was done. A good number—mostly nominal Christians, with two or three Hindus—professed quietly to find the pardon of their sins. Many of the same seekers came up again and again; but the whole number of them for the week was about twenty-five.

On Saturday evening, November 4th, we had a concert of native Christian music in the chapel, which attracted a crowd of Hindus. The narrative of the prodigal son in poetic measure was detailed in short chapters and then sung by a choir of native singers, accompanied with several instruments. Some of the missionaries said at the close, "We hope to see the day when we shall have as many Hindus to come and hear the Gospel preached as have come to-night to hear the singing." To their surprise we had a similar crowd of Hindus on Sunday, Monday, Tuesday, and Wednesday evenings of the ensuing week; and about a hundred of them became regular hearers henceforth, as I have learned since, some few of whom have been saved. The missionaries expressed themselves as greatly pleased with the results of our meetings, but I was not.

I arrived again in Bombay on Friday, the 10th of November, 1871. Rev. C. Harding, under the American Board of Commissioners for Foreign Missions, met me at the station and drove me to his house in Byculla. I commenced a series of Maratti services in Brother Harding's chapel on the following Sabbath, the 12th. Rev. Vishnu Punt is the pastor of his native church, but Brother Ram Krishna Punt came from Ahmednuggur to interpret for me in Bombay. I preached at 9 a.m. to a congregation of thirty persons.

Monday, 13th. At 7 a.m. twenty-seven hearers ; at 6.30 p.m. about fifty.

Wednesday, 15th. At 7 a.m., fifty-six hearers.

At 6.30 p.m. about one hundred hearers. God is with us ; but I apprehend His workers in this city are but few and feeble.

One good man met me at the door as I came out and exclaimed, " Except the Lord build the house, they labour in vain that build it.'

"True ; but He needs builders, nevertheless. He has never yet built a house among men without the labour of human builders."

Then he quoted, "Thy people shall be willing in the day of Thy power."

"Exactly so ; and if we can only secure the fulfilment of that prediction—the willingness of God's people to witness and work for Him—then we shall see His saving power manifested in this city."

On Thursday, 16th. 7 a.m., sixty-four out.

At 3 p.m. I preached to the schools of the Free Church of Scotland ; about one hundred and twenty present. At half-past six again in the American Chapel, to about one hundred and thirty, including a few Hindus and Mohammedans, who had not been coming before. There was a deep seriousness ; and I believe the Spirit of God applied the truth.

Friday, 17th. It rained this morning, but we had thirty-seven hearers. At 6.30 p.m., after preaching, we invited believers to come forward and unite in praying for power to do the work God wants us to do. About thirty came ; after which three or four spoke with great feeling. A native editor prayed, weeping all the time, and said many striking things to God, among which were the following : " As hot iron thrust into the water is hardened, so our hearts, heated by Thy Word and Spirit, thrust into the chilling waters of worldliness, have been hardened. The many prayers we have said are such poor things that we do not know whether to call them prayers or not ; I think we should change the heading !"

Friday, December 1st. Two services, as usual. This evening closed a series of eighteen days. Fifteen persons who came forward as seekers testified publicly and clearly. I heard of a number of members of different churches who professed to have found pardon under the preaching by quietly receiving Jesus in their pews. The wife of a native minister professed to get pardon at these meetings, though a nominal Christian for fourteen years. It was a hard fight, with some victories on our side.

I then arranged for a series of English services in the Institution

Hall, in connection with the school of the Free Church of Scotland; with morning services in the Scotch Orphanage for native girls.

Wednesday, 6th, Good service with the orphans. In the evening I preached on holiness; and, what seemed strange, the Hindus present were much more interested in that subject that any I had brought under their notice. Their eyes sparkled, and frequently they gave manifest expressions of approval, which they are apt to do when pleased.

Thursday, 7th. Had an extraordinary meeting with the orphans this morning. Sixteen of the young women came forward, and with great penitential weeping received Christ and found pardon. Each one afterwards stood up and gave a clear, plain statement of the facts in her experience. I visited during the day and prayed with families.

Friday, 8th. At the orphans' meeting Brother Dhanjibhai interpreted. Thirteen girls came forward and told the simple story of their awakening and salvation. I did not, however, see the same degree of interest expressed by the heads of the institution as was manifest the day before.

I afterwards talked to them. They confessed that they had not the least ground to doubt any one of the girls who had professed to find peace, but thought it possible among so many that some of them might be mistaken. I replied, "It is possible that some of them are mistaken; I don't pretend to know the heart of any one of them; but to show suspicion and doubt in our conduct toward them is to give help to Satan in his first assault. The very first thing the devil will say to all who are truly saved will be, 'Take care that you don't say anything about this, for you may be mistaken; and to make a false profession will bring you into the shame and disgrace of a hypocrite. Indeed, you are mistaken. It is all excitement and will soon pass away.' God's plan, when a babe is born, is to put it to the breast of a healthy, hopeful mother to get nourishment; your plan is to put it out into the jungle, among the jackals, to see how it will get on in the world."

They all received my talk as it was meant, in great kindness, and theoretically gave in; but they could not at once get rid of the dark shadow of their education on this point. Twenty-nine of the orphans professed to find Jesus, and Rev. S—— said the testimony of every one was simple, natural, and clear. Dr. Wilson baptised a number of them.

Friday evening in the hall we had a large crowd, but no break here yet; but it dawns upon my mind that God will lead me to organise many fellowship bands in the houses of the people who will be saved at my meetings. We cannot have an organised, witnessing, working Church without them. I have no plan and don't intend to have any, except to discern and follow at any hazard the Lord's plan, as He may be pleased to reveal it.

Saturday, 9th. By invitation of Mrs. Major Raitt I took tea and spent the evening at the house of her mother, the Widow Miles, a Christian Jewess.

Saturday, 30th. This evening, in the house of Mrs. Miles, I organised the first fellowship band, or class, ever organised in this city. I appointed Brother Bowen leader. At this, our first meeting for fellowship, twenty-eight persons told their Christian experience, most of them young converts. In circumstantial detail, variety, simplicity and point I never before heard better testimony for Christ.

New Year's Day, 1872. At 7.30 p.m. I went to the house of Brother George Miles, to organise Band No. 2. We had a blessed fellowship meeting. Sixteen spoke in charming simplicity. Not a technical, commonplace remark; not a single old fogey to teach them any!

Brother Christian said, "Brother Morris came into the bank and told me that Jesus had saved him from sin and was preserving him from sinning daily. It brought forcibly to my mind two facts: First, I have never had an experience of that sort; second, if Mr. Morris has got it, why cannot I get it? That was my starting point."

He described the struggle of last night which precluded sleep, and the visit to me in the morning and the final struggle this afternoon. He was called to dinner, but did not cease his pleading with God for pardon.

He proceeded to say, "I said, 'What is the matter? I can't believe.'

"The Spirit said to my heart, 'What is it that you can't believe? Do you not believe that God is able and willing and ready now to save you, if you will but receive Christ?'

"I said 'Yes, I believe all that.'

"'Well, then, why not receive Him?'

"I said, 'I will, I do receive Him.'

"I did receive Him, glory be to God! and He saved me, and I went at once and told the joyful news to my dear parents and sister, as they sat at the dinner table."

Captain W—— and his wife had both yielded to temper and brought darkness into their souls. We all immediately kneeled down and prayed for them, and they both received a renewed application of the pardoning blood of Jesus, verifying what is written, "Confess your faults one to another, and pray for one another, that ye may be healed."

CHAPTER XXXII

WORK AT MAZAGON AND AT NEW OUTPOSTS

I PREACHED at Mr. Thomas Graham's, in Mazagon Road, January 2nd, 1872, at 7.30 a.m. House well filled and good attention. At 7.30 p.m. preached in the library room of the Peninsular and Oriental Company's dockyard. About one hundred and thirty hearers.

Wednesday, 3rd. At 7 p.m. we met in the library room half an hour before preaching, to practise singing from our new book, "Hymns New and Old." This became from that time a regular part of each evening's service, and thus our people became rich in the acquisition of choice hymns and tunes. About one hundred and fifty present; deep attention, and several brethren gave a good testimony for Jesus.

Thursday 4th. Good meeting at Graham's; fifteen seekers, and fourteen of them professed to find the Saviour.

Friday, 5th. Good work at Graham's. At 7 p.m. our meeting was in the Peninsular and Oriental Company's Theatre, instead of the library room, the former being larger and better suited to our purpose, which they kindly lighted with gas, and gave us the free use of the whole.

Saturday, 6th. Prayed an hour with Major Raitt. He had a hard tug to get rid of self. Good fellowship meeting this evening at Mrs. Miles's house. Several more joined the band.

Sabbath, 7th. Preached at a private house at 7 a.m., and to eighteen vagrants at 3 p.m. Twenty were shipped for England last week, including the one who received Jesus last Sabbath. At 7 p.m. we had a great crowd in the theatre; eight seekers, and two professed to find Jesus.

Monday, 8th. Four seekers this morning at Graham's. Glorious fellowship meeting to-night at Brother Miles's. Mrs. Harry Wilcox received Christ at it and was filled with joy. Several months afterwards she died, sweetly resting in Jesus.

Tuesday, 9th. Good meeting at Graham's. A man was deeply awakened, and wept much.

"Will you not submit?" said I to him.

"Yes, but not to-day; I want to wait and bring my wife with me."

He was so convinced of sin that he went and sought reconciliation with several men with whom he had long been at enmity, and spoke freely of me and my meetings as the means of his awakening.

At 7 p.m. eight seekers, and one man professed to find the Lord.

Wednesday, 10th. Good meeting at Graham's. At the theatre about two hundred hearers; eight seekers, and four professed to find the Saviour. It is a hard pull all the time; God is slowly but surely developing an infant, witnessing, working Church from the foundation.

Friday, 12th. No conversions at Graham's this morning. A dozen seekers and four saved at the theatre. Major Raitt bore a distinct testimony to the saving power of Jesus in his heart.

The tide of opposition is rising, and the papers are beginning to open fire upon us. Our people are evidently gathering strength proportionate to the increasing pressure from without.

Saturday evening I organised Fellowship Band No. 3 at Mr. Graham's and appointed Brother Harding leader. Sixteen joined at this our first meeting.

Sabbath, 14th. I preached at Berkeley Place at 9.30 a.m. Four seekers. Arranged to organise a fellowship band there next Sabbath at 8.30 a.m. A fine class of our converted men and women live near and will join it. At 3 p.m. organised Fellowship Band No. 4 in Mazagon, and eleven joined. We are establishing the custom of weekly fellowship thank offerings.

Preached at the theatre at 7 p.m. Large crowd; a growing spirit of work among the young converts. Six persons professed to obtain remission of their sins to-night.

Monday, 15th. Twenty at the fellowship band at George Miles's at 7 a.m. Marvellous simplicity and candour in the mutual confession of their faults one to another, and sympathy and prayer for each other.

The progress of the members in the knowledge and love of God is very manifest. Their testimony is full of variety and incident.

Six new cases of conversion to-night in the theatre.

Tuesday, 16th. At 7 a.m. preached in Balassas Junction Road. Again at the theatre at 7 p.m. None found the Lord to-night that we know of. Timid seekers quail before the rising floods of opposition. Two daily papers have opened their batteries, and several ministers are preaching against the possibility of sudden conversions.

Sifting will do us good. God is leading, and we will follow.

Wednesday, 17th. Thirty hearers at Junction Road at 7 a.m., and a good prospect. Major Raitt tells me that he has succeeded in his application to the Government Committee of the House of Correction to allow me to preach to all the European prisoners who may desire it.

The chaplain will go into fits. He had one the other day when he saw my name on the visitors' book, which I signed by request when I went to preach to the vagrants. When the chaplain opened the book to sign his own name, on his next visit after I had committed the grievous offence of preaching to the vagrants, to whom he did not preach, he saw my signature, and shouted out, "What! has that man Taylor been in here?"

"Yes," said the deputy, "he has been preaching to the vagrants."

He got into a dreadful rage, and stormed as but few even high ritualists could do. This chaplain has some good points, but is a victim to his own hot temper.

Thursday, 18th. Preached at 4 p.m. to over fifty prisoners and taught them to sing a hymn. Many of the poor fellows wept as they sang,

"What a Friend we have in Jesus."

" Dear friends, you are indeed weak and heavy laden, burdened with sin and sorrow, hard toil and no pay. This Friend from heaven speaks to you. He says, ' Come unto Me, all ye that labour and are heavy laden, and I will give you rest.' He will not interfere with your disjointed relations to society and the legal penalties of British law; but if you will take His yoke and receive Him as your Saviour He will plead your cause before the throne of His Father, and the penalty of eternal death entered in the books of divine justice against you will be cancelled."

Friday, 19th. Several seekers at Junction Road at 7 a.m. In the evening we had a great crowd at the theatre. Among the seekers were Mrs. Captain O—— and Colonel A——'s daughter.

Saturday, 20th. Visited Mrs. Captain O——. She had found the Saviour. The colonel's daughter was there in great distress. Just as I was commencing in family worship to show her the way to Jesus, Miss P—— came in, saying, "I have come for you, Miss A——. Here are two letters from your pa. He is coming in the train and wants you to meet him at the railway station."

She talked like a governess, but I did not yield the floor, and she sat down ; then I proceeded with my instructions to the penitent young lady.

We kneeled and had a season of silent prayer, and there upon her knees Miss A—— gave her heart to God and received the Saviour. Miss P—— also broke down in penitential tears, and soon after at her own home professed to find forgiveness of sins.

Sabbath, 21st. Organised a fellowship band at Berkeley Place at 9 a.m. Fifteen joined. Those who joined seemed very promising cases but recently converted in the theatre. At 11 a.m. opened a little Sunday-school in the theatre. Organised a new band at the theatre at 4.30 p.m., and preached there at 7 p.m. to a crowd, and had a few saved. Thank God !

Tuesday, 23rd. Opened morning and evening services at a private house in Falkland Road. I closed special services at the theatre, and told the people to go home and rest a week ; in the meantime I made this quiet arrangement for a work in a neighbourhood in which we had not done much. We had twenty-four persons in the morning and thirty-four at night, mostly new cases.

At 3 p.m. preached again to the spirits in prison, and had sixty-five hearers. Major Raitt witnessed for Jesus, and exhorted the men earnestly, " Submit to God, and receive Christ as I have done, and you will, like me, obtain the pardon of all your sins."

An application for the use of the town hall for my meetings has been before the council for some time; but through the opposition of two ministers, as I learn on good authority, the matter was staved off, and finally referred to the governor and refused, though freely accorded to Keshub Chunder Sen, the Brahmo. Of course I know that I am in a great pagan city, and that the authorities, naturally enough, try to conciliate the natives as far as possible; and I have nothing of which to complain.

Newspaper war waging fiercely. George Bowen is responding to their guns splendidly, both in the *Guardian* and in the *Times*. Most of the editors seem disposed to deal fairly; but correspondents say what they like, and many of them have no regard for the truth.

Thursday, 25th. Preached at Falkland Road at 7 a.m. and at 3 p.m. to seventy hearers in the prison. A military prisoner was found to be under awakening, and Brother Harding and I took him into a room assigned us by Major Raitt and prayed with him till he professed to receive Christ.

Friday, 26th. Three letters in the *Times* to-day, two against the revival and one on our side. I have not read any of them; I seldom ever read what the papers say about me, but I hear of these things from others.

Visited two of the Peninsula and Oriental Steamship Company's sick men to-day. Mr. Macey is near his end, but is resting in Jesus. Smails is recovering. He is one of the company's divers, and has recently returned sick from Galle, where he had for some time been engaged in raising the passenger's luggage and the mails of the steamship *Rangoon*. He says, " She lies on a beautiful plain of very white sand one hundred feet below the surface of the waters. The pressure of the water at that depth is so great that all the divers got sick; indeed, it nearly killed them. Two men had to do most of the work. We raised four hundred and thirty mail bags. I never saw so many fish in any one place in all my diving experience as I saw there; fields of them in every direction. I saw many sharks, but they were always near the surface. I saw a most beautiful serpent of many colours, about nine feet long."

Tuesday, 30th. Preached in the prison at 3 p.m., and one prisoner in the seekers' room professed to find Jesus.

At Falkland Road this evening three professed. We had with us my old friend Barker, from Sydney, New South Wales. He gave us a good account of the progress of the work of God in Australia. He is on his way to England.

February 2nd. Discoursed this morning at Junction Road on Christian fellowship—showing the ground, the Scriptural authority, and true bonds of fellowship—and gave notice that I would, the Lord willing, organise a band there next Sunday morning at seven o'clock.

Preached at Falkland Road at 7.30 p.m. Had several hopeful cases of conversion to God, and gave notice that I would organise a fellowship band there next Sabbath at 9 a.m.

A very curious thing occurred one night there after one of our preaching services. A number had just been saved, and I gave them an opportunity to bear witness for Jesus. After half a dozen new converts had spoken just to the point in their newborn simplicity a very red-faced, burly-looking man, whom I had never seen before, stood up and gave a long detail of twenty years' experience of miraculous deliverances which God had wrought for him, stating that he loved the Lord with all his heart. Finally Rev. George Bowen rose to his feet and the man sat down. Bowen knew him well as a man who had just lost a good appointment under the harbour master on account of his habit of getting drunk. He was well read in the Scriptures, professing high attainments in religious experience, and most pious when drunk. Here he was in our meeting, vitiating the testimony of true witnesses. Bowen was horrified, and prayed that God, without injury to him, would shut his mouth; and from that time the man could not speak a word for some weeks!

Sabbath, 4th. At 7 a.m. we organised Band No. 6 at Junction Road. Ten joined it, and I appointed Brother William Ashdown the leader.

At Falkland Road, 9 a.m., twenty-one joined, and I appointed Major Raitt the leader. I shall, of course, continue to lead all the bands; but I appoint leaders to help to bear the responsibility of caring for so many newborn souls, and thus train the leaders to be efficient subpastors.

Preached in the evening in the theatre on Christian perfection. Brother Barker, from Australia, was at several of our fellowship bands to-day, and witnessed a good confession to-night. Brothers Bowen and Raitt also spoke right to the point.

Monday, 5th. Brother Bowen has rented Framji Cawasji Hall, belonging to the Parsees, for our services. We opened there on Tuesday, the 6th, at 7.30 p.m. About two hundred and fifty persons in attendance, including a good sprinkling of Hindus, Parsees, and Mohammedans.

Sister Morris first, and a number of others at different times, asked me what I should do to provide for the pastoral care of all these converts. I advised them to pray to God, but say nothing about it till we should see more clearly the Lord's leading in that matter.

We have been advising the converts to continue to go to the churches they had been most inclined to attend. But pastors who will not allow me to preach in their churches are not the men to nourish and lead to usefulness those who have been saved at my meetings. It has long been manifest that I must in some way provide for them, but I have not been clear as to whether or not it is the will of God that I should take the responsibility of organising a Church.

CHAPTER XXXIII

METHODIST CHURCH ORGANISED IN BOMBAY

On Thursday, the 8th of February, 1872, Brother George Miles drew up for himself and others the following letter or petition relative to the founding of a Methodist Episcopal Church in Bombay, and addressed it to me:

"To THE REV. WILLIAM TAYLOR—DEAR BROTHER,—We, the undersigned, who have by God's mercy been awakened through your preaching to a sense of our sins, and who have found the Lord Jesus to be our Deliverer, are desirous for the establishment of a Methodist Episcopal Church in this city.

"We are satisfied, from all that we have yet learned, of the Scriptural authority for the methods practised by the Church to which you belong; and we therefore unitedly invite you to take the necessary steps for the accomplishment of our wishes, and to act yourself as our pastor and evangelist until such time as you can make arrangements with the Home Board for sending out the necessary agency to this city."

Brother James Morris the same day showed the paper to a number of the converts, and thirty of them signed it; so in the evening, when he came home and showed me the list of signatures, I said, "Now, before you go any farther with this business, I must read our General Rules in the bands, that they all may know what we shall expect of them and act intelligently." So by Monday morning, the 12th of February, I had read the rules in the seven bands we had up to that time organised. Brother Morris, meantime, had increased his list of signers to eighty-three, and on Wednesday, the 14th, I formally accepted their call by a letter, which was published in the *Bombay Guardian.*

It was from the start distinctly stated and unanimously concurred in by all our members that ours should be purely a missionary Church, for the conversion of the native nations of India as fast and as far as the Lord should lead us; that while it should be true to the discipline and administrative authority of the Methodist Episcopal Church it should neither ask nor accept any funds from the Missionary Society beyond the passage of missionaries to India, nor hence come under the control of any missionary society, but be led directly by the Holy Spirit of God and supported by Him from Indian resources.

We are not opposed to missionary societies, or to the appropriation of missionary funds to any and all missions which may require them. Our ground on this point is simply this: There are resources in India, men and money sufficient to run at least one great mission. If they can be rescued from worldly waste and utilised for the soul-saving work of God, why not do it? All admit that self-support is, or should be, the earnest aim of every mission. If a work in India, the same as in England or America, can start on this healthy, sound principle, is it not better than a long, sickly, dependent pupilage, which in too many instances amounts to pauperism? I am not speaking of missionaries, but of mission Churches. We simply wish to stand on the same platform exactly as our Churches in America, which began poor and worked their way up by their own industry and liberality, without funds from the Missionary Society. The opening pioneer mission work in any country may require, and in most cases has required and does require, some independent re-sources which the pioneer missionary brings to his new work before he can develop it or make it self-supporting. Thus St. Paul de-pended on his skill as a tentmaker; I depend on mine as a book-maker, and missionaries ordinarily have to depend on mission funds. Ten times the amount of all the money now raised for mission purposes would not be adequate to send one missionary for each hundred thousand of heathens now accessible.

While we accept nothing, we, on the other hand, do not furnish homes, or compounds, for our converts. On this principle we may not for a while get so many native converts; but they will make up in quality any lack of numbers. To insure sound instruction on this subject we seek no native agency from other missions, and, as far as practicable, discourage all native Christians from joining our mission.

We state our principles to the Hindus, Mohammedans, and Parsees, and they approve of them. They are all familiar with the newspaper reports of lawsuits, and many of them have footed the bills involved by them to recover their sons from the compound of the missionary; and from their standpoint they can but regard the man of God as a kidnapper.

We say to them on all suitable occasions, "We claim for your wives, children, or servants, as for yourselves, liberty of conscience. The laws of the British Constitution and the laws of God support this claim; but, on the other hand, we recognise your rights of prop-erty to the persons of your wives, children, and servants, and we pledge our word and honour that we will not infringe your rights. If we can get your wives, children, or servants to receive Christ and salvation we will baptise them and send them home to you. You must not suspect that we will hide them: we will not. We will send them back to their friends and kindred, and we will require of you that you treat them properly and not interfere with their conscience."

Our mission in the north was begun in 1857. I have always taken the ground that, as it was planted in the new provinces of Oude and Rohilcund, it was quite proper for us as a Church to found educational institutions, orphanages, printing establishment, etc., and do from the foundations what older missions have done for nearly all other parts of India. I have always, from my arrival in India, done what I could to advance their work. I knew that in planting a mission on these plain, old-fashioned principles I should be misunderstood and misrepresented by many, and have not been disappointed or for a moment discouraged.

The following is a copy of a petition which I addressed to the General Conference which held its session in Brooklyn, New York, commencing May 1st, 1872 :

" TO THE GENERAL CONFERENCE OF THE METHODIST EPISCOPAL CHURCH.—DEAR FATHERS AND BRETHREN,—The God of our fathers has planted Methodism in Bombay.

" I have been but three and a half months in this city, and the first month was devoted to the Maratti natives through interpreters ; but you may see from enclosed Circuit Plan an indication of our growth. This is a city containing a population of nearly a million of souls ; Moradabad, the seat of our recent session of the India Mission Conference, is about fourteen hundred miles distant ; hence this mission cannot in reason be appended to that Conference. Moreover, we believe that God intends to run this soul-saving concern on His old Pauline track, which must pay its own running expenses and help ' the poor saints in Judea ' as well ; and therefore we cannot be tacked on to a remote dependency.

" We have asked our Missionary Committee, through Bishop Janes, to send us two young men, to arrive in November of this year ; but it is already manifest to us that God will raise up ministers here from the recruits He is now levying. One young man had over thirty seals to his ministry before he was two months old. We have nine classes, in which more than one hundred and thirty new converts meet weekly ; and others are being added daily. Nearly all these speak the different native languages spoken in this city ; and God will lead us down upon the native masses as soon as we are sufficiently developed and equipped for such an advance. We shall want the facilities for initiating and organising into a regular Methodist ministry the men whom God may call in Bombay for this work.

We therefore respectfully ask the General Conference at its present session to grant us a charter for the organisation of a Bombay Conference, not a Mission Conference. If we stand alone on our own legs, by the power of God, and draw no mission funds, why call it a Mission Conference ? We have a number of spacious places of worship in our circuit, named in the accompanying Circuit Plan ; but we are also raising funds for the erection of a Methodist Episcopal Church. For further information I refer you to Rev. R. S. Maclay, D.D., and Rev. Henry Mansell. As it regards myself, I am subject

to the Master's orders, to stand at this post till He shall release me
and order me to some other.

"Your Brother in Christ, on behalf of the Methodist Episcopal
Church in Bombay,

"WILLIAM TAYLOR.

"BOMBAY, *March 4th,* 1872."

You naturally inquire, What was the result of the petition ? Well,
the Committee on Foreign Missions were about to consign it to the
waste basket without even reading it, when Brother Mansell, who
had recently passed through Bombay, and was a member of that
committee, called for the reading of the petition. It was read and
laid on the table, not to be taken up again. The idea of man laying
the foundations of a Conference in a heathen country in the short
space of three months !

Since we organised our young members have been put to a severe
persecuting test, but most of them stand undaunted. Many of the
pulpits and the press are denouncing us, but God is with us, and we
will not fear what man may say or do.

After special services for three weeks in Framji Cawasji Hall, the
details of which I have not given, we engaged the hall for Sabbath
services, morning and night, for thirty-five rupees per week.

On Sabbath, March 3rd, we held our first sacramental service, and
had sixty-five communicants. Brother Harding said that it was
much the largest communion in the city ; and yet, owing to the great
distance of our extreme wings from this centre, not more than half
of our people could be present.

Held a successful series of services of over a fortnight in Morley
Hall, in Colabba. Krishna Chowey, a young Hindu, was awakened
there.

Mirza Ismael, a Persian Mohammedan, was a regular hearer at the
Parsee Hall meetings, and in Morley Hall, on March 7th, he came
out as a seeker. In his penitential struggle, while I was talking to
him and praying for him, he had a sort of vision. He saw before him
a beautiful garden. He wanted to go through a gate into that lovely
place, but could not advance. In every attempt he went either to
one side or the other, and could not reach the gate. In his fruitless
struggle a charming-looking man appeared at the gate and beckoned
to him to come, and he believed that he could ; and in the effort he
recovered proper consciousness and heard me saying to him,
"Receive Christ ; He has come to save you."

"I did in that moment receive Him," he added, "as my Saviour ;
and I was filled with light and happiness."

We had no facilities for baptism at the hall ; so Ismael came home
with us to Brother George Miles's, and there I baptised him. He
was thirty-one years of age, and was teacher of the Persian language
in one of the schools of the city. He took our advice to go home to
his place among his Mohammedan friends and proceed with his
school duties as before.

" Why baptise him so quickly ? "

Because I have learned in heathen lands, as I never did before, the importance of following strictly the apostolic precedent in this as in everything else.

Our dear Ismael had been under instruction for weeks, had seen many souls brought to God, and had publicly come out himself and received the baptism of the Spirit ; then why any distrust or delay ?

March 11th. Organised Fellowship Band No. 10 in Middle Colabba, appointing Brother James Shaw the leader, and appointed Captain Winckler leader of Shaw's soldier band at Captain Christian's.

" Why note so many details of this sort ? "

All my facts and details belong to the early history of a mission that is to span this empire and has been the subject of rejoicings in the presence of the angels of God ; yet I can only in my limited space insert illustrative examples of large classes of such facts. I am so familiar with them that I feel the danger of undervaluing them and of leaving out many that should be written.

Sabbath, 17th. Preached to the soldiers in Colabba at 9 a.m., and again at 7 p.m. to the best congregation we have had. Contributions in the boxes at the door, thirty-one and a half dollars ; a little gush of one of the streams on which to float our self-supporting mission.

Monday, 18th. Had a glorious fellowship band at Brother Miles's to-night. Brother Mirza Ismael was present. He is very happy, and gave a rupee as a fellowship thank offering. He gave a full account in the band of his penitential struggle and the vision that had helped him to receive Jesus.

Tuesday, 19th. Regular visiting day with Brother George Ainsworth. He gives me one day in the week for a certain round of about eighteen families. He is in the customs department, and was saved at one of our meetings at Falkland Road.

Sabbath, 24th. Commissioner Drummond, from Rohilcund, was present at Framji Cawasji Hall this morning. He afterwards told me that he came early to the hall, and the first one who came after him was a Hindu, with whom he had the following conversation :

" Salam, babu ! "

" Salam, sahib ! "

" What is your religion ? "

" I am a Hindu. "

" What have you come here for ? "

" To hear Padri Taylor, sahib. "

" He's not a Hindu ; why do you come to hear him ? "

" Well, sahib, there is a very mysterious work going on here in connection with his meetings. Many men, whom I knew to be drunkards, swearers, and dishonest men—tyrannical men, too, who were before always abusing the natives in their employ—have been entirely changed at these meetings. They are now all teetotallers ; they are honest and true in their dealings, and speak nothing but words of kindness to everybody ; and instead of hating and abusing their servants they show real love and sympathy for them and are all the time trying to do them good. I have looked into these things closely, and know that what I tell you, sahib, is true; and this kind of work is going on all the time at Padri Taylor's meetings. I don't understand it, but I feel so anxious to know more about it that I can't keep away."

We don't ask anybody to seek religion. Everybody in this country has religion of some sort; and it requires too many words to define the kind you wish him to seek. We urge people to seek *salvation*, to seek redemption through the blood of Jesus, even the forgiveness of sins. They thus obtain pure and undefiled religion.

None of our people are instruments; they are all intelligent, responsible agents. God never by word or by implication calls a man an instrument, a mere tool. Men may be sovereigns, subjects, slaves, ambassadors, witnesses, workers, kings and priests unto God, children of God and heirs of eternal glory, but not instruments.

On Friday, the 10th of April, I said to a number of our young workers, "Sisters and brothers, I have for months been absorbed in our English-speaking work; the margin of the available stuff of that sort is very narrow, and we seem to have cut through it; but we have got out of it a good working force. It is now upon my soul specially to seek power from God to lead this band of workers through the heathen lines."

Monday, 13th. Heard Brother C. W. Christian preach this evening at Mrs. Miles's. He has had many children saved at his meetings, and now leads two juvenile fellowship bands. Though only converted to God last New Year's Day, he is an earnest preacher, whom God has called.

Tuesday, 14th. At 7.30 p.m. I commenced a series of special services in the Old Strangers' Home building, in middle Colabba. Brother Bowen has been preaching here four evenings per week for three weeks, and has had some very interesting cases of conversion. This evening we had about eighty hearers and several saved.

Krishna Chowey came out as a seeker this evening, and after a weeping struggle surrendered and received Christ. He has been under awakening for months, but never came out on the Lord's side till to-night.

Wednesday, 15th. Brother Shaw and I visited Brother Krishna and his two brothers, Trimbuck and Ana, and prayed with them. Krishna told me to-day that when I was leading him to Jesus last night the things that other missionaries had told him about me kept ringing in his ears and were a great trouble to him; but finally he got the victory and accepted Christ, and is now resting in Him. Glory be to God!

16th. Good service as usual in the prison at 3 p.m. We have it twice a week.

The chaplain is in great difficulties. He opened his mind freely to Major Raitt, and said, "Taylor is a dreadful man; he has driven me out of the prison, and also out of Mazagon!"

The major tried to show him that he was quite mistaken. "Taylor has got some people saved in all these places, but that has not affected you in the least. I know that so far as the prison is concerned he has greatly increased your congregation. Before he came here this prison was a bedlam. It was almost impossible to get on with them, they were so profane, so quarrelsome and insubordinate; but now I have no trouble with them, and from morning till night they are singing Taylor's hymns; and I believe that more than a score of them are truly converted to God."

"They ought not to be allowed to sing in prison," rejoined the chaplain.

Paul and Silas were allowed to sing in a Roman prison.

In visiting the hospital the chaplain said to one of our converted Romanists, "What made you leave your mother Church and go and hear this foreigner?"

The convert pointed him to his Bible and said, "You will find my reasons in this Book."

The chaplain administered the sacrament to our prison converts, they being members of his Church. We led them to Christ, but did not interfere with their Church relations. He never could have got them to the sacrament before, and did not attempt it. He thus unwittingly indorsed our work among them, but afterwards saw that he had committed himself, and tried to get out of it by telling them that having been baptised and confirmed they had always been Christians. Prisoners, convicted by the judges of all the crimes known to the law, locked up here in the interests of society—a rare lot of Christians!

Friday, 17th. Three men came out as seekers to-night; one of them was Trimbuck Canaren, Krishna's brother. After meeting I walked with Trimbuck on the beach in the light of the moon. As he was fresh from the ranks of Hinduism I asked him what he thought of missionary operations generally.

He spoke very intelligently and kindly of the missionaries. "But," said he, "they cannot succeed, because they lack confidence in themselves, in their own methods, and in the natives."

Sabbath, 19th. On my way to Colabba I met Trimbuck, with the said native minister, on their way to the service of his missionary. I had a few words with him, and he said Mr. —— had been talking to him till midnight about being baptised by him or his missionary.

It had been arranged that Krishna should be baptised at our 11 a.m. service at Framji Cawasji Hall; but they have been labouring with him till he was inclined to postpone. He called on me in my room before meeting hour to advise with me and know if it would not be better first to write and consult his uncle.

I said, "In matters of conscience toward God we must find out His will and do it. To make our obedience hinge on the dictation of man is to ask God to defer to man. You know the mind of your uncle now as well as you can know it after writing him; and to provoke his prohibitive order and then act in opposition to it will be interpreted into direct disobedience and greatly complicate your case."

Monday, 20th. Early this morning Krishna came to my room in great distress.

"Brother Krishna," said I, "what is the trouble?"

"Well, after I left you last night I met Rev. —— and his wife, and she said, 'Krishna, where have you been all day?'"

"'I have been in the right place; I have become a Christian.'"

"'Yes; but you are not baptised yet.'"

"'Yes, I am; Mr. Taylor baptised me to-day.'"

"'Why did you not consult me?' said the padri."

"'In matters pertaining to God and my conscience I don't follow any man.'"

"'But did you not consult Mr. Taylor and Mr. Bowen?'"

"'I got instruction from them in regard to my duty to God; but when I saw my duty I did it unto God, and not to any man.'"

"'Why did you not let us know? and I would have had all our native Christians there to witness the ceremony.'"

"'Mr. Taylor doesn't want any show and parade about such things.'"

"God gave me words of wisdom to reply to all his questions," added Krishna, "and he was quiet for some time.

"Then he said, 'Krishna, your uncle will be down upon you like a shot. You must leave his house instantly. Your life is not safe there, and I cannot stop any longer in this neighbourhood; I must take my family away from here, and you must go with us. I will give you a home and protection in my house.'"

Poor Krishna, knowing so well the positive character of his Hindu uncle, yielded to fear and lost his peace, and now came weeping and saying, "What shall I do?"

"Do that cowardly dodge and you will bring disgrace on our cause that we cannot wipe off in months to come; and it would be an insult to your uncle that you never could explain away. It would be saying in effect, 'My uncle is such a bloody monster that I had to run for my life and hide in a mission compound.' Go right home, my brother, and write to your uncle and tell him that you have received Christ and become a Christian, and that you are stopping in his house, and with his permission will remain there."

He wrote accordingly, and gave Chowey a general account of the great work of God in Bombay, and how he and many of his old friends in this city, whom he mentioned by name, had received Jesus and had been saved from sin; that though called Christians when he knew them they were not real Christians then, but now had got hold of the right thing, and that he was happy to inform him that his nephew, Krishna, had become one of his Christian brothers, and was very happy.

Thus, while we have no rupees to offer, and no compounds in which to hide away native converts, we give them all the moral support we can to help them to stand firmly in their home relations and fulfil all their home duties. I am sure we are right, according to apostolic precedents and principles.

22nd. Visited Krishna and his brothers. Had a serious talk with Trimbuck and Ana and prayed with them. Preached at half-past seven, but no definite result. Arranged for a series of prayer meetings specially for the conversion of the heathen; that is, to pray for wisdom and willingness to work together with God in the fulfilment of His purpose concerning them.

A glorious fellowship band at our place this evening. Brother Krishna told a good experience. He says he is ready to die for Jesus now; indeed, he would glory in dying for Jesus if He should so order. I am sure he would, not from natural courage at all, but from heart loyalty to God and the martyr spirit inspired in him by the Holy Ghost.

Sabbath, 26th. I preached there at 6 p.m. and administered the sacrament to ninety-two communicants. Our circuit is seven miles long, so that only about half of our members can get there.

As we came out from the meeting I saw Krishna's tearful, smiling face in the moonlight as he exclaimed, " Oh, I have received my blessed Lord Jesus, and I would not give Him up for ten thousand worlds like this ! "

Monday, 27th. Preached in the open air near the queen's statue at 6 p.m. Had about one hundred and fifty attentive English-speaking native hearers. We had the moral support of Sisters Raitt, Morris, Ainsworth, the Misses Miles and other sisters, and a number of our brethren.

Tuesday, 28th. Preached again at queen's statue at 6 p.m. to about one hundred and fifty hearers. After explaining the Word of God I called for testimony for Jesus from a few of our witnesses.

Thursday, 30th. Had over three hundred at our outdoor service. Brothers Christian, Shaw, and John Fido followed with their testimony.

Rev. Dhanjibhai also spoke; but while speaking in Hindustania Parsee flared up, saying, " I know you ; it's all humbug," and went on with abusive words till Brother Bailey, inspector of police, took him aside and said to him, " You would not allow us to disturb your gatherings for worship ; why disturb ours ? "

Supposing that Bailey was going to arrest the disturber, there was a rush of the Parsees, composing about half of our audience to the spot.

I started a hymn, and all our party joined in singing,

> " God is my strong salvation ;
> What foe have I to fear ? "

In a few moments we had them all back, and many more. Both those native ministers were learned, good men, and able ministers of the Gospel ; but at that time debate and disputation with learned natives was characteristic of all the bazaar preaching of India ; hence, even at my meetings, where debate was out of the question, they could not keep out of it.

Thursday, 6th. A little late in getting to outdoor appointment, and on arrival I found some three hundred Hindus and Parsees waiting for the preacher to come. God is giving me favour with this people.

Wednesday, 12th. Over three hundred at outdoor preaching. One Parsee and a few Hindus at the after-meeting.

Thursday, 13th. Outdoor work about the same as yesterday. The editor of the *Bombay Guardian*, in a notice of our outdoor preaching, makes the following observations about our English agency :

" The writer has been preaching for twenty-four years in the vernacular in the open air in Bombay ; but it is a new thing to preach with a body of Christians, ladies and gentlemen, European and native, giving the moral force of their presence and prayer, uniting in singing and ready to bear their personal testimony to the value of a true faith in Christ. It is not easy to over-rate the importance of this kind of demonstration."

Monday, July 1st. Had Quarterly Conference at 5.30 p.m. at Mrs. Miles's, and love feast in the evening in the large hall of her new residence in Falkland Road. She tenders us the use of this hall, thirty feet by ninety, without charge, except twenty rupees per month for lighting and attendance. The Quarterly Conference recommended Brother James Shaw for licence as a local preacher. Hall crowded at the love feast.

A Parsee, who had been twice to see me for instruction, and was under deep awakening through the agency of Brother Jurain, stood up and told us that he had just received Jesus, and had got his sins forgiven.

At the close of the sacramental service George Mann and Arajee, the said Parsee, came forward and were baptised ; after which Arajee again spoke and said he was very happy, and asked the people to pray for him. The Parsees have been hitherto more inaccessible than the Mohammedans, but I believe that many of them feel their need of a Saviour, and that God will lead them into the light.

Our meeting closed at 10 p.m., and after many had gone, as I was passing out I saw Trimbuck and Ana, Krishna's brothers, lingering at the door in deep distress. I warned them of the danger of delay, and said to Ana, "If you wish we will go back into the room and pray for you , and if you will submit to God and accept Christ you will get forgiveness of your sins this very night. Will you ? "

" Yes," said he.

" If you get the pardon of your sins is it your wish also to be baptised to-night ? "

He hesitated and declined to answer. I then made a similar appeal to Trimbuck, and he consented.

With twenty-five or thirty sisters and brothers who had not gone away we had a prayer meeting for about half an hour, when Trimbuck obtained peace with God. After testifying to the fact of his pardon he added, " Now I want to be baptised. I want to be baptised to-night, for I know not what may be to-morrow."

So I baptised him. As soon as I said amen he started off in haste, I knew not whither, till I saw him sit down by his brother Ana.

Very soon he brought him to Jesus. We then prayed with Ana till he got rest for his soul, and at his own request I baptised him. I then administered the Lord's Supper to them. What a blessed night! All glory to God, the Holy Trinity!

The Parsee is a mechanic in the Great Indian Peninsular Railway Works, and has a wife. The two Hindus are single men, in the custom house service, sons of well-to-do parents, and pretty well educated.

Sabbath, 7th. Preached at Framji Cawasji Hall on perfecting that which is lacking in converts' faith. This afternoon Trimbuck took me to see an old Hindu sceptic. Trimbuck got two days' leave of absence from business after his baptism, and spent the time in visiting his Hindu friends to tell them what a dear Saviour he had found; different from the old plan of this country—of hiding a young convert to keep the Hindus from killing him! Trimbuck spent six hours on this sceptic, who expressed to me his gratitude to the young man for the interest he had manifested on his behalf, but remained unmoved.

At 6 p.m. Brother Bowen preached and I exhorted; a Mr. Bennett was saved. Krishna, Ana, Nourosjeé, and Arajee all stood up voluntarily in turn and testified for Christ. A number of Hindus and Parsees were listeners, and some of them, I am told, were spies, and will give trouble to our native converts.

Monday, 8th. As I was retiring, at 10 p.m., two Parsees brought a letter and handed it to me and hurried away. It purports to be from Brother Arajee, expressing regret that he had been baptised. I know it was not written by him; and if the signature (which is in quite a different hand) is his I am sure it was not his own voluntary act. His wife is at her father's house, and but two days since gave birth to her first child. Arajee told me that his wife was favourable to his being a Christian and would come with him to our meetings as soon as she should recover. The persecuting wretches have, no doubt, in her low, nervous state, driven her into hysterics, and under the terror of her cries and their taunts forced him to do, to save her life, what he never would have done to save his own.

Tuesday, 9th. Had but few Hindus at our lecture to-night, but a good gathering of our own people. Met Brother Jurian this afternoon and inquired about Arajee. They work in the same shop.

He said, "A messenger came yesterday afternoon in great haste for Arajee, saying that his wife was dying. Arajee said to me, as he passed out of the shop, 'Brother Jurian, pray for me, and go to Mrs. Miles's and ask them all to pray for me. I shall be beaten and perhaps killed. If they beat me I'll bear it; if they kill me I'll go to Jesus.'"

Friday, 12th. Called to see Brother Jurian, to inquire about Arajee. He said, "For several days he did not return to business, but has been there the last day and a half, guarded by three Parsees to and from the shop; and is closely watched while he is at work. In all that time I only got about a minute's talk with him, and he said,

'My wife was dying. I was imprisoned for three days and threatened with death, and now you see I am under guard. What can I do?'"

Arajee subsequently stepped aside with Jurian and said, "Brother Jurian, sing softly about the bleeding Lamb;" and Jurian sang in a low tone:

> "My Saviour suffered on the tree:
> Oh, come and praise the Lord with me."

When his guards saw him with Jurian they came and ordered him away. About fifty men in the shop—Parsees, Hindus, and Moham-medans, led by a few so-called Christians—with dreadful curses and threats made a set upon Jurian for getting the Parsee to change his religion; but Jurian witnessed for Jesus, saying, "You know what a vagabond I was before I received Christ; and you have been with me here every day since, and have seen the change in me. Jesus Christ saves me from all sin and preserves me from sinning, and has taken away from me the fear of death. You can kill me if you like; I am ready." They sneaked off and left him.

CHAPTER XXXIV

CAMPAIGN AT POONAH AND CALCUTTA

I said to some friends at Major Raitt's, "Suppose I go to Poonah a few weeks during these heavy rains?" It was quite a casual remark. I had no serious thought of going soon, for I knew of no friends there to visit, and could not see my way to leave Bombay in the midst of so interesting a native work as was opening up daily. A few minutes after this remark was made Brother Henry Bailey, inspector of the E Division of Bombay police came in, and said, "I am going to get two months' leave of absence and take my family to Poonah," and invited me to go!

I considered the matter prayerfully, and on the 16th of July went second class (one hundred and nineteen miles) to Poonah. Brother Bailey met me at the railway station and drove me to his house.

Wednesday, 17th. Went with Brother Bailey to market, and afterwards spent several hours at an auction, where over three thousand rupees' worth of household stuff was bid off. I had been worked nearly off the hinges; the change of scene was rest and the earnestness of the auctioneer refreshing.

18th. Brother Bailey drove me out to make a few calls. Colonel Field received us very kindly. He and Colonel Phayre, both earnest Christian men, led the expedition into Abyssinia. Colonel Phayre surveyed the warpath, four hundred miles, to Magdala; and Colonel Field's forces made the road and led the van. Two African youths, educated by Rev. Dr. Wilson in Bombay, showed them the way in.

Called at the manse of Rev. J. Beaumont, minister of the Free Church of Scotland; he was not in, but sent me a note inviting me to conduct their Thursday evening service in his church, which I did, and had an interesting time.

Poonah is high and healthy, nearly four thousand feet above the sea. It is a large military station and an old Maratti Brahman city of one hundred thousand population.

Back in Bombay for Sabbath and Monday and Tuesday appointments, and returned to Poonah on Wednesday, the 24th of July, accompanied by Krishna, who got four days' leave of absence from his work and paid his own travelling expenses, that he might tell those Brahmans about the Saviour he had found. On the evening of our arrival I lectured in the Institution Hall to about two hundred Brahmans on the experimental evidences of Christianity, and Krishna witnessed for Christ by an account in detail of his awakening and conversion to God.

Thursday, 25th. Preached this evening at six in the Free Church, which was well filled.

A lady in Bombay told Krishna of a vagabond young native in Poonah whose father was for many years, till his recent death, a native minister of the Society for the Propagation of the Gospel Mission, and, giving Krishna his name and address, requested him to hunt him up and try to get him saved. So this morning Krishna found his house and called at his door.

The response was, " Who's there ? "

" My name is Krishna Chowey, from Bombay."

"What do you want ? "

" I have come by request of a friend to see you."

" Go away from my door ; I don't want to see you."

" I promised my friend that I would see you, and I must see you."

"Well, I tell you to go away. You shall not come into my house."

" I am not going away till I see you. I'll sit down here at your door and wait till you come out or let me in ;" and down he sat.

After a little delay he was asked to enter. He showed the man a card on which his name was written by the friend in Bombay, and inquired, " Is that your name ? "

"Yes ; sit down."

Krishna then opened up a friendly conversation with him and gave him a history of his own life as a Hindu and an account of his conversion to God.

By the time he had finished his narrative his hearer was weeping bitterly and exclaimed, " There it is ; you were born and brought up a Hindu, and now you are a child of God—a Christian in deed and in truth ; I was born and brought up a nominal Christian, and now I am worse than any heathen. Oh, God of my father and of my mother, what shall I do ?" Krishna wept with him, and they kneeled together and prayed.

On my return to Bombay I went to stop again with Brother George Miles, his wife and family having returned from England. Glorious meetings at Framji Cawasji Hall.

I wrote Brother Beaumont in regard to intended special services in Poonah, and proposed to do what I might be able, to help him build up his own Church ; but the many beyond his lines whom we hoped to get saved at our meetings should be at liberty, without any afterclaps or reflections, if they in their judgment and conscience should so elect, to organise themselves into a Methodist Church, as so many had done in Bombay.

Tuesday, August 13th. Took the train for Poonah at 10 a.m. Brothers James Morris and Walter Winckler accompanied me to help in the work.

We commenced operations at 6 p.m. on Wednesday, the 14th of August, 1872.

Sabbath, 18th. Preached morning and evening in the Free Church to about one hundred and fifty hearers.

Monday, 19th. Bombay reinforcements (Brothers Shaw, Krishna, and Jurian) arrived, and the work went on vigorously. Among the first fruits outside of the orphanage were Angelo De Sauza, James Cristie and his wife and her sisters, the Misses Mulligan, and their cousins, William and Arthur Wright. These, with a host of others, all became earnest and effective workers for God.

I had to spend every other Sabbath in Bombay; but Brother Bowen alternated with me, and the siege of Poonah was steadily kept up. Many soldiers and civilians professed to find pardon at our meetings who did not become members of my Church. It is a principle with us not to persuade, nor directly to ask, any one to join us. Those voluntarily unite with us who are convinced that it is their duty by the force of our Bible teaching and the leading of the Spirit of truth.

Saturday evening, September 28th. We held a fellowship meeting at the house of Brother De Sauza. Over thirty young converts spoke very clearly of the saving power of God in their hearts. I had not decided in advance to bring up the question of Church organisation to-night. Several had mentioned it before; but I wished them to have sufficient opportunity by our daily preaching and work and our weekly fellowship meetings to know their bearings properly and to form an intelligent judgment as to their duty and privilege in the matter; but at the close of the speaking I was convinced that it was the will of God that we should wait no longer. So I explained that I had all through desired to build up the Church in whose place of worship, kindly tendered us, they had been brought to God; and " that no member of that Church would feel it his or her duty to join my Church. But, according to the written agreement with their minister, I was at liberty to give an opportunity to any saved outside of his lines to be organised into a Methodist Church if they should so elect." I explained briefly what would be required of them as members with us, and reminded them of the persecutions they might expect, and that they must be fully persuaded as to their duty, and if not clear on that point take further time to consider it. Brother De Sauza brought paper and ink; Brother Winckler took down the names, which were distinctly announced, without any personal prompting Dr. Fraser stood up first and gave in his name. Thirty-seven names were recorded that night. Others took further time for consideration.

Having secured a place of worship for our own Church and congregation in Poonah, we had our first sacramental service on Sabbath evening, the 13th of October. We had about one hundred and thirty hearers and sixty-four communicants. The *Deccan Herald* of the next day stated that the like was never seen in Poonah before.

The Church in Poonah has from the first to the present been a living, working, growing Church, and has a thrifty branch at Lanowli, forty miles to the northwest, where they have built a commodious chapel and paid for it. When her Majesty's Fifty-sixth Regiment was transferred from Poonah to Sinde, beyond the Indus, our converted soldiers were accompanied by their minister, Rev. D. O. Fox, and laid the foundation of our witnessing, working Church in Sinde.

On the 15th of November Brother James Shaw resigned his appointment of army Scripture reader and became an itinerant preacher in our mission, unquestionably called of God to this responsible position. He came to us with a good wife, a native of Bombay, to help him.

About the same time Rev. George Bowen joined us. He came to India over twenty-five years before as a missionary of the American Board of Commissioners for Foreign Missions. After a couple of years' service here he became convinced that to succeed in establishing a native Church in India on a sound, healthy basis would require greater self-sacrifice and a closer assimilation to native life on the part of missionaries than had been generally supposed to be necessary.

On the 22nd of November, 1872, Rev. W. E. Robbins, a deacon of the Indian Conference, arrived. He was a graduate of the Indiana Asbury University, and was three years in the Federal army during the rebellion. He commenced his ministry in California, but on account of the death of his father returned to Indiana and joined that Conference. He read my *Call for Preachers*, and not falling in with a mission secretary or bishop came on his own account, and paid his own expenses to Bombay. He learned to preach in the Maratti language before he was a year in India.

On the 1st of December, 1872, Revs. Albert Norton and Daniel O. Fox arrived in Bombay, also in response to my *Call*, but appointed and sent by the Missionary Board.

January 1st, 1873. Had a glorious lovefeast and watchnight service last night. At our Quarterly Conference, in the afternoon, Brothers Morris and Christian were recommended for licence as local preachers.

On Tuesday of next week, after holding a Quarterly Conference in Poonah, with the concurrence of all concerned I am to start for Calcutta. Brother Bowen will be preacher in charge of Bombay Circuit.

Krishna Chowey has never wavered for one minute. The day after his conversion he went on with his work in the customs, and after enduring much persecution there for a few weeks he was transferred to another department and put with a lot of very bigoted Brahmans. He was trembling with apprehension when he told me of this change in his work, and feared that he could not stand against them. I said, " Go, my brother, and do your duty. What you most fear is just the discipline your Father sees that you need, and has hence sent you to hold out your light to those Brahmans. Never fear. The Lord Jesus hath said, and had it written, that when brought even before governors and kings you have no need to take thought beforehand ' what ye shall say : for the Holy Ghost shall teach you in the same hour what ye ought to say.' He will give you the right words for those dear fellows who don't know our Jesus."

He went, distrusting self and trusting God. The Brahmans badgered him fiercely for about a week. Then they gathered round him and said, " Krishna, what does all this mean ? We never treated anybody so badly as we have treated you. We have tried every way possible to exasperate or intimidate you. You have shown no fear, nor ill-feeling, nor resentment. We can't understand it."

" Oh, my dear friends," replied Krishna, " I show no fear because I am not afraid ; I have quite made up my mind to die for Jesus if He shall so appoint. I show no ill-feeling because there is none in my heart. I show no spirit of resentment because I have none. The religion of Jesus is a religion of love. All this week I have been loving you and praying for you. I love you all now, and want you to be happy, as I am."

From that day those young Brahmans vied with each other in their attentions to Krishna. A year afterwards, at the Esplanade preaching, when the mob beat Krishna and stamped upon him with their feet and left him for dead, one of those very Brahmans ran in and, taking him up in his arms, carried him away and got water and brought him round.

When Krishna recovered consciousness, supposing himself to be passing through the gates of death, he said, " Thank God for the privilege of dying for Jesus. Oh, I am so happy to die for Jesus, He died for me ! "

The Brahman stood over him and wept like a child. Several of those Brahmans came to the meeting, and came to see me. One of them wanted to teach me the Maratti language without charge. I believe I should have led them to Jesus could I have remained in Bombay. I said in my heart, " We shall get them saved yet. Let all Christians join me in prayer for Krishna's Brahman friends."

Some months after Krishna's conversion, however, he was tripped. A prating Hindu came into the office where he was and used very abusive language against him ; he paid no attention to that, but endured it meekly. Then he dealt out some dreadful epithets against me, which cut to the quick ; for Krishna loves me because I led him to Jesus ; but he took it patiently. Finally the mad heathen began to utter the most vulgar and blasphemous charges against Christ. Krishna could not stand to hear his Master belied in that way, and with evident temper replied, " You wretched man ! You are worse that a brute to talk so."

His friends looked sorry, and said, " Ah, Krishna ! "

He confessed to them his sorrow that he had allowed his feelings to get the better of his judgment. Three days afterwards Brother C. W. Christian was driving home from the bank, and saw a native walking before him apparently weeping. Coming closer, he heard him sobbing, and wondered who it could be—a sight so unusual. On coming up, to his surprise he saw it was Krishna, and exclaimed, " Oh, Brother Krishna, what is the matter? Come, get up in the carriage with me."

Krishna got in and told him all about the unhappy affair that occurred three days before.   Brother Christian took him into his own room, and they together pleaded with God till the light of His face again filled Krishna's soul.

"Well," says one, "I often get into such a temper and think but little about it."

"But you don't often lead poor souls to Jesus.   I am sure you could not win a heathen to Christ.   'He that ruleth his own spirit is greater than he that taketh a city.'   It requires great men of that sort to do great things for God."

Krishna's Uncle Chowey, who was in the habit of coming to Bombay every year in May or June, delayed his coming this year for a couple of months; and thus the three nephews had time to grow and gather strength.   They finally heard that he was on the way, and were looking out for the vessel to arrive.   They were at our Sabbath afternoon prayer meeting at Major Raitt's when the ship was telegraphed. They went in haste, yet with trembling, to meet him before he should land; but when they reached the ship he had landed and gone. Then they went to his house, in which they lived.   Not knowing what might happen, Krishna went in alone, while the younger brothers remained without.   After a little while, hearing no row, they followed. They stood mute in his presence, as in boyhood they were often obliged to do; and he looked at them some time before he uttered a word. Then he angrily charged them with neglecting to do some unimportant thing, and they explained away his point.   Then he surveyed them closely, and in a softened tone said, "Why, you look just as you looked when I saw you last!"   (He expected to see them dressed in European clothing and looking as though they were foreigners from a far country, according to what he had so often seen.)

"Our missionary is different from any you know," they replied. "He don't require us to change any outward custom, but simply to give up all idolatry and sin."

But little more was said then.

When he afterwards got Krishna alone he said, "Now, Krishna, I am getting old, and not so well up to business as formerly.   I want you to resign your situation in the customs, go with me down the coast, take your wife and settle in a good home of your own. I'll make over all my business to you, and the property will all be yours in the end."

Krishna replied, "Uncle, if that means any compromise of Christian principle I cannot touch it."

The uncle then got into a very bad temper, and abused Krishna very much.   Afterwards he hinted to Trimbuck that if he would resign his place and go and take charge of his business he would cut Krishna off and make him his heir.

Trimbuck, but two months out of heathenism, replied, "Uncle, if you are of a mind to give us anything we will thank you; but if your offer means that I am to give up Jesus Christ I look upon all your possessions as dung."

The uncle was evidently taken aback. His fortune—the accumulation of his life of toil—going a-begging and treated, as compared with the despised name of Christ, as worthless *débris !*

He took a peremptory course with Ana, and said, " Ana, sit down here, and write your resignation before me, and come with me down the coast."

The young fellow, who had always before been dreadfully afraid of his uncle, modestly told him that he could do nothing of the sort.

The uncle had spent thirty years in Bombay, a bitter enemy of Christianity, but otherwise a fine man, and had many friends. The young men expected his friends to stir him up against them, but to their surprise, so far as they could learn, all except an old teacher of theirs—to whom the uncle would not listen—took their part and told the uncle what good nephews he had.

Before going to Calcutta I wrote to Rev. John Richards, the Wesleyan missionary there, with whom I had laboured in South Africa, and whom I had often met in England, and proposed to give him a week of special services ; but after that I should be free to follow providential leadings beyond his lines, and if God should give me a people in Calcutta, as he had in Bombay and Poonah, to organise them into a Methodist Episcopal Church. In his reply he said, " Of course I accept your offer of a week's services. When I wrote to you before you were strictly an evangelist ; now you seem to have changed your plan. Well, if you can come, and through God's blessing be the means of creating some healthy religious excitement among us in Calcutta, I shall greatly rejoice. Come and welcome, and I will work with you to the utmost of my ability."

Dr. Moffitt, of Cawnpore memory, had, by removal of her Majesty's Fourteenth Regiment to Calcutta, become a resident in this city, and had invited me also.

Thursday, 30th. Preached in the Wesleyan chapel nightly for two weeks. About twenty persons publicly sought and professed to find the pardon of their sins. Most of these were members of the congregation, and will probably join Mr. Richards's Church. On my arrival his English-speaking Church consisted of eighteen members, according to the books. Their numbers have doubled and their working effectiveness has greatly increased.

Sister Richards and Brother Fentiman tried to persuade me to limit my labours in Calcutta to their Church. I explained to them our principles to the effect that, as our doctrines were the same, when we found the Wesleyan organisation adequate to the demands of the country, wheresoever established, we should not feel at liberty to organise on the same ground. " But here in Bengal," I continued, " there is a population of sixty-six millions, and this little Church is the only representative of Methodism in this great Presidency. You have been working here for nine years, and you now see what you can do and what you cannot do. The style of agency necessary to secure a great work of God, adequate to His purposes, is also necessary to conserve and extend it. It is not the work of a passing evangelist, simply, but requires the enlistment and combined struggle of millions of martyr spirits for a hundred years."

They felt the force of my argument, and gave in, but not without manifest regret; and I was very sorry that I could not yield to their wishes.

I was now an outsider, but I procured the use of one hall after another, and weekly family services, six or seven each day, extending into about forty families, neglected East Indians, followed by preaching in a hall every night.

February 2nd. About a year ago I wrote my patient wife that I should probably be detained in India beyond the time I had appointed to return home, and desired her to consult the boys and give their mind about it with hers.

Two or three days after writing I received a letter from her, written two months before, anticipating my question, saying, "As you have laboured sixteen years as an evangelist, helping to build up other Churches, if God has given you the opportunity of demonstrating in a heathen country the saving power of the Gospel from the foundation, you should take time to do it. We are most anxious to see you, but we will wait. Don't hurry on our account."

Last Friday I wrote her again on the same subject, saying, "I am here in Calcutta, the Paris of India. If God shall open this city to me, and give me a Church, as in Bombay, I shall have to man it before I leave. That will detain me some months. Then I could go home for a couple of years and return; but what shall I say for my dear wife and boys, whom I so long to see? Tell me what to do."

Yesterday, February 1st, 1873, I received a letter from her, in which she says, "I have never yet dared to call you home. It is likely you are too poor to come, and we are not able to help you; but if your work will allow it we should wish you to do so, if but for a year. Perhaps your people will give you leave of absence."

Saturday, February 22nd. Mr. Harris, the druggist, gave us the free use of his residence for our fellowship band meetings. Captain Jones, who was converted to God and joined my Church in California in 1855, rendered good service in Calcutta. Rev. Mr. Kerry, a Baptist missionary, is the principal of a native boys' school, also superintendent of some native Churches in and about the city. He showed me his school, containing over two hundred lads, and Mrs. Kerry's girls' school; he then conducted me into his native chapel, forty feet by sixty, and said, "I don't know what this chapel was built for except the anticipation of getting many of the native students to become Christians, which, I am sorry to say, has not been realised. We have a small native congregation and Church which worship here Sabbaths at 7 a.m. and 4 p.m. Beyond that we have no use for it, and if you can make any use of it you are welcome to it."

It was not well located for my English-speaking East Indians, but no other place seemed available, so I concluded that God had opened that as the best to begin with, and we made quick preparations, advertised extensively, and opened regular services there the following Sabbath (February 23rd, 1873), and kept them up in that chapel for about a year. Rev. Brother Kerry exerted himself on all occasions to advance our work. We held special services there for more than a month, often with great promise, but with very little permanent fruit.

The hardest work of my life, I believe, was in the streets of Calcutta, under the greatest discouragements. For months it seemed very doubtful, by all outward indications, whether we could raise a working force at all. I became more and more convinced that a great work of God was what Calcutta least desired and most needed, and that a more convenient season would never come; so I determined, as the Lord should lead, to push the battle and win or die at the guns.

Sixty-six millions of perishing souls in this Presidency! Most of them have heard of Jesus and hate His name immeasurably more than they hate the name of Satan. They won't listen to what His friends have to say in His favour, but drink in foul, blasphemous lies against Him from the lips of Mohammedans and infidels. The books of French and English infidels—most of whom are now realising the realities of Bible truth in the regions of the dead—are more extensively read, I believe, by educated natives in India than anywhere else. Tom Paine's "Age of Reason," for example, sells for a shilling in India, and nearly all the wretched infidel fallacies which, in Christian countries, have been refuted a hundred times are now sown broadcast here, with no antidote in the form of refutation.

"Why do the heathen rage, and the people imagine a vain thing? The kings of the earth set themselves, and the rulers take counsel together, against the Lord, and against His Anointed, saying, Let us break their bands asunder, and cast away their cords from us." This is just as true of the Indian rajahs and the great masses of their people as it was true of old Pilate and Herod and the murderers of our Lord's human person.

God has sent me here to organise at least one body of witnessing soldiers for Jesus, who will endure hardness; and by the power of the Holy Spirit I must succeed or die in the trenches of the enemy. God help me! It is all for Thy glory and the salvation of these poor, perishing millions, in love and pity for whom my Saviour died.

About the 9th of April, for the first time in Calcutta, I gave an opportunity for the converts who were attending our fellowship meetings to enroll themselves as candidates for membership in my Church, and thirteen gave in their names. A very small beginning after two months of so hard work; but, thank God! it is a germ of His planting, and will become a banyan, with branches and trunks innumerable, and millions will yet repose at the feet of Jesus under its shade.

Soon after this we got the use of a room in Bow Bazaar for Sabbaths at 7 a.m. and two nights weekly. I began to feel the support of workers ready for any call of the Master. Unfortunately for the onward progress of the work, we had to give up the use of the hall in which God so blessed us, and could not get another till we built one in Zigzag Lane, in the same neighbourhood.   A dear brother in Bombay offered ten thousand rupees toward the erection of a Methodist preaching hall in that city ; but as we have large bungalow halls there suitable for our present purpose, and none such here, our dear friends in Bombay said, " No, give it to Calcutta ; " so it was sent to a bank in this city subject to my order, for the purpose of building a Methodist hall here.   But we were in need of a place at once, and hence found it necessary to put up a temporary hall for the extension of the Bow Bazaar work, while a more perma-nent chapel was being constructed, requiring all the funds our people could give, in addition to the liberal gift from Bombay.

From about the 1st of September I was absent from Calcutta a month, holding quarterly meetings in Poonah and Bombay.

CHAPTER XXXV

REVIEW OF MY INDIAN MISSIONS

OUR quarterly meeting in Poonah was an occasion long to be remembered. The Quarterly Conference was held on Saturday night, just before a public preaching service, and was composed of a score of humble, valiant men of God, instead of three, as when we organised it eight months before. Our brethren and sisters from Deksal, about one hundred miles south-east, and from Lanowli, forty miles north-west, had come in force to attend the quarterly meeting, representing Churches which had meantime grown up in those places. At this meeting a building committee was appointed to put up a Methodist chapel in Lanowli, which has since been completed and paid for. Brother Geering, one of our converted railway men there, paid twelve hundred rupees for its erection.

Our love feast was on Monday night. The speaking was superb. About eighty persons in the space of an hour witnessed for Jesus. Brother Fox, our minister there, on that Sabbath baptised two Hindus, cultivators from a village ten miles out ; and at a later period of our services that week two Brahmans, both school-teachers, one in a government and the other in a private school. I spent a week in Poonah on this trip, and had a few new cases brought to God.

I then spent a week in Bombay. During my absence of eight months the work of God in that city had wonderfully developed and extended. In addition to a large increase of English and East Indian members over a dozen Hindus and three Parsees had been saved and baptised. All these converted Hindus and Parsees were abiding among their people, according to the avowed principles of St. Paul's mission and ours as well.

One of our Parsee converts, Brother Ruttonji Merwanji Metta, was then (1875) planting a mission in Khandwa, Central India. Another was in Christian work with Narrainsheshadra, in Jalnah. Another was Brother Manekjee Mody. His high social position and his bold testimony for Christ at our outdoor services on the Esplanade exposed him to great persecutions. In his boyhood he went for a short time to a Sunday-school in the kirk, which made it easier for him to come to a Christian place of worship; but he remained a staunch Zoroastrian till awakened at our meetings. His testimony, which he repeated again and again in different languages to the masses at the outdoor preaching, was substantially as follows:

"Friends, you know me. You know what a sincere zealot I was for the Parsee religion. After the death of my wife I got up at three o'clock in the morning, and, with my incense and sandalwood, went, in those dark hours of the night, to the Tower of Silence, and there, near the bones of my ancestors, where my own father and my own dear wife had been given over to the vultures, I burned my sandalwood, and in the odour of my incense offering mingled my prayers and groans and tears from a broken heart. Let no man doubt my sincerity; I was sincere. Every morning at three o'clock, when you were all asleep in your beds, I repeated this daily for two years, but found no rest for my sin-burdened soul. I have no quarrel with my nation, and I don't abuse our great man Zoroaster; but he was not a saviour. Our Parsee religion has no saviour to offer to our dear, struggling people; hence, I could find no relief from it. Then I was led to examine the claims of Jesus Christ. From the records of the Bible and the testimony of His people I became convinced that He was indeed the Saviour sent by God to deliver poor sinners from their sins. I sought Him, and in Forbes Street Hall I submitted to Him and received Him as my Saviour, and at once He delivered me from my sins and gave rest and peace to my soul. Now I know that I am a child of God, and that the Lord Jesus abides with me and preserves me from sinning and sustains me under all my trials and persecutions."

An infidel Hindu raised a mob to beat my preachers on the Esplanade. The next day the commissioner of police held a court of inquiry to investigate the affair. Brother Samuel Page was called on for evidence, and gave a full statement of the facts in the case. He had witnessed the affair, and knew both the circumstances and the motives.

One of the officers inquired, "What sort of people are these Methodists?"

"Well," replied another, "they are a curious people. I heard Taylor tell of one who got his sins forgiven in a quarter of an hour."

"Bosh!" rejoined the other.

Then said Page, "Well, gentlemen, you know I would not tell you a lie; though I was long under awakening it was not till the 21st of last September that I came out as a seeker; and then in less than a quarter of an hour I received Christ and got all my sins forgiven."

"Very well, Mr. Page," said the commissioner, "we will not discuss that subject. Why don't these Methodists, like other people, appeal to the law for protection?"

Page replied, "They don't disclaim their legal rights; but under all ordinary wrongs and this opposition to their work they prefer to suffer the greatest wrongs and injuries rather than appeal to the law."

"Why, they have no spirit!" said the commissioner.

"Oh yes; they have the spirit of Christ their Master. They are not cowards. You will find them, in spite of the wrongs done to them to-day, preaching in the same place to-morrow, quite undismayed."

"Why, they might get killed!"

" Oh, they would not mind that at all ; they are not afraid of death ! They are a people who wish only to know their duty, and that they will do or die in the attempt."

" Well, then," said the commissioner, " we must protect them."

The court then decided that without partiality they would protect any orderly person who wished to preach in the streets—Christian, Hindu, Mohammedan, or Parsee ; but for the sake of order they must have their preaching places half a mile apart. If a Mohammedan establishes a preaching place no Christian will be allowed to open one within less distance than half a mile. The Hindu who has for nearly a year and a half been giving so much annoyance on the Esplanade must be arrested at the next meeting. He must not be punished at once but warned ; and if then he repeat it, punished. The same warning must also be given to the Mohammedan at the fountain.

This order was faithfully executed ; thus, after patient suffering for a year and a half, our outdoor preachers got protection unasked, but none the less appreciated.

Krishna's wife was sent to him by his uncle. He got her well instructed, converted to God, and baptised ; and then they were united in Christian marriage. He is now a licensed local preacher in our Church, and believes that he is called to devote his life to the work of the Christian ministry. I believe so too; but as yet he is pursuing his business in the customs and devoting his leisure to study and active soul-saving work. He has had eight of his kindred saved and baptised, and hopes soon to get all his family connection into the Kingdom of God. Trimbuck preaches well and was recommended for licence at our District Conference a few months ago ; but, wishing a better preparation, begged the Conference to let his case lie over till their next meeting.

The number of native converts in the Bombay Circuit—mostly from Hinduism—was in 1875 about sixty. The great break in their lines had not come yet ; but a grand preparation of the field and of the workers was daily progressing, and God was about to give these heathen to Jesus for His inheritance. I expected to see many thousands of them brought to God before many years should elapse.

On my way back to Calcutta, Brothers Krishna, Trimbuck, and Manekjee, and other native brethren, accompanied me eighty miles to Egutpoora, where we held a number of services.

I spent two days in special services at Allahabad with Brothers Thoburn and Osborne. Dennis Osborne laid the foundations of our Church in Allahabad soon after his own conversion to God in Lucknow. My tour from Calcutta to Poonah and Bombay and back involved 2972 miles of railway travelling, by first-class ticket, going and returning, would have cost two hundred and sixty-seven rupees fifteen annas. I went with the native masses by third and intermediate class carriages at a cost of sixty-one rupees four annas. That may illustrate one of the ways by which we run a self-supporting mission. Of course the mission has nothing to do with my own expenses. We do not oblige any of our preachers to travel third class, but my example makes it easier for those who wish to do so; and I believe all of them travel third class, except those who preach much to railway people and have a first-class ticket given them.

Before I left Calcutta for this trip we leased a lot in Zigzag Lane, and let out to contract the building of a plain chapel thirty feet by fifty. We had trustees and a building committee; but as Sister Freude, a thorough business woman, lives near, the responsibility of superintending its erection was left with her and she did her part faithfully.

We also bought a lot in the best centre of the city, in Dhurram-tollah Street, near Wellington Square, for four thousand six hundred rupees, and let out the contract for building a permanent brick hall forty feet by eighty.

At the opening of our new chapel in Zigzag Lane the place was crowded, and God was with us. It was at this opening service that Koshenath Borooah, a high-caste Hindu from Assam and a student of the Calcutta Medical College, was baptised. He was brought to Jesus during my absence, in the following manner: two Singhalese native medical students—Brothers Everts and Fry, who were converted to God at my first series in Calcutta—brought Koshenath with them one night to a fellowship band. He was a bitter hater of Christianity. He had a young brother who had been a short time in a Christian school, but died at the age of fourteen years, and requested, when dying, that there should be no Hindu ceremonies performed over his dead body. No one knew why he made such a request. Well, Koshenath sat down quietly in the fellowship class meeting and heard twenty-seven men and women tell that they had received Christ and had been saved from their sins, and that Jesus was with them, and that He was giving them power daily to resist temptation, and was preserving them by His own almighty hand from sinning.

Koshenath listened, and thus reasoned with himself: "These are intelligent men and women. They are not speaking about creeds or opinions, nor telling of things hoped for, but testifying to facts within their personal knowledge. These are credible witnesses, whose testimony would stand in any court of justice. They speak of Jesus not merely as a historic character of the past, but a living person of the present. They say, though invisible, they know Him and have daily communication with Him. They say they received Him by faith; a thing which I have considered nonsense before, but how reasonable it seems to me now. How could they receive Him except by faith?"

So he stated his case to the band and asked them to show him the way to Jesus. Dr. Moffitt and others gave him words of instruction, and they all prayed for him; and before the meeting closed he testified that he had then and there received the Lord Jesus as his Saviour, and that He had filled his heart with light, love, and peace.

We begged the missionary secretaries to send us missionaries to supply the growing demands of our work in India, but this year they did not send us one. My mission, and the principles which render it peculiar, have to pass, as I expected, a severe ordeal of criticism and opposition. Every new steam engine or boiler has to be tested ere it can be trusted; and so with every other new thing—though like our mission, having no novelty but the new application of old principles. The misapprehensions of friends on both sides of the world, the mis-statements of those not friendly, the fallacies of speculators, and the long letters written, would make up material for a very curious but very uninteresting book, which I don't intend to write.

We heard of Bishop Harris's episcopal tour round the world, holding Conferences on his route in Japan, China, India, Bulgaria, Germany, Denmark, and Sweden, and we were awaiting his arrival with pleasure. While the bishop was at Ceylon he telegraphed to Dr. Thoburn in Lucknow to meet him in Calcutta; so Brother Thoburn came in advance of his arrival and gave us valuable help in our work. I was told afterwards that the good bishop had an apprehension, from the many things that were rumoured about my mission, that I was going to set up a new sect—a thing entirely out of the question from the first, both with myself and all my people—and thought he might need Thoburn's advice. Every document we had, and the trustees and deeds of our property in Calcutta, were all proofs of our entire loyalty to the Church of our choice, though refusing first and last to yield a single principle or plank in our platform as a mission. All intimations against our bottom motives were unfounded and gratuitous.

When the bishop and his party arrived I met them at the ship and invited them to stop with me.

As soon as we left the ship, and the bishop and I got into a carriage alone, he said, "Now, Brother Taylor, we want to bring your mission into a closer connection with our Church, and we want you to become officially and in name what you are in fact, its superintendent."

I replied, "I received a very kind letter from Bishop Simpson proposing the same thing, and at the same time a letter from Dr. Eddy, containing a similar request from you. I immediately wrote, in reply to Bishop Simpson and to yourself, stating that while I was not at all ambitious of any honour or official position in the gift of the Church, yet as God had opened and organised this mission through my agency, and had thus made me its superintendent, I should not object to your official confirmation of His appointment, provided there shall be no interference with the peculiar principles on which our mission was founded."

"I had left New York before your letter got there, and never received it," replied the bishop; "but your principles are very clear and sound. Where the Missionary Society appropriates the funds of the Church, of course they are responsible for their proper disbursement; but where they give no money, as in the case of your mission, what have they to do with its internal management?"

So the whole thing was arranged in less time than it takes me to write it. It was agreed, as a matter of convenience, that I and my ministers, until we could organise a Conference of our own, should join the India Mission Conference; but that the said Conference should not have an official relation to the Bombay and Bengal Mission, any more than the Baltimore Conference has with our mission in Japan because Rev. R. S. Maclay, its superintendent, happens to remain a member of that Conference.

All the Indian Empire outside our India Mission Conference was assigned to me under the title of the Bombay and Bengal Mission.

At the ensuing Conference, in January, 1874, in Lucknow, these arrangements were all completed; and contrary to my expectations, and to my great joy, Rev. J. M. Thoburn, D.D., resigned his work in the India Mission Conference and joined my mission. He had resigned his salary a year before, and had fully adopted the principles of our mission. Brother C. W. Christian had resigned his situation in the Bombay Bank some months before and become my assistant preacher in Calcutta; George Gilder, also of Bombay, and C. R. Jefferies, of Calcutta, had been duly recommended for the itinerant work; so that our lack of helpers from the Mission Board was being made up in part in India. Our members and probationers in Calcutta and Kidderpore now numbered over one hundred. The whole number in our mission then was about five hundred; and our appointments, as announced by the bishop at the close of the Conference session, stood thus: Bombay—George Bowen, W. E. Robbins, James Shaw. The Deccan (Poonah, Lanowli, Deksal, etc.)—D. O. Fox. Central India—Albert Norton, George K. Gilder. Bengal (Calcutta)—J. M. Thoburn, C. W. Christian.

We had at the same time a cause developing at Secunderabad, through the agency of Brother Walter Winckler, a nephew of Mrs. Miles. When but four months converted to God he gave us valuable help in the Poonah siege, and was then appointed by government as a civil engineer to Secunderabad, in the Nizam's kingdom, to build a section of the government railway. He arrived there an entire stranger, but soon commenced witnessing for Jesus to a number of soldiers in a cowshed. Next he went among the civilians, and got some of them saved. Then he was taken ill, and Dr. Trimnell, the civil surgeon, a good man in his way, came to see him; and by some sort of mutual improvement society the Lord used the doctor to cure Winckler's body and used Winckler as a witnessing agent in getting the doctor's soul into the hands of the great Physician, and he was healed.

During the year 1874 Brother Bowen visited Secunderabad and organised our Church there, of which Winckler, under God—daily hard at work making the railroad and preparing the way of the Lord as well—was the founder.

Later in the year Brother Shaw spent a few months there and greatly extended the work. Later still I spent a few days there, and found a healthy, growing, working Church of God, of more than one hundred members and probationers, besides scores of converts who had not joined our body. We had one hundred and twenty communicants at the sacramental service which I held among them. Dr. Trimnell, my kind host, told me that becoming a Methodist—and hence a total abstainer from all intoxicating drinks—he has daily done two hours' more work than before with less fatigue. He was what is called in many circles a temperance man before, never known to be the worse for liquor; but he thought he could not get through with his excessive work without artificial stimulation, especially when up all night with the sick. Now he finds that he was quite mistaken before, and instead of loss he has gained a greatly improved condition of nerve, muscle, and brain, with a clear gain in time of two hours per day. He gave me the testimony of a Mohammedan merchant concerning the Work of God in Secunderabad, as seen and noted by the Mohammedans.

An army officer owed this merchant a bill, and seemed more disposed to lay out his money for drink than to pay it. The Mohammedan said to him, "If you will give up drink like these Methodists I'll give you the amount of your bill. These Methodists are all teetotallers. They are willing to pay a fair price for an article, with but words few about it, and always pay their bills."

Brother Vale, our recording steward there, gave me similar testimony from a Parsee merchant, who had a very large general store in Secunderabad. The Parsee said to a man who came into his shop, "Have you joined the Methodists yet?"

"No; I have not."

"Well, I advise you to join them, for they are a very good people. They don't want an article for less than it is worth, and they always pay their bills."

"But," replied the man, "they are all teetotallers, and don't buy any of your wine and spirits."

"Yes, I know that; but though I sell them to other people I know the Methodists are right; and, moreover, spending no money for grog, they have the more to lay out for things of value to them; and I never have any trouble with Methodist bills, for they are always paid promptly."

On my way to the said session of the India Conference in Lucknow I called at Cawnpore to see my friend James Condon, M.D., civil surgeon of that station. He has a brother in Madras, surgeon in her Majesty's Twenty-first Fusiliers, E. H. Condon, M.D. Dr. James had long been in correspondence with his brother about the work of God in connection with my ministry; and now, when I went to his house, he read to me a letter he had just received from his brother in Madras, stating that for months he had been trying to get the missionaries of that city to invite me to go there, and that Rev. Mr. Barton, of the Church Mission, warmly favoured it, and brought the question of inviting me before the January meeting of their monthly Conference, but that it was not concurred in, and that he would invite me on his own responsibility, and deputed Dr. James to urge me to go, as the need of a stirring up there was the greatest need of that city.

I replied to Dr. James Condon : " Having Calcutta on my hands, I cannot possibly promise anything, and certainly cannot go to Madras for months to come."

But when Dr. Thoburn joined me and was appointed preacher in charge of our work in Calcutta I suddenly found myself foot-loose, and told the doctor to write his brother that, the Lord willing, I would go by the first steamship from Calcutta.   Having hastily put Brother Thoburn into line, I sailed by the Peninsular and Oriental Company's steamship *Indus* for Madras.

I paid my own fare, first class, one hundred rupees.   I was nearly used up by excessive work, and the best accommodations were the cheapest for me.   By the mercy of God the voyage restored me.

Before sailing, however, I received a letter of invitation direct from Dr. E. H. Condon, asking me to make his house my home while in Madras, adding that Colonel Goddard, Dr. Vansomeren, and Mr. Bowden were associated with him in asking me to come to Madras, and would back me to the utmost of their ability, but that he hoped I would not organise a Church there.

I replied : " I will leave that entirely to the Lord's leading, as He may manifest it clearly, not only to me, but to you and your friends. I cannot certainly anticipate His will in the matter, but must leave myself entirely free to accept His decisions and yield obedience to His will as He shall make it known to us."

CHAPTER XXXVI

MADRAS, BANGALORE, AND ONWARD

THE city of Madras was a small Hindu village, in which a plot of ground was marked out by the Rajah of Chundergiree as a trading post for the East India Company. They erected a factory in 1639, which in the intervening centuries has expanded into this great city. At that early period, to give confidence to the native merchants, a fortification was built and twelve guns mounted upon it; and they named it Fort St. George. This is the fort in which my brother and hospitable host, Dr. Condon, his estimable wife, his sister, and two little daughters resided. I found my way to their happy home on Tuesday, the 4th of Febuary, 1874.

On Thursday, the 6th of February, Dr. Condon introduced me to all the Nonconformist ministers of the city, the missionaries of the Church Mission, and a few of the more liberal of the Establishment, in their own houses.

Rev. W. Miller, of the Free Church of Scotland, gave us permission to use their Evangelistic Hall for our first series of special services, to commence on Monday night, the 10th of February.

Monday, 10th. This evening we commenced our series of services in the Evangelistic Hall, which seats about three hundred persons, and was packed with attentive hearers of all sorts, including twenty or thirty Hindus. After preaching I went with Dr. Condon to the monthly Missionary Conference at the house of Rev. Mr. MacDonald, of the Church Mission. The regular topic for the evening was postponed, and I was invited to occupy the time. I gave them an account of how God had led me in the organisation of the Bombay and Bengal Mission, and of its peculiar principles of self-denial on the part of its ministers, self-support by its people, and the self-reliance of its converts. I gave them a number of examples of converted Parsees, Hindus, and others, illustrative of the practicability of carrying out the Gospel principle of self-reliance, under which Jews and Gentiles alike were expected, when converted to God, to go home to their friends and tell them what great things the Lord had done for them.

It was but a month before that an invitation to Madras was refused me; now I stood among them as a sort of wonder. But they received me as kindly as they could, some with real pleasure and some in meekness, as they would other inevitable visitations. I had, upon the whole, a very good meeting with these dear men of God, and with their wives, who were present as well.

Tuesday, 11th. Hall again crowded this evening and a great awakening. I called for seekers to come to the front, where I could get access to them to instruct them, pray for them, and lead them to Jesus About thirty came, a large proportion of whom afterwards testified that they had obtained the pardon of their sins and peace with God. These services were kept up four days in the week for three weeks, and preaching every Saturday evening for the New Town Prayer Meeting Committee in the Baptist chapel for three months.

We went from the Evangelistic Hall to the Memorial Hall, built in memory of God's mercy in preserving Madras from any outbreak in the mutiny of 1857. It is a fine hall, to seat about six hundred, centrally located, and is, as the Exeter Hall of London, available for all religious and other popular assemblies. We had that hall well filled four days in each of four weeks. We next got the use of the London Mission native chapel, in Pursewakum, a very populous district of this straggling city of Madras. We afterwards rented that chapel and established regular Sabbath preaching services in it. Later Dr. Condon and his friends built, seated, and lighted (at the cost of one thousand rupees) a pandal, forty feet by sixty in size, on the Esplanade. The city authorities would not give us permission to occupy the site for a longer period than three months, but it became such a place of popular resort five nights in each week, and productive of so much good, that they kindly renewed our free lease, to run on indefinitely.

Each night of our services I wrote down the name and address of each person professing to find Jesus, and next day, or as soon as possible, called to see the converts. Those whom I found to be connected with the Baptists or Wesleyans, or wherever they were likely to be well cared for and do good, I advised to remain, and discontinued my pastoral visits to such, amounting to perhaps a couple of hundred persons ; but all such as were not actual members of any Church, or merely nominal members, especially of ritualistic Churches, with not much probability of pastoral nurture such as they needed, I organised into fellowship bands in private houses. Eight bands were organised within about a month of my arrival in Madras.

In addition to the special services six days per week in different parts of the city I led these eight bands weekly myself for five or six months, till I could develop leaders for them from among our newly converted men.

Our first advance out of the city, early in May, was to Perambore, famed for its great railway works and for the wickedness of the mass of its people. About twenty persons from there received Jesus in our meetings in Pursewakum, and walked three miles each Sunday afternoon to attend fellowship class. I saw clearly that God would have me organise in their own town rather than have them walk three miles weekly to meet us in the city. They soon after bought a lot and built a place of worship, and with a little help from the city paid for it, and there that beautiful prediction of Isaiah had another fulfilment, " The wilderness and the solitary place shall be glad for them ; and the desert shall rejoice, and blossom as the rose."

Mr. John James, of Salem, two hundred and seven miles from Madras, on the line of rail to Baypore on the west coast, who had formerly lived in Perambore when it was considered the vestibule of perdition, hearing of the marvellous change in so many of his old friends there, came to see what it was, and found that the half had not been told him. While there he submitted himself to God and received Jesus as his Saviour. He returned to Salem and opened his own house for meetings, and, though he was at first laughed at and jeered, within a few weeks he got ten of his neighbours converted to God, and now we have a living, growing Church of God in Salem Station.

About the middle of May, by invitation of Chaplain Grove, I went for a few week-days eleven miles out, to Palaveram.

Palaveram is a military station especially for the residence of veterans, who, having fulfilled their term of service, have their choice to go home to England, or settle down in that place and do light military duty and receive rations and pay. Many, having married East Indian women, prefer to remain. So in a short time we had a great work among the veterans and their families.

Among the many good men God has given us in Madras I make grateful mention of Philip B. Gordon, Esq., a Scotchman by descent, a lawyer by profession. In addition to his successful attention to his legal profession he has for thirty years been a diligent student of the vernaculars of Southern India. He received Christ about the 6th of July, and at once was drawn out by the sympathy and love of Jesus to devote all his leisure to preaching to the natives, and preaches with marvellous power in Tamil, Telugu, Canarese, Hindustani, and English ; a most valuable worker for God.

In the month of June we bought a small lot for two hundred and seventy-one rupees, in Pudupet Road, in Madras, and built a pandal at a cost of two hundred and fifty rupees, forty-six by sixty-seven feet ; the seats and lights made an extra cost of about two hundred rupees. Brother and Sister Fitzgerald were the leading workers in getting up this pandal, and the native school in it, the banner school of our new system of education in India, namely, the Sunday-school principle applied to every day in the week except Saturday : voluntary unpaid teachers ; school from 7 to 9 a.m., giving half an hour longer to all who wish to learn to sing Christian Tamil lyrics.

The pandal is covered over with about three inches of clean sea sand. The little Hindu children sit down in it, and each one smoothing a little square in front of him writes as instructed by the teacher in the sand with the forefinger.

During my absence at Bangalore and other new fields, before I could appoint a minister to take charge of the Madras Circuit, it was worked for a period of over two months by their own lay agency, with Sister Raitt to use the circuit horse and carriage in visiting, who made steady onward progress in every department of the work.

Before leaving Madras I baptised six Hindus who had publicly come out as seekers and professed conversion to God.

Bangalore is the capital of the native province of Mysore, a large native city and military station.

My first visit was about the first of August, in company with Lawyer Gordon, who owns property there.

I found that St. John's Hill and Richmond Town were very populous centres about two miles apart, and the only places of worship near either were high ritualists or Romanists; so I asked Brother Gordon to secure a lot for a chapel in Richmond Town, and my friend J. D. Jordan, Esq., to secure a lot on St. John's Hill. They each succeeded in getting a good church lot on reasonable terms in very good localities.

I deputed Brother Jordan to secure a hall and make arrangements for a house for special services on my return. In due time he wrote me that Judge Lacey, of Mysore, had tendered me the use of Clarendon Hall, a mansion with a large central and transverse front hall, giving sittings for about three hundred persons.

The rains continued to pour in heavy torrents through September, so that I did not return to Bangalore till about the 25th of that month. Brother Gordon and I arrived on Tuesday morning. Brother Jordan was confined to his house with illness, so that all arrangements for seating and lighting the hall had yet to be made. It was still raining, and the lookout was very gloomy, but we went to work, and before night we had borrowed seats and bought lights and had the hall all ready. Owing to the uncertainty of the weather and other conditions, no announcement had been made of our services. Dr. Condon had some large posters printed for Bangalore special services, and we had them posted the first day, but they were torn off the walls, so that I never heard of but two or three that were seen by the people who would be likely to come; so the first and second nights I had only twenty-four persons in attendance, but when the news of our services got out we had our hall crowded. Up to Friday night we had more than twenty persons forward as seekers, and a few saved. Then I returned to Madras for the Sabbath— distance two hundred and sixteen miles. That was the Sabbath of our second quarterly meeting in Madras, and a glorious meeting it was. Many had come into the light and liberty of assured discipleship.

Meantime the contract was let for building a cheap chapel on our lot on St. John's Hill, thirty feet by seventy. I appointed Rev. James Shaw, one of our ministers in Bombay, to the charge of this new circuit, and initiated him into the work before I left the field; and soon after his wife and three children joined him. The preacher in charge and his family were all well provided for by this new organisation.

From Bangalore I returned to Madras and remained nine days,

including two Sabbaths, and then, accompanied by Brother Haudin, spent a week on the Madras railway line, and organised a society at Arconam, another at Jollarapet, and another at Salem Station (where John James laid the foundations), distant respectively from Madras forty-two, one hundred and thirty-two, and two hundred and seven miles. Thence we went to Secunderabad and spent a few days in Walter Winckler's circuit, and had one hundred and twenty sisters and brothers at the sacrament of the Lord's Supper. Thence Haudin returned to Madras; and I proceeded to Poonah for a few days, and thence to our District Conference in Bombay.

As usual we had a glorious lovefeast in Bombay, as we had in Poonah the week preceding, at each of which about eighty persons told of their trials and triumphs in the service of God. On this occasion, in Bombay, three more of Krishna Chowey's kindred were saved, and I baptised them at the lovefeast.

Part of my business in Bombay at this time was to meet three missionaries from New York, sent us by our Mission Board. I expected to return to Bangalore and Madras, and thence, *via* Calcutta, to Shahjehanpore, to the annual meeting of the Indian Mission Conference in January; but on account of delay in the arrival of our new missionaries, and a change in the time of Conference session (from the 14th to the 6th of January, 1875), I was unable to return south.

Our dear brethren, Revs. C. P. Hard, Frank A. Goodwin, and John E. Robinson, arrived in good health the day after our lovefeast; but we extemporised another, and had a grand rally of our people, who were greatly refreshed by the rich testimony of our new men and their grand singing, all being good musicians and singers. They arrived on Friday and left for their work on the ensuing Monday.

The brethren did not know how they would get to their work, as they, according to agreement, came to us "without purse or scrip"; but when the time came to start each one found his bedding, new and clean, all strapped and ready, tickets for travel, and funds for the journey put into their hands by our stewards. The missionaries were so surprised by such things that they came and told me all about it as news for my information.

From the Conference in Shahjehanpore I went to Lahore, *en route* to Sinde; but in helping my Presbyterian brethren, I was detained in that city till I received an invitation to come to London. The letter containing it, written in December, was sent to Madras, and had to be forwarded to me in Lahore, nearly two thousand five hundred miles distant; hence it did not reach me till the middle of February. I was so intent on pushing my work in India that I did not for a moment entertain the thought of leaving at that time; but the next day I saw it was God's will that I should combine that with my visit to my family, and come away at once. The following, containing some confirmatory evidence from the pen of Rev. George Bowen in regard to our mission, is clipped from the *Bombay Guardian* of February 27th, 1875:

"The Rev. William Taylor has received a letter from Mr. R. C.

Morgan, editor of *The Christian*, in which, after giving an account of the plan of Messrs. Moody and Sankey to carry on a preaching campaign of four months in London, he says :

" ' Mr. Moody has requested me to write to you, in the hope that the Lord may give you to hear in this invitation the cry, " Come over and help us." Of course all expenses will be guaranteed. I may remind you that London is the metropolis of the world, and that to move this mighty city as it never has been moved is worth any effort which any number of men of God can put forth. . . . We fervently hope that it may be our Father's good pleasure to appoint you as one of His ambassadors in this great work.'

" It is seven years and a half since Mr. Taylor has seen his wife and children. His wife is a woman of kindred spirit to his own, taking the deepest interest in the work which the Lord has been accomplishing through him ; nor has she ever once asked him to leave this work and come home till now ; in the last letter received from her she for the first time expresses the desire, not for her own sake so much as for that of his sons, now fast growing to manhood. . . .

" During the last three years Mr. Taylor has given himself heart and soul to this antecedent and preparatory work of raising up, through the blessing of God, a witnessing and working Church, embracing men and women of all nationalities, but mostly using the English language, with this idea dominant in the hearts of all, that they are commissioned of God to show forth His saving truth to the Gentiles among whom they live. . . . The converts have been mostly among the middle or lower classes ; yet there has been no lack of funds. Six missionaries came from America to join the mission work superintended by the Rev. Mr. Taylor, and the expense of their passage from America was all that the Missionary Society was asked to defray. . . . The total disbursements amounted to 7733 rupees. This embraces expenditure, not only in Bombay, but in a number of places where the work was in its infancy. The receipts were 7042 rupees. A surplus at the beginning of 1874 supplied the deficiency. Of the receipts 3291 rupees were collected in fellowship bands, 2735 rupees in the congregations, and 1012 rupees by subscriptions and donations. Mr. Taylor has taken nothing from the Churches which he has been the means of raising up in India, not even his travelling expenses. Just so far as these Churches shall be animated by the same self-renouncing spirit they may expect to accomplish the end for which they have been raised up."

PART SEVENTH

MY MISSIONS IN SOUTH AMERICA

CHAPTER XXXVII

WORK FROM CALLAO TO IQUIQUE

I SHALL now narrate the circumstances attending the greater part of my work in South America. Glimpses of the countries and peoples holding the central and southern parts of our continents have been caught in many of the preceding pages of this volume, and still more fully in several of the books which I have previously published.

On the 16th of October, 1877, I bought for myself and for my brother, Rev. Archibald Taylor, a through ticket from New York to Callao, Peru, and embarked on the Pacific Mail Steamship Company's steamer, the *Acapulco*, bound for Aspinwall.

By sending missionaries to my work in India, together with heavy travelling and family expenses, my funds were so far spent that I was obliged to go third class to see my South American cousins, or not go at all, paying, as I do, my travelling expenses out of my own pocket, and not out of the pockets of my friends. A first-class ticket from New York to Callao costs two hundred and seventy-five dollars in gold; a third-class ticket, one hundred dollars. I believed, too, that my dignity would keep for eighteen days in the steerage. I have made over sixty sea voyages first class, at the cost of enough of my hard-earned dollars to give my sons a university education and keep me comfortably the rest of my earthly pilgrimage.

Ninth day out, "Land ho!" See, in the twilight of morning, the dense foliage of the Isthmus of Darien; the soft, fleecy clouds drink in and reflect golden rays from the Orient; the dolphins sport round us; we are nearing our first port of debarkation. Here we are in "Colon," the Spanish name for Columbus.

But the stay is not long. Our ship's company soon bestir themselves for departure from Colon. Rail train leaves for Panama at 3 p.m.

"Brother A. T——, if you'll stay 'with the stuff' I'll take a hundred copies of 'Hastings's Illustrated' and make a pastoral tour in the town. Yonder is a coloured cousin of ours, with his truck, waiting for an honest job; I'll begin with him."

"Good morning, sir."

"Good morning, captain."

"Can you read English?"

"Oh yes, sah."

"Let me hear you read a little from this paper."

He reads readily, and I give him the paper to keep.

"Where did you learn to read?"

"In Jamaica, sah."

"In what part of Jamaica did you live?"

"In Kingston, sah."

"To what church did you belong in Kingston?"

"Coke's chapel, sah; de Wesleyan Church, sah."

"I have preached in Coke's chapel many times."

"Oh, dear sah, we glad to see you here. If you are come to hunt for de place where you are needed de most, den you has found de field you is huntin'."

Here we are in the railway station at Panama trying to get our portmanteaux from the luggage car. Nobody in this latitude seems to be in any hurry to push business.

We can carry everything we've got in our own hands, but here are two strong fellows waiting for a job, so we'll give them a chance.

"Where did you come from?"

"From Jamaica, sah."

"How long have you been here?"

"About twenty years, sah."

"Have you made your fortune yet?"

"Make a livin', sah. Times very dull here now, sah. Fortune out ob de question wid me, sah."

"What church did you attend in Jamaica?"

"De Wesleyan Church, sah."

"What religious services do you have here?"

"None at all, sah, except de Roman Catholic, and we don't take no stock in dat concern, sah. We had a minister here some years ago, but de white people want to read de prars, sah, and de coloured people want to sing, sah, and de two parties couldn't agree, sah, so de preacher he done gone away, sah."

Light ahead—the city of Guayaquil. What an extraordinary light, brighter and brighter! It must be an illuminated house, but at this distance it presents the appearance of a great sheet of flame, reflecting what appears like a stream of fire far along the surface of the placid waters.

Halloo! they are taking down our bunks; what does this mean?

"All the third-class passengers must gather up their luggage and go to the after part of the hurricane deck." So all are busy collecting their luggage and preparing to go.

"Why do they want to clear us off this deck? We are getting on well here."

"They want space for two hundred bullocks, to be taken aboard at Payta."

What a bleak coast! Not a shrub, not a blade of grass, not even a cactus!

Here come the bullocks. I am surprised at their gentleness. A Cholo goes walking over their backs!

"Yes," replies the first mate, "they seem gentle enough cattle now, but if you had gone into the corral where they were lassoed, you would have seen them in another mood. I went one day to get a dozen choice bullocks for the ship. The owner told me to go in and make my own selection; so I walked in. They made a furious charge, and if I had not succeeded in leaping the fence they would have gored me to death."

On they come, each one suddenly pulled up, and passing through the same experience of surprise and terror in the ascent, and of manifest relief when they feel themselves standing again on their legs. Two hundred and two beef cattle are thus stowed away as closely as they can stand in our late quarters.

While we are watching this scene the new passengers from Payta have squatted on every foot of vacant space on the after part of the hurricane deck. Happily our sleeping space was covered by our blankets and portmanteaux, and our claim had not been jumped; but since the days of Noah who ever saw the like of this scene? I have travelled with crowds of Mohammedan pilgrims in the Mediterranean, but they had left their live stock at home. Only behold how our cousins travel! Each family has its small premises on the deck. The bed is usually in the centre, surrounded by boxes, bundles, and bags, on and around which are the parents, children, servants, dogs, poultry, and pets of every kind.

On Thursday, the 3rd of November, we woke up at anchor in Callao harbour. I can truly say, as regards wholesome fare and improved condition of health, it was the best voyage of my life! Callao, a city of about thirty thousand population, is the port of entry for Lima, the capital of Peru, with a population of about two hundred thousand.

My brother Archibald and I tarried in Callao for the greater part of two months. We preached according to our opportunities, but did not establish a mission. By the end of the year I made up my mind that a more auspicious field lay farther south.

I accordingly sailed from Callao for the south. I arrived in Mollendo, Saturday, January 5th, 1878. Mr. R——, the British Consul, received me very kindly, and I had my headquarters with him at the house of my friend, Mr. S——, the Pacific Steamship Navigation Company's agent, who had recently buried his wife, leaving him and little Pat, their youngest, in very lonely bereavement. In company with Mr. B—— I visited most of the people Saturday night, and preached to a small but attentive congregation on Sabbath. On Monday morning, assisted by my friend Mr. B——, I made up a subscription for passage and guarantee of support for a man of God from the United States.

I had brought some little blank books with me from New York.   In one of these I wrote the following simple proposal :

" Believing a school-teacher, being also a Gospel minister, to be greatly needed in Mollendo, I propose to send hither a competent man, combining in himself the twofold character of teacher and preacher, the first engagement to cover a period of at least three years.   I respectfully ask the friends of this movement to contribute the funds for passage and a guarantee for support till the school shall become self-supporting.   It will require three hundred and thirty dollars paper currency, for passage, and at least one hundred and fifty dollars per month for sustenation.

"Respectfully submitted,
"WILLIAM TAYLOR."

"We, the undersigned, concur in Mr. Taylor's proposal, and agree to pay the sums we here subscribe for the purposes named, and do all else we can to make the undertaking a success."

My first call was on an American railroad contractor.   Said he, " I am a Roman Catholic and don't wish to put down my name, but I will give fifty dollars to bring the man out and one hundred dollars more if you require it, and thirty dollars per month for his support."

That was my first financial stroke in South America.   I next went to another extensive contractor, a Scotchman, in whose family I enjoyed a generous hospitality.   He said, " I'll guarantee one hundred and fifty dollars per month to support a man of the right sort myself."

" I am greatly obliged by your kind offer, but I want to interest all the people of the town in him ; and the only way to do that from the start is to let them take stock in him."

We then called on shop-keepers, railway men, and others, who subscribed the passage money required, also the monthly stipend, leaving my liberal friend but twenty-eight dollars instead of one hundred and fifty dollars per month to pay.   I wrote in the little book my thankful acceptance of their liberality, naming three gentlemen as a committee and school board to collect the fund and make all necessary arrangements for carrying our plans into effect.

I subsequently appointed Rev. Magnus Smith and his wife to the work at Mollendo.   Brother Smith was a graduate of Williams College, Massachusetts, and, having studied in Germany also, was a good German scholar.   He had symptoms of lung disease, but knowing of persons similarly afflicted being restored to health and long life in South America, and the climate of Mollendo being very mild and equable, I took the risk of sending him, being a man of unostentatious but of very superior talents and attainments, with a wife to match.

For a time his health improved and he was very hopeful ; but he became ill, and while in that condition Mollendo was bombarded by the Chilian gunboats, and poor Brother Smith was hastily carried a distance of two miles to get him beyond the range of the guns. The shock, in his low estate, if it did not cause his death, at least hastened it, for he fell asleep in the arms of Jesus soon after.

On the 8th of January we swept through the roaring surf at Mollendo and embarked on the steamship *Ayacucho*, and in fifteen hours we cast anchor in the roadstead of Arica, five hundred and sixty miles south-east of Callao. I presented my papers to George H. Nugent, Esq., British and American Consul, a tall, commanding, fine-looking man. He received me very kindly, but could see no hope of employing either school-teacher or preacher in Arica, and thought it impossible for me to do anything in Tacna. But having heard in Callao that the merchants of Tacna were an enterprising, noble class of men, I could not consent to pass them without an effort to do them good ; so at 3 p.m., on the 9th of January, I took the rail for Tacna, thirty-nine miles distant, at an elevation of two thousand feet above sea level.

It was hot, dusty travelling across a desert, from which we saw in the distance the green gardens and orchards of Tacna, a town then of fourteen thousand inhabitants. Living streams, fresh from the Andes, flow through some of the principal streets and water the neighbouring vineyards and gardens. It is an oasis in the desert.

We arrrived at 6 p.m. I had a letter of introduction from our consul at Arica to Mr. A——, of Tacna ; so I engaged a boy to carry my portmanteau and conduct me to his house. We had gone but a few rods when my porter employed a smaller boy to do the carrying business, while he, as the original contractor, should play the gentleman and get a fee for himself and another for the little cholo who carried the load. Coming to a hotel, I left my luggage and went beyond the town and found the man I sought. I gave him the letter and explained to him the object of my mission. He was kind but quite unbelieving. He was quite sure that I could do nothing in Tacna, so I left him and returned to the hotel. At the supper table I made the acquaintance of a young English gentleman, and tried to find out how many English-speaking families resided in the town and what the prospect for educational work. He could give me no encouragement. Later in the evening I strolled down town to the plaza, where many gentlemen and ladies were promenading and others reposing on the public seats prepared and waiting for the weary ; so I sat down on one beside a German, who informed me that there were a few English and many German families in Tacna, and he believed that a good English school was one of the great needs of the city. I was glad I met with that German ; he did me good.

I returned and retired to bed at 9 p.m., but not to sleep. It was one of those nights of waking visions such as I used to have in Bombay, when God made known His way to His poor, ignorant servant. I don't mean miraculous visions, but an intelligible manifestation of God's will, showing me my path of duty through unexplored regions where there were no signboards nor blazed trees to indicate the right way. The revealings of that night widened my field of operations, narrowed my work, and shortened my stay for the present in South America so as to put me back to New York early in May of the current year. My way was widened so as to enable me to send good school-teachers where preachers would not be received at all ; my work narrowed so that instead of staying to plant Churches, as I did in India, I was first to send men to lay the foundations, and then, after a term of years, return to build ; time shortened by extending my preparatory work rapidly along the coast and hastening home to find and send the workers.

Tacna was to be my first departure from the old lines of purely evangelistic work to the new line of school work simply, where nothing more is at present possible. I had it all mapped out before morning, and hence the first thing was to write my proposal for the merchants of Tacna to found an English school. I had it clearly stated, so that they could see the object and the way to attain it at a glance, and have nothing to do but subscribe the funds and sign the papers. I went into the coffee-room and sat down by a young man who I thought might understand the English language. I found him to be an intelligent gentleman of French extraction, but a native of Minnesota. He was my providential man for the moment.

I laid my case before him, and he said, " I don't think you can do anything in Tacna, but the man whom you should see is Mr. William Hellman. If you can get him to see as you do you'll succeed. He'll not come to his office till 11 a.m., but I am just now going down town and will show you his place of business."

At the hour designated I presented myself to Mr. H——, and stated my object and showed him my written proposals.

He replied, " It is a thing very much needed here, but this whole country is badly demoralised, and I fear that nothing can be done."

" Well, my dear sir, you are hardly prepared to turn them all over to the Old Scratch without at least one more effort for the education of the rising generation. If you can succeed in giving a good education and a good moral training to one boy of thousands who are running wild around here he may be the coming man of mark to raise this country to a higher level. What I propose, too, is not like a great railroad venture, involving a hazardous outlay of funds, but a very economical enterprise, with promise of large returns for the good of the country."

" I have brought out governesses at different times from England, but they get discouraged and do but little good."

" Now, last of all, you had better try one live American to help you found a good English school in Tacna."

" But I am not the man to lead in such a movement ; you should go to Mr. Outram."

" Very well ; if Mr. Outram leads will you follow ? '

" Yes ; I will do my part."

" Shall I go alone to wait on Mr. Outram, or will you go with me ? '

By this time he had put on his hat, and said, "Come, let us go."

Just outside he met the banker, Señor Don Basadre, and began to explain the project to him. I said, "Bring him along." So on they came, and I was introduced to Mr. Outram, a merchant prince. My friend, Mr. H——, saved me the trouble of telling my story by stating the case himself and advocating it eloquently.

In a few moments a Mr. Jones came in, and Mr. H—— said to him : "Mr. Jones, you remember we were talking the other day about the great need of an English school in this town, and were devising how it could be brought about. Now, here is a benevolent gentleman who has come to help us in this very thing."

Mr. O—— said, "How long can you remain with us?"

"I expect to return to Arica to-morrow morning."

"This is our mail day for Bolivia, and we are all extremely busy, but we think well of your proposition, and I think we will write you a favourable response to Valparaiso, if that will do."

"Thank you, sir; that will do if you cannot do better; but this is a very plain case, which need not consume much of your time, and my success here will help to open my way along the coast."

He made no reply, but took up his pen and signed the articles of agreement.

Then Mr. Jones signed. Meantime Mr. H—— made some allusion to California, and said that he lived in San Francisco in 1853.

"Do you remember a man called Father Taylor, who preached every Sabbath afternoon on the plaza to the masses?"

"Yes, I remember Father Taylor very well."

"That same Father Taylor has come now to help you here in Tacna."

We both rose up and shook hands as old friends. So we proceeded and completed our preparatory business in about half an hour more. I asked for a subscription of thirty pounds sterling to pay passage of a single man from New York to Tacna, and the guarantee of one hundred dollars per month for his support till the school could be made self-supporting to the extent of at least that amount. Eight generous gentlemen signed the papers, obligating themselves voluntarily to give ninety pounds sterling for passage, and two hundred dollars per month guarantee for a male and female teacher, a good man and his wife, our engagement to cover a period of at least three years.

On Monday, January 14th, as the sun in grand, reflected radiance was sinking beneath the horizon of the great waters of the West, we embark on Captain Taylor's steamer *Maria Louisa*. She has a freight of eighty-five thousand gallons of pure water from Arica wells, bound for Iquique, distant one hundred and eight miles.

As we near our anchorage at Iquique on Tuesday morning, the 15th of January, Captain Taylor points to the wreck of a ship he lost there last year. This can hardly be called a harbour; it is a road-stead, protected on the south by a little island on which a steamship lies high on the rocks. She was anchored there quite unbroken by the tidal wave of the 9th of last May.

Captain T—— introduced me to half a dozen leading gentlemen

of Iquique, who gave me but little encouragement. All admitted the great need of a school, and some thought a preacher might do some good ; but the thing had been tried in good times, and the result was utter failure, and now in these hard times it was all nonsense to attempt such a thing.

Iquique has a population of about twelve thousand. Its principal export is nitrate of soda, or saltpetre. It is brought from the coast range of mountains, back of the town. The villages of Limena and La Noria, thirty-four miles distant, are large sources of supply. I visited those diggings, and the rocks that cover hundreds of acres of those dry mountains are of pure white salt.

Iquique was the place we had read about that was swallowed up by an earthquake in 1868. It was not indeed swallowed up, but it was terribly shaken to pieces ; the tidal wave swept over a large portion of it, and of its thirteen thousand people it was supposed that one half of them were drowned. The town suffered terribly also by the earthquake of May, 1877. The people fled to the hills and escaped the tidal wave, but the kerosene lamps left burning in their houses were upset by the violence of the shocks and set the town on fire. There were three fire companies in the town, two German and one English. They rushed out with their engines to quench the flames. The tidal wave saved them that trouble, but swept away the engines and hose of both the German companies, and the English company made a very narrow escape.

Ralph Garratt, a kind-hearted Canadian, who was the station-master of the railroad, extending nearly one hundred miles inland, secured for me a furnished room and a free welcome to his table. His family consisted of a kind, gentle Peruvian wife, four children, an African nurse, a Chinese cook, and seven dogs. Mr. G——, with a religious education, had not heard preaching for sixteen years prior to my visit ; not unwilling to hear, but how could he hear without a preacher ? He was anxious for a school, and for preaching as well, and offered to subscribe liberally at the first mention of my mission.

The following is a copy of my proposal to the people of Iquique and of their reply :

" The city of Iquique being in need of an English school of high grade, for the education of the children of English, German, and the better class of Peruvian families in all the branches of a good English education and the classics, and also of a good Gospel minister for the English-speaking population, travellers, and seamen in this port, I propose to send hither a competent man combining in himself the twofold character of school-teacher and pastor. Religious creeds not to be interfered with nor taught in the school.

"I therefore respectfully ask gentlemen interested in this good enterprise to subscribe the sum of thirty-five pounds sterling, to pay his passage to Iquique, and a monthly subscription amounting to an aggregate of one hundred silver dollars per month for his support, until the school shall become self-supporting. Passage subscription to be paid by the middle of April of this year, the other monthly, after the arrival of the teacher. This agreement to cover a period of at least three years.

"Respectfully submitted,
"WILLIAM TAYLOR.

"IQUIQUE, *January* 17*th*, 1878."

"We, the undersigned, concur in Mr. Taylor's proposal, and agree to pay the sums we here subscribe, and do all else we can to make the undertaking a success.

"IQUIQUE, *January* 17*th*, 1878."

This was followed by a record of fifty names, with subscriptions exceeding the amount required.

At our meeting at the British Consulate, Mr. G—— was appointed to provide a preaching place for me during my sojourn in the town. He furnished the railway station with seats and lights, and I preached there on Wednesday and Thursday evenings of that week, and at 1 and 7.30 p.m. the following Sabbath. Our congregations did not exceed forty persons, but they were very attentive, and there was some awakening of real religious interest, like the outside melting of an iceberg. It required more time than I could command to secure a thorough soul-converting work.

The most striking incident of my visit to Iquique occurred on the evening of the 23rd of January. Mr. G——, a young Englishman struck by Gospel truth at my meetings, came at different times to have me talk to him and to pray for him. His wife was an interesting Chilian lady.

Well, on the evening of the 23rd he was in my room; I talked to him about an hour and then prayed with him. Just as I was closing my prayer, while yet on my knees, the bottom seemed to be going out. The foundations of the earth were shaken, and it appeared as though the mountains might be carried into the midst of the sea.

My man sprang to his feet, saying, "We must get out of this."

"Never mind; I suppose it will be over soon."

"No; if we don't get out at once the door will be jammed, and then we can't get out."

With that he went and tried to open the door. It was already jammed, but by pulling and jerking he got it open and went out. I looked about the room and got my hat, and was going out of the door when I remembered what my friend had told me half an hour before about the earthquake of last May overturning the lamps and setting the town on fire; so I returned and blew out my candle. The motion meantime was that of sudden jolting, like a waggon on a corduroy road. When I got out into the verandah I had to go a distance of fifty feet to get to the stairs leading down and out. I could hardly keep on my feet. It was like walking the deck of a ship in a chopping sea in the Bay of Biscay. Descending the stairs I held on to the railing and thus kept up. My friend was waiting for me below. By the time I got on to the ground the violent shocks abated, followed by vibrations every few minutes. We already saw lights on the hills and others moving rapidly up. Every dog in town seemed to expect the engulfing sweep of the tidal wave, and with the people ran to the hills, making the darkness hideous with their barking.

Mr. G——, said, " Excuse me ; I must go and look after my wife and children."

I then walked up to Mr. Garratt's. He and his family, with the help of some of his watchmen, were busily engaged providing bedding, water, and provisions for lodging on the hills.

Said Mr. G——, "This is heavier than the earthquake of last May, and the sea will be upon us in a quarter of an hour if we don't get away to the hills."

So I got my Bible and a wrapper and went with them. It was very dark, and, except for the hideous barking of the dogs, awfully quiet.

"Ah," said Mr. G——, "this dreadful stillness precedes the tidal wave. It will sweep this town in ten minutes."

It was awful to think of forty ships grinding each other to pieces and dashing and breaking up amid the ruins of the town. Never having had my nerves shaken by such scenes before, I did not feel half the alarm that the residents manifested, but I quietly prayed to God to spare the town and the shipping. I thought of Abraham pleading for Sodom, and begged the Lord, if there were not ten righteous men in the place, possibly there might be three, and to spare it for their sake ; and if not three, then in mercy to give the place a chance to benefit by the ministry of the man of God to be sent to Iquique. We waited on the hill about an hour, when Mr. G—— and I walked back. He stopped at his house, and I went to his office and met a number of leading gentlemen of the town. The earthquake had stopped the clock in the railway office at three minutes to 8 p.m., so we thus knew the exact time of the shocking event.

About 10 p.m. I went to my room and retired to bed. Happily the sea remained quiet, but all seemed to be painfully apprehensive of a recurrence, and perhaps the next time the earth might open her mouth and swallow the whole town.

I searched to see that I was wholly submitted to God, and quietly entrusted soul and body to the care of my Saviour. I could not call to mind one act of my life on which I could base any hope of heaven, but, sweetly resting my all in the hands of Jesus, I had sweet assurance that all was well. As I was dropping off to sleep I counted ten shocks that caused a creaking of the timbers of the building, but I soon fell asleep and waked up in the clear light of a peaceful morning.

After reaching New York, in June of 1878, I learned that Mr. J. Martin, secretary of our committee in Iquique, had collected and forwarded the requisite money for the passenger fares of such as I wished to send to the front. I accordingly appointed to the Iquique station Professor J. W. Collier, B.A., and made arrangements for him to sail late in July of that year.

24

THE people of Iquique made ample provision for both educational and evangelistic work in that city.

I proceeded thence to lay the foundation of self-supporting missions at Antofagasta, also in Caldera, Copiapo, Coquimbo, and Concepcion. We established a self-supporting seaman's union Bethel in Valparaiso, where unhappy seamen might find a welcome. Minute details of this work may be found in my book entitled " Our South American Cousins."

Arriving at Concepcion, February 22nd, 1878, I was welcomed to the spacious home and hospitality of William Laurence and his accomplished wife. They had emigrated from London to Concepcion thirty years before. As a leading merchant in the town, I depended on him to introduce me to the men of means. He appointed the forenoon of the 24th as the time for our effort. He was not hopeful of my success. Soon after noon he returned to his house, where I was waiting, and with him came Henry Bunster, Esq., to whom I had letters. Bunster was my providential man for that moment, and had come sixty miles from his home, on other business, to be sure, but the Lord arranged to have him help me. I gave him my letters and he at once recognised me. He was an old Californian, and had heard me preach on the plaza in San Francisco many times, and could never forget the scenes of those pioneer days in the history of San Francisco. I showed him my book, and he at once put down his name for fifty dollars. That struck a spark of hope in the heart of my kind host, and in ten minutes we were off to see what could be done. We called first on the intendente, the mayor, a noble native gentleman, and he unhesitatingly signed his name for fifty dollars.

Several leading native gentlemen subscribed each fifty dollars, and we should have easily raised one thousand dollars, the amount we asked to bring out the teachers and initiate the school work, but most of the men were absent on summer vacation.

John Slater, an American railway king, introduced me to men returning from their summer resorts, and we reached a figure that guaranteed success, and arranged to open a school, to commence with forty scholars, with good prospects of increase and permanence.

I made a short visit to Talcahuana and preached twice one night aboard two ships. The shipmasters, Mr. Van Ingan, a merchant from the United States, and a wealthy native gentleman were all anxious that I should send them a missionary to teach school and preach, giving part of his Sabbath services to the fleet, and pledged themselves for his support. Talcahuana is ten miles south-east of Concepcion, and its port of entry.

I took the cars in Concepcion for Santiago on Monday morning, the 4th of March. The skies were bright, the air balmy and bracing. The wheat harvests had been gathered, and the dry stubble fields gave the country a barren appearance, but this was relieved by the orchards and vineyards opening to view on every hand loaded with fruit.

I travelled that day one hundred miles to Chillan, and put up for the night at the French hotel. Chillan was then a town of twenty-two thousand population. There was no passenger train going north-ward next day ; so my friend, Mr. C. H. Laurence, the railway pay-master, gave me permission to go with his assistant, Señor Cheveria, who went through to Talca—one hundred miles—with engine and tender, to pay monthly dues to all the employees on that section of the road.

Tuesday morning, the 5th, we rolled out about three miles to the river Nuble. The railway bridge across it, about a quarter of a mile in length, was swept away by the great floods from the Andes last June ; indeed, they swept away all the bridges on the line from this place to Santiago. The Nuble is not large enough for steamboat navigation, but at its flood too large for the safety of any improvements within the breadth of its sweep. The new bridge was nearly finished. We walked across it amid a crowd of workmen hastening its completion. Here we got on to a much larger tender, run before the engine, so that we escaped the sparks and smoke. Our driver was a Mr. Allen, from Paterson, New Jersey. He had his wife and four children residing at Linaris, a town of six thousand people, on the line. He was taking his tea as we came up, and kindly gave me a horn, literally a pint of tea in a cow's horn. He kindly offered me bread, but having a supply I simply accepted the horn of tea with thanks. Now the real interest of the day began, the payment of dues to the railway employees. About every ten miles, where gangs of men were at work, the tender stopped. The men came running and each responded to the call of his name, and received his money. The scene can't be transferred to paper. Close by the paymaster stood a vulture-eyed fellow who every now and again grabbed a lot of the money. Just as it was passing into the hands of the hardy son of toil who earned it that fellow laid his hands on it and put it into his own pocket. There was one who had but two dollars of his fifteen left in his hands. There stood another with empty hands, and gazed at the man who pocketed his pay. His eyes said, " It is too bad, but what can I do ? "

I said, " Mr. Allen, who is that man who is gobbling the pay of these poor fellows ? "

"He is the boarding-house master."

"Oh, yes, I see. He's the man who gets the workmen round the board, ostensibly to eat, but really to drink up their wages before they are earned."

Our seeming thing of life blows its great whistle again, and we are off for another stage. The interest kept up all the way. The most popular man on the road was the paymaster. They all seem so delighted to see him. We crossed some of the rivers on a temporary side track, to be used till the bridges could be rebuilt ; others, which were larger, we had to cross in boats, and take another tender and engine waiting for us on the farther side. We reached Talca about 3 p.m. and put up at Hotel de Colon.

Talca is a pretty town, near to a river. There are a number of American and English families residing in Talca. I was cordially received by Mr. Holman, the miller, an American, and Mr. Bennett, the banker ; but I did not propose to open a mission in Talca, as an American missionary was trying to plant a mission there. Later he left that field, and my people founded a college in Talca.

Wednesday morning, March 6th, I took passage on a regular train, one hundred and sixty-five miles to Santiago, a city of one hundred and eighty thousand, and arrived at sunset of that day and put up at Hotel Oddo. After dinner I mounted the upper storey of a street car and went for a call on Hon. Thomas A. Osborn, American Minister to Chili, who received me cordially. He was formerly Governor of the State of Kansas. He combines good abilities as a statesman with the modest, genial qualities of a gentleman and friend.

Thursday, 7th, accompanied by Mr. Osborn I went to call on his excellency Señor Annibal Pinto, the president of the republic, who received me with great cordiality. Next to the president, the minister of justice and of public instruction for the nation, Señor Amunategui, was most hearty in expression of friendship for me and my work.

The president is a man of medium size, not corpulent, but in good condition, with smooth round features, keen black eyes, with an appearance of great amiability and kindliness of heart, and a model of simplicity. He was seated at his desk examining some documents as we entered, but arose and shook hands with us very cordially.

Mr. Osborn told him about me and my mission to his country, and that I had a letter of commendation from President Hayes. His expressions of pleasure, congratulation, and assurance of support in regard to the English schools I was preparing to found on the coast were very emphatic.

He inquired particularly about Señor Guillermo Laurence, of Concepcion, and other patrons of my work there. That is the city to which the president belongs, and his cousin, Major Pinto, is the treasurer of my school fund in Concepcion. After this conversation his excellency asked to see my letter from President Hayes, and read it over with close attention, evidently not on my account, but because it was from the hand of the president of the great republic. We did not ask or desire any government funds for the support of our work, simply recognition and co-operation on the principle of business equivalents.

In my long journeyings from place to place in foreign countries and during my voyages at sea I recall many pleasing incidents and reminiscences out of my past work. On my way to Santiago there comes into my mind what happened when I was riding in the rail cars one day in India. I fell into conversation with an intelligent Roman Catholic, and as I was older than he I invited him to hear me for my cause.

"Very good, sir," said he, "I will listen with pleasure."

I proceeded to give him a conversational sermon by the way, teaching him about the animal nature that is in us ; about the soul with its instincts and appetencies ; about the higher spiritual nature that unites us with God ; and in particular about the Bible, the Book of God. I showed him how the Bible is to the soul what the light of day is to the natural eye ; that there must be a book of spiritual revelation to the inner man ; and then recounted my own experiences with respect to the Bible. I told him that I had found that the Bible is the only book that sets up any tenable claim to be of divine authority. I elaborated on the commandments, and then on the New Testament doctrine, with the revelation of God in Jesus Christ as the Saviour of men ; and so on until the journey was ended. When the train stopped and I arose to leave, my Roman Catholic friend grasped my hand, with tears in his eyes, and said, "It is a most fortunate circumstance that I came on this train and fell in with a man like you. I never heard such good news before. I am sure I shall never forget your words, and I am greatly obliged for your kindness in telling me these things." My heart was full of love and sympathy for him. I learned afterwards that he received Jesus, and testified to a personal experience of salvation in Him.

Santiago was not then ready for the introduction of my work. The English people were committed somewhat to a Church of England minister stationed there at the time, and Mr. Osborn, a true friend of our work, advised that it would be safer for our cause to wait for a change in the local condition of things. I concurred in that judgment, and did nothing there but spy out the country. About a year later, when we needed new fields in which to plant our fleeing refugees from Peru, the English minister resigned his charge in Santiago and returned to England. When he went out our man La Fetra, from Valparaiso, went in, and after that a congregation and a college in Santiago were established and were run by my people. They had regular preaching services and a Sunday-school. The Santiago Female College was founded by Miss Addie Whitfield, who became the wife of Rev. Ira H. La Fetra, so that the superintendency of the institution devolved on the two of them from its foundation.

On the 24th of March I embarked at Coquimbo on the Pacific Steamship Navigation Company's steamer *Loutera*, eighteen hundred and forty-eight tons register. I spent a few days with my brother at Callao, and gave him help in his arduous work. He is an able

Gospel preacher, and had an interesting work of salvation among the English-speaking people of that city. I sailed thence for Panama, three thousand miles from Valparaiso, April 30th, 1878, spent one day in Aspinwall, and got a subscription of eighty-six dollars per month toward the support of a minister to labour in that needy field.

My whole fare home, first class, cost a little less than my outward passage in the steerage. I arrived in New York on the 3rd of May, six months and sixteen days from the date of my departure for South America. During my brief absence, by the mercy of God I travelled about eleven thousand miles, and opened the twelve centres of educational and evangelising work described in these pages. On my visit to the Boston University, a few days before my departure, I requested Rev. A. P. Stowell, one of the graduating students, to act as my recruiting sergeant for the enlistment of first-class workers for South America. During the first week after my arrival Professor Stowell sent me the names of eight candidates who were ready for orders. I felt a desire that, in addition to all other qualifications for their work, they should be singers and teachers of vocal music. It turned out that they all, in that, as in everything else, were just the men for this most delicate and difficult work. The ladies, too, were well educated, experienced teachers in all desired branches of education, including instrumental music.

To fill my first order to supply the twelve new fields I had opened I required twelve men and six women. I had just returned from my pioneering tour on the west coast, and had not a dollar of passage money in hand. I refused to receive money, either for passage or support. I had confidence in the committees I had organised at the front. I wrote a book on my homeward voyage entitled "Our South American Cousins," giving the facts in detail, illustrative of the whole movement so far. I had my book in the press before I had received a cent of passage money. Satan accused me of being the greatest fool out of the lunatic asylum for involving such risks on the faith of committees composed of Roman Catholics and of English traders, who are more nervous with fear of foreign intrusion, which might affect their business, than are the educated Romanists themselves. I had faith in God, and faith in man. Treat a man as a dog and he will bite you, unless he in Christian meekness returns good for evil, and makes you feel like a cur kicked for snapping at its master. I had a dozen classically educated candidates nearly ready to sail before a cent of money came to hand.

The first draught I received—and it came in due time—was from my purely Roman Catholics patrons of Tacna, Peru, passage for man and wife, amounting to four hundred and thirty-six dollars, ninety-five cents. Meantime I arranged after my return to send a young lady music teacher to Tacna, additional to the man and his wife.

The same mail that brought the check from Tacna brought a letter from the chairman of my committee at Concepcion, stating that he feared that the movement would raise a row between the two great political parties of the country, and, being a merchant, his business would be imperilled, and, therefore, he had ordered my collector not to collect the subscriptions. That slip indicated plainly the necessity of a transit fund at home; and from that time I allowed friends who desired to do so to give something for the passage of my missionaries; and I hurried round and sold books and managed to get enough for steerage passage for my learned and refined people.

I sent a man and two ladies to Concepcion. Their arrival was a great surprise to my English friends in that city; their astonishment was equalled only by their indignation against me for sending them teachers after receiving the letter foreclosing the whole movement, as they supposed.

My missionary man replied, "You can look at your subscription book and articles of agreement with Californian Taylor, a plain business transaction between two parties, which cannot honourably be dissolved without consent of both parties. Mr. Taylor has so far fulfilled his part of the agreement, and expects you, as gentlemen of business integrity, to fulfil your part." When the intendente or mayor of the city, who had, on my application, subscribed fifty dollars, heard of two Englishmen who had subscribed fifty dollars each and and declined to pay it, he said, "Put me down for one hundred had fifty dollars. This thing has got to go in." It went in.

My work in India meant my own direct evangelising work, till by the power of God, according to His Gospel, I succeeded in organising self-supporting Churches ready, at once to receive and support the pastors required.

In South America, owing to my limited time and the amount of of track-laying work essential to great success, especially among the natives, the opening of a field meant a very different thing. I had to work my way right in, book in hand, containing a written proposal of what I wished to do, with articles of agreement to be signed by the people, with the amount of money they would pledge —first, to pay the outward passage of the missionaries, and, second, the amount to be paid monthly for their support. As before stated, I refused in every case to handle a dollar of their money. For more than thirty years I paid my own expenses and wrought for the love of God and souls without any compensation from men.

From an official report of our school work of Chili District for the year 1892, made to Bishop Newman, I extract the following facts and figures, indicating the measure of the movement before it was added to the work of the Missionary Society:

	STUDENTS.	GROSS RECEIPTS.			STUDENTS.	GROSS RECEIPTS.
Talca College	... 94	$7597.40	Coquimbo		... 63	$4,930.45
Santiago ...	... 305	43,460.45	Serena	...	... 71	1,901.00
Iquique ...	... 210	22,446.30				
Concepcion	... 214	25,531.96	Total		... 957	$105,927.56

The land and buildings free from debt are held in trust for our Church by our Transit and Building Fund Committee. Their estimated value in gold is two hundred thousand dollars. A portion of this property value came from the net profits of our school work; the larger proportion came through our Transit and Building Fund, from our friends and patrons, especially from the munificence of my old friends Richard Grant and Anderson Fowler. All these institutions are centres of evangelistic work among the Spanish-speaking people. Our evangelists whom we train and send out are of the same race and language. Dr. Kanut is called the Martin Luther of Chili. He says that when a student in a Jesuit college he "became acquainted with California Taylor on his first visit to Chili, and from his plain talk and testimony to the saving power of Jesus I was led to surrender myself to God and to receive Jesus Christ, and was saved. I completed my college course of study, then took a medical course, and finally gave myself up to the Gospel ministry." He was stoned while preaching in the streets of the city of Serena. He picked up some of the stones hurled at him, and said to the mob that he would have them built into the walls of a Methodist church.

Some will say, "What about the failures and abandonment of stations partly opened?" We were compelled to suspend organised work in a number of places from various causes, but we did work for God in every field we entered, even for a short time. It was a great work to open such fields and bring light and love to the people, who to this day, so far as I can learn, speak kindly about us, and would welcome us back, and we or others expect to go back and to be kindly received through the doors we opened. The light of eternity will reveal the fact that we did a good, soul-saving work for God in Callao and other fields which I have not named in this showing, where we did not attempt Church organisation. My brother preached in Callao nearly a year, Brother Gilliland and wife wrought a good part of a year in Lima, where there was a congregation of over forty, and Brother J. Baxter and wife laboured over three years in Callao and saw good results, and were supported by the people saved. Finally, on account of failing health, he retired, and our Missionary Society took up that work.

If an ambassador tarries but for a night in a neglected field he leaves a blessing to some needy soul.

I sent two German missionaries to the German colonies in southern Chili. They wrought there for several years and got many Germans converted. My men became overworked and ill and returned to the United States, but the fruit of their labours remained. All my missionaries in South America are, and were from the beginning, supported by the people whom they served, but received liberal help from home for the purchase of school outfit and land, and the erection of schoolhouses and houses for Gospel preaching and religious worship.

I will add a few incidents that recur in the retrospect relative to my missionary labours in South America. One of my fellow-pioneer missionaries in California was Dr. J. A. Swaney. He was subsequently employed for six years on the coasts of Peru and Chili, where he served as chaplain for the American Seamen's Friend Society. It was he who first interested me especially in the South American field; and by him I was greatly helped in the very difficult task laid upon me by the Holy Spirit of planting self-supporting missions in that great country. I was also aided by the President of the United States, who kindly sent me, over his own address and signature, a letter of introduction and commendation to the good people of South America. It came about on this wise:

My old friend Chauncey Shaffer, Esq., of New York, was pleading a case before the United States Supreme Court in Washington, and, meeting with President Hayes, told him of my contemplated visit to South America to open fields for educational and evangelical work. The President replied that he had been well acquainted with Mr. Taylor's work for many years past. That letter met an emergency when I needed a friend, just the time I always get special help from God, often, as in this case, through unanticipated agency. I never thought of applying to the President of the United States for a letter. I applied to our Church authorities on behalf of South America, and tendered my services without any cost to the Church; but they seemed to think that the time had not come, so that I had to proceed wholly on my own responsibility, as I had done in India, not breaking any law of the Church, but proceeding so far beyond organised lines or established precedent as to be considered "out of order." Having no authority from Church or State to proceed on a mission to South America, this unofficial letter of friendship was very opportune.

When Satan saw that I should succeed in founding self-supporting missions in South America he got very angry, and moved one of his servants to kill me. My brother is a practical and scientific geologist, and for our needful exercise we often strolled on the south beach of Callao, gathering rare geological specimens of volcanic rocks.

On the morning of December 17th, 1877, as we sat by the seashore, we saw about half a mile east of us a trooper dash up to the bluff, followed by armed foot soldiers. They came by, two and two, about every hundred yards, evidently intending to cover the whole line of coast back to the city.

As we sat watching their movements, not suspecting personal peril, two soldiers with their breech-loading rifles came to the bluff opposite, and distant from us about forty yards. They halted and stood looking at us. In a few moments two more came to view west of us and distant about seventy-five yards. As soon as they caught sight of us one of them, an intoxicated Indian, cocked his rifle and in a half-bent position, with his gun elevated ready for an aim, ran down the ridge of rubble stones toward us till he reached more level standing ground, and then stopped and took aim at us. We sprang to our feet and held up our hands to show him that we had nothing and were unarmed. He then ran about ten steps toward us and took aim from his knee. Not satisfied with that chance for a sure shot, he ran about ten steps nearer and aimed at us again, and then about ten steps still nearer, bringing the savage within thirty steps of us. There, with a rest from his knee and as deliberate an aim as a soldier maddened with rum can take, he levelled his rifle at us. His fellow and the two soldiers opposite stood looking to see him shoot one or both of us dead on the spot.

I saw from their look and attitude that if we should attempt either to run or to resist the whole quaternion of them would fire at us. This was all the work of a minute. I could not get my nerves shaken with fear in so short a time, but I thought fast. I did not believe that God would deliver either of us to the bloody and deceitful men, but I had to do something, so I advanced rapidly on the Indian aiming at us. I curved a little to the left to avoid his direct range and crossed with quick steps to the right, passing the muzzle of his gun but a few feet distant, to give me vantage ground for seizing him. When nearly within arm's length he sprang to his feet and I grasped the barrel of his rifle. My impulse was to wrest it from his hands and throw it into the sea and lay him level with the ground, and I knew I had the power to do it; but I felt certain in such a defence of myself the other savages would fire on me, so as quietly as possible I simply controlled his gun so that he could not shoot either of us Meantime I said, " Amigos, amigos "—" Friends, friends." He then trailed his gun in his left hand and shook hands with me, but immediately drew up his gun to get a pull at my brother, who had followed close after me ; but I again seized the barrel of his rifle, and would not allow him to get an aim, saying to him, " Este mi hermano ; este mi hermano "—" That is my brother ; that is my brother." He then sprang back and tried to get another aim at me, but I closed upon him and held his gun firmly, saying, " Americanos amigos ; Americanos amigos "—American friends ; American friends."

He seemed intent on killing at least one of us, especially as the others were looking to see him do it ; but now he was cornered and shook hands with us both. Then he let down the hammer of his rifle and began to jabber to us in a lingo that we understood not, when one of the soldiers on the bluff, who had watched the whole transaction, called him, and they all marched off together. We sat down and waited until the coast was all clear and returned to our quarters We learned afterwards that they were in pursuit of thieves. To excite their valour, as in a revolutionary expedition, they must needs get furiously drunk, and, not finding any thieves, the next thing was to kill an honest man or two. If they could have got an excuse by our resistance or attempt at flight for firing on us they would have had a great story to tell of how they routed and despatched the thieves. No thanks to them that life and reputation had not both been sacrificed together. No coroners in Peru—it is enough to know there that a man is dead. If I had had my way with them I would have had them all converted to God. They needed it !

It was in May, 1878, on finding myself short of funds to pay even the steerage passage of my noble band of missionaries before described, that I opened a blank book in which I stated the facts of the case and began to enter the receipts of the free-will offerings of my friends who desired to help me to provide a transit fund. In the following August at Mansfield camp meeting, in Ohio, Brothers Inskip and McDonald espoused my cause, and mainly through their appeals at the camp meeting and through their papers, first the *Christian Standard*, of Philadelphia, and later the *Christian Witness*, of Boston and Chicago, they became my most effective financial agents, and the same periodicals are still abiding helpers on the same line. It was not till after my ordination as Bishop of Africa, in 1884, that I organised my " Transit and Building Fund Committee," consisting of Richard Grant and wife, Anderson Fowler and wife, Rev. Dr. Asbury Lowrey and wife, and a few others. For about six years preceding I had no incorporated organisation, but had grand administrative and financial helpers. Richard Grant was my treasurer and Mrs. Anderson Fowler was my secretary, and both were most efficient workers and liberal givers ; but as it was feared that I should within a few months find my grave in Africa, and believed that in that case my self-supporting missions, both in India and in South America, would be safer under the guardianship of an incorporated committee, hence the organisation as above stated.

Five years later we divided the work of supervision, assigning, specially, to my Transit and Building Fund Committee our missions in South America, and as far as practicable in India also, giving special personal attention to the many-sided and most difficult work in Africa, the one field officially assigned to me by the General Conference of our Church. Whatever may be said of the success or otherwise of my part of the work, I can say gladly and truly that my committee have displayed admirable Christian zeal, liberality of money-giving, and administrative effectiveness. I expect to hold them in loving esteem for ever.

The next year after my first trip to the west coast of South America, as before described, I opened a few fields for missionary work on the Brazilian coast. Some good was accomplished at several important cities, but thus far the only permanent success was made under the leadership of Justus H. Nelson, B.A., and his good wife at Para, on the Amazon.

Every new departure, especially in methods of Christian work, is subject, and very properly, too, to close scrutiny and sharp criticism. There was nothing new in my methods of work in India or South America except the audacity of raising up self-supporting Churches in foreign mission fields. The pros and cons of my missions in South America were discussed by the General Missionary Committee in 1882. I was not present, and knew not what was said, but received a telegram requesting me to meet a sub-committee composed of about a dozen of our ablest high officials, men whom I honoured and loved. After opening the meeting with prayer the chairman proceeded to state that my missions in South America were out of order, and that I should resign them to the Missionary Society; otherwise all my missionaries in South America connected with Conferences would have to return to their Conferences or locate.

" How will that affect my self-supporting missions in India?" I asked.

" They are organised into a regular Annual Conference by action of the General Conference, and do not come within the province of the present inquiry."

" Prior to that action they were as much out of order as my South American missions are now, and neither infringed the geographical boundaries or jurisdiction of any of our organised missions; so I will refer the case to the next General Conference. I will take the first steamer for South America, and not return till the time for the General Conference of 1884, so that the Church shall not be disturbed by any discussion of the subject."

I was at that time, as all the Methodist world knew, a member of the South India Conference, and under God the father and founder of it, and prized my relation to it most dearly; but I would not have my dear fellows in South America forced to a humiliation that I would not voluntarily submit to on their account. If I had possessed a grain of worldly policy in my make-up I should have reasoned thus : " To present my appeal to the General Conference I must be a member of it, and my hope of being a member of that body is to be elected and sent by my Conference, which will be impossible if I locate." Regardless of consequences, through love for my heroes in South America, I said by letter to South India Conference, " Grant me a location without debate;" and thus I became a located minister.

So I was off again for Peru and Chili by the first steamer, to share the humiliation of a location with my itinerant brethren in those countries.

Such was the logic of the case as it appeared to me then. I left it all to the Lord, and took rank with my located ministers who should abide with us at the front.

Every one of them was loyal to our Church, and only one decided to leave our work and go home rather than be located. He was a good preacher, successful missionary, married a good young lady in Chili, and was every way well adapted to our Chilian work. But he shipped for home with his wife and two children, *via* California, took ill, and died on the voyage. His widow returned heart-broken to her people.

On that trip I visited the most of my stations in Chili and spent about ten months as preacher in charge of Coquimbo Circuit, which comprised, besides Coquimbo, the head of the circuit, Guayacan, Serena, and the copper mines in the mountains, seven miles by horseback beyond Serena. The preacher in charge was taken down by illness, requiring home medical treatment; so he and his wife and children went to the United States, hoping to return, but never did. I appointed Rev. W. T. Robinson, M.A., principal of the boys' school in Coquimbo and to assist in the pulpit work, which never had there financial connection with the school work ; so I received the minister's salary of one hundred and twenty-five dollars per month, and combined it with some help from home and bought a good lot, and with my own hands and native help put on it a college building sixty-eight feet front, two storeys high.   That was our first venture of buying and building in Chili.

Before our building was quite completed I received official notice of my election by South India Conference as a lay delegate to the General Conference to meet May 1st, 1884, in Philadelphia.   That was a surprise to me, for it had never struck me in the forty-two years of my ministry that I was a layman ; but my dear spiritual children in India were sharper than their father.   I saw that my Lord meant that I should be there ; so when the General Conference roll was called, in May, 1884, I answered, " Here."

On the fifth day, when petitions and prayers were being sent in, I sent in mine, which was in effect as follows :   " That this General Conference shall declare whether it is lawful and right for an American Methodist minister to get people converted to God outside of the United States ; and whether it shall be lawful and right to organise them into Methodist Churches according to our Discipline ; and whether on their fulfilment of probationary conditions they have not a right to membership in the Methodist Episcopal Church directly, without the sponsorship of a missionary society."

My petition was read and referred to the Committee on Missions. I was a member of that committee, and observed its silence in regard to my business for three weeks, up to the day appointed for the committee to rise.   Meantime the Lord had put me through on a fast train into the missionary episcopacy, with authority to open missions and develop Methodist Churches on my own missionary methods anywhere in Africa.   So a sub-committee was appointed at once, with instructions to prepare and report amendments to the Discipline bearing on the case.   The General Conference did accordingly make the changes prayed for, and the same were incorporated in the Discipline.

PART EIGHTH

MY AFRICAN EPISCOPATE

CHAPTER XXXIX

ELECTION AND OUTGOING

At the General Conference of 1884 the problem of African evangelisation came up for solution so far as it related to the Methodist Episcopal Church. During her occupancy of the Liberian field for more than half a century many precious lives of martyr missionaries had been poured out in that torrid zone. But as for extended missionary work among the heathen nations we had not up to 1884 a single station in a heathen tribe, except the beginning of one in Kroo Town, Monrovia, by Mary Sharp. During said half century two coloured bishops, Roberts and Burns, had been ordained and sent out.

Two of our American bishops had been sent over to extend the work among the heathen; but it was considered a risk of their lives. In each case a ship was kept at anchor during their sojourn in which they should lodge, and not risk their lives for a single night on shore.

Such was the aspect of the case as it came before the General Conference of 1884. I ventured to say on that occasion that were I disposed to lay a scheme for killing bishops decently I would advise that by all means they should avoid the highlands of the interior and spend all their nights in that deadly climate down on the water level in the lower strata of the malaria! If I were to prescribe for the preservation of their lives and effectiveness I should advise that they proceed to the field directly to which the Lord called them, eat where they labour, sleep where they eat, commit their way unto the Lord, trust also in Him, and allow Him to bring to pass results worthy of His own wisdom and preserving power.

I had not then the most remote idea of having to swallow the pill that I was prescribing for others more honourable. I was not a candidate for any office in the gift of that venerable body. Subsequently, when nominated for the missionary episcopate of Africa, I hurriedly inquired of a number of the leading members of that body whether or not that meant any interference with my self-supporting mission work ; if so I should certainly refuse to have the nomination submitted. They assured me that the General Conference had no such design, but just the opposite ; that they wanted me to introduce self-supporting methods into Africa ; and that fact was compressed into the short sentence of " Turn him loose in Africa."

The adjournment for noon recess was moved and passed immediately, and, as I sat near the door of the great hall in which the Conference was in session, I skipped and was out of sight before any one had a chance to ask me any questions or to make any suggestions.

Immediately on the return of the Conference from their lunch the question was submitted and passed without discussion, so that as I was entering the hall a member of the Conference said to me, " You are Missionary Bishop of Africa, by a vote of 250 for your election against 44 for your highest competitor."

The nomination, election, and ordination all passed within less than twenty-four hours, so that there was no time to entertain intermediate pros or cons, and nearly the whole Conference seemed to perceive and admit that it was the Lord's doing and marvellous in the eyes of all concerned.

I do not pass from the episode of my election without subjoining the following letter from Rev. M. D. Collins, of the Des Moines Conference. He entitles his contribution to the editor, " How William Taylor Came to be Bishop of Africa : "

" Among the providences which have marked the pathway of this man of God none have been more clearly identified than the marvellous train which led to his election to the office of bishop in the Methodist Episcopal Church. It was my fortune to be a member of the General Conference of 1880, which met in Cincinnati, Ohio. In the assignment of committee service I was placed on the Committee on Episcopacy. A petition came before that committee from the Liberia Conference asking for a missionary bishop to reside among them. This petition was discussed for some time, but with the feeling of great paucity of knowledge as to the real needs of the case. One day a member of the committee suggested that William Taylor was in the city, and that it would be a good idea to have him come before the committee and give us information we so much needed. Accordingly he was sent for, and soon appeared before that body. The chairman, who, as I remember, was Dr. Joseph M. Trimble, of Ohio, explained our dilemma to Brother Taylor, and he gave answer to all our queries and shed much light in a brief time on the whole question, and closed up the matter with remarks to this effect : ' It is no use to elect a bishop for Liberia. Liberia is a very unfortunate approach to Africa, being hedged in by hostile and warlike nations, and cannot be made an acceptable gateway to the continent. If you could find some man like Livingstone, who would open up Africa, it would be wise to elect such a man, but otherwise it is useless to send a man to live there in episcopal service.' The conclusion of the committee was adverse to the petition of the Liberians, and the matter of missionary bishops went over another quadriennium.

"Four years later, in the General Conference of 1884, which met in Philadelphia, it was my good fortune to be in membership and a witness of the marvellous scenes that transpired there. The matter of missionary bishops had received a large discussion through the Church press before the meeting of the Conference, and came before it upon petitions and memorials among its first presented business. The whole matter was thoroughly discussed before the committee, and very exhaustively presented on the Conference floor. The conclusion of the wisdom of these four hundred representative clergymen and laymen of Methodism was that '*we will not elect any missionary bishops this quadriennium.*' At this point in the proceedings I think, so far as I could measure the pulse of this ecclesiastical body, that all parties accepted it as settled that nothing would be done in this direction for at least four years, and many thought perhaps never should we have missionary bishops in Methodism again. But lo, a sudden and marvellous change came upon the whole body unexpectedly to any, and most so of all to the prime movers in its execution.

"Saturday morning, before the ordination of bishops on the following Sunday, came, with the quietus of the missionary bishops subject still on us. Dr. Curry had long treasured a desire to see a coloured man on the Board of Bishops, and had laboured for this end at the previous General Conference, but the failure to find a man who could carry the suffrages of the delegates had caused its failure then. Now Dr. Curry thought he had discovered his man, and in joy thereof consulted the Board of Bishops and obtained their sanction of the project of bringing him forward. The only way to meet all the difficulties of the case was to present him as candidate for Missionary Bishop for Africa. Hence on Saturday morning Dr. Curry got the floor, and without bringing the matter before the Committee on Episcopacy, of which I think he was chairman, he presented it *de novo* and nominated his man. This was a new and unanticipated turn of affairs. The nomination was seconded; another coloured man was nominated and seconded. Then Brother Olin, of Wyoming Conference, rose and said about this: 'I think when a bishop for Africa is to be seriously considered all minds must instinctively turn to the man, the only man, God's man for that place; I refer to William Taylor.'

"This proposition of Brother Olin fell on the Conference like a clap of thunder out of a clear sky. It was received at once, as thunder follows lightning, by a storm of enthusiasm and tide of approval that was utterly irresistible. But this was not at all what Dr. Curry desired, and that veteran of a thousand parliamentary contests exhausted his store of tactics in vain endeavours to stop or sidetrack a movement he had unintentionally set going. The Conference would do nothing but vote, and vote they did to such effect that the first ballot elected William Taylor, lay delegate from South India Conference, Bishop of Africa by an overwhelming majority. Within twenty-four hours he had been nominated, elected, and ordained a bishop in the Methodist Episcopal Church for Africa against the previously declared wisdom of that body expressed after one of the most thorough canvassings that any subject ever had at the hands of a like body. Without premeditation, without knowing whither they were moving, until they were at the very point of landing, this body of as strong men as Methodism ever gathered in council, when the proposition flashed like meridian sunlight out of Egyptian darkness, received it as the will of God, and heartily, determinedly gave it their approving votes. In a whispered canvass of our delegation and those about us I found one sentiment—*It is of God, and we must not withstand Him.*

" These are the facts as I recall them after these years, true, I am sure, in all essential particular ; and having been an actor in them I feel it will be for His glory whom we serve here to record them."

The election to the episcopacy brought with it a twofold responsibility : first, to administer for the Missionary Society in their organised Liberian work ; second, to found missions of my self-supporting plan anywhere within the radius of the African continent.

The fundamental principles which I adopted from the start were, first, to attend to my own business and not to interfere with the business of other people ; not to encroach on the territorial boundaries of the missions of other Churches. Second, my plan of missionary training should embrace the industries necessary to the self-support of civilised life for all those whom we got saved and civilised. A development of that plan will in due time create self-support for the mission itself and its missionaries. Third, in every station where we shall have a competent missionary matron, to establish a nursery mission composed of children adopted from heathendom before they shall be old enough to become heathens, and have them at the first stage of responsible life submit to God and receive Jesus Christ, be justified by faith and regenerated by the Holy Spirit, and train them as witnesses and workers for God from the time they are six years old.

Soon after the adjournment of the General Conference the celebrated German explorers, Dr. Pogge and Lieutenant Wissmann, published a report of their explorations of the head waters of the Kassai and thence across the continent on a line of six or seven degrees south of the equator, in Lake Tanganyika, a vast country hitherto unknown to civilised nations, possessing a dense population, with large towns and fruitful fields approaching high up toward the standard of civilised life. So I was led to believe that that should be an object-ive point of my missionary movement, starting in through Angola, where Pogge and Wissmann came out. Dr. Pogge, the dear fellow, got no farther than St. Paul de Loanda, but died and was buried there. Lieutenant Wissmann continued his African explorations and afterwards gained great celebrity.

But while I selected the Bashilange country, at the head waters of the Kassai, as an objective point, more than a thousand miles inland from our port of entry, I could not determine in advance whether the Lord would have us go in a thousand miles to begin, or have us begin at the place of entry and found a chain of stations extending inland as fast as possible, and keep up communication with our base or port of entry.

The question of supplies, of missionaries, and money to pay their expenses had to be considered. I had an efficient committee, consisting of Richard Grant and his wife, Anderson Fowler and his wife, Rev. Asbury Lowrey and his wife, Stephen Merritt, besides Mrs. Jennie Fowler Willing and other ladies as remote helpers in the selection of missionary candidates. Mrs. Emily Fowler had for years past been my missionary secretary. It was supposed, as I have said, by a large number of my friends that I should die in Africa the first year; therefore, to give stability and authority to my committee, we had them incorporated under the title of Bishop Taylor's Transit and Building Fund Committee. They had long been doing grand service; the incorporation was not to increase their efficiency, but to provide for the possibility of my becoming a victim of the African fevers.

For the supply of missionary men and women, and money to pay their expenses, and for building up mission stations we had to depend mainly on the Lord. We have tried from the beginning, as opportunity served, to keep the subject before the people, but have no travelling solicitors for funds. The Lord has wonderfully helped us, both in regard to working agency and the building of mission houses, school-houses, and places of worship. Our plan of work opened a wider field for a greater variety of the Lord's workers than any other mission. We require some educated ministers, but for our extensive educational and industrial work we furnish an ample field for many workers, male and female, who are not ministers, but are better adapted to our plan of work than very learned ministers would be likely to be. Paying no salaries, and having in prospect poverty and sickness and death, it was supposed that we could get but few persons willing to go; but we found immediately—and it has been true ever since—that we have twice as many candidates considered suitable as we have been able to employ.

We did not, as is usual with missionary societies, receive any for a limited term of five or ten years. We tried to be assured that every candidate was called by the Lord to that difficult work, but we could not anticipate the Lord's time limit, if He had any, so we put them in on their profession that they are called by the Lord for His work. If they get sick and discouraged and find themselves wanting in adaptability to the work, the sooner they leave the better. If they have health and success and blessed fellowship divine, we could not drive them away if we were to try. Moreover, we require heroes and heroines for such a work. One essential condition to that is freedom, freedom at the front.

Before the end of that year (1884) we had accepted about thirty volunteer men and women, with about a dozen children, and supplies in all suitable varieties to put us comfortably through the first year.

Brother Anderson Fowler had written in advance to Fowler Brothers, of Liverpool, to afford me and my party every facility possible. J. H. Brown, of that firm, became our most kind and efficient helper. One of the first things he did was to provide in advance a good hotel where our missionary party could be accommodated. He selected one for convenience of location and informed the landlord that he wanted hotel accommodation for a few days for about forty missionaries on their way to Africa. The hotel keeper bristled up and said he wouldn't allow a lot of niggers to come into his house at all. So Mr. Brown bade him good day, and went next to Hurst's Temperance Hotel, accessible and commodious. Mr. Hurst said, " Certainly, Mr. Brown ; I'll be glad to entertain your missionaries ; I don't stand on colour or nationality, and will entertain a black man just as cheerfully as a white man if he behave himself."

So when our missionary party arrived Mr. Brown conducted them to Hurst's hotel. Mr. Hurst was surprised to find that there wasn't a coloured man among them, and Hurst's hotel has been the stopping place of our missionaries passing through Liverpool ever since. The hotel keeper who refused to entertain us got very angry at Mr. Brown for not informing him that the missionary party was made up entirely of white people. After such a display of his hatred of the coloured man Mr. Brown would not have sent him any missionaries on any account.

I went on a few weeks in advance of my party to Liverpool to make arrangements for their transport. I ascertained that there were two companies, the West African Steamship Company and the British and African, and that one or the other sent a steamer through to Loanda every month. The only steamer suited to our time belonged to the West African Company. Accompanied by Dr. Summers, one of our medical missionaries, and Heli Chatelaine, our best missionary linguist, we went on a month in advance of our party, so as to hold the Liberia Conference and preach a few days in Monrovia, Grand Bassa, and Cape Palmas, and at the last-named station waited for the arrival of my party for Angola. In the meantime I sent Summers and Chatelaine directly on to St. Paul de Loanda, the port of entry of Angola, with a letter to the Portuguese Governor General of Angola to apprise him of the coming of our missionaries and to procure by rent a capacious house in which they should find comfortable quarters during their sojourn there.

But before we left Liverpool, in making arrangements for steamship accommodation for my party on their arrival, I learned that the president of that company, Mr. Bond, resided in London ; so I made it my business to go and see him. I informed him that I wanted passage for about forty-two men, women, and children aboard one of his steamers to Angola. He said the price, first class, was thirty five pounds ; second class, twenty-eight pounds. I replied, " We are not in the pay of any society, nor flush of funds, and we can't come up to either of those figures."

He heard my statements, and was very gentlemanly and kind, and said, " I'll write you a bill of fare, and if that will suit you I'll tell you what we can do for you."

So he wrote out a bill of fare for three meals each day.

I replied, " That is entirely satisfactory, good enough for anybody."

" Well," said he, " we'll say nothing about class, but will give you the liberty of the ship—saloon, cabins, everything—and will charge you but twenty-five pounds a head for your adults and half price for the children under twelve."

I informed him that we had one boy a few months past the age of twelve. He said. " All right, put him in at half fare."

So by that transaction we saved about two thousand dollars on the passage from Liverpool to Loanda.

CHAPTER XL

WE had a blessed work of salvation in Monrovia, Grand Bassa, and Cape Palmas, both among the Liberians and semi-civilised heathens from without. In due time my party arrived in the steamship *Biafra*, and I joined them at Cape Palmas. On arrival in St. Paul de Loanda we were received cordially by the head of the firm of Newton, Carnegie & Co., the only English firm in that city, and were conducted to the house procured for us, in a high part of the town, and large enough for our accommodation.

We learned that the governor general had received my messenger kindly, and expressed a strong desire that I should establish missions in Angola, and that it would be his pleasure to give us in fee simple any quantity of land we might require up to a thousand hectares (twenty-four hundred acres) for each station. In the meantime he had gone down to Mossamedes, and would not be back for three or four weeks.

While waiting his return most of our party were taken down with fever. On the governor general's return I made arrangements to take a few of those of our party who were able to travel and to proceed into the interior to select mission sites and make preparation for occupying them. So I waited on his excellency at his office to inform him of our contemplated departure from the coast. He welcomed us to make any selection we saw proper, but warned us against taking women and children into the interior. He gave me an account of three attempts of the Portuguese government to establish Portuguese colonies in the interior, but they failed utterly; many died, others yielded to discouragement, and from one cause or another the whole of them disbanded, and the attempt proved a failure. He begged me to send the families to Mossamedes, four hundred miles south, where the climate is genial and healthful.

I replied that our objective point was the Bashilange country, a thousand miles in the interior, and that we only asked permission to travel through his country; but to honour his generosity we proposed to open a chain of mission stations through Angola and on easterly into the far interior.

Then he inquired, " Are you going into the interior yourself ? "

" **Yes**, your excellency; I expect, in company with half a dozen

389

young men, to start to-morrow. We will leave all our sick folks and our women and children and go inland to select mission sites and make arrangements for our families."

"All right, then," said the governor general; "you take the risk, and I'll render you all the service I can."

And he did, writing to all the commandants along the line to render us every facility possible.

When subsequently we succeeded in opening stations and settling our families, who, in the main, are enjoying good health, it revived a forlorn hope in his heart and in the hearts of the Portuguese people generally. Soon after that they commenced the construction of a railroad into the interior, and laid on water from the Bengo River, five miles distant, to supply the city. Most of our party remained in St. Paul de Loanda three or four months, on account of sickness. One of them died, and eight or ten more, through illness and discouragement or otherwise, left us and went home. We had not brought with us much money, expecting to proceed into the interior, where money was not taken, but goods instead.

By our long detention in the port our money supply was quite exhausted in a few weeks. We had tons of goods in great variety, but they were not available on expense account. John Terry, of London, had said to me, "If you get short of funds you may draw on me for five hundred pounds;" so half of that amount paid all our expenses through and the other half purchased and paid for our Nanguepepo property, with spacious mission house accommodation; and so the Lord led us gently, kindly, and in that campaign we opened a mission station at Dondo, two hundred and forty miles from Loanda by steamer, the head of steamboat navigation on the Coanzo River, a town of five or six thousand inhabitants, natives, with a few foreign traders; thence by footpath fifty-one miles we opened Nanguepepo Station; thence by trail twenty-seven miles to Pungo Andongo; thence sixty-two miles to Malange. Thus on our first tour we opened and manned five stations. I appointed Rev. A. E. Withey presiding elder of that district. He has made a grand record on the line of holiness to the Lord and hard work in its variety in building up missions. He and ten others of the pioneer party of 1885 are at the front to-day, and have never been out of the country since their first settlement as missionaries. Since then we have added Benjamin Barratt Station, Canandua, Munhall Station, and are preparing to build Pegley Station, sixty miles north-east of Malange.

Seven volumes of our monthly *Illustrated Africa* conducted by my son, Rev. Ross Taylor, give but very brief illustrative examples of this work in Africa, and our present space will allow us but a brief index to the unwritten facts. For example, I appointed S. J. Mead, and Ardella, his wife, and Bertha, his niece, in charge of Malange Station, in September, 1885. He writes under date of May 28th, 1888: "Our health is as good as it would be in New England under the same amount of pressure and care. The prospect is glorious and success sure. We need a good Portuguese teacher and an ordained preacher, who could give their whole time to the work, and we will see that they are well fed with our kind of food." He became an ordained preacher in due time; Ardella, his wife, Bertha, his neice, and half a score of our converted natives constitute his teaching corps in Portuguese, English, and Kimbunda. Mead goes on to say: "We have a good supply of books. We use from seventy-five to one hundred Sunday-school picture papers each Sabbath. Our regular attendance for morning service is from eighty to one hundred and twenty, and about thirty-five in the afternoon. Our class meeting consists of nine coloured boys, besides the members of our missions." His classes contained an aggregate of about sixty in 1894.

All our Angola stations are provided with comfortable, permanent houses, some of stone, others of adobe. My work in South Africa, nearly thirty years ago, was in a prepared field, where faithful missionaries had been preparing the way of the Lord for forty years. But our party landing in Angola, as before stated, we could not utilise the English language. The Kimbunda, the language of the people, had not been reduced to manuscript, much less to printing, and we had no interpreters; so we had to sit down and pick the words out from between the teeth of the heathen. But in less than five years we had a grammar and the Gospel by St. John printed in the Kimbunda, and all our pioneer missionaries could witness and teach and preach in the language of the natives. In connection with all this all the stations of Angola became self-supporting, and have so continued to be.

Dr. Summers was the only one of our party that pushed through to the Bashilange country, for the reason that we all, except the doctor, interpreted the will of God to be our establishment of a chain of stations as before intimated. The doctor had intense energy and impulse in a weak body, "sword too sharp for its-scabbard." So I gave him perfect freedom to select his own field, and if short of supplies to let us know and we would supply his wants. It was needful that the bodies of men should have treatment as well as their souls, and the frail doctor had medicine for both. I copy the story of his adventure from his letter to Rev. Dr. Sims, at Leopoldville, dated,

"LULUABURG, *March 28th*, 1888.

"At our Conference in Angola, Bishop Taylor appointed me as medical missionary at large, so gave me a big field. My original idea (and I am sure I was divinely led) was for our mission to push on to this country as soon as possible.

"My·prospecting work being done, at request of friends I settled for a time at Malange, the most inland trading town. I waited, prayed, and watched to know God's will, healed all the sick, collected vocabulary of Ambunda, etc. The merchants almost quarrelled as to who should be my host, and finally I had a large room which served as everything, even to a hospital, from one, took *café* with another, breakfasted with another, and dined with another, and in a couple of months had my boarding rearranged at houses of still others. Sickness was great at the time I arrived, and they had no sensible treatment. They used all the quack remedies advertised. My treatment was very successful, many times to my own surprise; so my name spread till I had patients even from Loanda. As my needs were supplied I made no charges, and as a fact I did my work for the influence I could obtain over these poor, neglected Portuguese.

"In February, 1886, Germano arrived in Malange from the Bashilange country (generally called Lubuko). I found he had to return in May with some fifty loads for Lieutenant Wissmann. I laid the matter at the feet of Jesus, and was soon assured that my path was ahead. But I had not a cent; hardly a change of wardrobe, medicine scarce, and not a yard of fazenda. I arranged to pay Germano twenty dollars to act as my interpreter on the road and look after my men, of whom as yet I had none. So I was now in for it, certain it was God's way and sure He would provide. One day Germano brought three carriers; I engaged them, and promised to pay later on. I told my friends of my intention of going to Lubuko, and then, day by day, cash came in, and carriers came, till at the end I had increased my wardrobe, bought one hundred dollars' worth of medicines, paid carriers, and had seventeen boxes of material for paying my way and future use, and three loads of rations on the way; the other loads being books, boxes of medicines, stationery, private materials, etc., one load of biscuits and one of dried salt fish, the two latter given me by a patient, a mulatto gentleman, who, when on the journey, wound up by giving me a riding ox and saddle! On the journey I never mounted the ox; I found walking so much to my taste that I walked the whole way, and never had a day' sickness.

"Of the journey I will say nothing but that it was full of interest and that the road is perfectly open; but being a white man I had to pay right of way to the principal chiefs, who, by the way, are anxious for white men to live with them. We arrived here in one hundred marches, the marches averaging six hours. Here my heart was overwhelmed at the reception I everywhere got from the Bashilange. Every hill is dotted with large and beautiful villages, the country teeming with people who have abandoned fetichism and are waiting for what the white man can bring them; all anxious to learn, intelligent, have now some idea of God, want to know about everything, faces always smiling, and every one polite. Go anywhere over this country, and great villages meet the eye. The population is enormous, and is marvellously thick. Truly, 'the harvest is great, but the labourers are few.' Few! One only, and that one worth almost nothing. When I came I found that if I wished to work in the State I must first ask for building land of the administrator general, as the chief here had no power to let me build a school or a house; so I immediately wrote, and the letter went by the steamer of December, 1886. Then 'patience and water gruel.' I pitched into the language, but with no suitable help it was dragging work.

"In the beginning of December I had a sudden attack of pleurisy and pericarditis. Next day Lieutenant Le Marinel went down with hæmaturic fever, and I had to leave my bed to treat him. The third day I had the fever under control, and on the fourth convalescence set in. It was sharp work ; it was a bad case. My leaving my bed these days left its mark upon me ; the pleurisy extended ; there were adhesions in several directions; the pain was fearful, and there was much *angina pectoris*. These continued with steady high fever for two weeks, then septic fever to wind up. By the end of December convalesence had set in, but temperature never went lower than before the pericarditis. I was a perfect skeleton. I gradually gained in flesh, but not strength. To-day I cannot walk a mile.

"A few days of terrible sickness ; three days in bed, unable to eat ; no one visited me, no cooling drink for raging fever ; in great despondency, as I thought, no one but my boy Chico cared a cent for me, when all at once I had a remarkable manifestation of Jesus, as He said, 'I will never leave thee nor forsake thee,' ' Lo I am with you alway, even unto the end of the world.'

" I cried for holy joy as I communed with my elder Brother, and my boy thought it was from pain. On this day, in my dark hour, I had thought of running away by first steamer, but now I felt assured I must stop and finish my building. I had no medicines, so I laid my case in the hands of the great Physician. My faith would not rise to ask for a cure ; I asked Him to modify the disease.

" Work out your opinion, and if possible try and give me some relief. If possible, I want to stay here till the bishop sends some one to take up my poor thread ; but then I cannot get away, as I have no forty dollars to pay passage. I have not a cent, but am now sending to Dr. Dowkontt for cash, which I can well repay with ivory. With all our cattle and goats we can get no milk, and this to me would be of great value.

" God bless you in your labour, dear doctor, and give you abundant success.

" I remain, your brother in Christ and for Africa,

"WILLIAM R. SUMMERS."

The wearying delay of Dr. Summers in getting permission to build was owing to the great distance to Boma, the capital, and no regular mail communication, and probably time lost in delay of his excellency in getting communication with me in person. I met him at Vivi, and he inquired of me to know who Dr. Summers was.

I informed his excellency that Dr. Summers was one of my missionaries, a good doctor, and every way a competent, reliable man. The governor general replied that he would take pleasure in giving him land, and authorised him to proceed in putting up his mission buildings.

In all the vast regions explored by Dr. Pogge and Lieutenant Wissmann the people gave evidence of industry, peace, and plenty, and not a track of an Arab trader to be seen. A later communication from Lieutenant Wissmann to the Royal Geographical Society brings to light a painful contrast between the expectancy of kings and people that Godmen were coming to teach them and the Arab raids that did come. Lieutenant Wissmann, whose acquaintance I made in Madeira, told the Bashilange people that I was coming and bringing teachers for them. A doctor, who was an eyewitness to the scene, told me that the good news caused great rejoicing among the people, and that they brought quantities of their heathen greegrees and threw them into the river. A summary of Lieutenant Wissmann's letter is as follows :

On the first occasion, in 1882, he was welcomed by a prosperous and contented tribe, whose condition and occupations bore ample evidence to the existence of its villages for decades in peace and security, free from the disturbing elements of war and slave hunts, pestilence and superstition. The huts of the natives were roomy and clean, fitted with shady porches and surrounded by carefully kept fields and gardens, in which were grown all manner of useful plants and fruits, including hemp, sugar, tobacco, sweet potatoes, maize, manioc, and millet. A thicket of bananas and plaintains occupied the back of each homestead, and shady palm groves supplied their owners with nuts, oil, fibres, and wine. Goats, sheep, and fowls abounded, and no one seemed afraid of thieves. The people all had a well-fed air, and were anxious to trade, their supplies being plentiful and extremely cheap. A fowl could be purchased for a cowry shell, and a goat for a yard of calico. Everywhere the visitors found a cheerful, courteous, and contented population, uncontaminated by the vices of civilisation, and yet not wholly ignorant of its arts.

Four years later Lieutenant Wissmann chanced to be in the same district, and after the privations of a toilsome march through dense, inhospitable forests, rejoiced as he drew near to the palm groves of the Bagna Pesihi. A dense growth of grass covered the formerly well-trimmed paths.

"As we approach the skirt of the groves we are struck at the dead silence which reigns. No laughter is to be heard, no sign of a welcome from our old friends. The silence of death breathes over the lofty crowns of the palms, slowly waving in the wind. We enter, and it is in vain we look to the right and left for the happy old homesteads and the happy old scenes. Tall grass covers everything ; a charred pole here and there and a few banana trees are the only evidences that man ever dwelt there. Bleached skulls by the roadside and the skeletons of human hands attached to poles tell the story of what has happened here since our last visit."

It appeared that the notorious Arab, Tippoo Tib, had been here to trade, and in the course of that process had killed all who offered resistance, carried off the women, and devasted the fields, gardens, and banana groves. Bands of destroyers from the same gang had returned again and again, and those who escaped the sword perished by the smallpox and famine which the marauders left in their train.

The whole tribe of the Dene Ki ceased to exist, and only a few remnants found refuge in the neighbouring state.

Such must be counted among the results of Arab trading in Africa, and if it is at such a cost that the blessings of Mohammedan civilisation are purchased by the native races it is no wonder they are not considered a desirable acquisition. Even if it be true that Christianity is sometimes tardy of operation in its beneficent effects on the blacks, Christian missionaries and Christian traders can, at least, boast that they have never wittingly acted otherwise than beneficently toward them.

Having settled my pioneer party of missionaries in Angola by the middle of September, 1885, I made a hasty tour to Lisbon and to England, and returned to the session of the Liberia Conference in January, 1886. I went from Loanda to Lisbon in the Portuguese steamship *St. Thomas.* At the island of St. Thomas some French army officers were added to our passenger list, all dressed in their military costumes except one lean, tall man, very straight and symmetrical in his proportions, dressed in the plain style of camp life, and accompanied by a huge dog. He looked as though he was a servant to those finely dressed officers. When the bell rang for dinner the plainly dressed man took a seat next to me at the table. He was very affable, and I soon began to talk to him in English, and was pleased to find that he could converse intelligently in my language, and soon, to my agreeable surprise, I found that I was conversing with one of the most celebrated African explorers and builders of military stations of this wonderful age of African exploration and occupation, Lieutenant De Brazza, now Governor De Brazza. He had then spent about thirteen years in opening and occupying that vast region known as French Congo, of which he is now the governor.

Excelling in gentlemanly affability and kindness, he became my principal travelling companion throughout the rest of the voyage. He insisted on paying my boat fares at Madeira, and went with me to call on Lieutenant Wissmann. He was very communicative, and from the details of his extraordinary African experiences I learned many valuable, practical lessons.

Arriving in Lisbon, I made myself known to our honourable American minister, whom I found ready to render me any service desirable.

I asked him if he could introduce me to the King of Portugal. He replied that he would take pleasure in doing so, but it would require over a week, according to the etiquette of the court, before I could get audience with him. I answered that I could not possibly spend more than three days in Lisbon. That was late on Friday afternoon, so I bade the minister good day and returned to my hotel. But on the way I inquired of a fellow who was showing me around, " How far is it to the palace ? "

" About two miles."

" Will you kindly come to-morrow morning and show me the way to the palace ? "

" Yes," he replied ; " I'll be at your place about 10 a.m. to-morrow."

So at the time appointed we went to the royal residence of his majesty the king. Happily the man who met me in the reception room could speak English; so I told him I wanted to see his majesty the king, and gave him some letters I had, one from the Portuguese ambassador in Washington, and another from President Hayes. So I sent in my name and my letters of indorsement, and requested an interview with the king.

My man was gone but a few minutes and returned my letters, saying, "His royal majesty says he'll be very glad to receive you to-day or to-morrow or any time which will suit your convenience; but the etiquette of the court requires that you be accompanied by the Minister Plenipotentiary of the United States."

"Very good, this is Saturday; too late to arrange for that to-day; to-morrow is the Sabbath and the day for rest and religious service; so we'll set Monday forenoon, when I'll be here with the United States minister."

He said, "Very good, sir; let it be so understood."

So I reported the facts in the case to our minister. He said, "Very good; you come here Monday morning and I'll have my carriage ready, and we'll drive to the palace."

On Monday morning it was raining, but I came to time, and our minister's carriage and pair were awaiting us. So we were driven to the palace and I was introduced to the king, and was agreeably surprised to find that he could converse freely in the English language. And he asked me so many questions about my missionary work in different countries as to afford me a good opportunity of giving him a brief history of my self-supporting missions in India and in South America and in the Portuguese province of Angola. He seemed interested and pleased, and bade me welcome to work under the flag of Portugal. I asked no favour of his royal majesty, but was nevertheless favoured by his good will in all our subsequent intercourse with his Angola government officials, from the governor general down.

Our minister remarked as we returned to his office that he had introduced many Americans to the king, each requiring at least a week of preparatory etiquette; but the king gave me ready audience and longer in time than in any case within the minister's knowledge.

As Lieutenant Wissmann had just explored the Kassai River from Luebo to its mouth on the Congo, seventy-five miles above Stanley Pool, opening a waterway direct to the Bashilange country, we were led to believe that the steamer route up the Kassai was preferable to the route from Angola. Having that in mind, I made it my business on that tour to England to call and see the patron sovereign of the Congo Free State, Leopold II. So on my arrival in Brussels I reported myself to the American minister, and asked him if could see the king. He replied, "I don't know; I came here last January with all the papers requisite to my official position, and it took me twelve days to get a sight of the king. I don't know how long it will take you. I advise you to see the minister at court who represents the Congo State."

So I proceeded at once to see the said honourable minister, and was glad to find that he was familiar with my language, and he received me cordially. I showed him a pamphlet I had just published in London, giving an account of my missionary methods of work and our chain of new stations in Angola, and our contemplated hope of reaching the Bashilange country by way of Congo. I handed him one of my pamphlets; he glanced over it and said, "Can't you furnish me with a bundle of them? This is just the thing we want to see. I want to furnish one to all the heads of different departments of the Congo State here. I want to give a copy to the king."

I said, "Oh yes; I can give you as many as you desire," and handed him a bundle of them which I had under my arm.

"This is Wednesday; to-morrow I shall be extremely busy; but I will make arrangements for you to come to see the heads of departments and the king on Friday afternoon."

I went accordingly on Friday afternoon. I was kindly received by all the different officers of state, and about 4 p.m., the time appointed, I was conducted by a servant to the royal residence of his majesty. A line of soldiers along the way leading to the reception room stood with their caps off as I passed through, and the king himself opened the door and received me.

He conducted me to a seat and sat down near me, and we talked forty minutes. He said he had been long wishing to know how he could introduce American industry and energy into Congo State, and proffered to render us every facility possible in planting missions in that country; and we have ever felt the benefit of that interview in our effort to plant missions there.

Our objective point was the Bashilange country, the same that we had in contemplation through Angola. The south side of Lower Congo, extending from the ocean to Stanley Pool, was preoccupied by the Missionary Society of English Baptists and the American Baptists' Missionary Union, and others. Not wishing to intrude ourselves on preoccupied territory, and presuming that the organised transport facilities of the government, and of the missions by the way, could be depended upon for the transportation of our mission supplies to Stanley Pool, we settled on Kimpopo, twenty miles up the east side of Stanley Pool, as our transport station and port of embarkation for the upper Kassai countries. I accordingly led our pioneer party up through the mountains to Stanley Pool, and planted a mission in Kimpopo, which had been used as a government station. The government kindly allowed us to occupy it and rendered us valuable help in opening it, and we depended confidently on getting passage at the Kassai in a government steamer the same season. Only one or two steamers per year went up in those days. If we had succeeded in executing our plan we should have reached Luluaburg about the same time that Dr. Summers struck that point from Angola. But the government steamer was overcrowded and could not afford passage for even one of us. Moreover, we found great difficulty in securing adequate transport even to Stanley Pool. There were two mission steamers at that time on the Upper Congo, the *Peace* and the *Henry Reed*, but neither of them was available for our purpose.

The logic of events had led us to the conclusion of building a steamer of our own for the Kassai River. At that time the government was organising a transport force which they considered would be adequate for the transport demands of the government and all the Congo missions, and I accordingly arranged with the government transport agent to take charge of our steamer material in man-loads immediately on its arrival at Banana, at the mouth of the Congo. So we ordered the building of a little steamer. According to contract the whole was to be in man-loads of sixty-five pounds, except four pieces which required four or six men ; but by a mechanical mistake a large portion of the steamer material came in bulk suited to a traction engine instead of the shoulders of men, on the assumption that a traction engine on Stanley's turnpike would be just the thing. The proof of that was supposed to be found in the fact that the steamer *Stanley* had been taken up in sections on great carts made for the purpose. It took a thousand men to work them, at a cost of fifty thousand dollars. There were no turnpike roads, and they ascended the mountain by means of great cables which were drawn up the steeps by man force and carefully let down the steeps on the opposite side.

On our arrival with our steamer material at the mouth of the Congo we learned that the government had not succeeded in organising a transport force of carriers beyond their own requirements, and Mr. Stanley's expedition, having passed up the Congo but a few weeks before, had gathered up all the available carriers of the Congo, so that we were struck. After innumerable delays and disappointments, utterly despairing of getting our steamer stuff transported to Stanley Pool, we had her built and put on to the Lower Congo, a first-class steamer, eighty feet long and sixteen feet beam. At that time Banana was the port of entry, and freights for the Upper Congo were carried up by river steamers to Matadi, the starting point of the Congo Railroad. With that arrangement our steamer would have soon refunded the money invested in her, and would have yielded a large income for the establishment of missions. At that time there were no missions on the north bank of the Congo, so that without intruding on anybody we concluded to open a line of stations on the north bank. But, happily for the transport commerce of the country, the ocean steamers gradually felt their way up the Congo until they made connections—boats of the ocean steamers—with the railroad at Matadi. That in a measure precluded the work of the river steamers, so that our steamer is not so productive as was hoped.

Upon the whole our missions on the Congo, though in a great measure self-supporting, are not a success compared with our missions in Angola. During the last few years one good woman and six of our best men have died in the Congo work. Our women on the Congo stand it better than the men, and are mainly holding the fort at the present time. I am not writing a history of Africa, nor of our work in Africa, but furnishing facts to illustrate the story of my life.

Our third chain of mission stations was on the Cavalla River, within the geographical boundaries of Liberia, but remote from Liberian settlements. The Cavalla, a beautiful river, nearly as large as the Hudson, running between high banks through the midst of a hilly country of great fertility, flows into the Atlantic Ocean about eighteen miles south-east of Cape Palmas. J. S. Pratt, a zealous layman in our Church at Cape Palmas, had two trading stations about eighty miles up the river. In 1886 Pratt spoke to the kings and chiefs of Tataka Tabo and of Gerribo, where his stations were located, about Bishop Taylor's proposal to plant missions at those places on his return in 1887, and they assured him they would gladly assist in every possible way.

Meantime a war scare swept over the Liberian coast, which seemed to shut us off from the Cavalla River country. It came on this wise: In 1874 the Half Cavalla tribe of Grabo natives rebelled against the Liberians, and drew twenty-seven tribes into a war for their extermination—not a living Liberian was to be left at Cape Palmas. The Liberians hastily built a rude stone fort at Tubmantown, three miles east of the cape, and after seventeen battles the war-making tribes signed treaties of peace, and all of them kept the peace except the Half Cavalla tribe and two little tribes under the power of the Half Cavalla tribe. This belligerent tribe tried in 1886 to draw into rebellion the whole force of the rebellion of 1874.

The Liberians were fearful that their efforts in that direction might succeed and bring on a great war, and when I came in 1887 the country was in a high state of excitement, and a panic had seized the Cape Palmas people. I arrived in the midst of this trouble, and it was said, "Bishop Taylor can't go up the Cavalla. The Liberians can't travel there now, and the Half Cavallas won't allow missions to be opened up that river."

I said, "I see no sufficient reason for being frightened away by the rumours of war;" so I arranged as quickly as possible to be off for the Cavalla River country.

On Sabbath, the 14th of March, 1887, I preached thrice in our church at Cape Palmas, and fifteen children came forward as seekers, and ten of them professed to find Jesus in the forgiveness of their sins.

On Monday, the 15th, we got the use of a surf boat, and secured seven Kroomen as sailors, and set sail for Cavalla at 2 p.m. On our passenger list were myself, J S. Pratt, Amanda Smith and her companion, Sister Fletcher, and my two interpreters from Monrovia, Tom Nimly and Saco. They had been converted to God and baptised at my meetings in connection with Mary Sharp's mission.

Tom was a man of almost giant proportions and good natural ability, and could read a little in the Testament. His Christian name was Africanus. Saco was a youth of about eighteen, with a fair English education. The captain of our little craft was a powerful Krooman and a good seaman, though of a quiet, even temper.

The bar at the Cavalla mouth was dreaded. We reached it a little before sunset. It seemed impossible for us to get over it, but probable that we should get under its fearful surf. Amanda could not bear to see the recoil of the river current and the swell of the Atlantic Ocean, and so buried her face and hands in her lap; but I knew she would hold on hard to God, and we all believed in the power of Amanda's prayers.

Africanus, being himself an old sailor, displaced one of the ordinary men and took his oar, so we made for the entrance into the river. Urged on by the shouts of our captain, our dear fellows pulled as for life; but before we got halfway through the breakers we had to "about ship" and pull seaward or be swamped. We made a second abortive attempt, but the third time we entered safely and were glad. The heroic pluck and pull of our Kroo boys brought tears to my eyes.

Tuesday, 7.30 a.m., we took to our boat, and after a heavy pull against the current for eight and a half hours we put up for the night at a native village called Barabo. The people were very kind to us, and wanted to know why we should pass by them and not give them a missionary.

I was gazed at by a crowd of women and children till I gave them to understand that I wanted to retire for my night's rest. Just as I was getting into my first doze of sleep a man called me to come and partake of a feast he had prepared for me. I thanked him for his kindness, and respectfully declined to get up; but my party were on hand.

Wednesday we were off again at 7.30 a.m. Our brave boys pulled against the stream all day. At 4 p.m. we had a thunderstorm and heavy rain, which gave us and our stuff a pretty thorough wetting.

About sunset we tied up near the town of Eubloky. The people received us hospitably and prepared for us a good dinner of boiled rice, palm butter, venison, and fish. We passed a pleasant night, I, as usual, sleeping in the open air, and all my party in the native huts.

Thursday morning the kings and chiefs insisted on our having a mission palaver. They were entirely unwilling to let us pass them otherwise. So we had an assembly of the kings, chiefs, and people, and the whole plan of an industrial school for "book and plenty of hard work and God palaver." I drew up articles of agreement, binding them to give us all the land we might need for school farms, to help to clear the ground and plant, to carry all the heavy logs for pillars to elevate the mission house six feet above ground, and to carry all the timber for frame, and the plank, shingles, etc., and binding us to send the missionaries, and to do all our part of the agreement. There were two kings in the town, one very old and

infirm, the other the active ruler. The articles were signed by
Dings, Nebby, and Pacey, and Chiefs Enyassah, Toa, Phae, and
Tahara, Pacey to be head man of our mission farm till the arrival
of the missionaries. So we were allowed to depart in peace, after
making a selection of our farm lands.

We came in the afternoon of that day to Tataka Tabo, the first
town for which we had started to fulfil the agreement for a mission,
and submitted by Brother Pratt the year before.

Before reaching Tataka we passed the town of Yawkey. The
people hailed us and asked the usual questions put to strangers in
Africa: "Who are you?" "Where did you come from?" "Where
are you going?" "What are you going there for?"

When such questions come from the ruling authorities of a town
the right thing to do is to stop and answer them, and see that you
answer them straight.

When we had answered they refused to allow us to pass unless
we would agree to give them a missionary, the same as Tataka
Tabo; so we promised them that if they allowed us to pass we
would come back to-morrow or next day and have a mission palaver.
Then we were allowed to pass, and we went on to Tataka. Kraharry,
King of Tataka, never would believe that Bishop Taylor would
"come and make mission for his people," but now he shouted,
"Pratt's mouth no tell lies. Pratt say bishop will come, and bishop
has come!" He gesticulated and shouted and danced for joy; then
ordered to the front a file of soldiers who fired four or five rounds
of musketry, and the whole town was in a buzz. The king would
have us "sit down next day," and "no leave him yet." So we
remained over Friday. In the afternoon we had our big palaver,
and selected a beautiful site for our mission on high ground, in view
of, but over a quarter of a mile distant from, the town. We held
service at Tataka, and tried to preach a little to the people, but
found the broken English of the heathen sailors, which served as a
medium for interpretation for simple business purposes, quite inadequate to our purpose of Gospel teaching.

Saturday, March 20th. This morning early Tom Nimly, of Yawkey,
came with his canoe to take us back to fulfil our promise to "make
mission at Yawkey." Tom has a very pleasant countenance, has
been at sea for years, and speaks intelligibly in English. We had
the palaver, and King Wahpasara and Chiefs Jawa, Wahney, Krura,
Tuba, Taba, and Teah signed the articles. We selected our site
for mission buildings and farms and got back to Tataka by noon.

At 2 p.m. the same day we were off for Gerribo, but we had to
pass the town of Beahboo, and had to go through the "shorter
catechism" of the country, as we did at Yawkey, and made a
similar pledge to return from Gerribo and have a mission palaver
with them.

We reached Gerribo on Saturday, a little before sunset, and were
welcomed by its ruler, King Grandoo.

Sabbath, the 21st. In the morning I preached in Pratt's store, from

John's Gospel, i. 2, to all that could understand English. At night we had a meeting in a native house, with Grandoo and as many of his people as could get into the house, and an interesting time it was. Tom Will, our captain, was my interpreter. He knew the language of the Bush tribes. Africanus and Saco were not sufficiently familiar with it, though much of it they knew, and helped Tom Will out when he stuck. At the close of the preaching, such as it was, Africanus seemed to get the mastery of the language, and told his experience, and exhorted the people earnestly to turn to God. Saco told his experience also, and Amanda Smith talked in her wonderful way, and Africanus interpreted. Then the king and two chiefs talked calmly and sensibly. The substance of what they said was that they were ready to give up all their greegrees and devil worship and turn to God as soon as they could get light enough to see which way to go. Amanda rose up and sang, and shook hands with all in the house. So ended the first religious meeting ever held among the people of the Gerribo tribe.

Monday, March 21st. We went back this morning to Beahboo to redeem our pledge. Articles were opened, too, for the planting of a mission there, signed by the two kings, Yahsanoo and Tahley, and by the chiefs.

To the five stations on the river above described we subsequently added Barraroba, higher up the river, and Wissika, below Enbloky, a total of seven stations on the river bluffs—five on the west side, and two, Tataka and Barraroba, on the east. I have never before put up missions so close together, but each town in which we have arranged for a station represents a different tribe, and some of them at war with each other. They have severally fought their way to the waterside, giving them canoe access to the sea, as many of them are sailors, and have a water frontage sufficient for their river town ; but the big towns and big kings and the great body of their people are back in the interior. The big town and king of the Gerribo tribe are about twelve miles back. The town is called Wallekay, which has two big kings, Sahboo and Sabo, who sent messengers inviting us to visit them, and then sent a dozen carriers to take us to the great place. They wanted to carry me, but, as in every other place in which I had travelled in Africa, I preferred to walk, and respectfully declined the honour of being toted on the shoulders of men. Amanda, not being very well, was carried in a hammock. Julia Fletcher walked, and I and Brother Pratt, Africanus and Saco took it afoot. We passed westerly, back of a range of mountains, and thrice crossed a large creek in canoes, and waded several smaller mountain streams of clear, cold water. We passed through two towns on the way. At the first we rested, and the people prepared for us a good dinner, to which we did ample justice. We reached the second town just in time to get shelter from a heavy rain ; but afterwards the bushes bending over our path were dripping with water, and we got our clothes as wet as if we had been in the rain. We passed through large rice fields, one of which contained at least twenty acres of young growing rice. The women engaged in its cultivation generally ran like deer at our approach ; but having heard of our coming they soon got over their fright, and many of them approached us shyly and allowed us to shake hands with them.

When we got within a quarter of a mile of the town we heard the big signal drum giving notice of our approach, and we arranged there, as at the other places named, for founding a mission at Wallekay, the big town of the Gerribo tribe.

We opened next a chain of stations on the Kroo coast, Pluky Garraway, Grand Sess, Piquinin Sess, Sass Town, Niffoo, Nana Kroo, and Settra Kroo, and subsequently established ten more stations in the midst of the Liberian work in Sinoe District, Grand Bassa District, St. Paul's River District, and Monrovia District. These ten stations were in 1893 turned over to the Missionary Society, being in the midst of their organised work and manned by Liberian ministers. Of the twenty stations opened on the lines indicated we have lost over half a dozen through the wars, but have added more than that number of sub-stations. Some of our stations grow grandly, especially on the lines of education and salvation. Others progress slowly.

CHAPTER XLI

FAREWELL

In addition to chains of stations we have opened on the Liberian coast and Congo country I appointed a man of extraordinary adaptability to the work, Rev. E. H. Richards, to plant and develop a chain of mission stations in South-east Africa, starting at Inhambane and to be extended into South Zambesi.

The early summer of 1895 I spent in reading the proofs of this "Story of My Life" and in supervising the publication. On several occasions I was absent to preach—once I went to Philadelphia and once to Boston. In these avocations and excursions I never lost sight of my own special work, and my return thereto was only postponed to a fitting time of the year.

After the September and October Conferences, which to the number of ten or twelve I attended in the fall of 1895, I hastened my departure for Africa, and early in November I sailed from New York to Liverpool; there I stayed for a season and preached. I also visited Sunderland and Southport and preached in those towns. Finishing this work, I took ship in the steamer *Boma* for Monrovia, where I arrived in the first days of the new year. The Christmas holidays I spent at sea.

It was my duty to hold the Liberia Conference at an early date, and for this I arranged to begin on the 22nd of January, 1896. The interval I spent in visiting our stations and in preaching. The winter months in Liberia are very mild, and afford opportunity for carrying forward all manner of enterprises, religious and educational work included.

According to the calendar which I had prepared, I opened the Liberia Conference in Monrovia on the 22nd of the month. The work of that body extended over eleven sessions, at all of which I presided. The Conference was completed with the reading of the appointments on the evening of the 28th.

After the conclusion of my work in connection with the Conference I visited several of our stations, preaching at Mount Scott Church, at Tubmantown, at King Hodge's Bigtown, and at Plukey. I also presided at our Sunday-school celebration at Mount Scott, where we had 284 children in attendance. Afterwards I walked fifteen miles to Barraka Station, which was in charge of Miss Grace White and her sister Annie, our missionaries. I opened in connection with the work in this part of the country two sub-stations and left them in a promising condition.

My episcopal visitation to Africa at this time brought to my mind many things to be noted in a general survey of the field. Facts and reflections numberless arose, many of which I used in my report to the General Conference four months afterwards. I will here recapitulate the substance of what I gathered on this trip and used in my third (and last) quadrennial report, made at Cleveland in May of 1896:

When I went to the General Conference in 1884 the prevailing sentiment seemed to be that our missions in Africa were such a failure that they would have to be abandoned. Official action on the subject was delayed, in the dread of the disgrace of failure, until they settled on a scapegoat, or a Joshua, to solve the problem. Our dear fellow-workers of the Episcopal Church still appropriate thirty-two thousand dollars a year for their Africa work. The fact is that our liberal appropriation of over thirty thousand dollars a year was applied to the Americo-Liberia work, incidentally striking a few notable cases of conversion among the natives; hence, when I went there I did not find a single Methodist mission among the raw heathen; and concluded, therefore, that the liberal appropriation to the Americo-Liberia work, however important, furnishes no fair test of our Gospel possibilities in direct work among the heathen.

Although I have given due attention to the Liberia Conference work proper, all my new mission stations have been planted among the raw heathen. In every new field I entered the way of the Lord had to be prepared just as necessarily as the grading and track laying of a new railroad. It requires toil, time, and great patience. When I went as an evangelist to South Africa in 1866 I entered a field in which preparatory work had been going on for forty years, so that, according to the report of the missionaries, in less than a year over seven thousand Kaffirs experienced salvation, and the whole movement was put upon a plane of direct and continued effectiveness.

A little over eleven years ago I led my pioneer party of missionaries for Africa to Angola, south of the Congo. The English language was not available at all; the Kimbundu had not been reduced to manuscript, much less to printing, and we had no interpreters; so we had to sit down by the naked heathen and patiently pick the words one by one from their mouths, and write them down according to their sound as best we could. In less than five years from that time we printed a Kimbundu grammar and the gospel by St. John, and our pioneers had learned to talk and preach in the native language. That was slow business, but if we had had command of money and men adequate we could by this time have established a thousand stations, and had them well on toward self-support.

In opening a station we make it a point to secure a good, high, healthy site, and good land for agricultural purposes, and make simple industries, involving self-support, an essential part of education. Our plan is also to establish a nursery mission in every station in which we have a competent missionary matron. Instead of a few hundred children under training, we could accept from the hundreds of godly women who are offering for our work missionary matrons to train a million children separated from heathenism before they could become heathen. It was, however, several years before we could successfully establish our nursery missions, owing to the difficulty in obtaining the young children.

I learned my first lesson on the necessity of gaining the marriage dowry control of the little girls to be adopted by a conversation with Rev. David A. Day, of the Muhlenberg Mission. Said he : " Over twenty years ago my wife and I, on a visit to Boporo, became acquainted with a native family in which was a beautiful little girl. We fell in love with the child, and begged the parents to give her to the mission. So they gave her up without urging very strong objections, and we brought her home with us, and loved and educated her just as if she had been our own child. She was a lovely child, and became a good musician and a good Christian. As she grew to womanhood she received the attentions of a young man educated on our station, and they expressed a wish to be united in marriage. The fact was communicated to her parents, who gave consent and they were married. Soon after messengers came from the parents stating that her marriage dower had been paid by an old man when she was a child, and they must conduct her to his house. We were horrified, and begged for time, and in response to our importunity the parents finally agreed to permit the newly married couple to live in peace. A few months afterwards the parents begged to have their daughter and her husband visit them. So accordingly they proceeded to Boporo ; but on entering the town a mob, led by her parents, attacked the young man and killed him, and tied the young woman to a tree and gave her a whipping about every hour for a whole day, and thus compelled her to promise to go and live with the old heathen who had paid her marriage dower when she was a child."

That was my first lesson on the marriage dower, by which no child can be enslaved, but their selection of marriage is controlled. No marriage dower is paid for slave girls ; they are bought and sold like cattle. We never procured any as slaves. We adopted about forty little girls to be our daughters under the same kind of training we give to our own children.

Later, as the people have become acquainted with us and our work, we have the offer of all the children we can take care of, for the most part orphans. So we have nearly ceased to redeem children by paying the marriage dower, much to the disappointment of our friends who wish to redeem and name the children. Some time ago a big native man came to our mission at Malange with a little girl about three years old on his shoulder. She was, as is usual with the children in that country, almost entirely nude, and covered from head to foot with fresh marks of smallpox. The man laid her down on the floor and said, "Three months ago the mother of this child died at Loanda. When dying she said to me, 'When you see me put in the ground, carry my child to Malange and give her to the missionaries.' [From Loanda to Malange is about three hundred miles.] So," said he, "when the woman died and was buried I laid the child on my back, but when about halfway on the journey she was taken with the smallpox. I nursed her for a whole moon until she was able to travel; so to-day I finish my task, and put her in your care." Americana, a little girl who had been with the mission for three years, went and looked closely at the little girl and said, "What is your name?" The little one replied, "My name is Lubina." Americana pressed her to her bosom, exclaiming, "Oh, she is my sister!" The mother had formerly lived near Malange, and became acquainted with our missionaries there and gave them her older daughter when a baby.

We have in our work purely among the heathen twenty-seven principal stations and nearly as many more sub-stations, manned by forty-eight white missionaries and some hundreds of natives under training. The best material for evangelising agency in Africa is the raw material, and the best place for its development is where it was born. Already the Lord is indicating His chosen vessels among our converted natives, who will surpass in Gospel effectiveness those who under God dug them out of heathenism.

Rev. George Grenfell, of the English Congo Baptist Mission, spent a few days with us at Malange. One day, having listened to one of our native men preach, he said, "Mr. Mead, where was that man educated?" "He was educated here in my school," replied Mr. Mead. Mr. Grenfell said, "That cannot be. I never heard such preaching before. That man was well educated before you ever saw him." He was a freight carrier from the interior, and when he came to the mission he did not know a letter in the book. In one of our meetings he was awakened and converted to God. Then he came to Mr. Mead and said he wanted an education. Mr. Mead said that he was short one pit sawyer, and if the man would come and work in the daytime he would pay him regular wages and teach him at night. The big Ambundu, a powerful man, said he would not take any pay for his work, but would work every day and study every night. He subsequently married one of the mission girls, and they are doing effective work for God in one of our sub-stations in Angola.

Visiting Barraka Station a few years ago, Miss White, our preacher in charge there, said to me, "I want to consult you in regard to our man Jasper. He is my best farmer, my best preacher, and my most successful soul-saving worker. But he is beaten by the natives whenever they can get near enough to him, and I am afraid they will kill him. I have waited for an opportunity to consult with you as to what we had best do." "The best way," I said, "is to let Jasper decide for himself." So he was called in, and the case stated to him, and his prompt reply was: " I was born here; these people who want to kill me are my people; they have the same hatred toward Christ and Christians that I had before I found Jesus; so I have no quarrel with them. I patiently bear their unmerciful thrashings, and if the Lord wants me to die for Jesus I prefer to die on my own native soil."

A year from that time Jasper's name was sung among the heroes in their war songs. The Barraka nation, to which he belonged, had been at war with a neighbouring nation for over a hundred years, and any one of either party crossing the dividing line met his death. But about a year ago Jasper crossed the line, walked straight to the royal house of the belligerent nation's king, and, hailing him, said : " My name is Jasper. I belong to the Barraka nation, and I bring to you to-day a message from God. It is very simple. God wants you to open to me and my fellow-workers a house in which to hold a prayer meeting in your town." The king, without hesitation, consented, and Jasper and his praying band came on immediately. Then, after three nights of prayer, he called on the king again with another message from God, which was to ask the king to call a peace palaver in his own house, to be conducted by the king and his counsellors on one side and by Jasper and his praying band on the other. They prayed twenty-eight nights, and on three occasions all night. The joint parties talked peace twenty-three days, and made a settlement, according to the laws of the two nations, establishing a permanent peace. There have been since two or three occasions of disturbing the peace of the two nations, but they were promptly settled by arbitration. Suppose our friends had given us money to establish a thousand such stations, each one turning out a Jasper, we could begin to see the culmination of our evangelising work in the Gospel conquest of the nations of Africa.

As it is, despite the devastating wars all along our lines, especially on the west coast, our official statistics indicate our progress from 1892 to 1896 as follows :

	1892.	1896.	Increase.
Probationers	202	528	326
Full members	3064	4403	1339
Preachers	54	62	8
Children baptised	85	234	149
Adults baptised	75	190	115
Churches	31	42	11
Probable value	$28,526 25	$53,684 8	$25,158 285
Parsonages	1	8	7
Probable value	$75	$6040	$5965
Sunday-schools	38	84	46
Officers and teachers	320	510	190
Scholars	2750	3072	322

Of these scholars 1070 are members of our Church.

After completing the work of the Liberia Conference, I spent the remaining interval of my stay in visiting the West Coast mission stations and in establishing our new missionaries in their respective fields of work. I was thus occupied during the greater part of February and March, 1896. It was necessary for me to return to the United States in time for the General Conference, and I finished my outside work, returning to Cape Palmas late in March, from which place I embarked for New York. The following month I spent in preparing for the meeting of the General Conference and occasionally preaching in places near the city.

The General Conference of 1896 convened at Cleveland on the 1st of May. I was able to attend in my usual health and spirits. I prepared my report, which was read before the Conference on the eighth day of the session. As usual at our General Conferences, the discussions turned, on several occasions, to the relations of the bishops to the work and economy of the Church. The debates on this topic broke out from time to time. Our people are a free people, and their representatives in General Conference have their opinions and their "views" about all questions affecting our denomination and denominational usages.

Many are the notions which prevail as to the policy that should be pursued regarding the general superintendents. In our day the discussions have turned upon the nature of the bishop's office, upon his time of service, and especially upon the question of his residence or location. Many of our people think that the term of the episcopal service should be limited to a period of years. Some advocate the policy of locating bishops here and there, as is the usage in the Church of England. Some go farther than these and probe the bishop's office to the bottom, renewing the old discussion as to whether our *episcopoi* constitute another order, or what they do constitute.

Debates on these questions were heard at Cleveland; but most of the discussions subsided into nothing—*except* that which related to the retirement of some of the bishops on account of their advanced age. I was included in this number. Of my brethren on the Episcopal Board only Bishop Bowman and Bishop Foster are my seniors; I come next; and then Bishop Andrews and Bishop Merrill, who are my juniors by a few years. It was thought, however, that I was, on the score of strength, as near the point of retirement as Bishop Bowman and Bishop Foster. Most of our bishops have died in office. A few have been excused from further active service. In this case, the matter came to an open proposition to "retire" the three of us, who were thought by the brethren to be less "effective" than we had been. The contemplated action was precisely analogous to that so many times taken at Annual Conferences for the superannuation of preachers.

A resolution in accordance with this policy was adopted at an early date in the Conference with respect to Bishops Bowman and Foster. A like action in my case was suspended until late in the session, but that policy at length prevailed and I was relieved from further active service—that is, I was relieved from further *official* service as a bishop, although this action could hardly affect my own purposes as regards the prosecution of evangelistic work. The missionary cause has been *my* cause, and must continue to be so to the end of the journey.

The action for my retirement from active duty resulted from a report emanating from the Committee on Episcopacy. Of that committee, my friend, Dr. J. M. Buckley, editor of *The Christian Advocate*, was chairman. On the 25th of May Dr. Buckley made an address before the Conference, incorporating in his remarks the second recommendation of the committee, as follows:

"After protracted consideration we find ourselves compelled to report that William Taylor, Missionary Bishop for Africa, is non-effective. With a deep sense of the intrepid heroism which has characterised his career as a pioneer missionary in the early days of California, in Australia, India, and South America, in Africa prior to his appointment as missionary bishop, when past sixty years of age, and for twelve years since that appointment; his fervour and power as a preacher; his astonishing success as an evangelist, and the permanency of the fruits of his labours; and also with an affection for him personally which has been increased by every hardship he has endured, we profoundly regret that the same fidelity to our convictions which has always characterised him compels us to report that he is non-effective."

This report was adopted, and by the action I was relieved of my duties as Bishop for Africa. The office I had held for twelve years. It was given by the free choice of the Church, and by the purpose of God, in 1884. Now I was relieved from the bishop's duty and left once more to my own motions and resources. The action of the Conference did not contemplate the abolition of the office of Bishop for Africa, though that question was discussed. There was an active debate, re-opening all the vital questions about the missionary episcopacy. The committee decided that Bishop Thoburn was effective and should be continued in office. It was also decided to elect a new Bishop for Africa to take my place. The matter was taken up two days afterwards—that is, on May 25th—and Dr. Joseph C. Hartzell was chosen to take my place. He had already been re-elected Secretary of the Freedmen's Aid and Southern Education Society, but the Conference decided to transfer him to a more responsible station.

The action of the body relative to myself was not erroneous or distasteful to me personally. Many of my friends, however, were for the time aggrieved, but not I. The servant of God accepts what comes in the order of Providence, and makes neither comments nor complaints. Owing to the murmurs of my friends I deemed it best, as soon as opportunity offered, to compose the following brief general letter, under the title of " No Mistake ":

" Many of my friends think and declare that the action of the General Conference which kindly put my name on the honourable list of retired heroes, such as Bishop Bowman and Bishop Foster, was a mistake. No such thought ever got a night's lodging in my head or heart. I have for fifty-four years received my ministerial appointments from God. If any mistakes were made, through the intervention of human agency, they did not fall on me. For the last twelve years God has used me in Africa as leader of a heroic host of pioneer missionaries, in opening vast regions of heathendom to direct Gospel achievement, which will go on 'conquering and to conquer' till the coming of the King, if no bishop should visit them for half a century; but the General Conference has appointed as my episcopal successor a tried man of marvellous adaptability.

"Bequests and deeds to mission property are made to Bishop William Taylor, or to his 'living successor.' Bishop J. C. Hartzell is now my 'living successor.' If he should die, or superannuate, then the episcopos appointed by the General Conference to take his place would be my 'living successor.' I bespeak for Bishop Hartzell, on behalf of my work and faithful workers at the front, all the loving sympathy and financial co-operation of my beloved patrons and partners in this great work of God. 'And you are going to lie on the shelf?' I am not a candidate for 'the shelf.' I am accustomed to sleep in the open sparkling of the stars, and respond to the bugle blast of early morn. At present:

> "God calls me from mudsill preparation—
> John the Baptist dispensation—
> To proclaim more widely the Pauline story
> Of our coming Lord, and of His glory.

Under this call of God I expect to lead thousands of Kaffirs into His fold. In an evangelising campaign of a few years through Southern and Eastern Africa, I will, D.V., strike the warpath of the grand heroic leader of our Inhambane and South Zambesia missions— Rev. E. H. Richards. I will, D.V., go directly from New York to Cape Town,' South Africa, by S.S. *Wilcannia* to sail on the 18th inst. Any communications designed for me may be addressed to Rev. Ross Taylor, 150, Fifth Avenue, New York City.

"WILLIAM TAYLOR."

June 24th, 1896.—This is the morning of my departure. Our steamer lies at the Atlantic Dock in Brooklyn. It is the crisis of a beautiful summer. Of summers I have now seen in this world seventy-five. My wife, my son Ross, and some other friends accompany me to the wharf to bid me farewell. I go to the Kaffirs. May God give me success among them, and enable me to reclaim, in the name of His Son, ten thousand souls!

I here renew the dedication of this "Story of My Life" to my Divine Sovereign, whom I serve, and to my fellow-subjects of His spiritual kingdom.